A PLAGUE OF DEVILS

BY

M. GARFIELD

Pennaeth Publishing
Wilmington, Delaware

Cover illustrations by Catherine Haverkamp, www.catherinehaverkamp.com

Cover design by Evren Bilgihan

The cover is inspired by *The Bayeux Tapestry* which hangs in the Musée de la Tapisserie de Bayeux, 13 Rue de Nesmond, 14400, Bayeux, France. www.tapisserie-bayeux.fr/

Family Tree and Map designed by Virginia Ruths, touchstonepubs@gmail.com, www.touchstonepubs.com

contact@pannaethpublishing.com

ISBN 978-0-9964136-3-3

For My Father

ACKNOWLEDGEMENTS

First of all, I would like to thank everyone who had anything to do with the publication of this novel. The noted artist Catherine Haverkamp provided me a spectacular illustration for the front cover of A Plague of Devils. We worked beautifully together—thank you so much, Kat. Evren Bilgihan, my publisher and the artist who drew the cover for A Domesday Tale, digitized Kat's art into the cover of the book. I'm grateful, Evren, for your artistic brilliance.

And to the three most special people who, with their intense and also delicate editing, helped make this book readable. Thank you with all my heart—Eric Levine, Susan Walls, and Rachel Garfield-Levine.

To my immediate family and extended one, particularly Marty Garfield-Levine, Paul Levine, Anne Bilgihan, and Terry and Bob and Aryn Garfield for reading and/or listening to me babble on endlessly about A Domesday Tale and A Plague of Devils. Your support and discussions helped me to see myself as a good author, and I am grateful to you for that precious gift.

Odette Trellinger. I am deeply in debt for your interest and support for my novels and writing. And Debra McKrola, my great friend and physical therapist—I could not have completed this work without your help, especially keeping my troublesome body in somewhat decent working order.

Again, I must mention our writers' group—Lindsey Flewelling, Reneé Prud'homme, Rachel Rozdzial, Rachel Garfield-Levine, Eve Grina, Patrick Callier, and Erica Haseman-Hawks. Your inspiration was priceless in the writing process. I'm beholden to you ladies and gentleman.

A special thank you goes to my husband, Eric Levine, who actually read out loud to me the entire novel, A Plague of Devils, while editing. It was quite a feat! He gave each character a silly name, and I will eternally think of this book as the love story of Stanley and Monique. He also graded my book with an A! I love you, Eric.

I also need to include in my thanks my amazing Facebook friends, who gave me support and confidence from their wonderful reviews of A Domesday Tale and their desire to read A Plague of Devils.

Last, but, of course, not least, my forever and deepest thanks goes to my mom and pop, Mary and Wayne Garfield, who have passed, yet still love and look after me every day. I love you two and miss you terribly.

*****

A PLAGUE OF DEVILS

The Family
of
William the Conqueror

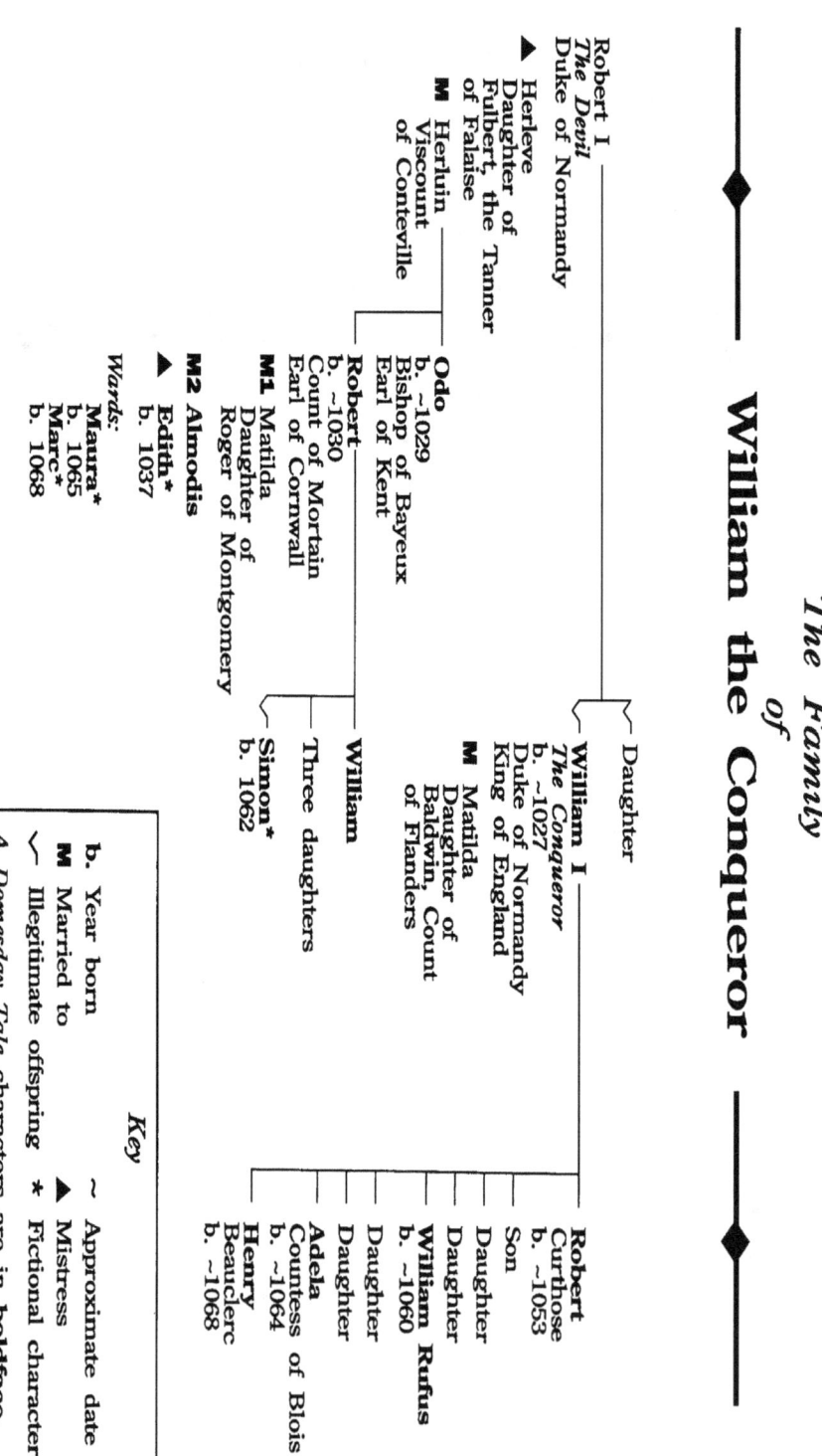

Robert I
The Devil
Duke of Normandy

M Herluin
Viscount
of Conteville

▶ Herleve
Daughter of
Fulbert, the Tanner
of Falaise

Daughter

Odo
b. ~1029
Bishop of Bayeux
Earl of Kent

Robert
b. ~1030
Count of Mortain
Earl of Cornwall

M1 Matilda
Daughter of
Roger of Montgomery

M2 **Almodis**

▶ **Edith***
b. 1037

William

Three daughters

Simon*
b. 1062

Wards:
Maura*
b. 1065
Marc*
b. 1068

William I
The Conqueror
b. ~1027
Duke of Normandy
King of England

M Matilda
Daughter of
Baldwin, Count
of Flanders

Robert
Curthose
b. ~1053

Son

Daughter

Daughter

William Rufus
b. ~1060

Daughter

Daughter

Adela
Countess of Blois
b. ~1064

Henry
Beauclerc
b. ~1068

Key

b.	Year born	~ Approximate date
M	Married to	▶ Mistress
⟨	Illegitimate offspring	* Fictional character

A *Domesday Tale* characters are in **boldface.**

England and Normandy
Principal Locations in *DOMESDAY TALES*

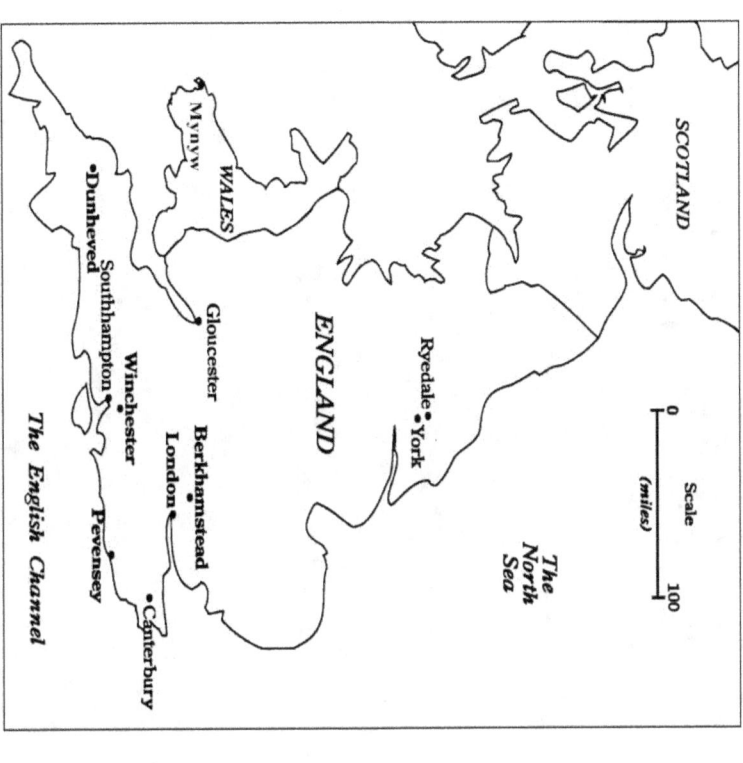

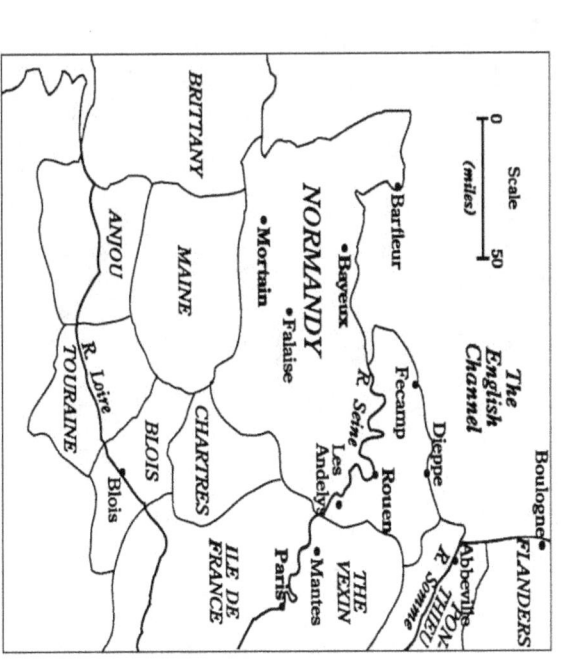

A PLAGUE OF DEVILS
CHAPTER ONE - PASSED OVER

"Curse you, God!" railed Henry, thrusting his balled fist to the arched beams high overhead. An explosion of fluttering wings answered as swallows darted and dove from their rafter nests in company with his tirade. "He worshipped you! Every miserable day of his life he got down on his knees and begged for *your* mercy, *your* love, *your* guidance. And now you've deserted him, sent the Devil to torture him! Four weeks he's screamed for deliverance. Four weeks! Why? My God, tell me why! Why have you forsaken him?!"

Agonized groans rumbled from a nearby chamber, drowning Henry's entreaty. He slumped into a chair, buried his head in his crossed arms upon a table, and wept again as he'd done for days. His mind screamed at him to run from this Hell! But his body refused to budge; it stayed leaden and stuck in the chair to suffer the harrowing sounds of his father the King's final fray with death. This was Henry's punishment for impudence and disobedience. He heaved from the table and staggered about the Refectory of the Priory of Saint-Gervais in Rouen. He clamped his hands tightly over his ears to escape the droning torment, but it continued its abuse from somewhere deep inside his mind, pounding, shaking his skull, destroying his sanity.

A swipe of Henry's arm sent four empty wine flagons soaring from the table and crashing to the soiled rushes below. The stained linen cloth draping the table shredded between his balled fists; he next attacked the seat, hurling it against the stone wall. A splinter shot from the chair's arm, stabbing his cheek and flaring his distemper. He lurched down the stairs to the tables below and stumbled into a wall cloaked with a tapestry. He groped at the dense material and twisted himself in its folds, hoping to lose himself in the embossed pastoral scene. But its serenity proved brutal; the weaving tore from the wall and swallowed him up. He thrashed beneath its weight, gasping for freedom, for air. And when at last he found the light again, his body refused to rise; his head lolled in the rushes as the rafters, nests, tables, torches, and candles whirled madly before his eyes. He hugged his belly as it cramped from a lack of food and surfeit of stale wine, clenched shut his eyes, and moaned a prayer to end the madness. His entreaty was promptly answered, and his surroundings faded away to nothingness.

"My Lord...my Lord..." A cautious voice intruded on Henry's peace. He shifted away, but a jostling touch barbed the request. "My Lord, wake up...Your father asks for you...my Lord."

Henry opened stinging, bleary eyes to a youthful female face brimming sympathy. "Are you ill, my Lord?" she asked, helping him to sit.

He hid his wretchedness behind his palms and sadly wagged his head. Then as his fingers raked their way through his thick, black, tousled hair and settled on his bushy black beard, a self-assured spark replaced the lost look in his huge, umber eyes; his tone lost its crack and took on a tenacious ring. "He asks for me?"

"Yes, my Lord, and seems quite anxious. You'd best hurry."

Henry didn't need further prompting. With effort, he shoved up from the rushes, wavered a long moment, and once he'd found his balance, bounded toward King William's cell. Soldiers, advisers, and relatives crowded the door. Henry roughly shouldered his way through them, jabbing and cursing, "Let me pass, you stinking vultures! Can't you spare him a moment's peace?" Suddenly his father's face appeared before him, contorted with misery and disease, almost unrecognizable. William's skin sagged gray and loose from his jaws, not a strand of hair remained on his head, and only a few clumps of tangled gray tufts sprouted from his chin. His lips, cracked with bloody scabs, dribbled and spewed foam as he attempted in vain to speak.

The cramping returned and Henry's knees wobbled at the obscene sight of his father's bloated belly, buried beneath a pile of pelts. Injured from a fall upon his saddle's pommel while razing the town of Mantes, the doctors had said. And the injury had spread with a torpid malignancy, torturing, killing.

Henry swallowed dryly and risked a tentative touch to his father's gnarled fingers. William opened yellowed eyes to the tender stroking and strained a grin and greeting, "Henry..."

"Father, I was told you wanted me."

William's hand muzzled Henry's and gripped tight, making Henry cringe and forcing him onto the bed. "Get me Simon," William rasped. "Only *he* can save me now. Get him and bring him here."

"I...I...can't," sputtered Henry, prying from the King's hold. "He's far away, Father, and can't help you. Only God can save you by releasing—"

"No!" roared William, rising an inch from his pillow. "Simon will come, he always comes, he'll brew me a potion, take away the pain. He'll make me well again. Find him!"

While Henry floundered for a placating answer, he glanced across the slim, modest bed, and beheld his Uncle Robert. At the mention of his son Simon's name, Robert had suddenly become attentive, and he leant forward to catch any secrets Henry might spill. "You fiend," snarled Henry. "You pressured him to ask for Simon, encouraged him, so you could discover Simon's whereabouts."

"No, Henry," countered Robert. "This is the first he's mentioned him. He's been delirious, spouting gibberish. Why does he ask for Simon? How can he help?"

"You won't induce me to divulge a thing, you shriveled old worm!"

But in fact, Lord Robert, Count of Mortain, Earl of Cornwall, and half-brother of King William wasn't shriveled, nor did he appear old. Remarkably preserved at the ancient age of fifty-seven years, he stood at average height, with a slim and rigid posture. His face, its skin bronze and taut and bones structurally sharp, displayed scant emotion. A band of white hair circled low on his bald pate, and his piercing pale blue eyes betrayed the emotion his expression lacked. "If Simon can help ease his misery, then he must be found! You know where he is, Henry and you'll tell me."

"Never," sneered Henry.

The King's groans stifled the argument and their attention returned to him. When his pain eased a bit, he spoke with rampant urgency, "Bring me Rufus, Archbishop William, Gerard, my chancellor, and my clerk. I will make confession now and distribute alms."

Rufus, the King's middle son, sat in a corner hidden by other members of the King's household. His powerful though portly body was sprawled across a padded chair, his fat bottom lip was thrust out in supposed deep thought, and his hard gray eyes focused on nothing. The call of his name disturbed the emptiness that cloaked his mind, and he came alive. He stood, brushed crumbs from his wrinkled tunic and braies, and ran greasy fingers through his shoulder length, stringy, golden locks. His choleric complexion colored a richer scarlet at the thought of listening further to his father's demented ramblings. Perhaps, he hoped as he lumbered toward the bed, now he'd finally receive what was rightly due him—great prestige, wealth, the duchy of Normandy, and yes, even the crown of England!

"Father, I'm here..." said Rufus, appearing at the side of Lord Robert and taking on an expression of mawkish submission. The chancellor, Archbishop, and clerk, armed with parchment and quill, shuffled in and positioned themselves round the bed.

The King struggled to sit and directed his atonement to the Archbishop, "I ask God for absolution for all my sins, mostly those committed in pursuit of the duchy and crown. To ensure the Lord's forgiveness, I require those who have injured me and reside in prison, with the sole exception of my traitorous brother Odo, be released..." His eyes shifted briefly to his brother Robert who had opened his mouth to object. William raised a hand to quiet him. "A special distribution of alms will be bequeathed to the clergy of Mantes, to restore their village."

But Robert could not contain his upset and intruded, "My Lord, how can you forgive all but Odo? Five long hard years you've kept him confined. He loves you, prays for your recovery and your soul! Don't forsake him, release him! He has humbly paid his debt to you and to God. His sole desire upon release will be to keep harmony amongst your kin and in your kingdoms."

"No..." answered William.

"God will not take kindly to any vindictive actions on your part, my dear Lord," reminded the Archbishop. "To enter Heaven, your soul must be free from any cruelty. To be forgiven, you yourself must forgive."

"No," repeated William.

In a rare show of desperation, Robert burst out, "Let him go! He's suffered enough. After your death, I'll need him, as will your sons, to restrain the heathens that inhabit England and Wales. They will revolt and only strong leadership can subdue them! You know well Odo's strength."

"Too well," muttered the King.

"He'll wield a strong arm and tame the traitors," continued Robert. "To appease God, and secure your kingdoms, you have little choice, Brother. Let him go!"

William dropped his hand back on his pillow, and closed his eyes. All present piqued to the action, and awaited his next retort with bated breath—but nothing came. A long while passed, and Robert gently prodded, "Your Grace, my dear brother, what is your decision? Will he be set free?"

Too weary to raise his head, William pried open his bleary eyes, and croaked a broken and reluctant, "Ye...yes. But take warning, Robert, he will wreak havoc wherever he treads. Keep him well reined and you, and *only* you, must take all blame for his wrongdoings. Is that clear?"

Robert dropped to his knees in subjugation, gushing, "Yes, your Grace! I thank you, he thanks you. Your generosity—"

"And if you so much as slap your son, Simon," William cut in grimly, "who is dearer to me than my entire brood combined, I vow to haunt you forever and make your life Hell on earth!"

"I doubt God will grant me the gift of seeing him again," said Robert. "I swear to you, dear Brother, if given my wish to ask his forgiveness in person, I will treat him kindly. Your generosity will be forever in our thoughts and prayers. Thank you, Brother, thank you."

"Enough of your groveling. As for my treasures, a good portion is to be distributed among the English and Norman abbeys and to the poor. The Kingdom of England, having been acquired not by hereditary right but by conquest and at the expense of countless lives, I leave to God, but I pray God will grant it to my son, William, to whom I bequeath my scepter, sword, and crown. Rufus, come close."

William Rufus wavered a bit at his father's pronouncement. Being the second son, he had expected to receive his father's English acquisitions, but what the King had spouted about leaving the Kingdom of England to God had confused him. What exactly was meant by, 'I pray God will grant it to my son, William'? Did William mean him? He was his son and a William as well. Hell, why couldn't his father speak a bit more simply? *Who is all this ridiculous drama directed at*, Rufus wondered; it certainly didn't impress him. "Father," he spoke, wiping mucus from his bulbous nose with his sleeve, "is England mine? Will I rule as King? As second son, it is my right. And what of Normandy?"

"Take this letter to Archbishop Lanfranc at Canterbury." William motioned for and received from the clerk a sealed letter addressed to the Archbishop. "He will crown you."

"But you've yet to say, what of Normandy?"

"Your Grace." The King's chancellor Gerard stepped forward and reminded, "You have promised Normandy to your eldest, Robert Curthose. By many he is already called Duke Robert."

"Yes," railed William, "he who strikes at me at every opportunity, conspires with the King of France against me, and cannot drag his loathsome self to my deathbed! He's unfit to rule a pig and gets nothing!"

"You once told me, your Grace," said Gerard, "that ruthlessness was a necessary trait of a successful ruler. Robert Curthose has expertly shown this skill, as have all your sons. They require a strain of cruelty in order to survive your death and their enemies. You cannot renege on your pledge, Sire. Normandy belongs to Curthose."

"Heed my advice, William," cut in the Archbishop, "forgive all who have done you injury."

"Forgive...forgive," muttered William, his head lolling with indecision. "I'm glad I will soon leave this wretched place, for I see it crumbling beneath you bumbling fools. Normandy will go to Curthose. Rufus, depart for Canterbury without delay, for I want no question or lapse in the ruling of England."

Rufus brightened and his cheeks and chest puffed with satisfaction and pride. He was a bit miffed at Curthose getting Normandy, but he'd best not argue, he'd snare it at a later time. Rufus smirked at Henry as he nudged him aside and sat by his father, took his hand, and said with resounding compassion, "I'm wholly grateful to you, Father. My love and complete homage will be with you for your remaining time on Earth and forever in Heaven." He then kissed William's hand and cheeks, and clutched the King's frail form in his huge embrace.

Once out of the gloomy chamber, Rufus' pompous grin reappeared. He motioned for his men, sitting in wait in the rushes, to rise, and he began his triumphant journey to England.

"What's left for me, Father?" asked Henry, resuming his spot by the King.

"Money...I'll give you money."

"But I'm a mere bachelor knight, and have no land on which to keep it."

"You've forgotten your mother's lands. You are her heir and may retain her dower lands in England."

"How much...how much money?"

"Five thousand marks of silver will be yours. Share your wealth with your cousin Simon. His loyalty and love should not go unrewarded. And ensure his protection after I've gone. Swear you will carry out this small request."

"I swear, Father," said Henry with deep disappointment.

"Strive to be a good lad and behave yourself. Be true to your brothers, and help them temper their contrary natures. You alone have the wisdom and calm nature to guide them."

Henry received but did not return his father's kiss. He stood and dropped his embarrassed gaze to the floor. He had to leave the room before the sniggering began! The Archbishop stepped forward to administer communion and last rites, and Henry ducked behind him and scurried for the exit. William's words, 'Be a good lad and behave yourself,' pounded in his ears and rouged his cheeks. He was no lad, but a man of nineteen years, a knight, a constant soldier, a diplomat, and owner of a shrewd mind! Yet, to his father, he would forever be a baby. Passed over! He'd been passed over for a fat, effeminate brute and a stumpy, feckless toad.

His ire bubbling, Henry roused his men with kicks and curses, and gathered up his few belongings. First he'd stop at Rouen Castle and the Royal Treasury to claim his gift, then attend his father's funeral and act the loyal son. He must then find Simon and warn him of the King's demise and his loss of protection. Yet his cousin would get none of the measly pittance allotted by his father. Claiming his mother's lands might prove tricky, but Rufus, idiot that he was, could easily be duped. He'd continue to play the fool, the intellectual, the brave and loyal subject to both his brothers, and juggle his allegiances as long as necessary till the time arrived for him to conquer all! As he strode from the abbey of Saint-Gervais, he lifted his face to the warm rain, and reflected on his raving tirade to God that had preceded his visit with the King. *Lord*, he prayed silently as he mounted his steed, *I have but one final request—make Father suffer awhile longer.*

The King spent the night of Thursday, the eighth of September in the year of our Lord 1087 in tranquility, and woke at dawn to the sound of the bells of Rouen Cathedral.

"What is that noise?" he mumbled.

One of his attendants replied, "Why, it is the bells of the church of St. Mary, my Lord."

William lifted his eyes to his bed's canopy, and decreed with raised hands, "I commend myself to Mary, the holy Mother of God, my heavenly Lady, that by her intercession I may be reconciled to her Son our Lord Jesus Christ." And then William the Conqueror, Duke William II of Normandy, and King William I of England, shut his eyes and expired.

After the Archbishop had confirmed the King's death, the assemblage of magnates quickly departed to secure their own property. His inferior attendants, being left on their own, turned crazed with greed. They stole the silver candlesticks, the wine flasks and cups, the gilded communion plate and wafers, and jeweled vanity items. In their frenzy, they dismantled and carted away the furniture and pilfered the linen bedclothes. When their thieving arms could barely hold more, they shoved their majesty from his bed, stripped him of his silk robe, rings and slippers, and left him nearly naked and alone on the floor of the cell.

*****

Inside Rouen Castle, the only outward sign of excitement Lord Robert allowed himself as he waited outside his brother Odo's prison chamber door was a shifting from foot to foot. Yet inside his sturdy body, his heart pounded to burst, the contents of his belly churned, and a tingling rushed through his veins. At last his beloved brother was to be released! Unjustly imprisoned, unfairly ostracized, and denied a defense, Odo had been confined five years to a Spartan but comfortable cell in the King's palace at Rouen. His supposed crimes—seduction of the Lord's vassals and intended tyranny directed at the Pope—had in Robert's estimation been a ludicrous accusation. Being a member of the clergy himself, Odo had always aspired to the most admirable behavior, and demanded no less of his soldiers. Granted, there had been problems of allegiance with the numerous 'popes' of late, but still, Odo's fealty to the head of the true church remained unsullied. The guard fumbled with the keys and Robert's impatience swelled. "Hurry, man! I would see my brother, now!"

"I'm trying, my Lord," answered the sentry, and Robert sighed as the tumblers cooperated and the thick wooden door swung wide.

Odo sat at a modest table, scribbling fiercely upon a scrolled parchment; many more skins sat stacked by its side. He guessed the intrusion was merely his breakfast and didn't bother to raise his head. A shadow fell across his scripting, and the long graceful fingers that splayed upon the table were unmistakably those of his brother, Robert. He lifted limpid blue eyes to his brother's beaming expression. Bliss erased Odo's look of confusion, and he stood with an exuberance that rocked the table and scattered the parchments to the rushes below. "He's agreed," was all he uttered.

"Yes," replied Robert as tersely.

They embraced, a huge hug tense with relief. Odo pulled back slightly to ask, "Is he gone?"

Robert simply nodded. Odo performed a quick sign of the cross, then slipped his arm in Robert's and announced with suspense, "Then we have much to do...I will bathe in the royal bedchamber, and when I'm done, we will share a meal there, and discuss...our future."

As they strode from Odo, Bishop of Bayeux and Earl of Kent's cell, Robert gazed admiringly up into his elder brother's face, a face as changeable as Odo's capricious moods. Now it betrayed a triumphant serenity—his mouth relaxed in a thin grin; his cheeks slightly puffed; his brows arched pleasantly; and his eyes pale, gentle, and reflective. How naive, minor, and at times bumbling Robert felt in his brother's majestic presence. Exalted Bishop, valiant soldier, and genius scholar were Odo's honors, and bravely had he acquired them. A need to repent overtook Robert and he mumbled meekly, "I tried to visit five months past, Brother, but I was barred from your cell."

"Yes...William's orders. He had the gall to accuse me of planning a course of seditious acts with his son Curthose. I'm so harassed by his suspicions that I feel him hovering now, ever listening..." They reached the King's bedchamber and, entering, found it freshly made up as if awaiting their arrival. Odo strode to the bed, knelt, and swiped his arm under the elaborately carved hunk of furniture. His smile widened as he extracted a small jeweled box. Under the lid he discovered a handful of rusted coins which he passed to Robert with the instructions, "Go and purchase me a gay suit of clothes, and one for yourself as well. We must dress for our roles as senior advisors, so make the tunics long and of the richest cloth—the shirts, braies, and hose are to be tailored in silk. I will burn my prison garb, and soak awhile. Return here in but an hour's time." Robert nodded, added the coins to his money bag tied to his belt, and turned silently to obey. Odo's blurt, "And Robert..." made him pause in the door and turn. "I am eternally grateful to you for your persistence...concerning my freedom. On your market jaunt, think on how I can repay your loyalty, for no matter how difficult or costly, the task will be done." In response, Robert grinned awkwardly and left his sibling swaggering about the great room as if he'd always inhabited it—and in Odo's mind he always had.

Odo freed himself from the drab, knee-length woolen tunic, patched linen shirt, worn woolen braies and hose that had branded him a nonentity, a misfit, and a criminal. After loudly demanding service for his most urgent wants to the servants, he patted neat his slightly receding silver gray hair and, as his hand caressed his square jaw and dimpled chin, he acknowledged he could do with a trim and a shave. He sat as a wave of ecstasy wobbled his knees. The thought of having power again was dizzying, yet it would most certainly come to pass. He congratulated himself for his forethought in having his nephew, Robert Curthose, sign a writ declaring Odo his chief advisor upon Curthose's ascension to the duchy. Odo had no doubt that Curthose was now indeed Duke, William having never reneged on a promise, at least to his knowledge. But what of England? He prayed to God that William hadn't made the dire calamity of bequeathing it to Rufus—that repugnant excuse for a man. He gazed down at his belly, and noticed that years of forced inactivity had produced quite a paunch on his otherwise trim and burly figure. Well, he decided, the vigor needed to bring these ravaged countries to some sort of order and rally together his avaricious kin would most certainly carve away the unwanted fat.

Robert stood in the dribbling rain with his band of men, staring down the market lane. The street was empty, and the stalls tightly trussed. He chided himself for not realizing that the town would be in mourning for the King's death. He didn't feel much like mourning himself, and of course suffered guilt because of his lack of emotion. But for the past four years, he had spoken little to his brother the King. If the truth be told, he'd been frightened to, afraid to face the punishment he duly deserved for trickery and mistreatment of members of his immediate family. He was glad the market was closed; he knew nothing of bartering, his wife usually tended to such trivial matters. *My wife,* he worried silently to a chronic cramp in his belly—*where is my wife?*

"Closed?" Odo asked Robert, who stood tentatively in the bedchamber's doorway.

Robert nodded and, to Odo's inviting wave, ventured forward. He joined his sibling at a table, resplendent with roast quail doused with the most delectable sauce and framed with apples and pears. A plump loaf of bread, a huge hunk of cheese, and a bowl of thick, fragrant butter decorated the cramped space as well. Robert grasped a silver goblet and gulped the claret, trying to tame his nervousness. It helped only a little.

"I should have realized as much," commented Odo. "After all, someone should mourn his departure."

Robert gazed with pained confusion at his brother, and Odo swiftly replied, "I'm jesting, Robert. Of course, I feel sadness. Now eat up. It would be a sin to waste this sumptuous feast. As for the clothes, William's wardrobe should suit us fine, after everything's been altered, that is."

"Where did you find those?" asked Robert, eyeing the striking outfit Odo now wore.

"The servants borrowed them from Curthose's chamber. The braies and tunic are a bit short, but a mantle will hide that. It appears he's already installed most of his belongings here. And what of our dear brother's final distribution of wealth? Who gets what?"

"Rufus—England, Curthose—Normandy, and Henry—money," Robert answered with perfunctory blandness.

"Damn," muttered Odo, "Why divide the countries? Surely, he knew what mayhem would ensue if—"

"Rufus was dear to him."

"How could he be so blind to Rufus' abominations?"

"He chose simply not to hear or see." The jittery state of Robert's belly caused him to abandon the quail and munch instead on a hunk of bread.

"Then we'd best visit England soon to see how we can remedy matters."

"What matters?" Robert mumbled.

"I'd rather not say, as yet..." Odo switched thoughts with a buoyant question, "And where is the harlot you call wife?"

Robert cringed to the slur, then answered petulantly, "Her name is Almodis, and, at the moment, I know not her whereabouts."

"So you've misplaced her—again?"

"Not exactly."

"Robert, don't speak riddles. You are such a bumbling fool when it comes to women. They are simply wards of the Devil and should be treated as such, locked away and taken out only for decoration or when one wishes to indulge in a bit of sin."

"I've sent her away for safekeeping."

"Safekeeping? From whom?"

"My son."

"Simon?!"

"No...Will."

"Don't be preposterous!" scoffed Odo. "Will's harmless. He talks brazenly, yet never acts out his treachery. He's a simpering coward and a leech, who lives richly on the plunder of your heroics. Yet he does own a shrewd mind, and that at least is worth preserving."

"Will wants my child killed."

"Child?!" Odo exclaimed. "What child? What *have* you been up to, Robert?"

"Almodis was pregnant when I sent her away."

"Pregnant?" Odo threw back his head and burst out a raucous cackle. "Oh my dear, dear brother, she has indeed muddled your weak little mind. That whore has coupled with the entire male population of Normandy, except myself of course, and, I suppose, England as well. Your child..."

"It is mine!" stressed Robert. "She swore as much, and she did care for me!"

With a discounting look, Odo resumed his meal, then stopped mid-chew to suggest, "Then our first mission will be to find her and the child and bring them back safely to your loving bosom."

The sarcasm that laced Odo's words stabbed like knives. Robert closed his eyes and saw again the forever haunting vision of Almodis, her dark beauty blighted by despair as she wailed a plea for her life and the life of her child—their child—and begged forgiveness for her lies, her adultery. He'd come to accept that he'd been a cuckold and a fool, but still his affection for her endured, and each day grew ever more painful.

"And what of your wayward son?"

Odo's question disturbed Robert's grief. "Pardon?"

"Your carnal mistake, what's become of your bastard?"

Robert self-consciously splayed his fingers across his pate and answered with a shrug.

"You've had five blasted years to do away with him!" castigated Odo. "And as always you've failed! Every day that vermin walks freely upon this earth is a slight to me! Well, I see what our second mission is to be."

"Simon won't be bothered," countered Robert.

"What is this? Do I detect a hint of caring in your voice?" Odo's fierceness erupted and quaked and strained his words. "I do hope you know, if I intend something, it is done. And the vengeance I intend on your bastard, I have rehearsed well these long, hard years. He put me behind a locked door, and will suffer as I've suffered, no, he'll suffer worse! You can accompany me in my search for him, or pretend that we never mentioned the reechy, vile cretin. Whichever—my revenge will be done!"

Robert heaved up from the table and stood to leave. Being reminded of his gross inadequacies as husband, father, and brother was excruciating and he could bear no more.

"Robert..." Odo forced his voice gentler, "We'll speak no more on this especially sordid subject. Stay with me awhile longer. I've missed you."

"No..." said Robert faintly. "I'm tired, I need sleep and time to consider matters...alone."

"Yes, I think that wise," relented Odo. He stood and collected his brother in a firm hug. "I am truly grateful for all you've done for me. We will find your wife. You need her sweetness and beauty to comfort you. Go now and rest." Two wet kisses placed neatly on Robert's cheeks sent him away to his craved solitude.

*****

8

During his stay at Rouen Castle, Henry availed himself of a splendid feast, pampered himself with a tumble with a nubile servant girl, and after he'd kicked her from his bed, enjoyed a restful night's sleep. This morning he had carefully removed his 5,000 marks of silver from the treasury, extracted a bag of marks for his immediate needs, and stashed the remainder in a separate locked box in the treasury's vault. He'd had his barber snip his coal-black shaggy locks to a more respectable fringed style and trim his beard snug to his fine baby-like skin. Henry then donned his most pretentious suit of clothing—silk shirt, light woolen tunic, linen braies and hose, leather laces, and short boots—and went wandering the halls in search of another willing wench. He found only his Uncle Robert, looking especially somber.

"Uncle Robert! Why so glum? I'd imagined you'd be twittering with glee. You have let Odo out, haven't you?"

Robert stopped, gazed up, and muttered dumbly at Henry's unexpected intrusion, "What are you doing here?"

"I've come to claim my pittance."

"Well, I'm still angry with you, and don't wish to waste my time—"

"Angry with me?" interrupted Henry. "Why ever for? You can't be referring to our romp at Pevensey."

Robert nodded curtly.

"But that was such great fun! I actually had you believing I'd be the next Duke of Normandy! What an exquisite actor I am, don't you agree, Uncle?"

"Not actor, Henry...liar."

"No one knew for certain...Father could have granted me Normandy."

"But he didn't, did he? I don't wish to talk to you...not now, not ever. Now let me pass."

"Now *you* lie, Uncle. You want very much to talk to me, because you're dying to know what's become of Simon and Maura. Your ward was in quite a wretched state when you last saw her."

Robert hesitated; his body and voice seemed to shrink. "Is...Is she alive, is he?"

"Yes...I'll tell you that much, and that they are at last wed. Their holy union was blest by Lanfranc, which makes it impossible for you or anyone else to sever their bond. I left them healthy and astonishingly happy."

Robert swallowed in relief, then chanced delving deeper, "Why did William ask for Simon? How could he have helped him? I know they were close, yet—"

"You are so ignorant, Uncle. I've always made a point of intimately knowing my supposed enemies, to determine whether it would be to my advantage to fight them or befriend them. In not knowing your son, you've wasted a valuable ally. Simon is a revered physician and mediator. Father simply wanted Simon to heal him as he'd done countless times before."

"I know about the mediating, but physician? When did he become—"

"No, Uncle Robert. That is all you deserve to know. If you want more, you may have to speak to Simon yourself, though I doubt you have the temerity to risk such a confrontation."

"Would he forgive me, Henry?"

"I sincerely hope not. Now, I'm off."

"Will you see him?"

"I may."

"If you do, will you warn him of Odo's release? It seems he's determined to find Simon."

"He won't. I'll see to that."

Robert nodded in gratitude and slumped away. Henry called after him, "But if I fail, and Odo does find him, always remember it was at your insistence that he was freed..." He then watched till Robert's miserable figure faded into the shadows, pondered a moment the bit, '...he's determined to find Simon', then strode on his way.

*****

The clergy of the monastery of Saint Stephen's in the town of Caen stood assembled in eager anticipation of the arrival of the body of King William. Their See had been selected to be the site of the late King's funeral. William's daughter Cecily stood with the congregation, having joined them from her sister house of the Holy Trinity in Caen, where she was abbess. She squinted severely down the high road leading through town and wondered at the delay. There was no rain to hamper the procession's progress; on the contrary, the clear sky was marred with but a few wispy clouds, and the sun shone huge and hot. She caught sight of a group of horsemen riding toward the monastery and, as they drew nearer, she recognized the handsome lad at the fore as her younger brother, Henry. She beamed and, with wide arms, hurried down the stairs to greet him. He stayed awhile in her comforting hug, then let go to gaze on her engaging face, framed by a starched, ponderous veil. Tendrils of auburn hair had escaped the hood, accenting her youthful, innocent visage. It seemed to Henry that her doe-like eyes always smiled, no matter what her mouth chose to say, and they smiled now as she suggested, "You'll wait by me for Father's arrival?" He nodded and joined her on the stairs. "Henry," she asked, "do you know what might have stalled the procession?"

"No, but if they don't arrive soon, I'll ride back to find the problem." He took her hand, and her tender touch instantly quelled his upset. Of all his sisters, Cecily reminded him most of his sweet mother Matilda. He recalled his heartbreak when his parents had given her to the abbey of the Holy Trinity as reparation for their sin of consanguinity. Her calming presence never failed to coax from him his innermost desires, fears, and troubles and he easily asked, "May I stay awhile after the mass, to talk?"

"Of course," said Cecily. "You are welcome to stay as long as you like, Henry. But I'm worried, they should have arrived by now. Will you ride back?"

Henry nodded and, taking a guard, journeyed back along the potted high road toward the village gates. He cantered past a gathering crowd and crooked, enmeshed buildings and saw smoke billowing above. Henry rounded a tight curve and reined his mount sharply to dodge shards of burning wood shooting from the collapsing wall of a blazing stable. He leapt from his saddle and, catching up a bucket from a villager, joined in a frantic attempt to douse the flames. Not far from the chaos sat William's funeral procession, waiting impatiently to proceed.

Henry's arms ached and burned from the effort of passing and wielding water-filled buckets. Ash, mud, and sweat smeared his face and had all but ruined his clothing; he hacked and gagged from the dense black smoke. At long last the fire began to dwindle, more from lack of fuel than from the villagers' efforts. Henry struggled to remount his steed, wiped his face as best he could with his sleeve, and joined his kin leading the procession.

"Is it safe to continue, Henry?" worried his Uncle Robert.

"I believe so." He sighed and aimed a smug smile at the erect figure straddling the horse next to Robert. "Uncle Odo. You look remarkably fit and regal in my father's clothes."

"And you, Henry, look very dirty. Next time let the peasants do the toiling. Remember your title and birthright."

"Haven't you heard, Uncle? I've no birthright and have been stripped of my title. A King's brother is nothing...but then you know that only too well." Henry's puzzled gaze shifted to a rather stiff looking, though comely, youth riding beside Odo. Tall and gangly, he appeared to be near Henry's age, perhaps a few years younger. He possessed a head of thick black hair, ashen skin, gaunt features, and startling dark eyes.

Odo noticed Henry's interest and explained, "Henry, may I introduce my clerk John. He was schooled at Bayeux and has exhibited great promise. Perhaps you can take him under your wing, introduce him to influential people, and share with him the peculiar workings of our family."

Henry burst a derisive laugh, jerked his horse around, and waved the train forward. Inside the cathedral, the priest droned on far too long, the air was thick and stifling with moisture, and Henry had the bad luck to be stuck beside his sister Adela, the formidable Countess of Blois. They hadn't spoken since they'd last traded profanities at Rouen shortly before Easter. A quick glance her way revealed a thick blond braid escaping her veil, curling over her shoulder and—unfortunately, thought Henry—failing to hide her priggish scowl. His critical eye strayed to her swelled belly. She was again pregnant, for the third time, he reckoned. He tried but failed to contain the barb that slipped from his smirk, "Well, Adela, you've become quite the brood mare." Her glower stayed on the priest while she ground Henry's toes with the heel of her boot. He barely restrained his howl as he shoved her; her harsher shove hurled him out into the center aisle. He scrambled to his feet, intent on drubbing her, pregnant or not, but a commotion at the back of the church ended their scuffle. All heads jerked to a man in peasant garb, flailing and raging at a slack-jawed cleric. Guards hustled the villein out the door, and the priest conducting the service begged all to return their eyes and thoughts to the late King. Henry and Adela exchanged snarls as her husband, Count Stephen, stepped between them.

The service done, a group of church attendants ventured forward to lower the King's body from atop its pedestal to a marble coffin set on the floor below. The four wavered beneath William's ponderous corpse as they fumbled to fit him in the too small casket. The congregation shifted in distress to the attendants' strained grunts and grumbled complaints. Then their grumbling abruptly ceased; they swiftly slid the marble slab atop the coffin, clamped hands to their mouths, and scurried away. The priest's face colored green, drew a swift sign of the cross in the air, and hurried after the attendants. The mourners shared bemused looks, then sniffed hesitantly at the air. In unison, their eyes bulged and skin paled. They masked their noses and mouths with handkerchiefs and hands and fought their way from the chapel.

Henry spilled out of the church, tripped down the stairs, and staggered behind a grove of lilac bushes. He fell to his knees and retched violently into the grass. When convinced his belly finally empty, he flopped limply to his side, coiled his body, and squeezed shut his eyes. His lids fluttered open to a cool, welcome touch on his brow. Cecily smiled wanly and explained, "The attendants burst Father's body forcing it into the coffin. That's what caused the stench."

Henry swooned and grasped her helping hand, then shook from his weakness and asked, "What was the commotion with the peasant?"

"He claimed he owned the land where the grave had been dug. They paid him and he went away. Will you attend the burial?"

Henry shook his head and Cecily insisted, "Then you'll come to my cell where I'll warm you milk and hear your troubles. I imagine you have a few...You look wretched." Henry nodded in assent and humbly trailed his sister to the Abbey of the Holy Trinity. Once there, they retired to a tiny yet comfortable cell furnished with only a modest bed headed by a crucifix, two rickety chairs, and a table built for one. Cecily and Henry snubbed the chairs, preferring instead to lounge upon pillows set on petal fragrant rushes. A small tiled fire pit centered the room, and as Cecily stirred its coals, a thin thread of smoke wound its way from the ashes upward and out a hole in the ceiling. She roused a few meager flames and hung a pot of milk over the pyre to warm. "So tell me, Henry, were you with Father at the end?"

"No, I left him the night before he died."

He spoke with scant emotion, and she probed, "Your final words...I hope they were friendly."

"I suppose." He shifted for comfort, his expression twitching with mystery.

"Then why are you angry with him?" said Cecily insightfully.

"He passed me over, gave me nothing."

"Five thousand marks of silver isn't nothing," said she.

"How do you know—"

"I heard a rumor. Is it true?"

"Yes...but the way he spoke to me...like I was a mere babe and incapable of—"

"Henry, I apologize for interrupting again, but if you could let go of your pride for just a moment, you'd see that to Father you *were* a mere child. And as long as you know you're grown, why does it matter?"

"But I'm wiser than either Rufus or Curthose, I read and write, and I'm far braver. Father became Duke at seven, so why am I not old enough at nineteen? He never let me prove my worth...never!"

Cecily rested a calming hand on his flailing arm. "He often came here and confessed his devotion to you and his need to protect you, not that you necessarily needed protecting. He didn't want you to rule."

"Why not?"

"Father wanted you to be a priest. When he realized how ludicrous that notion was, he was unsure what to do with you. Believe that he loved you, Henry, and wanted you to be happy."

Henry flushed at her too simple answer and lapsed into a sulky silence. Cecily strove to sway his mood by wondering aloud, "Last visit you spoke of a woman you claimed had stolen your soul. Have you got it back yet?"

Henry swallowed dryly and shrugged.

"Then perhaps," she went on, "you should go to her, talk to her. She may be able to comfort in ways I cannot."

"I will see her soon."

"Good, and will you tell her your feelings?"

"I can't."

"Why not?"

"She's married and won't accept my affection," argued Henry. "She cares for me simply as a friend and a..."

His guilty look prompted Cecily to sit taller and press, "A what?"

"Cousin."

"Henry, of whom are you speaking?"

"Maura."

Cecily hesitated a moment, her mind searching for the name, the face. And when they came to her, her jaw dropped, and she sputtered, "Ma...Maura, Uncle Robert's ward?"

Henry nodded.

"But she's Rufus' wife!"

"No...that marriage never took place," said Henry, "and Father annulled her next betrothal to a peasant soldier from Yorkshire so she could marry...Simon."

"Robert's son, Simon?"

"Yes..."

"That was kind of Father."

"She prefers Simon to me," snorted Henry.

"Well, I must say it is fitting though rare to prefer one's husband," commented Cecily. "Henry," she sighed with a censuring look, "why make your life so confusing? You're always wanting things that don't belong to you. I suspect if she returned your ardor, you'd lose interest quickly enough."

"No...Not this time!" he extolled with passion. "I've never known a woman like Maura. Once when we found ourselves in the midst of a siege, she fought for me, saved my life! I've told her secrets I've shared only with you. She's brilliant, beautiful, brave—"

"And she chose him."

"Why?" he whined, his despair rising.

"I think you know that answer. You and Simon have always been close. You worship him, everything that is his you covet, including now his wife. Simon is a fine man and an excellent mentor to you. I highly recommend you do nothing to jeopardize your bond. If you do, Henry, you will never forgive yourself."

Yet Henry did not hear her warning, for his mind had wandered back to when he'd last seen Maura—her beauty so simple, so warm; her eyes brimming with tears as she'd begged him not to leave angry, that she and Simon loved him and owed him so very much. All the while jealousy had chewed at his gut. And when she'd kissed him farewell, the kiss had burned, and he still felt the sting.

Cecily noticed his lids drooping and offered a cup of milk and the suggestion, "Now drink this and sleep. Your troubles will seem gentler in the morning." Henry gulped the milk, settled himself in the rushes, and gratefully accepted from his sister a blanket and good-night kiss.

Cecily stayed in the rushes awhile and watched Henry till he slept. Of all William and Matilda's nine children, she considered Henry the prettiest. Comely like his mother, tall like his father, one moment his expression reeked the sweetest innocence, the next devilish mischief or solemn maturity. If only he acted the latter a bit more often, Father might have seen him in a sensible light and bequeathed something more enduring than coins.

Dawn broke, chilly and dripping. Henry enjoyed a leisurely meal with Cecily and purposely steered their chatter toward the light and trivial. Then, after cramming her gifts of food into his saddlebag, he bade her farewell, rallied his guards, and departed for Abbeville, a village northeast of Rouen. There he would rest the night before traveling on to Bologne, Westminster, and, dare he consider...Wales?

On his journey, Henry kept his mind busy, for any reflection on the past fortnight wracked his soul with tremors of remorse, shame, and hatred. He distracted himself by concocting an ingenious plan to disgrace and discredit his kin, in particular the two dunghills that were his brothers. And only he possessed the wisdom and guile to carry out such an endeavor while pretending to be each one's most loyal, cloying subject. They would most certainly attempt to destroy each other, and he'd readily do battle for each, flitting in disguise between the opposing forces. They'd never realize his ruse, they were far too dim. Yet try as he might, he could not shake off the heavy pall of emotions that continued to knot his belly and wrench his heart.

The dripping turned into a tempest, dumping rain into puddles the breadth of ponds. The puddles sucked at Henry's stallion's feet and grating winds hampered his pace. He suspected something else amiss yet couldn't quite locate the cause. Then as he stopped to watch one of his men dig mud from his steed's shoe, it came to him. Somehow, he'd gained an extra guard! He dismounted and slogged from mount to mount till he discovered John of Bayeux. "Why are you following me?!" he barked over the noisy deluge.

"I got bored and escaped. Besides, Bishop Odo mentioned you were the one I ought to emulate. How can I do that if I don't follow you?"

"You might have asked."

"And you might have said 'no'. Now, I'm certain your benevolent nature won't desert me in this bog. When we reach shelter, we'll talk, and if you don't like me, you can leave me there."

"And if I don't care to talk?"

"Then we'll sing. I hear you own a lovely voice."

Henry couldn't help but smile; John reminded him a bit of himself, years back. Wearily, he nodded and said, "You may follow, but not intrude. Is that clear?"

"As air, my Lord," muttered John, as Henry released his horse and tramped back to his own, already regretting his too swift surrender.

It was far past nightfall when the troop arrived before an unassuming residence on the outskirts of the village of Abbeville. Exhausted, drenched, and chilled, Henry slipped from his saddle and passed his mount's reins to John. "See to my horse's care," he ordered, "then join me inside."

"Why stop here?" John said, askance.

"Ralph, the owner, offers his home to travelers for a coin. It is familiar and comfortable."

"How's the food, my Lord. I'm famished."

"My interest doesn't lie with the food," smirked Henry.

John struck a confused expression and led Henry's steed away. Henry staggered stiffly inside the dimly lit cottage. A majority of the lodgers, mostly soldiers, had finished their fare and found themselves cozy spots amongst the rushes to sleep. Ralph, a wiry, blemished man, intent on shooing the late visitor away, looked up harshly from scouring a huge trestle table. But seeing the beleaguered FitzRoy, he softened his expression and spoke with deep compassion, "My Lord, we received the tragic news from your brother, Robert Curthose. Come, drown your sorrow with a tankard of ale and have a bowl of stew. I'll have your room made ready and—"

"I'll see Sybil," spouted Henry.

"It's past time for her to be awake and—"

His eyes cruel, Henry demanded, "Bring her to me now!"

"I don't think that wise, my Lord. Much has happened since your last visit."

"One further argument, Ralph, and you'll have no hand to scrub those tables with, nor will you have any tables, nor a home. I'll see her and I'll see her now!"

Ralph had suffered the Prince's tantrums many a time and harmless they always were, but a hardness had captured Henry's expression, frightening in its intensity. Ralph haltingly motioned toward the chamber kept ready for distinguished visitors, and said with a quaver, "Set...settle yourself, my Lord, and I will send my daughter in to you."

"Do so and quickly!" shouted Henry as he sidled the tables, rounded a plump cauldron burbling a greenish stew, and marched into the minuscule chamber. His squinty gaze strayed to the room's sole window. A slim leather thong holding the shutters together strained against a raggling gale. Rain spit through the slit between the shutters, dampening the rushes and muddying the ground. A slim candle, a chamber pot, and a full tankard of ale flanked the larger of two mats. Henry's lips curled in a leer as he recalled the countless times he'd lain upon this mat, nuzzled up against Sybil's long, leggy, voluptuous form. No wench was as accommodating to his carnal needs as she. He never knew why, nor had he asked; he hadn't really cared.

14

Henry flung his soggy cloak in a corner and flopped down upon the mat. The ale he guzzled gratefully, leaving its foam to mingle with his beard. The door creaked, and a trail of light crept across the ground. When it reached him, he pushed up on his elbows. She stood in the doorway, her figure in shadow, and appearing a bit more voluptuous than he'd last remembered. "Sybil," he whispered loudly, "is it you?"

"Yes, my Lord," she whispered back.

Never had she called him 'my Lord' at least not when they were alone, and her tone betrayed a twinge of trepidation. Henry cocked his head quizzically and made himself sound caring, "Come inside, my sweet. I need your comforting. You've heard about my father?"

"Ye...yes..." she sputtered, not moving from the doorway.

His confusion grew; he patted the spot by his side. "Come here beside me. I need your touch."

"No, Henry."

Had he heard correctly? He burst a surprised guffaw, then turned dreadfully serious. "Enough games, my dear, come here now."

"I can't, Henry," she whined.

"And why *can't* you?"

"Because...I...I..."

Her diffidence riled Henry. He rose and strode the few feet to her side, and when her face became visible he saw it wasn't his imagination, it was rounder, as was her belly. He lost his fingers in her thick black tresses and a charming smile filled his face. "And so, we've made another one." His arms circled her waist, and he licked, then murmured in her ear, "You needn't fret, my sweet, I'll be gentle with you, and I love how your breasts swell when you're with child—"

"It's not yours, Henry," Sybil bluntly announced, detangling from his clutch.

"What?"

"You didn't father this child."

"If not I, then *who* may I ask did?"

"My...my hus...husband," she stammered and flinched away.

"Your husband?" he said incredulously; but after his puzzlement ebbed, his bile surged. "You have no husband. No one would marry you, you ugly, fat, lying bitch!" He caught her arm and wrenched her close. "You'll lie with me this night and give me all I ask for. I'm in no mood for discussions."

"Sybil?" The deep disembodied voice reverberated through the chamber like thunder and for a moment wilted Henry's command. He eased his grip and peered warily beyond Sybil to the door. In its frame loomed a beast of a man who stood at least a head taller and a whole body thicker than Henry. His voice struck terror as it boomed, "What is the trouble here?!"

"Nothing, Herbert," squeaked Sybil, wriggling from Henry's hold. "I was only speaking with an old friend."

"Old friend, my arse!" shrilled Henry. He jerked her back and stupidly taunted, "This whore is mine, and will always be mine, as is this child, and all her other brats. She'll do for me this night, for I am brother to the Duke and the King and have what I want when I please and you, you gross, slimy hog won't dare do a thing to stop me! Now leave us, I've missed your wife's charms, pig that she is. Unless, of course, you care to stay and watch?" He forced open her robe, exposed her breast, and roughly fondled her nipple, pinching till she cried out in pain. She shrieked and beat from his grasp. Her sound box to his ear reeled him backward, but he swiftly recovered his balance and struck her jaw, knocking her to the mat. Ralph elbowed past Herbert, stopped short and stood aghast as Henry dove onto Sybil, ripped off her robe and forced her still with his weight. While his knee wedged apart her legs, his mouth smothered hers and tasted blood.

"Stop him, you bumbling oaf!" hollered Ralph to Herbert. Yet the oaf didn't move, he stood swelled up, dumbly puffing raspy breaths, and waiting...

And what he waited for and had suspected all along soon occurred. The fight left Sybil and Henry. Her lips, arms, and legs clamped him in a vise-like hold. She broke from their kiss and breathlessly mewed, "It is your child, they're all yours. You swore you'd take me from here, you promised, but you ran after the red-headed girl and didn't come back! What could I do? Herbert's kind to me...but...but Henry...oh, Henry," she wailed, "I missed you so!" Naked, wet, and willing, her lusty gyrations excited Henry to the point that he didn't care who watched. He couldn't tear his mouth from hers as she tugged at his tunic, and he grunted, cursed, and struggled with the waist cord of his braies.

Herbert's huge hand grabbed a fistful of tunic and shirt and easily lifted Henry a few feet above Sybil's splayed and panting body. Henry squirmed, swam for freedom, and howled as Herbert dragged him by the hair into the main hall. There was no time to muster strength, scream for help, offer a prayer! Herbert's fist struck Henry's face once, twice, and the force of the third blow catapulted Henry backward over two tables, crashed him into a chair, splintering it to kindling, and flung him up against the opposite wall where his flight at last ended. He slumped, unconscious and bleeding, to the rushes. The snoring hulk beside him never stirred.

*****

CHAPTER TWO - A PORTENTOUS VISITOR

"I do hope this isn't the behavior I'm supposed to emulate," noted John as he wiped blood from Henry's lip. "If so, I aim to return to Bayeux. It's quieter there."

Henry struggled to rise and batted away John's helping hand. He strained to focus on his surroundings, and spit a tooth as he stammered, "Where...where's Sybil. I'll *have* her..." He paused to swallow blood, then finished with vigor, "...now!"

"She was hauled away at least an hour past. Took three men and her brute of a husband to restrain her. She seems quite enamored of you…but you're in no condition to have anyone just now. Rest awhile. I'll fetch ale." He waved and mouthed his request to a nearby serving maid who looked astonishingly similar to Sybil.

Henry managed to rise to his knees before tipping again into the rushes. His head felt about to burst, vomit mingled with the blood in his throat, and every inch of him ached. "Am I going to die?" he moaned.

"I doubt it. Sleep is what you need, a spirit induced sleep to dull the hurt." The maid handed John the ale. He supported Henry's back and pressed the rim of the cup to Henry's mangled lip. "This is the most potent brew Ralph could find. He fetched it specially for you. I'm amazed he's let you stay, considering. And I believe, though I can't say for certain, he muttered something about one of his other daughters entertaining you in the future."

"I don't want his other sluts, I...I want Sybil," sputtered Henry between slurps. The last drop of ale passed between the Prince's lips and John carefully lowered him back to the rushes. He balled up his cloak to serve as a pillow, plumped and tucked it beneath Henry's head, then mentioned to the overly attentive maid, "The FitzRoy could do with a blanket, please."

"Stop fussing over me," harped Henry, swatting at John's fidgeting.

"But I've trained my whole life to serve," said John emphatically. "I know nothing else."

Henry considered this bothersome youth hovering above him, bloodied handkerchief in one hand, the other bracing the cup. Perhaps he did need someone to take on the perilous task of looking after him, for he admittedly owned a penchant for attracting potentially lethal situations. Henry sighed in torment and cringed as he shifted for comfort. "You may stay with me..." he muttered low and added with suspicion, "granted you don't order me about or attempt to steal my women."

"I don't know how to order about, and your women won't interest me, my Lord."

"Are you saying you suffer from Rufus' malady?" spat Henry in disgust.

John scoffed a laugh, "No...but, I have no knowledge of women, intimately or otherwise. And at moments like this, I wonder if I indeed want any knowledge."

"God's breath, man! You've been under Odo's rule for far too long...and that's downright unhealthy. I've heard he loathes all women. But I'll share a secret—while training at his castle at Rochester, I caught him a number of times *not* loathing them," Henry sniggered, then added, "Perhaps you should strive to emulate my behavior of awhile past. Tumbling with a wench livens the blood, puts a bounce in your step—"

"You're not exactly bouncing now," noted John.

"The difficulty I suffered here was a rare occurrence—for myself. And why did it occur? Because Sybil preferred me to her bullish lout of a husband. Listen well to my advice, boy, for I am expert on the topic of females."

"I will gladly heed your counsel, my Lord."

"Perhaps," noted Henry slyly, "if you perform your new office as my master butler with aplomb, decorum, and discretion, there are a few *friends* I might be willing to share...We shall see."

"I will handle my temptations discreetly. I must say, my Lord, your vocabulary is highly impressive."

"That's Simon's doing."

"Who?"

"Simon, my cousin and the most remarkable member of my family. He's Uncle Robert's bastard, half English, half Norman. Very learned. On our missions together, he prided himself on improving my diction."

"Well, I applaud his efforts. I assume that you two are no longer together?"

"No...He's embarked on a new life of wedded bliss in Wales. I'm on my way to warn him of Father's death. There are scoundrels about who intend him harm."

"Then I look forward to meeting your cousin...Simon."

"I'm surprised you've not heard of him," said Henry.

"Why should I have?" wondered John.

"Odo despises Simon. Claims he was the cause of his incarceration. I'm surprised he didn't try to poison your mind against Simon."

"I've spoken little to the Bishop. I spent most of my time at Bayeux in the company of my fellow clerks."

"Yes, well. I don't want details of your *doings* with the clerks. I've heard you're a perverse lot. I require only your complete homage."

"You have it, my Lord—Henry."

"Now I will sleep. Stay close...I may want for something in the night."

"I won't leave you, my Lord."

A flutter of doubt tickled Henry's belly as he shifted away from his newly appointed butler and squeezed shut his eyes. The boy, though dreadfully naive, did seem sincere. Yet he, Henry, was such a wretched judge of character, except, of course, when it came to Simon. How terribly he missed his cousin, especially his companionship, nagging guidance, and loyal affection. In truth, Henry felt lost without his mentor, and snuggling down in the rushes, he imagined their joyous reunion, replete with a bit of wrangling, cheering tales, jesting, comfort and—The tickling in his belly intensified as an enchanting vision intruded on his fantasy...Maura.

*****

Gael crouched her petite self down by Simon's curled up form and reached to shake him awake. But she hesitated a moment and studied him instead. He appeared angelic in sleep, a bushy angel with a copper colored beard, and abundant, gold, tousled hair. Then his lean, long, body coiled tighter, his pristine expression turned worried, his slightly pouting lips tensed, and his slim brows merged to an all too familiar brood. A shudder took him, and he muttered fearfully.

She rescued him from his fretting dream with a shake and soft call, "Simon...Simon, wake up."

He did so, too quickly and, still caught in his nightmare, cried out, "Maura! Maura, where—"

"No, Simon..." Gael cupped his chin and lifted his frantic gaze to her soothing one. "It's Gael. Maura's back home at Mynyw. Prince Rhys asks for you."

Simon wiped slumber from his pale blue eyes and sat with a shivering yawn. It was always dark in the Prince's longhouse and he asked, "How long have I slept?"

"A few hours. Not nearly enough."

Simon unfolded himself from the rushes and raked hair from his eyes. "How does he seem?"

18

"Better...His gruffness has returned, he's asked for food, and..."

"And what?" asked Simon, concerned.

"He pinched me."

"Then he's definitely healed." Simon managed a pert smile while helping Gael up. "Perhaps we'll be allowed to return home."

"You go. I want to stay on a day more. I haven't had the time with my sister that I'd hoped for."

Simon nodded, and as they trod upon a carpet of rushes toward a dividing tapestry Gael wondered, "What was your dream?" Simon shrugged, but she pressed further, "Tell me. It upset you."

"I've...I've had an inkling ever since last evening that something's amiss at home. And my dream confirmed my suspicions."

"Simon..."

"I shouldn't have come here, Gael, or stayed this long," he muttered bitterly. "I should not have left Maura alone."

"She's not alone, she has the villagers and Gruffydd."

"He's but nine years old!"

"My son is very capable," said Gael with umbrage.

"I'm not arguing that point, but my place is with Maura!"

"You've pledged to be the Prince's physician, and in doing so agreed to come here whenever he's in need of your services."

"Well I've made him better and now I want to go home."

"He won't deny you that," said Gael.

"He might..."

"Why would he?"

Yet she didn't get her answer. Simon shoved his soiled, wrinkled shirt in his braies, swatted an irksome lock of hair from his eye, then shoved aside the tapestry and determinedly approached the Prince's bed. Prince Rhys ap Tewdwr, ruler of the Kingdom of Deheubarth in south Wales, sat propped by pillows upon an unadorned bed wedged in a corner of the timbered llys called Dinefwr, home to his dynasty. Dawn filtered through cracks in a shuttered window above his head, casting a halo round his thick black curls, broad furrowed brow, plump jocund cheeks, and well cropped mustache and beard. The fever that had plagued him a full week had left his eyes, and now their blackness shone with a grateful glow as he clutched the pelts atop his round belly and boomed, "Simon, my lad, I'm much restored this morn. You mix such magical potions! When can I rise?"

Simon rested his slim backside on the bed and answered with a touch of sternness. "You're not to rise till the day after tomorrow. Allow your body the time it needs to heal."

"I swear to obey. Now I expect you'll be wanting to return to your gem of a wife. Oh how I envy you! Tell me again why she didn't accompany you? Her comforting way would lighten any man's troubles, especially my own."

Simon smiled knowingly and related, "Not long past, she experienced pains and some bleeding. She seems well enough now, but we felt it best if she remained home. As you can well imagine, I'm anxious to see how she fares."

"Yes, indeed. When is that child of yours due to arrive?"

"Shortly after Christmas."

"Then we will have the grandest feast to celebrate both the birth of Our Lord Jesus Christ and your little one as well! You are free to go after you've instructed my servants how to brew up your curing draughts."

"Is that all you require?" Simon chanced asking.

"Yes, I believe so. But tell me again that wonderful word you used to describe my tortured belly."

"Oh yes...borborygmus."

With a hearty laugh Rhys mimicked, *Bor...bor...rigmus*! Such a funny word. And tell me again, Simon, how did you fill your marvelous mind with such jeweled words?"

"Studies. Lots of studies." Not wanting to discuss his entire life of schooling again, Simon gifted Rhys an appeasing grin and prescribed, "Remember, stay abed one day longer, then take care not to tire yourself. Drink the draughts till your nausea calms completely."

"I will...and..." Rhys performed a sly wink and requested, "Kiss her for me, a long wet one."

Simon blushed scarlet, bowed his head, and rose to leave. He had almost reached the tapestry when the Prince's ebullient voice called, "Simon...wait." He tensed, knowing what was to come next—it always did, and he dreaded the words. "I've quite forgotten," added Rhys, "I've payment for you."

That wasn't what he expected to hear, and Simon glanced back, puzzled. "I don't ask payment."

"I can offer, can't I?"

Simon shrugged and sputtered, "But...I...I don't need—"

"Take this," Rhys insisted, extending his balled fist. Simon held his hand beneath the Prince's, and Rhys dropped a ring into it, gold and embossed with intricately entwined circles.

Simon turned the ring over in his palm and questioned, "I don't understand?"

"It was to be my eldest son's, but he doesn't seem the least bit interested. I'm weary of seeing it in its box so lonely and have decided of all the people I know you would be its most worthy owner."

"This is far too gracious," humbly countered Simon. "I can't accept—"

"You can and will. You and your sweet wife have brought much gladness to my household and peace to my territory and are deserving of a great deal more than a simple band of gold."

Simon studied the ring more closely. "The pattern, does it have significance?"

"Yes, it stands for benevolence and perseverance. The attributes of a fine ruler. Which is fitting, don't you think?"

"I'm no ruler," scoffed Simon.

"You rule over my health! No more arguing, take it, give it to Maura, wear it yourself, sell it if you like. I do hope, though, that you'll choose to keep it."

"I'm grateful, Rhys."

"As am I."

Simon tried again to leave and was halfway beneath the tapestry when the usual cringe worthy order sounded, "Simon, you will visit Nesta before you go. She's been a mite peaked of late and has asked for you."

His eyes closed, his shoulders slumped, and his lips formed a curse. He started to argue but thought better of it. Whenever the Princess' name was mentioned, arguing instantly became futile. "I'll see she's taken care of," muttered Simon as he ducked away.

Gael sat at a trestle table in the spacious open hall, opposite the partitioned rooms, plaiting her sandy blond hair. Her child-like features pinched in distress at the sight of Simon storming across the hall. She rose and gasped, "What's happened?!"

"Only what I dreaded..."

"Has he gotten worse?"

"No, it's not to do with Rhys. He's ordered me to see to Nesta."

Gael didn't catch the problem, shook her head slightly, and prompted, "And..."

"I won't see her!" groused Simon.

"Why ever not?"

"She's not ill," Simon continued with petulance. "She's never ill. She's asked for me so she can practice her seduction tactics."

"Her what?"

"She parades for me."

"Parades for you?"

"Yes...naked!"

Gael stifled a guffaw, and tried to sound as severe as her raving friend. "Simon I do believe your lack of sleep has dulled your sanity. What *exactly* is your complaint?"

"I won't play her games. I want to go home!"

"But every time you've come before, Maura's come with you."

"Yes, and on several occasions she's witnessed the parading as well," said he. "We're not entirely certain which of us Nesta's trying to entice."

"This is too silly to be believed."

"I agree, that's why *you're* going to talk with her."

"Me? Why me?"

"You're better at this sort of thing."

"What sort of *thing*?" asked she.

"Taming wayward girls."

"I'm grateful for the compliment, Simon," she noted sarcastically. "But what exactly am I supposed to say to the parading Princess?"

"If I knew *that*, she'd have stopped long past."

"I don't feel sorry for you," snorted Gael. "Most men would gladly suffer your problems."

"Then you find those men," flared Simon, "bring them here, and let her strut for them! I haven't time for her nonsense."

"Yes, my Lord. Whatever you say, my Lord," mocked Gael with a curt bow.

"Fine, I'm going home," Simon stated decisively as he squirmed into a patched light woolen tunic and slung a saddlebag across his shoulder. Then he hesitated, scowled another "Damn," and whined a plea, "Will you please tell Rhys' cooks how to brew the draught? I've left a week's worth of the clove pink, anise-seed, and fennel."

"I will, and take care. Kiss my son for me. Tell him I'll be back very soon."

"We're thinking of giving Gruffydd the colt," mentioned Simon, "if you agree, that is."

"That's very sweet. He'll be ecstatic."

"I do appreciate your staying," said Simon meekly.

"Yes, yes, I know you do. Now go. And I'm certain Maura will laugh when you tell her your dream."

"I pray you're correct."

They kissed cheeks; she smirked and waved him off, then watched fondly as he trod from the room and out the house. As she completed her braiding, she recalled wistfully how Simon had come into her life. After the puzzling death a year past of her husband Rhodri, the Pennaeth of Mynyw, she and her son Gruffydd had suffered a dire loneliness. Then one glorious day in June, Simon had arrived to fill their emptiness with his indulgent friendship, a friendship that had been forged five years earlier when Simon, disowned and banished, had sought refuge in South Wales. After he'd completed his medical training in the village of Myddfai, he'd settled in Mynyw and resided a happy year with Gael's family. Then to her family's great sorrow, Simon's uncle King William had ordered Simon back to England to act as mediator and he had grudgingly complied. Yet he'd sworn they'd be together again, and had honored that pledge, returning to seek sanctuary in the one place that had wholly accepted him. He was of her Saxon blood, spoke her language, and acted as loving guide to her son. And to Simon, Gael was heartily thankful for the present of Maura, who had grown to be as dear a companion to her. For a short moment she recalled Simon's portentous dream, but then spying his bow lying in the rushes, a worry cut short her musing—he'd left alone and without protection! She hurried to the main door of the llys, leapt puddles out to the gate, and peered down the winding road, alight with a rising mist and the glow of the waking sun. He was nowhere in sight, and she was certain he hadn't waited for the escort of Prince Rhys' guards. *Oh Simon,* she chastised to herself, crossing her arms with a huff, *will you ever learn to take the time to consider your own safety?*

*****

Maura sprawled languidly upon a mattress of sumptuous feathers, her flame red hair splayed like a shimmering veil across a pillow, her sapphire blue eyes fixed on a vent in the timbered thatched roof, and her mind atangle with worry. Six days he'd been gone; two days too many! When he'd left for Dinefwr, bow strapped to his back, he'd assured her with a nervous grin that he'd carried the weapon solely for catching them a rabbit or quail. But she'd known better and now feared the worst.

Each morning she allowed herself a time for lamentation over her husband's absence before attending to her many chores. This being their first separation since their marriage, she had not been prepared for the regret and upset she felt over her insistence that he go without her. And he'd taken her next-closest companion, Gael, who had wanted to spend some long overdue time with her sister who was a servant in Prince Rhys' household. Maura was grateful for Gael's son Gruffydd's perky presence and over-enthused assistance, but their conversations had proven fairly limited, and centered mostly around his mother and Simon's return, his whittling, the colt, and when Simon would take him fishing again.

As she caressed her belly, she rejoiced in the feel of its slight bulge. And then, for the first time in her pregnancy, the babe inside her ever so softly returned her touch. Bliss flushed Maura's freckled face and bolted her upright. She swiped at an ecstatic tear, sucked a breath and waited. Again, the fluttering came, stronger this time. Maura swooned with joy and hugged her belly, bubbling to herself, *It is real, he's real or...she. I must tell Simon, he'll be so thrilled!* She scrambled up from their bed and, in her zeal, stubbed her toe on the cradle Simon had finished crafting before he'd gone. Pain awoke the truth—he wasn't anywhere near to tell and despair sank her back to the bed. How terribly she missed him, every bit of him, and a whispered prayer trembled her lips, "*Please* Lord, let it be today. I do so want him back—today."

A knock and tiny voice intruded, "Maura...May I come in?"

She snatched up a sleeveless unbleached woolen tunic lying at the base of her bed, and tugged it over her translucent linen chemise. "Of course," she mumbled as she smoothed the tunic's skirt and adjusted the long clingy sleeves of the chemise.

The door cracked ajar wide enough for Gruffydd's head, topped with a shock of auburn hair, to pop through. "Are you sick?" he asked with a hint of worry.

"No," she assured, waving him inside. "Why would you think that?"

"I remember how the mornings used to be for you," he said as he gingerly entered, fumbling self-consciously with the skirt of his too large, loosely woven tunic.

She grimaced to the memory. "And the afternoons and the evenings. I was quite wretched, wasn't I?"

"Not really." He gazed at her with vague uncertainty, while adding, "I heard you cry out."

22

"I stubbed my toe on the cradle." She knotted a braided girdle slightly below her thickening waist and, with one hand splayed protectively over her belly, knelt to find her slippers. As she searched she considered sharing the movement of the baby with Gruffydd, but not keen on adding to his confusion surrounding her pregnancy, she decided against it. Irritation gripped her as she crawled through stale rushes and hunted beneath assorted piles of discarded clothing. She happened upon a chewed soup bone, and the solution to the missing slippers came to her. "Henry's taken them...again."

"Taken what?" asked Gruffydd.

"My slippers. Have you seen him this morning?"

"No."

"I'm certain he's buried them. Do you remember where his hiding spot is, Gruffydd?"

"I think so."

"Then we'll fetch the trowel and go dig them up," she grunted, rising. "I hope he's not buried them too deeply. Last time, I was so pleased with rescuing them that I didn't think to look inside and slipped my toes into a nest of worms!"

Explosive laughter doubled Gruffydd over. Maura tried to stop her smile while plaiting her hair and mildly chiding, "So you think that's funny, do you? Well then, when we find them, I'll allow you the honor of scooping them out." She wrapped a linen veil round her head, fastened it securely beneath the two thick plaits, and wondered, "Is it very late?"

The boy ignored her question and asked instead, "Why do you wear that? My mam never covers her head."

"Her head doesn't broil in the sun like mine does." She wandered to the wall flanking her bed and drew open the shutters. The sun warmed her cheeks as she drank in the heavenly scent of wild roses, iris, and blue-bells. Noting the high position of the sun, she turned and inquired, "Why didn't you wake me?"

"There wasn't need," said Gruffydd. "The chores are done."

Her mild tone sharpened with bother. "Gruffydd, you're not to do everything. I'm not an invalid."

"What's an invalid?"

"Someone who's sick and needs to stay abed."

"But Simon said—"

"I know what Simon said." Maura splashed her face with water scooped from a washing bowl set upon a rickety table by the bed, then mumbled into a linen towel, "You've reminded me countless times what Simon said. I must keep my hands and mind busy. If I don't, I think too much, then I start to—"

"Worry?" he finished for her.

"Yes."

"So do I." The brightness faded from his pale greenish blue eyes, identical in color to his mother's; he pursed his thin lips and whined, "How long till they come home?"

"I wish I knew. I've offered prayers for them to come today." She beckoned him close, bent to his level, and grasped his hands to assure, "I'm certain it will be soon. Have you left me anything to do?"

"You need to cut the herbs and mix the poultices."

"Good. If we keep each other busy the time will pass more swiftly, and before we realize, they *will* be back. Have you eaten?"

"Yes...I've cooked oats. There's some warming for you."

"You are a wonder," she sighed and, with joined hands, they strolled through the door into a larger room. Maura paused before a tall trestle table set under a broad window, its shutters drawn wide. Dried flowers and greenery crowded the table top and

23

dangled from the window frame and rafters in the ceiling. She reached past a marble slab, a mortar, a strainer, a silver balance, and pots filled with honey and lard to fetch a thick crudely bound book. Flipping to its marked page, she browsed over the columned scripting till she found the correct date's entry. "There's not much to prepare this day," she noted to Gruffydd. "When I'm done and the poultices are delivered, would you care to walk on the beach?"

"Yes! Oh yes, we'll go to the beach!" he exclaimed with a little jump. "And can we bring Henry? Please?!"

"If he's not too much of a nuisance."

As if he'd heard his name, a tricolor mutt of a pup, who seemed to be all feet and ears, came loping through the opened main door of the cottage. Not known for grace, he immediately collided with a stack of bowls stocked with bulbs of onions and garlic. Chaos erupted as the bulbs rolled and he chased after them. Maura caught up a broom and barked orders, "Henry, stop! Out! Get out now!" He barked back in glee, shot past her swipe, then skidded round a tiled, smoldering fire pit hung with a plump cauldron, and escaped beneath another larger trestle table pushed up along the side wall. "Come out from there now!" yelled Maura, squatting and wielding the broom handle. A few pokes to his bottom dislodged him and Gruffydd, laughing and using a shriller, more congenial voice, coaxed him out the door. "Get him to lead you to my shoes!" called Maura after them. "I'll join you after I've mixed the poultices."

After retrieving the bulbs, she scooped oats from the cauldron into a wooden bowl, added milk from an earthen jug gracing the trestle table, and took the bowl and spoon with her to the physician's table. She perched herself on a high stool, spooned and stirred honey into the gooey mixture, and ate contentedly while reviewing medicinal recipes. When full, she abandoned the bowl and began crushing a clove of garlic in the mortar. Occasionally, she raised a loving glance to the young ones rollicking amongst wildflowers and gnarled oaks. The site of their property, spread over a plateau topping a sheer hill, provided a generous view of the commote of Mynyw, including its cathedral and the sea, this day blinding in its serenity. When the air was particularly clear a peek of Ireland was possible. The damp heat of summer had persisted through the first two weeks of September and, as Maura wiped sweat from her brow and swatted a bee from the rim of the honey pot, she longed for the brilliant hues and crispness of autumn.

Her fingers ground the pestle to the clove and her thoughts snuck back to the lusciousness of her bed and her husband. She closed her eyes and felt again his warm lips tasting hers, then creeping their way down her neck and along her body to secret places that yearned to be caressed and nibbled. A crash jarred her rapture and she looked to the floor where pieces of mortar lay strewn in the sparse rushes, with garlic pieces scattered everywhere. "God's breath," she cursed, then moaned, "Come home, Simon! Only with you near can I keep my mind on work."

"Maura!" Gruffydd's cry, spiked with alarm, thrust her from her seat and to the door. "Maura, there's someone..." he yelled, racing toward her, his hair blowing every which way, eyes bulging, and mouth gaping. He skidded to a halt before her, gasping and stammering, "A man...a man on a Norman stallion...not Simon...climbing the hill...coming here!"

Her heart leapt to her throat and pounded there as she yanked Gruffydd inside the cottage, snatched a dagger from a sheath nailed high up on the door's frame, and stuck the knife in the back of her belt. "Stay quiet and still," was her terse order.

"No, I'll come. I can help!"

"No, you must stay here!" Fear quavered her voice as she added, "I...I will greet our visitor."

"But Maura...Simon said—"

She halted his argument by slamming the door and rolling a tree trunk used for chopping wood before the thick barrier. Henry's spiraling bark announced the visitor's approach. Maura swallowed her terror, steeled herself, and propelled herself across the sea of wildflowers toward the path that wound up from the lane at the base of the hill.

*****

As Simon traveled along the road that wove among the southern foothills of the Cambrian Mountains he fought to clear his mind of vexing thoughts. Gael was correct; perhaps he shouldn't take his dream of impending death seriously. Yet *whose* death, he couldn't clearly recall. He shook from his fretting and gave an affectionate slap to the neck of the gray beast he straddled. Up to a month past, Fulk had been an overly tempestuous percheron stallion—until he'd undergone the trial of castration. Fulk's former owner, Henry FitzRoy, would be highly displeased when he heard of Simon and Maura's unanimous decision to geld the beast. Because of lack of pasture, Fulk had to be corralled with Simon's Welsh mare, E'dain, and their colt. He hadn't taken kindly to the foal, and keeping him required drastic measures which had remarkable results. Fulk had immediately mellowed and thus became a far more productive member of their burgeoning family. Simon chuckled when he thought of a number of human acquaintances who would reap benefit from such an operation...for instance, his half-brother Will. He wondered to himself, *Where is that snake of a man and what is he plotting?* For Will was ever plotting vengeful schemes against Simon and Maura. *When will he surface again?*

The sun scorched the top of Simon's bare head; sweat trickled down his brow and stung his eyes. Closing them, he felt exhaustion weight his shoulders. A grove of blue-bells surrounded him, assaulting his senses with a sensual lightness and flinging his mind back to his cottage at Mynyw and to Maura. The same heady aroma lingered in the room where they loved. He craved so the heat of her embrace, the silken caress of her hair, the delight of her lips locked with his...but his desire ebbed as his weariness stole her image and slumped his head to his chest. The reins went slack and Fulk continued to plod along.

The sound of a clearing throat startled Simon awake. The placid scene of sun and blue-bells had uglied. Black malefic clouds threatened, and thorny, sinuous branches stretched out to prick and rip. He forced wide his eyes and beheld three hirsute individuals astride shaggy ponies, all the men sporting evil expressions. "Who are you and where are you headed?" growled the fiercest looking one.

Simon eyed his inquisitor's bow aimed at him, and his thick stock of arrows, and realized to his chagrin that he'd left his behind. His parched mouth begged for moisture as he strained and stammered in Welsh, "I...I'm Simon. My...my home is at Mynyw." A gibing laugh followed his answer. He shifted uneasily, tautened his grip on Fulk's reins and tried, "Please allow me to pass..."

No one moved or spoke, and the suspense was excruciating. Finally, the spokesman ribbed, "Your accent is wrong, but you speak our words well. It's your horse that betrays you...*you Norman pig!*"

Panic wrenched Simon's gut and he lashed out, "I've come from Dinefwr. Prince Rhys was taken ill, and I was summoned to care for him. I am his physician, not your enemy!"

"What shall we do with this pretty lad?" asked the leader to his troop of mute companions. "If he speaks the truth, which I doubt, he could prove quite handy. We could use a stitcher. But I suspect he's either headed for or returning from trouble. What say you men?"

"Take him," blurted one.

"Shoot him," sneered the other.

25

"I'd much enjoy carving him to tiny pieces and feeding him to the crows," concluded the leader. "Then I'd stick his head on a pole at the border as warning to others to stay away."

Simon forced his expression blank while madly fumbling for a conciliatory reply. His body reacted before his mouth and a sharp kick lurched Fulk ahead. He bolted between the skittish ponies, yet one pony was quicker, and bit the gelding's flank. Fulk reared; Simon wrestled for control, and the taunters grabbed their weapons.

Simon squeezed shut his eyes; his mind screamed prayers to a screeched command containing the word arrows, and the dire sound of bow strings being drawn taut. And so he was about to die...by these miserable thugs, in this miserable place, in this miserable way. Never again would he see, touch, or kiss his wife; never would he know or hold his child. He tensed for the strike, the pain, the blackness. Instead he heard a new strident voice, demanding, "Wait!"

The order froze all, including Fulk. Simon didn't dare run or turn, but strained to hear the discussion.

His woolly savior, a smallish man possessed of an eminent presence, emerged from behind a scrub of hemlock. "We're here to hunt food, not Normans," grunted he. "Besides..." He glanced pensively at their target, and said in a distant irked tone, "I believe I recognize your victim, and if so, he speaks the truth. Lord Rhys would not be pleased if it be known that *we* cut down his prized physician. Let him go, he's no use to us, for he's a lover of peace."

Simon recalled the snide nasal voice yet failed to attach a face to it. Squabbling followed; Simon's sudden rush of relief almost dropped him from the saddle. He fought to still his shaking, scolded himself for not being prepared for such an encounter, and mightily kicked Fulk. The steed bounded forward in a full gallop and Simon encouraged his frenzied pace till their menace was far, far behind.

*****

Atop the path, Maura hid at the back of an ancient wind-bent oak and, with great trepidation, watched the rider and horse climb the hill. Distance obscured the man's features. He rode slouched upon a black stallion, his arms not guiding, but swinging loosely. The stallion trudged along, dragging his feet, his nose dusting the ground. The scene before Maura did not shout danger, it screamed for help. She left the safety of the tree and hesitantly started forward, her steps lengthening as she drew nearer. The horse stopped to wobble; his knees buckled and he collapsed in a heap. The rider rolled to safety, then rocked to a halt and lay gravely still. His features came clear and Maura stopped. Blood rushed from her head to her toes as she wavered a moment, then stumbled ahead, screaming, "Marc!"

Gruffydd heard her cry as he rammed his body for the hundredth time against the door. His protective fervor made him abandon the door and clamber onto the physician's table. He scrambled through the open window, hit the ground at a run, and dashed to Maura's aide.

Maura fell to her knees by her brother, gently cradled his head, and used her skirt to swab away his sweat and dust, and her tears. "Marc, oh Marc! It's Maura. Open your eyes...Talk to me!" He stirred to her touch, his head lolled, and he moaned through cracked, foamy lips.

"Who is it, Maura?" panted Gruffydd, appearing beside her.

"My...my brother, Marc," she stammered, trying to mask her alarm. "He's come from Normandy and his long journey has made him ill. We must get him inside." She scrambled around to his head, squatted, and gripped under his arms. Her face pinched with pain as she yanked.

"No, Maura!" Gruffydd yelled. "Simon said you're not to lift anything!"

"I can't leave him here!" she shouted back.

Maura's effort proved futile; her mind swam with dread and she barely heard Gruffydd's suggestion, "Don't try to pull him! I'll fetch Sulien."

"Sulien?" Maura looked up hopefully and urged, "Yes Sulien...hurry. I'll bathe his face, perhaps that will wake him. Hurry, Gruffydd!"

The lad floundered his way down the path, and Maura dashed back to the cottage to fetch water, sloshing it from her washing bowl on her hasty return to her brother. Joy and distress clashed within her to produce copious tears as she soaked a linen cloth and pressed it to his brow, cheeks, and lips. Marc's mouth pursed, seeking more moisture, and his lashes fluttered, as Maura's tender voice lit the darkness. "Marc...hear me! It's Maura...You've found me, you're home. Please open your eyes...See me!"

Marc was trying so hard to do just that, yet nothing would move...Water, he felt water and his mind screamed, *More, give me more, let me drink!* As if she'd heard, Maura cupped the water and brought it to his mouth. His eyes stayed closed, yet his lips parted ever so slightly to accept the palmful. The liquid's saving effect proved instantaneous; his arms stretched, his fingers flexed and groped, his legs twitched. She bathed his face, then offered more water which he hungrily gulped. Then to his sister's clear delight, he blinked open his eyes and croaked, "Ma...Maura."

"Yes, oh yes, Marc, it's me, it's Maura!" she gushed. "You're home and you're safe."

Not fully believing the miraculous vision before him, he clutched at her arms, yanked her closer and tried to sit.

"No..." Maura insisted, "lie still. Sulien will be here soon to carry you inside. Sulien will soon come..." He surrendered to her assurance and, nestled in her hold, went limp once more.

From the east, black petulant clouds tumbled toward the siblings, and Maura's thoughts slipped briefly to Simon and how elated he'd be at Marc's arrival. Yet as she bent over Marc's body to shield him from fat splattering drops of rain, she silently fretted—*Why exactly had he come?*

*****

"He doesn't seem feverish," remarked Bishop Sulien, a balding, aged, giant of a man cloaked in monkish robes. He shifted closer to Marc's body stretched long upon Maura's bed, and examined intently his patient's sedate expression. One of Sulien's broad hands was splayed thoughtfully over his shiny pate, while the other lifted each of Marc's eyelids. "And he's not lost consciousness," he discovered. "Rather he's sleeping. Exhaustion...exhaustion and hunger, that's what he suffers. I suspect Simon will discover more, but till he returns I prescribe food, ale, and rest."

"Are you positive that's all that's wrong?" pressed Maura worriedly.

"Not positive, but near enough." He noted her ashen countenance and urged, "Don't harry yourself so, Maura. You need to take care." His concern suddenly turned wary. "It's not only his health that makes you fret. Confess what else." She wrung her hands, shook her head, and turned away. He reached out and pressed further, "What upset does he bring?"

Maura slowly turned back an anguished look and quavered, "He...he's here because his homage to the King is done, which can mean only one thing—the King is dead."

"Did he say as much?"

"No...I only guessed."

"Then you mustn't panic, especially for the child's sake. Perhaps there is a simpler reason for his arrival. He tired of war or—"

"He wouldn't have deserted," she countered.

"Come..." He stood and settled a comforting arm round her shoulders. "You spoon him a bowlful of whatever is in your cooking pot, for when he wakes, which will be soon, he's certain to be famished. I'll try to remove some of his clothing to make him more comfortable."

Maura nodded a ruthful glance Marc's way, then left him to Sulien. During her frenzy to get Marc inside and tended to, she'd all but forgotten Gruffydd. She spotted him crouched in a corner of the hut, a look of simmering terror haunting his eyes. "Gruffydd?" she asked concernedly, hurrying to him and crouching as well. "Gruffydd, what is it?"

"Has he come to steal our land and kill us?" he answered in a small strangled voice.

"Who?"

"Marc?"

"God's breath, no!" ardently affirmed Maura. "Why would you think that?"

"He's a Norman soldier...Norman soldiers steal our land and kill us."

"Marc has no intention of harming anyone. He's here to see me and Simon. I believe he's done with war."

"But Owain says," whined Gruffydd, "there's no Norman that's good and we should—"

"Owain?" Maura interrupted, askance. She searched her recent memory and Owain's bushy vision quickly appeared, the belligerent Welsh mountain raider who despised everyone. "When did you last speak with Owain?"

"After Mam left, when I went home to fetch my whittling knife, he was there."

"And what was he doing *there*?"

"Letting his horse drink from the trough by the lane. He asked me questions."

"About?"

"Mam...and the village and my tad and Simon."

She guided him from the corner, sat cross-legged, then patted her knee and delved gently, "What about your father?"

Gruffydd perched on her knee and answered in a tremble, "He asked if I thought someone had...killed him on purpose."

Maura spat her shock, "Why...what...how dare he question you about something that personal! What did you answer?"

"I didn't know what to say. I've heard Mam when she thinks I'm not listening tell people that she's sus...susip..."

"Suspicious," offered Maura.

"Yes, about Tad's death."

"What else did he ask you, about your mam?"

"If she cared for my tad, if they fought, if she kept company with other men, and where she was—"

"Other men!" burst Maura. "This is totally outrageous. Gruffydd, if ever you see Owain again, you don't speak to him. Instead you run to your mother, to me, to Simon, and tell us where he is. Is that clear?"

Her severe tone fed his fear and he clutched at her. "Yes, but I believe him...about the Normans. He said they'll hurt my mam, and burn our home, and my beasts!"

"Gruffydd," said she, stroking his hair, "you've forgotten one very important thing...about Normans."

He gazed up. "What's that?"

"I'm one, and so is Simon."

"I know that," he shrilled, "...and I told *him* that! But he said in time even you would turn bad. I don't want to believe that part, Maura, I don't want to!"

28

"And you mustn't," she murmured with a hug. "I love you, I would never hurt you, or your mother, or your beasts. And Simon...do you truly believe he would—"

"No...no," he blubbered. "I told Owain about Simon, how he heals people, not hurts people. I told him he's doctor to the Prince and then he looked at me so strange."

"Has he talked to you before...about these things?"

"Yes, many times."

"Does your mother know?" she queried, using the hem of her skirt to swab his tears.

"No, he told me not to tell her."

"Was he mean to you?"

"No." Embarrassment dropped his eyes and hushed his voice as he admitted, "When he lived in Mynyw, sometimes I wished he and Mam wouldn't fight so. And that they'd become friends, like you and Simon are. She was lonely after Tad died."

"I know she was, but..." She cupped his chin and met his guilty look to warn, "Not Owain, Gruffydd. Don't waste your dreams on Owain for no friendship will ever form between him and your mam. Now come, forget for awhile all you've heard about Norman soldiers, and help me heal my brother. For I'm certain he will become as dear a friend to you as Simon is."

"Really?" brightened Gruffydd.

"I'll guarantee it."

"What does guarantee mean?"

"It means...promise."

"Maura..." Sulien's lilting voice drifted from the sleeping chamber. Maura looked up, her expression pinched and expecting the worse. But he smiled at her and murmured, "He's awake and calls for you."

She beamed and firmed her grip on Gruffydd's hand. "Will you come with me and meet the kindest man I know."

Gruffydd held back a moment, then cracked a nervous grin as he clambered up to follow.

Maura surged forward to Marc's weak smile and into his opened arms. They sat caught in a tight clutch for a long while, then Maura eased their hug. "I...I don't believe you've finally come!"

"Nei...neither do I," Marc answered in a raspy crack. "The last mile was the hardest. I was afraid if I collapsed anywhere else but before your hut, I'd be cooked up for supper."

Maura laughed at his healthy show of humor and passed him the ale cup that sat on the side table. He drank freely and arched a questioning brow at Gruffydd's timid approach. "Marc," announced Maura proudly, gently tugging the boy forward, "this is our dear friend, Gruffydd. He's watching over me while Simon's away."

"Away?" Marc's posture and voice tensed. "Away where?"

"He's tending to the Prince...Prince Rhys fell ill and—"

"He shouldn't have left you alone! It's not safe here!"

"But I'm not alone," she argued with a calming touch. "I have the villagers, Gruffydd, and Bishop Sulien. You've met Sulien, he's Bishop of Mynyw, and a good friend. I'm never alone."

Marc's bluster waned, his eyes shut, and his head lolled. Sulien hurried forward to help as Maura eased Marc further down in the bed, plumped another pillow behind his head, and covered him with a crudely woven woolen blanket. "I'll fetch you oats," she said. "How long since you've eaten?"

"I don't remember," mumbled Marc, forcing his eyes open.

"No more questions," she soothed, smoothing his brow, "and no more worries."

"But, I..." Marc gently urged her aside and balanced on an elbow to search. A movement behind her skirt prompted his smile. "*Griffith*," said Marc faintly, "I was rude...I'm sorry and would like to say I'm quite honored to meet you, and grateful to you for keeping my sister...safe." Gruffydd peeked from behind Maura, grinned shyly, and reached out tentatively to accept Marc's hand.

Marc sank back upon the pillows. Gruffydd stayed by the bed, still gripping Marc's fingers while narrowly studying him, and Maura and Sulien retired to the main room. They were still only feet away and Marc could clearly hear their gibbering, for that was what it sounded like, queer, terse grunting sounds. He stole a glance at his sister through the doorway. She had changed so since the last time they'd been together, still too thin, but a radiance had replaced her gauntness of before, and more freckles, and something else he couldn't quite put words to...yet. He shuddered to think what he must look like. There wasn't much left of him, in mind, body, or spirit and he cringed to think how she'd react when he told her why he'd come. If Simon were here, it would be easier. Life was always easier when Simon was near.

Maura, barefoot and bowl in hand, stood a moment in the doorway to consider her little brother, who stared vacantly at the vent in the roof. She clearly recalled his knighthood ceremony not a year past; how proud she had felt, how enthusiastically robust he'd been, so young, virtuous, and trusting. Now she barely recognized him. His once vibrant blue eyes had grown dull and harsh. His golden brown curls looked like clumps of straw, and a dark stubble mingled with the filth and scars that marred his innocent visage. A deep scowl that seemed permanently carved into his skin made him appear bitter and ancient—at the tender age of nineteen. She sagged with sadness, then straightened with hope. Somehow, they'd nurse him back to the Marc they'd known before when their world had been carefree and glorious. He'd be well again, and whole again, she'd see to it. Her heart ached to his needy look, and she ventured forward, suggesting, "Now you'll eat, but not too much. Your belly won't take much."

"What were you speaking?" he asked.

She pondered the question, then realized that she'd been able to switch from Welsh to English without a thought. Simon would be so pleased. "I speak Welsh whenever I can."

"To Simon as well?"

"No, not to Simon," she smiled. "I thought it would be such a chore to learn, but it's proven quite simple."

"You look happy," he chanced.

"I am, exceedingly so."

"But," he added, "you're still too thin."

"Not for much longer." She beamed, then smoothed her skirt over her bulging belly, and buoyantly answered his quizzical look, "I'm to have a baby around Christmas time!"

Her announcement dizzied him; she grasped Marc's outstretched hand as he struggled to sit and sputtered, "You...you were married?"

"Yes, this past Easter, at Canterbury by Archbishop Lanfranc."

"Good...I had prayed...Tell me."

"Not now. Now you'll eat. I'll help you and, when you find the strength, I'll tell you and also, everything that's happened to us you can read in the letters I wrote to you. Simon's written you quite a few as well."

"I'd like that," said he.

"I'm so glad you're here!" she burbled, lifting the spoon to his lips. "We've missed you so."

He pushed aside the spoon and muttered gravely, "I need to tell you, Maura, why I've—"

"No," she cut in curtly, "you'll eat first."

Yet her order went unnoticed and he bluntly spilled, "The King was injured at the start of August. He's very ill and may not live. I felt no allegiance to anyone else, so I decided to heed your advice and left. If I'm found I will be executed for desertion."

She gulped, then stated, "Then you won't be found."

"And if *you're* found?" he asked with trepidation.

Maura squeezed his hand, dropped her tearing eyes, and was silent.

*****

CHAPTER THREE – INTRIGUING PROPOSITIONS

𝕳enrʏ, with John tight on his heels, sauntered into the great hall of the Palace of Westminster, his belly grumbling from their perilous journey across the waves—wine would surely tame it. He peeled off his gloves and shiftily surveyed the massive room, roofed with high arched timbers, floored with dirt and rushes, and furnished with one raised table and several trestle tables crowding the area below. As he sidled past an empty tiled fire pit, his belly griped once more, and he bellowed, "Rufus! Where in God's breath are you?"

A sudden swarm of sentries answered his gruffness, storming toward him at a treacherous pace. He fumbled for his dagger, and his squeak, "Gua—" was cut short by a sword tip pressing into his neck. The lead soldier briskly stripped him of his weapon, wrenched his arms to his back, and trussed his wrists with leather.

William II, King of England, emerged from the royal bedchamber and swaggered his robust self into the hall. His ponderous silk robes staggered his stride, and a crude crown of gold, perched lopsided upon his thick skull, parted his long greasy yellow locks.

Despite his awkward station, Henry fought to suppress a chuckle. In matters of fashion, Rufus always faltered—badly. Then his bile erupted and he carped, "Dearest Brother, what, may I ask, have I done to deserve such an amicable welcome?"

Rufus, so nicknamed because of his choleric complexion, plopped himself into an elaborately carved throne centering the dais, threw back a goblet of claret, and directed a flagrant belch Henry's way. He swabbed his mouth with his sleeve as he leant forward and sneered, "By the holy face of Lucca, what are you doing here? Last time we were together, you weren't very nice."

"By the holy face of what?!" Henry wondered, fuddled.

"It's my oath. Now answer my question."

"At...at Father's deathbed?"

"No. At Pevensey," Rufus specified.

After an explosive "Ha!" and a cringe as the blade dug deeper, Henry argued carefully, "But...but we had such great fun."

"I lost," sulked Rufus.

"Even *you* can't expect to win every tussle, and I did, after all, have Simon on my side." Henry took on a wounded air and sniveled, "Please, your Grace, kindly have your brutes ease their hold and untie me. The blade makes it difficult to speak."

To Rufus' brusque nod, the guards retreated one step. Henry shook from his binding and pried loose his collar, while John, pale as snow, rose warily from his cower and hid in his master's shadow. Henry started forward, then hesitated with a wary, "May I advance, your Grace?"

"I suppose," said Rufus mordantly. "But keep a safe distance, I don't trust you."

"Why ever not?"

"You swore you'd tell Father all those wicked things about me."

"But I didn't, did I? And it wouldn't have mattered if I did. He would have given you England anyway. You could at least offer me wine." Henry inched cautiously round the end of the dais and stood awaiting Rufus' permission to sit. When the limp wave came, Henry sighed, sat, and plopped his feet on the dais, wondering brightly, "How does it feel to be King at last? Are you enjoying yourself?"

Rufus' smiles always betrayed something other than pure joy, and this time his fat lips brimmed haughtiness as he muttered, "Immensely so."

"I'm glad to hear it," said Henry with effusive giddiness, "for that throne is where you truly belong, your Grace."

"And where do *you* belong, Henry?"

"At the moment, I'm not quite certain." He nodded in thanks to a serving boy offering wine, gulped heartily, then chided, "I believed I'd be received warmly by *you* but—"

"I must take care," interjected Rufus, "...*always*."

"You must indeed, yet I threaten no harm, your Grace." Henry's tone reeked submission. "For I love you and pledge my complete allegiance."

"What of Curthose?" probed Rufus.

"What of him?"

"What do you pledge him?"

"Not a thing."

"Yet..."

"Never—" Eager to end their circular wrangling, Henry steered the conversation from loyalty. "Tell me of your court. Where is wily Will? I imagined he'd be offered the post of chief adviser."

"He's not fit to be chief dung slinger," sniggered Rufus. "I've asked Rannulf Flambard to guide me. He's considering the offer."

"He served Father well," conceded Henry. "I congratulate you on a shrewd choice, Brother. And such an eloquent oath! How did you think of it?"

"Father took me to the church of Saint Lucca in Italy. I liked her name."

"I'm impressed by your memory and love of saints. And will you marry?"

"It's not likely."

"Yet it is your duty to produce an heir, and you've become quite the dandy in your resplendent new wardrobe. Surely there has to be some vapid maid somewhere who would be willing to take on the perilous role of your queen."

Rufus pouted a whine, "I wanted to marry Maura."

"Oh Rufus," burst Henry, "surely you jest!" His boots dropped to the ground and he lunged forward to steal Rufus' goblet. After a bolstering swig, he boldly ventured, "She wouldn't have survived your wedding night, and you must admit Simon did win her fairly."

"I didn't kill her then?"

"No. You gave her a wretched scar though," winced Henry, illustrating with a swipe to his neck. "At times, you can be such a brutal fiend." As punishment, he gave his brother a brisk slap on his pimpled cheek.

"Only to those deserving abuse," parried Rufus, and his return swat almost unseated his brother. He swiftly collected himself and huffed a grunt, "Where is Simon? He promised himself to me."

"He would have promised anything to pry Maura from your lethal clutch. And he knew well your frailty. You've always lusted after his taut little backside. Where are your boys?" Henry spouted waggishly, scanning the room. "I miss their putrid, giggly presence." Rufus snarled and Henry dissolved with laughter, "Here's a marvelous trick—with a wig, some face paint and a frilly gown, one could act your blushing bride. You could buy a baby and—"

"Shut your gob, Henry," warned Rufus.

Henry wisely swallowed his joke.

"At least I haven't," noted Rufus, "like your slimy self, spawned an army of tiny monsters, who will give me grief when they're grown."

"I strive to prove I'm not afflicted with your perversities."

"You've outdone your proof, Henry," scorned Rufus. "Who's he?" His gray glare shifted to the skinny black-haired lad, still standing in the center of the hall, looking terribly lost.

"Oh, that's John, my new butler. Uncle Odo gave him to me," answered Henry. "Pretty isn't he? But you can't have him, he's all mine, and he grovels so slavishly."

"Enough of your drivel. What do you *truly* want, Henry?"

"Mother's English holdings," Henry stated blandly. "They were willed to me."

"Who has them now?"

"I'm not entirely sure." Henry rested a few fingers on his lip, tilted his chin in a docile pose, and dripped his next words. "I had hoped, your Grace, that you would allow me to search out the title documents for the land."

His brother's meekness softened Rufus and he gently rumbled, "From what I've heard, all land title documents are stored at Winchester."

"Then you won't mind me taking a slice of your territory?"

"You mean *caring* for a slice of my territory," clarified Rufus. "It will be titled in your name but will remain mine...for it all belongs to me, including yourself if you choose to reside in England. Is that clear, little brother?"

"As air," simpered Henry.

"So, do you still propose to lay claim to my land? It will cost you dearly, and not only monetarily."

"If you let me stay this night and sample your rather odd brand of hospitality," responded Henry, "I swear that directly before I depart, you will have my answer."

At that, Rufus abruptly ended their banter with a smug nod and a motion for food.

*****

Gael smoothed escaped wisps of pale hair from her damp brow, and rehearsed her speech to Nesta in a low mutter as she approached the Princess' partitioned corner of the long house.

On the other side of an exquisitely embroidered tapestry, Nesta, daughter of Prince Rhys ap Tewdwr, sank her perfectly sculptured, nude form down upon her feather bed, and grumpily yanked a wood-toothed comb through her lush chestnut locks. Her intense green eyes gleamed victorious at the sight of the swaying tapestry and a delicious grin parted her plump, sensuous lips. She flopped back upon her pillows, arranged herself in an inviting pose, and breathed, "Come...Simon."

Gael balked at the little girl voice and giggle, but inhaled deeply, wiped her sweaty palms on her shapeless tunic, and forged ahead. What greeted her took her aback. To call Nesta comely was an insult; to anyone, male or female, her fairness was highly intimidating. Gael dropped her blush to the floor and stuttered, "Nes...Nes...ta, please cover yourself."

Nesta's twittering turned coarse. "Where's Simon?" she scowled, hurling the comb and yanking a coverlet over her breasts.

"He...he's gone," said Gael as she stole a look, sighed relief, and took a bold step forward. "I've come to tend your illness."

"What illness?"

"Your father mentioned you were ill," Gael reminded.

"Oh...oh, yes, indeed I am. But I trust my health only to Simon."

Gael folded her arms across her chest and muttered crossly, "Well now you'll have to trust it to me."

"Where's he gone?"

"To where he truly wants and ought to be—home."

"With Maura," added Nesta snidely.

"Yes...with Maura. So, tell *me* your problem."

"What problem?"

"How are you ill?"

"Oh, my belly aches, like my Father's."

"Then I'll have my sister mix a curing draught for you. Simon left the ingredients and—"

Nesta's whine shortened Gael's speech, "Why doesn't he like me?"

"Who?"

"Simon."

"He doesn't *dislike* you," replied Gael.

"But he doesn't want me."

"Want you?"

"My body."

Gael had a bad feeling as to the direction this exchange was swaying. She wanted to leave, yet felt the need to defend her friend, so she stated in a tone that suggested this would be her final comment, "His interest lies elsewhere."

"With Maura," Nesta griped on.

"With Maura," echoed Gael, cursing herself for encouraging the pesty Princess.

"Why?" Nesta shrilled. "I hate her! She's old, she isn't particularly pretty, and she'll soon be big as a horse! Why does he want her when he can have me?"

"Because he loves her desperately, her mind and soul as well as her body!" Gael railed. "All he needs from a woman, he gets from her, and more. And I find it very difficult to imagine anyone hating Maura!"

In a goading gesture, Nesta kicked her coverlet away. "*No* one, including Maura, owns a body as exquisite as mine," she bragged. "Don't you agree?"

"I...I...can't really comment," Gael gibbered and, nonplussed, snatched up a wrinkled shift at the foot of the bed. She thrust it at Nesta, jabbering, "And...and Simon sees naked bodies, men's and women's, every day. I suppose after awhile it numbs one's perception."

"Has he seen yours?" Nesta teased.

"Par...pardon?" stuttered Gael in disbelief.

"Your body, naked."

"No."

"Do *you* want him?"

"What?"

"Do you want him?"

"No!" yelled Gael in exasperation.

"But you have no man."

"And at the moment," railed Gael, "I don't feel a dire urge or need *to* have one!"

"But he's *so* handsome and kind. A bit blunt at times, but he has the most gorgeous..."

"Stop this, Nesta. I didn't expect a discussion on lust. I don't have time—"

"Oh please..." Despair robbed Nesta's sneer. "I have these feelings, almost a hurt—" She clutched at her belly. "Here. No one will listen. Simon's the only man Father will allow near me. I so want him to touch me, but he always brings *her* along."

Nesta's graveness touched Gael; she softened, rested herself on the bed, and probed, "How old are you?"

"Near to fifteen."

"Yes, that could mean trouble."

"Trouble how?" wondered Nesta.

"The feelings you have are perfectly normal, just a bit misplaced. Have you asked your father why you're not allowed to meet with a man—chaperoned of course?"

"No."

"Then maybe you should. I suppose he'll be considering your marriage soon and if there are a number of worthy applicants, you could perhaps spend time with each, then have your pick."

"I don't want to marry before I know what true pleasure can happen between a man and woman, because if I'm unlucky in marriage, I may never know."

"That's understandable," Gael conceded, then cautioned, "but it could also prove dangerous."

"Do you know?"

"Know what?"

"What true pleasure is?"

"It's not your business, Nesta."

"Your expression says 'no'."

"Nesta..." Gael paused for patience; she felt herself being drawn into absurdity again and raised her palms in objection.

The gesture was lost and Nesta harped further, "I heard Father discussing you this past evening. He's still searching for a Pennaeth for Mynyw and means to marry you to his choice."

"You lie," scoffed Gael.

"I don't. Ask him yourself."

"I will do just that."

"Now tell me more about lust," burbled Nesta in wiggly anticipation. "Who owns yours?"

"No one, and I'll say no more. Your mother is who you should be discussing this matter with, not me."

Nesta paled and her reply hinted terror. "You won't tell my mother that I asked!"

The intensity of her plea piqued Gael and she answered, askance, "I hadn't intended to."

"Please don't. Swear you won't!" wailed Nesta.

"Swear you won't what?" came a commanding voice, feminine yet gruff. Nesta's mother, Gwladys, swept between the tapestries, her face creased with irritation, her mouth set in a rigid frown, and her cold green eyes leery.

Gael hung her head and performed a short bow, while greeting, "My Lady." Then she raised her eyes to the tall, lissome, mysterious figure, seldom seen at Dinefwr. A veil wrapped too securely about Gwladys' head and brow accentuated her glower and made her appear nun-like, and Gael realized she had never seen the color of the lady's hair. Perhaps when younger Gwladys had possessed her daughter's beauty, but now all that was visible was a distant, bitter woman, tired of her family and the world, and old before her time.

Nesta covered herself and cowered to her mother's scolding, "Why aren't you dressed? And you shouldn't be abed at this late hour, you lazy, impudent creature. Now get up and tell me what you swore!"

Gingerly, Nesta emerged from beneath her coverlet and swiftly tugged an unadorned woolen shift down over her head and ample curves. Her prissy look vanished and her silent plea to Gael reeked of despair.

Gael rescued her with a stuttered lie, "I...I swore not to tell you a rather bawdy story I was sharing with your daughter. Though I ought not to have and—"

"Why are you here, Gael?" Gwladys asked with distaste. "I thought your husband dead."

"I assure you my Lady, he is dead and long since buried. I came to visit my sister."

"Well she's gone missing nigh on a week. This isn't the first time she's bolted and if it happens again, I will be forced to send her back to your family in Shrewsbury."

"Don't you believe that rather harsh, my Lady?"

"No, her duty is companion and servant to my daughter. And in return for her service, she receives food, shelter, and protection. If this agreement is not fulfilled, she can go elsewhere!"

Nesta paled to her mother's swelling ire. Gael noticed her pallor and was suddenly beset with a sickly sense that Gael had played out this drama before. A retort did not readily come and she acquiesced, "I will inform her of your warning, my Lady, and will take my leave."

She tried to do so, but was distracted by Nesta's mewed plea, "Gael, perhaps you can visit again...*please*."

"Perhaps," she smiled stiffly, then left. The ache in her belly sharpened when a flurry of horse's hooves, rough bantering, and lewd laughter sounded outside the main entrance. Gael backed into a shadow and craned her neck to watch what chaos would erupt next. But instead she heard the appalling sounds of screeched reprimands, blows being struck, and Nesta's screams for forgiveness. A rash of unbidden tears blurred Gael's sight and obscured the identities of four hulking males barreling their way through the door. They flung an assortment of blood-soaked beasts into a far corner, near to the fire pit. Then the men, garbed in fur and resembling beasts themselves, shook rain from their hirsute bodies, shoved each other about, and laughed uproariously at, from what Gael could discern, nothing at all. Their chortling drowned Nesta's misery, but escalated Gael's. All she wanted was to go home, to her hut, her son, and her friends; but what if Nesta's claim about marrying the new Pennaeth was true? It was crucial she speak to Rhys before—A harrowing sight wandering through the door gagged her upset. She choked into her palm and retreated further into the recess. Owain! Why had he come, and why now? How overjoyed she'd been three months past when he'd decided her village not worthy of his exalted vigilance and disappeared. The rascal, lacking any tact or manners, took pride in disrupting the tranquility of the commote. He'd claimed to have been sent by Rhys to protect them, but his protection had taken the form of harassment aimed especially at her. She'd hated him then and still did now as she watched him plop himself down churlishly on a bench.

The prospect of marriage could be dealt with later she decided as she mustered a saving breath and snuck from the dark in the direction of her shoes set by the door. Slip into them and keep walking, out the door to the stable, borrow a guard, and start for home. Yes, that's all she had to do and she needn't acknowledge him at all. Yet her shoes no longer sat alone; by them rested a pair of muck soaked, scruffy, burr-dotted boots and they weren't empty. Her wide eyes crept the length of Owain's rumpled form and stopped at his squinty eyes, moss brown and mean. She stood transfixed by his filth—tousled hair and beard clotted with grease and mud, skin encrusted and black. The furs and rags that hung on him were worn and shredded, and her eyes grew rounder at the astounding sight of some plant actually climbing a leg of his leather breeches. All the nastiness she'd saved exclusively for him burst forth in one explosive barb, "Don't you ever wash?!"

His companions howled in raucous laughter, and Owain joined them, his chuckles more calculating. Yet his gaiety abruptly stopped with a grunted inquiry, "Why are you at Dinefwr?"

He deserved no explanation and she retorted, "I am welcome here!"

"So you're to be his next," he sneered.

Gael bristled at the Welsh's inability to complete sentences, before asking, "Whose next what?"

His knowing nod directed at Rhys' partition clarified his accusation.

"You...you believe I'm to be his mistress!" she sputtered, aghast.

He arched a brow and muttered, "We've heard as much."

"I've come to see my sister," she countered firmly.

"So, have we."

Her belly lurched, and pulse quickened as she pressed, "What would *you* want with her?"

"We've watched her travels these past weeks and wish to ask her questions."

"Regarding?"

"If she's selling the Normans anything other than her body."

Gael grew faint at the prospect. She knew her sister to be confused, impetuous, and greedy, but whoring and spying for the enemy? Never would she disgrace herself or her family by engaging in such depravity! "I will answer for her, *Sir*," she snipped. "She is innocent of your accusation and is merely visiting relatives."

"Oh, I didn't know you had Norman kin," he said with exaggerated politeness. "If I had, I'd have been even more disagreeable to you."

Gael's control faltered, and she screamed, "I don't have to explain anything to you, you slimy turd! Move so I may pass."

"Not till you confess her whereabouts!"

"I told you her whereabouts...or are you as deaf as you are stupid?"

"And you lied. So, I can conclude that you not only know the truth but may also be involved in her crimes. It would not surprise me in the least—"

Her gob of spit splattered his cheek. He didn't flinch and parried his gob as expertly. She scoured her face with her sleeve and groaned, "Damn you vile pigs!" at her audience of jeering, hooting laggards.

Owain bent to fetch something and, straightening, thrust Simon's bow into her hand. A look of disdain began his tale, "And as for stupidity, a short while past your physician friend wandered off the road into hostile country. I rescued his hide from impalement, but I don't expect gratitude, not from you or him. Only his wife seems well bred. Tell him next time he chooses to roam about not to forget a weapon, not that he's capable of using one."

Suddenly muddled, she dropped the bow, and felt her sickness resurge at the dire image of Simon's murder.

"Lady Gael..."

She jerked her head to the welcome intrusion and hurried toward Rhys' servant. Yet before she ducked beneath the tapestry, she stole one last seething glare at Owain, now crouched in a corner as if purposely distancing himself from his crude comrades. His fingers absently picked globs of mud from his breeches, while his expression had taken on a somber reflective guise. She despised the emotions this man evoked in her—rabid rage, paralyzing fear, and most upsetting, something insidious and elusive that dwelled—Her hand pressed her belly to console the ache and the simple act conjured up Nesta and her confession, 'I have these feelings, almost a hurt...here'. As if scalded her hand leapt from her belly; she whimpered a prayer for calm and disappeared behind the cloth.

Rhys sat upright in bed, sporting a grin that suggested impish innocence. Gael stopped, bowed slightly, and returned a grin, though a bit forced. Her trepidation swelled as she saw they were alone and there were no chairs about. He beckoned her with a crooked finger; she haltingly advanced and stood next to his bed, looking as staid as her nervousness would allow.

He patted the spot by his side and said, "Please sit, my lovely Lady."

38

She did so, yet kept herself balanced on the bed's edge with both feet planted solidly on the ground.

"What is it, Gael?" Rhys asked worriedly.

Not willing to disclose her fright that Owain could possibly have been correct in his ludicrous claim, she gabbled, "I...I've just spoken to Nesta, and our visit was upsetting."

Rhys tensed, and his eyes grew round with concern. "Her ailment, is it serious?"

"No...I don't believe she's ill at all."

"Did Simon tend to her?"

"No, he was in such a hurry to leave, I offered to see her instead. Nesta wasn't pleased."

"She's fond of Simon."

"*Too* fond," Gael mumbled beneath her breath.

"What did you say?"

"Noth...nothing."

"I'm sorry for her rudeness and will speak to her," said Rhys.

"I don't think that's necessary. Your Lady wife is with her now."

"So that's the cause of all the shouting."

"Yes...Are they always that way together?" wondered Gael.

"They've never been friendly and most times it's not a problem. Gwladys resides elsewhere."

"Why?"

"Because *we've* never been very friendly..." Rhys cleared his throat and continued with a waver, "And Gael, it is precisely because of our rather tenuous bond that I've asked you here."

Now the Prince seemed restive, a side of him that Gael had never witnessed. And curiously his discomfort served to quell hers. She gazed down at his fidgeting fingers and carefully prompted, "Rhys, you were saying?"

"Yes, I do apologize. I'm not skilled at speeches, so I'll be brief. My former mistress decided to wed and has left me—lonely. I offer to you the privileges of my home, my bed, and my attentions if you are so obliged."

Gael shut her eyes, bit her bottom lip, and strangled her skirt. *How did Owain know? How had he heard?! How dare he know my future before I do!!* Perhaps he was the sort she'd heard tales of...those gifted with the sight...but no, he was far too vile—

"Gael," called Rhys, "are you well?"

"What?" spurted Gael, turning too quickly and tipping off the bed to the floor. Embarrassed, she accepted Rhys' helping hand and clumsily struggled to her feet. This time she remained standing.

Her dour expression prompted his comment, "Does the idea of us together not give you pleasure? It does me!"

His eager expression begged an answer, and her fluster babbled forth, "Oh Rhys, I suppose I'm flattered. I do care for you. Since Rhodri's death, you've been overly kind to me and Gruffydd. But I didn't expect...I came here to see my sister!"

"And have you seen her?"

"What?"

"Your sister, have you seen her?"

"No."

"We haven't for a while either," said Rhys with a slight scowl. "She'd best show herself soon. Gwladys is incensed."

"I've heard. What of your Lady wife, Sir? How would she view our *friendship*?"

"With indifference, perhaps even relief." Rhys shifted closer and lowered his robust voice to divulge, "Gwladys has always viewed the physical bonding between man and woman with repugnance. I'm amazed we've managed to produce the children we have. Gael, I don't expect an immediate answer to my request."

Recklessly, she blurted, "If I don't accept you, will I be returned to Shrewsbury?"

Rhys shunned her worry, grasped her hand, and insisted, "Gael, this is not meant as a punishment, or an ultimatum. It is a compliment! You are a lovely, kind and intelligent woman. I appreciate your company and long for a more intimate arrangement."

She pried from his grip to answer impulsively, "But I was brought from Shrewsbury to be wife to the Pennaeth! I am no longer that, and I sometimes wonder what *is* my purpose at Mynyw."

The playful spark in his dark eyes faded as he mumbled, "I do have another proposition for you to ponder. You might have heard that I am seeking a new Pennaeth for Mynyw. Your son, of course, has a hereditary right to that office when he comes of age, but till that time, I will assign someone temporarily to protect Gruffydd's welfare and guide the commote. If you choose to shirk my own invitation, I would like you to consider marrying the man I pick for Pennaeth."

And so Nesta was correct as well. Gael sighed in defeat and sagged onto the bed. "And if I don't agree..."

Rhys spoke with wrenching bluntness, "Gruffydd will stay with me and you will return to Shrewsbury."

His reply wasn't surprising; she had anticipated and dreaded this moment for the entire past year. He knew too well she would never risk losing her son and would agree to anything for the joy of keeping him. Her freedom had been fleeting and wondrous and now it was to be taken from her and given to whom? "Rhys," she questioned with hesitation, "have you anyone in mind?"

"Not as yet. There are quite a few in waiting, though I plan to offer the title to my favorites first. I suspect you've been lonely."

"No, not particularly."

"But with no man to warm your bed."

"I've kept myself sufficiently warm."

"I will strive not to burden you with an old man," said he. "There are quite a few young lusty lads vying for the honor of Mynyw and yourself."

The compliment was lost on Gael, and she duly muttered, "At your pleasure, my Prince, I would like to leave for home."

Rhys turned her glum face to his, and assured, "I will not make my decision rashly, and neither should you. Consider carefully my propositions and choose what you believe will suit you best. If you like, over the next few months, I will send the final contenders separately to Mynyw, to woo you and the villagers. And if I'm unable to make a decision, perhaps I'll allow you to sway my choice."

Gael nodded vaguely and rose to her feet with a faint request, "May I borrow two of your guards for my journey home?"

"Of course. When and if your sister returns, I will send her to you for a much needed reunion. Does that please you?"

"Yes, my Prince. I'm grateful for your kindness and your audience. May I take my leave?"

He again took her hand and gave his permission in the form of a lingering kiss placed purposely in the center of her palm. She reclaimed her hand and, with another nod and awkward grin, departed. To her profound relief, Owain was nowhere to be seen. She grabbed Simon's bow and arrows, hurriedly crammed her feet into her slippers, and left the hall. The courtyard was crowded and boisterous; tradesmen's thatched huts dotted the grounds enclosed by a steep wooden fence; sheep, hogs, and cows roamed and grazed freely on scant tufts of grass sprouting by bogs of mud. A dull grayness had stolen the sun, and a thick smoke cloud disgorged from the llys and huts hovered stubbornly above the enclosure. Its sting teared her eyes; she rubbed them, blinked, and quickly spied a familiar guard. He gladly assented to her request for protection and left to fetch her horse and a companion while she idled about the main gates. Her gaze absently wandered the grounds as her mind raged with uncertainty. She would take the whole of the tranquil journey home to sort out the prospects, so there was no need to panic...yet. And of course, she would seek Simon and Maura's advice, and anyone else who cared to offer. And Gruffydd—his opinion would be vital to her final decision. Yes, perhaps this confusing edict could somehow be turned to her advantage. Her brief sense of triumph was interrupted by the sight of the communal tub, teeming with naked romping men. She was jealous of their carefree way and for an instant was tempted to strip and join them, but she craved more the solace of home. The guard's voice startled her, "Lady Gael...your horse."

She accepted the reins with a stammered, "Tha...thank you..." and turned to mount, but she hesitated and cast another envious eye on the happy tub. One fellow had clambered over the planked wall and stood facing her, his face buried in a towel. She couldn't help but gawk a moment at his unclothed self; tan and expertly formed, his chest and arms rippling with lean, glistening muscles, and his legs wet and sinewy. His towel fell away, and she abruptly dropped her embarrassed gaze to her feet. Something, though, made her look up, and what greeted her were Owain's eyes, no longer mean. But realizing the identity of the on-looker, they flared again; his hands hid his loins, and he darted behind the bath.

Owain felt ashamed and wounded, ashamed she'd seen him this way—so vulnerable—and wounded by her accusation that he'd never bathed. Of course he did, daily, well at least once a week. He'd been a bit more attractive before he tumbled into the bog, yet she deserved no explanations, she deserved only contempt! He rooted madly through piles of clothing, searching out his own, and frowned when he found them thoroughly spoiled. They'd never do for an audience with the Prince. The shirt and breeches sitting nearby looked fairly clean and fitting. He swiftly leapt into the pants and wriggled into the shirt, then whipped the wet from his hair and smoothed it away from his face. And as he loped toward the long house, he hoped the owner of the clothes wouldn't mind their loss, and also that Rhys wouldn't suggest for the hundredth time that he become Pennaeth to Mynyw. He would gladly choose death to being shackled forever to a hysterical harpy.

*****

Marc opened his eyes slowly and carefully, praying his arrival at Maura's was not just a dream. His prayer's happy answer came in a vision of the hut's ceiling vent, dripping from a steady, pattering rain. All was quiet save for a queer shuffling noise. He pushed up an inch and searched the room; the shutters were slightly parted, showing the day darkening and ushering in a moist sweet smelling breeze. A brown and white ball of fur hugged a soiled doll and snored at his feet. Maura's old, tattered trunk sat in a corner, piled high with rumpled clothing. Mounds of well-thumbed bound parchments crowded the space beneath the window; and neatly stacked wood logs adorned the wall opposite the bed, which was nothing more than a wide box cushioned with a mattress stuffed with feathers and draped with linen sheets and a wondrously embroidered quilt sewn in hues of blues, reds, and purples. He sat up taller and caught the stark contrast between the sheets' whiteness and his soiled skin. Glancing longingly at the washing bowl gracing one side table, he wondered if he'd ever be clean again. The other table held a lit candle, a cup of reviving ale which he immediately downed, a bowl of congealed oats, and a batch of letters tied with a ribbon. His interest roused, he wiped

41

his lips and took up the folded parchments, eased off the ribbon, and read the date of the first, 10 April 1087. It began...

'Marc, I am alive and recovering in an abbey somewhere between Pevensey and Canterbury. How I got here or what occurred immediately before I was taken from Pevensey I can't wholly recall. Henry and Simon have offered little to refresh my memory, but I do clearly remember being captured in a chamber, Will's I reckon, Rufus restraining me, Will attacking...It is all too horrid to write. Then, somehow, I acquired a knife which I promptly stuck in Will and as he reeled, I almost escaped. Rufus stopped me. I hung a long while in his clutch, his dagger digging at my neck, while familiar faces, good and bad came and went. Then there was Henry and Simon and scuffling— candles, tables, and chairs tipping. Someone trod on me and whisked me away. I saw a fist, then darkness. And I awoke here to Simon, and Henry, and freedom...'

So, that's where the ghastly scar on her neck came from, thought Marc, looking up to see a blur of red. And there she was, standing lovely in the doorway, veil gone, hair loose, smiling so big it seemed every one of her teeth showed.

"How do you feel?" she murmured, coming closer.

"Better, and actually hungry."

"Good. Do you think your belly can handle bread soaked in melted cheese?"

"I'm willing to chance it." He stared curiously at the front of her tunic dusted with chaff. "What have you been doing? I've heard strange noises coming from the outside room."

She swatted futilely at the dust. "Replacing the rushes. They were getting a bit rank. Gruffydd was helping me, but sometimes his help hinders, so I encouraged him to go play in the puddles."

"Who does he belong to?"

"Gael, our closest friend here," she explained while fussing with his blanket. "When Simon lived here before, he lived with Gruffydd, Gael, and her husband, Rhodri, who was Chieftain. Rhodri died near a year past and is buried out by Simon's herb garden. Gael traveled with Simon to Dinefwr to visit her sister, Ella. This must sound dreadfully confusing."

"Yes...it does," he admitted.

"In time it will all make perfect sense. You do plan to stay, don't you?" she cautiously asked.

"As I see it, I have no other options. I don't know what I'm good for, though."

"Don't be ridiculous," she asserted. "While I was laying the rushes, I thought of when Simon bragged about your adventures in Normandy, how you handily took on the task of physician's assistant. Once our child arrives I'm sure the time I spend helping Simon will be needed elsewhere. He'll be wanting a new helper, and there's no reason why you can't start training now."

"Does he still serve as mediator?"

"No. I've taken on that rather exasperating task."

"You?" he asked, surprised.

"Yes. I admit to causing some interesting reactions when called on to tame an upset. But at times my gender can prove quite effective. More often than not, the enemies are so stunned to see a woman they promptly forget their argument." She took up the bowl and cup. "I must fetch your food."

"You needn't wait on me," he said, striving to rise, yet as his foot hit the ground, he realized that, light as he was, he lacked the strength to stand. He flopped back and huffed, "I don't much like being this way."

"I know," she soothed with a light touch to his cheek. "Have some patience and I predict, with rest and a dose of Simon's invigorating tonic, you'll be up and about by tomorrow. You haven't said—" she added expectantly.

"Said what?" he wondered.

"Would you like being Simon's helper?"

"It is what I'd hoped for."

The pattering on the roof increased to sustained drumming, and Maura gazed up worriedly. "I must get Gruffydd inside, before he catches a chill."

"Maura," Marc called to her back. "How fares my horse?"

She turned in the door and confirmed, "He's fine. Last I visited, he was up and contentedly munching."

"And my saddlebag, did you rescue it?"

"Yes, why?"

"Inside is a letter from Edith."

Excitement stole Maura's breath and thrust her back to the bed. "Did you see her?"

"No...I was guided to her hut, but she wasn't there, nor was she at the market. On the table inside her cottage I found a letter lacking only a signature. I left a note and took the letter with me."

"Have you read it?"

"I haven't had a chance."

"Then I'll fetch it and Gruffydd and we'll read it together."

A short while later and back on the bed, Marc munched on his cheese, while Maura helped strip Gruffydd of his wet clothes, bundled him in a blanket, and hoisted him upon her knee. Gruffydd reached to stroke the puppy and asked, "Who's Edith?"

"Simon's true mother, and adoptive mother to Marc and me," replied Maura.

"What's adoptive?"

"When you are raised by someone other than your true parents, they are your adoptive parents." His look betrayed more confusion and Maura added, "If Simon and I instead of your mam were to raise you, we would be your adoptive parents."

"But why would you do that?"

Maura silently begged Marc for counsel and he kindly intervened, "Perhaps we'll talk of this further when your mam returns."

"I heartily agree," sighed Maura.

Gruffydd pressed one more question, "Why was Edith *your* adoptive mother?"

"Because our parents died," answered Marc.

"Like my Tad?"

"Yes."

"Oh, I see," he said and, snuggling in Maura's hold, listened politely.

"Some of this is blurred," Marc began, "but I'll do my best to decipher it...'Dearest Son and Daughter, I'm writing this letter not knowing whether you'll ever receive it, yet as I write I feel I'm closer to you and that is comforting. A bard passes through Dunheved each spring and fall, so I'm hoping he'll agree to deliver this to you. I am well, as is Arthur, who sends his love and has become, not surprisingly with his charm, the most sought after merchant at market. We are happy together, at last. Simon, your brother Adam has grown at an astonishing rate, and is simply adorable. Almodis' and Alan's bond appears to have strengthened each time I visit them, which is often.'"

Marc paused to look up in question. Maura dismissed him with the waved assurance, "I'll tell you later. Go on."

"'Maura,'" resumed Marc, "'Rose is as grumpy as ever, and so is perfectly fine. But she does miss you terribly, and if she didn't have Almodis and the baby to look after I feel she might wither up and die of sorrow. Speaking of Rose, promptly after you left, she confessed her suspicion that you might be pregnant. I pray every day she's correct and if she is, I advise you take care not to keep too busy. I know for you that will prove difficult. I thank God that as yet, there has been no sign of Robert or Will, or anyone else intent on treachery. With winter drawing near, the chance of our journeying to you dwindles, yet by spring we expect to have saved enough coins to take time to travel to Menevia. I pray you're blissful and safe and I cry when I think of our parting.'"

Marc set aside the parchment and, while Henry gnawed on Gruffydd's fingers, brother and sister sat, quiet and wistful, musing over how intensely they missed their adopted family.

*****

With a look of sublime joy, Edith crushed the ripped slip of parchment to her breast and sank onto a bench that flanked her trestle table. Marc...He was alive and well and on his way to Wales, to Simon, to Maura! How grieved she was to have missed him, yet elated for his thoughtfulness. She inhaled a joyous breath as a multitude of tender memories flooded her mind and heart. She saw clearly her children embarking on one of their many jaunts—Marc, a pudgy babe crowned with pale curls, struggling to keep pace with Simon, gangly and mussed, and Maura, striding briskly, determined to keep her lead. And then would come Marc's frustrated whimper and Simon's instant surrender as he returned to gather up the boy. Maura would stop, hands on hips and irritated but, in little time, she too would succumb to her brother's cries, waiting where she'd halted with her arms wide and beckoning. What a happy time that had been— happy and simple, as her life was presently. Her lifelong friend and now husband, Arthur, had taught her much about herself in their few months of marriage. He had instilled in her a sense of worth and pride, reminding her daily of the goodness she possessed and bestowed, not only on him, but on all those fortunate to own her friendship. And she had come to acknowledge, rather reluctantly, her invaluable role in the upbringing of three most remarkable individuals. Arthur...How grateful she was for his endearing devotion, and how wholly she adored him...yet try as she might, she could not douse the faint flickering in her heart that persisted for Simon's father, Robert, her one great passion. She still mourned his change from nurturing partner to treacherous fiend, and loathed those who had urged his turnabout—especially Robert's brother, Odo, who concealed his bigotry and ruthlessness behind Bishop's robes.

The date on Marc's note read September 7th and, since a week had passed, Edith was certain the three were together again, for she could somehow sense their joy. She sighed contentedly and rose, wiping her palms on her tunic's skirt. There was no hurry to prepare supper; Arthur was away, purchasing cloth in Gloucester. His absence often made her feel lost and uncertain as to what to do next, which was confusing for she had lived on her own for a long, long while. Rain fell steadily, prohibiting a walk; her mending was caught up, the beasts fed, her baking done. She did feel a bit weary and could do with a nap. A straw pallet, broad enough for two, graced a corner of her modest hut. She knelt by its side and unbraided her silver and chestnut hair. It broke from its taut confinement, tumbling down past her shoulders to mingle with the perfumed rushes. Edith peeled off her sleeveless tunic, and stayed clad in her linen shift as she spread pelts evenly over the straw and plumped her pillow. Satisfied with its softness, she stretched out her sturdy, slim body and nestled herself beneath a sumptuous quilt. She pressed her face into the pillow and her eyes, dark and glinted with gold, closed as sleep came quickly. Her slumber though was vexed by troubling dreams loud with pounding hooves, neighs, bellowed commands, kicks and splintering wood. Then she drowsily realized the sounds came not from a nightmare but from somewhere outside her hut! Alarm forced her awake and up from the pallet; her mind and body froze with throbbing terror as she beheld the door to the cottage being battered inward. Where to run?! The stable! She'd escape through the back door of the stable! She made a lurching dash through the adjoining door and past the stalls. In the dusky light, her fingers clawed at the door's unyielding latch, then found and grabbed the bolt, yanking upward. Her hurled weight flung the door wide, and she bolted directly into the paralyzing embrace of a hauberked soldier. A choking gag muffled her scream, a black hood blinded and smothered her. The soldier thrust her to the ground, wrenched her arms to her back, and twisted her wrists with his forceful binding. Next, he trussed her feet, hoisted her over his shoulder, and hauled her, writhing and bucking, round to the front of the cottage. He threw her in a cart and forked straw over her. The grass' weight pressed her still and, though her mind raced with panic, she paused her fright to listen, feel, and smell. Her kidnappers' mutterings were unintelligible, but the lane's ruts told much. The cart headed south, maneuvering over squeaky planks that bridged sections of the eroded lane. Beyond the smell of straw came the stench of manure—the village common—they passed the common, then turned east onto grass, and a sudden coolness suggested trees. The forest encircling the rear of Dunheved Castle! And so she was to be Robert's prisoner. The thought seemed ridiculous, almost farcical; he hadn't the gall to incarcerate her! She wrestled with her bindings and whimpered at their biting assault. The cart plodded on, round the circular curtain wall. Edith jerked to the jolting sound of the drawbridge dropping, and the screech of the portcullis being wound up into the attic of the gatehouse. Again came clopping hooves and squeaky planks, then the murmurs of strolling tradesmen. The bailey she remembered vividly, and she mentally identified each hut they passed—the forge with clanking hammer; the kitchen with heady aromas; the stables with neighs and the high-pitched voices of grooms. The cart came to an abrupt halt; the straw was shoved aside and a blanket was thrown over her. Roughly swathed, she gasped for breath, and felt herself dangling again from a shoulder. A door groaned open, then slammed shut. She bounced as the soldier trotted down a tightly wound staircase, her head whirling from his rapid descent. He stopped and she fell the long way from his shoulder to the hard, bruising ground. She moaned and rolled as the blanket was brusquely whisked away. Footsteps climbed and dwindled; a damp and dreadful cold descended and sharpened her quaking, the gag tore at her mouth and she retched to the taste of blood. She knew precisely where she'd been abandoned. It was the one place in Dunheved Castle she could never bring herself to go, for she believed the prison to be—Hell, where damned souls were tortured with hot iron, starved, flogged, dismembered, and murdered. She reckoned this was not the end of her torment, only the beginning. Whoever her kidnapper, he not only wanted to steal her freedom, but also her secrets. What she knew was worth great value to some—the whereabouts of Simon, Maura, Almodis and Adam. She tried to sit, but any movement only heightened her agony. Instead, she lay limp and still, and prayed, more desperately than she'd ever prayed before, not for her own deliverance, but for the salvation of her family.

It seemed a long time had passed and perhaps she had slept, when Edith suddenly came alert to a command—cool, distinct, and exact, "Remove the hood." The hands that performed the deed were different from the ones that had abducted her, smaller and gentler. At first, removing the hood made no difference, all remained black, yet gradually her surroundings crystallized, and their malevolence stoked her panic. Instruments of torture and confinement decorated the moldy, dirt walls punctured by torches. The cave stank of urine and excrement, and crawled with insects and vermin. Her body ached so she could barely move, let alone locate her abuser. Again came his order, "Truss her in the chair." The voice was derisively nasal and unmistakably Odo's. So, at last he was free to wreak vengeance on those he believed had wronged him, no doubt including herself.

45

Instead of being dragged, she was surprised to feel her feet and her gag being untied. Then strong arms lifted her to her feet, and guided her into a crude, thickly crafted throne. Her eyes watered furiously from the glare of the torches' flames, and through tears she looked up to the guard with the kindly touch. Recognizing him, she could barely mask her shock as she quickly shifted her eyes to Odo. She saw he was not much altered from when last they'd met; perhaps he was a bit more wrinkled and stockier. The evil in his pale eyes had endured and intensified. His cleric's robes, sewn in the most vivid violets and reds and lavishly embroidered with gold and silver threads, seemed garish in this putrid pit. Everything about him was pompous and impeccable, especially his expression as he greeted her with a pert bow, "My Lady Edith, during my confinement I prayed endlessly for our glorious reunion and I am thrilled my men were so swift to locate you. My spies tell me you've done quite well since my brother came to his senses and tossed you out. That you sell baked goods at the market and reside with a fellow burgher and Saxon, a cloth merchant by the name of Arthur. I've also discovered that my hapless brother does not tax you, but he has always been burdened by weaknesses. Now, I suppose you're wondering why I've brought you here."

Edith mimicked his mocking tone, "Not really."

"Fine...then let's dispense with trivial chatter and move on to more crucial matters. Where is Simon?"

"I don't know."

"You lie."

"Perhaps, perhaps not."

"I want only to speak to him."

A guffaw exploded from Edith and she viciously returned, "It is impossible for you *'only to speak'* with anyone!"

A gruesome grin prefaced his proposition, "If you cooperate, you will be returned to your cozy abode immediately. But," he cruelly added, "if you persist with your foolish resistance, you will reside here indefinitely and be introduced to a host of crudities. I will discover where he is, my Lady—if not from you, then from your man."

"You won't touch Arthur!" she wailed, lunging upward and wrestling with her binding.

"And so I've found your frailty," he sniggered, knocking her back into the chair. "That is usually all that's needed—one frailty—and you, being so pitiful, have so many—"

"Where's Robert?" she spat, sick of his drivel.

"He's searching out his beloved wife and child." He studied her reaction, hoping for a wounded sign. She betrayed nothing. "I'm certain your son blabbed to you the news of Robert's marriage, he's quite good at blabbing things. The Lady Almodis is a lovely creature, genteel, far younger than you, and she has gifted Robert with a legitimate son, highbred and pure, not base like your brat." Odo's taunting failed to produce the desired upset, and he bristled, "Tell me where he is!"

"No."

She spoke too calmly and he wondered where her brazenness came from, for surely she knew the dire consequences of obstinacy. "I'll leave you to a bit of coercion, then return and ask again," he threatened.

"Why waste your precious time?"

"Because I have precious little time left on this earth, woman, and before I go I will have my revenge!"

"Then I'll pray for your rotted soul, and for your conscience to prevail, if you indeed own one. If you need to harass someone, go harass Lanfranc. It was he, not Simon, who betrayed your crimes to the King—"

46

His fierce slap stole her breath. Rage quaked his bulk, flushed his face, and fired his eyes. "You dare slander a man of God, you...you Devil's bitch!" He slapped again, harder, cracking her head against the back of the chair, and frothed, "You bewitched Robert, convinced him the bastard was his, robbed his strength and will!" Eerily, his choler quickly cooled and he spoke as if reciting a sermon, "Now the time has come for penance to be exacted. And God has commanded that I deliver yours. It will be done. While I'm gone," he coarsely directed to the sentry, "you can have her if you wish. She was my brother's whore for twenty-odd years and, I dare say, relishes depravity of all sorts." With a grand huff, he spun on his heels and left, slamming a dense, barred door behind him.

Edith closed her eyes a moment, let go a long bitter moan, then managed a smile at the youngish, guilt-ridden face of her once loyal servant. "Benjamin!" she cried. "How is it you?!"

"My Lady!" he answered as buoyantly, dropping to one knee. "I didn't know it was you he confined. If so, I would never have agreed to come with him!"

"I thank God you did!"

"I cannot release you, Madam, I have no authority, nor a key."

"I would never ask you to endanger yourself," she said with urgent clarity. "When the deliverer of my penance arrives, run and find Lord Robert. Tell him of Odo's treachery and send him here. Do you know my cottage?"

"Yes, my Lady."

"Leave a note there, informing my husband Arthur of my whereabouts. Insist he not attempt my rescue, for he would most certainly be killed. Robert will see to my deliverance. I'm sure of it."

"I will my dear Lady! I will!" he gushed.

"And please hurry!" she begged. "Please, Arthur will be home shortly and he will go mad with grief and attempt something foolish!"

"If I leave you alone, you will be tortured!"

"There is no escaping that fate. I pray it will be short-lived when Robert is alerted."

"I will at least untie you," said Benjamin. She turned and he grunted and struggled with the knots, finally freeing her hands. Her heart ached to his misery as he whipped off his tunic and fumbled to swab the blood from her wrists.

In thanks, her trembling fingers touched his ginger curls and rested on his rouged cheek. "Bless you, Benjamin," she ardently murmured.

"Many of the soldiers in Lord Robert's guard still hold you in the highest regard and miss you terribly." He cloaked her shoulders with his stained garment and kissed her fingers, vowing, "I will personally see to your freedom, Madam. And what of your son?"

"I can say little, there are too many ears about. I *will* tell you he is well, safe, and happy."

"The thought brings me joy. He was a dear friend."

His confession coaxed from her tears and wistful words, "Yes, I remember well..."

As Odo trudged the stairs, he paused every so often for air and to consider another odious plot. The trouble with Edith was that she would gladly die for her brat, and thus shorten his fun. And yet, he decided wickedly, whether or not he managed to extract from her Simon's location, it was possible to draw out her turmoil—indefinitely.

*****

CHAPTER FOUR - A FINE WELCOME

𝔍𝔫 the early hours before dawn Marc and Gruffydd slept soundly upon the bed, with Henry the pup sprawled between them, belly exposed and feet dangling in the air. A brisk moist breeze forced its way between the closed shutters and fanned the coals in the main room. Maura thrashed fitfully on a mat close by, trying desperately to escape the wind's smothering warmth, her blanket, and her horrific dream...

Abandoned in the courtyard of a long house, she twisted and flinched in terror, screaming for her parents' rescue. Marc, just a babe, wailed along and clung to her skirts. All about them flaming birds dove from the sky, igniting everything they lit upon. Silver-clad beasts raged upright round the enclosure, chasing, hacking, and battering; dense smoke cloaked and strangled. Maura's mother raced toward Maura, her gold hair swept up by the hot wind, her mouth wide and yelling something Maura could not hear. She motioned furiously at the long house. Maura snatched up Marc and slipped and struggled through limbs and hewn bodies, the faces of dead friends and kin gaping up at her. Whimpering, she squeezed shut her eyes and pitched forward through the gore. Marc's head thudded against the ground, stopping his wailing. Maura's whimpering spiraled to hysterics as she scrambled to her feet, clutched him tighter, and ran on to the house. But the beasts ran after her, their heavy boots quaking the ground, stomping closer while the door seemed to grow smaller and move farther and farther away...

The thought of Maura's welcoming embrace, and water and oats, spurred Simon and Fulk down the lane that entered the commote of Mynyw. Fulk handily took the sharp turn that led up the steep path to their home, and snorted happy breaths as he bounded through the wildflowers and reared to a stop before the door. Simon sprang from the saddle, but his foot caught in the stirrup. Both horse and rider danced, Fulk from excitement at being home and Simon from crazed frustration. His curses roared through the night as he hopped about, clawing and struggling for freedom. Finally, his boot fell from its shackle and he landed with an abrupt thump on his bottom. Fulk took off for the stable while Simon sat a bit stunned, swabbing sweat from his brow, and gazing with loving relief on his humble cottage, barely visible in the moonless night.

Inside Maura's nightmare flared on...She reached the long house and stumbled through the open doorway. She saw her father engulfed in smoke and lolling in a far corner. He reached out a desperate hand and she hurried toward it, leaping clumps of burning rushes. His face appeared through the mist, dark blue eyes pleading, copper hair and beard seared and blackened; along his neck, a long gash gurgled blood, and his expression convulsed with pain, terror, and love. He gripped her ankle and dragged her and Marc into the corner with him. His head dropped to the rushes, and his body went limp, yet his clutch held fast. Flames surged the walls and devoured the rushes; shards of burning wood shot from crumbling timbers, stabbing and singeing her skin. Maura fought to flee, kicked at his hold, screamed at him, "Let us go!" But he didn't answer, didn't move. The smoke briefly parted and she beheld her mother, wrestling with a silver beast—not a beast—a soldier! Maura screamed, "Here! We're here! Save us!" Her mother spun to her squall and, at her lapse, the man unsheathed his sword. "No! The man!" cried Maura, but the crackling pyre drowned her shriek. The sword neatly sliced the smoke and cut her mother to the ground; her head rolled close to Maura's feet, the mouth still twitching from the quick throes of death. The man charged for Maura. She bundled Marc and shrank deeper into the corner. He drew himself to an ominous height, his reddened sword poised to strike. She challenged his smoke-veiled glower and dropped over Marc. The blade plummeted...

Maura screamed as Simon tripped on her foot and crashed head first into the wall. He slumped dazed to the floor as she rose up, howling so pitifully, shivers shot up his spine. He tackled her back to the mat, but her screams only heightened. She raked and beat at his face and shoulders, thrashed and arched beneath his weight.

Marc's feet hit the rushes by the bed and his legs instantly crumpled beneath him. His hands groped and climbed the wall, hauling his useless body up. He lurched through the door and, squinting through the blackness, saw Maura's attacker. Crouching, he swiped out blindly, grabbed a fistful of cloth, and punched; the scoundrel toppled listlessly into the rushes. Marc felt for Maura but found the mat empty and heard the front door bang shut. He kicked the man aside and somehow mustered the strength to charge out after her, over the flattened wildflowers, and onto the path. Her white flapping figure came into view, racing wildly ahead. He followed, then to his horror, he saw her stumble, fall, and roll down and down the hill. Faster he chased, chest heaving, throat burning, head whirling and, when close enough, he dove to his belly, caught hold of her skirt and rolled with her. A nettle bush sharply stalled their descent, and together they lay, tangled and still.

Henry yelped, dashing back and forth between the bed and the door, leaping at the latch, scratching at the wood. Gruffydd, eyes huge with fright, sat at the foot of the bed. He quaked and wrung his hands, panicking inwardly, *Why don't they come back and fetch me?!* He'd sworn to protect Maura and she'd screamed, but Marc went to help instead. *Why doesn't Marc come back and say everything is fine, that Maura is fine? Where did they go? Is someone still outside the door? What will they do to me?!*

Henry at last managed to paw the door open enough to squeeze through. He discovered a body not far from the fire pit; its familiar odor made him yowl and whine, nuzzle and lick. Simon let out a long achy groan and attempted to raise his head; the resultant hurt made him groan louder. He floundered to sit, to see, yet nothing but clouds swirled before his eyes, thick clouds of pain. The dog, the damned dog kept licking; he hated the dog licking his face. He shoved Henry away, and the pup wedged his way back through to the bedchamber, making such a racket that Gruffydd grudgingly left the bed to find its cause. Peeking through the crack in the door, he saw a moaning lump lurching about the floor. He promptly closed the door and pressed his back against it to keep it shut. Over his heart's rapid pounding, he considered, *Maybe the lump outside is Marc and someone has stolen Maura! It is my duty to help Marc rescue her!* Henry nipped at his toes; he nudged him away, and crept to the side table to fetch a candle. He boldly ventured out beyond the door and, as silently as possible, he tip-toed past the lump and knelt by the fire pit. He chose an especially brittle rush and pressed its tip to a coal, then blew fiercely. A tiny flame leapt to the rush and he touched it to the candle's wick. The miraculous sight of Simon, sitting cross-legged in the rushes cradling his head, came clear. "Simon!" Gruffydd cried and crawled close, setting the candle nearby. Henry joined them, squirming and yapping. Simon woozily peered through the mist, searching out the owner of the greeting, and smiled vaguely at Gruffydd. Gruffydd sensed something queer—Simon's eyes looked strange, he was usually much cheerier, and his head flopped a bit. The strange sight brought on a memory of a time not long past when Gruffydd had gone with Simon to tend some men who'd been in a fight. One acted like Simon did now. Simon had waved an open jar under the man's nose, making his arms flop and his head jerk. Then the man had started yelling. If only he could find that jar! Gruffydd scrambled off the floor and onto the stool flanking the physician's table. He grabbed up jar after jar, opening and sniffing, but everything smelled good; the jar Simon used before smelled awful. He hopped down and rooted through a trunk stored beneath the table. His hunt grew more fervid till one jar produced the shock he wanted. Its stench snapped his head back and knocked him on his seat. He shook from its blow, smiled, then confidently squatted by Simon, who hadn't budged and still moaned. Sucking a bracing breath, he thrust the jar in Simon's face.

Simon flew backwards, flailing and gasping such horrible gasps that Gruffydd screamed and began sobbing. He waited for Simon to say something, but Simon lay still and quiet and, certain he'd killed him, Gruffydd's bawling intensified. Simon opened his eyes and found the clouds gone; the events of the last hour struck with an intensity that bolted him upright. He fought to slow his panic when he saw Gruffydd racked with misery and hugging his belly. "Gruffydd, Gruffydd," he murmured gently, clasping the boy to his chest. "I'm here and you're fine. You must stop crying and tell me who hit me. Where's Maura?! What happened? You must tell me!" But the child cried on and Simon's stuttering turned desperate, "I...I must find her! You stay here, you...you'll be safe. I'll lock the door. *Please* don't leave."

"No!" wailed Gruffydd, his hold strangling. "Don't leave me! Marc hit you, Marc did it!"

Shock made Simon stand and drop the boy, only to sink to the rushes once more and choke, "Ma...Marc! No...it...it can't be. Not Marc!"

"Yes!" Gruffydd cried. "Maura swore he'd hurt no one, but he hurt you!"

"Where've they gone?"

"I don't know!"

"We'll find them!" Simon frantically decided. He swung Gruffydd up in his arms, wavered a few steps, then found his balance and sprinted out the door. It was dark, too dark, and his eyesight hadn't sufficiently cleared. But terror that Maura and Marc lay at the bottom of the cliff, their necks broken, propelled him on—across the path and beyond.

With a jolting groan, Marc flipped over and gasped at the ghastly sight of Maura caught fast in the nettle's stinging limbs. He touched her softly so as not to startle; she moved slightly, yet failed to wake. Help, he needed help, but who and where? No one knew or could understand him. There was Sulien, but Marc didn't know the way to the Bishop's home and he couldn't, wouldn't leave her alone, not with her attacker so near! And the boy, what would happen to Gruffydd?! Never had he felt this powerless as he tugged at the branches. They refused to let go and stabbed back at him. He sucked blood from his fingers, and tried but couldn't stop his tears. Held back for so long, they flooded forth, washing streaks of dirt from his cheeks, and doubling him to the ground. He prayed as he sobbed, prayed she was not dead, for if she was, he'd die of heartbreak and shame. *It's my fault she slept on the mat in the main room. If she'd been in her own bed, I could have stopped her attacker, stopped her before...*

Panted breaths and a low, soothing voice drifted through his dirge. "Marc...Marc...It's Simon. You must help me get her free." A warm touch joined the whispered entreaty, "Marc, are you able to help me?"

"Yes..." The strength of his reply surprised Marc. Though the dark was still dense, he could clearly see his friend, a hairier Simon, but Simon nonetheless, and he reached out to take his hand. Their firm clasp paled their knuckles.

A necessary calm had claimed Simon. He knew its saving effect would be brief, so he took advantage of the rare moment to issue orders. "Gruffydd has gone back for a knife. When he returns, I'll cut the branches and you work her loose." He noticed Marc's bloodied fingers. "I see you've found how nasty the hairs can be." His bolstering tone seemed to ease Marc's confusion, so he encouraged on, "You've done nothing wrong, Marc, nothing wrong. I would have done the same. Once we get her back to the hut, she *will* be fine."

"Are you certain?" whimpered Marc.

Simon confidently lied, "Of course."

Gruffydd appeared, out of breath with dagger and hooded candle in hand. He kept shy of Marc, squatted by Simon, and shifted a wary eye between the two men.

Without further talk, Marc and Simon began their tricky task. Simon sliced carefully, while Marc eased Maura from the plant's grip. They sighed in unison at the sound of the last cut, then Simon gathered her in his arms, rubbed his cheek to hers, and called softly, "Maura..."

Marc noticed him tense to her silence, and gently reminded, "Once we get her back, she will be fine."

They made what seemed a long journey to the hut. Gruffydd, first to enter, flitted about finding and lighting candles till both rooms blazed brightly. Simon held Maura while Marc straightened the bed, apologizing, "I've mussed it."

"It's no matter," Simon dismissed. He lowered her carefully upon the covered feathers, and blanketed her with the quilt.

Marc helped to bundle her, then watched Simon's expression wrench with worry. "What should I do now, Simon?" he wondered loudly. Yet Simon stayed quiet and grave, and Marc knew it was his turn to bolster. "You know better than anyone how to help her, now let me help you. Tell me what to do."

"Ale," Simon whispered, then croaked louder, "warm ale...and water and a towel to bathe her face." He gulped, then quavered the question, "Did she fall?"

"Yes...and rolled."

"Then...then I...I must check her for bleeding...the child...She had trouble before." Simon's calm crumbled, his fists clenched, and his despair exploded. "Marc, she can't lose this child! She'll die if that happens! I'll die! What happened? Why did she scream and fight me?! Was she ill? Why are you here? Tell me!"

Marc felt unbearable alarm. He wanted to scream as well, curse, wail, and hurl things, but instead he mumbled, "I'll warm the ale and fetch the water, then tell you all I know, which is very little."

Simon watched him leave and fought crazed ramblings that threatened his tenuous control. He focused on the serenity of Maura's expression, yet saw and heard again the Welsh raiders growling, their bows being drawn, Maura's scream, Gruffydd and Marc's tears...then felt his own wetting his cheeks, choking his murmurs, "Maura, it's Simon. I'm home. You're safe and the ba—" His hand reluctantly left her warm cheek to move aside the quilt and blanket. No blood stained her chemise. He tentatively lifted its hem and thanked God aloud when he found none on or between her legs. "The baby is fine," he assured her, spreading his fingers over her belly and kneading slightly. He felt no hardening. Her sedateness didn't leave, and he sadly realized he shouldn't force her waking. It was best she be kept still and warm, and that she sleep...something he hadn't done properly in three days. The corner of his eye caught Gruffydd striding toward the head of the bed holding a jar exuding an odd odor, the same odor— "Gruffydd, no!" shouted Simon, grabbing his wrist, and knocking the jar to the floor. Gruffydd sobbed again. Simon picked him up, hugged him tightly and consoled, "I'm sorry, Gruffydd, but that ointment would wake the dead."

"Is Maura dead?!" the boy cried.

"No," Simon soothed. "She's only sleeping and needs to sleep more."

"Where's my mam?"

"She stayed behind to talk with Ella. I'm certain she'll return by tomorrow dusk. I'm to give you her love, and this." He kissed the boy's brow, and Gruffydd burrowed deeper in his hold. Simon imagined the tumult he must be feeling and lauded, "You were smart to know how to wake me, and so brave to return alone to the cottage for the dagger. Now you must rest..." He patted the foot of the bed. "Here...help keep her warm." After settling the boy beneath the quilt, he added a last cheering remark, "Your mam's agreed to let you have the colt." Gruffydd glowed and wriggled with joy, which prompted Simon's gentle chide, "Keep still now. Where's Henry gone?"

"I don't know...Why did Marc hit you?"

"He didn't know it was me. He thought I was hurting Maura and he stopped me."

"He *seems* nice."

"And he is."

As if their praise conjured him, Marc appeared sporting a bated look, and carrying a steaming cup and bowl.

"There's no blood," Simon swiftly affirmed.

Marc's expression eased and, with a weak smile and nod, he set down the crockery, sat opposite Simon, and readily spilled, "I arrived early yesterday morn. It took me a full month to travel from Mantes. I made good time till I left Dunheved. I was robbed, not that I had much to steal. Amazingly, they left me my horse. Then I got lost, and there was no water, no villages. It was so hot. I don't remember much, but I must have asked directions because I soon found the cathedral. Then came the sea and the village, the road to your hut, and Maura."

"My mother and Arthur, did you see them?" Simon asked anxiously.

"No...but I've brought a letter. They are fine. And Maura was as well. Very bubbly, worried about you. I don't know what happened, Simon. She insisted I stay in your bed."

"Marc, I'm thrilled to see you, especially now, yet I must know—"

Marc knew his need and related, "Just before I left Normandy, the King was injured in Mantes. He was taken to Rouen to recover. There was nothing and no one left to fight for, so I came here."

"And he *will* recover," stated Simon emphatically.

"I'm not certain of that, Simon."

"*I* have to be..." As Simon glanced ruefully at Maura, then down at the boy now sleeping, he was suddenly stricken with a weighty weariness that pressed him to the bed. His jaw throbbed, the room spun, and he mumbled, "How hard did you hit me?"

Simon heard Marc's faint, "*Very* hard," and, before all went black, he briefly pondered what had happened to spoil his much anticipated—fine welcome.

*****

Marc arranged Simon neatly in his bed, and then Gruffydd comfortably upon the mat in the main room, stoked the meager fire, then took the stack of letters, a candle, and a cup of ale to the trestle table. There he sat and, for a long peaceful moment, reveled in the glorious silence. The earlier commotion had rendered him too awake for sleep, and he decided to use the remainder of the night to discover more about Simon and Maura's recent and tumultuous past. He spread one parchment flat, weighted its corner with the candle holder, and read...

'15 June 1087. Marc, one word most completely describes our wedding...resplendent! And credit for its success rests entirely with Henry, for he arranged the entire celebration. I know it's hard for you to think kindly of him, but he does have his giving moments. Archbishop Lanfranc performed the rites which was fitting for he and Simon are very close. But our short time at Canterbury was not without upset. Lanfranc disclosed that it was he and not Simon who had betrayed to the King Odo's scheme to usurp the Pope. And that disclosure alone led to Odo's

52

imprisonment. And so Odo falsely accused Simon for the sole purpose of destroying Robert's and Simon's bond and so, so much more.'

Marc paused a moment, wondering at the '...so, so much more.' Maybe the more would appear later he hoped, as he eagerly ventured further...'We spent an exquisite month traveling, visiting old haunts and discovering new ones, then stopped in Dunheved to stay awhile with Edith. To our joy, we found with her our dear friend Arthur. He had journeyed from Winchester to Dunheved just to woo her and was quite successful in his mission, for within the week, they were wed! While riding to Rose's son's manor home, I could hardly contain my excitement, and it erupted at the astonishing sight of Almodis and Alan! It seems Almodis and her then unborn child were being stalked by Will. He wants no contenders to his inheritance. In a bold move, Robert sent her away secretly with Alan for safekeeping, and Alan very wisely brought her to Rose. During our stay, Almodis confessed to me her tender feelings for Alan and that they are heartily returned by him. Also during that eventful week, Almodis gave birth to Adam, a robust, black-haired, dark-eyed angel.'

'It was devastating to leave our family, but we knew our destiny lay elsewhere, hopefully in Mynyw. When we arrived here, we were met by Gael, whom I admit to being jealous of till I was assured her and Simon's past was only friendly. We were not immediately welcomed by the villagers, but I was so sick I didn't wholly realize the dire consequences of our not being allowed to stay. Simon did and in his intensely special way he managed to convince the villagers that we would be giving and peaceful neighbors. And, Marc, a miracle has happened! As I sit beside my sleeping husband, here in Gael's cozy hut, I caress my belly and our child. I cannot properly describe our bliss, for we both had grave doubts that we'd be blest again. And no one, no one will take this one away—ever!'

Marc drank long from his cup and stared off curiously into a dark corner. What did this '...blest again,' mean? He remembered Simon's hysteria over the child's well-being. Had there been *another* child? And had it been taken from them? But when and how? Was it a tragedy too terrible to tell? In the morning, he'd seek out Simon—alone—and ask him of the mystery, but he must do so gently, for at times Simon had a tendency to react rather severely.

*****

With rising terror, Edith watched the bulky, mail-clad jailer roast iron rods over a fire pit. She studied his face—dead of emotion, wrinkled, flabby, and swarthy from, she imagined, endless hours hovering over flames. The rods were meant for her; a means of coercion, but the exact method of application escaped her. As she watched, her thoughts flitted about, grasping at anything distracting. She wondered what sort of person came to be a torturer, and if indeed they had a choice in the matter. Such a sad, horrid life. She wished Benjamin was with her now, but she was more pleased he had managed to slip out unnoticed when the jailer and his men had entered, and was this moment on his way to Robert. She prayed her Liege not far away, and then considered the lies Odo had spouted in his attempt to weaken her resolve. He could not have known Almodis' child's gender, nor that Adam had actually survived birth. And Almodis...how shocked the Bishop would be to hear that Robert's wife was in fact Edith's dear friend and confidante. Edith shuddered to think of the punishment planned for Almodis if she were discovered. Yet then again, Robert had sent Almodis away with Alan specifically for safekeeping, and according to Almodis, he had been aware of their closeness. They made such a curious pair—Almodis, an outlandish, petulant woman capable of enormous generosity; and Alan, unassumingly direct, yet deeply emotional. On several occasions he had been rescuer to Simon, who was known to all for his impetuousness, and Edith was forever in Alan's debt. The rods at last glowed red, and she wondered

53

sadly and briefly, if Robert didn't come to *her* rescue, there was an excellent chance she would never see her friends or family again. The misery she had fought so hard to contain streamed down her cheeks, and she cried out, "No, in God's name, please have mercy!" as the hood darkened her world once more.

Edith prayed for strength to endure her torment, and heard the ominous query, "Will you betray his location, Madam?" With the wag of her head came a pain so fierce its location eluded her, the stench of burning flesh filled her head. She arched in her seat, strained against her bindings, retched and gagged on a violent scream rumbling from her gut. And then a miraculous cocoon of lightness surrounded and lifted her from her suffering. Her limpness prompted the jailer to remove the rod from the sole of her foot and mutter a curse, "Damn the bitch. She could at least have stayed awake for one more application. The Bishop will not be pleased."

*****

Benjamin rode through the night in furious haste toward Robert's coastal residence at Tintangel. He was welcomed at dawn by a grueling wind, a spitting rain, and a host of snoring guards sprawled about the unbattened guardhouse. The bailey's inhabitants were scarcely awake and took no notice of his flurried figure weaving between their huts, vaulting puddles, and clambering the steep steps of the timbered keep. He surged across the modest hall and banged repeatedly on the Lord's bedchamber, rousing the squire sleeping at its base. "Sir...Sir," the boy stuttered, "Who...why are you here?"

"I serve Lord Robert at Dunheved and bring urgent news. He must be woken at once!"

Benjamin's fluster thrust the boy to his feet. He wrestled with the lock and shouldered his way inside the chamber, shrilly calling, "My Lord, a messenger with urgent news requests your audience. My Lord!"

Startled awake, Robert fumbled for words and the dagger beneath his pillow. He clutched his pelts to his naked chest and peered into a shadowy grayness, faintly demanding, "Who's there?" The puzzling scene brightened at his squire's strike of a flint, and Robert saw by the side of the bed a man balanced on one knee with bowed head. The boy scuttled about the scantly furnished chamber, lighting candles, which Robert stopped with a swipe of his hand and the order, "Go, Thomas, and round up my guards. Now, who are you?" Benjamin's hood fell away; he lifted a harrowed expression, and Robert gasped, "Benjamin! What's happened?"

Benjamin stayed submissive and silent while Robert scrambled off the tall bed and swiftly pulled on his braies, shirt, and tunic. Then he spoke passionately, "Your brother, Bishop Odo has taken the Lady Edith prisoner. He aims to torture her, my Lord, lest she tell him Simon's whereabouts!"

The news dizzied Robert; he hugged the bedpost, cleared dread from his throat, and spoke staidly, "You were correct to come for me. Follow Thomas, ready my mount and a small contingent of soldiers. I will join you shortly in the bailey."

With Benjamin away, the enormity of the situation struck Robert, slumping him to the bed. And so Odo's scheme to destroy Simon had already commenced. It had taken too many years, but Robert had finally come to accept his son's innocence in the Bishop's debacle, and guilt over their shattered bond endlessly plagued him. And now Edith was to fall victim to Odo's madness! No, he would never allow that, not after his disturbing meeting with her near a year past, when he'd discovered his fondness for her still alive. He hesitated at the door and slumped again to the dire thoughts, *Can I stop Odo's treachery? Can anyone?*

*****

Arthur led his pony in the rear door of the stable connected to his home of three months, a modest, cozy daub and wattle cottage in the borough of Dunheved. After settling the beast in its stall and providing water and oats, he called out for his dove of a wife, Edith. He received no answer, and wondered why she was so early gone. Perhaps she had left for the market, he thought, as he wandered in the main room, opened a back window to allow in the morning's dim light, then sat a moment at the trestle table. There he noticed a clumsily scribbled square of parchment, weighted by an earthen jug. He wiggled it loose, turned the note over and over in his palm, and realized the scribbles were not from her hand. Then slowly he mouthed the terrible words, "'Edith taken prisoner and held at Dunheved. Do not attempt rescue or you both shall die. Lord Robert will be alerted'."

Rage shook Arthur's stout and robust figure; he heaved from the table, raked fingers through his long silver hair and raved, "Alerted!" to the soot-stained ceiling. "Alerted to what?! How truly fiendish he can be!" He snatched up his cloak and stormed staunchly toward the door, yet paused and read again the warning, 'you both shall die'. What good would he be to her dead? And if *her* death resulted from his single-handed attempt at rescue, he would never be able to forgive himself. Hadn't he lectured Simon many times of the dangers of impulsivity? Yet, in spite of *his* recklessness, Simon was still alive, and residing happily with his love. He'd always been a bit jealous of Simon's foolhardy tendencies. And it had been precisely that jealousy that had driven Arthur's successful mission to woo and wed the Lady Edith! As he kicked his way out the battered door, he rightly decided he'd not lose her, not now, and never to that monster, Robert!

Edith's consciousness wavered. She forced open her eyes and saw only blackness, but a coolness touched her face and she knew the hood was gone. She lay on what felt like straw; its stench was overpowering and all about her were faint rustlings. Her shift was soaked, she supposed, from her own urine, and her foot burned as if set ablaze. A clinking sound and louder rustlings intruded. A resonant, sickeningly familiar voice boomed above her, echoing eerily, "Will you endure more pain or confess? I have little patience, my Lady."

She felt her mind slipping away again, and fought the fog to rasp, "Do what you will. I'll never say where he is...never...never to you."

Odo's ire spewed forth in a booming trail of curses, rumbling together and off the dank walls. Edith allowed the fog again to save her from his horror, for even in her deluded state, she knew Odo would torture her only if he were granted the pleasure of her screams.

Arthur's repeated attempts to enter the bailey were met with grunted rebukes from the guards. If, as they stated, Lord Robert was not in residence, then who had her, and where? His despair kept him near the entrance, squatting behind bushes and waiting...for what or whom he did not know.

It was near noon when hoof beats shook the ground and started Arthur from his anxious stupor. He rose, strained to see, and swiftly recognized Lord Robert, riding at the fore of a small contingent of soldiers. He recalled that same stony look twenty-one years past, on the fateful day Robert had forced his way into Arthur's home to steal Edith and Simon away to Dunheved. Arthur stormed out from his cover. Weapons were loudly and rapidly unsheathed as the troop circled closer. Robert's steed reared to Arthur's flurried advance, almost unseating his royal rider, who struggled for control and swung his crop high to strike. But Robert stopped mid-swipe, and gaped curiously at the preposterous sight of Arthur, flourishing a piece of parchment, plump face flushed scarlet, bulk quaking, and lips sputtering, "If I owned a weapon, I'd carve out your frigid heart, you heinous pig! Give me back my wife!"

Robert shook from his fuddle to ask, "And *who*, Sir, may I ask is your wife?"

"The good Lady Edith..."

Again Robert almost toppled from his seat as he blurted in disbelief, "*Your* wife?"

"Yes...I found this note."

Robert snatched it up and futilely tried to comprehend the script. He offered it back, mumbling in embarrassment, "Tell me what it says."

"That she's been taken, and I shouldn't attempt rescue, and that you'd be alerted! Well I'll alert you now, my *Liege*, that if she's not set free immediately, you'll know the wrath of the entire village..." Arthur's fists shook the sky and his wail touched all, "for she is as dear to them as she is to me!"

Robert looked to his men's disquiet, swallowed his own, and asserted, "Believe me when I say it was not I who kidnapped her. And in fact, I have just returned to right this wrong." There was something disturbingly familiar about Arthur. Robert briefly scanned his memory, and one eye narrowed to his question, "Might you be called— Arthur?"

"I am!" answered Arthur with ire.

Robert straightened to the retort, then answered indignantly, "Then follow along, *Arthur*, and we shall find your Lady wife!"

As Arthur bustled along, struggling to keep pace with the horses' trot, he wondered at Robert's uneasy air. Perhaps, in truth, it wasn't he who had taken her, but then Arthur recalled Edith's grueling rendition of their last not so congenial meeting and bristled inwardly, *Of course it was Robert! Who else would wish harm to Edith—a saint!*

Arthur followed Robert's men into the keep of Dunheved Castle and along dark, tortuous passageways to the great hall. There, Robert's hollering sent his men scurrying in every direction. "Fetch every guard and the jailer. Find who's in residence and bring them before me—at once!" He pitched into his throne, massaged his brow, and closed his eyes. Arthur boldly stood opposite and, studying the tormented soul before him, pondered Edith's long-lived fascination with the rake. In looks there was no comparison, Robert was still sharply handsome, and he...well, God had not been so kind. Knowing Edith, there had to be more—some spark of humanity that would have deserved her devotion for so many years. She claimed Robert now to be a cold, vicious beast; looking more closely, Arthur was not convinced of her accusation—this man was deeply troubled—clearly not the reaction of a vicious beast. Robert lifted a flat expression to suggest, "You may sit. Would you care for wine?"

"Wine!" Arthur raved. "How can I—you sit when she could be this moment—How can you do nothing?!"

"I've sent my men. They will find her presently."

"Point the way to your prison!" demanded Arthur. "I will go!"

Robert answered his offer listlessly, "No you won't. Your blustering will only worsen matters."

"What matters?!" shouted Arthur accusingly. "You *did* know of her capture. Who is in residence here?"

"I'm not certain but I believe it to be my brother."

"The King?!" exclaimed Arthur.

"No, the King is dead. My brother...the Bishop."

Arthur stood agape and stunned. The King dead! The devil Odo released! He couldn't have imagined a more bodeful turn of events—Simon and Maura's protection gone with the King, and the Bishop free and bent on revenge and treachery. Oh, the odious tales Edith had spoken of Odo's endless capacity for deceit, avarice, treason, and...murder!

Robert interrupted Arthur's dread with a light question, "When did you marry her?"

"Wha...what?" started Arthur.

"When exactly did you wed the Lady Edith?"

"June of this year."

"You failed to ask my permission."

"What?"

"My permission," repeated Robert. "And mind how you speak to me, *Sir*! You chose to move here and become my subject. Any marriage performed in the borough of Dunheved requires the Lord's blessing, or is considered null."

Arthur grew crazy with rage. He wanted to pounce on this *Lord*, rip off his smug grin, bloody his face, pound his wiry form to nothingness! At first, the only response he could muster was a sputtered string of curses which finally merged and strengthened to a thunderous rebuttal, "The only Lord *we* answer to resides high above, and *He* wholeheartedly blest our union! *You*," he challenged with wielded finger, "never owned the decency to marry her...you...you filthy, scheming, lecher!"

"Scheming? Scheming how?" postured Robert.

"You brought Edith here to taunt her...and me. You can't endure the thought of her with another man, happy and contented."

"You spout nonsense. As I claimed before, I did not take her, nor do I envy your happy, contented union. I have better."

"Better what?" retorted Arthur, then he realized Robert spoke of Almodis. He almost burst a guffaw, yet swiftly stifled it for Almodis' sake and his own.

"My Lord," interrupted Thomas, Robert's pocked, baby-faced squire, "the Bishop Odo is in residence and is occupied elsewhere.

"Have him occupy himself here."

"But my Lord," Thomas sniveled. "He won't listen...He's in a foul temper and—"

Robert raised a hand for quiet and rose with a bitter sigh. He didn't want to, but haltingly offered, "Then I will fetch him. You stay here with this...this...*Saxon* burgher. I don't trust him. He may steal away with all my treasures." He threw one last sneer Arthur's way before striding off. Arthur wagged his head in disgust at Robert's accusation. Treasures! Their stable's dung heap held more treasures than this squalid pit.

Robert tread more slowly as he neared the base of the prison's staircase. Perhaps the sight of Edith's suffering would enable him the gall to reproach his brother. Yet his advance halted as he grappled with doubt and wondered why someone else couldn't handle this nasty mess. Maybe he should have sent Arthur ahead to fuddle Odo; he seemed a fearsome adversary. But Odo was rarely fuddled. He braced himself to expect the worst, and indeed saw just that, as he rounded the corner and stood aghast before the travesty. Odo paced in front of the torturer's throne muttering curses spiced with religious fervor; the jailer squatted and roasted irons; and Edith sat slumped upon the chair clad only in a filthy shift. Her head hung in a queer way to the side, her eyes blazed with fevered misery, and her lips were swollen and cracked. They had trussed her bloodied wrists to the chair's arms, and her feet, soles blackened and blistered, were bound together to a stool. Robert was not prepared for the wrenching guilt and compassion that attacked his insides and made him groan. He jumped to a touch and whisper at his elbow, and sternly whispered back, "Benjamin, don't scare me again!"

"I won't my Lord. I wondered if I might be of service."

"Yes...Stay by my side," he directed feebly as he took a broad step forward, and tried to distract his brother. "O...Odo." Odo's unbroken tirade drowned Robert's piteous squeak so he spoke again, louder, "Odo!" The Bishop paused, whirled, and his fierce countenance struck Robert dumb. He gulped his fright and inched nearer to stammer, "Odo...I...I demand you cease this...this..." He struggled but couldn't summon a devious enough name for his brother's villainy, so finished weakly, "punishment at once!"

"Why are you here?!" Odo blared back.

"I do own this castle and reside here from time to time," Robert noted pointedly. He glanced at Edith's face, her eyes now closed, and felt his mettle surge. "I am the only baron authorized to take, keep, or torture prisoners in this hole and...and I demand you leave here immediately!"

"Fine..." Odo appeared ruffled by his brother's rarely seen mastery, yet rebounded with greater force. "I will go, but I take my prisoner with me!"

"No! She resides in my village and is my subject!"

Odo reeked sarcasm. "And I suspect she also resides in your bed, you weak depraved worm, slave to debauchery...licentiousness..."

"Enough!" demanded Robert and to Benjamin he swiftly ordered, "Rally my guards to escort the Bishop *out*."

"They are rallied my Lord, just beyond the door."

Robert cast his servant an awed look and waved a limp hand in the air. The gesture instantly issued forth the band of hauberked men and Odo's mastery and curses quickly faded. He grinned and spread his arms in surrender, slowly wove his way through the pack, then trudged the stairs in defeat. Robert motioned for the jailer to go, then nodded toward the throne. Benjamin and another guard freed Edith's arms and carefully unbound her feet. "Take her to my chamber, quickly," issued Robert. "Fetch my physician and servants to tend her." Benjamin swept her flaccid form easily into his arms and hastened, as if he carried nothing at all, away and up the steps. The sentries followed and Robert held back a moment to survey the nasty mess. He had never spoken to Odo as he'd done moments before and felt a twinge of pride. But the twinge was quickly squelched by the realization that his brother would surely take his revenge; he always did, and Robert shuddered as he wondered when and how it would be exacted.

*****

Edith twisted in delirious torment. She heard voices wavering, wrangling, and sounding vaguely familiar. And when she opened her eyes, a tiny gasp left her. She briefly recalled her mother telling her Heaven was a place where one relived the most joyous moments of life. Well then, she thought, this must be Heaven. She felt warmth, heard the lulling crackle of flames, touched pelts, and was dry. Yet the pain still raged. There would be no pain in Heaven. Then she must be in Hell—condemned there for her illicit time with Robert, to suffer for eternity, here in this austere chamber on the bed where they had loved and been so close, for so very long.

A face hovered above her, a pudgy face brimming adoration and sympathy. "Edith..." it whispered, "can you speak? Talk to me, my dove!"

She strained to sit and rasped, "Arthur? Why...why am I here? I don't want to be here. Please take me home. I want to go home." Another face sharpened opposite Arthur's and her confusion and misery soared as she babbled, "Robert? Where's Simon? Did I say something I shouldn't? Where is Odo?!"

Arthur gathered her close, stroking her hair, gently cooing, "No, my dove, you said nothing and Odo is gone. Robert sent him away. A physician is fetching supplies to treat your wounds. You're feverish and must try not to upset yourself."

"I want to go home!" she wailed.

And I'll take you there after you've been bandaged."

Edith tried but could not move her feet. Rage shook her tiny bulk as she turned a simmering glare on Robert and grittingly asked, "What...what did Odo do to me?"

He sucked a ragged breath and looked away.

"What did *you* allow him to do to me?!" she shrieked, pushing off Arthur, and lunging for Robert. Her fists missed him and instead beat the pelts as she let fly her fury, "You knew he'd come here to find Simon...and me! You knew yet did nothing! You coward—"

"No!" Robert vehemently countered. "I am not responsible for this! Odo acted on his own. *I*, Madam, rescued you and can just as easily throw you back down that hole—"

"Stop!" railed Arthur. But Edith didn't hear his order, for her pain and Robert's threat sent her swooning, and she collapsed senseless to the bed.

Robert lurched forward to help. Arthur stopped him with a murderous glare and sneer, "You'll not touch her...not now, not ever again. We'll leave here."

"But you can't!" stressed Robert. "She could lose both her feet if they're not tended to properly."

"The village leech will tend her feet."

"Wait at least for the binding, man!"

"This place and you give her nothing but grief," growled Arthur. "If her welfare concerns you so, you may send your physician to our hut. Don't come with him!" Arthur searched for something to wrap his wife in, and humbly asked, "May we borrow a blanket or cloak? The air outside is chilled."

"Yes," Robert mumbled. "Take what you need."

"We'll only need the blanket." Arthur carefully swathed Edith, then lifted her and started for the door.

Robert looked on amazed and asked, "Do you actually intend to carry her the entire distance to town?"

"I haven't a choice, my Lord."

"My...my man, Benjamin, stands outside," stuttered Robert. "Tell him to fetch you a padded cart. He will return you to your hut."

"I'm grateful, my Lord, as will be Edith when she wakes in more friendly surroundings. May I speak freely, my Lord?"

"Nothing has stopped you before," muttered Robert.

"I have for you some advice. I've heard of Odo only through Edith, yet I feel I know his wickedness well. This day you've only slowed his vengeance. You'd best devise a way to stop it permanently, before he finds and murders Simon, Maura, their child, and..." Arthur paused, unsure how to phrase his final strike, but Robert's tortured look emboldened him, and he warned on, "your wife and child. For you know eventually he will find them and, I dare say, after them, comes you."

Robert scowled disgust and torment, yet before he could hurl a retort, Arthur and Edith left. The thought of Maura pregnant swirled his head with repellent memories. And Arthur had mentioned '...*your* wife and child'. Did that mean he knew where Almodis was, and that the child—his child—had been born alive? He must find Almodis before Odo did, for he could not stand the thought of her beauty—marred. "Thomas," he muttered sharply, and his squire instantly appeared. "Have the couple followed and their hut watched...for their protection. And I would know immediately if they leave their dwelling, for I wish to join them on their journey...unseen." Thomas bowed, then dashed away.

Robert sat awhile on the bed to consider his wretched day. His wish to appear Edith's valiant rescuer had failed miserably and he wondered with petulance, *How can she prefer that fat toad to me?* As his fingers sensually stroked the fur, he allowed himself a swift moment to reflect on a time long past when he and Edith had laughed, cuddled, and loved beneath these pelts. Then pushing up and away, he chastised himself for his many weaknesses...especially the one that eternally longed for her and Simon, and the life they had shared before—Odo.

*****

59

Simon in a half sleep pried wide his eyes and wondered briefly where he was, then the wondrous sight and feel of Maura, tucked up by his side, elicited from him a loud rapturous sigh. His fingertips brushed her cheek and he prayed for her waking, but she didn't respond. Frowning, he raised up on his elbow and noticed through the parted shutters faint flickerings of sun. The foot of the bed was now empty and only one candle remained lit. How thoughtful of Marc to allow them some privacy. He suddenly felt cold and lonely, and wiggled beneath their lavishly embroidered quilt, the one Arthur had gifted them before their wedding, closed his eyes again, and snuggled closer. To his nearness, he felt her stir. Joy thudded his heart! He moved slightly away to implore, "Maura...it's Simon! Please wake up. I need to talk to you, and feel you hold me. I miss you so. *Please!*" She woke gradually and he wisely kept his short distance while murmuring, softly, tenderly, "You're safe and in our bed. You needn't fear. No one will hurt you...no one..."

Maura's eyes opened slowly and focused uncertainly on his, and then they beamed as did her face and it seemed her whole self as she gasped, "Oh, Simon!"

They clung together, each trying to touch every part of the other, their hair, fingers, and lips mingling, as they sputtered between deep, desperate kisses...

"Oh, Simon don't go away again, swear you...you'll never go away again, swear it!"

"I...I won't, believe me, I'll never leave this house without you again, ever!"

They forsook the tumultuous events of a short while past to relish again the feel of each other, and share a second rash of kisses, these more amorous than before. Finally, questions began to sift through Maura's exaltation; she placed fingers between their lips and asked, "Simon...Simon, how did I get here? Why didn't you wake me? Where's Marc gone? You *do* know he's here?"

A part of Simon didn't want to answer, wanted to keep fondling, kissing, wanted the whole debacle simply to fade away, but it wouldn't. All the disturbing, puzzling images flared to the fore of his mind, and he balanced back up on his elbow. "I know he's here and why. When I entered, I didn't see you sleeping on the floor. I tripped on your foot and you screamed and fought me and ran away. Marc reacted as Marc would, he hit me—hard, then raced after you. I found you both by the nettle bush, you were unconscious and—"

"The baby!" Her fright was blatant, paling. "The baby...nothing's happened, has it?! *Please* say no, Simon...please!"

His soothing smile curbed her fretting. "No. There's no blood. Have you any pain...here?" he asked hesitantly as his fingers splayed over her belly and tenderly squeezed.

"No..."

"Any tightening like you had before?"

"No..."

"Good. I don't think any harm's been done. But maybe you should stay abed a day or two, to make certain all is fine."

"Gladly," she smirked, "if you stay abed with me."

He gently wagged his head. "I mean that you stay still and calm."

"That's quite impossible with you by my side," she smiled.

"And so I should leave?"

"No Simon," she whined and gripped tighter, "I'll be good...I promise!"

"But can I?" he added with a wry wink.

"I'm certain of it..."

Their lips gently joined, lingered to taste, and parted as Simon soberly asked, "Maura, why did you run?"

She thought back and recalled tensely, "My nightmare, it's come back!"

His jaw fell slack, then closed to object, "It can't have! You remembered everything except the man's face."

"Simon, it was different. Before when I dreamt, I was in a cottage. This time I was in a courtyard, the buildings resembled those of Dinefwr."

"A bailey?" he questioned.

"I don't know. All the houses were timbered, and the wall as well..."

"When you were five and this happened, your father's keep would have been timbered."

"I don't know," she cried, "I just don't want it to haunt me again."

He spoke confidently, "It's come back because Marc's here."

Maura could not hold back her dread and tearfully spilled, "I don't want to hide, I want to stay right here, and love you and our baby forever!"

"There's nothing to fear, my love...no one to hide from..." Simon purposely skipped the 'yet' and strengthened his hold.

A faint fluttering brought back her smile, and she guided his hand to her belly and gushed, "It moves, I feel it! Do you?"

She frowned to his pensive silence. He quickly brightened, suggesting, "No...not just yet, but I will, very soon. She only needs to get a bit bigger."

She stroked his cheek and snuggled closer as another flutter made her glow inside and out. "Are you certain it's a girl?"

"Positive..."

"But how?"

"A doctor knows these things," he said with a playful grin, "and...she told me."

They chuckled together, but at Maura's broken confession, "And she...she missed you so very very much!" their laughter ceased and they hugged again, this clutch full of passion and also melancholy—as if it was to be their last.

*****

61

CHAPTER FIVE - ALLUSIONS TO A TRAGEDY

𝕴𝖓 the stable of a modest manor home not far from the village of Dunheved, Almodis sprawled languorously across the straw. The bodice of her tunic was purposely parted to expose her breasts, and the skirt was hiked high to display the rest of her long lissome self. Alan, a burly, blue-eyed gentleman with dark brown hair and beard, knelt over her, struggling fitfully to remove his tunic and shirt, complaining, "Why here, Almodis? I feel I'm sixteen again."

"That sounds promising," she sighed with sultry allure. "Hurry, any moment now Rose will find us! And Adam seems to know instinctively what we're up to and starts crying whenever we're away." She huffed impatiently and sat up to help her suitor, then chafed vigorously at the tiny bumps that erupted over his now naked arms and back.

"I'm too old to hurry, and it's too cold to do this here!" he griped on. "What's wrong with the bed?"

"It's boring, and Rose is always listening!"

"Why should that bother *you*?"

"It doesn't really, it's just that you feel the need to be quiet when she's about, and it's hard to do what we do quietly!"

"It's also hard to do it frozen—" Almodis stopped Alan's banter with a ferocious kiss and his chill quickly melted as she sank back and caught him between her raised knees. Lust glowed her olive skin, fired her black eyes, and she gasped as his lips left hers to taste a nipple. "Sometimes I feel I'm suckling two babes," she chuckled softly.

He raised an eager face and slipped to her side, where they both struggled frantically to undo the cord that secured his braies. A cleared throat stalled their fervor. Alan grabbed his tunic to cover his chest and the excitement that tightened his trousers. Almodis didn't bother to hide anything, and sneered disdainfully at Rose.

Pernicious and crow-like, Rose stood posturing in the stable's doorway, holding and jiggling a red-faced, black-haired, screaming infant. Her bark was cold and direct, "Your son is hungry and he smells."

"Certainly you can handle it, Rose!" flared Almodis.

"I can handle one of the problems, not the other, and I refuse to handle either! I'm done with mothering, and if you insist on behaving wantonly wherever you choose and continually shirking your responsibilities, *I* will have no choice but to *insist* that you reside elsewhere! And Alan, I am appalled at you for—"

"At me!?" he burst out. "What wrong have I done? I'm the one who's responsible for the upkeep of this entire manor, and, I might add, I handle that job quite competently! I deserve some time for...for recreation." Almodis turned on Alan a look of astonished pride. She'd never heard him speak to Rose with such tenacity and squeezed his hand in tender appreciation.

"Recreation?" snorted Rose. "Name it correctly, Alan—adultery—pure and simple adultery. You'll both be damned to Hell!"

"Give me my child!" shouted Almodis, scrambling up and posturing herself. "You're jealous," she hurled, "you frigid, tight-lipped bitch! You're jealous because you have no man of your own. And no sane man would dare touch a hideous slug like you!"

Rose slapped Almodis with a force that staggered her backwards. Almodis wielded her fist for a return strike and Alan leapt up to intervene, but his jaw caught the brunt of her swing. He wavered a moment, counting the stars that flitted before his eyes. Both women stood agape and ashamed, and the babe continued to scream. "Rose," said Alan carefully as the stars slowly faded, "let me have Adam. I think it's best if you go inside and we'll join you shortly."

"Alan...I didn't mean to—"

"Please go."

Rose murmured endearments to the child as she passed him to Alan, then hung her head, and muttered her way out the door.

Almodis gasped guiltily and planted sloppy kisses on Alan's jaw while taking custody of the child. "Oh, Alan," she blubbered, "why did you get in the way?"

"Because I hate it when you two fight."

"Then you must hate it most of the time," she quipped.

"Yes I do," Alan sharply agreed, "and it only seems to get worse."

They both sat down hard on a bale of straw. "Rose and I weren't meant to live together," Almodis snipped as she arranged herself and her son more comfortably. The child's misery swiftly ebbed at finding her nipple.

"You could if you tried harder!" fumed Alan. "Consider why we came here."

"I thought you took my side of the argument."

"I take *my* side! I don't understand why you two can't live together civilly. I swear, sometimes it seems you live to harp!" She took on a wounded air, and he instantly atoned, "I'm sorry, Almodis, I'm tired and cold and hungry. Let's go inside."

"Not right away," she said wearily. "Stay with me awhile." Her fingers twirled her son's black curls as she wistfully confessed, "At times I resent being stuck here in this hovel, and not in Mortain or Berkhamstead, where I was surrounded by luxury." Her hand left Adam's hair to turn Alan's sulk her way. She stroked his cheek and said with a breathy passion, "But with you I've found a luxury I've never known before, in bed or out...and that is love. I'll fight anyone to keep it *and* you...and that includes the indomitable Rose."

His anger vanquished, he kissed her palm and lips and suggested, "Maybe all we need is a change of scenery. Would you like to visit Edith and Arthur?"

"Oh yes!" beamed Almodis. "I so enjoy their company, and perhaps they've had word from Simon and Maura. I miss them terribly..."

"As do I..." mumbled Alan.

They sat in a clutch for a long, reflective moment, then Alan wriggled into his clothes; Almodis loosened the sleeping infant from her breast and, flashing a yielding smile, accepted his hand to leave.

With supper done, and the child cleaned, fed, and cradled, Almodis, Alan, and Rose lounged about the tiled hearth that centered the timbered hall. The earlier battle seemed forgotten, and all spoke cordially. "Won't you come with us Rose?" said Almodis sincerely, "Otherwise Edith will be greatly disappointed."

"No, I cannot. My son Richard is due back tomorrow, and I must remain here to greet him. I do pray Edith has had word from Maura."

"If she has we will memorize every detail," assured Almodis. Her hand caressed Alan's knee, and they shared a fawning look.

Rose ruffled with discomfort at the sight, stood, and sighed, "I'm to bed, as I'm sure you're to be before long. Try not to wake the child." Her request went ignored, as their fondling increased and was soon accented with noisy kisses. Feeling rather invisible, Rose sighed again and shuffled off to her corner of the huge room, partitioned by a thick, worn tapestry. She stiffly peeled off her tunic, left on her chemise, and heard her old bones creak as she settled painfully into her downy bed. Thoughts of Maura quickly visited. How desperately she longed for her charge's sanguine presence; Maura never made her feel resented or neglected. Well, she had once, when they'd squabbled about Simon, but it had lasted only a short while. More often than not, their quarrels were

63

quickly resolved. She sorely craved their sprightly banter, for with Maura she always felt alive and capable; with Almodis she felt old, infirm, and bitter. Yet thinking back over the past five months, she had to admit to moments when the Lady had reduced her to giggly tears. And when she listened deep in the night to their soft moans of passion, her disgust was sometimes replaced with a yearning that there might be some man, somewhere, who could make her feel as exquisitely loved as her husband had done so many, many years past. She wiped a tear, snuggled down beneath her pelts, and shifted her thoughts to Richard. How happy she'd be to have him home again, and how pleased he'd be to see how improved the manor was, thanks immeasurably to Alan...and, she grudgingly acknowledged, to Almodis.

"You must apologize to her," insisted Alan as he whipped off his hose and slipped beneath the pelts into Almodis' eager embrace.

"For what?" wondered Almodis.

"For what happened in the stable."

"But she was vile to me!"

"As you were to her. Besides she's weary of tending the baby for you."

"If I lived at Berkhamstead, he'd be tended to."

"Then," returned Alan, irked, "perhaps you should consider returning to Berkhamstead...and Robert." Her pout made him melt with remorse, and he quickly consoled, "If the King would grant me a baronage, I would gladly give you every luxury you could possibly want or imagine. But I'm only a guard, and a banished one at that. I'm not meant to be anything else."

"No, not only a guard," she argued sweetly. "You are infinitely kind, fair, brave...and gentle. I don't know why you endure my tantrums."

"Because I love you," he answered almost bluntly.

"Yes you do, don't you?" she said in wonder. "And love seems so natural for you. It wasn't till a very short while past that I was able to feel any emotion other than hate."

"When you met Maura?" he asked.

"Yes. I believe it was then. She taught me much."

"And me...as did Simon."

"Do you believe we'll see them again?"

"I pray we will." Alan sought to sway her somber mood with an enticing invitation. "Now that it's warmer, and we needn't hurry, what do you require of me, my Lady Countess?"

"Would you mind just holding me?" she responded with a hint of embarrassment.

His heart ached to her want and he gladly obliged, cuddling her near and rhythmically weaving his fingers through her hair, for he knew the immense comfort the simple act brought. As he delighted in the warmth of her, he wondered what he would do when he lost her. For in time, and perhaps a short time at that, he surely would. Lord Robert wouldn't allow her absence for much longer and he'd be wanting his son. And if not Robert, there was always Will, forever plotting trouble and murder. In choosing not to serve Rufus, Alan had willingly disobeyed the King, and thus could never return to William's service. He briefly thought over his lifetime of blind duty to William, and readily conceded that at the grand old age of forty-one, he much preferred thinking freely and being called on to manage things. Perhaps he'd stay on here permanently as seneschal. That is, if he wasn't executed for his time with Almodis, which was a distinct possibility. Yet he'd have no regrets, for he did love her more than life itself.

When she was sure of Alan's slumber, Almodis carefully rose and slipped on her robe. She checked her son's breathing, then crept silently across the drafty hall to Rose's bed. She stood a moment and studied her landlady from a short distance. In truth, Rose *was* ugly, with her long hooked nose, gaunt hollowed cheeks, dark accusing eyes, and perpetual scowl. Almodis likened her to a hovering black thundercloud. Despite her disagreeable looks and temperament though, she had allowed them the comfort of her son's home in which to hide, and on several occasions had acted kindly. Alan was correct as usual, she must apologize, so she bent close and nudged Rose's shoulder. Rose woke with a gasping jolt, and startled Almodis who raised her finger to her lips and insisted, "Hush! You'll wake Adam!"

"Why are you here?" asked Rose, staying flat and shielding herself with her quilt.

Almodis remained standing, hands tightly clasped before her, and began with great difficulty, "I've...I've come to apologize for what I said today...about you...in the stable."

"I've forgotten it."

"No you haven't. I wouldn't have."

"Well that's another way that we're different," said Rose strictly.

"I disagree," countered Almodis. "Our problem lies in the fact that we're far too alike. We're both overly stubborn and overly proud."

"If you've come to slander me again, Almodis, I will ask you to leave."

"No...I can't sleep...and I do need to apologize. I do it rarely and if I'm willing, you should also be willing to listen and accept—"

"Almodis, go back to bed," said Rose, as she shifted away and pressed her head into her pillow.

But Almodis plopped herself on the bed, rocking Rose back around, and asserted loudly, "I'm not your daughter, Rose! I am not Maura."

"What?" grunted Rose.

"I said I'm not Maura...I will never be Maura. Stop trying to make me Maura...I can never be that good!" With an incredulous look, Rose pushed up in bed. "I've never accused you of—"

"Oh yes you do!" Almodis retorted. "You eternally judge and compare."

Rose opened her mouth to protest, then shut it slowly to the realization that the Lady might in fact be correct. "I didn't know...I didn't mean to put undue pressure on you, or make you believe that when I occasionally spoke of Maura—"

"She does everything better."

"Maura is no saint, Almodis."

"Compared to me she is."

"I'm weary of your drama," scorned Rose. "With Edith, I raised Maura, and up till four months past, we'd not been separated. I miss her and so I speak often of her. If you choose to take that as a personal affront, do so, but don't blame me for your inadequacies. You've been pampered far too long. I don't pamper."

"You did Maura," refuted Almodis.

"No...never. Well once I did, when Robert...hurt her, but I'm sure she told you that tale."

"Barely...she said that Robert had taken her child, and she didn't know where."

"Almodis," corrected Rose, "the child was killed while still inside her."

The brutal truth made Almodis' antagonism falter and her posture and voice shrink. "Tell me Rose, tell me Maura's tale."

Rose's bile likewise ebbed, making her stutter, "I don't want to...I can't...remember that time. It's all too horrible."

"I order you to tell!" commanded Almodis. "Robert is my husband. I will know what atrocities he's capable of committing!"

"No! I won't," Rose answered as adamantly, "not when I don't know if I'll ever see Maura again! Just before I left her to come here, she confessed that she had dreamt of her child and seen him dead. And I'm certain she's pregnant now and I have a fear, a constant fear that it will all happen again. And if it does, will I be there to hold her, to love her?"

As Rose paused to swipe a tear, Almodis saw more deeply the unbreakable bond that existed between Rose and Maura. How lost and shattered Rose must feel without her, how utterly useless, and she admitted inwardly that her contrariness had, no doubt, heightened those feelings. "It won't happen again, Rose," comforted Almodis, coming closer and resting an arm round her shoulder, "it couldn't...Simon is with her. He will protect her, hide her away if needed. He'd never allow anyone to hurt her or their child."

"He believed he was saving her before when he left Dunheved...I love Simon dearly, but he is no match for Robert's army, not if they come for her."

"Robert doesn't want her back!" cried Almodis. "He's accepted their marriage."

"You know how volatile he can be," said Rose. "What he accepts one day, he condemns the next. His avarice is guided by the Devil. Maura was his last opportunity to acquire land through marriage. If the possibility of a beneficial alliance arose today, he'd not hesitate one moment in seeking her out, annulling their union, and passing her to the highest bidder."

"No!" Almodis adamantly continued, "I don't believe that...He's changed, softened! He sent me away to safety from Will."

"For the sake of the child, Almodis, only the child. You are dispensable, as is anyone who gets in the way of his greed."

"Then I'll not return to him, ever!" Almodis stated soundly.

"You speak as if you have a choice," scoffed Rose. "I'm certain at this very moment he's seeking you out...and the child. You'll not escape him or his wrath. No one does."

"But Rose, it was *his* decision to send me away."

"And that decision he's conveniently forgotten," finished Rose.

Almodis tried but could muster no response to Rose's final assertion. She removed her arm, and with a limp pat to Rose's shoulder, returned, shaken and humbled, to her own bed. Alan woke to her vise-like grip and saw in her eyes a crazed look, fearful and desperate. Her strained plea, "Love me now," alarmed and excited him.

Confused, he rose up over her splayed and willing form, murmuring, "Of course, but something worries you...what—"

"No!" she cried, yanking him closer, "we won't talk, I don't want talk, I want you—now!" She clamped his waist with her legs and rubbed against him with a coarse insistency that dizzied. He shut his eyes and felt himself floating, then falling. And when next he dared look, she had straddled him, her lush dark hair a tousled halo, her eyes wild and body still rubbing, writhing, searching. She found him ready and, rising up on her knee, impaled herself upon him. Unexpectedly, he called out to her as her frenzy invaded him, making him grip her hips and anything else he could grab hold of and drive into her with an abandon he'd not known before. He filled her again and again, and she moaned as a jolt of pleasure shook her, and then another, and another, but it wasn't enough—he'd come closer than any other man to quenching her desire—but it was never enough! Their lips crushed together as their urgency culminated in one explosive spasm that sent them reeling and almost toppling off the bed. For a long while, their hold didn't loosen, nor did their bodies part. Then Almodis shifted away. Alan molded to her back and nuzzled her neck, and she welcomed his arms around her waist. The tumult he felt was immense, as was his fondness for this captivating creature whose sexual hunger he could never quite satiate. Nevertheless, he vowed to himself, he would gladly perish trying.

Almodis basked happily in his warmth and love, yet then what she most dreaded came quickly. Insidiously the cold emptiness returned, a dank hollowness that gnawed endlessly at her gut and that nothing and no one could heal. Sometimes she felt it was her heart, forever bleeding, and soon it would shrivel away to nothingness, and she'd feel no

more need, no more guilt. Perhaps then, she thought, choking back tears, her life would be easier.

*****

Marc knocked but received no answer. He'd left Simon and Maura alone for a whole day and night, and now felt a dire need to discover if they were indeed still alive. He nudged the door and peered through the crack, yet the grayness of dawn didn't allow him clear sight, so he haltingly entered and crossed the room to open the shutters. Sunlight sliced through the gray and he turned to see upon the bed a tangled mess of arms, hair, and blankets. He came closer, striving to distinguish where one body began and the other ended. Then the bright intrusion caused them to stir and cringe and Maura to cover her head with the quilt. Simon stiffly sat and shielded his eyes to the ghostly figure standing at the bed's side. "Marc..." he croaked. "Is that you?"

"Yes."

"Come near...I can't see...the glare is too harsh."

When Marc did venture nearer, Simon almost gasped, for before him stood the true Marc, not the dirt-encrusted, pitiful soul he'd encountered a few hours past, but the Marc of years past—his ivory skin scrubbed clean and slightly rouged, his stubble gone, his golden brown hair gleaming, cut short and wispy, and his dark blue eyes vibrant. Yet what pleased Simon most—though Marc always considered it a curse—was the look of perpetual innocence that glowed once again.

"Ma...Marc..." Maura appeared bedraggled from beneath the quilt, and said sleepily, "Marc, thank you for catching me." As she woke further, her eyes widened with the same astonishment Simon felt, and she spouted, "You look...wonderful!"

Embarrassment darkened Marc's already pink cheeks and jerked his eyes downward. "I...I found the well and the soap and some of your clothes, Simon. I hope you don't mind my borrowing them."

"No. Take all you need. We have stacks of Arthur's cloth in the stables, and there's an excellent seamstress in the village who can stitch you up an entire wardrobe in practically no time at all. Now...I'll get supper together and—"

"But Simon," cut in Marc, "it's dawn."

"Dawn!" gasped Simon. "It can't be!"

"It is...You both slept a whole day and night. I supposed you needed the rest and didn't dare wake you."

Both Maura and Simon tensed; Simon floundered up, shoved his shirt in his braies, and mumbled worriedly, "The animals must be ready to revolt! Where's Gruffydd?" Maura started to rise but Simon insisted, "You'll not be getting up!"

"Simon, I feel perfectly well...really there's no need."

"There is...one more day and then we'll see. And you must eat. God's teeth, you've missed a whole day of food!"

"Simon," Marc calmed, "I've fed the animals and Gruffydd. He's outside playing with a friend, and there's a stew bubbling in the pot."

Simon cracked a relieved smile. "Why thank you, Marc. Maura, I'll fetch you a bowl and some oak beer. Marc, you stand guard and make certain she stays put."

When Simon was gone, Marc commented, "He still loves to worry, doesn't he?"

"I don't mind," Maura said with fondness.

"Oak beer?" Marc asked skeptically, resting on the bed.

"Yes, it's quite tasty and makes a wonderful tonic. I suggest you sample some yourself."

"I will. You seem better."

"I am," she asserted. "I know you're most likely wondering about the other night. What I ran from was a dream. Do you remember the nightmare I suffered at Dunheved?"

"Oh, yes," he readily replied.

"It comes back whenever I feel worried or threatened. But it won't return now that Simon's home."

"And a fine home it is. Was it already standing?"

"The foundation was, but the rest was in ruins. We rebuilt it and added the extra room."

"You and Simon rebuilt it?" he asked with a dubious smirk. "That I find hard to believe. When you were younger any task you took on together ended up a disaster."

"Well I'll admit to a few disagreements, but when he worked at one end and I worked at the other, all stayed fairly peaceful. Of course, the villagers helped."

"They accept you now? I read in a letter that when you first arrived you weren't warmly received."

"That's true," she said, scratching at a rash of nettle bites that mottled her forearm. "Luckily, Simon already owned a marvelous reputation here, and it didn't take long to sway the few contrary souls to our staying. Then," she beamed, "we discovered I was pregnant."

"I know, I read that as well."

"I can feel her move," she burbled and rested a hand on her belly to show where. "No one else can as yet, but soon..." To his deep blush, she tempered her cheer and phrased her next thought carefully, "And how do you feel about becoming an uncle?"

"Very good. You said 'her'. How do you know?"

"Simon's convinced it's a she. He talks to her a great deal and claims she told him. I know he's only playing—"

Her elation shone brighter as her husband returned, balancing a bowl, a mug, and a book. Marc stood to help and took the book, while Simon bustled round the bed and set the dishes on the table by Maura. "What's in this stew, Marc?" he asked skittishly, spooning up some and letting the clumps drool back into the bowl.

"Anything I could find that seemed edible."

"It looks intriguing," complimented Maura.

"And smells so too," added Simon, giving her a sly wink.

"Gruffydd liked it," said Marc.

"Gruffydd will eat anything," blurted Simon without thinking, then quickly relented, "Not that I mean..."

"I won't mind if you hate it," mumbled Marc.

Maura chanced a taste, and her doubting look eased into a pleased one. "No, Marc. It's different, but nice...very nice. Here, Simon, try." He did so and, while chewing, grunted in agreement. "Perhaps, Marc," said Maura, smiling, "we should let you cook for us always."

"Please no!" objected Marc. "I don't like to cook, and I'm no good at it. What's this?" he asked, paging through the book.

"My recipe book," said Simon. "I write in it the patients' medication recipes, and when they need them delivered. If you still want to help me with my doctoring, the book's an excellent reference."

"Yes I do. You don't mind if I study it a while?"

"Not at all. I've memorized all of the recipes, and the deliveries are current."

All became hushed as Maura and Simon, murmuring and chuckling, fed each other stew. Marc watched amused for awhile, then feeling rather intrusive, rose to leave, excusing, "I promised Gruffydd I'd chase him and his friend...*Kunan*."

"That's correct," Simon lauded. "Cynan speaks no English but I suppose that makes no difference in play." Simon paused a moment as a word Marc had said echoed loudly in his mind, and he spouted ecstatically, "Chase! Marc, I had almost forgotten...You're able to chase?!"

"I chased Maura, didn't I? Yes, Simon, thanks to you, my leg healed beautifully. I suffer from a slight limp, that's all."

"I'm pleased. Very pleased!" beamed Simon.

"As am I," beamed Maura. "Simon told me how severe your wound was and he doubted you'd ever recover full use of your leg."

Marc approached the door and turned to praise, "My brother-in-law is an excellent physician."

Maura's eyes and words sparkled with pride, "And so is my husband."

Simon blushed deeply and swiftly switched the topic. "Marc, when we finish here I'd like to check your teeth. They usually have a lot to say about the rest of one's health."

"I used the awful paste the army provided us, but I ran out before I left Normandy. I've been mostly using twigs to scrape them clean. They've been bleeding."

"We've a wonderful paste here," noted Maura. "It's made from gelatin, sage, and mint. Your teeth will shine so, they'll be blinding!"

Marc nodded and left Simon and Maura to go and find the boys. He emerged from the cottage into an ebullient scene of children squealing and tumbling over a carpet of green grass and vividly colored wildflowers, with Henry the pup bouncing and yapping along. At the sight of Marc, the boys and dog changed their game and exuberantly charged. Marc kept up the chase several times round the green, but eventually his laughter cramped his side and tripped him to the ground. The boys pounced, howling in triumph as they wrestled with their new-found friend and tickled him to the brink of agony. Their vivaciousness quickly faded as Henry dashed off, yelping his particular bark that meant someone was arriving. The three untangled and rose, Marc only to his knees, then Gruffydd screeched, "Mam!" and sprinted away toward the path. Cynan loped behind, and Marc stood and remained where he was, straightening his mussed clothes and hair. He squinted from the glare of the new sun to see—Gael. She was nothing like he'd imagined, not oldish and matronly, but a small wisp of a woman, with a mass of pale crimped hair framing a pretty, impish face, alight with joy as she caught her racing son in her arms and gleefully swung him round and round. Gruffydd struggled for freedom, and Gael followed his tug, laughing in answer to his insistent commands, "Come Mam, hurry! There's someone you must meet. He's very nice and chases us, and he was a knight in King William's army!" His last tribute slowed her pace and, with a slightly daunted look, she strained to recognize the young man standing feet from her, fiddling with the hem of his tunic, and betraying a stark look of embarrassment. She inched forward, then to Gruffydd's yank, stumbled closer to Marc. "Mam!" he shrilly introduced, "This is Marc. He's Maura's brother."

"Ma...Marc!" stammered Gael in happy relief, lurching forward and thrusting out a hand. "I never thought...that you...I mean I'm surprised and delighted to meet you! Simon and Maura have spoken of you once or twice," she said with a wry smile. Her unabashed stare only intensified his chagrin; finally, she realized her rudeness and asked, "Where are they? Simon did make it home safely, didn't he?"

69

"Ye...yes," sputtered Marc. He touched only her outstretched fingers, then swiftly let go. "They're...inside."

Gruffydd tugged on her tunic sleeve and vibrantly related, "Simon came home two night's past and tripped over Maura while she was sleeping. She ran away but Marc found her after he'd hit Simon. I woke Simon up and then we found them by the nettle bush."

"What?" she laughed, thinking Gruffydd's vivid imagination had suddenly exploded. "Save your tales for your friends, Gruffydd," she gently chided.

"No, Mam! It really did happen and Simon said I was brave to wake him."

"He speaks the truth," said Marc.

"But...why?" asked Gael.

"Perhaps Simon and Maura should explain. It's rather complicated."

"It does sound so. I'll go in then." She paused an uncertain moment and asked, "Is it safe for me to go in?"

"Yes...I'll stay with the boys."

"I appreciate you chasing them."

Marc grinned and nodded and Gael, clutching Simon's bow and arrows, gingerly stepped inside the cottage. Her eyes darted about hunting for signs of bedlam, but instead she saw almost everything in its rightful place. She tapped softly upon the bedchamber door, heard nothing, and her fretful curiosity urged her to crack open the door a tad. What she beheld made her snort a laugh and roll her eyes in exasperation— They sat, propped up against pillows, lips and bodies locked in a tender embrace. They slowly sensed her presence and without breaking their kiss, shifted only their eyes to the door. "Don't you two ever tire of slobbering all over each other?" scorned Gael with affection. "Gruffydd made me believe you were near death!"

Their broke their kiss and exclaimed in unison, "Gael!"

Simon started to rise, but Gael stopped him with a gesture. "No, stay." She sat at the foot of the bed, pressed Maura's hand in greeting, then Simon's and asked, "So tell me what happened two night's past."

"Simon returned to a rather rude welcome," answered Maura.

Gael anxiously pressed, "Is everyone well?"

"Yes...very," confirmed Maura, squirming for comfort.

"And my son—did he behave himself, and was he of help to you?"

"Oh yes, immensely!"

"And so Marc's come. Why?"

"The King was injured in Mantes," replied Simon. He used his pillow to help Maura sit up taller, fussed with her blanket, then continued, "He's recuperating in Rouen, and Marc felt there was no one left to defend, so he came here."

"He deserted?" asked Gael, shocked.

"I choose to call it acting intelligently," quipped Simon.

"*You* would, but it's not you he answers to. He seems very sweet, and *very* shy."

"Painfully so," remarked Maura.

"Will he be staying?"

"Yes, he'll be helping Simon with his doctoring."

"Gruffydd seems quite fond of him already," said Gael distantly, wandering to the window and drawing the shutters wider. She drank in the aroma of blue-bells and mumbled to no one in particular, "The blossoms have all but fallen away. Cold will come soon."

They waited while she continued to stare dreamily out at a pure blue sky. Her mumbling faded so only she could hear. Simon and Maura exchanged worried looks, then Simon questioned, "Is there something wrong, Gael?"

"No," she replied abruptly. "It was a long, boring journey home, and the weather was vile." She left the window and, crossing her arms, perched herself on a stool close to the bed. "I heard, Simon," she noted dryly, "that your journey was anything but boring."

Simon scowled, yet Maura straightened attentively to probe, "What haven't you told me, Simon?"

"Nothing," stressed Simon. "I happened upon a band of belligerent Welsh raiders. Who told you?" he asked Gael.

"How belligerent, Simon?" Maura insisted.

"They hurled a few threats, that's all. One recognized me as Rhys' physician and let me continue on."

"Who recognized you?"

"I don't know. I couldn't risk looking back, but his voice was...familiar."

"It was Owain," offered Gael flatly.

Simon's dropped jaw prevented speech, and Maura shouted for them both, "Owain!"

"Yes, amazing isn't it? He told me of your meeting, Simon, and asked that I tell you not to be caught anywhere without these." She scooped up his bow and arrows from the bed and shoved them in his direction. "Sadly, I have to agree with him."

"But I don't understand?" questioned Maura. "Those arrows *are* yours."

"I...I forgot them," Simon sputtered.

To Maura, Gael explained, "He left Dinefwr rather impulsively."

"Simon..." scolded Maura.

Simon looked perturbed and fuddled, and asked Gael, askance, "Are you certain it was Owain who stopped the others from—"

"From what?" demanded Maura. "What were they going to do to you?!"

"Not to worry, Maura," calmed Gael. "Owain told the tale rather loudly and his version agrees wholly with Simon's. They taunted and teased him a bit, that's all. Now Simon why don't you go romp with the boys. I would speak to Maura alone."

"Why must I leave?" he asked, pouting.

"In time, you'll no doubt hear it all, but I need to discuss a rather sensitive matter with Maura first."

Captivated by her mystery, Simon remained seated. Gael prodded him up from the bed and, with a poking finger, urged him toward the door. "Don't look so glum," she appeased. "It's not about you, and she *will* survive."

Simon turned back and glowed to Maura's blown kiss. He started to blow one in return, prompting Gael to help him out with a shove, shut and bolt the door, and snort to Maura, "You two are so syrupy it's sickening."

"Yes, we are, aren't we?" Maura agreed with a silly grin.

"If everyone is *so* well," Gael said, returning to the stool, "why are you still abed and why was he fussing with the pillows and such, and isn't that your meal on the table?"

"Yes. The past evening, I fell. Simon ordered me to stay abed till we're certain the baby's safe."

"And is the baby safe?"

"Yes...and moving."

"You feel it?"

Maura nodded.

"What a precious moment that is when it first happens," said Gael wistfully. "It makes everything glorious and real."

"I wholeheartedly agree," Maura gushed, hugging the quilt closer. "And how is Ella?"

"I didn't see her. It seems she's missing, and since this isn't the first time she's bolted, and I'm certain it won't be the last, I'm not overly concerned. Rhys promised to send her here when she returns."

"That will be nice."

"Not really. She can be extremely maddening." With a disgruntled huff, Gael switched thoughts. "Your brother is certainly handsome. Doesn't favor you much though, except in the eyes."

"He arrived starved and spent three days past," said Maura, "but he rebounded quickly enough, as is his way."

"I expect his presence will be questioned by the villagers," Gael stated ruefully, then scoffed, "but since they're so pleased with the two of you, I doubt he'll have any trouble being accepted."

"That is, if Owain doesn't return."

"Why do you say that?" Gael returned sharply. "What have you heard?"

Maura answered mildly, "Nothing...I was only jesting. Why would he come where he's so disliked?"

"He enjoys being disliked."

"Gael...besides him telling you about Simon, what else happened between you two?"

"We had words."

"Well it's done and you're home with friends," said Maura. "Try not to let it bother you further."

"It's not that simple, Maura," Gael countered. "Owain wasn't the only disturbing part of my visit."

"What else happened?"

"I had a talk with Rhys."

"And..." Maura prompted carefully.

A long uncomfortable moment passed, then Gael rapidly spilled her woe, "He presented me an ultimatum. I'm to become his mistress, or if that doesn't suit me, I'm to marry his choice for Pennaeth for Mynyw. If I refuse either, he will take Gruffydd from me and send me back to Shrewsbury."

Maura gaped and sputtered, "But...but surely he can't insist that—"

"Indeed he can, and will! After all he is—*Prince*."

"What did you say?"

"I don't remember. I blathered a bit, but gave no answer and he's giving me time to consider my choices."

"Could you care for Rhys?" asked Maura.

"I do care for Rhys."

"As mistress?"

"How can I comment on something I know nothing about?" Gael said evasively.

"I don't believe that, Gael."

"It...it's true," Gael foundered. "I...I've never felt...felt...that way about any man."

"What of your husband?"

"When it came to *that*, we did our duties to each other...very infrequently. Perhaps that's why we had no more children. I loved him, respected him, and was devastated when he died, but I felt no pleasure when we..." She suddenly grew quiet, hugged herself, and averted her pinched gaze to the window.

"Gael, it seems difficult for you to speak of this—"

"No Maura...I want to. I *need* to speak of this!" anguished Gael. "I don't know what to do, only that I will do anything to keep my son!"

Maura offered as solace her cup of oak beer and advised, "Here, drink some of this, it will help soothe you."

Gael heaved a morose sigh and obeyed, gulping all the beer. Yet it only made her feel worse; nausea joined her wretchedness, and two tears began a torpid journey down her cheeks.

Never had Maura seen Gael this shaken and tearful, and she wondered aloud, "How can Rhys be so hardhearted that he would threaten taking Gruffydd from you?"

"He's not being hardhearted." Gael wiped away her fluster with her skirt and sniffled, "In his mind, Gruffydd belongs first to Wales, then to me, and me being a Saxon makes our bond even more fragile."

When Gael seemed calmer, Maura strove to lighten the mood. "Well then, let's try to see this dilemma in a more rational light. Do you find Rhys attractive?"

"In a cuddly sort of way."

"That's a promising start."

"But," Gael bemoaned, "I don't want to live at Dinefwr! I don't want to leave here, leave you and Simon. And I don't care much for Rhys' family, especially his wife and daughter, nor his *guests.*"

"Meaning Owain?"

"Yes...and the insipid louts who follow him everywhere."

"I'm afraid there's something further you need to hear about Owain."

"What's he done?" asked Gael, her upset rising again.

"He's been...questioning Gruffydd."

"About what?"

Anticipating an explosion, Maura replied dully and quickly, "You and Rhodri, you and other men, whether his death was in fact murder."

"How dare he badger my son and slander me!" lashed out Gael, springing up from the stool with a force that toppled it to its side. "That pompous, despicable turd!"

"Now Gael," Maura said, pressing the air for calm. "Perhaps there's well-meaning behind his mischief."

Gael threw up her arms and raised her voice in exasperation, "Oh Maura, why do you insist on finding goodness in every piece of shit you encounter?"

"And why do you work so hard at hating him?" Maura retorted.

"He makes it *so* easy," sneered Gael.

"I'm not going to fight you about Owain," said Maura. "If you two are destined to make peace, you'll do so in your own way and time. Now back to Rhys. Will you accept his proposition?"

Gael's bluster turned to bother and she muttered bitterly, "I don't think so. I'm content with our friendship and don't wish it to change...I've almost decided to meet the candidates for Pennaeth, and see if any one of them is to my liking—whatever *that* means." Her disquiet drove her back to the bed and she asked faintly, "Maura?"

"Yes?"

"Feel free to tell me if I'm...if what I'm asking is too...oh Hell, was Simon...I mean is...has he been your only lover?"

"The answer is no."

"No?" Gael blurted.

"You're surprised?"

"Yes, a bit...Tell me."

At first Maura hesitated, then she began slowly and deliberately, "Simon was my first lover, and the only one that's ever truly mattered. The love and passion I feel with

73

him I could never feel with any other man. But when he first left me at Dunheved, I hated him with good reason or so I thought at the time. I went to live at Winchester, and when my outer wounds had healed, Queen Matilda introduced me to an older gentleman, a widower, and we became *close*."

"How *close*?" coaxed Gael with intrigue. "I mean, did you? And if you did, was it pleasurable with him?"

"Yes, we did, and yes, somewhat, but nothing like I'd known before. He had loved his wife dearly, and was lonely, as was I. We had needs that wanted tending."

"And then it was done?"

"He wanted more from our dalliance than I did and we parted. I heard later that he'd remarried."

"You didn't love him?"

"Heavens no!" said Maura. "I was soured on love, and wanted nothing more to do with it. For me love hurt and killed."

"And after the older gentleman?"

Maura shifted and self-consciously tugged at the embroidery decorating the quilt. "You would have me tell you all?"

"Please."

"The other tryst I'm not overly proud of, for he was younger, and very vulnerable. He seemed to be searching for a goddess, and picked me to play out his fantasy. I admit to using him to please myself, and when I told him I was tired of our game, he was...hurt. I still carry guilt over that time."

"*You* would...Is that all?"

"And then there was Will..."

Gael's chin almost hit the ground. "Not Simon's evil brother! You didn't! Not with him!"

"No, but we came mighty close. He is charming, handsome, and an expert at seduction. I'd seen him several times at Winchester, and then we became reacquainted at Christmas Court in Gloucester shortly after I'd been betrothed to Rufus. I needed a diversion, and he was more than willing to grant my every whim."

"What stopped you?"

"His eyes."

"I don't understand..."

"It...it's to do with the time right after Simon left me at Dunheved," explained Maura with a struggle. "Will was there."

With bulged eyes, Gael chanced, "He wasn't one of those who—"

"No, but when we were no longer friendly, he told me he'd wanted to join the guards, and was in my chamber, hiding behind a tapestry, watching while they—I remembered only his eyes."

Gael was well acquainted with the horrid tale, and also was acutely aware of the turmoil caused by recounting the event. So, she didn't press the issue, but interrupted Maura's pained silence with the comment, "Does Simon know all this?"

"In a way...He didn't want the details, except about Will. I refused to tell him for fear he'd do something rash. And I'm not overly eager to hear the intricacies of his doings while we were apart."

"He's always loved only you," insisted Gael, "believe that, Maura."

"I do...but I suppose he got lonely as well."

"Not while he was here."

"Gael..." Maura reached out long to clutch her hands. "Talk to Simon about Rhys and the others. Perhaps he can help—"

"Would you tell him?" Gael interjected plaintively. "Then send him to me."

"Of course I will," answered Maura, straining a faint smile.

*****

Simon stood bare-chested in the front door of his cottage, brusquely toweling his wet hair. "Cynan!" he yelled to the red-headed lad sitting atop Marc. Cynan snapped to the summons, waved, and scurried to Simon's side. "How fares your cough?"

"It's mostly gone," said Cynan. "Mam's wanting more mustard and figs."

"Certainly."

"Will you play with us?" Cynan asked excitedly.

"Maybe later. I haven't had a chance to speak to Marc. Could you send him in while I prepare your remedy?"

Cynan nodded and dashed off. When he reached Marc, he muttered, "*Simon moyns chi. Ydy tu mewn.*"

Gruffydd ended Marc's bafflement with a quick English translation, "He says Simon wants you inside."

"Oh...Thank you Gruffydd, Cynan," Marc said, scrambling up and promising, "We'll play more later."

At the door, Marc encountered Simon wriggling into a clean shirt. "No, stay outside," Simon suggested. "I want to show you round our home." He waved a cloth bag in the air and Cynan skipped by and leapt high to whisk it away.

"They're quite feisty," noted Marc.

"Not unusually so," replied Simon, grunting and hopping into his short, soft, worn boots. "Though I'm glad to see Cynan so sprightly. He suffers from a meddlesome cough. I pray it's finally cleared."

"I didn't hear one wheeze," noted Marc.

Simon snorted a smile and tilted his head toward the stable. "First, I'll introduce you to the livestock."

Once inside the thatched, timbered structure, they inspected each occupant, and when they came upon the stall housing Fulk, the massive gray percheron, Marc commented with scant belief, "Henry gave you his stallion!"

"Henry won't be pleased to discover he's a stallion no more. But yes, Henry presented him to us as a wedding gift. E'dain was pregnant and wouldn't allow me to ride, so Fulk carried us to Wales."

Marc glanced over at Simon's roan Welsh pony, E'dain, and muttered, "That was kind of Henry, I suppose."

"Marc, he is capable of such kindness."

"So you keep claiming."

"We're giving E'dain's colt to Gruffydd," Simon said purposely to distract. "They've become quite good friends."

"He's a fine lad."

"I agree. Maude here," Simon announced fondly, as he stroked the head of a black, cud-chewing bovine, "was a gift from Arthur, as were the swine, though I'm convinced he was glad to be rid of them. They're an ornery lot. Maura handles them with a firm hand, and the sharp toe of her boot when needed."

"Will you slaughter them come November?" asked Marc.

"A few...and I'll leave that task to Maura as well."

"Simon," Marc berated, "that's terrible."

Simon draped his arm round Marc's shoulders and feigned distress, "But you see I have this problem. If I cut one, I'll only feel obligated to sew him up again."

"A flimsy excuse for cowardice," simpered Marc, squirming out of Simon's hold.

"Well, if you're so brazen," Simon snipped, "then we'll allow you the honor."

"I won't mind," shrugged Marc. "I did it all the time in Normandy."

They left the stable to wander along the paddock's fence. The boys had abandoned the green and now gamboled inside the fence with the colt. "How did you pick this spot for your home?" asked Marc.

"Gael's late husband Rhodri and I came here often to talk," explained Simon, "and the former cottage's remains formed a solid foundation for the new hut. We love it here. It's secluded, yet not difficult to reach, mostly quiet, and it belongs to us." They came upon a large tilled area, dotted with buds and leaves of every hue, and each separate plot diligently tended. "And here lies my garden," Simon proclaimed, proudly swiping his arm over the toft and a modest wooden cross. "And Rhodri lies serenely in its center. I rely on him to watch over the herbs and liven their growth, which he does quite nicely."

"Simon..."

"Come," Simon whispered and beckoned with a finger. "I'll show you our secret."

Piqued, Marc trailed Simon through a dense thicket of oaks, their leaves tipped with the warm shades of autumn. He stopped short to Simon's firm gesture and warning, "No further, or you'll meet with a damp surprise." He squatted, gripped up a handful of turf, and peeled it and a collection of woven branches and twigs back to reveal a large, circular hole, lined with leather and filled with water. A faint mist hovered over its surface. Simon scooped up a handful and encouraged Marc, "Feel."

He did so and marveled, "It's warm!"

"There are several wells located about Mynyw, some warm, some not. They're noted for their restorative properties, and are considered sacred. We've not told anyone of this one, because we want to keep it to ourselves, for washing, soaking, and..." he smirked, "other amusements. You are welcome to enjoy it any time you please."

"Gladly," grinned Marc. "I found the one closer to the cliffs. It's cold!"

"You found St. Non's well. She supposedly gave birth to St. David, for whom our cathedral is named, directly on that spot. Come," said Simon, covering the tub, and eagerly waving Marc on. "I'll take you to the best seat on the hill."

A sheer cliff and Marc's dizziness stalled their stroll. The view was precarious and splendidly vast; wild flowers and heather sprouted abundantly beyond the tree line and clung to the cliff. The expansive sea swelled and glittered, gently caressing the rocks below. To the south, an island sprouted up from the sea. Their steep location gave them ample sight of the various inlets and heads and even a hazy view of Ireland.

"It's amazingly beautiful, Simon."

"If tomorrow's still this warm, we'll ride down to the beach for a swim and a race. Would you enjoy that?"

"Oh yes...very very much!"

"Good. Sit and rest awhile, and tell me of your last days in Normandy. Did you see the King injured?"

"No..." Marc sat cross-legged and requested instead, "Before we talk of Normandy, I'd like to ask some questions."

"Certainly," agreed Simon, sitting himself and gathering up pebbles to lob off the hill.

Marc decided it was best not to ramble, so he leapt directly to the crux of his confusion. "Maura gave me her letters to read. One was recently scripted, and told of your arrival here. In it she mentioned the baby...and also wrote something about 'being blest again'. Can you explain what that means, Simon?"

The question blanched Simon's expression; his gaze, suddenly narrow and troubled, drifted to the sea. He didn't want to think on that terrible time and said, pebbles slipping from his grasp, "I thought she told you of our past."

"Not all. I need to know all."

His eyes were near to angry when they peered back at Marc. "Why?" he asked sharply.

"Last autumn I tried to get Rose to confess why she and Maura were so angry with you. She constantly claimed I was too young to hear. But I'm not, Simon. I'm as old as you were when it happened. And I want to hear it all—from you."

"And you deserve to...hear it all," Simon replied with brittle calm. "But it's hard for me to tell. I've not told anyone the whole tale. Only Maura knows."

"I understand that, Simon. *Please,* can you try?"

Simon sighed loudly in submission, plucked up a violet blossom and twirled it between his fingers. His brow creased a frown as his thoughts turned inward. "We don't speak of it, yet now that the King is ill that time is always on our minds...If William should die, our protection dies with him, and we're not entirely certain who intends us harm."

"Perhaps it would easier to start at the beginning—" urged Marc with care. "When you were banished from Odo's castle at Rochester. That was in '82?"

"Ye...yes," Simon stumbled, then grudgingly began, "It's hard to imagine five years have passed since I spent that mid-summer holiday with Uncle William at Winchester. One evening, late in our visit, he deliberately filled me too full of wine and coaxed me into betraying Odo's plans to travel to Rome with his own garrison and extra men from the King's bastion. I'd been told the only purpose of the crusade was to seek guidance from the Pope. It wasn't till much later that I discovered Odo's true design—to steal the King's legions and do battle with the Pope. Odo claimed it was my slip of tongue alone that caused his arrest and imprisonment. I was denied my knighthood, and banished from Odo's castle in Rochester to Dunheved to await my father's judgment on the matter."

"Did being denied knighthood upset you, Simon?" wondered Marc.

Simon looked aghast. "I was devastated, as you would have been, or any young man who had spent four long hard years training for that honor!"

"But now you seem so opposed to war."

"Yes I am, unless there's a damned good reason to wage one!" Simon hotly returned. "And acting as a mediator I've heard every reason *not* to wage one. When I took my oath as physician, I swore, and these are the exact words—*to never slay, but preserve from what would slay, and to be in accord with peace, and not with the rage and enmity of man to his fellow man.* And that vow has at times been horrendously difficult to keep."

"Like when you fought Will in Normandy?" reminded Marc.

"Yes...and stealing Maura away from Rufus."

"You didn't actually harm either one of them."

"That may be true, but my rage at times proves too huge...almost rabid. I've always envied you in that sense."

"Why me?" asked Marc, surprised.

"You have always had expert control over your emotions."

"On the outside perhaps, never on the inside. Don't waste your time envying me, Simon. Tell me about when Robert returned to Dunheved."

"I don't waste my time," noted Simon tersely, then he sucked a bracing breath and continued more staidly, "He didn't, at least not immediately. He stayed in Normandy consoling Odo, and didn't return for an entire year." He broke a plaintive smile to the blissful image of his next memory. "Yet Maura was always with me at Dunheved and, since I'd left, she had changed from a gangly girl into a lovely young woman. You know I'd always loved her as my closest companion, and I wanted more...I wanted her body as well as her soul, yet was afraid my want would repulse her, so I kept silent.

Then one magical night in March, she confessed her desire for me. Edith and Rose were gone from the castle on visits to friends and family and we found ourselves alone. We quickly became lovers and were reckless and blind to anything but each other. Edith returned in October and we tried to keep our secret by staying apart, only that led to quarrels and we separated further." His tense posture, clasped hands, and pale knuckles all betrayed his surging upset. "I felt so torn, so frantic! I had never craved anything the way I craved her, and to be forced apart was such torture! Then Maura took ill. I was convinced she was dying. Edith refused my attempts to see her and in turn, I suppose, realized all was not as it was before." Crushed petals fell from his fingers and anguish tripped his too rapid speech. "Soon after Maura was confined, Father arrived at Dunheved and, without allowing me one word in my defense, condemned me for Odo's incarceration. He...he said the Saxon in me had betrayed our family, that I spoke the Devil's tongue and he would never hear me again. Maura came to me that last night, crying as I wanted to, and I tried to stay strong...for her. She wouldn't confess her woe, and we held fast to each other through the night. Just before dawn she returned to her room. I heard her scream and when I got to her chamber, I found Edith beating her and screaming obscenities."

"Edith, obscenities?" Marc doubted. "Simon, that's awfully hard to imagine."

"She was...she was crazed with panic!" Panic began to overtake Simon as well, flushing his skin, knotting his fists, making him shudder and stammer, "She...she knew that Robert planned to punish me, but knew not how, and finding Maura and me together drove her mad. She threatened to have Maura cloistered, then left us. I chased after her, to explain that we'd done nothing wrong, that we loved each other. I found Robert and Edith fighting in their bedchamber. He knew Maura and I were lovers and blamed Edith. He was hurting her! I struck him—his head hit the wall, he slumped to the ground. There...there was so much blood." He covered his eyes so not to see it again, then his fingers tugged and raked at his hair, as he raised a tortured gaze to Marc, chilling him more. "Mother screamed at me to go, to run away, but I couldn't, wouldn't leave Maura! She warned if I stayed or took Maura with me, we'd both be murdered. She said Mynyw would hide me, and swore when things were calmer, she'd send Maura there. I believed her, she'd never lie, not to me! To get Maura to stay behind, I had to make her believe I felt nothing for her, but she knew I lied and refused to let me go. We were wrestling in the hallway and a guard attacked, his broadsword aimed at Maura's back! I heard again Edith's claim, if I stayed we'd both be killed. I pushed Maura from the guard's path and I tumbled backwards down the stairs. I don't know how, Marc, but when I got up I...I ran away, from everything and everyone I'd ever held dear, everything I loved. I ran away with Maura's screams pounding my skull. I—" Simon's tale abruptly ended as his head sagged to his chest and his eyes closed.

Yet Marc wouldn't be dissuaded and blurted, "Was she with child?"

Simon didn't immediately answer. Marc believed his silence intentional, and grabbed his shoulder to force the answer. His roughness shook from Simon great rumbling sobs of guilt, "Robert tried to murder the child by ordering his guards to rape and beat Maura! That failed, so he sent Maura to an abbey, where the nuns forced her to eat herbs that killed the baby and almost killed her!"

Marc seized Simon's other shoulder and yanked him close. "How could you leave her?!" he wailed. "How could you go knowing—"

"I didn't know she was pregnant!" Simon cried back. "Maura never told me! Edith suspected it, yet dared not say, for she knew I would never have left had I known the truth!"

As quickly as it appeared, Marc's anger vanished. He eased his grip and struggled to hear as Simon mumbled, sad and listless, "I didn't go far. I returned for Maura that evening and found everyone gone except Will. He said Maura had been taken to Normandy to marry, and my mother had left to visit her family. I know now every word was a lie. Then I came here to hide. I was accepted, almost coddled. I'd studied medicine when I was with Lanfranc, so they sent me to the village of Myddfai to learn more from a family of physicians that lived there. I stayed here for two years, doctoring, then Alan arrived to take me back to England and the King. I became William's emissary and when not peacemaking, I searched everywhere for Maura...in vain." Simon raised his eyes, wretched and red from misery, and faintly asked, "Do you remember last Martinmas?"

"Vividly," answered Marc in a numb, faraway voice.

"That was the first we'd seen of each other since we parted," mused Simon, wiping at tears. "She hated me then, yet in the months that followed, she found a way to forgive and love me again...I can't imagine how, but then I'm not capable of such goodness."

"I disagree," soothed Marc.

"But Marc," Simon choked, "I'm responsible for every horrible thing that's ever happened to Maura, for the death of our child and—"

"What else could you have done, Simon?" Marc vehemently objected. "If you had stayed at Dunheved, it would have made no difference for you and she would be dead."

"There had to be some way to save them...from Robert, from Will! And I harbor the same dread as Maura, that it will all happen again, and when it does, Marc," he despaired, gripping Marc's arms and begging assurance, "will I be able to protect them? Will I?!"

Marc enclosed Simon in a bolstering hug and quavered, "I remember when we were together in Normandy, my leg was mangled and you shielded me with your body the whole night through. You swore to me then you'd never allow anyone to hurt me ever again, and no one has. Now I swear the same to you, for as long as I'm able, no one will harm you, nor Maura, nor your child...I swear, Simon," he repeated, gripping tighter and shedding tears himself, "I swear!"

*****

79

CHAPTER SIX - REJOINED

𝕱or a long while, Marc and Simon sat quietly numb, striving to restore their calm, Marc more successfully than Simon. The sun, now directly overhead, glared and stung. Simon wiped sweat from his brow and blurted, "I want to go back."

"Yes, we should," agreed Marc. He rose and extended his hand. "We've been away far too long. They'll be worrying about us."

With Marc's aid Simon scrambled up dizzily, saying, "I'm worried about Maura."

"I don't think you need be if Gael's with her."

"I'll see for myself that she's fine."

Marc struggled to keep pace as Simon hurriedly ducked, skirted, and wove his way through the dense grove, round the barn, and shouldered his way through the cottage's closed door.

Maura, sitting at the physician's table, spun to the sudden intrusion, then tensed to her husband's pallor. She shoved up from her seat and caught him in a clinging hug. Their clutch lingered, then he pulled back slightly to take her face in his hands and question, "Why are you up?"

"Because, my love, I'm perfectly fine and so is our child. What's happened to you?" She glanced to Marc for a clue, but received only his shamed look in response, and her fretting spiraled. "Someone tell me what's happened! Have you heard something about Uncle William? Please tell me."

"Nothing's happened," said Simon.

"I don't believe you. You left here happy and returned sad. I'll know what's happened and I'll know now!"

"We only talked, Maura," mumbled Marc.

"Talked about what?"

"It's not important," said Simon.

"Don't coddle me! About what, Marc?"

"About when you two parted, five years past."

"Why would you talk of that time?"

Simon swallowed dryly and answered, "Marc had some questions—"

"I gave you the letters," Maura snapped at Marc. "The letters told all!"

"Not all, Maura."

"All that needed to be told!"

"I don't want to discuss this again, not now," stated Simon with finality. "I have remedies to mix and deliver."

"I've mixed them," said Maura.

"Then I'll go."

"May I come, Simon?" asked Marc.

"No...Please Marc, I'll go alone. I shouldn't be long. There's only three to take. Where's Gael, Maura?"

"She took Gruffydd and went home."

Simon nodded stiffly, grabbed up three woven bags, the names of the patients and herbs carefully scripted on each, and turned to leave.

"Simon..." Her hand's slight pressure stopped him as Maura murmured, "If you need to, go slowly. We'll be fine."

He nodded again and slipped away, leaving Marc muddled and Maura dismayed. She immediately busied herself, straightening herbs and cleaning mortars, while he fidgeted with various items topping the larger trestle table. And when she could no longer contain her fluster, Maura coarsely muttered, "I won't have him pestered about that time!"

"I didn't pester him, Maura," Marc scolded back.

"Then why ask?"

"I had questions. I thought it would be easier for him—"

"What questions?"

"About the first child."

"But the letters—"

"Never said!" he volleyed. "Why didn't you tell me?"

"I...I..." She paused to muster her composure, then somberly said, "Because it was only a short while past that I remembered what happened to our child. I'm sorry."

"As am I."

"Please Marc," she implored, "I am reconciled to our past, Simon is not. It's very hard for him to remember or speak of it...God's forgiven him, I've forgiven him, but he's not yet able to forgive himself. When he told you, were you angry?"

"I was till he confessed not knowing of the child. I swear I won't mention it again."

"I'm not asking that of you...only if there's anything else you need know, please come to me."

He breathed a solemn, "Yes," and slumped onto the bench flanking the table, picked up the remedy book, and traced with a finger the wrinkles branching across the worn leather binding. She came up behind him, settled her hands on his shoulders and kissed the top of his head. His hand left the book to squeeze hers.

*****

On their walk, Henry yapped and nipped at Simon's heels, provoking Simon to wag a threatening finger, and bark back, "You'll behave or spend the rest of the day in the stable!" But his bluster didn't faze Henry in the least, and the pup continued to bother. "I've always believed," sighed Simon, "that all dogs were trainable creatures, till I met you. You've certainly lived up to your name." He gazed fondly down at Henry, who had paused to lick beneath his leg, and laughed, "You're exactly like him!" It felt good to smile again, and as Simon slapped his thigh and indulged his furry friend's antics, he grudgingly admitted that on a few occasions he missed his cousin, Henry. For despite the FitzRoy's outward gruffness and pomposity, Simon felt sure that somewhere inside lurked a salvageable soul. Simon supposed that a visit from Henry was imminent, and again his mind lapsed into its desperate chant, *Uncle William will recover, he can survive anything...he will recover!* But when his attention returned to the present, he found himself not at his patient's hut but at the door of the small chapel connected to St. Davids Cathedral that offered services mostly to the villagers. His craving for comfort and contemplation had lured him here—Maura had known his need when she'd said, '...go slowly'. But then she always knew his needs, oft times long before he did. The intense solitude drew him swiftly inside. He closed the door on Henry's eager panting and, after a whimper, the pup resignedly curled up on the stoop to wait. The humble chapel boasted scant furnishings, few icons, a modest altar, and a single crucifix. Simon rested on one of the four benches, shut his eyes and, letting loose a long, ragged sigh, allowed the solacing ambiance to calm and nurture. Very soon the disorder vexing his mind began to lift, and he had an overpowering sense he was no longer alone. He opened his eyes and found his suspicion true, for there, filling the curved doorway leading from the chapel to the refectory stood Sulien, his expression matching the black of his robes.

"Simon?" he called, just above a whisper, "I didn't know you had returned. Are you needing me?"

81

Simon grinned meekly and Sulien joined him on the bench. The Bishop had the uncanny gift to hear one's worry before it was spoken, and asked, "So...if King William dies what will you do?"

"We won't stay if threatened," Simon replied staidly. "We won't endanger the commote."

"I dare say if the King dies, we'll all be endangered. The truce forged between Rhys and King William is a fragile one, and if William Rufus is next to claim the English throne, I don't believe our lease of this territory will be honored. But I can and will rightly say for the entire commote, that we are prepared to protect ourselves and your family from any adversity. For you belong to us, Simon and we've missed you." The Bishop broke from his seriousness to inquire lightly, "How fares our Prince?"

"He seems much improved."

"Such glorious news, and well worth a celebration! Tomorrow evening, join me and my wife at the long house for a gathering. A bard will attend, there will be a feast of tales, food, ale, and music, and we'll all indulge in a bit of much-needed play. It will be an excellent opportunity to introduce Marc to the village. I'm certain he'll be warmly accepted, for I've done a bit of canvassing on his behalf. I do fret, however, once the ladies get a gander of him, he'll not have one moment free."

"I don't think he'll complain much," answered Simon. "You look tired."

"I am...I'm tired of being Bishop and Pennaeth, when I'd rather just be a husband and father. Has Rhys chosen Rhodri's successor?"

"He didn't mention anyone in particular."

"Well he'd best hurry. I'm far too old for such a frenzied existence. I'm thankful you're here to doctor, or I expect he'd be wanting me to tend to that as well. I see you have your bags." Sulien quickly read the names on each bag, including the one that Simon attempted to cover. "Let me guess, Bleddyn gets centaury to boost his appetite, you've mixed something for Hywel's hoarseness, maybe plantain in goat's whey, mugwort, and nettles, and for Angharad..." He paused and finished in a censuring tone, "black thorn."

"When she misses her flow," Simon stringently defended, "she doctors herself from her own stock of herbs—too severely, and then it falls on me to stop her hemorrhaging!"

"All she need do is lock her door to that wandering rogue she calls husband!" declared Sulien.

"She doesn't want to lock her door to him, and she needn't suffer for letting him in!" Simon returned.

"But, it's not right, Simon!"

"Perhaps not, but it's not my place to moralize."

"But it is mine...and in this instance I've failed miserably. Well," Sulien sighed, using Simon's shoulder to hoist himself up, "I won't argue Angharad's plight with you now, for I'm certain the topic will arise again...after his next visit. Go, dispense your remedies, and then get a decent night's rest, for you look every bit as weary as I do. We'll expect you and your family tomorrow evening at nightfall."

"We will be there, probably early for Marc's sake. He's slightly shy."

"Fine."

The Bishop released Simon's shoulder to leave, but Simon stopped him with a last thought, "Sulien, the infirmary...Do you need me there?"

"All the beds are empty...thank God."

Simon smiled in agreement, watched Sulien disappear, then took up his bags to go. Looking inwardly, he found that what he'd come for had been delivered—he felt needed and capable once more. And as he strolled away, he offered an extra thanks to the quiet.

*****

Arthur snapped his head in the direction of the stable door and heard again the soft rapping. His fearful gaze darted back to the village leech, who knelt by Edith's feet, carefully applying a salve to her festering soles. "Should I answer, Elva?" he asked pleadingly.

"I can't say," replied the grizzled, white-haired woman. "If you do or don't, she'll be no worse."

"It may be Lord Robert's physician."

"He'll do no good here, and if you let him in, I leave."

"I won't let him in, but...Lord Robert mentioned he might come," said Arthur struggling up, and moving slowly toward the halved door leading to the stable. Should he or shouldn't he? He knew their hut was being spied upon; he'd noticed the stranger loitering across the lane. But desperate for sympathetic company, he decided to answer the summons. Arthur's discovery that the knocking came from the rear door of the stables bolstered his decision, and he whispered through the barrier, "Who's there?"

"Alan...and—"

Arthur didn't need to hear more; he thrust open the door and hustled his three friends inside the stable, beseeching, "Quick...You'll be seen."

"By whom?" blurted Almodis, shaking back the hood of her cloak.

"Robert's men..." Looks of dread struck Alan and Almodis, and Arthur's next words, "Edith's been hurt," forced their frowns longer. They threw off their wraps and followed him inside the main room. Arthur immediately returned to his unceasing vigil by Edith's head.

When Almodis beheld Edith, so miserable on her mat, her grip on Adam faltered, and she called out, "Alan, please take Adam! Alan!" He whisked the child from her arms, and Almodis lurched to her knees beside Arthur. "Who...who's done this?" she sputtered frantically. "Was it Robert? It was, wasn't it? It was Robert!"

"No..."

His whisper only heightened her alarm, and she burst, "Will? Was it Will?!"

"It was Odo," Arthur muttered with hate.

She grabbed his shoulder to halt the room's spinning. "Ho...ow...He's imprisoned."

"No more. William is dead, Odo is free."

"But you said Robert...You said Robert's men would see us."

"I believe he's watching out of benevolence, not malice."

"Damn your riddles!" flared Almodis. "Tell me what has happened here!"

The sharp tones roused Edith from her fevered sleep; delirium and a sweet-smelling, hovering smoke hindered her sight. "Ar...Arthur...who's there?" she groaned, groping through the mist.

"It's Almodis, Alan, and the boy, my dove. They've come to cheer you." His reply helped ease her turmoil, as did his caress of her limp hand and kiss to her brow.

Alan settled Adam in a cradle kept handy for his visits, then rejoined Almodis and Arthur. He stared in fascination at the healer's ministrations to Edith's feet. The woman hadn't acknowledged their arrival with speech or gesture, so Alan asked, "Who is she, Arthur?"

"The village leech. She's called Elva. I called for her immediately after we returned from the castle, and she has been here ever since. She rarely rests or eats, and speaks less, but her treatments seem to bring Edith comfort."

Almodis resumed her prodding, "What has she said of Edith's recovery? How did this happen, Arthur? Why did it happen?"

83

When he was certain Edith was asleep, Arthur motioned Almodis and Alan up from the floor and over to the trestle table. "I've only stale ale to offer," he said, emptying a pitcher into three cups. "If you're hungry, there is a little bread and dried meat."

"No," snapped Almodis, "stop lagging and tell me—"

"Almodis!" flashed Alan. "Can't you see his trouble?"

"His trouble may be our trouble, and we need to know precisely what that is! Arthur, I apologize for my harshness. Can you try to say what's happened?"

Arthur sagged forlornly onto the bench, Almodis and Alan sat opposite, and Arthur shakily divulged to his rapt audience, "Odo's men captured her near a week past. I was in Gloucester. She was held and tortured till Robert arrived to set her free."

"Why was she captured?" asked Alan.

"Odo wants Simon's whereabouts."

"And does he know them now?" panicked Almodis.

Arthur looked appalled. "No...she'd die before betraying Simon to Odo."

"Will she die, Arthur?" asked Alan tentatively.

"No...but when or if she'll walk again is questionable."

"I must warn them," stated Alan.

"Warn whom?" queried Almodis.

"Simon and Maura."

"No!" she shouted, rising an inch from her chair. "You...you can't leave me alone!"

"You won't be alone...Rose will—"

"Rose may be a tyrant, but she can't protect me from Odo or Robert!"

"Neither can I," Alan argued.

"I must go to Edith," blurted Arthur, eager to escape their wrangling.

Alan had the same purpose when he suggested, "Arthur, you need rest and sustenance. I'll see to Edith. Almodis, please fetch him some food."

Almodis gaped at Alan, then shook from her selfishness, and rose to search out something palatable. She had been forced to cook on rare occasions at Rose's manor, and had done so reluctantly; she was used to being waited upon, yet was a very adequate cook if needed. A cauldron resting by the fire held a gelatinous mixture wafting a pleasant aroma. Before setting it atop the flames, she thought first to ask the healer, "Madam...will I bother Edith's treatment by warming this stew?"

The woman shuddered which Almodis took to mean 'no', and she hung the handle of the pot to a chain dangling from the vented roof. She stirred the mixture once, then returned to Arthur, who looked more mournful than before. "Arthur," she said, striving to cheer, "after you've eaten, you'll rest and not worry. We shall handle—"

"That's quite kind of you, my Lady, but I've no intention of resting," he answered abruptly. "And besides, I can't close my eyes, for each time I do, I imagine different ways of murdering the two brothers."

His fierceness took her aback. She studied her elder friend a long moment; his usual jolly countenance had vanished, leaving his bushy brows knitted with worry, his jowls hanging morosely, and his usually twinkling green eyes dull and grave. His ash-gray locks were disheveled and clumped, and his long, belted tunic was rumpled and stained. How woeful she felt, peering at his distress. Her fingers wound round his and patted, while she consoled, "She will be fine, Arthur, and she will walk again. No one can defeat the noble Lady Edith, certainly not Odo. Surely God will allow her a while longer to revel in your adoration. And if you happen to dream up a murder that's both heinous and feasible, please provide me the details."

He raised up the slimmest of smiles, and Almodis left to fetch the stew and fresh ale from the stable. She spooned Alan a bowl, checked to see that Adam was content, and settled again by Arthur. Elva rose shortly after to pronounce, "I've done all I can for now. I will return once a day to apply the poultice. Keep her quiet and warm, and faithfully burn the herbs. She should wake more fully by morning, but don't allow her to walk. If she does all my work will have been for naught."

Arthur rose as well and extracted three coins from a small pouch hanging from his belt. He pressed them to the healer's palm and nodded, "I am obliged to you, Madam, as is my wife."

The woman shoved the coins up her sleeve and hobbled away through the stable.

"Strange creature," remarked Almodis with disdain.

"Strange, but skillful," noted Arthur, returning to the table. "How fares the boy?"

Almodis softened to Arthur's thoughtfulness and answered, "He's perfect, and so polite."

Arthur glanced toward the child's cooing, and saw his tiny fingers dancing in the air. "I can see that," he commented. "Edith and I have sorely missed him. And what of Rose?"

"She's continually grumpy, and her son, Richard, arrives tomorrow," groused Almodis. "I can't abide him, he's disgustingly self-righteous."

Arthur couldn't help a chuckle. "Sometimes, Almodis, I wonder what you say of us when we're not near."

"I utter nothing but compliments," she assured with a fond wink. Again his spirits sank and she struggled to think of a way both to distract and comfort. She looked at Alan and warmed to his expression of deep caring; Edith remained quiet, as did the child, so she sighed loudly and asked, "Tell me about Edith, Arthur."

"What?" he asked, bemused. "What can I say that you don't already know?"

Almodis turned round her request and spilled, "I first heard the dear Lady's name mentioned at Berkhamstead in late December of last year. Will and I were still friendly, and Simon had arrived unexpectedly on his way to Gloucester for Christmas Court. It was a queer night. The brothers had yet to become stalwart enemies, but there was already a sizzling animosity between them. When Will introduced Simon as his half-brother, I almost choked. No one had informed me of Robert's long-lived dalliance with Edith and I was a bit miffed. Will told Edith's tale, quite eloquently as I recall. He began in '51 when King William, who was then only Duke, had traveled to Winchester to secure his ascendancy to the English throne from King Edward...Edith was fourteen..."

"And simply lovely..." Arthur took over the telling and related wistfully, "She was servant to Edward's Queen and so excited that the Normans were visiting. There were to be feasts and games."

Encouraged, Almodis rested forward on crossed arms and suggested, "You knew her then?"

"We had met on her twelfth birthday, when her parents had sent her on her own to our stall to purchase lace for a new frock. Our cloth stall had survived generations, and at that time my grandfather and my parents tended the stall, and I apprenticed. We became fast friends and I loved hearing her gossip from the castle, and when we could get away from our chores, we'd hike everywhere and talk of everything. Few know it, but she has a mischievous streak."

"I see it reflected in her son," remarked Almodis.

"Yes, I agree," smiled Arthur. "I loved her then. I suppose I've always loved her. There was no one I felt closer to. And then *he* arrived and nothing was the same. It seems at one feast Edith served Robert, and he believed she would make his first wife, Matilda, a fine gift, so Edward presented her to him."

"And how did Edith feel about that?"

"Honored. She was infatuated by William and Robert, especially Robert. Her talk became thick of him and I grew more and more impatient and jealous. When I told her I'd heard enough, we had a grievous fight. But before I could apologize, she was gone to Normandy."

"So you were reunited a few years past, when Robert banished her?" asked Almodis, entranced by the heartrending story.

"Oh no," said Arthur, absently stirring his stew, then fiddling with the grip of his tankard. "She wrote to me regularly after arriving at Mortain. The letters would come to the castle and then were passed to me. She seemed content in her role as servant, for at the start, that's all she was to Robert. It wasn't till after Matilda and Robert's final battle that he and Edith became lovers."

"I don't understand, Arthur," pressed Almodis. "Their 'final' battle?"

"Robert and Matilda hated each other, and their fights turned physical. Their priest threatened to annul their union if they didn't part. So they did. Robert lived in Mortain with Edith and Robert's three daughters, and Matilda and Will went to live in Belleme with her parents. Mostly, Robert's family frowned on the union and snubbed Edith, especially Odo. Only William seemed agreeable. I hadn't sensed trouble between them in her letters, but one fine day in June, I came out from behind my stall to serve a customer and there she stood...Her hardship spoiled my bliss, for she soon admitted that after discovering her pregnancy, Robert had decided to return her to England for her safety. Her family had since moved to Sussex, and she had sought solace from them, only to be cast away. So she came to me and my father, my mother and grandfather having died. We welcomed her, and she became one of our family. Simon was born the first of October that year and made us complete. If you believe him a joy now, you should have known him when he was little. He was so bright, full of mettle, and like his mother, born kind."

"And what of Robert?" asked Almodis, confused.

Arthur seemed hesitant to return to that facet of the tale, but grudgingly assented, "Yes...Robert. Four years after Edith came home, we were conquered by William, Robert, Odo and the others. My father was killed in battle, and our trade almost ruined, but we managed to scrape together a pittance to survive. Six months following the Conquest a lone knight rode up to my stall and I saw in Edith's face the look I was never gifted with. Robert took her and Simon away to Dunheved—not that she wasn't appreciative for what I'd done for her, and for Simon. She loved Robert."

"And Simon? He must have been upset...being removed from the only father he'd ever known," guessed Almodis.

"He was too young to know what had occurred or why. Once a year, Edith brought him for a visit, and I felt blest to have them near, and glad that he spoke fondly of his father. Then a few years past, as you know, the great debacle occurred, and Robert tossed Edith from Dunheved with nothing, not even her son. Her pride kept her from me...for awhile. And when she did come it was more for comfort than rescue. She returned here to live as a burgher and has managed quite well ever since."

"And how did you end up here?"

Arthur somehow managed a smile. "I'm sure you remember Simon's last visit to Winchester."

Almodis' expression shone the happiness of the memory. "Such a glorious time!"

"Yes, for all," concurred Arthur. "His doggedness to wed Maura inspired me to venture here to win Edith's hand."

"And victorious you both were!" praised Almodis.

"I had to agree to leave Winchester, a decision I was content with till a week past." He grasped her hand, urged her closer, and spoke secretly, "Almodis, I'll confess something to you...I've always believed, no matter how much she claimed to love me, if he happened to enter her life again, I would be alone. And it happened—Odo took her and Robert valiantly came to her rescue. He purposely had her taken to their old bedchamber, and, as if in competition, we waited for her to wake, I bracing one side of the bed, he the other. I was petrified for her to open her eyes, afraid for her to see him." He paused as grateful tears welled in his eyes and his grip strengthened. "But when she woke, Almodis, she looked to me, not to him. She begged me to take her home, and I did, and I won't lose her now that I know how she truly feels, and never to those devils!"

"You'll not lose her, Arthur," Almodis soundly asserted. "I feel sure of that. And I appreciate you sharing your life with me, not only your tale just now, but the past five magnificent months. And I'll confess to you something—many times at Winchester, I took a stroll through the market solely for the delight of visiting you."

He blushed so severely that for an instant she regretted her compliment. But she had meant every word; few could make her laugh as heartily as Arthur did and she so longed for his mirth. Adam's mewling turned needy and Almodis rose to attend him, murmuring to Arthur, "Eat now, then rest, and when you wake, we shall speak further."

Arthur grinned in submission and began picking idly at his stew. Alan continued to mop Edith's sweat-beaded brow, and Almodis raised up her son and settled opposite Alan. She favored him with a quick atoning glance, then, squirming among the pillows for comfort, commenced feeding the boy. Almodis' focus fell on Edith's feet, the scorching now hidden by bandages, and she thought of Arthur's bittersweet tale. As she recounted her neither bitter nor sweet history with Robert, she realized the one-year anniversary of their nuptials had recently passed. Personally, she knew little of her husband and had intentionally striven to retain that distance. To her, he had been charitable, most times genial, and adequate in bed. And with that she'd been content, for in comparison to the suffering she had endured with her three former husbands and countless lovers, her life with Robert she deemed ecstatic. And though her husband was to her a perplexing stranger, Almodis believed she knew why Edith had cleaved to him for so long. He owned a tenderness rarely revealed; Almodis guessed only Edith and Simon had been privy to his secret, concealed neatly behind an icy facade of propriety. And now that Odo was free, Almodis was certain, he would set about brutally destroying Robert's tenderness, for to Odo empathy was equal to weakness. She gazed lovingly down at her son...He too would inherit the beauty of the Mortains, but would his nature veer toward the diabolical or the genteel, and, she sadly wondered, how much influence would she be allowed to wield in his shaping? As Arthur had so aptly named them, the devils were near, so close their force stifled and strangled. Her belly lurched as she recalled Alan's dire assertion, 'I must warn them', and she blurted impulsively, "You cannot..."

He looked up curiously and whispered, "Cannot what?"

"Warn Simon and Maura."

"I must."

"You'll lead Odo directly to them and then you will all perish!"

"I'll elude him by leaving from the back—"

"He surrounds us, Alan," she countered, shuddering with revulsion. "I can smell his stench. I forbid you to leave this hut!"

"This hut or you?" he asked, peeved.

"I regret my selfishness of before, but I was afraid. Surely you'll forgive me?"

He appeased her penitent look with an outstretched hand. She removed the sleeping infant from her breast, crawled to Alan's side, and snuggled against him. At sight of the sickly Edith, an overwhelming glut of affection made Almodis swallow a whimper, and insist more frantically, "Don't sacrifice yourself attempting something that's certain to fail. Too many have suffered, Alan...far too many. Simon and Maura will hear of the King's death, and when they do they will take measures to protect themselves. We must stay here and see to Edith's recovery."

"And then?" wondered Alan.

Almodis shrugged and, with a somber sigh, lowered the boy to the pelts by Edith. "It will soothe her to wake with him near."

"A kind gesture, Almodis," complimented Alan. They heard snoring and turned to see Arthur's face buried in his crossed arms. The warm quiet lured them to steal one kiss, then another, and another, each one ripe with despair.

*****

"Simon's been gone quite a long while," mentioned Marc, idly watching Maura chop garlic.

"He spends a good amount of time with each of his patients," said Maura. "He believes that showing concern is the cause of most of their recovery." Maura chopped more sharply and mused, "Marc, do you remember anything of when we were separated from our parents?"

He searched a moment for the long past memory, then said, "I have flashes of being ripped from your hold, but I've never recalled our parents."

"I did," she said almost gleefully. "And I wasn't dreaming when it happened. Father was red-haired like me, Mother had flaxen hair. And when I saw them in my mind, their images were joined by the most wonderfully loving feelings..." Her hands splayed over her belly in a wiping gesture and she added with emotion, "They died saving us."

"I imagined as much," said Marc. "Lord Robert also saved us."

"Yes, I won't deny his sacrifice. But what I constantly wonder is—saved us from whom?"

"Does it matter, Maura?"

"It does to me. When I asked Robert about that time, he purposely lied about our attacker's identity. I believe he's protecting someone still alive and still dangerous."

"Perhaps he forgot or became confused."

"I don't think so, and I aim to discover the truth."

"How?"

"At the moment, I haven't an idea, but—"

Her resolve was disrupted by Simon's obtrusive arrival. He staggered through the door, encumbered by two lumpy sacks hanging from each shoulder. Maura rushed to help, glowing at his beaming countenance, and marveled at how well his doctoring visits served to heal him. He swiftly tasted her lips, and passed her the lighter sack. After depositing the other upon the table, Simon acknowledged Marc with a nod and smirk. "And what mischief have you two been up to while I've been away?" he asked, reaching inside the sack and pulling forth a plethora of food stuffs. There were bread loaves, blocks of cheese and butter, salted beef, eggs, and two plucked chickens.

"Mostly talk," answered Maura as she in turn extracted from her bag material goods, such as tailored tunics for both her and Simon, chunks of soap, flints, candles, wooden utensils and bowls. "Oh Simon, look at these beautiful tunics. I must thank Angharad personally. And how fare your patients?"

"Improving and awfully gabby," said Simon. "They're grateful for your deliveries while I was gone."

Marc looked astonished at their fortune and spouted, "Where did you find all that?"

"Payment for the medicine," replied Simon.

"God's breath!" he exclaimed. "They must be rich!"

"In appreciation," noted Simon, "not in coins."

"Then you're never in need of anything?"

"Not a thing," said Maura. "Especially not money. Soon after we arrived, we discovered our coins worthless, and we gave them to the monastery."

"I'm amazed," said Marc. "Life seems so simple here."

"Most times it is," agreed Maura, "except when Simon's gone."

"Well I won't be gone again. What, besides you, my love, smells so heavenly?" Simon asked, sniffing and peeking into a cauldron dangling over blazing coals.

"A stew of leeks, beans and onions. I'm just adding garlic and spices, and half this chicken will thicken it nicely." She deftly hacked off the naked bird's legs and wings with a silver bladed knife and tossed them into the aromatic concoction. "Take this, Simon," she suggested, pouring and passing him a cup of ale. "Sit, rest, and talk with Marc. I'll put away our gifts."

He kissed his thanks and, while the men conversed quietly, Maura flitted about, finding a place for each item. A loft provided storage for the goods they already owned; a bolted larder set into the ground in a corner kept the salted beef, butter, cheese and chickens fresh and safe from Henry; the vanity items she took to the sleeping chamber and placed them neatly atop the trunk. She switched stubs of candles with new tapers, hung pieces of strewn clothing on pegs jutting from the walls, and paused a joyous moment to attend to her baby's stirrings. The luscious sensation radiated further as she sat on the bed, and let her fingers skim their way over the crumpled bed clothes. She burned inside for the heat of Simon's touch and yearned for this evening to pass quickly, so that they might lie together and love again! It had been far too long, and there was no reason to wait longer, for the child was exceedingly healthy and happy. Wistfully, she glanced down at the ring of stones footing the bed. A similar ring had warmed the secret chamber at Winchester Castle where they'd been rejoined after being apart for so many years. The magic of that night would endure forever in their minds and hearts, and she prayed to God that he help them defeat any challenges to their future happiness. She shivered from an unexpected doubt and chill, hugged herself and her child, and rose to return to the main chamber and her men.

*****

When next Maura sat on her bed, all outside was dark, her belly was full of stew, and the new candle flickered gentle shadows about the room. As she wriggled from her tunic and unwove her braid, she thought back on the wondrous evening—a near perfect meal, gratifying conversation, and she and Simon had come close to laughing themselves sick to Marc's rendition of Simon's last visit to Normandy and joust with Will. She reveled in the satisfaction of having another near who shared her ideals, aspirations, and language. For, with the exception of Gael and Gruffydd, there always seemed an enforced distance between herself and the villagers, mostly the women. Each day it grew smaller, but she often worried if it would ever disappear completely. In contrast, Simon did not own this problem; his rapport with the villagers was excellent, particularly with the women. She wondered if jealousy prompted their coolness toward her, for the wars had left many widowed. Maura felt an annoying twinge of insecurity as she glanced down at her rapidly expanding figure. Simon's desire for her seemed not in the least deterred by the fullness of her belly, but what if—Heat on her neck stopped her concern; she felt the damp tickle of his lips, and gasped delightedly as his hands reached round to cup her breasts. Her head lolled back against his shoulder and her hands covered his. "Oh, Simon," she begged, "we needn't wait, don't make us wait more!"

"And what makes you think I want us to wait?" he murmured, urging her around, and drawing her into his arms.

"I thought your fretting about the baby's health..."

"You've amply convinced me there's no longer any reason to fret over her."

"Have I truly?"

He smiled at her doubt, kissed her full and long, then said, "Absolutely, and the feel and taste of you convinces me further that not attending to each other's pleasure will soon prove unhealthy for us both."

"You needn't talk like a doctor to me, Simon."

"And what would you have me say?" he teased.

"Tell me what I can do this night to please you most..." she offered temptingly, lacing fingers through his hair.

His instant blush brought from her an endearing chuckle.

"What's funny?" he asked, his head tilted innocently.

"It amazes me that after all our time together, my love talk can still bring color to your cheeks."

"And other places as well," he intimated.

They both laughed and sank to their sides. "Is Marc asleep?" asked Maura as Simon bared her shoulder and nibbled at her freckled skin.

"I left him reading," he mumbled, nudging her chemise lower and nuzzling the escaping mound of her breast.

"Then we must wait," insisted Maura, stiffening.

"Why?"

"Because he'll hear."

"Yes...I suppose he will if he chooses to listen, and..."

"Because I'll feel inhibited."

"Inhibited?"

"Yes."

Simon sat up, cradled his head in his hand a moment, then swept back his hair to ask, "Are you saying, our timing for this is dependent on whether or not Marc chooses to sleep?"

"I suppose," Maura answered.

"Maura, he's liable to be our guest for a long, long while and I don't see how we can arrange our loving to suit—"

Her eyes and face lit to the notion, "We'll go to the well!"

Simon looked agreeable. "A fine idea for now, but what about when the cold comes?"

"By that time we'll have thought of another solution." She tugged playfully at his tunic. "We'll escape through the window so he'll not know what we're up to."

"What if he needs for anything?"

"He's seems fairly self-sufficient," she said, swinging one leg over the window sill.

"Careful," he cautioned, "there's barely a moon. Let me lead."

She did and hand-in-hand they bobbed their way through thicket and grove, Simon cursing periodically when he stubbed some part of his anatomy on a low jutting branch. The ever-yapping pup appeared, squirming for a game, and Simon's curse blared louder, "God's teeth, Henry. Go back!" Henry's answer was as booming as he raced circles round Simon's legs. "Get away! Go!" yelled Simon, stomping for emphasis.

"Oh, Simon," sighed Maura with wag of her head. "Why do you bother? He never listens to you."

"No one does," sulked Simon.

"I mostly do..." said Maura, her tone beguiling. "Ignore him, he'll soon get bored."

Just then Marc's voice rang through the balmy dark. "Henry...Henry...Come in!"

The dog's ears instantly perked, and he tore off in the direction of the cottage. Maura and Simon exchanged bemused looks, shrugged, and gamboled on.

Maura sat herself upon the cushiony moss surrounding the well, embraced her knees and drank in the moist, tepid air perfumed by the sea and spiced by soot from the village fires. Entranced, she watched her husband peel back the well's cover. How thrilled she was by his beauty; what little moon-light there was glistened his hair and beard silver, burnished his bronzed skin, and lit his eyes limpid as the water. He sensed her approval and came to sit by her; moving very close, he touched her face. Passion leapt from his fingertips, and tingled its way through her. She whimpered for more and joined her lips forcefully to his. A sudden surge of heat made them groan and entwine further. Maura groped for the hem of Simon's tunic, finally grasping it and jerking upward, but Simon stopped her with the allurement, "No...wait...I'll go slowly..."

The look he lived for sparked her eyes; wild and fevered, they locked to his, impelling him to begin...He shed his tunic with a deliberateness that was near painful, but he relished this kind of hurt and prayed it never to end. As each garment fell away, her hand would reach out seemingly to help, but instead dangle just shy of its target. When at last his body lay bare, she pressed her cheek to his heart's fervid beat and breathed in deeply his warmth. As her fingertips traced each rippled muscle, a quivering anticipation overtook him. Reverently, he spread her back upon the moss and, hovering above, deftly peeled away her chemise. His lips kindled each bit of skin exposed, lingering to rouse the tips of her breasts, tickle the swell of her belly, nuzzle the down between her legs. And all the while, his hands roamed everywhere creating a luxurious tension that livened her breaths, stiffened her limbs, and plunged her nails into the dirt.

Simon suddenly slipped off her into the pool. Maura raised up on her elbows and cocked her head in wonder. "Come," he coaxed with open arms, "we'll play awhile."

Her lusty smile agreed; she kicked away her chemise and shoved off the spongy ledge into his huge embrace. They swooned from the shimmery liquid's snug caress, then Simon disappeared below the surface. Maura sucked an expectant breath and slapped at his trail of bubbles, tittering, "Simon...Simon, where've you gone to?" Currents rushed round her waist, spider-like fingers crept up her thighs; the bubbles burst and he exploded to the surface, spewing water, and mauling her with tickles. Heaved handfuls of water baptized her as sopping as he. Their delighted squeals trilled through the dark, but the laughter soon dissolved to blissful sighs as the tickles turned tantalizing. "I can do nothing right without you near to keep me...contented," Maura murmured, dipping fingers between his lips.

Simon nibbled the tips and chuckled coarsely, "How contented?"

"Marvelously," she beamed.

"Show me...marvelously..." he seduced.

"With pleasure," she parried and motioned for him to turn. Her hands took a rapturous while to knead the long length of his back, smooth his firm flanks, then creep round his legs to grasp and incite his already blatant excitement.

He gripped the rim of the pool to still his wooziness, and gritting, "My God, woman, I missed you!" whirled around with a vehemence that swelled waves beyond the ledge. Their crazed groping drove them back up on the ground where he entered her with an ease that made them both gasp.

They nestled quietly on their sides, Simon quietly enclosed and resisting the acute urge to probe deeper, for if he succumbed, his zeal would prove too great and end their coupling too soon. He saw in her eyes and tasted from her lips a fierce hunger, yet her tone dripped sympathy. "Simon," she said in a breathy whisper, "you needn't hold back. We have the whole night...and you know each time we love lasts that much longer." Yes, he did know, but each time he needed assurance from her touch, her words, and he heard her lure on, "Each night you were away I burned for you here..." She reached low to stroke where their bodies fit so perfectly together, and, molding nearer, chaffed her nipples to his. "I craved your swelling, you moving inside me, gripping me so strongly I feel my bones will break!" Gradually, he realized that what she spoke, he did, and listening to her sweetness drained his worries and prolonged their pleasure.

She felt so cherished locked beneath him, her legs bent and embracing, her body undulating and gliding to his steadfast rhythm. A swift rocking swirled the stars and trees, and when all was still again she found herself stretched over him. She paused a moment for breath, then slipped her knees to his sides, and rose up...

He reeled to the sensuous sight and scent of her—eyes still flamed, lips rouged and swollen, hair tousled and hugging her like a scarlet gossamer cloak. A proud toss of her head swept the drape away. He reached up to smother the richness of her breasts and felt her nipples go rigid against his palms. His touch then strayed lower, rubbing into her wetness, making her wail a throaty, "Oh Simon!" as a simmering tension erupted in her womb. She collapsed upon his chest and began again their exquisite churning. Her panting increased, his lunges quickened, their moans blending and spiraling as they wrestled wildly over a bed of sodden leaves. Frozen in ecstasy, he shuddered into her one final cry of elation.

They lay a while, dazed, sweat-coated and spent. Then with limp effort, he pushed up from the ground and chuckled wearily, noticing their clothing and the pool had moved a dozen or so feet away. Maura accepted his hand up, and dreamily they strolled back to where their play had begun.

A pinch to her backside propelled Maura back into the steamy liquid and, with a sound splash, Simon exuberantly followed. They sank and sat enmeshed; their faces almost touching and petting continuing as water lapped gently at their shoulders. "So...are you contented?" murmured Simon.

"Ever so..." she sighed, twining tighter. "And the evening's young yet..."

Simon marveled at her radiance and felt his own skin sizzle to her meandering touch. He flashed a dazzling smile and flattered, "You've blossomed since coming here."

"That's due entirely to you and...her."

"No," he strongly objected. "You've come into your own right with your mediating, and how wonderfully you help me. The villagers admire and love you. Today, on my rounds, they especially complimented your visits while I was gone."

Her uncertainty rushed forth and she uttered, "I wish I could believe that, Simon."

"And why don't you? I wouldn't lie."

"I know you wouldn't. But I suspect they're only being polite...to you."

"Polite they may be...but their compliments are sincere, except of course..." he scowled, "Hywel's."

"He can be so horrid," chuckled Maura.

"Can be?" scoffed Simon. "He's always horrid. He's convinced I'm a charlatan but that doesn't stop him from demanding treatment for every ache, scrape, broken nail, hair out of place..."

Maura laughed louder to his griping, muffled it with a kiss, and said, "Perhaps you're correct, but sometimes...not often, I feel a bit resented."

"Once you've mastered the language," he assured, "which is happening at an astonishing speed, and the child comes, you're bound to feel more accepted."

"And Marc?" wondered Maura.

"It will take quite a while before he's convinced he's done right by coming here."

"Helping you will make that come about quicker."

Simon shifted with unease and muttered, "Perhaps..."

"He idolizes you Simon...he always has."

"But how can I possibly live up to his exalted image—"

"Easily," she asserted.

He nuzzled his cheek to hers and avowed, "I do love you..."

"And I you..." she pledged as adamantly.

Guilt made him sputter, "And there's some...something I need confess. "I wasn't entirely truthful about my encounter with the Welsh raiders. They aimed to kill me and almost did."

"Owain stopped them?"

"Just..."

Then when next we see him," she stated in awe, "we...we must thank him..."

Simon nodded, then meekly asked, "Can we go in...I'm feeling chilled."

"Of course, my love," she answered. "I'll fetch your clothes."

"No...you stay warm. I'll fetch mine and yours."

She smiled, but swiftly caught his chill as he scrambled out of the bubbles. He dressed with shivering quickness, and beckoned her out of the water and into her chemise. Maura's dampness made the sheer cloth hug her taut curves like a second skin. The winsome sight set his blood to boiling again. He hurriedly covered the well, and hustled her along, eager to wrap himself in their quilt and once again round her luscious body.

A mournful howl stalled their climb through the window. Daunted, they peered intently through the trees, then started to Henry's shrill reply. "Wolves?" Maura asked.

Simon nodded. "I've never heard them so close."

"What's it mean, Simon?"

"An early winter, perhaps. They sound hungry." He swung her easily through the opening, and bolted the shutters. "We'll have to make certain the stables are securely locked and keep Henry inside at night."

"He won't much care for that," said Maura.

"He'll much prefer it to being some wolf's supper. Now get yourself snug. I'll check on Marc and Henry and fetch us apples."

"Lovely...I'm famished." Maura slipped out of her chemise and under the quilt, trying futilely to sweep away the terrible image of Simon's impaled body lying somewhere between here and Dinefwr. He wouldn't go again, she determined, not unless accompanied by an overly large contingent of Rhys' soldiers, and she would go with him, in a cart, litter, whatever, but they wouldn't be separated...ever!

Sporting an impish grin, he tip-toed in the door, mouthed, "He's sleeping," then latched it, and dove upon the bed. He disrobed madly, burrowed between the bedclothes, and surged into her clutch.

"What shall I eat first, you or the apple?" she asked with a luring grin.

"Definitely the apple," he proposed, "or your belly will grumble." He passed her the plump rosy fruit, and munching on his own, mumbled casually, "So what did Gael have to say that was so sensitive?"

"I'm proud of you, Simon," she said, aghast.

"Why?"

"It took you practically the whole day before you pestered me about it."

"I'm not pestering and besides, I was slightly busy," he argued, then prodded with suspense, "Now tell me all the juicy bits."

"None of it was juicy...On the contrary, it was all rather distressing."

Concerned, he rose up on an elbow. "What is it?"

"It seems she's been given an ultimatum by Rhys to become his mistress or marry his choice for Pennaeth. If she doesn't agree, Gruffydd will be taken from her and she will be sent back to Shrewsbury." Piqued by his lack of comment or surprise, she pushed up as well and asked, "Did you know, Simon?"

"No...but I sensed a portion of it. While tending Rhys, he constantly complained of his lack of female companionship, and pressed me for details about Gael."

"Such as?"

"If she were keeping company with anyone here, did I think she might be attracted to him, and other such nonsense, or so I believed. I answered what I knew, which was little."

"Why didn't you warn her?"

"Of what?" asked Simon, fuddled. "That he found her attractive?"

"I suppose."

"I saw no need. He regularly rambles, and as far as I can surmise, there isn't a woman alive that he doesn't find attractive. And I was so intent on healing him and returning to you, that I forgot. What will she do?"

"She doesn't know, but she did request a talk with you."

"Why?" he asked with caution.

"She wants to discuss her options."

"But how can I help?"

"Listen and encourage her in her decision."

"What if I don't agree with her decision?"

"Let her know gently," suggested Maura, "but don't try to persuade her to change her mind, for if she does and your choice proves disastrous, she will never forgive you."

"Then I will gladly speak to her...And it's perfectly clear to me why you're such a brilliant mediator."

"I haven't done much mediating lately," shrugged Maura.

"And that's good news," noted Simon.

"And so is the fact, that you're home safe and...intact." Delight glittered her eyes as Maura tossed her apple core to the rushes, stole his away and tossed it as well. She tasted the sweetness lingering on his lips, and enticed, "And now I'll prove to you...my thanks." Her lips ambled thrillingly downward, leaving in their wake a damp trail round his nipples, over his belly, and lower...

Simon came alive again beneath her mouth's stroking. He grabbed the quilt to keep from floating away and issued soft moans to encourage her fervor. In little time, his passion threatened to peak; he groped out desperately, imploring, "Come up by me, my love." She swiftly obliged, hugged her thighs round his, and guided him inside. Wound tightly, they moved with a leisurely ardor, pausing occasionally to praise, share caresses, and shift their bodies to make their loving endure. But they could not evade their mounting bliss forever. And when it crested, it jolted them with a stunning force. They strained together for an endless moment, kissing fiercely to hush their joy, then wilted to a moist and tangled heap. Slowly their panting eased and, unwillingly, Simon shrank apart from her. The breadth between them instantly cooled, making them both flail out, grasp up the quilt, and bundle beneath its sumptuous warmth. Pressed to her, Simon believed he felt their child's flitting, and he decided, "She seems pleased."

"She is," sighed Maura.

He combed fingers through her hair and mentioned, "There's to be a celebration tomorrow eve at the long house."

"Wonderful," she gushed. "Will there be a bard?"

"Yes, and music, dancing, and food."

"Oh, Simon," Maura replied, "I do love living here..."

"But," he prompted.

"Sometimes..." she ruefully admitted, "I miss Rose, Almodis and Adam, your mother, Arthur, and...Alan. I wish they could come live with us."

"I wish the same," said he.

"Did Marc tell you of the note?"

"What note?"

"The note from your mother."

"He did mention something about a note right after I arrived home," recalled Simon, "but with all the ruckus, I forgot."

"Then I'll fetch it," said she.

"No." His grip and voice tensed. "Don't leave me."

"I'll be only a moment."

Simon reluctantly released her with the request, "Would you bring my saddlebag as well? There's something I want you to see."

Piqued, she floundered out from under the ponderous blanket. A nipping breeze, sneaking between the shutters, raised bumps over her bareness as she skittered about, snatching up the crinkled parchment hidden under her tunic, and his saddlebag, thrown and forgotten in a corner. Her teeth chattered as she bustled back beside him. They half sat, propped on pillows, and Simon squinted to read the tiny blurred print. His expression switched rapidly from expectant, to cheerful, and, as he mouthed the closing, to solemn. She stroked his beard, and turned his sadness to hope with the consolation, "She's healthy and happy, as is everyone else and come spring, surely they'll visit and perhaps...stay."

He nodded, stared away a thoughtful moment, then dug into his satchel and produced the ring. "Rhys gave me this. He said it was payment for my doctoring, but I sense it's more than a trinket, that it's a Welsh symbol for royalty. I don't know why he gave it to me..."

"He has tremendous respect for you, Simon."

He seemed not to hear the compliment and rambled on, "He said I might give it to you. It's rather large, so if you choose to, perhaps you could wear it on a chain round your neck."

Maura pinched up the ring from his palm. The most mystical look filled her face as she scrutinized the gilded woven pattern. A paleness joined her mystery, and Simon fretted, "What is it, Maura?"

"I've seen this ring before, Simon."

"Where?" he questioned.

"I don't—" She squeezed shut her eyes and instantly flashing images sliced through the black, none complete—a flailing hand; graceful fingers singed with soot, glinted with gold, gripping, strangling. She jumped to Simon's touch, clutched his hand, and strained, "I...I can't remember!"

"If it troubles you, my love, maybe I should return it," he suggested warily.

"No!" she said with force, setting the ring on the side table. "I want to wear it and I will remember...Someday I'll remember all of my past."

"I won't have you upset," he persisted.

"Simon, the memories brought on by this ring don't come with upset."

"Are you certain?"

"Yes," she emphatically assured.

"Perhaps..." A yawn stifled his thought, then he finished sleepily, "it's best if you do remember all...Perhaps..." His eyelids drooped and she encouraged him further down in the bed. They cuddled together and, with a kiss and loving look, bid each other a sweet night.

Maura felt his breathing slow and waited for hers to follow. But it didn't, and couldn't, for her mind was again cluttered with scattered visions of her parents' death. She was certain the ring was a prominent piece of the vexing puzzle. But who wore the ring? The man who murdered her parents? It seemed likely...Yet why would Lord

Robert protect a member of Welsh Royalty? He had selflessly played the hero and rescued her and Marc from the raiding Welsh. Why would he lie about the incident and say the skirmish took place in Cornwall against the Saxons? And she was positive he had lied, for Rose's husband had perished in the battle, and she had recounted an entirely different story. Rose would never deceive her. If only there was someone who had witnessed or heard of the incident, who could truthfully and without bias relate the whole episode. *And if there is such a person,* she wondered, *how can I find him? Why am I so obsessed with my past? Why can't I forget as Rose insists?* But she had an inkling that the horror of her youth was somehow intricately linked with the danger of their present. And to find the freedom and safety that they eternally craved, she must and would discover—the entire truth.

*****

CHAPTER SEVEN - MERELY "NO!"

𝔍𝔫 the vague glow of morning, Maura shifted languidly and heard nearby the sounds of happy muttering. It wasn't Simon, for he still slept, his warmth molded neatly to her back and his arms limply circling her waist. Maura didn't want to wake, she wanted to stay snug to her husband and her glorious dream; a dream in which she and their child lay on the floor of a small weathered boat. Soothingly, the sea rocked them as Simon paddled the craft toward an island rising higher and larger beyond the slapping waves. The sun, huge and beckoning, glittered sweat on his brow and naked chest, and ignited within her the most brilliant sense of safety. He stopped paddling a moment to smile down at them, then laughter boomed loud and forced open her eyes. She snorted her discontent, and thrust her head beneath the quilt. But listening further, she wondered *Who is laughing?*

Simon wound tighter and nuzzled against her neck; she felt him lift his head slightly and heard him mumble, "What's funny?"

"I'm wondering that myself," she replied, straining harder to hear.

Simon swiftly forgot the noise and focused instead on the heady aroma worrying his empty belly. He joined Maura under the blanket and commented, "I thought Marc said he couldn't cook."

"Not couldn't," corrected Maura, "he said he wasn't any good at it."

"I disagree."

"So do I...and he's no longer alone out there."

"Henry's with him," said Simon.

"And it seems Henry's no longer a dog, but a woman."

"What?" spouted Simon.

Marc sat at the head of the trestle table with Gael at his right and Gruffydd on his left. "I peeked in a while past," he explained, watching Gruffydd twitch with impatience and hunger.

"Were they there?" asked Gael grumpily.

"I suppose it was them," smiled Marc. "All I saw was an overabundance of...bare skin."

Tired of their chatter, Gruffydd squirmed more and whined, "Mam, I'm hungry!"

Gael ignored him to sneer at the door, "Layabouts...Just wait till that child arrives. Then there will be no more lounging the days away." She grinned and resolved wickedly, "I know how to rouse them!"

"How?" Marc asked.

"Mam!" wailed Gruffydd, drumming his spoon for emphasis.

"We will be polite and wait for Simon and Maura!" she answered sharply, then she crouched and crooked her finger at Henry. "Henry, come!" He obeyed exuberantly, his tail's swishing almost lifting him off his feet. She scratched his ears and body, exciting him to fits, while practically squealing her request, "Maura and Simon desperately want to see you! Yes, they're in their bed, and they want you in there with them, licking their faces and wherever else you choose. Now...go get them!" Her eyes flickered delight, and she couldn't suppress a snort as she creaked open the door just wide enough for him to wriggle through.

Henry leapt from door to bed, eliciting as he landed a loud "Umph!" from both occupants. He dug furiously, trying to locate them, and bit at their squirming outlines. Simon stupidly emerged from his hiding place to yell, "Bleeding Jesus, Henry! Go away!" He was promptly attacked with licks, which made him flail and scream more,

"Henry! Stop...Go!" He shoved the pup away, but his harshness only increased the dog's gloppy affection.

The bedclothes soared from Simon's kicks. He groaned crazily and lurched on his hands and knees across the bed.

"Simon!" Maura gasped from cold and alarm. "Where are you going?"

"To kill whoever let him in!" he flared back.

"No. Wait!" she cried, scrambling after, and swiping out to stop him. She grabbed one foot, yanked back, and spilled him on his face.

"Let me go!" he hollered.

"But you've forgotten something!" she yelled.

"What?"

"Your clothes."

"Where are they?"

"I don't know. You tossed them somewhere."

He rolled off the bed and scurried madly about, cursing and heaving clothing and apple cores. Henry chased him, yapping hysterically, and nipping at his master's heels. Simon's anger blew; he ripped open the shutters and deposited the mutt outside. Next, he chucked out the apple cores, and stumbled into his braies, grumbling, "I'll kill whoever set that demon upon us. Even if it was Marc the saint, I'll kill him!"

Maura reached over the edge of the bed to retrieve the blanket. "Henry's not a demon," she noted calmly, bundling herself. "He's...he's..."

Yet she couldn't think of a suitable descriptive phrase and Simon raged for her, "A demon!" as he surged out of the chamber and slammed the door behind him. Simon's face popped out of his shirt's neck hole, and he stood a fuming moment, surveying the tranquil scene before him. Gael, Gruffydd, and Marc sat silently at the table, hands clasped tidily before them. In unison, they raised pleasant smiles and Marc greeted, "Good-day, Simon."

"Who let him in?" growled Simon.

"He's unapproachable in the morning," noted Gael to Marc. "Why, when he lived with us, we dared not say one word to him till at least—"

"I said, who let him in?"

Gruffydd readily divulged, "Mam did," then hoped, "Can we eat now, Mam?"

"Yes, my dear. And, Simon, I expect your mood will improve greatly after a bowl of honey and oats. Come join us."

Simon's expression stayed surly as he approached, jerked out a stool, and plopped himself down. Yet the heavenly odor of oats, honey, and milk interfered with his wrath, so he plucked up his spoon and thrust a heaping helping between his sneering lips.

"That's better," smiled Gael. "Where's Maura?" Simon glowered and refused to answer. "And what have you done with Henry?" she glared back. "You haven't murdered him, have you?"

"You didn't hurt him, did you Simon?" whined Gruffydd.

"No..." muttered Simon. "I put him outside." He waggled a threatening finger at Gael. "And I'll put you outside as well if you ever—"

She shoved his full spoon into his mouth and howled with laughter as he blustered and drooled oats. He aimed his bowl at her; she jumped from her seat and ducked beneath the table. Gruffydd leapt onto the bench, spitting oats, and inciting, "Get her, Simon! Get her!" Marc snickered quietly as he watched Simon loom over Gael, the bowl tilted precariously, while Gael groveled in the rushes and feigned torture.

Maura rushed into the discord, plaiting her braid, and wondering brightly, "What's happening in here?"

"Simon's going to dump his oats on Mam!" shrilled Gruffydd.

"Is she the culprit?" Maura asked Simon. He nodded sharply, and she huffed with crossed arms, "Then go ahead and dump!"

"No!" squalled Gael, scrambling from beneath the table. "I won't set Henry on you again, I swear! But you did promise Marc a race on the beach and if you'd slept any later, the clouds would have come and spoiled everything!"

"She's correct, Simon..." noted Marc.

"Did you promise, Simon?" asked Maura.

"Yes, I suppose I did," Simon limply admitted.

"Then I suggest," said Maura, settling herself before a waiting bowl, "we eat and go."

Gruffydd slumped down in disappointment, but Gael gushed in thanks, "Bless you, Maura," and warily slipped back into her seat.

"I'll have my revenge," groused Simon to Gael, "and you'll not know when or where I'll strike."

"You are evil," snarled Gael.

Simon simpered in response and all resumed eating.

*****

Gruffydd and Henry had to trot to keep pace with Simon and Marc as they led their war horses down the path to the beach. E'dain and her colt ambled alongside. Maura and Gael straggled behind, chattering merrily. "So, which one is the greater horseman?" asked Gael.

"They're fairly equal in skill," said Maura. "I suppose Marc has an advantage being so recently in battle, but once..." Maura paused to gaze longingly ahead at the massive steeds.

"But once what?" prompted Gael.

"I was the greatest."

"*Truly?*" Gael returned in an amazed voice.

"Yes...When I was younger, I trained as vigorously as they to become a—" Again Maura stopped, this time to blush.

"Become a what?" Gael coaxed.

"A knight."

They both chuckled, then Maura mentioned, "In a week's time, it will be Simon's birthday."

"And how old will he be?"

"Twenty-five."

"I thought him older," said Gael. "And since I'm twenty-seven, I expect I have the right to order him about. How old are you, Maura?"

"Twenty-two...I think."

"You think?"

"I didn't speak at all during my first year at Dunheved," Maura explained. "Rose says when they asked me my age, I'd hold up five fingers, so they took me to be five and made the day we arrived my birthday."

"And Marc?"

"Nineteen..."

"We think," they chorused, smiling together.

"He seems wise beyond his years," commented Gael.

"He is..." Maura said with great affection. They quietly walked on, then Maura mused, "I'd like to do something special for Simon, but I'm having trouble deciding what."

"He could do with a hair trim," suggested Gael.

"I like his hair the length it is," defended Maura.

"But Maura, at times he seems to have trouble seeing. On my husband's birthday, I used to offer him my body. You doing that for Simon wouldn't be special."

Maura looked appalled.

Gael hurried to repair her slip, "I meant to say unusual," and then she sputtered, "He...he does enjoy eating. Why don't you fix him his favorite meal?"

Maura hopeful looked saddened. "I'm not a very accomplished cook."

"I am! We'll do it together. It could be fun."

"Yes let's!" agreed Maura.

"What day?"

"The first of October. Did you hear of the feast this night?"

"Sulien stopped by this morning to tell us," answered Gael. "Will Marc come?"

"If he cares to."

"I do pity him," said Gael with a woeful wag of her head.

"Why?"

"The unattached women will surely devour him," replied Gael. "And perhaps some of the attached ones as well."

"Do you truly think so?"

"He's mighty handsome, and they're awfully hungry, Maura."

"And he's terribly innocent," added Maura protectively.

"I hear they like that kind the best," quipped Gael. "We'll keep a tight rein on him." Gael looked up ahead, and was surprised and pleased they'd reached the beach so quickly. Simon and Marc had already mounted their bare-backed steeds, and Marc was reaching down to take Gruffydd up with him. "Oh no!" Gael shouted out, sprinting to her son's side. "I'd like him alive for a few years more. You'll watch, Gruffydd."

Gruffydd strained against her hold and squawked, "No, Mam...I want to ride! Please let me ride!"

"He'll be safe with Marc, Gael," Maura assured, coming up behind her.

"I said no, and that's final! If you like, Gruffydd, you can ride E'dain."

"She's too slow," griped Gruffydd. He heaved a mournful sigh, and looked to Simon for solace. In response, he received a sly wink, and his expression beamed hopefully.

Simon and Marc urged their mounts away and cantered gracefully to the far end of the beach. Gael shielded her eyes and, with pinched expression, remarked, "They're so large!"

"Who?"

"The horses. Simon and Marc look as though they were born in the saddle."

"They practically were." Maura too had caught Simon's wink and suggested with innocence, "Come, let's move up closer."

The waves rippled mildly upon the shore, ushering in the rising tide, and billowing clouds whipped by a breeze cooled the sun's glare. The horses dodged and danced in anticipation, their ears flat, and muzzles snorting and sparring. Simon struggled to calm Fulk, then leant in close to talk to Marc. They glanced toward their audience and reined in their steeds. Gael gaped as Maura raised an arm, purposely waited an excruciating instant, and plunged her hand downward. Gael's jaw dropped ever lower as the horses thundered down the beach, spewing sand and spray in their zeal. She'd never witnessed anything travel that swiftly and the powerful sight and sounds dizzied her. Gruffydd screamed in excitement and darted forward. Gael caught the neck of his tunic, jerked backward, and screamed as well, "No. No closer!" She marveled at Maura's stoic veneer, yet peering nearer, she also noticed a gleam of envy in her narrow stare that flared, then dulled as the horses pounded by. "Maura," Gael offered with a tender touch, "you'll ride again."

Maura tensed a grin, and announced, "Marc's horse Noir won by near a foot. Fulk's defeat is probably due to his gelding. But they'll go again. Simon won't be beaten that easily."

Gael glanced back at the riders and shouted in amazement, "What's Marc doing? Surely he'll kill himself!" Marc rode back up the beach, standing on his mount's broad back. And what Marc did, Simon had to attempt.

"Marc won't die...but Simon just might," fretted Maura as she noticed him rise to his knees. She started forward, her hand raised in caution, but it soon fell limply to her side and her expression shone pride as Simon stood as steadily as Marc. They broke into a circular canter, and abandoned their reins. Gael dug her grip into Maura's arm, Maura's teeth almost drew blood from her lower lip, and they both rocked to Gruffydd's effusive gyrations. Then from the corner of her eye, Maura spied Henry dash by in chase of a scuttling gull. The bird soared from the ground and sailed low and directly for the horses, Henry still fast in pursuit. Marc noticed the danger and promptly plopped on his seat. Simon's attention, however, was fixed dreamily upon the sea. The attacking gull, Henry's bark, and Maura's yell, "Henry, no!" clashed together, spooking Fulk; he reared steeply and pitched Simon high up into the sky. Simon landed with a dull splat on his back in the sand. He closed his eyes to swirling clouds and felt cold water wash over his face. The tide retreated and was replaced by a sopping tongue and all too familiar yelping whine. "Simon! Simon!" He heard Maura's panicked call, then saw her as she dove to her knees with a splash. She gently raised his head above a rushing wave, and cried, "Are you hurt?!"

"No...no," he choked as he sat and swept his wet hair from his eyes. "Bleeding Jesus, Henry! You could've killed me!"

Maura shrugged, wagged her head, and offered her hand and the thought, "Perhaps we should go home."

"No!" Simon protested. "I've yet to win."

"You don't have to win."

"Oh yes I do...at least one race." He struggled up, wavered a moment, then gingerly hobbled to where Fulk stood. Turning to a line of wincing looks, he chided to Maura, who wore the most piteous face of all, "And don't you go telling Marc to let me win!" It took a number of attempts, and many grunts and moans, but Simon managed to remount. He motioned for Marc to do the same, then resolutely announced, "And this night we'll be having Henry for supper!"

The men repositioned themselves, braced for the second match, then nodded to the women and Gruffydd, who now hugged a writhing Henry. Maura's arm cut through the air, and the horses charged forward with increased vigor and intensity. Gael wondered, *How can they go faster?* She snapped her head to Maura to say the same, but Maura was gone as were Gruffydd and Henry. As Gael turned to find them, Marc veered Noir off the race's path and spurred him straight for her back. Too late she heard the hoof beats bearing down on her. She took flight and, with a jarring thud, found herself straddling the massive beast. Marc's arm cinched her waist and held her still, but the speed was terrifying! Each time she opened her eyes, she let out an involuntary scream! Exhilaration coursed through her veins, and water battered her face as they bounded into the sea. And then she flew again, this time landing on the peak of the wave. She promptly sank, bounced once on her bottom, and jolted back to the surface. With sagging relief, she found her bearings, only to be knocked to her knees by the oncoming tide. Marc guided his stallion to her side and flinched to her flailing tirade, "Of all the mean, cruel, and nasty things ever done to me, *that*, Sir, ranks as the worst! I'm shocked and angered and—" Gael grunted more curses as she stormed from the sea, leaving deep impressions in the sand. Simon, still astride Fulk, sauntered up before her, a goading smirk curling his lips. To his slyness, Gael abruptly halted; she whirled round, hands on hips, and to Marc brokenly declared, "And...and...I very much...enjoyed it! Can we do it again?!"

"As you please, my Lady," laughed Marc, thrusting out a hand.

"Simon," Gael yelled, "go get Gruffydd!"

Simon beamed and cantered to the squealing boy, who raced toward him across the beach. Maura stripped down to her chemise and ran into the water to await their arrival. Fulk, Simon, and Gruffydd won the next race, and Gael, screeching as exuberantly as her boy, forced her eyes open the entire length of the beach.

*****

"Dance?" Simon groaned dramatically as he flopped upon the bed. "How can I dance if I can't even walk?"

"It's your own fault," chastised Maura. "You and your cursed pride. I reckon if Marc suddenly decided to go flying off yon cliff, you'd go sailing off right after him, thinking *what marvelous fun*!" She hauled open the trunk and, on her knees, began rummaging through its contents.

"What are you doing?" asked Simon, rolling to his belly.

"Finding us clean clothes."

"We have to dress?" he whined.

"Were you planning to go naked?"

"No...but why change?"

"Because we're coated with sand and it itches!" For Simon, Maura plucked out an unbleached, knee-length tunic, its sides split to the waist, and embroidered at the neck, cuffs, and hem. She plunged deeper and found a linen undershirt and beige, light woolen braies and hose. As she stood, he surged up and caught her round her waist. They tumbled backward upon the bed and swiftly became entangled in clothes, sheets, and each other. Long brusque scratches to her back made Maura moan hungrily and beg, "More..."

"Gladly," he said. "We'll stay here tonight and I'll scratch every bit of—"

"No!" she retorted and abruptly sat. "It won't work, Simon. You had your fun this day, and now I'll have mine."

"At least let me try changing your mind," he purred, nibbling her earlobe.

"I...I'll let you try...for a...short while only...but..."

Maura's objections soon were reduced to sumptuous sighs. She melted to his kisses and his murmured comment, "You taste...deliciously salty." He hiked up her skirt to sample more spice on her knee and suggested with a whispery passion, "We'll do our own private dance upon this bed. I'll be your bard and tell you rousing tales of love and lust..."

As Simon's fingers and lips ventured further along her thigh, his inducements sounded more and more reasonable to Maura; after all, the weather was turning nasty, the food at such doings was notoriously poor, Marc wasn't keen on going, and the conversation was sure to be drab, not at all like Simon's. A polite rapping startled them both to sit and blurt aloud, "Yes?"

Maura swiftly rearranged her chemise as Marc poked his head in the door and announced skittishly, "If we're going, perhaps it should be soon. The sun's low and as you said Simon, they're expecting us round dusk."

"Dusk," muttered Simon, "I did say dusk, didn't I."

"Yes," answered Marc.

"Simon," said Maura buoyantly, "why don't you take Marc to the well to rinse off? And Marc, you'll look extremely handsome in Simon's new tunic. I'll wash and dress here, and swear to be ready to leave upon your return." With a pinch to his backside, she urged Simon off the bed and hung his shoulders and arms with clothing. She ushered them both out the door and said, smiling, "Now go and enjoy yourselves."

Once alone, she shook to clear her senses of her husband's lingering seductive presence, then peeled off her chemise and filled the washing bowl. While washing, she wondered what to wear. It seemed every frock she owned made her feel and appear not pregnant, but plump. Her new tunic was sewn in the Welsh style, simply described as sack-like, which would suit her figure in a few months' time. For now, though, she preferred the more tailored and clinging Norman fashion, even if she did stick out a bit in front. She dug again in her trunk and found a favorite tunic, its peach-colored wool lightly cured and almost matching the hue of her hair. Silk threads of royal blue edged the neck hole, elbow-length sleeves, and mid-calf hemline. She drew on linen hose and gartered them just above her knees with leather thongs. Next, she wriggled into a high-necked, billowy sleeved chemise, then layered on the tunic, and cinched the outfit with a braided rope girdle. Her hair she attacked with a wooden comb missing many teeth, and left it unadorned and flowing free. At last, somewhat content with her image in a tiny, cracked and smudged looking glass, she left the bedchamber to find a snack to munch on. In the main room, she came upon Henry, sprawled clumsily by the fire and snoring. She tip-toed so not to wake him, and admitted inwardly that despite his many foibles, she did feel great affection for the nettling pup, and marveled at how similar he was to his namesake.

At the well Simon grew concerned at Marc's paleness and asked while scrubbing sand from his arms, "You look a bit peaked. Are you feeling well?"

"Yes," answered Marc too quickly; he ducked below the water, and Simon smiled curiously. When Marc appeared again, he whipped the water from his hair, wiped his face with his hands, and asked impulsively, "Will there be many there?"

"At the feast?" asked Simon.

Marc nodded.

"For certain, Sulien and his wife Raythyen will be there and—"

"His wife?" interrupted Marc. "But Maura introduced him as Bishop."

"And he is. Here the clergy do not follow the edict of Rome and are free to wed. I suppose most of the commote will attend, for they do love celebrations."

"I noticed..." Marc paused to swallow and drag fingers through his sopping hair. "I noticed on our walk home today a great number of women about, but few men. Why?"

"The wages of war. Many are widowed, and many have been forced into remaining maidens, and few are pleased with their situations." Suddenly, the cause of Marc's anxiety dawned and Simon bluntly assured, "Marc...I don't believe you'll be attacked by the ladies upon entering the long house."

"Simon," Marc blushed and gibbered, "I...I didn't mean that, I mean I didn't say...What I mean to say is that I'm not very good at meeting people, especially women. I haven't had much practice. I don't even know how to say 'good evening'."

"Noswaith dda."

"Pardon?"

"Noswaith dda means 'good evening' in Welsh."

"Oh. Nos...wieth...tha?"

"Exactly. You'll do fine. Most of the women who live here speak adequate English. They'll be curious, perhaps even a bit forward. Accept and enjoy their compliments and, if you're not interested in their plans for you, don't hesitate to tell them 'no'. They handle rejection rather politely."

Simon spoke with a conviction that bulged Marc's eyes. "Have you had to tell them 'no'?!"

103

Simon barely nodded to the slim silver band gracing his hand and noted, "This ring doesn't deter all."

"Does Maura know?"

"Yes."

"Does it upset her?"

"If it does, she doesn't show it. If *I* were her, I'd show it."

Marc smiled and timidly asked, "How did you learn about women, Simon?"

"About women?" Simon asked back, puzzled. "Most of my life I've been surrounded by women, quite happily I might add."

"No, I mean in a courting sense," clarified Marc.

"Oh...I suppose Maura taught me, yet we didn't bother much with courting. We just sort of leapt to the learning part."

They chuckled together and Marc blushed at his next question, "Were...there any besides Maura?"

Now Simon's disquiet was obvious as he mumbled, "After we parted, there were very few and none that mattered." He paused to chastise himself, "No, that sounds cruel. They were very kind, but I wanted only to be with Maura. I suppose I tried to turn them into her and that wasn't very kind of me." Marc's daunted look reappeared and Simon wisely switched topics, "We'd best dry ourselves before we catch a chill. And Marc, tonight, if you feel at all uncomfortable, stay close."

Marc's tenseness eased and his indulgent smile returned. He accepted a linen towel from Simon, chafed his skin briskly, and hurriedly shivered into his clothes. As Simon turned to fetch up his shirt, Marc noticed the many thick ruby red welts running the length of his back. "Simon!" he gasped. "What happened to your back?!"

Simon sighed, turned, and calmly told his much repeated rendition of the cause of his injury. "This past January, my father had me whipped. He used Maura to lure me to Berkhamstead, then imprisoned and punished me for my many sins against him and our family."

"But how did you survive? The scars are terrible! And how did I not see them on your trip to Normandy?!"

"I kept my back from your sight. I owe my recovery to the devotions of a competent leech, Alan's family, my step-mother Almodis, her guard Godfrey, and your sweet, sweet sister." With an odd grin, he added, "It still pains me sometimes."

They chatted quietly on their stroll back to the cottage. "May I come along on your next rounds?" asked Marc as they approached the door.

"Of course! If you care to, I'll let you mix the remedies."

"Yes, please!"

Entering, both stopped to gape, Simon sputtering, "My God, woman...you...you are truly lovely!"

Maura colored scarlet, fussed with her dress, and stammered in return, "And...I...I'm honored to have such dashing gentlemen accompany me to the feast." She wove her arms in theirs and, after shutting Henry safely inside, they started for the commote of Mynyw.

*****

On their walk, Marc intently studied the village. Snugly bracing the skinny rut-filled road sat dozens of crude huts, haphazardly scattered, some with thatched roofs, some timbered. In the dusky light he noticed all sorts of beasts clogging the road and feasting freely upon a common pasture. Unlike the Norman castles perched high upon their mottes to loom over the villages, the only imposing structure in Mynyw was its cathedral. The immense timber and stone building stood bathed pink by the sunset, pestered by gulls, and peacefully secured behind a forbidding rock wall. Jaunty strains

104

of music reached their ears as they neared the llys or long house, constructed as its name implied. Smoke billowed from two vent holes cut from its angled thatched roof. Villagers loitered thickly about the entrance, spilling out into the fenced courtyard. Marc's belly lurched as they entered the yard and was wrenched further by dozens of piercing stares. Gratefully, he felt Maura's fingers lace between his own, and her grip firmed as she guided him through the prattling folk and into the house. The sights that greeted him there warmed his soul—the fire's flames dancing and crackling; ruddy faced children romping upon a carpet of green fragrant rushes; adults of both genders and all sizes and colors laughing heartily and swilling drink. A small band of musicians, hugging crude instruments, sat upon a broad straw-packed bed, strumming, bowing, and singing. Just inside the entrance, open barrels of mead braced the wall. Each reveler brought with him his own personal cup, and dipped it into the drink as they entered. A broad trestle table headed the room and held platters abundant with beef, venison, pork, and a colorful assortment of vegetables. Scattered between the platters were blocks of cheese and butter, bowls of fruit, and generous portions of flatbread.

Marc spotted and vaguely recalled the Bishop, steeply tall, balding, and owning the most gentle eyes and manner. Sulien approached arm-in-arm with his petite, pleasant-looking lady. "Marc," he welcomed warmly, "I've meant to visit but, alas, members of my flock have proven particularly needy this week. You look wonderfully well!"

Maura gazed with affection as Marc grasped Sulien's hand and acknowledged, "I am, thanks to you, Gruffydd, Maura and Simon."

Marc shifted his gaze to Raythyen and smiled kindly while being introduced in Welsh by Maura, "Raythyen, this is Marc, my brother, newly arrived from Normandy. He has yet to learn any Welsh, but he is eager for lessons, and is a quick study."

Marc confidently presented his hand and spurted his newly acquired knowledge, "Noswaith dda!"

All three stared in surprise, then broke into bright smiles, Maura complimenting, "Marc, how thoughtful! Who taught you?"

"Simon," he answered and she returned a knowing grin.

"I must steal away your sister for a short while," said Sulien, cupping Maura's elbow. "There's news from the Prince that she needs to hear. Don't be shy," Sulien directed, "eat, drink, enjoy yourself."

Maura cast Marc an apologetic glance as she was guided away. Raythyen and Marc exchanged awkward grins, and his quickly heartened as he spied Gael, hovering over the trestle table, helping her son fill his plate. He bowed politely to Raythyen and hurried to Gael's side where he received jubilant greetings. "Marc! I didn't see you when I arrived and I thought you'd decided not to come. I'm so pleased I was mistaken. Have you eaten?"

He stared an awed moment, entranced by her loveliness. Her bulky grey tunic could not hide the fine lines of her figure. A braided leather circlet tamed her crimped yellow curls, her sea-green eyes twinkled affectionately, and her smiling lips glistened as she repeated, "Have you eaten?"

"No...no...I've just arrived. Gruffydd?" Marc called.

The boy's attention was so focused on the food that he didn't hear his name. Gael nudged him, and tersely reminded, "You've been spoken to."

"What?" Gruffydd answered. Looking about dumbly, he discovered his new friend and his enthusiastic response rocked his plate's contents. "Marc! I've told my friends about today—the races. But they don't believe me and they want to hear the whole story from you!"

"Will they understand me?"

"Most speak English, and I'll fill in the parts they don't understand. Can you tell them now? *Please!*"

"Not now, Gruffydd," Gael argued. "Let him eat, hear some music and stories, then he can tell our tale."

"I don't mind," said Marc.

"No..." she insisted, ushering him away. "Once the young ones get you cornered there's no escaping. Where's Maura?" she wondered.

"With Sulien."

"And Simon?" As she spoke his name, they both caught sight of him, caught amidst a pressing crowd near the door, and Gael cursed quietly, "God's teeth...This always happens."

Marc peered closer and noticed everyone surrounding Simon seemed to be whining at once and clutching parts of their bodies. "What are they doing?" he asked.

"They're making him be doctor!" she answered curtly. "We'll have to rescue him, because he has great trouble saying 'no'."

"Not always," commented Marc as they headed for the door.

Gael elbowed her way through the crowd, grumbling in Welsh, "Leave him be! He'll see to your problems tomorrow. He's hungry and wants to dance, isn't that true, Simon?" she prompted, grasping and tugging at his arm.

"I suppose I do, yes..." he mumbled, tripping along behind her. Once free of the sniveling mob, he bowed and gushed graciously, "Thank you, my dear. Where's Maura gone to?"

"She's speaking to Sulien," answered Gael. "You and Marc find a secret corner where we won't be bothered and I'll fetch us food and drink."

Sulien spoke soberly to Maura, "There's been a rather serious skirmish just inside Brycheiniog's border between Rhys' forces and a Norman baron whose name wasn't mentioned. Rhys has arranged to meet the perpetrator here at the cathedral the first of the month and wishes your attendance and expertise. He will arrive early to discuss strategy."

"When is early?" asked Maura.

"Any moment now."

Simon grew concerned at Maura's pensive expression, and left Marc to investigate. "What is it, Maura?" he pressed. "Sulien?"

"Not to worry, Simon," calmed Sulien. "A message from the Prince. I'll let Maura relate the details while I mingle."

He left them and Maura swiftly assuaged, "Sulien was only informing me of the Prince's imminent arrival. He's to ask for my assistance with a mediation—"

She paused and he urged, "Between?"

"Sulien didn't know the name. He mentioned some Norman baron's skirmishes in *Brecknock*."

"Brycheiniog? That's curious. I'm surprised the baron has managed to encroach so far from the English border. Rhys doesn't expect you to travel there, does he?"

"No, the talks will be here."

"Well," encouraged Simon, "at last something to make your life a bit more exciting."

"You fulfill that role more than sufficiently, my love," she charmed, wrapping her arms round his neck, and offering her lips.

He partook of a kiss and noted, "And the night's young...yet."

She nuzzled close to his ear and tempted, "We'll beg exhaustion and leave early, for I fear those sore muscles of yours are in dire need of massage."

Her scheme dizzied Simon and he wondered, "Is now too early?"

"Yes, a bit," she agreed. "We'll insult Raythyen if we go without sampling the fare, and you did promise me a dance."

"Not here," he countered.

"We'll *start* here," she decided smoothly, then slipped her arm round his and, hugging close, accompanied him to a darkened corner already claimed by Marc.

Gael strode up behind them, stating, "You two look hungry," with a hint of distaste. They sat as one and Gael dropped a platter before them, interrupting their fondling with the command, "Eat!" As they began feeding each other, Gael huffed and plopped down beside Marc, carping, "At times, they do get boring. Does it bother you, Marc, all their petting and such?"

"No. Why should it?" Marc shrugged. "They've always been close."

"Certainly not the same sort of closeness they share now?"

"No...but this seems natural."

"You are overly tolerant, Marc." She presented a plate along with the enticement, "Eat."

"Thank you," Marc replied.

"And I thank you for today," she said sincerely. "I did *so* enjoy myself."

Marc blushed, fought to swallow a hunk of meat, then brokenly requested, "Te...tell me about the people here. Who's that?" He pointed to a young, darkish man, hobbling about on a crooked stick.

"Bleddyn. He was wounded in battle and retired to home. He seems constantly embarrassed by his fate. I don't understand why. If I were him, I would be glad to be home." She examined Marc's curious expression, then bluntly asked, "Are you glad to be home?"

"I don't really have a home."

"Of course you do, your home is here with your family. Why did you leave Normandy?"

He paled and food fell from his fingers, yet he had no trouble explaining, "After the King was injured, the ranks scattered. No one knew who was in command, or who would be. In my mind, there were only two choices. One is Robert Curthose, William's eldest son, who already calls himself Duke of Normandy. He's a cruel, witless coward, and for many years has been in league with the French King to destroy William. I felt no allegiance to him. And the other choice...You've heard of Rufus?"

"Unfortunately, yes."

"For many years, he battered my sister, many times almost killing her. It's difficult for me to see him as anything but a putrid beast, so I left."

"Isn't there another Prince?" questioned Gael.

Marc kindly corrected, "There is no word for Prince in the Norman's version of French. The son of a King is called FitzRoy."

"I didn't know. The only time I hear French spoken is when there's a mediation. Simon and Maura speak English to each other, at least when I'm around. But they've often mentioned Henry—a cousin, I think. They even named the mutt after him. Is Henry a rival to the throne and Dukedom?"

Marc sniggered derisively. "Henry? I doubt he'll be considered. He's a spoiled, snotty-nosed toad, who doesn't act old enough to wipe his own bottom."

Gael's jaw dropped at the intensity of his crudeness. "How old is he?"

"My age."

"Well, I see your problem."

"No you don't..." Marc returned curtly. "No one does."

Gael quickly realized his rudeness came from grief, not anger. She touched his arm, and tenderly consoled, "Some would call your actions cowardly. I believe holding true to your convictions and walking away took tremendous courage. Following blindly is the coward's way."

Marc turned his astonishment on her, and his tense expression relaxed into a radiant smile.

"Look Simon," said Maura, cracking an optimistic grin, "everyone seems to be staring at Marc...and whispering. I wonder what they're saying?"

"I have a good notion of what some of their comments might be," he said, then asked, "Will you introduce him?"

"No, not now...He'd be mortified. You can do that on your rounds. They do seem fascinated."

"Yes..." Simon glanced over at Marc and Gael, marveled at their nearness and animated expressions, and whispered, "And Marc seems equally fascinated."

Maura was referring to a covey of young women, collected near the door, nudging, pointing, and giggling. She prodded excitedly, "With which one, Simon? Tell me!"

The music suddenly turned bouncy, coaxing couples out onto the rushes for a jig. "With everyone," he quipped, and urged her up from the floor and into his arms. "And here's the dance I promised you."

She noted in jest, "We mustn't do those sorts of things in front of everyone."

"Why ever not? They'll love it."

"And so will I," she murmured. As he drew her past the band, she leant close to one member, winked and whispered, "Please, make it a long one."

"Oh dear," moaned Gael. "This is the part I hate."

"Why?" asked Marc.

"I'm not a dancer."

"Have you ever tried?"

"Yes, with tragic results. Have you?"

"A few times. Would you try again...with me?"

She balked at his offered hand. "I don't know, Marc. They tend to get fairly wild here."

"I'd never do such a thing."

The glint in his eye intrigued her and she hesitantly slipped her hand in his and rose. The dance began slowly with smiling nods and bows. Gael performed a graceful curtsy and lightly commented, "I rather like this." Everyone rose up on their toes, which she easily managed, and her movements began to take on grace and confidence.

Marc led her beside Simon and Maura. Simon snorted and lauded, "You are brave, Marc. I danced with her once and limped for two days after."

Gael aimed her foot to stomp; Simon easily dodged her strike, and waved his arm high. His signal drastically increased the music's tempo. Maura readily hopped into his arms; he flung her high into the air. Marc easily caught her, and tossed her back. The other women present squealed as they were in turn chased, grabbed, and hurled. "Oh no! You've tricked me!" wailed Gael as she lunged to escape, but Marc caught her waist and spun her furiously round and round. She dizzily joined in the hooting and laughter, struggling futilely to keep pace with Marc's rapid and expert stepping. "I can't, Marc," she whined, stumbling and doubling with laughter, "I'll get trampled!"

"Then come closer..." His grip firmed and urged her near, and then the most miraculous thing happened. She no longer needed to dance. Her feet dangled not an inch from the ground and he danced for her. It was just as exciting—no, more so, for when her toes did touch the ground she found herself in perfect step with the others. In wonder, she asked herself, how could this very slight and shy man possess such enormous strength and talent?

The volume and excitement surged and Gael reckoned she knew what was coming next. Effortlessly, Marc hauled her up and sent her soaring. With a loud, "Oomph!" she flopped into Simon's arms. "Oh...it's you!" she declared in panted relief. "And where will you send me?"

"Where do you want to go?"

"Back to Marc."

"As you wish, my Lady."

With a loud grunt, he heaved and she flew and landed limply back in Marc's arms. "This is becoming quite fun!" she spouted. "Throw me again."

"But Gael," regretted Marc, "the music's stopped. There's no one to throw you to."

"Oh, well," she frowned, sliding from his embrace. She tried her balance, but her feet failed her and she stumbled.

Marc saved her from falling. "Perhaps we should sit out the next one."

"Yes," she shakily agreed, "I'm feeling a bit light-headed. It's been quite an exciting day!" Gael sank to the rushes and gratefully accepted his passed cup of mead. She gulped heartily and found herself agape and thrilled by the surrounding melee. The children had joined in the next song, leaping and spinning, and she cheered and clapped at Gruffydd's tripping attempts at dance. Marc clapped as well, astounded at the crowd's flair for jollity. Then Maura and Simon stole everyone's admiring gaze. They moved with a bold and exuberant harmony, smiling and murmuring sweetly to each other. Gael rested her chin in her palm and sighed dreamily, "They are beautiful together. How do they know to do exactly the same steps?"

"Practice."

"I never learned such an art. Where did you learn, where did they?"

Marc wistfully replied, "A long time past, when we lived together at Dunheved, Lord Robert, Simon's father and our Liege, frequently held great feasts. Edith and Rose would shuffle us off to bed early, then we would sneak back down, get lost in the crowd, and dance for hours into the night. After we parted, I guess Simon learned to dance, as I did, preparing for knighthood, and Maura must have attended feasts regularly at Winchester."

"Well I envy them many things, and love them, and hope that they and you stay here for a very very long time..." Uncomfortable with her unabashed display of emotion, she pointed and blurted, "Look...by the door stands the Bard. An odd creature, I'm sure you'll agree."

Marc's wide stare concurred. A withered, white-bearded man, weighed down by dense black and purple robes and helped along by a gnarled wooden staff, made his way carefully to the center of the llys. Someone fetched a stool and cup. The throng politely parted and settled themselves about his feet. Simon and Maura struggled their way to Marc and Gael's corner. Both whispered praised for Gael's dancing as they sat; she blushed in response and dismissed them with a wave. Then, touching his lips, Marc encouraged them to hush. "Do you want me to translate for you, Marc?" muttered Gael.

"Later..." he answered.

She nodded, smiled, and listened.

"This night," the Bard began, "I tell the tale of the Countess of the Fountain. The Emperor Arthur was at Caer Llion ar Wysg, and one day he was sitting in his chamber..." The lull of the tale and the Bard's lilting voice transfixed his audience. Gael closed her eyes and lost herself in the romantic tale of Arthur, and his knight Kynon's strange journey to the otherworld, where he encountered every sort of wild beast, golden haired children, and a black man, keeper of the forest, no smaller than two men of this world, who had only one foot, and one eye in the middle of his forehead. Then suddenly the characters' identities changed. The knight involved had the name Owain, and Gael turned ashen as she heard the Bard relate, "In this state Owain saw through the join of the gate a road, and a row of houses on each side of the road, and a girl with curly yellow hair and a gold headband, dressed in yellow brocade and wearing buskins of mottled cordovan. This girl approached the gate and asked for it to be opened. 'God knows, lady,' said Owain, 'the gate will not be opened from out here, any more than you can rescue me from in there.' 'God knows, it is a shame that you cannot be rescued,' answered the girl. 'It would be right for a woman to help you, for God knows, I have never seen a better man for a woman than you. If you had a woman-friend she would be the best of woman-friends, and if you had a lover she would be the best of lovers; therefore, I will do what I can to help you...'"

Gael suddenly felt ill and desperately craved cool air. She pushed up and stumbled her way through the crowd and out the door. Marc started after her, but Maura stopped him. "Let Simon go to her. He knows this upset better."

"Gael," Simon called out of the door of the llys. The night had turned brisk, and he hugged himself as he searched the yard. "Gael! Where've you gone?"

"I'm here," she answered quietly from beneath a lone oak.

He hurried his approach, fretting, "Are you ill?"

"No..." She refused to look directly at him. "The dancing, the food, the heat, upset my belly and that's all."

"And the speech about Owain?" prompted Simon.

"Didn't bother me in the least."

"I don't believe you."

"And you shouldn't..." Her guilty gaze finally met his caring one. "Because I'm lying. Before I left Dinefwr, Owain and I had words."

Simon asked, askance, "Only words?"

"He spat at me."

"What!" flared Simon. "How dare—"

"After I spat at him."

"Oh..." Simon's anger sagged, then, trying hard to hide his smirk, he ventured, "And what would make you resort to gobbing?"

"He slandered my sister."

"How?"

"He claims she whores and spies for the Normans."

"Did you tell her he said this?"

"No, I couldn't. She's gone missing." Her hand darted out to take his as she despaired, "I'm afraid to tell her, because I fear he's right! He knew that Rhys would ask me to be his mistress. He knew before I did! I suppose Maura told you."

He returned her grip and confirmed, "Yes, about Rhys, not about Owain. She also said Rhys told you that if you don't accept him, you must marry the next Pennaeth or return to Shrewsbury."

"Without Gruffydd! Simon," she implored, "what am I to do?"

"I can't tell you that," he stressed back.

"I want you to!"

"And if I tell you wrong?"

"You won't."

"Did talking with Maura help? It always helps me."

She left his hold to shiver, pace, and mutter lowly, "Of course it helped, but at times, Maura can be almost too sensible. At the moment, I'm feeling anything but sensible. That's why I needed to speak to you."

"I appreciate the compliment," he said with a chuckle.

"It is a compliment! We are alike in the way we let our feelings rule us, Simon. We think more with our bellies than our brains! And you know too well what terrible trouble that can bring. You have Maura to tame you."

"As do you," he reminded softly.

"I don't want to bother her! She has enough worries. My entire pregnancy, I did nothing but worry, and she's already had problems—"

"She won't be bothered. She wants to help!" Gael hugged her arms as if to distance herself, and turned away. Simon sighed, and, shaking back his hair, struggled for his next words. When they came, he delicately asked, "Will you tell me exactly Rhys' proposal to you?"

Gael faced him and spilled her strife, "After he discussed his need for a new mistress, he said that if I chose not to live with him, he wanted me to consider marrying the man he picks for Pennaeth."

Simon's eyes brightened; he straightened and echoed, "Consider?"

"Yes! But he made clear the fact that if I shirk both invitations, Gruffydd would be taken from me and I would be banished."

"Who has he picked?"

"No one yet. He mentioned there were quite a few in waiting, and that he plans to send them here separately to woo the village and me."

"To *woo* you?" Simon repeated for clarity. "As I hear this, he's letting you choose."

His enlightened look rallied her angry reply, "Yes, between doing his bidding, or returning to Shrewsbury—"

"No," Simon soundly intruded. "He's letting you choose your next husband and the new Pennaeth!"

"Stop, Simon! You're confusing me."

"No I'm not! I believe Rhys confused you on purpose."

"Rhys would not do that to me," she defended. "He isn't that cruel."

Simon began to pace and spoke urgently, "I don't claim that, but he wants you badly, badly enough to present his other plan in a way to make you panic into accepting him as lover. After all, to you he's familiar, affectionate, entertaining, and attractive in a...a..."

"Cuddly sort of way," she duly finished.

"Yes, exactly! Isn't all that preferable to being forced to marry a stranger?"

"But I don't want to be his mistress!" Gael hotly returned.

"I know that, and he's not forcing you to become anyone's wife! Not yet, at least. He's sending them here to court you, and then he'll let *you* choose. You could presumably draw the betrothal process out for months, and let's hope there's at least one acceptable fellow in the bunch."

Gradually, Simon's insight lifted the gloom that had cloaked Gael's mind for days. "Choose my own husband?" she speculated in awe. "Not many are allowed that privilege."

"True. My legs pain me a bit," he said. "Can we sit?"

"Of course." She smiled faintly and asked while walking to the stairs, "Why didn't I realize his true proposal, Simon?"

"Because he threatened to take your son," explained Simon as he sat. "There's no way one can think logically when faced with that dilemma. I know how strongly I care for my child, and she's not even here yet."

"Care to wager on the sex?"

"Later perhaps...Do you feel any better?"

"Yes, but—" She squirmed and warily expressed, "I still have a fear. I'm afraid Rhys will send Owain."

"Why would he send someone the commote already despises?"

"Because he's fond of Owain."

"He's fonder of you," reassured Simon, "and as you said before he's not cruel and he's certainly not stupid."

"I pray you're right." Her fidgeting intensified and made her stutter, "I...I'll confess to you something, if...if you swear not to laugh."

"I swear," Simon promised, hand splayed over his chest.

"Right before I left Dinefwr, I saw a naked man drying off outside the communal tub. His face was buried in a towel, and...and I liked what I saw."

"Wonderful!" exclaimed Simon. "Perhaps he'll be one of the contenders!"

"It was Owain," Gael dropped bluntly.

Simon clamped his mouth so not to break his vow. Yet Gael noticed his shoulders quaking, and accused, "You swore, Simon!"

"I'm laughing because I'm happy for you!"

"Why?"

"At least there's something about him you don't hate. Did he see you gawking?"

She swallowed a chuckle. "I didn't *gawk*...and yes."

"Then," he asserted, "there's not a chance of him ever returning here."

Gael laughed out loud and hugged his neck. "Thank you! You've made me laugh, as always. And I do see things in a better light now."

Simon hugged back and when their hold at last eased, he said, "Before we go back in, there is one request we must ask of you."

"And what is that?"

"Maura and I have decided that...well, if any harm should come to us while living here, we would like you to mother our child."

Her emotions again engulfed her and made her quaver, "Of...of course I will. And I'm honored you asked."

She wiped one tear and Simon noted with a smile, "I'm certain the old one is done with his ridiculous tale. We can go back in now."

"And will you dance with me?"

"Do I have to?" he whined. "Last time you hurt me!"

"All you need do is lift me up like Marc did."

He groaned; she shoved him playfully, yet as they started to rise a frightened ball of fur dashed out of the dark and leapt into Simon's lap. Simon hugged the shaken pup and soothed, "Henry, where've you come from? We locked you up."

"He can escape from anywhere, Simon."

"I hope he's not dug under the wall." Both shrugged and climbed the stairs, Simon continuing to fret, "Do you think it safe, bringing him inside?"

"He obeys Marc and Gruffydd," offered Gael.

Simon nodded and the three entered the welcoming warmth, where a heartrending scene made them stop and stare.

In a far corner, surrounded by three highly attentive young women and numerous children of all ages, sat Marc. Gruffydd, snuggled in his lap, was fast asleep. Maura sat opposite, holding Cynan, who sporadically hacked into his palm. The group listened in wide-eyed wonder to Marc's adventures of this day and of his tumultuous year in Normandy.

Maura turned and noticed Gael and Simon. She whispered to Cynan and helped him off her lap, struggled up, and approached her husband and friend. Taking Gael's hand, she spoke brightly, "Your cheeks have color again! Did you tell him all?"

Excitement spiked Gael's response as she guided Maura to a corner. "Yes! And he explained everything so clearly!"

Over her shoulder, Maura gifted Simon a most loving look, then returned her interest to Gael, who gabbled on, "I...I'm to pick my own husband, Maura, and I'll take my time. If they're not to my liking, I'll send them back to Rhys and tell him to find me another. It could be fun, and will no doubt be fascinating!"

"I'm certain it will be both," chuckled Maura.

Simon and Henry wove their way between dancers to the trestle table. Simon crouched, set Henry down beneath the table, and lectured, "Now, you're to stay here. It's safe and warm, and I'll fetch you some food. If you come out, I'll have to put you back outside." The mutt continued to shiver, and licked Simon's hand. Simon wondered if he might be sick, but his eyes were bright, and his nose cool. He issued the order, "Stay!" and perused the food for Henry and himself. After delivering Henry's fare, which was ignored, Simon leant up against the table, munched on a hunk of cheese and buttered bread, and scanned his gay surroundings. One of the young ladies flanking Marc was now twirling a lock of his hair; another had rested her head upon his shoulder. Between the dancers, Simon spotted Maura and Gael engaged in an animated conversation. His heart swelled as his gaze rested upon Maura; he loved seeing her so happy, and prayed he could forever keep her this way. His eyes then strayed past the doorway to a blackened area beside the barrels. Someone stood there, purposely hidden, perhaps spying. Simon squinted to recognize the stranger, but a jostling knocked him off balance. A bite of cheese caught in his throat; choking, he grabbed the table's edge and snapped his head to berate the rude one. Nesta, Prince Rhys' nubile daughter, stood beside him, her eyes round with beguiling innocence, and her comeliness shrouded in what appeared to be a nun's habit. He regained use of his throat and sputtered, "Nes...Nesta, why...what—"

"I beg your pardon, Simon, but I had to get your attention," she said in rapt suspense. "It's dreadfully important what I have to say!" Her gaze swept distastefully over the repast, then stuck back on him.

She moved closer, too close, forcing him to step back and insist, "What do you have to say?"

"Come outside with me."

"No...You'll say it here, or not at all." Everything about her annoyed him—her forced femininity, her little girl voice, her compulsive touching, her inability to understand *no*. He moved further away and excused, "I'll be leaving soon, so I suggest you get on with it."

"And what might '*it*' be?" she said enticingly, batting her lashes.

He started away; she grabbed his arm and spun him back around. His ire was clear as he jerked from her hold, and gritted, "Get away from me."

"You won't mean that once you hear the wickedness your virtuous wife has been up to."

"Nesta," he warned, "I suggest you stop...now."

But she didn't stop; gleefully sneering, she yammered on, "Two evening's past, I listened to a Norman baron speaking to his servant, no—boasting to his servant, about knowing the saintly Maura, knowing her intimately, as intimately as two can know each other. The act took place in March of this year in Normandy. I remember clearly how he described their romp. 'She took me with force', he said. He did, Simon. He described her perfectly, all I've seen and more."

"Who said this?!" flared Simon.

"I didn't see him. Father wouldn't allow it."

"Then how did you hear?"

"There was a tapestry between us."

"You don't know French."

"I know enough."

"Why was this Norman at Dinefwr?"

"I know not," snipped Nesta. "I arrived just before he left. She's deceived you, Simon!" she loudly assailed. "That child she carries, it's not yours. I heard its father two night's past, or perhaps it was sired by someone else—Maura's tangled with so many." Somehow, Nesta had wiled Simon into a corner, where few could see. He was caught fast between the wall and her heaving, tempestuous self. Her scent smothered him, twisted his belly, and his head swam with a cacophony of her outrageous lies. Nesta's wetted lips dripped passion, "I'll tell Father...He'll gladly annul your false union, banish the whore, and tie you to me. For that is where you belong, by me for always. I love you, Simon, only you! You must know that I'll do anything for you!"

She was everywhere, touching, kissing; he couldn't breathe, couldn't speak, couldn't move! He lurched to the side and gasped for air and control and managed to stammer, "Get...get away from me...now!"

"Kiss me!" she commanded, and thrust her lips upon his. One firm shove dropped her to her bottom. She sat a stunned moment, whimpering and hiding her humiliation in her palms. Her veil had fallen back, revealing her closely shorn hair. Nesta's hands left her face and crept over her head; finding the veil gone sent her despair and wailing spiraling.

The dancing stopped and the floor instantly cleared. The stranger left his covering and stealthily approached the trestle table.

The fierceness of Simon's expression filled Maura with dread as she stood and started toward him. Marc laid Gruffydd, still asleep, on the rushes. He rose warily and instantly was joined by Gael.

Nesta saw Maura coming, scrambled up and lunged for Simon. Her arms strangled his waist, she clung to him and groaned, "No! You'll not have him. He loves me, wants me!"

Again she tried to kiss him; he jerked his head away, and screamed to himself, *I can't hit her, can't hurt her! Dear God, get her away from me!* Her strong slap knocked his head back against the wall. Before he could react, she slapped again, harder. Then Simon bit into his fist and howled a howl that struck terror in all present, especially Nesta.

Gael darted forward; Marc clamped her wrist and yanked her back, shouting, "No, don't!" She was confused and frightened, yet did as told, and her confusion soared to the astonishing sight of Owain, standing by the table, glaring at the insanity.

Maura approached Nesta's back, reaching out and speaking with forced calm, "Nesta, come away from him. *Please*..." Cautiously, she touched her shoulder.

The Princess shrieked as if scalded, whirled, and sliced her nails across Maura's cheek. Marc saw Simon surge for Nesta; he dove to stop him, tackling Simon inches from the cowering girl. Sulien rushed to restrain Gael, and Maura stood starkly silent, her hand cradling her cheek and blood dripping from between her fingers. The crazed din woke Gruffydd, who stayed near the ground, and cried out, "Mam...Mam!"

Nesta threw back her head and cackled hysterically at the frightened child; at Maura and Gael; at Simon, groaning and thrashing beneath Marc; and at her thunderstruck audience. Her audacity enraged Maura, dizzying her and blurring her sight, but not enough to deter her well-aimed blow. Maura's knotted fist shot out, neatly glanced Nesta's jaw, and easily crumpled her senseless to the rushes.

Without expression or word, Owain broke through the stunned crowd, hoisted Nesta over his shoulder, and disappeared. Gael chased after them; Sulien stopped her at the door, and yelled to Marc, "Take her to her hut, lock her in, and calm her down! I'll keep

Gruffydd here." Marc leapt up to obey and, gripping Gael's waist, hustled her out of the llys.

Simon's fury was far from gone, and his eyes darted suspiciously about as he clutched Maura fast to his chest. Sulien knelt by his side, and suggested with caution, "You must leave here quickly, get Maura home, and tend her wound. I'll explain all of what happened to Rhys. But I don't think it wise that you be here when he arrives. Hywel can help you."

"No," Maura said with effort. "I'm fine and I can walk on my own. Sulien's correct, Simon, it's time we went home."

Hywel, a bear of a man with a grumbly constitution to match, stepped forward and, to the dazed couple, muttered sense, "Now...now, my young Lord and Lady, you'll accept my aid, as I, on occasion, have had to accept yours."

Each time before, Hywel's greeting, 'My young Lord and Lady,' had been spoken with ridicule. Now, Simon heard fondness in his words. He grasped Hywel's hand and, with Maura still snug in his clutch, was easily hauled to his feet. Raythyen provided Maura a dampened linen towel and bundled her in a cloak. The crowd pressed close, offering touches and murmurs of condolence, as Hywel guided them out of the house and to his horse's side. "She's old and slow, but she'll get you home safely," he grunted, settling Maura in the saddle.

Simon climbed up behind her and, securing the reins, replied with weary affection, "We thank you, Sir." As they trotted away, Simon whistled over his shoulder to Henry. The pup dashed down the stairs of the house and loped along in pursuit.

Simon and Maura were too exhausted and stunned to speak, or to offer explanations, accusations, or excuses. The wind howled in their ears, rain spat at their faces; cold, confusion, and simmering anger made Simon tremble and urge Hywel's horse faster along the road and through the opened gate of the village. Flashes of distant lightning lit the way as the mare snorted and puffed her way up the steep path to their hut. Nearing the wildflowers, Simon noticed light shining through the closed shutters. He reined in the horse and slid from the saddle. "Stay here, my love, and try to keep Henry quiet," he warned, scooping up the pup and passing him to Maura.

"What is it, Simon?"

"I'm not certain. Stay...I'll return shortly." She reached out and grasped his shoulder. He loosened her fingers, kissed them, and assured, "I swear...I'll be back."

*****

As Geoffrey relieved himself on a bush flanking the cottage's door, he woozily wondered how much longer he and his other soldiers would have to drink this stale, diluted ale and endure their Lord's exaggerated tales of exploits in bed and on the battlefield. Hours had passed since they first arrived at this hovel—long, tediously boring hours. He was tired and near drunk and wanted to sleep, but his Liege kept insisting he might need defense against Welsh marauders, which was ridiculous. The only marauder they'd encountered since crossing the border three days' past was a rat of a dog, who'd bitten Geoffrey, and been rightly punished with a kick.

The lightning's glow intensified and Simon spied someone slouching by the door. As he stealthily approached, he noticed the man's back faced him, but he couldn't quite make out what he was doing or his intent. Who could it be? It wouldn't be anyone from the village; they were all present at the feast. The next lightening flash struck, illuminating the man's sword dangling at his side. Simon carried no weapon, yet he knew his bile was still boiling so hot that he'd not require a weapon to kill if the need arose. He lunged forward, seized the man's shoulder and whipped him around. Before the man's hand could reach his sword, Simon kicked his exposed groin. Geoffrey yowled in agony, grabbed his genitals, and jerked forward, smashing his face into

Simon's up-thrust knee. He slumped unconscious to the ground, yet Simon wasn't done. He lurched to his knees and raised a balled fist to pound the intruder further. Maura raced toward him and stalled his strike with the piercing cry, "Simon, no!"

The door flew open; hands, arms, and bodies shot out, capturing Simon, and dragging him, bucking and howling, into the hut. Maura pummeled her way through the chaos, shrilling, "Let him go! Release him now, or I'll murder the lot of you!" She yanked the dagger from its sheath by the head of the door, whirled, and swiped through the air menacingly, scattering the men and revealing their leader. She froze and blinked in disbelief as her jaw dropped, closed, then fell again to exclaim, "Henry!"

*****

𝔍𝔬𝔯 a terrifying instant, Henry didn't recognize the crazed woman posturing before him—flaming hair jutting out in all directions, face scarlet with rage, eyes fired with malice. Blood smeared her hands, face, clothes, and she flourished her knife with lethal expertise. Convinced of his imminent death, Henry shut his eyes to ask God's forgiveness, then heard the wild one squeak his name with Maura's voice! His fright faded and he gushed in relief, "Thank the Lord, it's you!" and hurried to greet his favorite cousin. Yet the knife still glinted at him. He halted, and heard his fear return in a cracked plea, "Ma...Maura...It's me—Henry. Please put the knife down. I'm here to visit, not to harm you."

"Make them release him!" she roared.

"Yes..." he speedily agreed, then ordered to his men, "Let the scoundrel go, or she'll murder the lot of us!"

The struggling on the floor ended. Maura, her dagger still brandished, glaringly watched the guards disperse. She counted six as they unfolded their hulking selves off Simon. One ginger-haired sentry, whom Maura believed she recognized, bent to help her husband. Even with assistance, Simon stood with great difficulty, then groaned as his knees buckled him back to the ground. The guard again offered his hand; Simon batted it away, shuddered to clear his head, and floundered up on his own. Henry squinted severely at the draggled, hirsute man hobbling toward Maura. "Is it you?" Henry muttered beneath his breath. The man's intensely blue eyes, eerily pale, confirmed Henry's suspicion; he burst out, "Simon!" and lunged forward to express his joy at finding them, but Maura still wielded that damned knife!

Simon peered blankly at Maura, then at Henry and his guards, and struggled to remember what exactly he was supposed to be doing. Sulien's command, '...tend Maura's wound,' echoed through his foggy mind. With resolute calm, he removed the knife from her hand, and slipped it back in its sheath. His arm embraced her waist as he guided her between the sentries to the physician's table.

Maura's fretting heightened to Simon's odd countenance, yet the reason for it was obvious—if he acknowledged Henry, he would also have to acknowledge King William's death. And with the recent turmoil still so fresh, his mind and body could take no more torment. "Simon," she spoke softly, sitting and watching as he dampened a cloth in their near empty barrel of ale, lifted her chin, and ever so tenderly bathed the four long scratches. The stinging silenced her; she sucked a breath, gripped his other hand, and cast a pleading look to Henry.

"Did my man do this to you?" Henry demanded.

"No," Maura answered wincingly, then she returned her concern to Simon. "Simon...Henry's come."

"What's wrong with him, Maura?" injected Henry.

She waved Henry off, and asked Simon, "Should I ask why Henry's here?" He quietly continued to dab at her wound, so she grasped his shoulder, shook him, and repeated, "Should I ask?"

"No..." he replied with scant emotion. "I know why he's here." And then the enormity of Henry's presence, and the pain caused by the scuffle with the guards struck Simon with debilitating force. He slumped forward; Maura caught him and strained to Henry, "Please help me!"

"What's wrong with him, Maura? What's happened?!"

"He's been trounced on by all your guards and has just realized your father's dead!"

117

"Yes...Father was old and sick," Henry hurled back. "Old and sick people die!"

"And Simon loved him dearly! It's been a hard evening, Henry. Help me!"

"It looks as though you endured the worst of it. What can I do?"

"That gray jar, there." She pointed with her nose. "Pass it to me, but don't remove its cork." Maura barely loosened the potion's lid and waved it slightly under Simon's nose.

In violent response, he jerked upright, his eyes flew open, and he gasped, "Gruffydd!"

"Who in God's name is *Griffith?*" wondered Henry.

"It's no matter, Henry. Simon?"

When Simon's moist eyes met hers, he practically clambered into her lap and arms, and as they hugged, the same dread infected them both. Simon eased back, and said alertly, "I must go to the long house and fetch...and fetch more...ale."

"Yes, Simon, go quickly."

"But how can I leave you here, like this, with these—"

"It's only Henry," she assured. "I'll be fine. You must hurry and tell Gael who's come."

"Who is Gael?" asked Henry, thoroughly muddled. Yet still he was ignored, this time by Maura as well.

Simon untwined himself, plucked up another jar from the table, and handed it to Henry. He rested his hand firmly on his cousin's shoulder, squeezed once, and succinctly directed, "Smooth this on her cuts while I'm gone. I'll hurry." Before Henry had a chance to say his name or share a hug, Simon walked away.

Henry stared slack-jawed at the door, and called in a wounded voice, "Simon, are you pleased to see me?" Simon stopped to glance back, nodded, and staggered away. Henry turned attentively to Maura; she sat stiffly still, her hand supporting her brow, and her eyes shut. "He said to spread this on your cuts," he muttered.

"I heard what he said," she whispered back.

"Should I do it, then?" he asked.

She wagged her head. Henry shrugged and glanced in the corner where Geoffrey lay, looking as dreadful as Simon, and mentioned, "Perhaps my man could use some of that waking ointment." Maura didn't object; her concern for Simon was so encompassing she couldn't hear or say a thing. So Henry took up the jar and went to tend his guard.

Simon, his mind in a fog, blundered aimlessly about their property. He came upon the horse, munching contentedly on wild flowers and, along with the lightning, memories began to flash—Hywel's horse, the feast, the Princess slashing Maura. *If I'd gotten hold of Nesta, would I have hurt her, but didn't I hurt someone else?* All he could remember was being captured and jumped upon by many huge men. And Maura holding a knife...at Henry? *It's not Henry, it can't be Henry. He's still in Normandy with his ailing father—ailing, not dead.* Then why was he out here, and Maura still inside, shut up with a group of mean and burly strangers? *Why does my head pain me so?* "Bleeding Jesus!" he howled in frustration, and his yell flushed the pup out of a nearby bush. He wiggled up to Simon. Simon squatted and Henry licked his face, but this time the licking didn't disgust Simon, it helped clear his mind, and he remembered—Marc. *I must get to Marc and warn him of Henry's arrival!* It took all the strength he possessed to stand, and no matter how hard he tried, he could not force his aching body astride the horse.

*****

118

The peaceful ambiance of the cathedral's infirmary was wasted on Rhys and Owain as they paced either side of Nesta, reposing unconscious on a cot, and hollered at each other. "I ordered you to watch her!" railed Rhys.

"I'm not a nursemaid!" parried Owain.

"Then kindly tell me exactly what you believe yourself to be?"

"A constant soldier."

"You're far too intelligent to be wasted on battling," said Rhys.

Owain knew what was coming and, heaving his arms to the sky, hotly stressed, "I won't agree to be Pennaeth to these mindless sods. They hate me!"

"If they do, you made it so! They are normally gracious people."

"Not any longer!" Owain countered. "He's turned the commote into a Norman camp."

"Who are you talking about?" Rhys demanded, trying desperately to regain his command.

"The doctor." Hands on hips, Owain glared and grumbled, "I saw their pretty dances, their fancy food and clothes. He's conquered this place and you, with false smiles and mind blurring potions."

Rhys snorted his response, "Owain, you speak nonsense!"

"No, I'll have my say at last!" Owain waited for the Prince's retort, but surprisingly none came, so he let his fury fly. "He's a wily coward, a traitor who grows flowers, and makes his wife fight his battles for him! I'm convinced he's poisoning you, slowly so no one notices...but you'll notice, the day you die!"

"Owain!" shouted Rhys. "These are severe charges, charges based on nothing but jealousy. Are you saying he should have hit my daughter?! Would you have hit my daughter?! And poisoned! How dare you accuse Simon of such a thing! I've never felt so fit since he returned!"

Bug-eyed, Owain choked, "Jealousy! Why would I be jealous of that pompous prig?"

"Because contrary to yourself, *he* is liked."

Nesta stirred and stalled their squabbling with a whispered sigh, "Simon..."

Her eyes fluttered open to her father's effusive concern, "My sweetness, it's Father! You're in the infirmary and safe, with me. How do you feel?"

Nesta struggled to sit, flashed a quick sneer at Owain, then struck a pitiful pose, and whimpered, "I hurt...here." She gingerly touched her jaw, then added with a pout, "Wine would help."

A hooded brother standing nearby received the Prince's terse order, "Fetch wine, quickly!"

Owain rolled his eyes in exasperation and flopped down upon the next bed. His clasped hands supported his head and, seemingly entranced by the planked ceiling, he listened in disgust to the Princess' drivel.

"Oh Father," she implored with dainty despair, "you'll arrest her, punish her with a whip, then marry her to the oldest, ugliest, and cruelest man you know!"

"Who?"

"Maura of course."

"But Maura's already married."

Nesta self-consciously fingered the ends of her cropped hair, while boldly asserting, "After you hear what she's done, she won't be much longer!"

"And what has she done?" asked the Prince.

"Well...many devious things, but I'll start with her nastiness this evening...She hit me! Without cause!"

While Rhys sat dumbly absorbing the accusation, Owain pondered Maura. What Nesta claimed was a lie, and he should say so, but why should he defend the Norman bitch? Perhaps because she wasn't a bitch, and was, as well as he could remember, the only person in the last six months who'd acted kindly toward him. Before he could dissuade himself, he started up from the bed, and spouted, "I beg to differ, my Prince."

Rhys twisted to find the voice; locating it, he frowned and barked, "I'd hoped you'd left. Why do you differ?"

"Because the Lady Maura had good reason to strike your daughter."

"And that cause was?"

"Nesta sliced her face with her nails!"

Rhys turned his shock and puzzlement on Nesta. "Why would you scratch Maura?"

"She threatened me because I discovered her treachery," she said in wiggly drama. "And I was in the course of telling Simon the torrid truth when she—"

"Ha!" Owain burst indignantly. "You were in the course of raping the man!"

To that, Rhys almost tumbled off the bed. Once he regained his seat, he stammered to Owain, "What...what are you implying?"

"I'm *implying* you'd best lock her up before she gets herself ruined or killed or both!"

"Father, don't listen to him," goaded Nesta. "He's angry because he wants me, but he's not of fine enough breeding to have me, and besides he smells and is mean."

"He doesn't smell," Rhys defended, "and he's only mean...sometimes."

Listening to the wretched child was painful; Owain's belly churned and he begged, "May I take my leave, Sir? I'm feeling rather ill."

"Yes, go."

"And I advise," Owain added, "if you want the truth, speak to the Lady Maura. She has no reason to lie."

As Owain barely bowed and strode away, he heard the Princess shrilly continue her crudities. "But she has lied, Father, she's lied to Simon, to everyone. The baby she carries was sired by another man, the Norman who slept at Dinefwr two night's past. I heard him talk of Maura in the most passionate and endearing terms. I believe it's Simon's right to know of her deceit."

"I ordered you to stay away from the FitzRoy!" raged Rhys.

"I heard his confession from behind my tapestry," she timidly divulged.

"Well then, I'll hear it from him and, if need be, from Maura as well in the morning."

Adulation spiked her reply, "The FitzRoy is here?"

"Yes," Rhys replied with reserve, "he's Simon and Maura's cousin, Henry, and has come to tell them of the death of his father, King William. I hear he's a flagrant liar, braggart, and rake. And well...Maura and Simon have proven their trustworthiness time and time again. We will gather all concerned in the llys tomorrow mid-morning, and there we will discover the truth."

Nesta's resolve faltered and she begged, "Father, I'd rather not be there. After all, you don't want me near this Henry, and I'm afraid Maura will strike me again. Her pregnancy has made her overly suspicious and, I fear, abusive."

Rhys ended their wrangling with an icy, "You *will* be there." While his daughter sipped her wine, Rhys grew quiet and pensive. Defending the Lady Maura would do no good, Nesta was set solidly against her. But why the strife? Always before, their visits had been courteous. And what was this nonsense about the FitzRoy's bragging...or was it more than nonsense? He was a renowned seducer, and according to rumor had acquired quite a harem, and scores of bastards. The idea of taking a cousin as lover wasn't all that outrageous. Well, whatever the outcome of the inquiries, the meeting

120

could prove quite fascinating. He wondered how he could induce Gael to accompany him, for he did want her to witness his skill as judge. By some, he'd been compared to the great Solomon for his wisdom and virility. His wisdom Gael seemed convinced of, but his virility still evaded her. A knowing grin crept over his lips as he realized—*Of course she will agree to come—she was witness to the dirty deed, and will surely relish the opportunity to speak in defense of her dearest friends.*

*****

"I want my son now!" yelled Gael for the hundredth time at Marc, who stood before the door to her hut, barring her escape.

"He's safe with Sulien," retorted Marc. "When you calm yourself, we'll go and fetch him. It will upset him to see you this way."

"He sees me this way frequently! And I am calm, see." She glided placidly about the hut, but her eyes still blazed fury, her cheeks still held a heated glow, and her lips spat more than talked. "I want to see Maura. Don't you?"

"Of course I do," Marc readily replied. "Simon's with her, so she's fine."

"Perhaps they've been arrested. Maura could be arrested for what she's done!"

"Simon will protect her."

"If you're so certain of Simon," Gael asked, "why did you have to tackle him to keep him from killing *her*."

"We've always watched over each other. And who is *she*?"

Gael snarled, "The Princess Nesta."

"Princess!" repeated Marc, aghast. "She doesn't act much like a Princess. Have you any idea why she did what she did?"

"Lots of them. The one that looms foremost in my mind is that she's mad, horribly, terribly mad, and needs to be locked away somewhere where she can't hurt anyone else. How dare she hurt Maura!" Gael fumed again as she paced. "Maura has always been kind to her, as has Simon. And what was she doing with Owain?!"

"Who's Owain?" asked Marc, still supporting the door.

"I'd best not start on that topic," warned Gael, "or we'll never be able to fetch Gruffydd. Please, Marc!" She gestured as if praying and begged, "Lock me in if you have to, but go get him and bring him here. He calms me, please!"

"I won't lock you in, only swear that you'll stay...swear!"

"I swear."

Marc suggested, "I read in Simon's prescription book that warm ale calms the soul. Would you please prepare some while I'm gone?"

"Yes," she gushed, "and thank you...again!"

Grumbling and snide remarks heckled him as Simon squirmed his way through the milling crowd and into the long house. He wished he could remember why he was here. The mood of the place had rotted. The room was stuffed too tight with Rhys' soldiers who had captured the food, the mead, and every inch of the floor. The musicians were gone and their stage of straw was now piled high with snoring men. Sulien, Raythyen, and Gruffydd were the only villagers remaining. As Simon made his way toward them, he was purposely harassed, shoved, and jostled, but he didn't seem to notice or care. Sulien, frightened at his dazed way, waved and approached, calling, "Simon, you look terrible. You'd best sit before you fall. There's a clear space over here."

"No...no, I can't. I must find Marc, warn him."

"He's taken Gael home. Warn him of what?"

Simon didn't say and reached for the boy. "Then I'll take Gruffydd and go there."

"You don't look able."

"I am...fine."

121

As he was lifted, Gruffydd clutched direly at Simon and begged, "I want Mam! Take me to her, Simon."

"Yes...I'll take you home." The boy was heavy and Simon's pain flared, making him moan and waver. Somehow, he managed to wobble with Gruffydd through the soldiers, but the weather only deepened his misery. As he stepped outside, the sky poured down rain, crackled lightning, and pounded thunder. Simon's attempt to hurry ended soundly with a slip and spill in the mud. The fall ignited Gruffydd's tears and panic; he rolled to his feet and, with tenacious tugs, yanked Simon up and along the drowning path. The sight of someone slogging toward them made them pause and scramble back in the opposite direction.

They almost sank back to the mud in relief as Marc slid to a stop next to them, swept up the boy, and yelled over the din, "Where's Maura?"

"At the cottage," croaked Simon.

"Why aren't you with her?" shouted Marc.

"I'll tell you when we get to Gael's."

They tumbled into Gael's hut, flustered and dripping. Gruffydd wrested from Marc's grip and raced into his mother's smothering hug. "Come, my sweet," she said, fighting back tears, "We'll get you dry and snug in your bed." Then she spied Simon, pressed tight to the door, ghostly pale, and trembling. "Si...Simon!" she stammered in shock. "Fetch him a cup of ale, Marc, and also one for yourself. Why are you here and where's Maura?"

"At the cottage...I have something to say to Marc. Then I'll return to her and—"

"What is it, Simon?" Gael asked with panic. "What's happened?"

"Henry's at the cottage."

"Good..." She sagged and sighed. "He shouldn't be out in this tempest, neither should we, or you."

"No...Henry FitzRoy. King William is dead."

Marc slumped heavily against the wall, sloshing ale from the cups. He suddenly felt faint and very cold. "Has he come alone?" he quavered.

"No...He's with six or seven guards."

"Did he mention me?"

"Not in the little we spoke."

Gael watched as Marc somberly offered the ale to Simon. She knew how Simon had been dreading the news of his uncle's death given how uniquely close the two had been. "Simon," she soothed from across the room, "I'm terribly sorry about your uncle." Then she asked with careful insight, "What's the other problem with Henry?"

"Henry and Marc fought together in Normandy," explained Simon. "If Henry discovers Marc is here, he could have Marc arrested and imprisoned for desertion, and—"

"Executed," Marc glumly finished.

"Executed!" repeated Gael, with wide eyes and a dry swallow.

"You can't come to the cottage," Simon insisted to Marc, "not this night, maybe not till he leaves."

"I will return with you," countered Marc.

"No!"

"Then, you'll tell him I'm here!"

"What?" asked Simon in disbelief.

"Tell him I'm here and my plans. If he is the caring, noble man you claim he is, he will let me stay. Tell him!"

"If I agree, will you promise, if Gael agrees, to stay here this night?"

With blushing discomfort, Marc argued, "I won't compromise the Lady. I'll stay at the long house."

"And what an exciting time you'll have there," noted Simon with irony. "The place is infested with near a hundred Welsh soldiers, hungry, and itching for a fight. You'll be safer here."

Marc studied Gael's expression; she seemed not in the least concerned with Simon's suggestion, but then she was busy ridding her son of his sopping clothes. Perhaps she hadn't heard his plan.

"Of course, you'll stay here, Marc," she affirmed. "It's valiant of you to be concerned about my reputation, but I won't be compromised."

"I must go," muttered Simon unsteadily.

"Take my horse, Simon," offered Gael.

"That's kind of you, but I can't get on one, or off."

"What's happened to you?" she worried.

"It's nothing serious. Come to the cottage in the morning. I'll tell you everything, and you can meet Henry. Don't bring Marc."

"I won't hide from him!" Marc intruded with ire.

"I know you won't!" returned Simon as forcefully. "I beg you stay away this night! We've just got you back, Marc. We won't risk losing you...not again...not so soon after you've come home."

After a long and troubled pause, Marc nodded, and took back Simon's empty cup.

Gael snatched her cloak from a peg on the wall and wrapped it round Simon's shoulders. "It will at least keep you from getting any wetter. Take care, Simon, and give Maura my love and apologies for everything that's happened this night." They kissed, hugged a tense hug, and then parted.

Simon turned in the open door to restate adamantly, "Marc, don't come to the cottage till Gael tells you it's safe. Please say that you won't!"

"I won't," Marc mumbled. He latched the door after Simon, threw back the ale left in his cup, and forced his eyes and thoughts to Gael and Gruffydd.

*****

Geoffrey gazed woozily at his Lord, who knelt before him and chastised, "You insipid fool! You're weren't exactly *on alert* were you?"

"He attacked me, my Lord!"

"Yes, bare handed while you had a sword!"

"Tis true, my Lord! I admit, I wasn't fully alert at the moment he struck, but..."

"Enough of your sniveling," carped Henry, throwing his man a damp cloth to remove the blood encrusted beneath his nose. "I pray we don't encounter any serious menace while in Wales, for you men are a sorry lot."

"My Lord," called John, hovering behind Henry.

"So I see you've finally squirmed out of your hole, you cowardly worm!"

John had grown used to his Master's odd style of camaraderie, and replied with a ruffle, "The Lady Maura has retired to the other chamber, and from the noises I heard coming from the room, I guess she's not well."

"Well, what am I supposed to do about it?" snapped back Henry.

"Perhaps she would benefit from your comforting company, words, and touch."

"Why me?"

"If her love for you is as extreme as you claim, my Lord, only your presence can adequately console her."

"Do I have to?"

"I would suggest it, my Lord," said John.

"If I see her puking," whined Henry, "I'm liable to do so myself!"

With a severe nod, John gestured toward the bedchamber door. Henry hesitantly rose; he'd walked only three steps before stopping to turn a hapless look. John waved him on and, stubbornly, he obliged. A peek through a knot in the door revealed a lone candle sitting on the floor, illuminating Maura on her knees, retching into a chamber pot. So, this was the woman he swore he worshipped above all others. In her present groveling position, she had little appeal, and he lamented to himself, *God's breath, why me?* as he knocked and gingerly entered.

Maura swiped at her mouth, sat back on her heels, and glanced up eagerly. At not seeing Simon, she tried but failed to mask her chagrin and said brokenly, "Hen...Henry...I'm a bit wretched at the moment. I...I will rejoin you in a—"

"No..." Henry interrupted, his voice brimming compassion, "You'll stay in here. If you're done, I'll help you up." Before answering, she rested her head on the bed. His heart ached to her pained expression, so ashen that the slice marks on her cheek appeared garish in contrast. "Come Maura," he gently urged, "let me help you."

As she raised her hand to his, a peal of thunder quaked the ground and the hut, and fear rocked Henry to the bed.

With a desperate reach, she faintly fretted, "Is there sign of Simon?"

"No..." he grunted, yanking her up from the rushes to his side. "I'm certain he'll arrive soon. Now...Simon told me to put this salve on your cuts, and I will do as his Lordship commands." Maura stretched long, lifted the candle, and set it on the side table to lighten his view. Henry didn't want to look in her eyes, yet his eyes found their way despite his worry. The upset he saw there wrenched his belly and, as he studied her distress further, her appeal returned with such intensity that he knew she still owned his affection and soul and so much more. "Simon didn't do this, did he?" he said, striving for levity.

She didn't bother replying to that and said instead, "There was a scuffle at the long house. I stopped it."

"Not soon enough. This might sting, so hold tight to my arm." Using a feather touch, Henry spread on the ointment; in response, Maura's expression betrayed little hurt, but her grip strangled his arm. Their quiet closeness allowed him a moment of fantasy—Simon and Maura's bond surely had splintered since he'd seen them last. And if she be lonely, bored with her husband, and disgusted at her forced poverty, he could offer her a new life—the life she'd been born to, alight with passion, riches, and perhaps even the title Countess! How could she resist?

"Henry...did you hear me?"

"No, I'm sorry, Maura...What is it?"

"I need no more ointment." She removed his hand from her cheek, smiled humbly, and whispered, "Thank you. You can clean your hands in the bowl." When his wash was done, she scrubbed blood from her palms and asked gently, "When did your father die?"

"The ninth of September. I attended his service and journeyed to England to spend a week with Rufus..." He knew she wouldn't care to hear the raunchy details of that peculiar visit, so he rambled on, "Then I traveled cross-country, picked up two of my guards in Gloucester, and we found our way to the local Prince's outpost."

"Prince Rhys?"

"Yes...that's the one. We sojourned there two nights and completed our journey to you."

The fury of the storm flared, driving open a shutter and Maura to her feet with the appeal, "Perhaps you could send one of your men to search for Simon! *Please*, Henry!"

"Yes, perhaps I should. Guy!" he yelled at the door.

The ginger-haired sentry entered, looking expectant. "Yes, my Lord."

"Search the grounds and path for Simon. Help him with any difficulty."

"At once, my Lord."

"Guy?" asked Maura, peering at him curiously as she thought, *Could this be the same guard who so loyally protected Simon during his imprisonment?*

Guy answered for her, "Yes, my Lady. It is a pleasure to meet you again."

"And I'm pleased to see you, as Simon will be."

Guy beamed; Henry shooed him out, bound the shutter close, and was about to relate the remainder of the news from Normandy, but considering Maura's present tenuous state, he decided against it, and asked instead, "Would you care for anything, my Lady? Food..." He glanced at the chamber pot and deduced, "No, not food...uhm...I'm afraid we've drunk most of the ale."

"Water...could I please have a cup of water?" asked Maura. "There's a full pitcher on the large table in the other room."

"Right away..." he appeased and, forcing an awkward grin, slipped away.

With Henry gone, Maura's polite posture slumped. She squeezed together her hands, paling her knuckles, and frantically searched for her scream. She could hear it resonating throughout her body, splitting her skull, and pounding her ears! Why couldn't it find its way to her throat and out her mouth? If she screamed her frustration, her fear, her hurt, she'd feel much better. Yet she'd also alarm Henry and his men, and they'd all crowd into this room, hovering and fussing over her. No...she'd hold on to her scream, keep it hidden for now. The door opened and at seeing Simon, drenched, swathed in a too small cloak, and hugging the pup, she heaved up from the bed, and freely exclaimed, "Oh, Simon!"

Simon passed the dog behind him to Henry, and surged into her fitful embrace. Still holding tight, they sank to the bed, and gazed gratefully at each other a while before speaking. Henry considered their mawkish expressions, and cursed inwardly, *Their looks are soppier now than they were before they were wed! How can that be? Surely, they're tired of each other by now!* And what was he doing holding this damn smelly dog?

"Did you tell Gael?" asked Maura cautiously.

"Yes...and she's eager to meet Henry—tomorrow. I'll need to tell him about her, tonight."

"Do it carefully."

"I will."

"Who is this Gael?" grumbled Henry, setting the pup down. "You mentioned her before." The dog scurried onto the bed and, as Henry loomed closer, hid behind Maura.

"She's our closest friend," Maura answered lightly. "She was wife to the Chieftain of Menevia, but he died near a year past. And she will be wife to the next Chieftain, if one is ever picked. She's curious about you."

"And what does this curious Lady look like?" asked Henry, piqued.

Slightly irked, Simon returned, "What does it matter, Henry?"

"Not much, I suppose. I'll be honored to meet her."

They looked up in surprise at his lack of argument. Simon then fixed his interest on Maura's face and noted with relief, "The scratches already look much improved."

"Henry applied the salve," praised Maura.

"Thank you, Henry." Simon rose and extended his hand to clasp, but instead Henry clasped the whole of him, and Simon ardently returned his hug.

They kissed cheeks, and Henry admitted, lowly so Maura couldn't hear, "I've missed you dreadfully."

"And I've missed you...surprisingly," smiled Simon. "We'll speak later of your father. Now, I need to help Maura to bed."

Henry stayed where he was, smiling contentedly as if he rightly belonged with them anywhere they were, at any time. They, in turn, squirmed as they searched for words that would kindly get rid of him. Maura found them first, and frankly stated, "Henry, I need to speak to Simon...*privately*."

He inched his way backwards and, embarrassed, gibbered, "Oh. I...I'm sorry, I didn't realize. I'll leave you now. If you want for something, you need only yell."

They grinned and nodded him on and once he was away, fell back into each other's arms. "Oh, Simon," Maura loudly whispered, "I was so afraid for you!"

"Why?"

"Because of the odd state you were in when you left..." She swept back a clump of his wet hair, and added fervently, "And the terrible storm! Did you ride?"

"No, I couldn't. I ache a bit, I think because of the guards sitting on me. The rain seems to have cleared my mind though."

"Good," she said. "Will Marc stay away?"

"Only for the night. He's insisted I tell Henry that he's here and what his plans are, which I'll do...later. Now, I'll help you to bed."

"Did you see Nesta?" she asked warily before letting him go.

"No..." he answered in confusion. "I wasn't looking for her." He glanced to the floor and noticed the full chamber pot peeking out from beneath the bed. His eyes bulged as he gasped, "Maura, you've been sick!"

"Yes...I suppose it was all the excitement and the worry. I'm sorry, Simon."

"Why should *you* be sorry?"

"For what I did at the feast."

"I don't understand..."

"I hit her, Simon."

"You had to."

"Did I?" She reached out to pull him back beside her and despaired, "What happened at Dinefwr to make Nesta act so bold? Why did she say those things about you...wanting her...loving—"

She couldn't continue nor could she stop her tears. They poured from her eyes, and upon his hand as he rested it upon her cheek. He pleaded to ease her turmoil, "*Please* don't cry, my love! I have no idea what happened at Dinefwr, nor why she behaved the way she did, or said those things about me. I didn't see her at Dinefwr."

"But she always asks for you."

"And she did again," he concurred. "Gael agreed to see her instead."

"That was kind of Gael," sniffled Maura. "I suppose we should ask *her* what happened. Nesta was very upset."

"Don't you dare defend her!" he returned.

"I'm not, but she acted as though she had cause to claim you!"

"Maura..." He knew Nesta's accusations were ludicrous, just the same, he was afraid to speak them, as if doing so would somehow afford them credence. Yet Maura had to know what libel was being blabbed about her, and he cautiously recounted, "Nesta said she'd heard a Norman baron talk of you as his lover."

"Who?!" Maura cried out, aghast.

"I don't know and neither did she. She had listened to him secretly behind a tapestry."

"She lies!"

"I believe, more accurately, that she believes *his* lies."

"Who, Simon?! Who—" She paused as joltingly the truth declared itself. Henry! He'd been at Dinefwr two night's past, and true to his dramatic flair, would have boasted to anyone present of his sexual prowess. And all too frequently he confused

126

what he wished had happened with the facts. She swiftly swabbed her eyes with her sleeve, squeezed Simon's hand between hers, and tentatively began, "Promise me you won't kill him?"

"Kill who?"

"Henry..."

"The dog?" asked Simon.

"No, the man. Promise you won't, and I'll tell you what I think may have happened."

"I promise—maybe. Now tell me."

"Henry was at Dinefwr before he came here. He may have bragged about the time I accompanied him to Normandy. He has several versions of the trip, and one involves us as lovers." Maura watched his breath quicken and his eyes harden. She petted his clenched fist and reminded, "You promised Simon."

"He's responsible for this tragedy!"

"Not entirely."

"Close enough to entirely!"

"Simon..." Maura excused, "he's troubled, his father's dead, and he's just spent a week with Rufus. That alone would make anyone act—foolishly. Please, if you're going to reprimand him about this, do so calmly."

"What I'll do to reprimand him is drag him in front of the Princess and force him to tell her the complete truth! That should be emasculating enough to make him think twice before he starts decorating reality again!"

"I'd like them to meet," said Maura with a hint of vengeance.

Simon's fuming ebbed as a disturbing thought emerged. Maura had been genuinely frightened, not so much of Nesta's erratic behavior, but of her words, 'He loves me, wants me'. "Maura," he asked haltingly while cradling her face in his hands, "You'd never doubt my love, would you?"

She swallowed dryly, and the rims of her eyes reddened as she shakily confided, "Sometimes, I'm afraid...what with all the attention you get from the ladies, that...someday...someone...will come along. Nesta's so lovely, Simon, and I grow fatter each day and she's so determined to have you."

He couldn't believe what he was hearing and spurted out, "I...thought only *I* had that fear!"

Puzzled, she asked, "That you'll grow fat?"

"That you'll discover someone more deserving and—"

"Simon, no!" she earnestly interjected and tensed her grip. "How have I made you think that?"

"No way, *truly*...It's just a constant worry I have—losing you—that doesn't warrant mentioning."

"Because it will never happen!" she vehemently vowed. "There is no one more deserving of my love than you...Always believe that. Always!"

"I will if you believe the same. Come closer." His smile was wide and warm as he helped remove her tunic, then spread his hands lovingly over her belly. His expression and words turned wistful, passionate, "She is ours, made from our love. We vowed never to let anyone take her from us, and I swear that no one will ever take my love from you. You've never been more beautiful, and with each day, you grow ever more so. I beg of you, Maura, never doubt me or my love."

"I won't," she tearfully professed.

As he did often for solace, Simon rested his cheek upon her belly as she, in turn, sifted her fingers through his golden locks. Then he raised his head with a start and his radiance brought back her smile. "I felt her. There's no question, I felt her!" he joyously exclaimed.

"And in three months, we will see her," whispered Maura.

They lingered in their hold, silently envisioning every aspect of their miracle, then shouts and bantering from the adjoining room returned them to the present. Simon eased away, promising, "Before you sleep, I'll mix for you the same potion I gave to Rhys."

He started to rise; her fingers lightly encircled his arm, and she lured him back with the murmur, "First, let me kiss you." In glad assent, he closed his eyes and relished the expressive touch of her lips on his. He then urged her back to the bed, covered her with the quilt, and sat a moment to stroke her hand. The pup, still subdued, rearranged himself on Simon's pillow.

"Simon..." she wondered wearily.

"What is it, my love?"

"Will we be banished for what I did to Nesta?"

"I don't believe so. There were many witnesses."

"But Rhys is so doting. Will he accept their word over hers?"

"We can only hope and pray. Most likely we will be summoned to the llys tomorrow to restage the debacle. Till then, try not to worry. I must fetch your drink."

"Then you must speak to Henry about Marc," she reminded.

"First I'll lie with you till you fall asleep."

She nodded and watched adoringly as he took up the chamber pot and disappeared into the main chamber. It was important that he stay till she slept, for if she were left alone, the disturbances of the evening might cause her to dream again—her nightmare.

*****

Henry knocked, cracked open the bedchamber door, and whispered, "May I?" Despite the meek glow of the bedside candle, he caught Simon's nod, and crept inside. He eased his bottom down upon the foot of the bed, and soberly asked, "Should I build a fire?"

"No," Simon replied, "the quilt serves us fine."

As Henry became accustomed to the dark, the sight of Simon and Maura entwined on the bed before him upturned memories of a stormy night six months past, when they had lain the same way upon a crude bed following their horrific encounter with Rufus. And he had sat at the foot of that bed, and talked with Simon while Maura slept, and had felt so wanted. "Do you remember when last we did this?" said Henry with fondness.

"Oh, yes," sighed Simon. "And what do you have to say that will make me feel as uncertain as I did on that terrible night?"

Henry slumped to his side, balanced on his elbow, and responded with blandness, "Rufus rules England, Curthose Normandy, and Odo is free."

Simon let go a long hissed and quavered sigh, and then asked, "And Will?"

"I haven't seen or heard of him, which is nice."

"I thought Rufus would surely appoint him to some exalted position in his council."

"No...in fact," replied Henry, "the way Rufus talks, it would seem their bond is fragile and near broken."

"That's curious," mused Simon. "And my father?"

"I spoke with Robert at Rouen, immediately after Father's death. He attempted to coax your whereabouts from me, but did not succeed. Simon..." Henry leant forward to relay carefully, "He asked me if I believed you would forgive him."

"And you answered?"

"I told him—I hope not. Would you?"

128

Simon glanced ruefully down at Maura curled in the crook of his arm and looking so peaceful; her untouched cheek rested on his shoulder, her leg lay over his, and her arm hugged his waist. His answer was a definite, "No," and he queried further, "And where is he now?"

"At Dunheved."

"Is Odo with him?" asked Simon.

"Not according to Guy, who was recently at Dunheved. Guy left a fortnight past for Gloucester to rendezvous with me and the rest of my men. I have a new man, John. He's my butler and rather vapid, but he's willing to take on the ponderous task of looking after me. I wish you still did."

Simon thought it best to disregard Henry's wish for now. "Is there a chance Odo might have had you followed here?"

"No," answered Henry assuredly. "He has no clue where you are, or who harbors that information. He's taken on the role as Curthose's chief adviser, and considering the amount of advising that imbecile requires, I doubt if Odo will be pestering you anytime soon. Yet the day may come when he decides to take England for Curthose. Till then I don't believe you need fret."

Simon hesitantly queried, "But...when will *then* be?"

"Perhaps never," said Henry. "Anyone who willingly takes on Rufus is an idiot and as good as dead."

"We did," reminded Simon.

"And amazingly we lived to admit our lapse of sanity." Henry's finger traced the circular patterns embroidered on the quilt, while he muttered in snide tribute, "Odo may be a sanctimonious pile of manure, but he's not an idiot. If you're worried Simon," he pledged, "you can return to Normandy with me. I'll keep you safe."

Simon shifted for comfort, and achingly asked, "Did William suffer long?"

"Grievously long and near the end he cried out for you, claiming only you could save him."

Simon's chin sagged to his chest, and he let out a long doleful sigh.

"He gave me pittance Simon," Henry griped. "Treated me like a mere babe. One day soon, I'll prove to everyone his horrendous mistake. I'll rule all and make those who doubted me rot in Hell!"

Simon lifted an astounded face to Henry's furious one and countered, "Henry, William didn't purposely slight you. To him, you *were* a mere babe, and you acted as such whenever you were with him."

"I did not!"

"Yes, you did! I see his excluding you as ruler a generous compliment. He did it to protect you."

Henry pouted and said, "That's what Cecily claims."

"And what an intelligent woman she is," praised Simon.

"She complimented you as well, but I still don't understand, Simon. How was he protecting me?"

"Think for a moment, Henry, how many pieces you'd be in if your father had snubbed Rufus and declared you King of England."

Henry did think and as he thought his eyes grew rounder, his skin paler; he trembled and admitted, "I never considered the consequences of such a thing."

"That's your most serious problem, Henry." Simon figured it was the perfect time to mention Henry's newest blunder and chided on, "You never consider the consequences of anything you undertake. For example, two night's past at Dinefwr, I believe you were bragging to your man John, perhaps, of your amorous exploits in Normandy...with Maura."

129

Henry's hand clamped his mouth, his eyes bulged again; he seemed to shrink into the bed, and gibbered, "What? What?! When did he say that? You haven't spoken to him! How do you know?!"

"Someone else heard you, Henry, and it was the wrong person."

"Who?" squeaked Henry.

"The Prince's daughter, Nesta."

"There was no one near, Simon! I swear! I'd had too much to drink and I was rambling, that's all. I can dream can't I?!"

"Henry, calm yourself or you'll wake Maura. Nesta was listening from behind a tapestry. And of course you may dream, if you do so asleep!"

"What harm can a little lie do?"

"It depends, Henry, yet your lies are never little and this prodigious one caused Maura's injury."

"No!" protested Henry, sitting upright. "You can't blame me! Maura said it happened at a long house. I was nowhere near any long house."

Vehemently, Simon countered, "Nesta scratched Maura after informing me that Maura had been another man's lover and, because of her infidelity, Nesta's father— Prince Rhys—would annul my marriage to Maura, and wed me to Nesta."

"Why would she spout such blather?"

"She likes me, Henry."

"And how do you feel about her?"

"At the moment," Simon gritted, "revulsion comes fairly close to describing how I feel about her—and you."

"Well it's not my fault she was lurking about!" groused Henry. "And I'm not the cause of her obsession with you." Then, feeling a twinge of anxiety, he wondered, "What do you intend to do about all this?"

"I suspect there will be a trial tomorrow," noted Simon. "You will accompany us, and tell the Prince and his daughter the entire truth concerning your time with Maura in Normandy. And you also erred on the date—it was the end of January, not March. When will you ever learn, Henry?"

Henry hung his head and mumbled, "I'm sorry, Simon."

"I'm not the one you need apologize to. You'll say the same to Maura in the morning. And if something similar happens while you're staying with us," added Simon stringently, "I will have to get angry."

Henry's assurance was barely audible. "It won't."

"Good," sighed Simon. "And I am pleased to see you."

Henry lifted a wan smile, and felt emboldened enough to ask, "My man John will have to sleep sitting up at the table. Would you mind if he bedded down on the floor in here?"

"No...unless he snores as loudly as you do."

"I don't snore," Henry sulkily returned.

"Yes, you do."

"So, I suppose you and Maura are still fond of each other."

"You're correct to suppose that," agreed Simon.

"And where did you get that mangy critter?" asked Henry, pointing to the pup, who was stretched out along Simon's side.

"He was the runt of a litter. Nobody else wanted him, so we adopted him. His name is Henry."

"What?!" Henry gasped and groused, "I don't appreciate the compliment."

"You have the same eyes," simpered Simon.

Henry snorted and rose to fetch his man. To Henry's weary call John entered timorously, his black eyes shifty, lips tense, and posture slumped. "Simon," Henry introduced, "this is John, an escapee of Bayeux, where he was imprisoned as clerk for far too many years."

Hearing the word Bayeux made Simon falter his greeting, "I...I am pleased to meet you, John. You're welcome to sleep in here with us."

Simon gestured to the floor by the bed, and Henry readily decided, "I'll settle down on the other side."

"There are extra blankets atop the trunk," noted Simon, thinking how interesting this arrangement would prove to be if Maura had to get up in the night to relieve herself, which in this phase of her pregnancy was quite likely.

"Would you pass me the candle, Simon?" asked Henry. "I can't see."

Simon did so. Henry used the flame to light the taper sitting on the table by Maura's side of the bed, then returned it to Simon and took the newly lit one with him to the trunk. He tossed one pelt to John, and the other to his side of the bed. Simon watched curiously as the extremely thin, dark, and fragile looking man squirmed for comfort beneath his skin. John sensed his interest and glanced up to say, "I thank you, my Lord, for your courtesy."

Simon nodded uneasily, and turned his ear to Henry's grunts and muffled curses. Suddenly, Henry popped up a beaming face. "Simon! What's this?!"

Maura shifted, and Simon scolded, "I told you to hush! What's what?"

"There's a...a...cradle down here."

Simon smiled as he realized he hadn't shared their happy news. "Maura's with child," he lightly replied.

Henry's excitement took on a suspenseful air, "How pregnant is she?"

Simon's smile grew larger. "Six months." He waited for Henry to finish counting, then heard what he expected.

"I was right! Do you remember, Simon?"

"Yes...You predicted she'd become pregnant on our wedding night, and by all accounts, you were correct."

"I always am. Father will be so pleased..." There was a lengthy pause, then Henry solemnly corrected himself, "Would have been so pleased."

Simon joined his sadness with the tribute, "Your father was a most remarkable man and will be remembered as such for a very long time to come."

"But Simon," considered Henry, "you two constantly argued."

"Just because we disagreed doesn't mean we didn't love each other."

"We argue as well."

"Exactly, Henry. Now settle down."

The light soon faded, as had the storm, and Henry's voice lilted with affection in his wish, "Goodnight, Simon."

"Goodnight, Henry," Simon returned in kind.

Hearing them, John grappled with discomfort inside and out. He hadn't expected to like this place, or for his host to be so unassuming and gracious. He'd heard differently. Perhaps tomorrow, he hoped as he drifted off, he'd discover something to despise about this perplexing young man and his lady.

*****

Marc heard pounding, but his mind fought to stay asleep upon this cushiony pelt, wrapped in this wool cocoon, and pressed against Gael's oh so warm—He started up as the pounding grew louder and he realized Gruffydd no longer separated them. With profound relief, he noted he was still dressed, as was she. He tried to rise but tipped

131

back to the floor. His head felt huge and about to burst, the scant contents of the room spun before his bleary eyes, and his belly lurched and grumbled.

Gael's hand stopped his next attempt to stand, as she gently and, with effort, urged, "Lie...lie back down. I'll answer." Once upon her feet, she noticed the ale barrel on its side, presumably empty, and was certain Marc felt as wretched as did she. She stumbled to the door, and cracked it only a tiny way open. Still the intruding brightness, tainted by rain clouds, made her moan, grip her belly, and rasp to the dripping, leather-clad soldier looming in the doorway, "What is it?"

"Prince Rhys," he announced, "requests your attendance..." With a nudge of his boot, the soldier widened his view of the inside of the hut, and added wryly, "and your companion's at the llys within the hour. Madam..." He bowed and abruptly disappeared.

She groaned inwardly, while repeating, "Within the hour? Marc...Marc." Turning, she gasped, for he stood directly in front of her, cradling his skull. "Did you hear?" she asked.

"Yes...where's Gruffydd gone?"

"I don't know, nor do I know when he left. I don't remember much of anything."

"Nor do I," said Marc. They peered at each other suspiciously, then broke into embarrassed grins.

"Mam! Marc!" called Gruffydd, wandering in by the back door.

His greeting blared at their sensitive ears, making them wince, and chide in unison, "Quiet!"

"I'm sorry," he said. "I've been awake for ages. I tried to wake you, but neither of you would budge."

"What have you been up to?" asked Marc in a strained whisper.

"Feeding my animals. Would you like to meet them?"

"He will in awhile," Gael answered for him. "First we must eat and then go to the llys." She paused, remembering, "Marc...we won't know if it's safe for you to go. Perhaps it would be best if you remained here with Gruffydd."

"Why do you think we've been summoned to the long house?" asked Marc.

"Most likely for a trial."

"Whose?"

"Maura's. After all, she did attack a member of royalty."

"Then I must go and defend her," he asserted.

"I think it likely that the entire village will come to her defense," assured Gael. "They don't much care for Nesta."

"Do you?"

"I pity her more than dislike her," she said, fidgeting with her mussed braid, and smoothing her skirt.

"Mam," cut in Gruffydd, "there's bread laid out, and butter, and some fruit. The ale's all gone."

"I know and thank you, my sweet." She smiled warmly while asking, "I guess you won't mind spending the morning with Marc."

"No, not at all. I'll quite enjoy it!" he said, enthused.

"And Marc, will you mind?"

"I'd be honored to stay with him."

Gael smiled with deep affection.

While eating, Marc let his clearing gaze wander the miniscule, yet cozy cottage. Dozens of expertly whittled beasts decorated the table, corners, and several trunks pushed up against the daub and wattle walls. Other than the trunks, table, and two benches, there was no other furniture, only thick pelts and vibrantly colored pillows strewn over fragrant rushes. Stacked bowls, which Marc reckoned held foodstuffs, topped a handled cauldron, and were stored beneath the table. The central fire, contained within a circular stone hearth, flamed merrily and swirled smoke through a vent in the thatched roof. Dried flowers and herbs hung by string, decorated the rafters. A halved door in the back of the house led to, as far as Marc could see and smell, a stable. Marc fingered a hunk of wood on the table and asked with acclaim, "Who's the carver?"

"I am," replied Gruffydd proudly.

"I'm very impressed," said Marc.

Gael chimed in to brag, "His father owned the same talent and sold his sculptures. Gruffydd won't part with his, unless he decides to give them away, which he does quite often. And what's your talent, Marc?"

"I don't own any," he said with a blush.

"Judging from last evening," she remarked, "I disagree." Marc's expression held a vague unease which Gael quickly cured, "I'm speaking of the beach and the feast...your riding, and your dancing, and storytelling. You excelled at all three and I'm certain you have many more surprises to unveil."

Marc wagged his head. "All I learned, I learned in training."

"Yet last evening before you fell asleep, you told me of all you learned before you went to live with the Montgomerys—" Gael paused to mention, "That's a very familiar name," then she lauded, "You took on reading and writing, mathematics, and the Scriptures all before you were nine years old!"

"As old as me!" spouted Gruffydd.

"And," Marc rallied, "your mother tells me you read quite well, and your script is near perfect."

"Sulien teaches me and my friends," said Gruffydd. "I get help from Simon and Maura, and Mam, you help too."

"Not as much as I'd like to. I was never fortunate to have structured learning. I was married at fourteen, mostly so my father would be rid of me."

"That's hard to believe," said Marc. "Was your marriage political?"

"Yes, Shrewsbury is an English stronghold on the border, and to ensure peace, I was offered and accepted as collateral. Not that I'm complaining. I was glad to get away and my husband was a dear and gentle soul."

"I must have said quite a lot last evening," guessed Marc.

"Not to worry," said Gael. "You didn't say anything too revealing or embarrassing."

"Good," sighed Marc.

"I must go," said Gael, rising and swatting crumbs from her skirt. "Pray for me and Maura and Simon."

As she brushed close to him, he chanced a kiss to her cheek. "For luck," he swiftly excused.

His skin burned red to her quizzical gaze. She touched her fingertips to his brow to check if he was as hot as he appeared. Then with a thoughtful grin, she left him with Gruffydd.

*****

Henry emerged from the bed-chamber, looking drowsy and tumbled. He raked all ten fingers through his hair and glanced about for food and drink and company. Yet he saw only a man sitting at a tall table; he guessed it was Simon, although the length of his hair, hanging near an inch below his collar, still puzzled him. And his beard! He'd never known a bearded Simon. His favorite cousin always did appear a bit misused, but he was normally reasonably trimmed. Henry stepped over Guy, still splayed and sleeping, and called out, "Simon?"

133

Simon turned a buoyant smile to Henry, and greeted, "Good morning, Henry. You slept well and loudly."

Henry simpered back, and asked, "Where's Maura?"

"Tending to the beasts."

"What are you doing?"

"Mixing remedies," said Simon. "I expect to be in the village today, and might as well drop these off."

"Rhys spoke highly of you as physician."

"That was kind of him."

"He seems a kind and just ruler." Henry watched a while, yet quickly grew bored and wondered, "Do you think Maura could use my help?"

Simon looked up surprised, then suggested, "You could ask her."

"I'll do just that," Henry brightly decided, snatching a cloak off Guy. Wrapped tight against a nipping breeze, Henry was pelted on his short jaunt to the stable by multi-colored leaves and frigid rain. He dashed inside the darkened, damp, and pungent structure and squinted all about for Maura. Her silvery voice singing a pleasant tune reached him, and her outline, in shadow, gradually became visible. She sat on a stool beside a huge cow; her back was to Henry, and then he saw that she gazed at him over her shoulder. He was elated to see her smiling and, patting down his hair, he boldly ventured forward. "Maura..." he called, his voice dripping sweetness, "I thought perhaps I could help."

"That's good of you, Henry, but I'm just finishing."

He could barely make out the scrapes on her uniquely, attractive face, highlighted by her abundant freckles; her eyes, large and of the starkest sapphire blue; and her lips, pale red and full. Her hair, the color of flames, was woven in one thick braid which curled round her neck, hugged the rise of her breast, and hung far beyond her thickened waist. Henry had wondered how his body would react when he saw her again in a situation where it was just the two of them, and the state of his cramping belly and the hardening of his favorite body part told him clearly—he still loved her. She grew uncomfortable at his gawking; he noticed her tension and shifted his fascination to the cow. "And who's this?" he questioned, tickling under the bovine's chin.

"Maude..." Maura answered with affection as she rose and patted the animal's rump. "She's a generous soul." She held out the bucket to show it over half full.

Henry nodded appreciatively and frantically searched the room for a topic of conversation. He spied E'dain in one stall, a colt in the next, and a large grey. "Fulk!" he cried out, and rushed to the gelding's side. "How has he behaved?" Henry asked as he stroked the horse's thick neck.

"Not so well in the beginning, especially after the colt was born, but since his gelding—"

"Since his what?!" Henry burst out in horror.

"His gelding," she duly repeated. "For him to continue living with us peaceably it was necessary."

"But...but..."

"But what, Henry?" asked Maura with arched brow.

"No...nothing," he stumbled and wisely switched topics. "Simon told me your grand news and I congratulate you. When's the happy event to occur?"

"A little past Christmas," she answered, grasping up a pail that held a stale odor.

Henry knew he could no longer postpone his apology. He trailed Maura to the pigsty, wringing his hands and fumbling for an alibi, but there was none to find. He watched her toss food scraps, and felt an affinity for the squealing, squirming piglets.

"I'm terribly sorry for the story I told at the Prince's house," he muttered directly. "Can you forgive me?"

She stopped tossing to pronounce, "I may consider it, though first...I have a special request to make of you."

"Of me?" Henry asked, flattered. "Anything you require, my Lady, will be yours."

"Hear me out before you begin making empty promises."

Suddenly, the largest boar stormed the fence, snorting and butting the littler ones away. Maura promptly drubbed him between the ears, and yelled, "Rufus...sit and wait your turn!"

Rufus reeled back on his fat haunches, and Henry exclaimed, "You're astonishing, Maura! He even looks like Rufus. Can I practice a few smites?"

"Later, if and when he's naughty."

"And if *I'm* naughty," Henry smirked and teased, "what will you do to me?"

"Don't chance it, Henry."

He laughed; she eventually chuckled with him, and he thought—*Oh, how I adore this scintillating woman, and won't she someday make a magnificent and fearsome Queen!* "So," he calmed to ask, "what is your special request?"

"I simply ask that when you see Marc, you don't question why he left Normandy."

"Marc is here?!"

"Yes," answered Maura pointedly, flinging the scraps faster. "He's come home to us to stay, and stay he will."

"Is he well?"

"Yes."

"Where is he?" wondered Henry.

"Last evening," she answered, "when we spoke of Gael, we meant Marc."

"There is no Gael?"

"Of course there is. Marc stayed at her hut last night."

Henry gasped and, feigning shock, staggered backward. "Marc stayed the night with a woman?! What wonders I hear!"

"Don't start, Henry," she warned.

He bowed lowly. "Yes, my Lady. Why did he hide from me?"

"He didn't want to, it was Simon's idea. Simon wanted to make certain Marc had nothing to fear from you. Will you do as I ask?"

Henry hung on the fence and spoke his tribute gravely. "Marc served my father well, and deserves an honorable retirement. I don't much care where he chooses to live, though the Montgomerys may."

"Why?" asked Maura, setting the pail of slops aside and wiping her palms on her apron.

"Maura, they own the border northeast of here at Shrewsbury, and may be the cause of the friction on the border of Rhys' domain."

"I know where they reside, Henry," she returned. "And so far they've kept their harassment confined to the area east of Offa's Dyke. So I don't believe they've encroached as far south as Brecknock, which is where the latest insurrections have taken place."

Intimidated by her astute knowledge of the Norman incursion into Wales, Henry floundered, "Oh...I...I see," then hurried to end the subject of which he wasn't as well schooled. "Well, they may still encroach and, if they do, they'll surely recognize Marc."

"If *you* believe his retirement to be honorable, why wouldn't they?"

"Because I suspect from the nebulous way his residing here has been alluded to—"

She held to his arm and insisted, "Henry, stop trying to impress me with your vocabulary taught to you by Simon and please speak plainly."

"Oh hell, what I mean to say is if he's hiding, he must have deserted."

She paused, then pressed guardedly, "And if he did, you don't mind?"

"Not really, and I suppose he did have just cause. I don't much care for my brothers either."

"Well then," she said with a relieved smile, "he can come home, and will you also promise to try to get along with him?"

Henry complained, "I always try, it's Marc who's so damned stubborn...and gloomy. And," he added with a leer, "why would he want to come home to you, when he has a woman to stay the night with?"

"Henry..."

"I'm only jesting, Maura."

Simon appeared unexpectedly and interrupted their smiles with an ominous look and announcement, "We've been summoned to the llys."

Henry tried but failed to mimic the spitted word, then asked, "Called to the what?"

"The long house," said Maura.

*****

One of Henry's guards helped hoist Simon onto Hywel's horse; Maura followed him up and, with Henry and three of his men striding beside, they headed for the llys. Nearing the long house, Henry became pale and pensive, and Simon muttered down to him, "You can end this interrogation very quickly by simply telling Rhys and Nesta the truth. We are depending on you, so don't disappoint us."

Henry's belly's loud griping drowned his mumbled, "I won't." He'd forgotten to eat and, in consequence, felt light-headed and trembly. Perhaps there would be food in this large house, or at least ale to numb his humiliation.

Simon limped behind Maura up the stairs; reaching the top, they stopped and stepped aside so Henry could enter first. Simon's severe expression weakened Henry's knees, yet Maura's bolstering grin garnered his strength. He breathed deeply and swaggered with his men through the door. The hovering smoke made it difficult to see. Squinting enabled Henry to make out four trestle tables arranged in a square around a second fire. He waited for Simon and Maura to join him inside, then together they approached the company already gathered and seated. All save one stood in respect and vacated three chairs. The three sat, Simon doing so slowly, and politely accepted passed cups of mead. Henry swept a curious gaze over the odd group. He recognized Rhys, his expression dark; the veiled young woman next to him with lowered eyes would be his daughter; the two husky bulls nearby he surmised to be Rhys' guards. The slight, pale-haired woman who scooted her seat by Maura's and whispered rapidly must be this Gael. There were about ten more unkempt creatures, male and female, in attendance.

As everyone sat, the Prince stood and grunted in Welsh, "I'm pleased my request for our gathering has been answered so promptly. I hope we can resolve this unfortunate misunderstanding as swiftly."

"Simon!" Henry leant near and whispered in dread, "How can I tell the truth when no one can understand me?"

"Most understand English, Henry."

"Why can't you say it for me?"

"Henry..." Simon strictly answered, then he requested politely to Rhys, "My Prince, may I rise?"

"Certainly."

Simon stood with difficulty, and eloquently began, "Rhys, Nesta, and dear friends— my wife and I have recently come upon information that, we pray, will accomplish Rhys' wish for a speedy resolution. My cousin, Henry, arrived at our cottage last night. Two evening's past he was fortunate to sojourn at Dinefwr, and after amply enjoying your hospitality, Rhys, he sat up late with his man and bragged of a time he spent in Normandy with Maura. Since I wasn't at Dinefwr or with them in Normandy, I will let Henry tell you what truly occurred. I beg of you, Princess, to listen to Henry as intently as you did at Dinefwr."

Simon sat, prodded Henry up, then searched for and found Maura's hand; they squeezed taut their grip as Henry haltingly declared in English, "I'm sorry for the inconvenience I've caused. I lied in my bragging. Though I wished it so, Maura has never been my lover. We were in Normandy on a mission to secure Simon's release from prison. And there, we accomplished our goal, and nothing more. The past evening, at Dinefwr, I imbibed too much of your fine wine, Sir, and—" He looked Nesta's way and glared, "I didn't realize I was being spied upon."

Henry's ponderous accusation rumbled through the group. Simon's wince twisted to a grimace, and Maura stood to restore calm. "I'm certain what the FitzRoy truly means is that he's used to walls separating bedchambers and didn't realize his gloating would travel so far." She directed her last words in biting French, "Isn't that correct, Henry."

Her harshness stung, and he lurched up to mumble, "Yes, that is exactly what I meant to say."

Content with the FitzRoy's testimony, Rhys shifted his doubt to Maura. "Why did you strike my daughter, Maura?"

All sitting straightened as a thick silence descended. Maura dropped her eyes to Simon's, received his confidence, then raised them boldly to Rhys. "I...I saw Simon struggling with Nesta. He had already suffered from two of her blows, and I knew he wouldn't hurt her. I was only trying to get her away from him. I suppose she thought *I* aimed to hurt her and she swung at me and scratched my cheek. The way she acted next made me believe she might hurt someone else, so I decided it was best to stop her— which I did as best I could."

"Nesta," grunted Rhys, "stand."

She did so, her fearful gaze penetrating the tabletop.

"Why did you hit Simon?"

A shudder took her, and she whimpered so no one could hear, "He slandered me."

"Speak up, child. Why did you strike him?"

"He slandered me! Called me a whore!"

"No, my Prince!" burst out Hywel, standing and striking the table. "Tis not true. I heard it all." He thrust a rigid finger at Nesta and accused, "It was *she* who slandered, *she* who called Maura a whore, and claimed you intended to end their marriage and marry her to Simon. She forced her affections on him. He had to push her away, but never did he slander her, never did he hurt her!"

Maura and Simon exchanged incredulous looks, then both gifted Hywel with grateful nods. Hywel sat, as did Maura. And when Nesta lifted her eyes, madness had replaced the fear. Her nails dug in the edge of the table as she raved, "I tried to kiss him because I believed he wanted to be kissed, for when past we met, he's always wanted to be kissed, and much more! He acts so innocent, so good, but, in truth, when he doctors me, he doesn't use herbs, he uses—"

Gael leapt up and loudly expressed, "Each time Simon has doctored Nesta, Maura has been with them! And knowing Maura as I do, I don't think she'd allow such doings to go on in her presence."

A few chuckles followed, then hushed as Nesta shrilly countered, "Last time he came without her!"

"That's true," agreed Rhys.

"And *I* saw you instead," hurled Gael.

"After he saw me!"

137

"You lie!"

"Gael," berated Rhys, "sit till you can speak civilly."

Gael snidely returned, "Some of us, my Prince, do not own a civil tongue."

"Bitch!" shrieked Nesta.

"Quiet, both of you!" commanded Rhys. "And I'll not warn again!" He paused for composure, then stridently directed, "Simon, rise." He did, and swept back his hair to look soundly upon the Prince and Princess. Rhys cleared his throat and said with a hint of regret, "We have allowed you and your sweet wife to reside here freely and without reproach, yet if you are judged guilty of committing the critical offenses of abusing my generosity and my daughter's affections, I'm afraid punitive measures will need to be taken. Hold that in mind when you answer these next questions. Have you had illicit intercourse with my daughter?"

Simon knew either possible answer would likely crucify him, still the truth was sacred to him, and to Maura, and their future, so he justly answered, "No."

"Have you intimated to her in any way that you desired her?"

"No."

"Did you visit her alone when last you came to Dinefwr?"

"No."

"Did she, last evening, force herself upon you, strike you, and call your wife a whore?"

Simon's steadiness faltered; he closed his eyes, hung his head, and sighed, "Yes."

Gael again rose with the comment, "I find Nesta's testimony confusing, my Prince, for when I met with her not one week past, she inferred that she'd not yet known any man, *intimately*. So if she has coupled with Simon, it's happened only in her dreams."

Nesta heaved contempt at Gael's breech of confidence, crushed her palms together, and spat furious curses beneath her breath.

Rhys replied with reserve, "Though I'm hesitant to resort to extremes, there is a way to confirm if in fact she has known any man...intimately. Nesta, you'll come with me to the cathedral's infirmary and we will discover if you are still—intact."

"No!" Nesta wailed. "They lie, they all lie! Father, believe me...I'd never deceive you. Please, no!"

"You'll come now or denounce your testimony!"

She gathered herself tall and glared at him in smug refusal. In response, Rhys grimly announced to the stunned crowd, "Everyone present will gather here again at midday, when I'll present my final judgment on this sordid matter." Rhys left the table, tugging his daughter behind him. She struggled little and, before disappearing out the door, cast Simon an ominously smug grin.

*****

CHAPTER NINE - LUCKLESS LIAISONS

Maura partly listened to her friends' grumblings as she sat in a shadowed corner of Gael's cottage. She felt drained of everything but worry and intense sympathy for her husband, who sat by her, hunched over with his palm supporting his skull. She wondered if he even heard Gael and Henry, who paced opposite ends of the room, seemingly oblivious to each other.

"That hateful bitch!" raved Gael in English. "She's bluffing. She has to be! No one would willingly undergo that sort of humiliation. Or maybe it's Rhys who's bluffing, one of them must be..."

"How dare those heathens doubt you!" Henry simultaneously railed in French. "I'll have my guards round up the whole stinking lot of them, and thrash the skin off their backs!"

"And Nesta," Gael growled on, "I wouldn't be at all amazed if she'd purposely rutted with one of her father's addle-brained, bug-infested drones so she could have the physical evidence to snare you, Simon!"

"I'd personally attend to the little whore's punishment," flourished Henry, rubbing his palms together in anticipation, "and take great delight in demonstrating what special torture is allotted spies and slanderers!"

Suddenly, Simon stood and reached for Maura; she scrambled up, took a firm hold of his hand, and hurried with him out the door. He broke from her grip, and turned back only his face. His eyes invited her to chase. She beamed and dashed off after him, down the main lane that wove between the cottages and past the cathedral. The road then shrank to a narrow furrow that cut across an emerald plateau to the sea. Maura stopped for breath and listened to the pounding of her heart as she watched Simon sprint toward the cliff, his cloak and hair whipped by a brusque wind. He seemed one with the oddly marked birds who sailed on wispy currents overhead. The sun's rays flickered through bleak, low-hanging clouds, sparkling patches of ground and the last blooms of summer carpeting Maura's way. She knew where he was headed and followed him over the plateau to the cliff's ledge. A well-trod path squeezed and crisscrossed its way between steep, viciously sharp rocks and ended only feet from where sea and coast savagely met. Salty sea spray rained over Maura, stirring her senses and desire for him. She turned and scrambled over biting rocks to where he stood, his arms opened wide in need. He pulled her into a hidden cove offering sanctuary from the ravages of princesses, and in their mossy hollow, they crushed bodies and lips and dropped to their knees upon his blanketing cloak. His fingers caught, tugged and tore at her braid, finally breaking its binding, and tumbling her hair down over his face and neck. They gasped frantic kisses and desperately groped and squirmed beneath layers of wool and linen. And when at last their bodies met, he groaned into her his frustration, his rage, his love. She caught his fury and their coupling rivaled the madness of the waves, pounding the rocks not feet away.

*****

"Where've they gone to?" asked Gael with a hint of alarm.

"I pray back to Normandy where civilized folk abide!" replied Henry.

"Please speak English!" she insisted.

"Was I speaking French?" he wondered tamely. "I hadn't noticed. I said I hope they've gone back to Normandy." He extended his hand. "I'm Henry, Simon and Maura's cousin."

"I figured so," answered Gael, politely extending her hand.

139

"And can I assume you to be...Gael?" asked he.

She nodded and swiftly removed her hand from under his lips. He looked muddled as she hugged herself, chafed her upper arms, and gazed worriedly out the lone window cut into the front wall of her home. "I hope they don't stray far," she said, tucking escaped wisps of hair under her circlet. "We're due back to the llys soon."

"This is your home?" asked Henry, gazing idly about.

"Yes."

"And do you reside here alone?'

"No, my son lives with me...Gruffydd. He's nine years old."

"I've heard him mentioned. Where is he now?"

"He's probably out somewhere with—" Gael caught herself, realizing she still didn't know whether it was safe to speak of Marc. "He's staying the day with a friend."

"A friend called Marc," Henry deduced with a wry grin.

"So they've told you?"

"Yes."

"And what do you plan to do to him?" Gael challenged.

"Do *to* him?" he repeated, then flatly answered, "Nothing."

"Last evening, he was fairly convinced you would arrest him."

"Marc tends to overdramatize trivial matters," explained Henry, "particularly when striving to lure the sympathies of a lovely woman. And did he lure yours?"

"Marc doesn't seem in the least bit—overdramatic," contested Gael. "On the contrary, other than his sister, he is the most candid person I've ever met."

"So he did lure your sympathy," Henry discerned glibly. He glanced toward the table strewn with breakfast scraps and asked, "May I?"

Gael shrugged in assent, hugged herself tighter, and continued her vigil from the window. Something about the FitzRoy irked her, something insidious. His guise was too polished, too polite, too pretty. He was indeed darkly handsome; his features, hands, and stature were delicate, but she sensed they masked a rigid harshness that might attack with little provocation.

As Henry ate he stared vigorously at Gael and smiled when he noticed her shift with discomfort. She was contemplating him, but contemplating what? He didn't know how long he'd have to remain in this boorish little town; he'd relish a bit of fun, and Gael looked like fun. Of course, his main goal was to convince Simon and Maura to return with him to Normandy. In order to achieve successful seditious acts against his brothers, he would need Simon's shrewd mind, and to distract him from his many troubles he would need Maura's fine body. Perhaps while here, the Lady Gael would be willing to enjoy his salacious company...Yet what about—Marc? There could be no serious competition there, for Marc was a pathetic joke, and now a freely confessed coward and traitor. Henry looked down to butter some bread and compose an entrancing quip, yet when he next looked up, Gael was gone.

*****

The calming effect of their frantic union was telling as Maura lightly stroked Simon's cheek and commented, "Your color's come back."

"With your help, how could it not?" praised Simon. He lifted his head from her supporting arm, and took a difficult while to sit. She followed him up, wrapped his cloak round them both, and leant close to him against the moss cushioned rock wall. He nestled his head on her shoulder, grasped her hand and, watching sea spray sneak its way into their hideaway, whispered, "Why is she doing this, Maura? We were never mean to her."

"Perhaps that's the problem," she considered with a bitter sigh. "She mistook your kindness for love. I'm hoping Gael is correct, and that they are both bluffing. Nesta will recant her charge, and all will be forgotten."

"No...not forgotten!" he blurted angrily. "I will never go near that woman again...ever!"

"If she truly needs your care, you will."

Simon didn't argue with what he knew to be true, and moved on to his next worry. "What if Gael's also correct in her assumption that Nesta found someone willing to provide her with physical evidence?"

"I believe Nesta's far too selective to stoop to that wile."

"Then I pray you're correct," he answered, then gradually realized, "We must return soon and discover what's to become of us. I'm so sorry, my love," he added with deep compassion. "I wanted so much to keep you safe...Now our home's been overtaken by a Norman garrison, I've been reviled as a lecherous liar, you've been attacked by a misguided child—"

"And..." she interrupted with a caress and small smile, "we will get our home back, you will be absolved, and Nesta and my scrapes will go away. We are safest here."

"How can you have such hope?" he marveled.

"One of us has to," she plainly replied.

*****

"I need to get down," said Marc to Gruffydd, as they rode together on a smallish, plump white mare along the path that hugged the cliffs. "I'm feeling dizzy." He slipped to the ground and took up the reins to guide the poky pony slightly inland. "That's better," he sighed. "Now I'm not looking straight down. Doesn't it bother you?"

"Oh no," replied Gruffydd. "I rather like it. Later, if you like, I'll show you a way to climb down."

"Climb down to what?" Marc asked skittishly, chancing a swift glimpse over the precipice. He saw nothing but a sheer wall and breaking waves.

"There are caves down there. Mam says smugglers hide stolen treasures in the holes. Me and my friends go down often to search. Once we found three gold coins!"

"I'm not good with heights, Gruffydd."

"My mam isn't either," said the boy. "You'd think she would be, with as long as she's lived here."

"Well, I thank you for the tour," acknowledged Marc. "Never have I visited anywhere as grand as here." He pulled his cloak tighter round his shoulders and, glancing above, noticed, "The clouds are darkening. Perhaps we should be getting back. I'm anxious to hear about Simon and Maura."

Gruffydd nodded and pointed Marc directly east. As they sauntered away from the sea, Gruffydd prodded excitedly, "You promised to tell me of Simon and Will's joust."

"Yes, I did." Marc snorted a laugh in remembrance and began, "I believe it was near the end of March when Simon arrived in Normandy to ask the King's permission to wed Maura, and King William sent us, together with Henry—"

Gruffydd intruded, "The *Henry* Simon spoke of last evening?"

"Yes...I suspect you'll meet him later today. The three of us were sent to spy on the King's eldest son, Curthose."

"Why?"

"He and his father didn't get along, and Curthose regularly sabotaged his father's battle plans."

Gruffydd twisted his face to ask, "Sabotaged?"

"Ruined," explained Marc.

"Oh, I see...go on."

141

"When we arrived at Curthose's castle, we found a melee in progress and watched awhile. Simon overheard his half-brother Will boast to his lady how he would be next to fight."

"Was Will there with you?"

"Oh no. Will was sitting on a raised platform that is especially constructed for members of the royal family. He was visiting his cousin, Curthose. Simon suddenly left us and at first we didn't know why. When next we saw Will ride out on the field behind him came a mystery knight, his identity hidden by his helmet and hauberk."

Marc wasn't surprised to hear, "What's a hauberk?"

"It's a shirt of chain-mail armor that's worn like a tunic." Gruffydd's look didn't betray further bafflement, so Marc told on, "Henry recognized Simon as the knight and was ecstatic, but I grew frightened that Simon would kill Will. He hates his brother. Have you ever seen a melee?"

"No, but I'd love to! Tell me all about it."

"Two armored, shielded, and mounted knights position themselves at opposite ends of a field and charge at each other with long lances. They attempt to knock each other off their horses, then fight further on the ground till one is downed. Simon promptly knocked Will from his saddle. Will stayed flat on the dirt, and Simon dismounted to leave. But Curthose was upset, I suspect because the melee had ended so quickly. He set his guards on Simon, and while Simon fought them, Will attacked his back. We warned Simon in time to turn, but Will managed a cut to his neck that dropped him to the ground. The guards aimed to kill Simon, then Henry threw himself between Simon and the guards."

Gruffydd jabbed Marc's shoulder and eagerly requested, "Would you stop walking and only talk now."

Marc obliged and smiled at the boy's round-eyed expression. He leant up against the pony's soft hide, and continued, hiking his voice in suspense. "Seeing his brother in danger made Curthose halt the games—"

"Is Simon his brother as well?" asked Gruffydd.

"No...I'm sorry...Henry is Curthose's youngest brother."

"What sort of a name is Curthose?"

"His true name is Robert...but there are so many Robert's in the Kingdom that he was given the nickname Curthose. He's not very tall and wears short hose. Curthose is French for short hose."

Gruffydd beamed proudly, "So I can speak some French!"

"I guess you can, and if you teach me some Welsh, I'll teach you more."

"That sounds fair. Now tell me more about the fight."

"Where was I?"

"Curthose stopped the games."

"Oh yes...Henry begged his brother to let the fight continue without the guards. Curthose agreed, and Simon and Will began again, this time on their feet. It took but a few swipes for Simon to down Will, and before he left the field, Simon plunged his sword through the material of Will's pants, just missing his skin, and stuck him fast to the ground." Gruffydd started to chortle at the image, and Marc laughed with him as he finished, "Simon left the field victorious, and Will was pelted and buried in garbage, which is fitting."

"Did Will know it was Simon?" asked Gruffydd.

"No, not when it happened."

"Do you know this Will?"

"Yes...though luckily not well."

They had almost reached the cathedral when the rain began again to trickle down. They both lifted the hoods on their cloaks, and the protective touch of the cloth emboldened Gruffydd to ask, "Marc, were you sad to leave your family when you were eight?"

Marc gazed gently on the boy. "Very sad."

"What did you do?"

"I cried," Marc answered easily. "My adopted mother Edith is as sweet as your mam, and I had to leave Maura and Simon."

"Simon was still at home?"

"Yes."

"But I thought him older than you."

"He is by six years. He wasn't sent away because he had more learning to do in order to become a priest."

Gruffydd gasped in disbelief, "Simon, a priest! Simon's not like a priest. He's funny and all. Not like a priest!"

"That's what his father wanted him to become. He soon realized though that Simon owned the skills of a warrior as well. So he was sent to train with his uncle, Bishop Odo, who is both Bishop and warrior, so he would receive the proper training for either fate."

"I'm confused, Marc," confessed Gruffydd.

"You needn't be. In the end, Simon didn't become a knight *or* a priest, not that he didn't deserve those honors and more...He's smarter than any priest I know, and his military talents are unchallenged."

"Do you mean he's good?"

"The best I know."

"That's funny," said Gruffydd. "The only military talents I've seen at their hut are when Maura helps me with my arrow shooting."

"She's very good as well."

"Yes, she is..." Gruffydd paused, then with bowed head confessed, "I'll be sad too, when I have to leave."

"And when will that be?"

"When I reach fifteen, I'll go to live with Prince Rhys, and train with his sons and soldiers."

Now Marc was the puzzled one. "Won't you someday become Chieftain to this village?"

"Mam says it's my right, whatever that means, but I still need to learn to fight. The word for chieftain in Welsh is pennaeth."

"Thank you Gruffydd...*pen nithe*. I didn't mind the learning part," Marc admitted. "It was rather exciting." He didn't wish to upset the boy with gruesome tales of true battles, so he brightly changed the topic, "When we get back, I'll tell you some tales of Simon, Maura, and me when we were younger and living together at Dunheved. Would you like that?"

"Oh yes! Marc, did you like staying at our hut last evening?"

"Yes, very much so."

"Will you stay again?" hoped the boy.

"I suppose that depends on your mam."

"I'll ask her then."

Marc didn't know whether or not to argue the point and, thinking how pleased he was to have Gruffydd's tacit approval, he happily tugged the pony quicker along the wetted path. And his smile widened at the sight of Gael, shrouded in a black cloak, scuttling their way. When she reached them, she asked, distressed, "Have you seen Simon and Maura?"

"No..." worried Marc. "Didn't they come to the llys this morning?"

"Yes...but Rhys postponed the trial till midday. I'm on my way back to the llys, as they should be."

"What happened this morning?"

"It's not good, Marc."

"Then I'll come with you," he urgently offered.

"I don't want Gruffydd there," she objected. "He's not old enough to understand some of the accusations, and I'm not ready to explain them to him. So, please, can you stay with him awhile longer? If the trial lasts more than an hour, I'll return home and send you in my place."

Marc's fingertips touched hers, and he watched concerned as she reached up to hug, kiss, and ask her son to behave.

Gael hastened toward the llys. On her way, she glared at her feet, muttering hatefully and, reaching the steps, vaulted them two at a time. Someone blocked her way and his boots were horribly familiar. She stuck her heated face in Owain's and muttered louder, "Aren't you a bit late?"

Owain didn't bother responding and stepped back for her to enter. She did and continued to harangue, "You were there! You saw what happened! You could have helped Maura and Simon, and your word weighs heavily with the Prince. Why didn't you come this morning?!"

"They don't need my help," he snarled.

"They need everyone's help!"

He wondered why her drama, but, then again, the Lady Gael was not known for subtlety. Her disgust instantly switched to gladness as she turned and noticed her spoken need had been amply answered. It appeared the entire commote had packed themselves into the llys, and she knew with whom their allegiance lay. She rushed into the crux of the throng to gush her thanks, and Owain slipped away out the door. He found dry shelter under a tree, and waited impatiently for the Prince and his daughter.

Simon noticed Owain and stopped short before passing through the gate. Maura searched for the cause of his hesitancy and also spied Owain, crouched in wait and glaring. She parted from Simon's grip, and boldly ventured forward. Squatting to his level, she presented her hand and said, "You'll get dreadfully wet if you stay out here longer. We'd like you to come inside and tell all what you saw the other evening. We've given our evidence, and we beg to hear yours."

"And does your husband share your request?" asked Owain narrowly.

"Of course he does."

"Then I'll hear it from him."

"Then stand and ask him—and not as his enemy."

Owain haltingly accepted her challenge. He stood and ducked from his refuge. Two broad strides brought the men nose to nose.

Simon spoke first and swiftly, "I'm grateful for your order to spare my life."

"What I ordered," scorned Owain, "I did only with the Prince's welfare in mind."

"I don't care why you did it, I'm only glad you did!" returned Simon as snidely. "Have you told Rhys what you saw happen at the feast?"

It hurt to admit, so Owain answered evasively, "I...told him...Yes, I told him what I saw."

"What did you say to him, man?!"

"Don't you yell at me! I'm not the cause of your dirty little problem!"

"How do I know that?! Perhaps you rehearsed Nesta's attack with her before you two came into the long house."

Owain responded with a murderous look and retorted, "And you were a damn fool to let her maul you! If you didn't want her, why didn't you shove her away?"

"I did!"

"Far too late!"

Maura loudly interceded, "Stop it! Both of you!" She shook with rage, and directed it at Owain. "We're not asking you for acceptance, for that we know we will never receive. We are asking you to be a viable witness and say exactly what you saw, not what you think was being said or implied. Can't you set aside your cursed pride long enough to put an end to this madness? And Simon...why are you trying so hard to alienate your defender?!" Neither man answered as they both dropped guilty expressions to the sopping ground. "Now I'm tired of standing in this blasted rain," she added, stomping up the stairs. On the top one she turned and more gently urged, "Won't you two come in with me?"

They collided in their rush to follow her. Simon stood aside and flagrantly waved his arm for Owain to precede him; Owain stepped back and crossed his arms in refusal. So Simon threw up his hands and hurried in behind Maura. Owain trudged up the stairs a ways after him. Once inside, he found his darkened spot beside the mead keg and slumped in a huff to the rushes.

*****

Henry heard voices coming from the rear of the property. He shut the trunk he was rummaging through, briskly stood, and swatted at rushes clinging to his clothes. "Gael?" he called out in an inviting tone. It was Marc who opened the halved door to the stable. In disappointment, Henry ran his hand over his beard, then folded his arms to his chest, and stiffly greeted, "Marc."

Marc glared at his unexpected visitor and his response sneered contempt, "Henry...have you come to take me?"

"I wouldn't want to take you anywhere, you're too damned morose!" scourged Henry. "I was waiting for Gael to return. We're due back at the long house."

"And that's where she's gone," said Marc.

"Without me?"

"Seems so."

"Well they didn't need me anyway." Henry peered critically at Marc. "You look...different."

"And you look exactly the same. Did Simon tell you why I came here?"

"No, Maura did."

"And?"

"I don't care what you've done or what you plan to do," sniped Henry. "Besides I have no power to arrest you. Father snubbed me in favor of those grubs he called sons."

"Rufus rules?" dreaded Marc.

"Only England."

"Then Curthose is Duke?"

"Yes..." Henry sat and heaved a bitter sigh.

"That means war," said Marc, holding to his rigid stance.

"Yes, an abundance of it I suppose," remarked Henry dryly, as he foraged for more food. "You were wise to get away when you did."

"And who gets your allegiance?" asked Marc, askance.

"I haven't rightly decided. I did get some money from Father, and I plan to purchase property and titles on both sides of the sea. Situate myself, so to speak, to have an advantage no matter who succeeds. You'll stay here?"

"If I'm able."

"Well, you're smart to take up with the wife of a Chieftain," noted Henry, munching on a piece of withered apple. "She can wield great influence on your behalf, granted your performance is worthy of her effort."

"I haven't *taken up* with anyone," answered Marc with spite.

Henry snorted, "Yet..."

"Besides she's no longer wife to the Chieftain," said Marc. "He died near a year past."

"Yet I've heard she's to marry the new one."

Marc tried unsuccessfully to hide his dismay; his command faltered as he sputtered, "Wha...what?"

"Simon and Maura told me Gael is expected to marry the new Chieftain, when he is appointed."

"You lie."

"Why would I lie about such insignificant drivel—"

"Because you always lie!" rumbled Marc, puffing up, and lurching a foot closer.

"Now, Marc," Henry appealed, his palms raised and fingers spread in defense, "calm yourself! Enjoy her while you can. She's a pretty thing, and from what I could surmise from my time with her, she's frisky as well."

"I think you'd better leave," cautioned Marc.

Stupidly, Henry didn't heed Marc's advice, and taunted instead, "Would you care to compete for her hand and, I dare say, the rest of her as well? I'll gladly accept the challenge, for I'm certain to win...I always do when the trophy is a woman."

Marc surged another intimidating step forward and snarled, "Get out!"

Henry stood abruptly and surrendered. "I'll go...but first, I have a warning for you. The Montgomerys live north of here on the border. I'd take care not to stray too close."

Gruffydd wandered in from the stable, immediately sensed the simmering strife between Marc and the stranger, and hid behind Marc's back. Henry grinned awkwardly and his unease was blatant as he stated, "You can come out, I don't bite."

Gruffydd poked out his head and asked forthrightly, "Who are you?"

"I'm Henry, and who are you?"

Gruffydd ignored Henry's question and asked in awe, "You are the Prince?"

"Used to be. You must be Gael's son...Grif—"

"Gruffydd."

Henry acknowledged the boy with a tilt of his head and an offered hand. Marc watched suspiciously as the boy gingerly approached, gave Henry's hand a quick squeeze, then retreated. *What an astute judge of character Gruffydd is*, Marc thought proudly.

Children bothered Henry; he couldn't speak freely in their presence, and none of them seemed to appreciate him. He really had to be getting back to the trial, and made his apologies, "I'll leave you two to whatever. I hope to visit you, Gruffydd, again very soon and, of course, your lovely mother as well. Marc..."

Marc sighed bitterly as Henry left, and Gruffydd complained, "How does he know my mam is lovely?"

"He saw her at the trial."

"Oh...I don't know if I want him to visit me, or my mam."

"Don't let Henry bother you, Gruffydd, no one should let Henry bother them. He's easily distracted."

"What?"

Marc shrugged and muttered, "Nothing...Didn't I promise you a meal and a tale?"

"Yes you did. I'll help with the food."

Marc wrapped his arm round Gruffydd's shoulders and gently firmed his grip. And to Marc's elation, Gruffydd beamed a radiant smile.

*****

In the llys, the waiting proved interminable. The room grew unbearably stifling; all swabbed at sweat, shifted with discontent, and grumbled what could possibly be taking so long.

What took so long was being staged concurrently in a private cell at the cathedral. Prince Rhys and his daughter sat on opposite stools. She stared down at her damp and writhing hands and her shoulders shook from hearty sobs. Rhys, his brow deeply furrowed, lay a comforting touch on her shoulder and begged, "Why did you lie to me, to everyone?"

"I love him, Father!" Nesta assailed.

"No you don't. And now I'm certain he hates you."

"No!" she wailed. "He loves me! I know he does. He would have married me, taken me away!"

"He doesn't now and never has loved you," Rhys adamantly countered, taking back his hand. "Simon was kind to you and that's all. He loves his wife." Wounded, he wondered, "And why would you want to be taken from me?"

"Not from you...I...I...What will you do to punish me?" she asked in a strangled whimper.

"I haven't yet decided. I may send you to your mother."

"No!" Her dire plea toppled her from the stool and to her knees. She gripped his hands and pressed her cheek to his palms, wetting them. "No...she...she..."

He urged her up and upon his knee, and despaired, "What is it, my sweetness?"

"She chopped off my hair, she makes me wear these robes...She beats me, calls me a whore! How can I be a whore if I know nothing of men?"

Rhys grew woozy and stuttered in shock, "What! Why didn't you say?!"

Nesta wagged her head and crumpled into hysterics, making her stuttering almost incomprehensible, "She...she said if I did say, she...she'd lock me away in...in a nunnery and never let me see you again. I love you, Father! Don't let her steal me away, please! I'll be good, I swear, I'll never try to get near another man till I'm wed, but please, *please* let me stay with you!"

He hugged her fast to his chest and frantically vowed, "She won't ever hurt you again, no one will. But you must promise never to lie to me!"

In his adoring hold, her tears began to subside. "I won't," she sniffled, "I promise I won't."

"And Simon will not treat you again...I doubt if I could persuade him to after what's happened. I pray he will still agree to tend me! You will apologize to him and to Maura. What you did to her was reprehensible. I doubt they will forgive you."

"But," she strenuously whined, "do I have *your* forgiveness?"

He paused a troubled moment, then blubbered, "Yes, my sweetness, you do as always. I love you and would die if you were taken from me."

She pleaded, "You won't tell Mother what's happened?"

"No, she needn't know. And she will never be with you alone again!"

"Bless you, Father...bless you!" She planted many tidy kisses over his fleshy face, and pertly decided, "I won't return with you to the llys, it would be too painful for me to admit my confusion before the entire commote. Yet I plan to travel to Simon and Maura's hut to present my apology in person."

"Take a guard along," Rhys urged.

"I will, but not Owain. And if you please, I'd like to speak to Gael alone, before I leave for Dinefwr."

147

"I see no problem," he consented.

"I want to encourage her to come live with us," she added with a beguiling wink.

Her father smiled broadly in gratitude, then patted, and kissed her cheek.

*****

All chatter promptly hushed as Rhys entered the llys—alone. Owain scrambled up and nodded his greeting; Rhys responded in kind. A path parted, and the Prince sheepishly lumbered his way to the tables. He sat in his chair, straightened his shoulders and hair, and dusted rain from his fur cloak.

"My Prince..." Simon stood and austerely asked, "Where is your daughter?"

"Recuperating," replied Rhys. "Not from the ordeal I threatened this morning. As I'd believed, we didn't need to resort to such a distasteful inquisition. Nesta freely confessed her deceit before we'd even reached the cathedral. I am pleased to report, Simon, you are wholly vindicated. Nesta is far too shaken by her improprieties to attend. You and your sweet wife will receive a formal apology from her by this evening. You receive mine now and I pray nothing more needs to be said of this lurid matter. So please all of you go home...I will meet with you all in a group before I return to Dinefwr, and I'm certain Simon and Maura greatly appreciate your loyalty and patience. Simon, Maura, and Gael, would you please remain with me awhile longer?"

When the last villager had filed out, Rhys pondered the three weary souls sitting near him at the table. It appeared relief had rendered them speechless, so he helped turn their thoughts to words, "Simon, you must have some comment on—"

"Why did she do it?!" Simon hotly demanded.

"It would take forever to explain."

"I have the time!"

Rhys ruffled slightly, then declared, "I won't say, not now—and not here, it's too intimate."

"And what assurance can you give that it won't happen again?"

"You won't see her again," Rhys simply resolved.

"That didn't work last time I visited!"

"Please, Simon...I sincerely apologize for her and for myself. I doubted her charges, yet she is my child and I had to be certain before condemning her. Surely, one day you will know of what I speak. Maura, I pray she didn't cause you too much pain."

Maura woefully wagged her head, and Gael stood to complain, "I've been away from Gruffydd all day. I really must return home."

"Before you go," said Rhys. "I want to try mending our rift by inviting the three of you here for supper."

"Not tonight, Rhys," Gael readily replied. "I, for one, can't take any more excitement."

"Then choose a better day."

Simon and Maura looked none too pleased with the prospect, so Gael decided for them all, "We'll make it the first of October and celebrate Simon's birthday."

"My, what a marvelous thought!" exclaimed Rhys, trying desperately to improve the doleful situation. "Do you two agree?"

Simon and Maura each looked to the other for an answer; not finding one, they both shrugged.

"Fine!" Rhys elated. "I'll have only members of my elite force attend...and of course Sulien and his sweet lady, and I hear you two have a family member visiting, whom I'm most eager to meet."

"Henry?" asked Simon, fuddled. "I thought you met him."

"No, Maura's brother. Sulien speaks highly of him. Will he agree to come?"

"Perhaps," answered Maura.

148

"And bring your cocky cousin as well. He was marvelous fun at Dinefwr. Then it's settled...In five days' time, we'll gather here at dusk to celebrate—"

"Where will Nesta be?" interjected Gael.

"Back at Dinefwr."

"Good...Please keep her there!"

"I will strive to. Before she leaves, Gael," mentioned Rhys with caution, "she wishes an audience with you."

"Why me?" griped Gael.

"Because she likes you."

"She doesn't act that way," Gael bristled, then curtly submitted, "Send her to my cottage later this evening."

Rhys' twittered reply, "As your Ladyship wishes," hiked Gael's misgivings, as did his grasp of her waist, and chuckled suggestion to Simon and Maura, "Wait for her outside. I'll keep her only a short while."

"Rhys, not now!" asserted Gael, wiggling to disengage from his roaming grope.

"May I come to your cottage as well?" he laughed and tried to kiss her.

"No..." She struggled harder, and had to yell, "Rhys let me go! I'm tired and worried about Gruffydd!"

Rhys released her with a pout, and begged, "At least tell me you've thought on my request."

"I haven't thought on much else."

"Good." His silliness returned as he burbled, "And when will I have my answer?"

"I can't say." His pout came back, which she instantly eased with the enticement, "Perhaps I'll say at the supper. And now, I bid you good-day, my Prince." She curtsied, then darted off, leaving him blushing with lustful anticipation. When Gael emerged from the llys, she was relieved to find the sun had returned and there was no sign of Owain, however another oddity piqued her attention—Simon and Maura and Nesta were crowded together in the cathedral's garden. Her wrath thrust Gael down the steps and toward the threesome, then she stopped and thought better of interfering. *Perhaps*, she prayed, *this meeting will put an end to the debacle.* Thinking further, she heaved a disgruntled sigh, knowing full well it wouldn't, for hadn't she just agreed to an audience with the infuriating Princess this very evening? Gael sulked her way from the yard and down the lane leading to her hut. She raised her weary eyes, and observed with annoyance that Henry strutted her way. Not eager for his bother, she hastened by him, and cringed to his snickered response.

Maura stood a few feet away, watching the curious and uncomfortable exchange between her husband and Nesta. Nesta stared at her feet, her hands clasped at her back, and she constantly swayed to and fro, causing Simon to feel nauseous. "I'm sorry for what I did, and said," mumbled Nesta. "Father says you're not to tend to me if I'm ill."

"I've never seen you ill!" grouched Simon to the top of her head. "If you're in true need of my care, I will agree to tend you...but never alone!"

His astounding response lifted her eyes to his, then warily they moved to Maura. Nesta showed no emotion in look or speech as she pronounced, "And I ask your forgiveness as well, Maura."

Maura didn't immediately answer her. To Simon she whispered, "Go fetch Henry. I have a final word for the Princess." Her hand brushed across his back as she urged him away and, once she was certain he could not hear, she willfully gritted, "I feel a need to advise you, Princess, that I won't hesitate to use whatever means necessary to protect my family from any danger, including yourself. And I pray, as should you, that we never meet again."

Nesta visibly shrank to Maura's frankness and the handful of posies she had plucked tumbled in pieces from her grasp. She threw away their stems, whirled, and dashed away to the llys. Maura was convinced, as she placed a loving hand on her belly, that Nesta was headed there to tattle and harp to Rhys. She shook her head at the unfairness of it all, and followed Simon, who'd been joined by Henry, home.

*****

Before entering her hut, Gael smiled contentedly as she secretly listened to Marc's tale from outside the window. "We discovered a burnt-out Saxon fort near Dunheved," he told Gruffydd, "and spent our entire free time there, defending ourselves against make-believe conquerors, dragons and sometimes real intruders. Sometimes, Maura and Simon would let me play baron, but mostly I was a guard, or serf, or baby. Still, it was marvelous fun." Her abrupt entrance drove Marc and Gruffydd to their feet, and Marc asked with bated expression, "What's happened?"

"It's over, and Simon and Maura have been found innocent." Gael added with a relieved smile, "I'd like you to stay longer, though I know you'll be wanting to hear all the details from them." She offered her hand. "I do thank you for watching over Gruffydd."

"He tells the best stories, Mam!" touted Gruffydd. "Almost as good as the bard's."

"And I'm certain I'll hear them all."

Marc pressed her hand between his own and asked with a pinched expression, "Did Henry find you?"

"I didn't let him."

His face lit to her knowing smile, and he babbled, "I...I should go."

"We would love to borrow you again soon," said Gael. "And I suspect the cottage will seem a bit cramped with Henry's entourage sprawled everywhere. How long does he plan to stay?"

"Not long, I hope."

"Will you visit us?"

"Yes, gladly."

"Good." Nothing more needed to be said as Marc released her hand, ruffled his fingers through Gruffydd's hair, and departed for home.

*****

As Simon, Maura, and Henry entered the cottage, Henry's guards scrambled up to attention, and John swiftly rose, slamming shut a book he was reading. Simon glanced surreptitiously between John's fingers and recognized his prescribing volume. But Maura noted John's disquiet and saw not far from the book a stack of her letters. They were still bound, yet she still felt a creeping uneasiness. Simon had told her of John's former career and home, and merely the mention of Bayeux and Odo had sent her heart racing. The pup's shrill greeting distracted her, and also the drudging prospect of cooking for this hungry horde. She was totally exhausted, and taking Simon's hand, she urged him into the sleeping chamber. "Simon," she whispered with remorse as he shut the door behind them. "I don't know if I can feed and entertain our visitors this night. I—"

He embraced her and she felt his shoulders shake. Concerned, she drew back, then beamed to his chuckling. "It's over!" he gushed. "Another catastrophe's been averted, and thank the Lord, our luck triumphed!" He kissed her with glee, then brilliantly stated, "I feel strangely invigorated. You rest as long as you like. Marc and I will make Henry help us cook." Maura laughed at the notion, and rested a moment more in his arms before climbing into bed. Simon helped her get settled, then promised, "I'll bring you your share of whatever we manage to stir together."

150

Maura pulled a face. "Only if it's edible." Then she beamed with admiration, watching him strip off his damp tunic. On its way off, his tunic yanked up his shirt and exposed his chest and belly. Her eyes bulged to the sight of horrible bruises mottling his bronzed skin. "Oh Simon!" she cried, surging to her knees, and reaching out to touch. "What's happened to your beautiful body?"

He looked down and winced at the degree of bruising, then tried to quell her worry by answering lightly, "I was sat on, remember?"

"I didn't realize...After supper, bring in your jar of rubbing lotion. I'll soothe the sore spots."

"And the not-so-sore spots as well?" he hoped.

"Everywhere!" she agreed. "And Simon...when you return, would you please bring me my letters? I'll feel safer with them in here."

He nodded, blew her a kiss, and left her to a well-deserved rest.

*****

While skittering about straightening her hut, Gael listened halfheartedly to Gruffydd yammer the tale of Simon and Will. And she heard, just as loudly, her inner ponderings—*Why has my life suddenly become so muddled and chaotic?!* Perhaps swiftly choosing a husband would prove calming, yet there was a larger part of her that relished the confusion and craved more. Then there came a rapping and she hoped Marc had returned. Opening the door, her expectant expression sank to a frown. "I thought..." she said to Nesta, standing meekly in the doorway, "that you were to come this *evening*."

"Father said to come now," answered Nesta. "He wants me to start for home before dusk."

"Well I won't argue that point." Gael waved her inside and noticed that Nesta all but ignored Gruffydd, who squinted at her with suspicion. "Gruffydd..." Gael wrapped her arms round his waist, kissed him, and gently persuaded, "Why don't you go keep company with your beasts awhile? The Princess won't be staying long, and later I'd love to hear more of Simon and Will." He nodded, but his narrow glare never left Nesta as he backed his way out of the hut.

"You've been a fool, Nesta," Gael lashed out. "You've made enemies of the wrong people."

"Simon's not my enemy," said Nesta. "He said if I were ill, he would treat me."

"He's too kind..." scowled Gael. "I've warned him countless times about his weakness, but he never listens. And has Maura forgiven you?"

"I don't think so."

"Good. Take care not to rile her again...She's far fiercer than he."

"I've noticed," agreed Nesta. She stretched her humble posture tall, cocked her bruised chin, and swept back her veil to address, "I've come to speak on another matter. Would you please accept my father's proposition and come live with us?"

"What?!" cried Gael, aghast. "You called me bitch!"

"It seemed the proper thing to say at the time. I don't really think of you as a—"

"Stop, Nesta!" insisted Gael. With heightened fervor, she continued to clean and grumble, "I won't play word games with you, not now. I'm far too tired and disgusted."

Nesta followed Gael, irritating her further by pestering, "Won't you accept Father?"

"I've not yet decided." She whirled round to face the girl. "Why do you want me at Dinefwr?"

"Your being there will keep my mother away," Nesta replied with rare verity.

The sights and sounds that had accompanied Gwladys' last visit flashed in Gael's mind, jarring her guile, and softening her tone, "Did this mishap with Simon come about because of something she said or did?"

Nesta tore off her veil for effect, and raved, "She cut my hair, beat me, and makes me wear these robes, all because she heard us talking about men!"

"Dear God!" Gael heaved concernedly. "What ails her?"

"I don't know. I don't see her often, but she warned me not to tell Father what she did, or she'll send me to a nunnery. I felt I had to get away and heard the story the Prince told about Maura. I believed him, why shouldn't I? And I thought if Simon knew, he'd leave her—"

"And go to you?" Gael finished dubiously.

"Why ever not?" Nesta asserted, "I'm far lovelier than Maura, and younger, and—"

"You are so ignorant, child."

"I wouldn't be if you came to Dinefwr and taught me," Nesta brightly coaxed.

"Taught you what?"

"Everything you know."

"There are better teachers, Nesta."

"But I like you."

"And I pity you," returned Gael grimly.

Nesta wrongly took Gael's sympathy as acceptance and vigorously pressed, "Enough to accept my father, and become my mother?"

"I really can't say...not now. And when I do, I will say only to your father."

"My father cherishes his mistresses, and gives them gifts and—"

Gael halted her tribute with a raised hand. "Praising your father won't change my mind, Nesta. I already know him and his generosity quite well."

"Then you'll accept?"

Gael flung up both hands as she loudly demanded, "Stop! I wish you to leave and not to bother me further on this issue."

Nesta sulkily surrendered. "As you wish..." At the door, she turned and reached for Gael's hand. Gael reluctantly obliged and with Nesta's touch came her rasp, "I need you."

Gael's upset swelled; she winced and shut her eyes, then opening them, she managed a crooked grin. "Rhys will be wanting you to leave soon." Nesta nodded and slouched away. Gael slammed shut and bolted the door, leant back against the coarse wood, and tried but couldn't stop the sobs; they wracked her mind and body, and forced her to her knees.

Gael's loud misery drove Gruffydd out from the stable to her side. He hugged her back, and cried out, "What is it, Mam? Did she hurt you like she hurt Maura? Tell me! Please, tell me!"

"No..." Embarrassed, she swabbed her tears with her sleeve, and sniffled in regret. "I'm sorry, my sweet...I didn't mean to scare you."

"But she hurt you!"

"No, she didn't hurt me. She...she makes me remember things, terrible things I want so much to forget."

"What things?"

"I can't tell you...You wouldn't understand."

"I would!"

"No...Someday I'll tell you, when you're older."

"Is it about Tad?"

Lovingly, she took his face in her hands and lulled, "No...There's nothing about your tad that I want to forget."

His pained look of puzzlement wrenched her belly more and his vow, "I won't let anyone hurt you, Mam...I promise!" made her tears flow harder. Gruffydd helplessly firmed their hold and, feeling as lost and lonely as she, cried along.

152

A curtain of rain blurred Almodis' view of the sentinel, forever vigilant from across the lane. He stood as still as a statue, dripping in the raggling wind, and she wondered for the hundredth time, *Why is he watching*? She closed and latched the shutter and sank down upon the rushes beside a sleeping Edith to await her waking. With each passing day, Edith grew cheerier and stronger, Arthur's bubbling mirth had returned, and Alan and Adam seemed contented. It was only Almodis who remained embattled and torn. No one knew, of course, for she was expert at hiding her emotions—perhaps too expert. As Almodis looked gently down upon her friend, she recalled their first encounter, and how prepared she'd been to go to war with the diminutive, yet ferocious Lady Edith. Who'd have ever guessed they'd become such fast confidants?

"Almodis?" called Edith, struggling to sit. "Did you hear me?"

"What?" started Almodis. Her glazed look relaxed to an indulgent one, and she entreated, "Oh, Edith, don't sit on my account."

"I'm not, I want to sit," said Edith as she foundered further. "I'm weary of lying down and sleeping and being waited on and—"

"Then," chuckled Almodis, squirming closer and offering her arm. "Let me help you."

"Thank you...Where were you a moment ago, and where are the men?"

"Pardon?" asked Almodis.

"You were somewhere far, far away. I spoke to you, but you didn't hear."

Almodis stretched to pluck up a thick, fleecy pelt, tucked it over and around Edith's legs and waist, and casually answered, "The men are in the stable and I was reminiscing about our first meeting."

Edith's smile broke wide. "I so wanted to hate you."

"As I did you. Would you care for ale?"

"Please."

Almodis rose and, while ladling drink from a keg into a cup, pondered aloud, "There's one aspect about that time that's always perplexed me. When we were glaring at each other, your hatred was focused directly on my belly."

"Yes," said Edith, "I admit I was jealous of your pregnancy."

"But why?" puzzled Almodis, passing the ale and lowering herself gracefully back to the ground. "With Robert, you had produced one of your own."

"Yes, I had...but I'd buried seven others."

Almodis jerked away as if struck, causing her cup to splash over her skirt. Feeling the damp seep through the wool, she slapped fitfully at the beads of ale, and sputtered, "I...I'm so sorry, Edith...I didn't know."

"And I'm sorry for the shock," atoned Edith, "but there was never any reason to tell."

"How did they die?" Almodis asked carefully.

"Five were dead at birth," said Edith, her eyes downcast, and fingers woven tightly. "Two lived but a week."

"How did you survive such tragedies?"

"With help from loved ones," answered Edith. "And I did have Simon, and Marc and Maura to ease my pain."

"I don't know Marc," mentioned Almodis.

"I pray someday you'll meet. He's such a tender soul," wistfully described Edith, "quiet and somber, like Alan, but less formal. Rose used to call him her saint. Maura's always been her angel."

"And Simon's her devil," smirked Almodis.

Edith twisted a grin and scoffed, "Of course, I don't agree with that compliment. But Rose felt obliged to act as Maura's mother, and she constantly blamed Simon for her *downfall*."

"And which downfall was this?" chuckled Almodis.

"Oh, she meant nothing specific by it. I believe she was referring to Maura's entire childhood. Rose envisioned Maura as a proper and frilly lady, and strove to make her so. And, of course, since Maura wasn't so inclined, Rose was constantly disappointed. She needed someone to blame and Simon seemed a reasonable and ever-present target."

"So you never acted as mother to Maura?" asked Almodis.

"We were more friends, sometimes contrary friends, and I do still feel tremendous guilt over the horrors she encountered after Robert banished me."

Almodis wondered if Edith's haunted look came from her present or past wounds, and she sought to soothe all her hurt by softly appeasing, "You needn't recount that terrible time. And surely only you with your losses could truly empathize with the death of her child."

"Almodis..." Edith's moist gaze asked for her hand, and her voice strained despair, "Now that Maura and I have made our peace, and we believe she is once more with child, I constantly fret that all will happen as before and I will be unable to save her, and Simon, and the baby."

Almodis clasped Edith's hand and chided good-heartedly, "It seems a common concern. Don't you have enough to fret about already, what with walking again, and returning to market, and caring for your wonderfully adoring husband? Let others do your worrying for you."

"Others?"

"I, my dearest Lady, will be honored to take on your woe," Almodis soberly professed.

Edith gazed curiously at her friend. Over the past three days, she'd frequently encountered Almodis' distant and troubled expression and yearned to help, as the Lady had selflessly helped her, but Almodis would never admit to any upset. Still she tried probing again, "Almodis, confess what vexes you?"

"Vexes me?" answered Almodis. "Nothing but the rain."

"It couldn't be Alan," quizzed Edith, "for he's been very attentive to you."

"As is his way," Almodis remarked offhandedly.

"He's a fine man."

"I agree..." Suddenly, Almodis flashed true sentiment as she despaired, "and as such he doesn't deserve me!"

"What?!"

"I bring him only bother," Almodis groused further.

"I don't agree!" returned Edith as curtly. "If that were true, he would have departed long past. He's not one to tolerate nonsense."

"Then it must be what my body offers that keeps him here."

"He needn't stay here to get that," dismissed Edith.

"I don't know why he stays with me, Edith," said Almodis, exasperated.

"He loves you," Edith simply answered.

"How could he love me?" Almodis raved back. "How could anyone? I'm a selfish, spoiled, hot-headed bitch!"

"I won't hear more, Almodis," Edith finished starkly. Then she softened, and shifted nearer to reveal, "Don't be afraid to believe what he tells you. I've never known Alan to speak falsely."

"Nor have I," Almodis said with a dark sigh. "But, Edith, you must know that the closeness I share with him, with you and your family, can't endure. To believe so would be absurd and perhaps lethal. Consider what happened to you—"

"What happened to me had absolutely nothing to do with you," countered Edith.

"You and your kin have done me great damage, Lady Edith," Almodis said, her smile sad. "You've made me want to care. My life was infinitely easier before the emergence of this irksome benevolence."

"Yes, I imagine it *was* easier," said Edith. "Caring requires great duty, yet it also brings untold rewards. Think on what I say when next you gaze upon your son."

"I want him so to know his brother, Simon," worried Almodis.

"Stay with us and he will," implored Edith.

Almodis' fingertip circled the damp spots on her skirt as she mumbled, "Rose and I will never find peace."

"Would it help if Arthur and I returned with you to the manor?" consoled Edith. "I will need time to recover, I miss Rose, it's quiet and hidden there—" Edith paused as she noticed for the first time, Almodis' eyes welling tears.

Almodis' voice shook with protest, "It's not only Rose, Edith...Don't you see—if that man stays across the lane—watching, neither Adam nor you nor anyone will ever see your son again!"

Edith failed to find an answer to the woeful prospect, a prospect she so far had refused to believe. Almodis understood her silence, touched her hand, and rose up in the midst of flickering shafts of sunlight, stealing their way between leaks in the window's framing. She hurriedly unlatched the shutter and flung it wide to welcome the warmth, and to her chagrin she again saw him, standing as still as before, staring...and she realized he'd always be staring no matter if they stayed here, or escaped to Rose's, or to Wales...unless—

"Almodis?"

Her hand was captured. She turned a furtive look to Alan, who fingered the silken tip of her braid, kissed her elegant brow, and lured her captivating smile with the greeting, "You are beautiful."

Her dark eyes and skin glowed to his homage, and she asked, "Does Adam need me?"

"He still sleeps. Supper is prepared and Arthur..." He paused as they both turned and smiled down upon Arthur, crouched by Edith and gathering her in his arms. "Let me," offered Alan.

Arthur waved him off. "And what would my dove think of me, if her husband couldn't carry her to sustenance?"

"I would think him wise not to risk rupturing himself," worried Edith.

"Carrying you is like carrying a feather," grunted Arthur, hoisting her up from the rushes.

Almodis snorted and lauded, "Well, I for one will welcome the addition of profound and spirited dialogue into our regularly boring supper discourse."

"What did she say?" chuckled Alan.

"I haven't a clue," answered Arthur. "Perhaps Edith does."

"I believe," Edith chimed in, "the Lady has given me a compliment."

Almodis humbled herself to translate, "What I meant to say is, I'm pleased you feel well enough to join us and share your immense wisdom."

"That's not much clearer," replied Edith, "but I do thank you, my Lady, and will strive to deserve your praise."

"You always do," Almodis said with forced cheer. "And I heartily return your thanks."

*****

In the early darkness, Alan and Almodis leant up against the back of the hut enjoying the stars and waxing moon, and some precious time alone. Cuddled together, they felt no cold, yet Alan sensed a frigidness in her hold, a vague distance in her gaze. Her reflective periods had lengthened of late, and it worried him, for she was rarely happy, and always before, Arthur and Edith's hut was the one place he could be assured of her happiness. "What is it, my love?" he murmured. She grew limp in response, and, feeling powerless, he drew her nearer. "How can I cheer you?"

"With every man I've known before you," she began, her voice rough with strain, "to receive a favor, I was first obliged to perform a favor. The only favor you've ever asked of me is to get along with Rose." She let out a little laugh, soured by sadness, then touching his cheek, soberly professed, "Always believe that I never wanted to hurt you, I only wanted to love you. I'm forever grateful for your sacrifice on my behalf, and I am, and will always be, immensely fond of you."

When her lips found his, Alan felt a sudden and uncertain dread, for her kiss asked not for his body, it begged for his soul. Much later, he woke to the comforting dirge of Arthur's snore, and felt a tingle of anticipation rouse his body, for they had taken to waking at this late hour to come together leisurely. And at times, in her dreamy state, Almodis would almost betray a true need and caring for something other than his body. As he reached for her, he prayed it would happen again this night, special in the way she had confessed compassion like never before. But he grasped only air, and searching further, crumpled nothing but fur in his palms. He started up; his round eyes darting about the hut, hunting for movement. Calling quietly, "Almodis?" he wriggled into his drawers, stood, and gripping the waist band, crept hurriedly about the hut. And what he feared most presented itself when he came upon the empty cradle. His eyes squeezed tight and his heart's pounding ached as he slowly opened one shutter. Tears blurred Alan's sight; he swiped them away and saw the sentinel gone.

*****

156

CHAPTER TEN - FORGIVENESS

The moon's incandescence lit their way as Almodis and Adam upon a horse, and Robert's man Benjamin leading by foot, approached the guardhouse of Dunheved Castle. Two sentries, started from their sleep, rose with effort and shuffled out of the house to see who rudely woke them at this very early hour. Benjamin reached up to take Adam; Almodis slipped to the ground and retrieved the infant, then stepped behind Benjamin to allow him the presentations. Almodis' face was hidden in the shadow of her cloak's hood, and the guards appeared somewhat impatient and irked. "Sirs," started Benjamin, "I pray that you will recognize..." Almodis took his cue, lowered her hood and stepped forward, as he announced, "the Lady Almodis, our Liege's good wife."

Taken aback, the men jerked to attention and scurried to raise the portcullis and open the gates. All had heard the peculiar tale of the Lady's departure, and did not expect to enjoy her presence again. Almodis, her expression noble, clasped her son tight to her bosom and glided into the bailey. She motioned Benjamin to her side, and quietly inquired, "How long have you served my husband?"

"I have been quartered at Dunheved since a young squire, my Lady. Near a month past, Lord Robert knighted me and made me his personal guard."

"Well then," discerned Almodis, "I expect we'll be seeing a great deal of each other since I plan to stay very close to my husband over the next few months. Benjamin...there are certain details concerning my absence that only I should divulge to my husband. I appreciate your escorting us back to the castle, and I also look forward to what I pray will be a pleasant association between us." Her voice suddenly took on a sharp edge, "Yet take heed, young man, I can and will make your life an absolute Hell if I discover that Lord Robert has received information concerning where I approached you, my whereabouts this past week, or any activities you may have witnessed taking place at the hut you were watching. Do I make myself clear?"

Benjamin stopped; a touch of his hand to her arm halted the Countess. "I understand completely, my Lady, but please understand *me*...My allegiance is and always has been to Lord Robert and the Lady *Edith*. I was watching her cottage to see that no further harm came to her. I don't know why you were there. Never would I cause harm to her or her family. Her son was once my close companion."

Almodis admired the lad's pluck and trueness, but not as much as his loyalty. She rapidly swept her admiring gaze over his ruddy curls and face and his trim form, clothed in crumpled leather tunic and braies; then she focused on his intensely pale blue eyes. An indulgent smile began her summation, "Then Sir Benjamin, I suppose we'll be the best of friends, for the Lady Edith and her entire family hold my complete allegiance as well. I have returned to enable their safety, as they enabled mine, and with your aid, I may succeed."

"I will do my best," answered Benjamin, performing a nod and profound bow. As he guided her across the remainder of the bailey, he stole one or two stealthy looks. She was indeed, as rumor told, a stark beauty with an acid tongue, and possessed of regal presence. Yet the smile she had kindly bestowed on him spoke of something more, compassion perhaps? Certainly he had heard the slurs of her baseness, but he would not let such gossip color his impression of the Lady; he would leave the coloring to her.

Adam woke grumbling for a meal as Almodis hesitated before the stone keep's door. She had never visited Dunheved and, from Will's descriptions, she'd imagined it a crude and repulsive tomb, lacking any comforts. And thus far, Will's description had proven exact—Dunheved appeared as onerous as Pevensey, Robert's residence on the

157

south coast of England. She had suffered residing there, thank goodness not for long, nor did she intend her visit here to be lengthy. Her intent was to persuade her husband, and more importantly his brother, to return at once to Normandy. Then perhaps Robert's former family could enjoy a most deserved peace, however brief and nebulous. But did *she* own the fortitude and wisdom to accomplish such a weighty task? Almodis briefly thought on her time with Alan and how, in his intensely subtle way, he had helped mold her tendency from greed to empathy. The pain she must have caused him struck her with force, making her waver and crave his stalwart presence.

Benjamin, standing staidly by, noticed her lapse and, supporting her elbow, asked, "Shall I take the child, my Lady?"

"No...I apologize for my weakness and I am now ready to enter."

"You needn't apologize, Madam, for many react the same as you before entering here." He yanked at the stubborn barrier's handle and, creakingly, it opened.

Almodis considered how proud Alan would be of her as she steeled herself, glanced to Adam for strength, then strode past Benjamin into the tomb. Torches jutted haphazardly from the walls of the low-roofed, too slim, rank hallway. Benjamin brushed by her, excusing, "I will guide you to Lord Robert's chamber, my Lady."

"Thank you, Benjamin," she sighed. He removed a torch and hiked assuredly down the passage. Almodis followed and babbled to mask her nervousness, "So, you are acquainted with Simon?"

"I was, quite well, my Lady."

"Then you must have known Maura as well," said she.

"Yes, she was a fine friend."

"As she was to me. They've wed."

"As they should be," said he.

"Odo wants to kill Simon."

"*That* I well know, my Lady."

"I will attempt to change his mind," she stated staunchly.

"I wish you luck," he replied, then wondered, "And the child, a brother or sister for Simon?"

Almodis beamed proudly. "A brother, whom I pray will know and emulate his brother."

"Whatever that means, my Lady, I pray for it as well."

"Thank you, Benjamin," she answered, slightly amused. "You remind me of a guard I once knew. Perhaps you've heard of him?"

"Who is that, Madam?"

"He was called Godfrey."

"No Madam, I don't know him." Her sudden sadness piqued his interest. "And where is Godfrey now?"

"Dead...because of my foolishness."

"Surely not, my Lady," he allayed.

They skirted between trestle tables crowding the great hall. Almodis cringed at the ominous rustlings of snoring, grunting sentries spread over the rush strewn floor, and scrunched in piles round the door to the Lord's bedchamber. She wondered why the extensive protection, and smirked, thinking her husband must be preparing for Edith's retaliation. "Benjamin," she said mildly, "I thank you again for your kindness and comfort. I will present myself."

"If you have further need of me, my Lady, I will be directly outside the door. Would you like me to find you a chambermaid?"

"That would be most helpful." Enlightened by a notion, Almodis further requested, "Did any of the servants abiding here serve the Lady Edith?"

"Yes, Madam, most did."

"Then send me the one who knew her best."

"I gladly will." He bade her, "My Lady," as he bowed, and left.

She sidled past bodies, tugged tentatively at the latch, and crept inside the chamber. The room was surprisingly bright; two candles burned on either side of the canopied bed, and the fire's flames danced high. The sparsely furnished room exuded much history, both cheering and malefic, and Almodis sensed the latter as she neared the lump reposing on the bed. Adam complained louder and, reaching out to prod awake her husband, Almodis hoped Benjamin would be quick finding the maid.

The bed's occupant snorted twice, jerked discontentedly, then started up, sputtering, "Who...who's there?"

The bedraggled man squinting curiously at Almodis was not Robert, but he was grimly familiar. "Odo!" called Almodis, upsetting Adam further. "Where's Robert?!"

Odo blinked furiously at the Madonna-like vision standing before him. Then her true vision came clear and he grunted, "Almodis...Why did you have to pick the middle of the night to return? But then you never were accommodating, at least not to me."

"What have you done with Robert?" she insisted more shrilly.

"I don't know where he's sleeping!" he said with petulance. "I needed this bed on account of my sore back, and he readily agreed."

Her jaw clenched and eyes flashing, Almodis heaved her command, "Get yourself from that bed this instant, and find me my husband!"

"You dare not speak to me in that fashion, my Lady!" he harshly retorted, flinging away the bedclothes and dropping down from the lofty bed. In his long shirt, he stood inflamed and posturing, awaiting her rebuttal. Yet instead of railing back, Almodis retreated a step and, taking in his plump form, burst into laughter.

Odo swelled larger. "What amuses you?"

"You ate well in prison...You've got fat knees!"

He snatched up a pelt to hide his naked limbs. "You poisoned-tongued witch, leave here at once!"

Almodis chuckles turned indignant. "No, no my exalted Bishop, I belong here, you do not. Benjamin!" she yelled, storming toward the door, and muttering, "Where is that cursed maid?"

"And so this squealer is your bastard?" sneered Odo.

"He," clarified Almodis, "is your legitimate nephew."

"He is the Devil's child."

"Well then, Odo, the Devil is your brother—Robert."

"Bitch and whore!" hurled Odo.

"What an exquisite and extensive vocabulary you have. Please find your braies and spare me any more of your knees and sanctimonious drivel." Almodis threw open the chamber door and screamed, "Benjamin!"

All on the floor scrambled up and searched about dumbly for the crisis. Benjamin squeezed through the pack, just ahead of a puffed-up, oldish, female servant, who brashly shoved the soldiers aside.

"My...my Lady, what is the problem?" called Benjamin.

"We seem to have misplaced Lord Robert. You can imagine my distress when I encountered that gross blob, Odo, occupying our bed."

"Bishop Odo! Oh, my Lady, I apologize, I didn't know."

"It's not your mistake, Benjamin," appeased Almodis. "Please help me find my husband. Is this the maid?"

"Yes...yes my Lady."

159

Alerted by Benjamin's uncertain tone, Almodis regarded the woman next to him with reserve. Her mussed appearance—wimple slightly askew, wrinkled tunic, apron untied—and ascetic manner told of an abrupt waking. Yet the sour creases in her jowly face lifted, and her hazel eyes twinkled at the sight of the mewling Adam. "Let me have him, Mam," said she, thrusting out both arms. "I'll find a wet-nurse to feed him."

"No..." replied Almodis brusquely, "I handle that chore myself, however you can wash him, find him some clean wraps, and bring him back to wherever my husband sleeps."

"It will be my pleasure, my Lady, and we are quite honored to finally be making your acquaintance."

"Yes...well..." Almodis waved away the woman's graciousness, grudgingly let go of her son, and strictly added, "I fear you need hurry, for Adam's patience wears thin. Benjamin, help me locate our Liege."

Odo stood in the doorway, smugly eyeing the disruption. When he was certain they'd gone and all was tranquil again, he yawned, scratched his crotch, and returned to bed, thinking how stimulating the household surely would become now that the great whore had returned.

One of the sentries quartered in the great hall offered to guide them to Robert's chamber. Almodis motioned for Benjamin to stay outside, knocked twice, and entered. Contrary to his brother, Robert slept in complete darkness and, as Almodis tripped on something soft and lumpy, she prayed it not alive. She stumbled back to the door, and whispered rapidly through the crack, "Benjamin, please fetch a candle." He dashed away and returned swiftly with her wish. She uttered, "Thank you," and disappeared again. Hovering over the bed, she held the candle near Robert's head, neatened her braid with her other hand, and studied him awhile in sleep. He appeared vexed by dreams, twitching and muttering, and she strove to rescue him from his trouble with a gentle shake and murmur, "Robert...Robert...wake up...it's Almodis." But he only flinched from her touch and dreamt more...

Baleful clouds hurled bolts of lightning as Robert rode in haste for Dunheved Castle. Simon, aged eight years, followed on his mount and, as the forest grew denser, Robert feared their speed too quick. He glanced back and saw in Simon's eyes the same raw fear he felt, yet his son kept up his valiant pace. The rain fell in torrents slicking the ground. He heard Simon scream and turned to the wretched sight of the horse bolting away and Simon sprawled lifelessly upon the ground. He leapt from his mount and sped to his son's side; crouching, he reached out to touch Simon's pale hair, matted with mud. His hand tenderly strayed to the boy's cheek, soiled as well, but as his fingers lit upon the mark, the dirt wetted to blood. Suddenly Simon was no longer a boy, but a man, unconscious, his shirt shorn in two, lying upon a prison cell floor, blood streaming from horrendous wounds thrashed into his cheek and back, wounds inflicted at Robert's orders! Odo loomed above them resoundingly reciting his threat, "And the vengeance I intend on your bastard, I have well-rehearsed these long hard years. He put me behind that locked door, and will suffer as I've suffered. No—he'll suffer worse!"

"No!" Robert cried, bolting up in the bed. "He's suffered enough. He'll not suffer more!"

Almodis recoiled from his wail, toppling the taper to the floor. She hurriedly snatched it back, and stamped on singed rushes, all the while appealing, "Robert...wake up! It's Almodis, please wake up!"

He snapped a lethal glare her way; she grew frigid with terror, and fleetingly recalled their turbulent parting. He'd been prepared to murder her then, why wouldn't he do so now? After all she'd been traitor and adulterer, and many had been executed for lesser crimes.

But the fire in his pale eyes gradually faded and was replaced by an incredulous stare. "Almo...Almodis?" he stammered, glancing about in alarm. *How can she be here,* he wondered frenziedly, *and where is here, and when? Has the past six months been nothing but a terribly long and ghastly nightmare?!*

Almodis' lilting words, "Robert, I've come back to you," and her touch to his white-knuckled fist, returned him quickly to the present. "Are you ill?"

Robert jerked from her touch, and said with suspicion, "I'm perfectly well. I didn't believe you'd ever return."

"I had no choice," she returned blandly.

He cast her odd reply a narrower look and, sitting taller, stuttered with dread, "What's happened? Where...where's the child?"

In respect, Almodis set the candle on the side table, hung her head, and clasped her hands at her back. She stood a safe distance away, and answered dutifully, "He...He's being washed and prepared to meet his father."

"Am *I* his father?" he curtly returned.

"Yes, my Lord."

"Is he well? Are you?"

"We are both quite fit, thank you."

"And his birth—"

"I handled well," she finished for him, "with appropriate help nearby."

"Help from whom?" he prodded, shifting attentively to the edge of the bed.

Almodis retreated a step and said with caution, "I don't know if it's safe to answer your query, my Lord."

"Enough of your empty blather, Almodis," he bristled. "Where were you and with whom?"

"And if I don't answer?"

He strove unsuccessfully to sound benign. "I wish to compensate your helpmates, not punish them."

"I don't believe you."

"God's breath!" he flared. "I sent you away for safekeeping, and I appreciate all who may have kept you from harm."

She arched a brow, and chanced, "Including Alan?"

"Did he return you here?"

"No...Benjamin did."

"Benjamin?" he said, muddled. "What were you doing in the village?"

Well-rehearsed, Almodis gracefully skipped through her reply, spouting only what she believed safe, "I was on my way here from Rose's. Her son Richard mentioned you were in residence and I felt it safe to return."

"How did you know Benjamin was mine?"

"I lost my way...It was the middle of the night. Only he was about, and I asked him."

"I find it hard to believe you would do something so reckless as to approach a strange man in the night."

Her politeness died, making her snap, "I don't care what you believe! I'm home...Be satisfied with that."

And now he raised a brow. "And Alan?"

"He bravely escorted me to Rose's, then promptly disappeared."

"Then my thanks for your well-being will go to Rose."

"Whatever you deem proper, my *gracious* Lord."

His body sagged to her blatant sarcasm, his fingers dug into his skull and, fitfully, he inquired, "Do...do you plan to stay?"

161

Her harping persisted, "Considering who I discovered in *your* bed, it appears my presence here is sorely overdue. How could you let him steal your bed?"

"His back was aching...What does it matter?"

"It matters much, my Lord. I hear on his visit he's already accomplished a great deal of harm."

"What did you hear?" he asked forcefully.

"The villagers' gossip. A tale of your former mistress, your brother, and heated irons. Will you allow him to torture me and our son in the same manner? For it seems your saintly brother is intent on destroying anyone who is or was ever tied to you."

"You are my wife," he answered with pained voice and expression. "I'll allow no harm to come to you, or to our child."

"Then my husband..." She at last felt secure enough to sit by his side. "We share a mutual goal and must rid ourselves of this scoundrel."

"I don't want to rid myself of Odo, and you are not his enemy, Almodis."

"Perhaps not, but plenty are," she reminded, "and they are in constant peril if he remains at Dunheved. If you cannot bring yourself to cast him out, then together we must convince him to return to Bayeux."

"I've tried."

"Obviously, not harshly enough." A prolonged disquiet followed, then Almodis calmed to mention, "I offer my condolences for your other brother's death, my Lord. And I need inquire...where is Will?"

"I don't know..."

Just then, there was a soft tapping on the door. Almodis' pride shone radiant as she hustled in the chambermaid and, with an expression of sublime joy, took up her son. "Stay a moment..." she pleasantly encouraged. "You are called?"

"Estrith, my Lady."

"I'm grateful Estrith, for your tending to Adam, and I would further appreciate if you would locate a cradle for him. Don't feel you need hurry, for he will sleep this night in bed with us."

Robert, clad in long shirt and braies, had risen and was skittishly inching closer, craning his neck to glimpse the infant; his shaky reach betrayed an urgency to touch. "Adam..." he mildly mused. "I would have liked to name him Herluin, for my father."

"His name will remain Adam," Almodis decreed.

With a submissive nod and arms partly outstretched, he said, "Then I'll hold— Adam."

Estrith stepped in shadow and mawkishly watched Robert's guarded posture and expression as Almodis offered him the wriggling boy. Yet once the child's warmth nestled in Robert's arms, his rigidness melted, and his lips twitched into an awkward grin.

Almodis approached the maid and whispered so only she could hear, "I have trusted you with my son, and will also trust you with my secret. I know dearly the Lady Edith, and have just stayed the week with her and her husband, Arthur. She recovers swiftly from her wounds, and surely affords you her most affectionate greetings. So, I beg of you, don't condemn me as her rival. I'm not her successor by choice, and while we are forced to reside here, my son and I crave your loyalty."

Estrith looked on perplexed, then returned with astute brevity, "I will care for the babe as if he were my own, and will gladly attend to your every need, my Lady."

"I'm most beholden," said Almodis in full voice. "Now if you could help us move to the Lord's bedchamber."

Robert heard her request and spoke up, "No...We'll stay the remainder of the night here."

162

"But, my Lord," Almodis sniveled in protest, "not here, not when—"

"I won't disrupt the entire household, not at this hour."

"Nor your brother," Almodis added snidely.

"Nor my brother," he bluntly confirmed.

She turned her disappointment on Estrith, who consoled, "No matter, my Lady. I will find a cradle and tomorrow freshen the Lord's bedchamber to your and the young one's liking."

"I appreciate your thoughtfulness, Estrith, and now you may go."

Estrith curtsied, cast one last longing look Adam's way, and then bustled her way out.

As Almodis peered skeptically at Robert and the child, she was slightly heartened by his intense interest in the boy. It was futile attempting to guess his thoughts; she had tried countless times and always figured wrong. He appeared no different from when they'd parted, his stature still wiry, his expression drawn and stone-like, and his pate sporting too little hair. Yet his intriguing visage did, as before, capture her admiration. She moved nearer and sweetly commented, "You seem pleased."

He looked up from his trance, and cracked a crooked grin. "I am...highly. He's quite handsome."

"As are all your children, Robert." Her compliment still fresh, she beguiled, "Must we stay here?"

"I've spoken my last word on that subject." He waited for her usual retort; receiving none, he cast her a quizzical look.

"As you wish, my Lord," was her simple answer.

She was close enough for Robert's scrutiny, and he felt a wrenching inside as he breathed in her fairness, unheralded for a woman of forty years. In contrast to her usual richly styled frocks, the tunic she wore was tailored of a coarse wool, her chemise, a loosely woven linen. And with her chestnut plaits unveiled and olive skin darkly tanned, her guise was starkly provincial, yet immensely enticing. Before he could censor himself, he blurted, "I've missed you," then dropped his shame to the loudly complaining boy.

Almodis beamed with confidence. "Let me have him, Robert. He's mighty hungry."

Again his questioning look appeared, when she threw off her cloak, deftly unlaced the front of her tunic and, from an opening in her chemise, produced a swelled breast. She rested back upon the bed, and cuddled Adam close; he quickly located his object of joy, and sucked vigorously.

"Almodis!" Robert spouted in surprise. "You needn't do such a thing. There are maids about who will—"

"But Robert," she interjected, smiling, "I enjoy doing such a thing. It gives us both pleasure and I've been told, performing this deed will delay my becoming pregnant again." Soberly, she included, "I don't desire another child."

"In that we are agreed. And," he considered carefully, "are you wanting to say that you will be wife to me in all regards?"

"I will, my Lord."

"How long does the feeding take?"

To Robert's eager look, Almodis chuckled, "Not long." She shivered and noted distractedly, "There's no fire in this chamber."

"Are you chilled?"

"No...The bed is small."

"We will fit," determined Robert.

"With the boy?" she teased.

"Comfortably with the boy."

His fingers cupped her chin and raised her face to his. The affection in his eyes stirred a vague warmness inside her, and she fondly recalled that their bed had been the one place where they most often agreed.

Not much later, as they shifted for comfort and traded casual chides, Robert ventured to ask, "Do you know where Simon is?" Her tense silence prompted him to affirm, "No one else will know."

"I won't say, not with Odo so close."

"Then won't you at least tell me if he's well?"

"I don't know, Robert, and that is the truth. I do pray so. He is a son to feel pride for."

"As this one will be," he commented.

"As this one *is*," she corrected, tenderly positioning the sleeping infant between their pillows and the head of the bed.

"I thank you for Adam," he stated.

"I'm grateful to you for my life," she responded, "and Simon's and Maura's—"

"And Alan's?" he asked, askance.

"Yes and Alan's."

"He is *truly* gone?" he probed further.

"Truly," she said.

The certainty of her tone emboldened him to take her in his arms, but there she stiffened, and he eased away in confusion. "We needn't," he said, "not if you're not wanting to..."

"I don't mind," she said distantly.

He touched his lips to her brow, and murmured, "I spoke the truth before, Almodis...I have missed you."

To his simple regard, he felt her resistance ebb, and heard allurement in her chuckle, "I imagine you did."

Almodis sat quietly still and allowed Robert to pare away her chemise. He understood her caution and wary eye, for their last time together hadn't been exactly genial. The sight of her exquisite nakedness, he imagined made more ample because of the baby, made him reach out in needy gratitude. He touched her face, and let his fingers linger upon her warm cheek, waiting while he wondered, *How did I come to be so blest? Why has she come back?* And she needn't have brought the child, she could have claimed him dead, and he never would have known his son. That would have been a just punishment for the atrocities he'd forced upon his family. But hadn't he also rescued Edith, pardoned Simon and Maura, and saved Almodis' and the child's lives, and for those gallant deeds, didn't he deserve a favor from God? And here sat his favor, so lovely, arousing, most times contrary, and in an odd way so very innocent. *My God,* he prayed inwardly, *let me keep her by me, and I swear, I'll treat her kinder, guard her and our son from harm, and strive to amend my many wrongs. Perhaps then, she won't stray, and you'll consider forgiving me...*

There was something bemusingly different in Robert's manner, a tenderness, a caring she'd not known in their past. It perplexed her, and heightened her stiffness as she considered the unbelievable notion, that she may have actually missed him and was this very moment feeling anticipation for what would soon occur between them. A short gasp escaped her parted lips; she covered his fingers with hers and guided them to her breast. Robert's mouth hungrily found the other, and he melted with her down upon the scratchy, wool draped mattress of straw. Her confusion swelled to the desire his fingers and lips elicited, and she pondered, *Do I desire the man or simply the physical act?* Had her time with Alan enabled her to see beyond the union of bodies, to the union of souls? But this man locked to her wasn't Alan...it was Robert—cold, exact, stone-faced

Robert—a shell devoid of feeling, and her heart froze to her next assertion, precisely like her.

*****

"What she did was not a slight to you!" Edith strongly related to Alan, slouched beside her and cradling his skull. To his tortured silence, Edith shifted despairingly against her propped pillows, and accepted Arthur's passed cup of ale.

Alan shrugged away the cup offered to him, prompting Arthur to suggest as he lowered himself to the rushes, "Please accept, lad. It might help soothe you, and Edith speaks the truth. The Lady's leaving was a selfless act done solely for our safety."

"Just yesterday," Edith cut in, "she spoke tenderly of her fondness for you, of how she wasn't deserving of your love."

"Love!" Alan lifted furious eyes and spat, "What could she know of love?! She lives by greed, hate, and lies! Her heart is as rotten as her soul."

"Alan!" chided Edith.

Arthur hushed her scolding with a look, and instead encouraged, "Get your anger out, lad, for not till that's done can you grieve her loss."

"And the child's," added Edith shakily. "We love you, Alan, and want you to remain here with us."

"No," he answered firmly. "I won't impose on your struggle."

"But where will you go?" implored Edith. "What will you do?"

"I don't know...I'm not good for much but soldiering."

"Rose would argue that," said Arthur.

"Poor Rose" anguished Edith. "Without the boy to tend, she'll surely die of woe!"

Alan's wrath boiled up again; he struggled to rise, and ranted as he paced, "When I think of the abuse Rose endured, all to keep Almodis and the boy safe and healthy! I must get back to the manor. She'll be crazed with worry."

"And she certainly won't take the news of the Lady's leaving calmly," said Arthur. "We'll return with you. The sentry's gone, but for how long we can't know. Now's our perfect opportunity to slip away."

"Rose's manor is secluded and comforting," heartened Edith. "It will be weeks before I can return to market and—"

Impulsively, Alan blurted, "I don't know if I want to go back there...without her."

"With our constant jabbering," said Arthur, "perhaps it won't seem so lonely."

Alan's slack look seemed to agree, but Arthur reckoned there was much more turmoil to come. He felt great affection and sympathy for this outwardly simple, yet inwardly complex man, and perhaps knew better than most the dreadful abandonment Alan must be suffering. And Arthur couldn't deny he would sorely miss the Lady as well. "Come lad," he urged with a clap to Alan's shoulder, "we'll collect a few belongings to take along on our visit, and stable the beasts with friends. And while we're away, my dove," he chided lovingly, "you won't attempt helping us."

Edith nodded to Arthur's forced grin and gave Alan's hand a pat as he rose to follow Arthur. He'd risen only part-way when he sank back down and confided in a rasp, "Edith, she asked me to be father to Adam, and I want him back."

"It will be hardest of all letting the boy go," Edith soothed, her hands resting tenderly upon his shoulders. She sadly searched his tortured expression and tried to console, "Alan, you must accept the fact that he is at last with his true father. And I trust that Robert will treat his son kindly and fairly, for Adam is his final chance to succeed as a father."

Alan reluctantly left her kindness to follow Arthur, and Edith sighed a glum and troubled sigh. The prospect of losing a son was an incessant heartache she had been suffering from for the past twenty-five years. And she did feel an ache in her breast as

165

she realized that today was the anniversary of Simon's birth, a day they had always striven to spend together. She missed him so! Had the sentry truly left? Could Almodis convince Odo to abandon his quest to locate Simon? It seemed unlikely, and if Odo succeeded, Edith would be without her son—a thought too horrendous to bear. But how could she save him? Her cup sagged from her hand, and spilt ale soaked her skirt and the rushes. She didn't seem to notice and wiped a tear as the solution to her dilemma became dreadfully clear. To save Simon she must purposely separate herself from him, from Maura, and from her grandchild. How could she survive such a sadness and how long must she stay away? Knowing well Odo's cursed determination, she imagined they'd be parted for the remainder of her life.

*****

Simon and Maura sat side by side upon Maude's stall fence, their postures identical, elbows on knees, chins in their palms, looking at nothing in particular, yet eyeing it sourly. Rain hammered the dripping roof above, and had sustained its relentless onslaught for a very long week. Vapor rose from the horses' stalls opposite as they stamped and snorted their displeasure. Ivo, Henry's stallion, threw back his head and, with lust-filled eyes, neighed his desire to Simon's mare, E'dain, which she shrilly returned.

"Oh Simon," muttered Maura limply, "why don't we just let them out in the pasture and allow them some fun? No one else is having any. They won't mind the rain."

"Because," he sensibly muttered back, "the other stallions would have at her as well. She might be injured, and I can't have her pregnant. I need her."

A bit wounded, Maura replied, "I'm still useful, aren't I?"

He sounded miffed when replying, "Of course you are."

Maura gazed at him an unsure moment, then curtly wondered, "Why did you say it *that* way?"

He broke from his vacant stare. "What way?"

"Meanly."

"I didn't!"

"You did!"

"I thought we came out here to escape the madness," he snapped back. "Now you're wanting to make some of our own!"

"I am not! It was you who stated the bit about not being needed when pregnant."

"What are you talking about?!"

"It's what you said, Simon."

"No I didn't!"

"Yes you did!"

He dropped heavily to the ground, spun to face her, and fiercely gripped the top rail. Anger shook and gritted his voice, "We'd best stop this before we start screaming, for that's what I've wanted to do for the past three days, scream at everyone to go away and leave me alone!"

"Do you want me to go as well?"

"No..." He softened, sagged and, taking her hands, helped her down. "For you, my love, are my only link to sanity."

She smiled weakly and murmured, "I miss you."

"And I you...And I'm *so* tired."

"Why does Henry snore so loudly?"

"I don't know," shrugged Simon. "I've tried kicking him, flipping him over, pouring water on him, nothing helps."

Maura took up a stool, rounded the fence, and approached Maude with a smile and gentle pat. The cow returned the kindness by slobbering on her shoulder. "You have no recipe than can handle the problem?" she asked, positioning her hands beneath the cow's udders.

"None that I know of, but I have been contemplating various poisons."

"You're not the only one considering murder, Simon. Henry's antics are turning us all into vengeful demons."

"What terrible thing did we do to deserve this?" whined Simon, slumping onto the fence. "Always before, I imagined only one, much tinier being intruding on our peace. Then Marc arrived and, well, he's no trouble, but how did we come to be invaded by seven gigantic trolls, one wispy clerk, and a bedeviling ex-Prince. And I truly believe that Henry's planning to stay and heckle us forever, and it will never stop raining, and we're running out of food, and—"

She stopped milking to fret, "Are we truly?"

"Yes...And when giants get hungry, they get grouchy, and I predict as a result—carnage."

Maura resumed her chore, wagging her head, and chiding with a chuckle, "Simon...don't exaggerate so."

"I'm not," he said, snatching up a pitch-fork. He used it to impale a bale of fresh straw from a low hanging loft, then stabbed at it to loosen the grass, while adding, "The guards...are beginning to make me nervous." Maura slowly raised a vexed look, causing him to stop stabbing and prod, "What is it?"

"Probably nothing..."

"What is it, Maura?" he insisted louder.

"Well it's interesting that you mentioned food, because the last two or three days, I've begun to sense that I'm being viewed as a morsel—"

He didn't let her finish and demanded, "What's Henry done?"

"It's not only Henry, Simon. His men sometimes look at me as if I've got nothing on."

"Have they been rude to you?"

"No, unless leering is rude. But they're so odd. They say nothing, and do less."

"And Henry? What he's guilty of?"

"Only pestiness...I've not had a decent wash this week. Every time I believe I'm alone and remove a piece of clothing, there he is!" Maude began to feel the brunt of Maura's complaints, and turned her head to issue a loud, low, complaint of her own. Maura instantly lightened her grip and tone, and patted the beast's side in apology. "He's amazing, Simon," she went on, "constantly chattering nonsense, and you know what happens each time we even think of getting amorous."

Simon raked viciously at the soiled straw in Maude's stall and muttered, "As you said, there he is, sporting his ridiculously silly grin. He's doing all this on purpose, Maura. Henry never does anything without a purpose."

"What do you think his purpose is?"

"I haven't a clue."

Maura asked, "Would it be impolite to ask him how long he plans to stay?"

"No. He has to realize we can't feed his entire entourage forever."

"They do nothing to help, well Guy does sometimes, but the rest, they only—"

"You needn't be nice around me, Maura," said Simon. "Say what you think."

Bluntly, she spilled, "They only grunt, belch, and eat."

To which he quipped, "Henry's men are not known for witty conversation."

Maura took hold of Maude's last two teats and dreamily watched Simon go about his work; focused and resolute, he swiftly cleared the entire stall, even the areas under the cow and Maura's stool, and deftly blanketed the bare ground with fresh straw. Over the past difficult week, they had spent little time alone together, and she relished having the opportunity to admire every fine line of his form and his graceful movements. Yet something seemed different, particularly his face. There was a gray gauntness she'd not noticed before, and his eyes were darkly shadowed by lack of sleep. She longed for his smile and strove to sway his mood by noting, "You seem to get along quite nicely with John."

Her attempt succeeded, for as she squeezed Maude's last teat dry, Simon paused his scooping and spouted brightly, "Yes...it's a wonder he's survived this long with Henry. He seems genuinely kind, and highly intelligent. He's offered advice on cultivating my herbs. It seems the clerks tend the sick at Bayeux. He's not directly involved with the infirmary, but has assisted the brothers with their gardening."

"I'm glad you like him. He's very polite, though seems a little frightened of me."

"You know who's handled this vile situation most successfully?" said Simon.

"Who?" asked Maura, setting her pail and stool outside the stall.

"Marc. He's memorized my entire book of remedies!"

"I'm not surprised." She gathered up two armfuls of grass to help him finish and added, "He's quite intent on helping you."

"And has done so immensely. We've gathered, dried, classified, and stored enough herbs to last the winter. I have a tall stack of bags that need to be delivered."

"Then you must go, but," she worried, "can you safely take the path? It's very slippery."

"I wouldn't chance riding E'dain down it," he said. "I suppose I could slide on my bottom to town."

She offered the point, "You could take the long way round."

He frowned. "Yes...I suppose I could, but I'm so weary of being wet. I must have mold growing on my body...somewhere. I itch everywhere!"

Maura tossed the last of her straw, swatted chaff from her tunic, and turned on him an alluring look and comment, "If you like, I'll venture a look."

As she approached, he grasped the pitchfork in defense and warned, "Don't Maura...don't start talking like that, for if you do and we do, he'll magically appear, and it's been so nice to have these very few precious moments without him skulking about."

"But Simon," she beseeched, "it's not natural being so close yet not being able to touch you!" Her fingers pried their way under his waist cord and explored lower. "Or kiss you..." Her lips wet the hollow of his neck and crept higher. "It's early," she encouraged. "He can't be awake yet. *Please!* I'll go mad if we have to wait much longer! And it's your birthday and this is my first gift to you! It's as if we prepared Maude's stall especially for us. She won't mind. Please!"

As her kisses lingered longer, his opposition drained; he dropped the fork, and followed her lure down to the straw. Ravenously they touched and, for a glorious while, they contented themselves with nothing more. Yet soon, Simon, desperate to see what he was fondling, gasped from her lips to tug at her tunic. "I need to see you," he vehemently implored. "Take it off, take everything off!"

"And you!" she begged. Her urgency ripped his worn tunic in two. He threw off the pieces and his shirt, kicked off his boots and braies, then helped her wriggle from her burden. They paused awestruck, as if this was their first time together, unclothed. She saw not a bit of mold on him, nor bruises, only bronzed, leaner than usual, rippled flesh, that quivered beneath her lips and fingertips.

He marveled at the rapid and voluptuous changes in her body, its flushed radiance, taut curves, and luscious mounds. With a hungry whimper, he urged her onto his lap. There, she hugged his waist with her legs, and moaned in delight as his bristled cheek nuzzled and tickled her breasts. His hands, gripping her hips, pressed her closer to feel him lengthen and harden against her belly.

In rapt appreciation, she let go a sultry laugh and tipped backward into the cushiony straw. He tipped with her, then sighed deliciously as he stretched himself over her entire winsome length. He had to raise up on his hands so not to press heavily on her belly, and blushed to say, "We won't be able to manage this way for much longer."

"Not to worry." She smoothed his hair away to kiss his brow and assure, "We'll always manage, for you fit so perfectly to my back, and I do so adore mounting you."

He grunted in response and buried his face in her neck. "My God, woman, I adore and crave you so much it hurts!"

And I crave you...inside me." Anticipation made her shudder, thrust her hips to his, and gasp, "Please Simon we can't wait! We may only have a minute—" With that news and scant effort, he found himself ensconced deeply inside her, wondrously warm and snug. He purposely slowed his passion to watch and feel hers quicken. Her head lolled as a fever emanating from her womb coursed through the rest of her, blushing and dampening her skin. Her toes stroked his buttocks and legs, her nails bit pleadingly at his back, and her lips whimpered for him to move faster. But he kept his unhurried, almost teasing pace. And she loved his teasing, nothing thrilled and incited her more. In a swoon, she rocked him from his support; he tumbled over her, and hugged securely between her legs, wantonly obliged her need. She writhed to meet his rapid pulse, their mouths moaning and crushing together. She felt she might scream, and when she opened her eyes, she did scream, not from ecstasy but from shock, for the huge brown eyes staring at them did not belong to Maude, they belonged to Henry!

Simon froze in terror, thinking somehow he had wounded her or the baby. Then his entire body wilted to the coarsely chuckled comment, "Don't mind me." A smoldering quiet ensued as Simon, taking care to hide Maura, carefully reached for her tunic. Maura's head was turned away, her eyes and jaw painfully clenched, her face crimson from shame. Simon worked the cloth between their bodies, and groaned as Henry ribbed on, "Perhaps you'd enjoy it more if I joined in?"

Once Maura was sufficiently covered, Simon rolled off her and, with his back to Henry, pulled on his braies. He knelt to tie the waist cord, sat back on his heels a pensive moment, then slowly rose and turned.

To Henry's devilish smirk, Simon swelled to the size of an enraged bull, huffed, and charged round the fence. Henry dashed away toward the paddock, cackling hysterically. Simon flew after him and, at the doorway, lunged and swiped for his tunic; he missed it by a thread. Seven stallions bounded from Henry's riotous arrival. He collided with one, bounced off and bounded into another. His laughing doubled him over, yet it was barely audible above the horse's shrieking neighs. Rain blurred his sight, and for a scary instant he lost Simon. Though, when he came into view again, Henry noticed there was little difference between Simon's countenance—eyes wild, lips tight, nostrils flared— and the disturbed beasts! Then came a rough nudge that knocked him toward Simon, and pain as huge teeth nipped his shoulder. Henry stopped laughing. He suddenly felt very small and very stupid. Simon's advance continued steadily, his arm steeled and hand balled to a fist. Henry's fists shot up in defense, but a hoof caught the back of his leg and hurtled him forward into mud and manure. He twisted and turned in terror as the horses crowded closer, stomping, biting, kicking at each other and at him. Henry felt hands grip his wrists and yank, and he slid from the menace, through the mud, and into the stable. His shirt's neck strangled him as he was hoisted to his feet, then roughly shoved up against a wooden wall. He managed somehow to slither away. Simon seized the back of his tunic and yanked him back. His fright turned frantic; he strained and squawked, "Let me go, Simon! You're hurting me. It was a joke, only a joke. I meant no harm!"

169

Simon's heaving, brutal silence spiked Henry's panic, and then from the corner of his eye he spied Maura. Maura would save him! She'd rescued him before, she'd surely do so now! Henry stared astounded as she stepped with amazing calm before Simon. Her hands covered and relaxed his fists, then smoothed the length of his arms and rested upon his cheeks. Henry strained to hear her whispered plea, "Simon, you must leave here...Take your bags and Marc and go to the village. You'll find a clean shirt and tunic on the trunk. It's best if you're away from Henry."

Simon spat and stuttered, "I...I won't leave you here, not with him, not with them!"

"I can handle Henry," she said, stroking his damp brow. "You need to get away...*please*. I'll be fine."

Henry prayed, prayed harder than he'd ever prayed before for Simon to listen to her. It was a good and reasonable thing to do, and Simon was most times good and reasonable. And his prayer was miraculously answered—Simon removed her hands from his face, squeezed them, then simply walked away. *My goddess! Yes, that's what she is, and a buxom, lusty goddess at that!* And he would fall to his knees and worship her and thank her for his life and—Maura whirled around; her flattened palm whacked Henry's cheek and for an excruciating instant his world went black. He shook from his blindness and saw bright dancing lights as he staggered about, screeching, "Stop...Maura, stop!"

But she fiercely followed, shoving him, and lashing out, "You putrid pig! How could you?! How could you do something so revolting? We've fed you, sheltered you, and this is how you show thanks, by humiliating us! I hate what you did, I hate it, and I hate you!"

He cowered, afraid she'd hurt him again, and groveled, "I...I didn't do it on purpose...I wanted to help...I thought only you were in here...and—"

"Quiet!" she yelled. "I won't hear your lies and I won't have you here. You take your stinking slaves and your man, gather your things, and leave!"

She stood silent, quaking and glaring and, just when he believed her ire would wilt to tears, she left him. He stupidly lurched after her, sniveling, "No, Maura. You must believe me. I'd never humiliate you! I...I swear I'll be good. Don't make me go yet, please don't, not till—" They were halfway to the door, when she spun back as if to strike again. He easily clasped her wrists still, shook her once, and grew excited to the glint of fear sparking her eyes. He felt strong and confident again and steadily finished, "Not till you let me repay you and your husband for your generosity."

"Let me go, Henry," she commanded in a quaver.

He did so quickly and took on a look of slavish innocence. "And I also need to stay long enough to make you believe me when I say—I'm truly sorry for all the wrongs I've done you and crave your gracious forgiveness."

She didn't understand his oily words or her dizzying anger and shame, and now there was this vague fear racing through her veins, turning her blood to ice. She believed she knew this man, could trust this man; hadn't he helped save her life and Simon's, swore he'd never hurt her, pledged homage to her! He'd always been bothersome, but never frightening, not to her. Had she been wrong to urge Simon to leave her here alone with him? Tentatively, she backed away, feeling blindly for the door and, once outside, raced madly through the deluge for the safety of the cottage.

In the cottage's doorway she turned to see if he'd followed. He hadn't. Inside, the guards were sprawled in their usual places, staring vacantly, barely moving, and barring her way to the bedchamber. As she stepped cautiously over and between their limbs, their refusal to budge and blatant leering scorched her cheeks scarlet. John, sitting and scripting at the larger table, cast her a meek grin, then resumed his writing. The bedchamber's door seemed miles away. She gasped a bracing breath and forged ahead, at last stumbling over a boot and through the door that had no bolt. They never felt they needed a bolt! She sank relieved across the bed, closed her eyes, and concentrated on slowing her heart and collecting her thoughts and strength. Then there came the knock, and the oh, so irritating voice, "Maura, it's Henry. Let me come in. I need to explain more—"

"No you don't," she hotly interjected. "You need to leave me alone!" She waited for his argument but heard only the thudding of her own heart. Time passed with no interruptions, and she fell into a fitful sleep. Abrupt pounding woke her; she sat too quickly, and gingerly shouted out, "Who...who's there?!"

"It's Henry...Prince Rhys has arrived and asks for you."

Had she heard correctly? Rhys? Why would he ask for her? It was a ploy, Henry's ploy to lure her out to the other room, where she'd be forced to suffer again his cow-eyed, soppy rubbish. No, she wouldn't surrender, and barked, "Go away!"

The gruff voice that answered, "I cannot, my Lady, for I am in dire need of your mediating skills," drove her up from the bed and to the door.

"Prince Rhys!" she gushed, and heartily welcomed his plump and jolly self into the bedchamber. "I'm so pleased to see you!"

His eyes were shifty with doubt and voice tremulous as he asked, "Do you think it wise that we speak here, Maura?"

"Here is fine," she burbled. "Besides, there's no room to move or breathe out there. Now what is it you need?"

He detected an odd shrillness in her speech, a wariness in her expression; her gestures were exaggerated and excessive, making him conclude, "Something's wrong."

"No, not a thing. You woke me, and I'm still a bit groggy."

Her explanation failed to quell his suspicion and he probed further, "Where are Simon and your brother?"

"Gone to deliver medicine. Believe me, Rhys, I am fine, just a bit perplexed by your visit...You've not visited before."

"No..." His confusion eased a bit and, looking about, he mentioned vaguely, "I'm pleased. Yours is a fine home, though a little cramped."

"Hopefully not for much longer," she said with a tight grin. "And I thank you for the compliment...Now, what's this about mediating?"

"Oh...The Norman Baron has arrived, with soldiers, and requests an immediate meeting. I'm having a tremendously difficult time understanding him, as is Sulien. We do need you, and quickly."

Her loud and rapid response, "I'll need only a brief time to wash and dress, then I'll join you outside," betrayed an over eagerness to leave.

Rhys, still fuddled, slowly lumbered from the chamber. Maura stood still a frantic moment, hands at her temples—thinking, then she began flitting here and there; snatching up a fresh tunic, chemise, hose, and boots; and digging furiously in the trunk for her long veil. She made do with the tiny puddle of water in the pitcher and managed at least to freshen her face and hands. Once dressed, she performed the arduous task of wrapping the too heavy veil securely, and checking in her looking glass to ensure all her hair was covered. After a final primping of garments, she gathered her calm, and emerged into the main room. Her formal guise dropped Henry's jaw, and brought the guards and John to their feet.

Rhys appeared satisfied, and praised, "Very nice, Maura. Now we should go."

"I'll go along," offered a beaming Henry.

"No you won't," gritted Maura.

171

"But I've spoken to the Prince," he returned, "and it happens that I know the Baron Bernard of Neufmarche personally. He was a companion of my father's, and a fine friend to my family."

"I believe it may be to our advantage to have the FitzRoy attend," concurred Rhys. "He'll bring prestige to the meeting and also the assurance that the present King William acknowledges my lease of Deheubarth."

Maura started her objection, "But Rhys, I don't—"

Rhys soundly cut it short. "Maura, he *will* attend. Now come, the Baron seems an easily agitated soul."

As they exited the hut, Henry complained to Maura, "Why are you wearing that ridiculously ugly veil?"

Maura ignored him to breathe in crisp clean air warmed by the long absent sun, and Rhys answered for her, "Since it is highly irregular for a woman to preside at mediations, we have Maura dress in a nun-like fashion, hoping our adversaries will see her as a bride of Christ and, thus, remember their manners."

Henry stopped a moment to snigger and consider how shocked Christ would be by his bride's doings of earlier. And he reckoned the Baron would relish hearing the tawdry tale. He hurried to catch up, bouncy with anticipation and the certainty that the fun of this morning wasn't done—it was only beginning.

*****

CHAPTER ELEVEN - A TROUBLESOME WHELP

They had almost reached the village when Marc stepped before Simon, halting his stormy pace and silence, and demanded "What did Henry do?"

"I don't want to tell you," Simon curtly answered.

"Why?"

"Because...you might kill him."

"Maybe he *needs* to be killed," said Marc. "I know you, Simon. If you don't tell me or someone else what happened, you'll carry your anger with you all day and you'll be grouchy to everyone except Henry. Him, you'll ignore, and that's not fair, especially to your patients."

"I'm never grouchy to my patients," Simon parried.

"Of course you're not, but you'll be even nicer if you tell me what he did."

Simon let out an involuntary groan, plopped his bottom down in the sopping grass, and sputtered irritably, "He...he...we were in the stable."

Marc crouched and prompted, "You and Henry?"

"No...not at first. Maura and I."

"And?"

"We haven't had much opportunity to be...alone...together."

"I know that," said Marc.

"Well, finding ourselves alone, we took advantage of the moment to enjoy...God's breath! Henry caught us being intimate!"

"Oh, I see." Marc sat as well to ponder the situation, and wondered, "...How intimate?"

"Extremely so."

"What did you do?"

It seemed a peculiar question for Marc to ask, and again Simon took offense. "What we do is private."

"No, Simon. I mean what did you do to Henry?"

"Oh...I don't wholly recall...Chased him, grabbed him, then Maura told me to leave with you."

"Are you certain that was wise?"

Simon snorted for effect and said, "If I'd stayed *I* would have killed him."

Marc began to wonder why he wasn't being understood, and deduced the confrontation must have severely shaken Simon. "No. I mean, was it wise to leave Maura alone with him?"

"What are you implying?" Simon asked, askance.

"I don't trust him, Simon."

"I know you don't, but I do."

Marc rose in a fluster. "How can you?! I've never understood why you endure his nonsense. He's a coward, a rake, a liar! Why are you so blind to his faults?"

Simon implicitly replied, "He is my cousin, and my friend, and has been helpful to me in the past."

"In the past," argued Marc, "not the present. Why is he still here? Has he told you?"

"He's...visiting."

"Visiting?" Marc railed. "He's driving everyone mad with his interfering and enjoying it. He has to go before he does someone serious harm or it's done to him! If you can't convince him to leave, I can and will."

Simon had rarely seen Marc in such a dither, though Henry did have the talent to turn even the most imperturbable soul into a raving zealot. "No Marc," he said with tenuous calm, "I'll handle Henry...somehow."

"And how is Maura handling Henry?"

A complacent smile joined Simon's hunch. "I suppose right about now she's walloping him."

His quip made Marc soften. "Good. Come, we'll see to your patients."

Simon accepted Marc's hand up, and on they walked. As they neared Cynan's hut, situated near the outer wall of the commote, Marc carefully inquired, "Simon...Do you think there's a chance we might visit Gruffydd's hut, I mean, as long as we're here in the village?"

"Gruffydd's hut?" asked Simon, one brow hiked high.

"Yes."

"The hut where Gael happens to reside?"

"You know it is."

Simon's smirk widened to Marc's disquiet and he taunted on, "Concerned about their welfare, are you?"

"Of course I am," Marc returned testily. "Aren't *you*?"

"Always."

"Then we'll visit?"

"I suppose we can manage a little time between patients."

"Good," Marc said with finality.

Yet Simon wasn't done. "You don't want to talk more about Gruffydd's hut?"

Simon's ribbing produced Marc's blush and chuckled reply, "Not really."

"Later perhaps?"

"Maybe." Marc swiftly retreated to the subject of doctoring. "What problems will we see at Cynan's hut?"

"No serious problems," said Simon. "His mother, Olwen, is eight months pregnant, and I can offer a few recipes that may lessen her discomfort. And you know of, and surely have heard Cynan's cough?"

"Oh, yes," Marc answered. "What cure do you have for him?"

"I've been easing his trouble with mustard and figs boiled in ale, yet his cursed hacking always returns. So this time, I've prepared a stronger concoction meant for a dangerous cough."

Marc studiously reeled off the ingredients, "Sage, rue, and cumin, pounded like pepper, then boiled with honey, and made into a confection. Take a spoonful night and morning."

Simon beamed and shook his head in wonder. Then with deep affection, he patted Marc's cheek and remarked, "You are indeed a marvel."

*****

Rhys and Henry, accompanied by two guards each, followed Maura through curious on-lookers and a throng of hauberk-clad Norman soldiers. For Maura, the sight of conical tents being raised along the road leading to the llys unleased a rash of disabling memories. And the sound of Henry's incessant gabbling further clarified the horrid time they had been caught in a castle siege in Normandy. The soldiers were blissfully unaware that their coarse comments regarding the fat Prince, his frigid mare, and his jester, were fully understood. And while Henry chortled, Maura's resolve faltered, and she wished Simon was near.

Bernard's contingent was already present and seated at the tables, set purposely in a horse-shoe fashion. They framed a blazing fire, and were adorned with linen cloth, silver candleholders, flagons of honey mead and platters of bread, cheese, and fruit.

174

Bernard, a huge, smug looking man, with gray closely-cropped hair and craggy features, rested his broad backside across most of one bench, shifted for comfort, and barked at his squire for more wine. The mead spilled over the linen as the Baron and his men were rocked from their seats by Henry's boomed greeting, "If it isn't Bernard—the bungler!"

Bernard's jaw fell slack and his beady eyes bulged as Henry elbowed his way between Rhys' men and strutted brashly up to his comrade. The Baron's firm, friendly cuff to Henry's cheek sent him reeling. Henry exuberantly returned the favor and, in an explosion of raucous laughter, the friends embraced and exchanged loud and sloppy kisses. "God's teeth, lad!" roared Bernard. "What a pretty sight you are Henry. But why are you here?" He jerked Henry close and tensely whispered, "Has news of my misdeeds reached Normandy?"

"No...I'm visiting Prince Rhys on a mostly political mission. Just this morning I heard your name and the mediation mentioned and talked him into allowing me to attend."

"Then," invited Bernard, "sit by me, have my boy pour you a cup of this heathen wine, and let us goad these hairy simpletons into believing I was only on a pleasure jaunt through their swamp."

Maura dubiously watched Henry and Bernard from the table directly opposite. She didn't care for the Baron's haughty manner, and Henry's gooey idolatry reeked of disaster. Beside her, Rhys rambled instructions, yet her fascination with the reunited couple interfered. Rhys noticed her distraction and groused, "Maura, I beg your attention, for this is a most delicate matter."

"I apologize, Rhys...I'm still questioning your decision to bring Henry along."

"He'll be fine. And look, he's readily put the Baron at ease, and that is to *our* advantage."

Maura quit her argument and asked, "What is it I need to know?"

They put heads together, and Rhys rattled the specifics of his force's clash with Bernard's men on the borders of Deheubarth and Brycheiniog.

Henry glanced their way, and his gaze stuck on the top of Maura's veil. The rousing image of her straining in heat beneath Simon came to him with such clarity that he felt beads of sweat pop out on his brow, prompting Bernard to worry, "What is it, lad? You've suddenly gone white." He followed Henry's stare and twisted a leer. "Ah, so the Lady's caught your eye."

"Not caught it," said Henry, "she's owned it and the rest of me for a very long while."

Highly piqued, the Baron sat taller and leant closer to gossip, "But is she not the Prince's wife?"

"I'm sure he wishes it so, but no, she's my adopted cousin, Maura."

"Is she traveling with you?"

"Sadly no. She resides in Menevia and acts as Rhys' mediator."

"She acts for the enemy!"

"Rhys is not our enemy," Henry asserted. "My father formed a pact with him in '81. For forty marks a year, it ensures Rhys' vassalage of the territory of Deheubarth, and Rufus has honored their agreement."

"Rufus!" Bernard snorted and scoffed, "He's too busy buggering his boys to care what we do on the border. Your father granted me my holding in Hertfordshire, and I aim to follow the ambitions of my neighboring barons and enlarge my tract."

"I wouldn't risk angering Rufus or...Rhys," warned Henry.

"I don't waste precious time on anger," said Bernard. "I intend to embrace, pacify, then destroy." Bernard eased Henry's daunted look by asking, "Is this Maura an abbess?"

"They would have you believe so, but this nun's halo is a bit tarnished...She's six months pregnant."

Bernard's expression lit in admiration. "Is it yours, lad?"

"Alas no. She's married to another relative of mine, and..." Henry whispered lewdly, "Would you care to hear what I discovered them doing in a stable stall this very morning?"

Bernard's eyes almost fell out of his head as he drooled, "Yes...please!"

"So..." Maura surmised, "You mean to tell him to keep to his property, and stop harassing your soldiers and civilians."

"Precisely," said Rhys. "And should another incursion occur, my forces will join with those of Brycheiniog and chase the scoundrel back to Normandy. Do you require more?"

"No," Maura answered steadily.

Sulien entered. Maura and Rhys stood in respect; Henry and Bernard continued their sniggering. Sulien acknowledged all with a kindly nod and asked for bowed heads as he blest those present and the talks to come, then seated himself at the head table. Maura and Rhys remained standing and Rhys pronounced in Welsh, "We welcome you, Sir, and your legion, and pray our discussions now and in the future will be civil."

In Norman French, Maura translated verbatim Rhys' greeting, and added, "Have you any opening remarks, Lord Bernard?"

Oh, do I, Bernard thought as he stood, *but not for Rhys*. He swallowed a guffaw, cleared his throat and said, "I am honored to have been invited to this lovely village to sample your gracious hospitality, Sir, and, like yourself, hope our talks prove fruitful."

After Maura relayed Bernard's greeting, all sat, poured and gulped one mouthful of wine, then braced for the hammering. Rhys ordered Maura, "Ask him why he was in Brycheiniog."

"The Prince asks why you were in Brecknock."

"We were hunting...and strayed over our border. We meant no harm."

"Hunting and they strayed," said Maura.

"Then why attack our border guards?" ruffled Rhys.

Maura interpreted and Bernard laughed back, "We mistook them for bears!" Henry howled along, but they soon quieted when they heard no one else appreciating their joke.

"Lord Bernard," addressed Maura pointedly, "Prince Rhys does not take kindly to ridicule. I suggest you show him proper respect or take your men and leave here at once."

Bristled by her insolence, Bernard blustered back, "I won't be lectured to by a woman!"

Henry jerked on the skirt of Bernard's tunic and lowly advised, "By this one, you surely will be. Now calm yourself and leave the jesting for later. Embrace the man and gain his trust."

Maura was carefully explaining the disruption to Rhys, "I've asked him to take the meeting more seriously or leave," when a movement to her right captured her eye; she turned to see Owain take the seat by Sulien. He acknowledged Rhys but not her, which wasn't surprising, and she boldly asked Bernard again, "Why did you attack Rhys' border guards?"

"When my men hunt," remarked Bernard, "they tend to get overly excited and shoot at anything that moves. Once or twice, even *I* have had to dodge their arrows."

Maura didn't need to censor his reply, and Rhys waved his cue for her to relate their rehearsed speech. "The Prince requires you to keep to your property and cease harassing his soldiers and civilians."

"My intent is not to harass but to befriend," appeased Bernard. "After all, Sir, we are family."

Maura snapped in confusion to Rhys. "He wants to be your friend and says you're related."

"What?!" bellowed Rhys, raging scarlet and rising an inch from his chair. "I have no Norman poison in my blood!" Maura flashed him a wounded look, and he quickly atoned, "I'm not speaking of *your* particular blood, Maura."

She sighed and stated to Bernard, "The Prince doubts your claim."

Bernard explained, "Our connection is by marriage and is close...*Griffith Lewellen*, your predecessor, and ruler of all Wales, was grandfather to my wife, Agnes, and uncle to your sweet Lady, Gwladys."

Maura told Rhys, "He says you're both related by marriage to Gruffydd ap Llywelyn."

"How does he figure that?"

She replied, "I believe your wife and his mother-in-law are first cousins."

Rhys sat, brooding and thoughtful, then lifted his head to submit, "He could be correct. Ask him the name of his mother-in-law."

"The Prince requests the name of your mother-in-law."

"Nesta, daughter of Griffith and wife of Osbern FitzRichard."

Rhys recognized 'Nesta' and muttered, "He's correct. Tell him, since it appears we are related, we should afford each other the respect due relatives, and strive to restrain ourselves and our hostilities within our own borders."

Maura complied, and Bernard and Henry commenced whispering. She waited and grew impatient with their rudeness. "Henry," she berated, "the Baron does not need your assistance with his answer."

Henry shot her a heated reply, "I was telling him that Rufus has—"

She cut him off as curtly, "Stand and say to all what you said to Bernard! This is not the place for secrets."

He cringed to her order and snidely muttered, "I won't stand or speak to these barbaric dolts."

Maura leapt up to the insult, and pointed rigidly to the door. "Henry, leave here at once!"

Rhys popped up to the altercation and demanded, "What did he say?!"

"It's no matter," dismissed Maura. "He's being rude."

"To you?"

"To us all."

Henry listened to their grunting and discerned Rhys would most likely agree with Maura and force him to go...But he didn't want to leave, not yet. He was enjoying himself immensely. So he gulped his pride and more wine, and stood to declare dashingly, "My dear Lady Maura, I deeply regret my rudeness, and will repeat in English my statement to Bernard. I was simply reiterating the pertinent truth that Rufus has agreed to honor my father's pact with Rhys made in '81, which secures the Prince's continued wardship of the territory of Deheubarth. Prince Rhys tendered me the lease payment of 40 marks during my stay at Dinefwr."

"Your point is well appreciated, lad," said Rhys.

With a grudging nod, Maura scorned in French, "I won't suffer more of your pranks, Henry."

Henry hung his head in submission, then raised an indulgent smile. "I'll gladly do your bidding, my sweet Lady, now and forever."

Bernard chortled and slapped Henry's back to acclaim, "What a silver-tongued devil you are, Henry! You've got her all aflutter." Then he urgently whispered, "What color is her hair?"

"Flame red."

Bernard practically swooned to Henry's answer, and proposed with delight, "You'll bring her to my tent after the talks, where we'll drink decent wine, lots of wine, and discuss her attributes in private. Please Henry, say you'll bring her!"

Alarming is the power this woman wields over men, concluded Henry as he considered the salivating dog at his side. He'd agree. Why not? It would certainly keep Bernard elated for the remainder of the day, and wasn't that beneficial to both parties? "I'll bring her," he complied, "and perhaps others as well."

Meanwhile, Maura sat with Rhys and muttered bitterly, "There's no point in continuing. The Baron is near to drunk, and Henry revels in being a nuisance. I suggest we meet again, late afternoon, without Henry and without the wine."

Rhys didn't answer directly, but looked to Owain. "What say you, Owain?"

Owain focused disgust on the prattling Normans, then answered in a noncommittal manner, "I agree."

"With what?" forced Rhys.

"With..." he haltingly admitted, "...the Lady."

"And Sulien, do you concur?"

"Fully," said the Bishop.

"Fine," decided Rhys. "We will regroup here late afternoon. I thank all of you for your presence, and Maura, for your patience. Please relate our decision to our guests."

She stood and announced, "Lord Bernard, it is the Prince's wish that we adjourn our meeting till late afternoon."

"But," he strongly objected, "I haven't had my chance to speak!"

"You will have more than ample time to speak your defense later and..." She shifted her glare to Henry and flared her finish, "you will speak it—alone!"

All stood to leave. Rhys directed Maura, Owain, and Sulien to stay behind. After promising to meet Bernard in his tent, Henry idled about, lurking and listening, but he could make no sense of the language spoken. Maura seemed not to notice him and, as he intently watched her alert expression and attended to her speech, he marveled at her elucidation of the grating gibberish. She had even mastered the accent! He knew that she'd not known Welsh before she settled here. Simon had and, of course, had taught her. Yet to have become so proficient in the short span of four months? It seemed an intriguing mystery...Definitely one worth pursuing further.

"Henry!"

Maura's call disturbed his whimsy. He snapped to attention. "Yes, my Lady."

"Is there something you need?"

"Not that I can think of at the moment."

"Then why are you still here?"

He fumbled for a reason. "I...I was waiting for...I would speak to you about the Baron."

"I don't care to speak to you."

His hurt was apparent in his pout. "Why are you being so vile to me?"

Austerely, she left the men and took Henry aside, where she lectured, "Henry, with your knowledge of the Crown's position on the ruling of Deheubarth, I can understand why you believed you could help this situation. But you have yet to show in your behavior a willingness to help anyone but yourself. The clash between these armies was not a harmless argument. Three of Rhys' soldiers were killed in the skirmish, and if a peaceful settlement is not reached this day, the result could be a full invasion, with many more dead. I don't want that to happen, and that's why I'm here. Kindly tell me *your* intent."

He stood dumbly pensive, then replied, "You don't know the Baron as I do. He's a ruthless, conniving snake. I was only trying to cajole him into admitting his crimes and recognizing the Welsh as a fighting force worthy of his respect and caution. I've done a fair amount of mediating myself—"

"With Simon," injected Maura.

"And alone as well!" Henry swiftly defended. "You and I use different techniques, yet surely we aim for the same purpose—peace. Who's to say which method is more persuasive?"

"*I* say, Henry, as does Rhys. He shares my decision not to allow your attendance at our next meeting. Now, please leave!"

It was as if she'd slapped him again, and Henry was growing weary of her impertinence. And in his parting glare, Maura spied the same coldness that had accompanied their altercation of the morning, when he'd held her still, and she'd known she couldn't break free. Her fear returned with a paling vengeance and, as the child lurched within her, she hunched over in pain, hugged her belly and swiped out for the edge of the table. In a flash, Rhys was at her elbow, demanding, "What's he said? What's he done?!"

Maura held him in suspense till her pain had ceased, then faintly answered, "No...nothing. He's done nothing."

"Are you ill, Maura?" worried Sulien. "Should we fetch, Simon?"

She turned on him a sublime expression and grinned. "The child kicked me, that's all."

"Come sit. Mead will help." Rhys guided her back to her spot on the bench, and fussed in his usual effusive fashion. "Now drink the whole of the cup, and I'll have Simon fetched."

Maura dismissed his fluster with a pat to his hand. "You needn't fetch Simon for I am perfectly well." She glanced self-consciously at Owain, reckoning her weakness would feed his objections to her participation in the accords. Instead, his expression betrayed genuine concern, and she promptly used this advantage to draw him into the conversation. "Owain, I believe Bernard's attack on your men was a blatant act of aggression, not a hunting accident. What say you?"

His answer was predictably brief, but effective, "I agree, and I see no worth in entertaining the brute. I suggest instead, doubling our border forces and encouraging the Lord of Brycheiniog to do the same."

"We will talk first!" said Rhys.

"Why?!" fumed Owain.

"Because," defended Rhys, "in the past four months, mediations have averted at least four potentially serious frays and thus saved countless lives."

"But..." Owain paused his countering briefly to study Maura. The sense that she shared his suspicion bolstered his confidence, and he spoke without reserve, "It's not the talks I question, it's the Baron. He's evil and aims to kill—you."

Rhys laughed off his prediction. "Owain, you are so morose." Owain dropped a vexed expression to the table top and Rhys resolved, "We will gather late afternoon, and strive once more to pacify the Baron. Our talk will focus on hunting privileges, territorial lines, and rewards for conciliation. And after we will have fun!"

"Fun?" asked Maura. "Fun with Bernard?"

"No," chuckled Rhys. "You've forgotten we sup together this night in celebration of your husband's birthday."

"Tonight?" gaped Maura. "Yes, I *had* forgotten. We will attend, gladly. We are in dire need of fun."

After farewells, Rhys and Sulien departed, leaving Owain and Maura alone. Owain wondered if she noticed he'd stayed, for she seemed plagued and distracted by worrisome thoughts. She sat perfectly still, her fingers pressed to her lips, her brow deeply furrowed. He was curious and broke her trance with the question, "Where's your husband?"

Her gasped reply panicked his heart, and he quickly atoned, "I didn't mean to startle you."

"I'd thought you'd gone. I'm sorry, what did you ask, Owain?"

"Where's your husband?"

"Attending to his patients."

"Why do you suffer the pup?" asked Owain.

Owain's abbreviated version of Welsh always seemed hardest to comprehend, and she returned in question, "Who do you mean?"

"The Norman Prince. He's obviously nothing but a troublesome whelp."

"Yes, that's partly true," she said with remorse. "But once, he was sweet to me, and helped save my life." Her last three words cracked her voice, and Owain felt ashamed, when she confided, "And I'm afraid...that he's somehow changed and—"

He waited but she didn't finish, and she needn't for he knew her fear, had seen it each time she'd addressed this Henry. The pup was a disarming liar, and capable of great harm. *But harm to whom?* Owain pondered. And then came a flash of insight— *The FitzRoy is no danger to the Welsh—the danger he poses is to his own kin!*

Maura was eager to switch thoughts and brightly asked, "Will you join our supper?"

"No," he bluntly replied.

And as he stood to leave, she answered his terseness with the compliment, "You are very welcome to come to our supper...*Sir.*"

*****

"How did you learn to speak to your patients?" asked Marc, as he and Simon trod from Cynan's hut onto the lane leading to the village common.

"Learn to speak to my patients," Simon repeated in a quandary. "How do you mean?"

"The courtesy you show," specified Marc, "how you put them at ease, gain their trust?"

"I don't know that I do anything special. I just speak to them with the respect and caring I'd speak to any acquaintance, and surely that's not difficult for someone like yourself."

"Simon, I've done very little talking since I was sent to the Montgomery's castle at eight years of age. There was always someone to do the talking for me."

"Practice...that's what will help," helped Simon. "Our next patient, Bleddyn, speaks fluent English. I'll let you talk to him."

"Maybe not the next one," Marc skittishly replied.

Simon understood his hesitancy. "Perhaps in a few days, you'll feel more comfortable."

"Yes...I'm sure I will. What's *Blethen's* trouble?"

"His war wound is paining him."

"And what relief do you have for him?"

"Bruised thyme boiled and thickened in ale as an ointment."

Marc was mentally rehearsing the recipe when he smelled, then saw smoke. Simon noticed it as well and they took off in a run for the center of town. They both stopped short as the conical tents came into view and, sharing the same dread, swiftly donned their hoods. They crept cautiously forward to examine more closely the camp, yet there seemed nothing foreboding about the gathering. The Norman soldiers wandered about, hauling pails of water, arm loads of wood, blankets, and pots. Villagers approached with peace offerings of food, milk, and ale. Then Simon remembered the mediation. "It must be the Norman Baron who's been harassing Rhys' troops on the north border. He's come with his troops to negotiate a truce, and Rhys has asked Maura to assist with the talks."

"Doesn't it worry you?" asked Marc.

"Does what worry me?"

"Maura being in the center of such a charged situation."

"Rhys assures her protection," said Simon. "Maura loves having the power to wage peace. Even if I was concerned, I'd never insist she stop, she's far too proficient at her task."

"As proficient as you were?"

"Immensely more. I haven't the patience," Simon noted distantly, while his squinted gaze swept down the bustling lane to the llys. He shielded his eyes and beheld Maura descending the long house steps. Yet once she reached the base, she was instantly swallowed up by the crowd. A sense of alarm propelled Simon forward and, with Marc trailing, he leapt, skirted, and searched his way through the encampment.

"Henry...no!" shouted Maura, straining to wrench from his grip. "I won't visit the Baron's tent!"

"He only requests you share a cup of his wine and a moment of his company," whined Henry. "It will be to your and the Prince's advantage to win Bernard's good graces."

"But according to you," she reminded, "he has no good graces."

"He does have, but they're deeply buried and only your beauty can revive his goodness."

"Stop!" she cried and rolled her eyes in exasperation. "You forget, I'm not one of your empty-headed women who's duped by every false compliment you drip."

"But...I *promised* him—"

"Promised him what?!" she yelled, yanking harder.

"My Lady...I'm grateful to you for agreeing to meet with me." Bernard stood by the door to his tent, smiling so his every rotted tooth showed. Invitingly, he gestured her inside.

"I didn't—" was all she was able to protest, before Henry nudged her from behind and into the tent.

Her discomfort raged and she tried to retreat, yet was halted by a guard barring the exit. "Rh...Rhys," she sputtered to Henry, "will be highly displeased when I tell him—"

"Tell him what?" goaded Henry in a strict whisper. "That you spent precious time between meetings uncovering your adversary's strengths and weaknesses? That is the work of a mediator."

"That is the work of a spy," she corrected.

"I'm only concerned with bettering your skills," stressed Henry.

Bernard turned from his trestle table, brandishing two cups of wine, and approached with the bowed offering, "Now we'll drink and you can tell me, my gracious Lady, how you came to hold such an exalted position as mediator."

Henry accepted his cup with a humble nod; Maura waved hers away and argued, "No...I want no wine, I *want* to leave."

The Baron's cloying expression soured as he thrust the cup into her hand and stridently ordered, "Drink the wine and take off the veil!"

Maura felt the tension of his fingers on the material as they crept upward. She jerked away, leaving the Baron with the veil, and lurched for the exit. At the opening, she tossed her cup at Henry, drenching his face and hair with claret, then threw her weight against the guard. He tumbled into the adjacent tent, and she darted away, her heart racing to the Baron's shrill commands, "Stop her! The lady with the red hair. Stop her!" The soldiers dropped their chores to their Liege's shrill cry, unsheathed their swords, and hunted fervently for the culprit.

Simon and Marc heard the orders as well and stormed their way into the chaos. "I see her!" hollered Marc, catching a glimpse of red wrestling with a sentry. Simon saw the same and pummeled his way through the resisting brutes. Reaching her, he leapt back to dodge the swipe of a blade; before his attacker could aim again, Simon butted his head to the guard's belly and dropped him gasping to the ground. He restrained the man with one hand and drubbed him senseless with the other. Marc pushed Maura to the ground, and knelt over her, his mind and body steeled to kill.

All mayhem ceased to a piercing whistle. The baleful sound of rushing boots answered as Rhys' entire contingent converged from every direction and advanced furiously down the lane. Spears and broadswords wielded, they jeered, hooted, and taunted, while awaiting their commander. He strode daringly between his men and, upon reaching their lead, thundered in rough and broken French, "Le...let the Lady go!"

Bernard scuttled forward to defuse the crisis, and was struck dumb by the bristling presence of Owain and not Rhys manning the troops. Owain brashly redressed Bernard's shock, "I said, let the Lady Maura go!"

"I...I don't have the lady!" shrilled Bernard. He grew light-headed at the looming disaster brought on by the brazen bitch. "S...so," he sputtered, "you may kindly disperse your men."

Owain had absolutely no clue what was said and took a threatening step forward. Maura heard and clearly realized the danger. She scrambled up and barreled her way between the Normans and toward Owain. Simon stumbled after her, finally catching her wrist, and forcing her still. "No, Simon!" she vehemently protested. "I must stop them. They can't fight, not because of my stupidity!"

He didn't understand, but promptly released her on the condition, "Then go...but I'll go with you." Marc joined them and they gingerly squeezed their way through the crushing throng.

The deadlock festered, the leaders snarling at each other, their soldiers bustling behind them, drooling for blood and poised to strike. At long last, Maura shoved to the fore of the Normans, and soundly ordered to Owain, "Call off your men, Owain! There will be no battle for my sake."

"You weren't abducted?" he asked.

"No."

"Nor harmed?"

"No...I am grateful for your concern for my safety, but there's absolutely no cause for this feuding. There is, though, an immediate need for more talks."

Simon, partially hidden, intently observed the drama from a short distance away, for Bernard appeared perilously familiar. He struggled inwardly with a zealous impulse to burst forth and remove Maura from the simmering stalemate. Yet he held back, knowing her command of the situation complete, and his meddling not needed. Marc readied for attack, studied Simon, and awaited a signal.

A path cleared and Rhys brusquely arrived, barking, "What goes on here?!"

"I believed the Lady Maura was abducted," related Owain, "and gathered your troops to force her release."

Rhys narrowly scrutinized the belligerent guises of all present, and assumed, "Well, it appears you've succeeded, Owain. Relieve these men before they become too riotous to control. Maura, tell the Baron to follow me and Owain to the cathedral where we will conclude our discussions."

She cautiously did as told, and was intent on accompanying the trio, when Rhys stopped her with a firm grip to her shoulder and the blunt dismissal, "No, Maura. I think it best you stay away, for your presence will only result in more discord. Sulien will translate." And they left her, squashed between the two volatile factions, her posture sagging and pride shattered. Another whistle sounded; the Welsh sluggishly disbanded, and the Normans resumed erecting their camp.

From behind, Simon's arms encircled Maura, supporting her disappointment, while he soothed in a murmured whisper, "We'll go to Gael's, where you'll rest and tell me all that's happened."

She was about to consent when she remembered Henry. "No!" she exclaimed. "First you'll come with me." He devotedly followed her tug back amongst the soldiers and into the Baron's tent. Once inside, he stared with her down to the ground at three dropped cups and port stained straw. She raised a pinched and ashen face. "Where? Where's he gone?"

"Where's who gone?"

"Henry..."

"I've not seen him. Come, my love," he gently urged. "If we stay, we'll only rile the troops more."

She hesitated, then limply assented. Marc had retrieved Simon's sack of remedy bags, and joined them on their trek to Gael's. As they ventured further from the llys, the villagers' interest in the Norman camp dwindled, and normalcy once again prevailed. The three soon spied Gael prodding her small team of livestock toward the common. Henry, the pup, merrily yapped along, nipping at hooves and tails, and narrowly dodging the cows' lethal kicks. Gruffydd, Cynan, and Cynan's younger sister, Nia, a sylphlike child with pale features, wispy yellow hair, and milk white skin, romped over the green, shrieking, tumbling, and clambering trees. Gruffydd spied the somber trio and exuberantly raced their way. His zeal was overtaken by the pup, who leapt into Simon arms and fervidly lapped his face.

"Stop, Henry!" sputtered Simon, then he lauded, "So this is where you escaped to. And I believed you dull...Now I see you've outwitted us all."

Noting their dour expressions, Gael hurriedly approached, insisting, "What's happened?"

In chorus they heaved a bitter sigh and muttered, "Henry."

"Why am I not surprised?" said Gael with a knowing smirk. "Come, enjoy the sun, sit, and rail a bit."

Promptly the men were captured and dragged off by the children to suffer the rigors of play, and Maura accompanied Gael beneath an oak, to sit and spill her upset of the morning.

Henry FitzRoy sat upon a wooded mound overlooking the Norman encampment, guzzling Bernard's wine and grumbling to himself. He'd hoped the clash of this morning would have resulted in a lively fray worthy of his interest, yet because of Maura's intervention, it had fizzled to nothing but a polite tiff. One of his goals, however, had been accomplished, that of retaliation. He grinned smugly, recalling the satisfying sight of Maura standing alone and humiliated while Rhys, Owain and

Bernard sauntered off to talk. And to himself, Henry vowed, *If I'm not allowed at the accord—then neither are you!*

*****

Simon, Maura, Marc and the pup did not return to their home that day. Marc and Simon finished their deliveries then returned to family, friends, and beasts to spend the time till supper on the green, where the ambiance and company were far more jovial than at the cottage.

After locking the pup inside Gael's home and escorting Gruffydd, Cynan, and Nia to Olwen's hut, the remaining four, feeling far less encumbered, ventured forth to the llys. They stopped before entering to consider the Norman camp, now fully erected and seemingly peaceful. The glow and ash of cooking fires penetrated the encroaching dark, perfuming the air and worrying their bellies. Gael and Simon readily scaled the steps, but Maura and Marc held back, uncertain as to the kind of reception they'd receive inside. Maura's doubt instantly was doused by the buoyant greeting, "Maura, get your comely self inside!" Rhys stood, his stoutness clothed in fur and leather, looming in the doorway, arms wide and begging to be filled. With a huge smile, Maura grabbed up Marc's hand, and dragged him into the long house, decorated in a formal fashion befitting a Prince. The trestle tables had been left standing, still draped with linen, and decorated with Raythyen's culinary excellence. Soft candle light, in contrast to the usual garish torch light, illuminated the festivities with an ethereal glow. Maura disappeared willingly into Rhys' hug, received two gushing kisses, and his ebullient apology, "I feel I left you this morning feeling frightfully worthless. That, my dearest Lady, was never my intent. The situation called for brisk action and calming words. Since the Baron seemed overly enamored of you, I felt your presence would cause Bernard to mince and strut further, and he'd persist in dismissing the matter at hand— the possibility of war."

"And was your talk successful?" she wondered hopefully.

"Not entirely, but I believe satisfactory to most concerned."

"Including Owain?" she chanced.

"Nothing is satisfactory to Owain."

His quip made Maura smile, and she heartily accepted his guiding hand to the tables. Simon stood by her chair, beaming at her improved mood, then he blushed to Rhys' wry comment, "And here stands your very old husband. I hope you will promptly inform me when he's no longer capable of servicing you as you rightly deserve to be serviced."

"And that will be never!" she passionately pronounced, embracing Simon and gifting him a most vehement kiss. Lusty exclamations followed, then cheers as most present approached Simon with congratulations on the anniversary of his birth.

Marc and Gael meandered about, perusing the food and the building, with Gael chattering tales of her time as wife of the Pennaeth. Rhys spotted them and grew curious with envy. He loudly advanced on the couple. "Gael! Who is your friend?"

His dubious look relaxed to her bright reply, "Oh Rhys, you haven't met Marc, Maura's brother. Marc speaks fluent English."

"Marc!" Rhys thrust out his hand, grasped Marc's firmly, and rocked his entire body with the greeting, "I've been ever so eager to make your acquaintance. So you were a member of King William's elite fighting force! How terribly exciting for you!"

"Yes, Sir. And I'm equally as honored to know you," said Marc, staring into one of the friendliest faces he'd ever encountered.

"You'll sit by me at supper and we will exchange tales of war!" enticed Rhys.

184

Marc's forced grin answered as he helplessly watched Rhys hustle Gael away and into a darkened corner. He didn't want to appear overly inquisitive so he kept to his place and, piqued, strove to hear.

"And so, my lovely," murmured Rhys, his hands and lips roving, "have you decided?"

Gael wriggled, tittered, and sputtered back, "No...no, not yet."

"Then when?" he whined.

"By the time I leave here this night, you will know my desire."

"I want to know and feel it now!" begged Rhys.

"Rhys stop!" scolded Gael. "Remember where you are."

"I don't care where I am, nor does anyone else!"

"I do," she firmly returned.

With that, he backed away, and resumed his polite mastery, "Then, my lovely lady, would you agree to dine with me?"

"I would love to," she said, "but I've promised to sit by Marc as well, so I will sit between the two of you."

Rhys scowled and blustered, "Is he my rival for your body?"

"Don't be crude, Rhys. My *body* is not a prize in any sense...at least not as yet," she teased with a chuckle, then left him to slip her arm in Marc's.

"Did he offend you?" was Marc's concern.

"Rhys?!" Gael scoffed in surprise. "Oh no, he rarely offends, he mostly amuses."

Rhys gloomily watched them stroll to the table. Marc was a mighty handsome man, and quite valiant, or so he'd heard. Yet he'd also been informed that the Norman knight had defected from the Montgomery's army. Such a soldier's experiences would be invaluable in helping Rhys devise his military strategy against the Normans. In doing so, however, Marc would need to denounce his countrymen and his morals and commit the sin of treason. Most would for a fitting bribe, and the perfect bribe was always a woman—though not Gael; he'd not have Gael. And if Marc did choose to cooperate, Rhys would strive to find him a lady as bonny and spirited as she.

Maura and Simon silently slipped onto the main table's bench. She noticed his shifty disquiet, and knew his dread. He worried that Henry would soon arrive; so did she, for she didn't know what to say to him, or how to behave in his obnoxious presence, or how *he'd* behave. Her thoughtful gaze swept fleetingly over the other revelers—Sulien, Raythyen, Rhys' two guards, Gael and Marc looked most relaxed and pleasant together—then her interest settled on a new face. A steeply tall, sandy-haired gentleman sat to Rhys' left, unassumingly attending to the various conversations. He was quite fine looking, with shaven face, gentle sloping mustache, sharply chiseled features, and piercing blue eyes. "Simon," she asked, tapping his shoulder, "Who is that man sitting by Rhys?"

Simon glanced over at the fellow, then dropped his eyes to ponder his identity. He met her gaze and wagged his head. "I don't know. I've never seen him before."

"I wonder..."

"Wonder what?" asked Simon.

"If he isn't one of the contenders for Pennaeth."

Simon's whisper agreed, "Yes...He could be just that!"

Both returned their curiosity to the young man and followed his trance-like stare to Gael. Gael also had noticed the stranger, and his intense scrutiny. Never before had she been the recipient of so many men's hungry looks, and she rather enjoyed it. She believed the time ripe for her to interrupt Rhys' rendition of one of his more gruesome frays, so she abruptly asked, "Rhys, who is your friend?"

"Friend?" he replied, bemused.

"The gentleman at your side."

"Oh, Taredd!" Rhys spouted in Welsh. "I've quite forgotten my manners. Gael, I present to you my advisor, soldier, and yes, fine friend, Taredd."

"I'm honored, Sir," she sweetly greeted.

"As am I, my Lady."

"And Taredd," continued Rhys, "this quiet, tolerant soul, sitting by Gael, is my mediator's brother, Marc."

The two men exchanged polite, though terse nods, Marc repeating almost in a whisper, *"Tareth..."*

Taredd mimicked his aloof style, and muttered back, "Marc."

Huge platters abundant with cheese, flat bread, thick, frothy butter, and blandly seasoned, yet still tasty meats, were set before the company, and the mead pitcher was passed around. All heartily indulged in the repast, and exchanged spritely banter that grew more animated with each emptied pitcher. The tables were cleared and, for amusement, dice and a chess board were brought out; a woman harpist from the commote magically appeared and proceeded to entertain with the most splendid melodies and ballads. Rhys strutted about mingling and exuberantly watching the matches. Though they could not understand each other's speech, Marc and Taredd nonetheless were heatedly engaged in a game of dice. Both kept their excitement hidden and were fairly equal in their luck; Gael loudly provided interpretation and encouragement. At the opposite table, Simon and Sulien engrossed themselves in a game of chess as they often did when Sulien and Raythyen visited the cottage. Maura offered suggestions to Simon, while vaguely listening to Raythyen's jabbering about cooking and babies. Rhys strode close to boast, "I believe this day I proposed to Bernard a most shrewd notion for taming the tensions between our two armies."

"And what was your proposal?" asked Simon.

"That we hold games," replied Rhys.

"Games," Simon echoed with doubt. "What sort of games?"

"Dice and chess?" wondered Maura.

"Of course not," retorted Rhys. "True games of skill—archery, wrestling, staff and sword play."

Simon set down his bishop and, after a grim sigh, inquired, "Do you think that wise, Rhys? Perhaps these games will serve only to heighten tensions."

"Nonsense," Rhys scoffed. "We are after all civilized creatures, no matter our heritage."

Simon and Sulien exchanged exasperated looks, then continued their match, Simon muttering beneath his breath, "Then I'd better thread up my needles."

Fingering the chain that held Rhys' ring round her neck, Maura suddenly recalled her family's mystery; she excused herself, rose, and taking Rhys' elbow, urged him away from the table and toward the door. "Rhys," she mildly asked, "would you join me outside for air?"

"Nothing would please me more, Maura," he gushed with twinkling eyes.

Outside, they roamed the yard, merrily taking in the stars and a plump moon. Somewhere close a pipe played a haunting tune. In fatherly fashion, Rhys held her arm securely in his and queried, "Where is your cousin?"

"I don't know, nor do I want to know," answered Maura.

"He's upset you?"

"I'm afraid it's a bit more than that, but I'm certain you don't want to hear the lurid tale."

Eyes wide, Rhys disagreed, "I do, indeed!"

"I'll tell you later," she promised. "Now, I have something to ask you about and thank you for."

Rhys' suspense burbled, "What...what is it?"

She pulled the chain holding the ring out from under her chemise, and held it up to his eye level. The gold shimmered in the moonlight, and Rhys beamed as brilliantly, "So, he's given it to you. I'm highly pleased!"

"As am I," offered Maura, "but I'm also wanting to know, Rhys, where would I have seen a ring of this type before?"

"I don't understand your question," said Rhys, leaning up against the yard's fence.

"When Simon presented me the ring, I had a distinct memory of a similar ring glimmering on the hand of someone in my past."

Rhys recalled, "You told me before of your memory of the Welsh attack on your family. Your parents were killed and you and your brother were rescued and adopted by Simon's father..."

He faltered for the name which she swiftly provided, "Robert."

"Yes, Robert. *Your* father, you believe, was a vassal of King William's residing on the north border of Wales."

"I do believe that," she concurred, "but I have been given two vastly different versions of my parents' deaths."

"Explain," prompted Rhys.

"My guardian Rose lost her husband in the skirmish that she insists occurred on the Welsh border. Robert told me the battle took place between my father—who was his favored knight—King William's soldiers, and a Saxon army in Cornwall. You can understand my bafflement."

"I can fully understand it and do indeed share it, my Lady."

"I believe Rose speaks the truth," noted she, "and Robert has reason to hide it. Rhys, do you know of any battles that took place sixteen or seventeen years past on or about the north border? If a Norman baron was killed, it would have been a war worth gloating about."

"Maura," Rhys answered, "at that time I was in exile in Ireland, and I can't recall a bard ever telling such a tale."

A slurred, dark voice interrupted their quandary, "If your father was a loyal baron of King William's residing on or about the north Welsh border, then your father is still alive."

Maura snapped her startled face to their intruder, a tipsy Henry, and sharply insisted, "What are you saying?"

"Only two barons have dominated the lands straddling the north border. They were there during the conquest of England, and they are still there today—namely Robert of Rhuddlan, and Hugh of Avranches. I'm to visit them after I depart here, for one holds a good portion of my mother's lands and I aim to claim them all for myself. There was one other baron. Directly after the conquest, William FitzOsbern, my father's favorite, occupied the area southeast of the north border, but he died on the continent, so you couldn't have been his child."

"I saw my father killed, Henry!" assailed Maura. "His neck was slashed, his body burned! He tried to save me and Marc, but his wounds proved too deadly. I saw my mother's head cleaved from her body. My parents are gone!"

Rhys listened to their squabble with an expression of wavering doubt. He'd known of child abductions, and how frequently they were committed by both Norman and Welsh armies. "Perhaps," he spoke up, "you were children of a murdered steward, and neither this Robert nor this Hugh wanted you, so Simon's father, feeling pity, took—"

187

"But the ring!" interrupted Maura. "During the fight, someone was wearing a ring, precisely like this one."

"That's simple enough to figure," offered Rhys. "Your parent's slayer wore the ring."

"I don't know," flustered Maura. "When I see the ring in my mind, I don't feel hatred, I feel love."

"I'm dreadfully sorry, Maura," excused Rhys. "I don't believe I can help. I can however make some inquiries."

"I would appreciate the effort, Rhys."

"And if it pleases you," piped in Henry, "I can ask Hugh and Robert what they know. Maybe you're not an orphan after all."

His light-hearted comment didn't quell, it only hiked her upset, and she wanly mentioned to Rhys, "I'd like to go in now."

"I will take you in," comforted Rhys. He cocked his head, and hushed the pipe's melody with a brusque command, "Owain...you will join us inside."

There was no answer, only sounds of grunts and scrambling, then Owain stepped into the light, glowering.

"How did you know he was there?" asked Maura in amazement.

"He's always lurking about, playing that blasted whistle. He needs to learn some manners."

Even in the dark, Maura caught Owain's blush. To ease his embarrassment, she hurried inside. Simon rose to greet her, but his jubilant look soured at the sight of Henry. Henry caught his displeasure, halted his advance, and slumped glumly down on a bench near Marc and Taredd. His admiring gaze at once found Gael, her prettiness ablush, and eyes gaily glittering. She let out a buoyant whoop as Marc defeated his adversary. Marc covered his smirk with his palm, and his eyes challenged Taredd to another roll.

Henry nudged the tall blond's shoulder, and muttered in English, "It's my turn." Taredd surrendered his spot, and Henry swelled with pomposity as he scooted up close and snipped in French to Marc, "And what's the prize to be? Or should I ask who's it to be? I propose the luscious and, I'm certain, hot-blooded Lady Gael."

"Don't be ridiculous, Henry," scowled Marc.

"Ridiculous?" chuckled Henry. "If you think you're going to acquire her any way but by chance, you're the ridiculous one."

Gael knew by Henry's flirty glances that he likely was maligning her in French. His crudeness made her snort in disgust and turn to leave, yet Marc stopped her with a gentle touch and request, "No, Gael, please stay, I want you to watch me trounce this scoundrel."

She relented and leant forward on her palms in anticipation of the rascal's swift defeat. His humiliation, though, didn't come as quickly as she'd hoped. Henry's luck persisted and his unabashed howls and gyrations quickly drew everyone's attention. All crowded around to witness the near equal match, Simon crawling upon the table to see more clearly. Finally came the moment when the game would be decided by a final roll, and Henry appealed to Marc, "If the impossible should occur and you win, and if the Lady is not to be given, what will be your prize?"

Marc, who throughout the entire match had kept his calm, answered assuredly, "I will challenge you to a competition."

"What sort of competition?" Henry goaded, his voice betraying a slight quaver.

"You'll find out when I win. And your prize?"

"I reckon you'll have to wait as well."

Marc grabbed up the dice and with a sure shake, dashed them upon the table top. Breaths stopped as they danced, rolled, and at last rocked to a stop. Everyone counted, but Henry's addition proved fastest, and he leapt up on the bench and crowed in triumph. Other cheers sounded, including Rhys' who slapped both men's backs and acknowledged, "A fine show, my young Prince, and what do you demand of your cousin?"

Henry twisted a sneer at Marc and flouted, "A race."

"Fine!" boomed Rhys. "I'll pick the ponies, and—"

"No, Rhys," interjected Henry. "A race on foot."

"Damn you, Henry!" shouted Simon.

Rhys looked confused and asked Simon, "Why your anger?"

"Marc injured his thigh in the wars," groused Simon. "Henry knows this. A foot race would be no competition."

Rhys turned a highbrowed, miffed look at Henry, and decided, "If you have no sense of fair play, Sir, then I will gladly take on the task of choosing the style of feat." A suspenseful moment lingered, then Rhys bluntly pronounced, "Swords at sunrise."

Maura believed Henry would faint. In contrast, Marc belied no emotion, though she did notice a dim spark of confidence light his blank stare. Henry's shock raged to fury when Simon clambered down from the tabletop and positioned himself at Marc's back, his hands firmly clasped to his shoulders. Gael joined Simon's show of loyalty at Marc's left, and Maura moved to his right. Henry, huffing in insult, cocked his chin high and barged his way out the door. Raucous laughter followed his exit, and Rhys took advantage of the noise to take Taredd aside to suggest slyly, "I believe dawn will bring a performance of genius from the Norman Knight. The Lady Gael is obviously enamored of his gentlemanly way, and will no doubt be nuzzling up to her champion by late morning. I think, for *you* to win the lady's honor, you should decide on a competition where your expertise will be unchallenged."

"But, Sir," puzzled Taredd, "you've made your desire for the Lady's affections blatantly clear. Why encourage my interest?"

"Because I love a game. And this game is turning highly intriguing. I didn't figure on a Norman rival, and if I lose her, I'll lose her only to a Welshman."

"Which Norman, my Prince. The room seems thick with them."

"The young lad you played dice with named Marc."

"Will you compete in the games, my Prince?"

"Of course...I aim to humble the Baron."

They both cracked smug grins and Taredd snidely wondered, "And what of Owain?"

"I don't..." Rhys paused as a mischievous notion fired his eyes. "Yes, I do know! Owain, come here!" he called giddily. Owain scrambled up from his spot by the mead keg and wandered forward suspiciously. He gave a vague nod to Taredd, and looked to his Prince for orders. Rhys laughingly spilled them, "On the morrow, you will compete against a Norman—"

"Oh no I won't," intruded Owain. "I've told you my objections to your idea of playing with the scum outside, and I refuse to join in."

"You'll compete if I say you'll compete. And your contender will be...Simon!" Rhys shouted, waving at the table.

Simon rose from his seat by Marc and strode over. "What is it, Rhys?" Then he spotted Owain, and his expression and tone turned wary, "Is there a problem?"

"No...no problem," chuckled Rhys. "No...none at all. I've just been considering a game between you and Owain here."

"Of dice?" asked Simon.

"Nothing so trivial," said Rhys. "The idea of a mounted race, as I mentioned before, still excites me. And does it excite the two of you?" Simon and Owain's eyes briefly met, then darted to their feet. The two men squirmed with indecision; Owain scratched absently at his bearded chin, while Simon rubbed the back of his neck. Rhys grew frustrated and commanded, "I'd like an answer sometime soon!"

Simon promptly replied with a tenacious glare to Owain. "I'm willing."

"Then so am I!" blurted Owain in return.

"Wonderful!" gushed Rhys. "Simon, I noticed a herd of lusty stallions in your paddock this morning. Can we perhaps borrow two?"

"They've been itching all week long for a good run," noted Simon.

"Then it's settled...You'll race tomorrow—midday."

Simon and Owain's sharp nods agreed and separated them. Simon's hopeful look prompted Maura to grasp up his hands and excitedly ask, "What did Rhys want?"

"A race."

"Between?"

"Me and Owain."

"And you agreed?"

"I did."

"And Owain?"

"He agreed as well."

"Are you pleased, Simon?"

"Yes...very, my love."

She caught his exuberance and beamed with him, and they shared a sweet kiss, which Gael interrupted with a snorted, "If you're able, I'd like to address the two of you with lips apart."

They obliged her request and followed her to the door, where she announced, "I expect the remainder of the evening to be drearily boring, so since Henry's away, I'd like to offer you, Simon, my gift. Maura, I believe you will be thrilled with my present as well—"

"Gael!" Simon laughed, "What is it?"

"I happily give you two the use of my cottage for the entire night and a bit of the morning as well. No one will bother you, especially not Henry, for no one but myself will know where you've gone. And I will not confess your whereabouts, even if faced with the threat of torture." She took their hands and added with great affection, "For your trial of this morning, you definitely deserve—"

Simon broke in to complain, "Maura, you told her?"

"Yes..." she retorted. "You told Marc!"

"She didn't go into great detail, Simon," defended Gael.

Their dander evaporated as the wonders of Gael's present suddenly took hold of their minds, hearts, and fantasies. Their gooey look made her snort again, and hustle them out the door. "Go, before you make me ill."

"But," Maura protested, "where will you stay?"

"Here. And I won't allow Marc to return to your cottage. I wouldn't trust him there with Henry—alone. I'll make certain he's safely sheltered."

"But," added Simon, "we must say our farewells to Rhys and the others, and—"

"I'll do it for you. No one will take offense."

"Thank you, Gael," Maura said with the deepest sincerity.

"Believe me, it will be my pleasure to see you two happy again." She received a kiss on each cheek from both, and Simon also planted one on her hand. As they scurried off, she called after, "I suggest you get some sleep! After all, we do have some swordplay to watch...at dawn." Watching them kissing and clutching at each other on their way out of

190

the garden, made her smile and sigh with satisfaction and also a bit of hope. Maybe she'd be indulging in some cozy walks herself in the very near future.

Gael sensed breath on her neck, and felt warm fingers lace between hers. She turned to see Marc, and smiled delightedly to his request, "Care for a walk, my Lady?"

*****

Marc briskly steered Gael away from the Norman camp and along the moon glimmered path that led to the cliffs. She noticed the further they ventured from the llys the more relaxed his posture became. "Do you have reason to fear the Normans?" she asked, breaking their intense quiet.

Marc stared thoughtfully at her for a moment, then replied, "I don't really know, and I'm not keen on finding out."

"But you've agreed to a duel with Henry. Surely, both armies will be watching and someone may recognize—"

"I'll be hauberked and helmeted."

"Oh...That is wise. And you do intend to beat him easily, don't you?"

"Easily?" he repeated in a question. "Not likely."

"I was under the impression that Henry was more than slightly inept."

"I wouldn't have agreed to the fight if we weren't of near equal skill. It wouldn't have been fair."

"No I suppose you wouldn't have," she responded. "Let's not go too near the cliffs. I get dizzy."

"So do I."

They rested themselves on two boulders jutting from the spongy ground halfway between the commote and the sea, and simultaneously gazed up into the crisp, star-dotted heavens. "It is beautiful here," sighed Gael, "don't you agree?"

"Yes, I do..." Marc replied, boldly capturing her hand. "When I lived at Dunheved, every summer the three of us would visit the sea. I'd so look forward to those visits, and racing the beaches, like we did a week past."

"And Maura would always win," finished Gael.

"How do you know that?" he asked in amazement.

She answered with a mysterious smile and wag of her head and questioned on, "Who do you think will win the race tomorrow?"

"I know nothing of Simon's contender, so it's hard to predict—"

"Unfortunately," she interjected, "I do...I figure he'll find a way to cheat his way to victory."

Marc shrugged and grinned shyly as her grip on his hand firmed. Gael smiled too, then intently studied her intriguingly handsome escort. The naiveté his comely visage held was misleading. Inwardly, she felt certain he would instinctively know how to react in any circumstance. But then again, she recalled Maura describing him as terribly innocent. *Innocent how?* she wondered, as she cautiously asked, "Marc...was there a woman you cared for and had to leave behind in Normandy?"

He seemed not surprised by her inquiry and readily assured, "No. The only woman I spent any time with was named Tilley. She nursed me after my accident."

"Accident...the one Simon mentioned, when you hurt your thigh?"

"Yes...We were caught unarmed in an ambush and hid under a dead horse, only I got frightened and lunged for Simon. My leg shot out and got trampled on." Gael clenched shut her eyes and clearly imagined the horrific vision. While she was so distracted, Marc studied her and wondered, *Why did she ask such a question? Is she about to tell me to let go of her hand and take her back to the llys for she will soon wed the newly appointed Chieftain, and there really isn't any point to our—*

"Marc..." she intruded, "is there something you're wanting to say?"

191

"Maybe we should return to the long house," he blurted.

"Why? The ones who are left, all they talk about is war...and I'm so weary of their boasting. You don't seem so inclined."

"Because I'd rather forget it all. Was your husband a soldier?"

"No," Gael related. "He had been when younger, and a fine one I'm certain, for he was elevated to Chieftain, which is a great honor. He spoke little of his time in battle. I believe, like you, it upset him more than most. He was a kind and gentle man."

Her wistful look made him falter his next question, "Did...did you love him?"

"As a companion, yes...but...there was no...no—"

"You needn't answer," Marc eased, "if it's difficult for you."

"I'd like to answer. As man and woman, there was no passion between us, no spark. Not that there needed to be..."

"But?"

"When I'm with Maura and Simon and see how they act, and touch each other, I do regret not knowing such an intimacy."

"You sound as if you'll never get the chance to know."

"I may not."

He guessed the announcement was coming and waited, but she said no more, and he hurried to close the slack in their conversation. "I've not known such an intimacy either." He was a bit shocked that he'd spilled his confession so easily, and found he could not hold back the others. "And I thought, that because you'd been married and have a child, and you always seem so confident, that you knew a great deal about...intimacy."

"Oh no, Marc. I may be confident about most things, but definitely not about the ways of love. I also believe that one can act quite knowledgeable about something simply to hide their ignorance."

He smiled and offered, "Like Henry."

"Yes, like Henry...and I dare say Nesta as well. Are you disappointed?"

"Disappointed...how?"

"That I'm not as knowledgeable as I seemed."

"No...I'm relieved."

She laughed a little and he beamed, and she'd never seen his smile so wide. And then she felt his fingers lacing through her hair and his lips touching hers, so warm, inviting, stirring, as if they caressed every bit of her. And she kissed him back, voraciously searching to feel what she had missed, had imagined and dreamt, and she found it and would hopefully find so much more. And then they abruptly broke apart as if they were frightened of spoiling their magical moment by venturing further. Their hands clasped together more tightly than before and, quiet and dreamy, they started back to the long house.

As they entered the llys, Gael mentioned, "I promised Simon and Maura that I'd not let you return to the cottage alone with Henry. Sulien and Raythyen will welcome you staying the night here."

"Where will you stay?"

"Here as well."

He started to argue, "But..."

"There's no impropriety in us sleeping under the same roof, Marc. We did so the night Henry arrived."

He nodded ashamedly, then they both started to a bellowed command.

"Where have you been?!" Rhys railed toward them, red-faced and mean. Marc protectively darted before Gael. Rhys shoved him aside, but Marc lunged back as

192

ferociously, and with a quick twist of Rhys' arm, and a sound kick to the back of his knee, sent the Prince sprawling face down upon the rushes.

Rhys' guards charged Marc, and Gael screamed, "No! Don't you dare touch him!"

They halted to her brazen order; one rushed to help his master, and the other stood by, gaping drunkenly. Rhys swatted away help and rushes, as he rose with difficulty, sputtering and grousing under his breath. Marc narrowly eyed his every move, braced to do battle again. Yet Rhys didn't strike, rather he gruffly surveyed the stern faces of Marc and Gael, and his haplessly inebriated guards, and started laughing. His chortling rapidly turned uproarious. Gael and Marc looked to each other in stark confusion, as all others present aped Rhys' mirth. The Prince approached Marc, slapped him brusquely on the backside, and lauded, "You, my lad, will prove a most worthy opponent. Now I would talk to the Lady, *alone*."

Marc wasn't about to retreat, till Gael assured, "It's all right, Marc. I will be fine and I do need to talk to him." She smiled so sweetly, he was convinced, and he left them to fetch some mead.

Rhys urged Gael into a corner, and his gay expression quickly soured. "Where did he take you?"

"He didn't take me anywhere in particular," she assured casually. "We walked and stopped short of the cliffs."

"And..."

"Rhys," she interrupted with insult, "you may be my Prince, but you are neither my father, nor my confessor—"

Rhys squeezed her arms too tightly and besieged, "I don't care to be your father—I want to be your lover! What did you do with him? Did he kiss you, touch you?"

She wriggled as if in pain and demanded, "Stop, or I'll leave!"

"You promised you'd tell me your decision tonight. Leaving with Marc, was that how you chose to tell me?"

"No...He asked me to walk with him. I saw no harm."

"Oh yes, my dear Lady. Any commingling between the two of you will cause you and him great harm. He is a Norman soldier. Any affection you show him is akin to treason!"

"No!" Gael fervently defended. "He's a soldier no more, he's kind and caring. He's not your enemy, Rhys!"

"This night, he eagerly became my enemy. You swore you'd tell me if you'll be my mistress. You swore—"

She wrenched from his grip. "I have decided...And my answer is no."

Her sharpness stung him, and he whined back, "But why?!"

"Because I want our friendship back! Before, you were never jealous, never demanding. I won't be forced to suffer your tempers, not when I don't feel for you here!" She pounded her breast, and lamented, "I always enjoyed visiting you, jesting with you, feasting with you, but I don't enjoy you now, not like this. I won't be your mistress, Rhys, and I'm not sorry or afraid to tell you so."

His blustering waned, and he softly answered, "I never meant for you to be afraid of me."

"I know you didn't..." she gently replied.

"I was concerned that you'd been gone so long, with what happened to Maura today."

"And I appreciate your concern, but I was safe with Marc."

The Norman's name again riled him, and he reminded, "I spoke of another condition to your remaining at Mynyw with your son. You do recall, don't you?"

"I wasn't likely to forget, yet since you mentioned your decision to marry me to the new Pennaeth, no one has arrived here to woo me or the village."

"They *have* arrived."

Her voice shook with dread. "Th...they?"

"I've narrowed my choice to two, and wish you to narrow it to one."

"And how long do I have to make my decision?" she asked, her voice trembling.

"I desire an answer by Christmas."

Gael tried to relaxed but failed. "Who are my choices?" she dared.

"Taredd, whom you met this night and...Owain."

She wavered, then mustered her failing courage in a stark reply, "Then there's no need to delay my decision...My choice is Taredd."

It was not the decision Rhys wanted, yet then again Taredd would suffice. And he knew how she and Owain despised each other, but never knew why, and he reckoned neither did they. He rested his hand on her shoulder and ruefully assured, "I'll pray for your happiness, Gael. Taredd is a fine man, and I beg for our continued friendship."

She patted his hand in reply, strained a grin, and glumly watched him lumber away. Marc promptly arrived at her side offering a cup of mead and his worry, "You're so pale. What's he done?"

Gael saw true caring in his eyes, heard genuine affection in his voice. Her belly cramped and she wanted to cry, but she wouldn't, not now and perhaps never. She'd keep her son...and that was most important. Gael smiled to ease his worry and stayed quiet, deciding not to tell Marc what had and would transpire; there really was no need to...yet. And later when all had bedded down on their mats, and she heard his breathing lengthen in sleep, she gazed longingly on his milk-white skin aglow in the moonlight. She thought of the moist pressure of his lips, and reached out to touch. His long lashes fluttered open to her finger's caress. He caught and kissed it, then gathered the whole of her in his arms, where she willingly remained the entire night through.

*****

CHAPTER TWELVE - GAMES

"Simon, sit still!" ordered Maura with a scowl and a huff. "How am I supposed to do this correctly with you squirming about so?"

Simon's bottom lip jutted out and blew a puff of air upward, and he spouted back, "You don't need to do it at all."

"No, I suppose I don't, but I won't be blamed when you crash into a tree because you can't see. Besides, Gael suggested this as a present to you."

Simon blew again, sending shorn golden hairs flittering through the slim space that separated them as they knelt face to face, each draped only in pelts. The window's shutter, cracked open less than an inch, ushered in a moist, chilly breeze, and revealed a brightening sky, prompting Maura's comment, "It will soon be sunrise. If you cooperate, I'll have this finished in an instant." She steered the shears round to his ear and was about to clip when he jerked away, clenched hold of her waist, and tackled her to the furry floor. "Simon!" she cried between chortles. "I could have taken your ear off!"

"And it would have been well worth it," he murmured in a growl, "just to repeat what we enjoyed last evening."

"We did repeat it, twice if I recall, and—" To his tickles, she lapsed into titters again, and as his lips began their immensely enticing journey down her neck, she sighed ecstatically and recalled, "How glorious not to be rushed, or spied upon, or interrupted, or...Simon," she gushed in earnest, "when do you think we'll get this opportunity again?"

He lifted a flushed face and smirked. "I've decided that Gael and Gruffydd should move to our cottage, and we will move in here, only till Henry's gone that is. I believe they'll happily agree, don't you?"

"Simon..." Maura laughed, and they shifted to their sides and proceeded to touch as they talked, each caress rendering their bodies more liquid. "When we arrived here, you were so twitchy," said Maura. "It took a good deal of intervention just to relax you."

"I figured Henry had followed us, but I did so relish your help." His eyes shone delight as he begged, "And I'm feeling somewhat tense now. Could you possibly intervene again?"

"Gladly, my love, if only we had the time. Remember, swords at sunrise."

"But," he implored, "surely we have time for just a bit of relaxing."

"Maybe we'll have a chance to sneak back here between the swords and the race," Maura suggested, squirming with hope.

"But how will I perform?"

"Magnificently as always!"

"No Maura, in the race."

Her lips nibbled his chin and nipped at the tip of his nose, and her fingertips stirred his loins as she breathed alluringly in his ear, "Would you care?"

He sputtered away from her teasing, "No...not in the least."

Their chuckling died as they melted together and stayed in a desperate clench till the creeping light touched upon their tangled feet. Then they grudgingly pulled apart to dress, and snacked on fruit, bread and ale, while Maura wondered aloud, "You don't think Marc will hurt Henry, do you Simon?"

"Marc has excellent control over everything he does."

"He doesn't when Henry's involved," reminded Maura. "Simon, I'm sorry I accused you of exaggerating Henry's obnoxious behavior at your mediations."

"He can be extremely taxing, and equally dangerous."

"You don't think he purposely caused the confrontation between the armies yesterday, do you?" asked Maura.

"I've considered the possibility, but I've yet to pass judgment."

"And do you still believe there's a purpose behind his foolishness?"

"I do..." said Simon.

"Well I hope we discover it soon, before he does himself or someone else serious harm."

Sharing the same plaintive expression, they rose to leave, and exchanged a loving hug and kiss before ambling for the door. "Simon," said Maura, "did you get an opportunity to speak to Rhys about our lack of food?"

"I spoke to Sulien...He said a cargo vessel docks today from Gwynedd with supplies for the cathedral and that we may have a portion to help us till Henry leaves."

"That's so kind of Sulien," said Maura with a grateful grin. "And I must insist you start eating heartily again. You mustn't sacrifice your health for me."

He patted her belly and answered with fond finality, "It is most important that you and she eat well."

She gratefully lifted his hand, kissed it, and switched thoughts with a whispered lure, "After Marc and Henry's feat, we'll congratulate the winner, tell Gael we're not quite done with her gift, and sneak back here to play more."

His dazzling smile more than agreed as they nuzzled cheeks and hastened away to the village common.

Gael wrung her hands and paced outside an outline of a huge circle cut into the grass of the common. Close by, Marc wriggled into a hauberk and helm, then crammed his fingers into thick leather gloves. Gael glanced nervously at the broadsword resting up against a tree, and heaved a ragged sigh. Never had she felt so miserably plagued by doubts. She should have told Marc last evening of her decision to marry Taredd, for she was certain he felt he was performing this feat for her—*his* Lady. She'd never be his *Lady*, she couldn't be his *Lady*! Yet, oh, how she yearned to be, if only for the three months left till her marriage. Across the circle, Henry glowered as he clumsily clambered into his armor, and Gael fumed with revulsion for the pretty fiend, sputtering beneath her breath, "If...if he dares hurt Marc, I'll take up a sword as wide and as sharp and gladly slice off his—"

The sight of Simon and Maura jogging her way halted her bloody vengeance, and she sprinted to meet them and comment on her fright, "I don't like the idea of this fight one bit! Marc told me that Henry is quite an accomplished swordsman, and the swords are not dull as I thought they'd be. There could be an accident."

"Gael," appeased Simon, "the fact that they *are* accomplished swordsmen ensures there will be no accidents."

"What determines who wins?" she worried. "The first head lopped off?"

"No," Maura explained. "The first to fall and stay down, or the first to step outside the circle loses."

"Oh..." Gael seemed slightly less fretful as she tugged them along to a spot that allowed the best view. To distract herself she halfheartedly asked, "And so, did you make good use of my cottage?"

"All went quite satisfactorily," smirked Simon. "And we were wondering if perhaps we could return there for another rendezvous between this fracas and my race with Owain."

Gael turned a gawk their way and marveled, "You're not done *yet*?"

"I pray to God we're never done!" exclaimed Simon.

And Maura pleaded, "We don't know when we'll get another chance to—"

"No, Maura...I don't require details. Yes, take all the time you need, but Simon, will you be able to ride—"

"Expertly."

Gael rolled her eyes. "I mean a horse."

"I know what you meant," he simpered, "...and the answer's the same."

Maura started to chuckle as she joined in his game, "Now I might not be able to straddle one for awhile but—"

"Will you two stop! You are disgusting! I ask only one favor in return."

"Anything," gushed Maura.

"That I'm allowed an audience with one or both of you before nightfall."

"Of course," answered Simon, concerned. He noticed the twinge of dismay in her expression and prodded, "Is there something—"

She brushed away his worry with a wave and blared announcement, "Look, there's Rhys...It must be time!"

A large and boisterous crowd had gathered, Welsh and Normans mingling in tenuous though polite harmony. Henry, helm stashed under his arm, strolled across the circle to the threesome, and greeted the ladies, "Gael...Maura."

Gael insulted him by dropping her eyes to her feet; Maura acknowledged him with a hesitant, "...Henry."

"Simon," said Henry, "I would speak to you a moment...alone."

Simon looked at Maura and, to her shrug, answered formally, "Granted. Come away from the crowd."

They walked away from the crowd, and paused beneath a sheltering oak. "What is it, Henry?" prompted Simon, folding his arms across his chest.

Henry kicked at the dirt and struggled, "I...I had promised not to make you angry. I broke that promise and wish to make amends."

"I wasn't the only one you slighted, Henry."

"I realize that and intend to beg Maura's forgiveness as well."

"We're getting mighty tired of suffering your mischief."

"But you've always forgiven me before!" countered Henry.

Simon briefly thought back on the countless times he'd been embarrassed, imprisoned, infuriated, and wounded by Henry's misdeeds and sadly related, "Henry, I believe it's more that I've forgotten, not forgiven. But can't you see," he emphasized, "you showed my wife disrespect, and that I can never forgive."

Henry looked about to cry as he beseeched, "What can I do to make things right between us again? I'll do anything for you, for Maura! I love both of you, and need you."

"Need us how?" asked Simon, askance.

"When I leave here, I need to know there's someone somewhere who cares for me. No one else does."

"That is not true, Henry!"

"Oh, but it is true!" Henry stressed, grasping and pinching Simon's shoulders. "I'm the forgotten son, and you know too well the consequences of that curse."

Yes, Simon did know and he felt a stab of sympathy for this irksome yet ingratiating youngster groveling before him. He stared away for a long while, then turned a tentative expression to say, "After my race—"

"Which you'll win, I've no doubt."

"Don't interrupt Henry," Simon chided.

Henry looked ashamed, and Simon spoke on, "After my race we'll meet, just the two of us, on some neutral spot, and wrangle out this dismal mess."

Henry beamed, almost leapt into Simon's arms, and spurted, "Thank you Simon and bless you!"

Simon took one step back to waggle a finger and warn, "Take heed, Henry. If there's one more incident, no matter how trivial, you will take your men and leave. Is that perfectly clear?"

"Oh, yes. I swear I'll show only the most admirable behavior for the remainder of my stay! I swear, Simon."

"And you *will* apologize to Maura."

"I intend to directly after my bout with Marc."

"Not then, Henry. After you and I talk will be a better time."

"Whatever you decide, Cousin. Now will you cheer for me?"

"I will cheer..." was all that Simon would reveal.

Henry kissed his cousin's cheeks, then strode away, a light-hearted confidence in his step. Watching him, Simon let out a rueful sigh, raked fingers through his unevenly snipped locks, and began to question the saneness of his considered pardon and his cousin. His intense concentration was jolted by a flying ball of fur. Henry the pup landed in Simon's arms and commenced slurping. Simon sputtered, "Stop...stop, Henry! Where have you been? No doubt up to mischief again." Then, as he gazed fondly into the pup's huge, sad eyes, Simon realized the dog was nothing at all like his namesake. He rubbed his chin on the top of the pup's head and murmured, "I propose changing your name to...Pup. For that's all you've ever answered to anyway." As he wandered back to the circle, he wrestled with Pup to keep him still, and warned, "Now, during the games, you'll stay in my arms. If you make a nuisance of yourself, we'll have to lock you in Gael's cottage." As if the pup understood, he suddenly became very still and only licked once.

Gael glanced across the circle and spotted Owain standing by Rhys. Flanking Rhys' other shoulder was Taredd, and she wondered if he'd been informed of her acceptance. The only emotion twitching his rather bland expression was an interest in the fray to come. Gruffydd, Cynan, Nia, and Olwen had joined Gael and Maura, and while Maura knelt to better hear the children's newest adventures, Gael left to speak to Marc. He stood armored, still and serene, awaiting the arrival of his contender. Though most of his face was covered, she could nonetheless sense his sanguine look as she grasped up his gloved hand, and said with great emotion, "I wish you luck, Sir, and ask you to swear to be careful."

"I always am," he affirmed, bringing the tips of her fingers to his lips.

She let them linger there till she heard Rhys declare in English, "Soldiers come forward!" then whisked her fingers and herself away to join the other spectators. Suddenly missing his warmth, she shivered, offered a silent prayer for his safety, and frantically sought out Maura's hand. Maura turned from the children as the knights started forward and to Gael's strangling hold cast her a quick questioning glance. The despairing look blanching her friend's face betrayed a multitude of secrets and, for a very confused moment, rendered Maura speechless as she considered, *When had this happened, and why didn't I notice?* Marc had said nothing specific, only casually referring now and then to Gael and Gruffydd. And if Simon had suspected a growing affection between the two, he'd kept silent.

Just then Simon wedged between the children and Maura, and draped the pup over his shoulder where he hung quite happily. Simon gifted Maura a most excited look; she smiled back, wrapped her arm in his, and gave Gael's palm a reassuring squeeze. They all jerked to blades scraping together as Henry and Marc took up their initial stances. Rhys' plummeting arm began their perilous dance and at first to Gael that was all it resembled. She recalled the dancing at the feast as she watched their mirrored footsteps, the perfectly attuned sway of arms and bodies. The men crept in an ever shrinking circle, and when they were but a sword's length apart, both abruptly swung their blades and struck uplifted shields. The dance ended and the fray ensued; they ducked, whirled, parried and lunged, brutally whacking away at each other's mettle and grace. Maura eyed her brother proudly, but also couldn't help but marvel at Henry's expertise. Frequently she stole a glance at Simon, whose expression and body subtly twitched and flinched and jabbed in rhythm with the contenders, as if he had left his skin and stepped into theirs. She saw the glint of longing in his eyes for the game he had once so loved to play and she felt a sudden sadness. A loud yowl interrupted her musing, and she snapped her head around to see Marc stumbling backwards; a slice in his leather braies exposed a gash and spurted blood. Her paleness rivaled Gael's as they both lurched forward. Simon blocked their advance.

As agony attacked his body, Marc struggled to straighten and braced for Henry's expected lethal charge, which came accompanied by a loud, long, and terrifying howl. He'd been a fool to allow Henry's wounding and frantically wondered how long he could remain upright. The only maneuver left was to exhaust the FitzRoy and Marc knew well Henry's compulsion for dramatics. He'd let him pound away till his strength left and the perfect moment arrived to swipe the final blow.

Henry couldn't believe his luck. No, not luck, skill! He was without question the superior swordsman, and would soon be done with this vexingly virtuous dunce. Then all would marvel and be humbled by his mastery, especially the women, and most importantly—Maura.

The battering that followed forced shut Gael's eyes and pained her heart, though her fright eased a little to Maura's quavered comment, "We mustn't fret. Marc's only been defeated once."

Gael gazed up quickly to ask, "By whom, the King?"

"No..." said Maura softly, "by Simon."

Gael gaped and dared to look again, but she couldn't comprehend Marc's strategy. It appeared he had all but surrendered, and was constantly retreating while Henry savagely clubbed at his head, shoulders, and shield. Yet she also noticed that no matter how vicious Henry's smites, Marc always kept within the circle. Her harried look began to brighten as she witnessed Henry's blows becoming more and more ungainly; they frequently missed their target, and staggered him with their intensity. One flailed strike broke Henry's balance and sent him spinning. Marc instantly delivered a precise blow with the virility he'd shown at the start—the flat of his sword slammed Henry's back, propelling him toward the boundary. Henry astoundingly stopped a boot tip short of defeat, and wavered there, his body arched and arms swimming furiously backward. Marc watched Henry's struggle for awhile, then limped forward. With barely a nudge to Henry's back, the hilt of Marc's sword spilled Henry just beyond the line. The crowd exploded in a sonorous roar and charged the victor. Yet the victor no longer stood; he had stripped off his helmet and sunk to the ground, woozy from exhaustion, hurt, and relief. Gael, Maura, Simon, and Gruffydd dashed immediately to his side. Gruffydd hugged his neck, Gael knelt to kiss his mouth, and Maura grasped his hand, while Simon ripped his braies to better view his wound. The pup barked crazily at Henry, who pushed with great difficulty from the ground and raised up a meek and needy look. He hoped to see Simon's sympathy gazing back at him, but instead he was rewarded with only his guards' bleak and vapid scowls.

"It will need a few stitches," prescribed Simon, glancing up at Marc. Marc wasn't listening, he was too involved in enjoying Gael's lips. The shocking sight made Simon choke his next comment, "And...we...we..." He looked imploringly to Maura for an answer, yet her expression held the same exasperation. *Well*, he thought, *with the threat of loss of blood evident, kissing could wait.* He interrupted the couple's celebrating by clearing his throat and announcing, "We'll take you to the infirmary where wine's available for cleansing." Still ignored, he had to resort to shouting, "Marc!"

Marc finally eased away from Gael's mouth to ask calmly, "Yes, Simon?"

Marc's enthralled look betrayed no pain. Simon smirked and asserted, "It's vital I get you sewn up. Take my arm, I'll help you."

The pride and affection Gael bore was so elating she felt as if she floated the entire way to the cathedral. Before entering, Simon guided Marc inside, and Maura urged Gael to stay outside. She panicked and strained against Maura's hold, till Maura reminded her, "Is this what you needed to talk to us about?"

"I will go to Marc!" Gael insisted.

"Yes, you *will* go to him," Maura spoke back as sternly, "but first you'll tell me your problem."

"I have no problem."

"You did have one a very short while past. How could it have disappeared so quickly?" Gael averted her eyes; Maura eased her grip, and slumped with bother. "You haven't told him, have you?"

"I'm afraid it's a bit worse than that," said Gael, meeting Maura's fitful gaze. "Last evening, I told Rhys whom I would marry."

"What?!" exclaimed Maura. "What happened to all the candidates coming to court you and—"

"Maura...There were only two candidates and one was Owain. What choice did I have?"

What choice did you make?" Maura cautiously asked.

"Taredd...the tall, sandy-haired stranger at the feast."

They both groaned and slouched down upon the top step to the entrance. "I didn't plan this with Marc!" anguished Gael. "It just happened."

With a hint of suspicion, Maura inquired, "Before or after you made your choice of a husband?"

"I didn't expect a lecture, Maura," Gael returned in defense.

"And you won't get one, but I will protect my brother!"

"It was before," confessed Gael. "I suppose it happened the day I came home from Dinefwr and I saw him standing there before your cottage. Actually, I don't rightly know when it happened, but I've grown quite fond of him."

"You will tell him, won't you?" pressed Maura.

"Ye...yes. Of course, I will."

"Soon?"

"Soon," confirmed Gael.

Maura pried further, "When will you wed?"

"Near Christmas."

"And till then?"

"I don't know, Maura." Gael vigorously wagged her head. "I don't know!"

"Perhaps," chanced Maura, "you should use the time to get to know your betrothed better."

"Perhaps...I should," Gael grimly agreed.

In the infirmary, Marc and Simon sat upon a cot, Marc sans his braies, blanketed, and propped up by pillows, with Simon deftly swabbing his gash with a wine-soaked linen cloth. Marc threw back a long swig of wine, and flinched at Simon's first tack, then croaked to distract himself, "Are you going to lecture me?"

Without looking up, Simon mumbled, "Have I ever lectured you before?"

"No."

"Then why would I start now?"

"But you don't approve," said Marc.

"Approve of what?"

"Gael and me."

Simon quickly countered, "There isn't any other woman I would rather have you infatuated with than Gael."

"Then why are you scowling?"

"I always scowl when I sew people up," said Simon, "and whatever you enjoy with Gael will be temporary and that makes me sad."

"Why temporary?" asked Marc, dreading the answer.

"Because she will wed the new Chieftain. I hope she has informed you of her plans."

"No she hasn't..." Marc hushed to breathe through a stitch, swallowed another few gulps, and then rasped, "Henry told me."

"No wonder you were bashing him with such vigor," lauded Simon. "You did fight brilliantly, exhausting him the way you did." He paused in his task, gazed up, and spoke earnestly, "Marc, I'm confident that you will do right by Gael and yourself. I don't want to see either of you hurt."

With a lost look, Marc confessed, "But I hurt already."

"I know you do," Simon soothed back.

Their dole was cut short by Gruffydd's breathless arrival. "Simon! Marc!" He skidded to a stop, gaped in awe at Simon's ministrations, and gasped, "Marc...does it hurt?"

"Ye...esss," slurred Marc.

"When Simon's finished, could you teach me how to swing a sword?"

"Maybe...in a few days' time."

Gruffydd conceded with an enthused toss of his head, and spurted more excitement, "The games have begun, and there's to be an arrow shoot! I want to compete, but I'm not sure Mam will agree. If one of you goes with me, I think she might say yes."

"No, Gruffydd," said Simon.

"But why not?" the boy severely whined.

"Because you might win."

Confused by Simon's strange reply, Gruffydd huffed and studied the scene before him. Marc had rested his head back upon a pillow and his eyes were closed. Simon was hunched over and seemed interested only in his stitching. With both men thusly distracted, Gruffydd felt emboldened enough to argue, "Then, I'll go alone."

Before Simon could react, Gruffydd had vanished. He called out angrily, "Gruffydd come back!" and then tried, "Gael...Maura!" But he got no answer, and noticed Marc was snoring. He couldn't leave him half-stitched, and as he dug the needle through the torn skin, he prayed someone would put a swift halt to the boy's foolishness.

Simon was removing the pillows from under Marc's shoulders and situating him more comfortably in the bed, when Maura and Gael arrived. "How is he?" they asked in a fretful chorus.

"Fine," sighed Simon. "And I'm certain he'll be up and walking in but a few hours. His head may pain him, though."

"I don't remember Henry hurting his head," noted Maura.

Simon smiled to say, "He finished an entire bottle of wine while I was stitching."

Gael was uncharacteristically quiet, hugging the side of the cot, her fingers rhythmically stroking Marc's. Unnoticed, Simon urged Maura away from the bed, and lowly recommended, "We'll leave her here and go find Gruffydd."

"What's happened to him?" worried Maura.

"I hope nothing. But a short while past he ran from here saying he was off to compete in the arrow shoot."

"What!" Maura exclaimed.

"Hush, Maura. Gael is in a fragile enough state without hearing her son is about to challenge and perhaps defeat a garrison of Norman knights."

"We must find him!" Maura stressed in a whisper.

Simon nodded, then cautiously approached Gael and rested a comforting arm round her shoulders. "Gael...will you stay with Marc awhile? I'm certain he'll much prefer waking to your loveliness than to my scowl."

Her pinched gaze questioned his sanity; he kissed her brow, and answered, "He cares for you." She lowered her harrowed expression back to Marc, and continued her stroking as Simon and Maura slunk away.

Pup greeted them at the door and loped with them to the center of town. Because of Maura's unfortunate incident with Lord Bernard, she stayed close to Simon on their search through the massed soldiers. All the contests in process seemed orderly and placid as they passed by groups pitching hatchets, hurling spears and daggers, and wrestling in muck. Simon heartened to the sight of Rhys, laughing with Taredd as they watched one muddy squabble. He sprinted to the Prince's side, tugging Maura along and, while she continued to look, he panted, "Rhys, have you seen Gruffydd?"

Rhys lost his smile, and fretted, "No. Is he lost?"

"Not if I can find where the arrow shoot is being held."

Displeased with the distraction, Rhys grunted, "What?"

Simon yelled over the din, "He wants to take part in the arrow shoot!"

Rhys nudged Simon aside to see the fight better, and distantly commented, "Fine. I'm sure he'll perform admirably."

"But it's far too dangerous!" argued Simon, agape.

The Welsh contender pinned his Norman rival in a paralyzing hold, eliciting clamors of praise from his audience. Rhys' nudge firmed to a push, and his hurrah sputtered to, "Simon...you worry far too much."

Simon bristled and was about to fling a retort, when Maura guided him away with the promising remark, "I think I see the archers!"

They hastened in her pointed direction and soon arrived at a spot crowded with sentries, mostly Norman, glowering at Gruffydd as he aimed his arrow at a tunic stuck by daggers onto a wall constructed of bales of hay. He let fly his dart, and squealed in triumph as it embedded itself precisely where the heart would lie if the garment were inhabited. Simon barged through the spectators, caught Gruffydd's arm, and dragged him, squawking in protest, out of the pack of maddened soldiers. "Simon," Gruffydd cried, straining and squirming, "let me go! I'm winning. Let me go!"

"No!" Simon vehemently scolded. He dropped to one knee, shook the boy to halt his hysterics, and gritted, "Are you mad?! I trained with men the likes of your fellow archers. I know their minds and their motives! Do you think they'll calmly allow you to humiliate them?"

"They won't mind!" yelled Gruffydd. "What does humiliate mean? They seem nice."

"Nice..." Simon rolled his eyes, and spoke carefully in Welsh so Gruffydd would be certain to comprehend the danger. "So nice, they may even suggest that you visit their camp, or ride with them, and they won't allow you to refuse. They're constantly searching for promising soldiers, and would steal you away in an instant!"

Gruffydd's eyes grew large with terror, his skin took on a ghostly hue, and he fell into Simon's hug, begging, "Don't let them take me, Simon! Mam wouldn't like it if I got stolen."

"No, she wouldn't and neither would we."

Having heard all, Maura eased alongside them, and softly petting Gruffydd's head, suggested, "There's no harm in your watching, Gruffydd. Only please stay between us."

"I will," Gruffydd sniffled, then asked, "Where's my mam?"

"She's watching over Marc," replied Simon.

"Good," remarked Gruffydd with a hopeful grin, and as they sauntered away, he added excitedly to Maura, "He said he'd teach me how to swing a sword...in a few days' time."

Maura narrowly eyed Simon; he shrugged innocently and directed them toward the hatchet throwers.

After watching awhile, Maura jumped to a hand on her shoulder and turned to see Henry. His eyes pooled with sincerity as he murmured, "My Lady, I would speak to you a moment...alone."

Her answer was to jerk away, and he tempered his whine to a dire plea, "*Please* Maura, kindly grant me a moment. Simon suggested I speak to you."

She reckoned he was lying, and looked to Simon, but his interest was so consumed in the pitching that he hadn't noticed Henry's arrival. Maura shook with exasperation and bent to whisper to Gruffydd, "You keep a firm hold on Simon. I'll return shortly. Tell him I'm with Henry."

Gruffydd didn't look away from the contest, but nodded vaguely to her request. She wandered off with Henry trailing at her heels, fidgety with nervousness and uncertainty. When they'd reached a fairly secluded area hidden by bushes, Henry took her arm and implored, "Here...We'll talk here. I must apologize—" He diligently began.

But she cut short his atonement. "No, Henry...You need not apologize. For I now know every word you utter is a lie, and you will hurt me, or Simon, or Marc again without a single thought to our feelings."

"*You* speak lies, Maura!" he shrilled. "You are my kin, and I might play a little with you, but I've never meant anyone true harm!"

She wondered if those were real tears welling in his eyes or did he own the talent to conjure them up anytime they were needed for effect? Yet his distraught look did touch her heart, and she gently chided, "At times you act as if you're younger than Gruffydd! We haven't time for your nonsense, Henry, and yesterday it came close to proving disastrous."

"I believed I was helping."

"Maybe you did, but you don't listen to anyone."

"For the remainder of my stay I will listen—keenly."

Her vexed expression met his, as she anguished, "I wish I could believe you!"

"My Lady...please do, please do!" Passionately, he grabbed up her hand, and crushed his lips to her palm. The devoutness of his act took her aback, and she started to pull away, yet he held tight and kissed again. "I'll do anything to regain your trust," he desperately emoted, "anything to have again your respect, your love!"

The lewd twinkle in his eye told his true aim. She shakily wrested her hand from his and sneered, "This is not one of your dreams, Henry. You've never had that sort of love from me, and you never will." Haltingly, she turned and walked several steps away before risking a look back. He stood where she'd left him, hunched and vanquished, his face shrouded by his hands. She felt sure his lamenting false, but worried when and how his elaborate charade would end.

*****

Marc raised his heavy head and blearily focused on Gael's fretful visage; her brows were deeply furrowed, she wrung his hand between her own, and bit her bottom lip with a severity that drew blood. He expected a question concerning his condition, and was surprised when she frenziedly blurted, "I'll marry the Chieftain come Christmas time, and it's to be Taredd! I wouldn't blame you for hating me, for I did encourage your affection and I should have told you, but Marc…I've been forced into this marriage to keep my son! Please can you forgive me?"

Struggling, Marc pushed up on an elbow, and tripped on pieces of words before stuttering, "I…I'm not angry with you. I'm grateful you finally told me. Have you a thought on what *we're* to do?"

She eased herself down on the cot, and continued to fumble with his fingers, while wagging her head and confessing, "Standing here, waiting for your waking, I've considered every possibility, and nothing seems feasible or fair…to you."

"I'll decide what's fair for me," said he. "What are the possibilities?"

She sighed then briskly related, "That we decide to be nothing but friends, that we continue to pursue our budding affection for each other till I'm wed, that we do what I've just said and keep on after I'm wed, or in final desperation, we take Gruffydd and run off somewhere."

"Where?" he asked.

"I don't know." She thought and spouted, "Normandy?"

"You wouldn't like it there."

"Then somewhere else…nicer!"

"But Gael…you love living here." His firm grasp stopped her fidgeting, and he ardently replied, "I'll always be your friend, and I'd love nothing more than to pursue our budding affection, but if I choose to love you I'll not love you casually, and I won't willingly break the commandments and neither would you."

"Then we'll run?" she ventured.

"There's nowhere left for me to go. Rhys would never allow you to take Gruffydd away from here and Henry may have already betrayed me to Bernard."

"He wouldn't!"

"Oh yes he would—happily."

"What's to become of us, Marc?"

In response, he heaved a defeated sigh and reached out in longing for her comfort.

*****

The sun neared its pinnacle and Simon and Maura shared disappointed looks as they realized they'd lost their chance to return to Gael's hut. The games were quietly disbanding as all sought out food, water, and ale. The heat was rare and relentless, and Maura and Simon had found refuge beneath a tree, and tiredly listened to Gruffydd's endless jabbering, "You'll race soon, won't you Simon?"

Simon glanced up, squinted from the glare, and answered, "Yes, I suppose I will. I'll need to fetch the horses."

Henry's loud suggestion intruded, "Bring Ivo and Marc's horse, whatever he's called."

"He's called Noir," said Simon.

"How gauche," remarked Henry, sagging down before them. "We'll insist that the Welsh lug rides Ivo. He'll not be able to control him, and the race will be done before it starts."

"His name is Owain," snidely corrected Maura, "and I expect he'll handle Ivo quite expertly."

"What's this, Simon? Your Lady flaunts the credits of another man in your presence. Is there reason to question her—"

"Quiet, Henry," cautioned Simon.

Henry pulled a simper, but obeyed. His presence had turned Gruffydd unnaturally solemn and Maura believed it was past time to return him to his mother. "Come

Gruffydd." She rose, smoothed her skirt, swiped her brow, and offered her hand. "I'll take you to your mam and Marc."

Gruffydd stood and burbled to Simon, "Could you bring Rhodri too? Cynan and I plan to follow you." He swiftly answered Simon's censuring look. "Not for the whole race, just the beginning."

Simon barely nodded; Gruffydd took Maura's hand and, once away from Henry, resumed his enthused commentary of the day's events. "Simon will win, won't he, Maura?"

"I believe so, but I don't know how well Owain rides."

"Welsh ponies are slow but easily tamed," said Gruffydd. "I think Henry may be right. Owain may not be able to ride his Ivo."

"We'll soon see."

"Is there something wrong with my mam?" asked Gruffydd.

"Why do you ask?"

Gruffydd worriedly explained, "When I passed you two on my way in and out of the infirmary, she didn't even notice me. She looks sad, and I thought she'd be happy when Marc won the sword battle."

"She was very happy for him," said Maura. "Maybe she's only tired."

"Yes, maybe she is," Gruffydd agreed. "I hope not too tired to watch the race."

"No...not too tired for that," assured Maura.

Back beneath the tree, Henry wondered, "Who is *Rhodree*?"

"The colt," said Simon. "Gruffydd's named him for his father."

"Oh, how thoughtful," said Henry off-handedly, then he struck a surly look and muttered, "I don't believe Maura accepted my apology. What did she tell you of our meeting?"

"*I* told you not to meet with her till after *we* talked," scolded Simon with little energy, then he related, "She said you hadn't much to say."

"That criticism applies more to her discourse than to mine," countered Henry.

"Henry," Simon said in a testy tone, "what does it matter?"

Henry inwardly replied—*It matters because I wish to do to her what you did to her in the stable*—but instead he convincingly stated, "I want to preserve our friendship."

"Maura doesn't retract her friendships easily, Henry. Perhaps if you show an honest effort to mend your wrongs, she'll forgive you."

"And if she forgives me, will you also do so?"

With extreme hesitancy, Simon uttered, "...I'll consider it."

Henry beamed and playfully punched his cousin's shoulder. Simon answered with a grunt and continued to fiddle with the grass at his feet as Henry swept his happy gaze over the common. His eyes lit suspiciously on the group of Norman knights clumped about the area recently used for the arrow shoot, all raptly attending to their Lord Bernard.

*****

At midday a boisterous crowd gathered at the gate of the commote's border wall. The throng's spiraling exuberance had infected the two stallions, exciting them near to uncontrollable. Two men wrestled to keep hold of each bare-backed steed, while Simon and Owain, bare-backed themselves, huddled with Rhys to learn the route. Henry took over custody of his horse and searched for the group of knights he'd spied before, yet they were nowhere to be found. His murmurs quieted the snorting beast, but his whispering turned gritty as Marc limped up beside him and took charge of Noir. "I'd wondered where'd you'd gone."

"I needed stitching."

"Next time I'll spare you any further pain by aiming for your neck instead of your leg."

Marc stoically ignored Henry's hassling, soothed Noir, and waited.

To Maura, Gael still seemed highly disturbed, yet Maura longed to hear all that had transpired between Marc and Gael in the infirmary. Instead of riling Gael more, she decided they could just as well discuss the episode after the race. Her attention drifted to Simon and Owain. She smirked with pride, and surmised that most likely every woman present was focused on them as well, for they both were exemplary specimens of manhood.

With sharp nods, Simon and Owain left the Prince and strode determinedly to the horses. Maura left Gael's side to join Simon and Marc; Gael mysteriously held back. Marc offered Simon a hand up, and Maura insisted, "You'll be careful and mind the mud. Promise?"

Simon bent low, took her face in his hands to kiss her firmly, then murmured, "I promise."

"When should we expect you back?" asked Marc.

"It shouldn't take more than an hour."

"Then in two hours I'll come looking for you," said Marc. "Good luck, Simon."

Simon smiled at Marc and gripped Maura's hand as Marc slapped the black stallion's rump, and started him forward to where the Prince Rhys stood.

Owain had no well-wishers to help him aboard Ivo. Only Henry stood by, brandishing a smug smile and the reins. Owain snatched them from Henry's taunting grip and steered Ivo toward Rhys. Gruffydd and Cynan mounted their ponies and, with the pup sitting between them, waited a safe distance behind.

Simon kissed Maura's fingers; she mouthed "I love you," stepped back and hugged herself. The riders steeled themselves for the Prince's signal. Rhys thrust his arms to the sky and as they plummeted, a sharp whistle pierced the suspended silence. Noir bounded away, but Ivo neighed and reared steeply to the shrill interruption. Owain soundly toppled off his back, and plunged with a spectacular splash into a puddle of muck. Henry hooted and roared with hysterical laughter; a number of Welsh soldiers laughed along, but the village folk sensed Owain's shame and stayed hushed. Owain scrambled up, shook off most of the mud, and surged for the horse. He seized the reins and, hurling curses, leapt on Ivo's back. A resounding kick sent them on their way. The boys and dog galloped after, whooping their zeal. When the last pony had cantered from view, the crowd slowly plodded their way toward the llys where promised refreshments awaited them.

An exhilarating wind whipped their manes and strained their lungs as Simon and Noir streaked up the road hugging the foothills. Simon felt sure enough of his lead to risk a backward glance. Puzzled at seeing no one, he eased Noir's speed and wondered where Owain had gone. He didn't seem the sort to quit before the contest had begun. Then just as he considered riding back, he spotted a gray dot, growing ever larger as it sped its way along the path winding from the commote; close behind came three smaller dots. Simon burst a spirited yell, dug his heels in the stallion's sides, and continued his sprint up the hill.

Marc and Maura led the crowd, Maura relaying the morning contests' results to Marc, and he, in turn, twisting to find Gael. Finally, Maura surrendered to his distraction. "It's no matter, Marc. I can tell you later."

"Where do you think she's gone to?"

"Perhaps her hut where she can be alone...to think."

Maura's answer elicited such a dour look from Marc that she instantly regretted voicing her thought. "Then again," she lightly added, "she may be waiting for Gruffydd's return and—"

Marc glanced up from his feet to press for a finish to her sentence. She stood still as a statue, intently listening. *Listening to what*, he wondered as he opened his ears and received his answer. All was still with an eerie quiet that shivered his skin and pricked up the hairs on the back of his neck.

Rhys stopped suspiciously behind them, and responding to their trepid expressions, asked, "What's happened?"

Marc only pointed to the lane before the llys. Maura felt Rhys' quick grip on her shoulder and heard his stammered fear, "The...the Normans are...are gone."

Rhys abruptly let her go, and barraged orders. "Go to your huts, slowly as if nothing's amiss. Bolt windows and doors and keep water close! Go quickly...go now!"

Most of the villagers walked stiffly away, leaving a small band of pilgrims without a home nearby, alone and unarmed in the center of the road. Rhys replaced Maura as leader, and his guards formed a taut circle round the others. "We will head for the llys very slowly," instructed the Prince. Marc continued his frantic search for Gael, and to his great gasp of relief, she elbowed her way through the group, and grabbed his hand. Maura assisted Olwen and her children Maredydd and Nia along as they cautiously crept their way forward. Finally, the steps loomed just ahead, and Rhys roared, "Ladies, run!"

The women broke from the group and dashed for the shelter. Inches from the steps, Maura froze to a dauntingly familiar whirring sound. Then she saw the flaming darts; they rained in hundreds from the sky. One pierced the ground by her side. She willed her feet to walk, then run and, once inside the llys, she took it upon herself to issue orders, "Bolt the shutters! Set a table against the rear door! Fetch sheets, mead, and mats, and collect all the water you can find!" No one questioned her; the women rushed to heed her commands. She flung wide the door and helped Marc, dragging an injured guard, enter. He was immediately followed by Henry Fitzroy, who helped Rhys haul in another casualty.

The women had hurriedly assembled a long line of mats. Marc got his man settled on one, then answered Rhys' request to help him gather weapons. They took up candles, lifted a plank cut from the floor, dropped down and tossed from below bows and arrows, a number of spears and swords, and thickly padded leather shirts. When they had exhausted the supply, they reemerged, and began distributing the weapons to the soldiers straggling through the door. Rhys suddenly realized who he was scuffling with, and sternly asked, "Marc, will you join with my men to fight your army?"

"No...not my army, Sir," stipulated Marc. "My loyalty lies with this village."

Rhys confidently thrust a bow in Marc's one hand, a quiver of arrows in the other, and suggested, "Don the leather shirt."

With a tense nod, Marc did as told and positioned himself beside a Welsh sentry securing a rear window. Henry paced in a vacant corner, wringing his hands and muttering crazily to himself. He paused his fluster a moment to study Maura wrestling with Gael near the door. Piqued, he inched forward to catch details of their discord.

"Maura!" wailed Gael, straining in Maura's hold. "I must find Gruffydd, let me find Gruffydd!"

Maura squeezed harder and clarified, "You step out that door and you're dead! He's safe out of the village and you taught him to hide if there's danger and stay hidden till found by one of the villagers. Owain and Simon are with him, they will keep him from harm." Gael sagged in hysterics to the floor; Maura knelt with her and was soon joined by Olwen, who offered a consoling hug.

Maura left the mothers to their dirge and hastened to tend the hurt. She knelt by the soldier occupying the first mat, offered him gentle words and a cup of mead, and ripped the shoulder seam of his shirt to assess his wound. The arrow's stick was broken off an inch or two from its head, which was deeply embedded in his muscle. She closed her eyes and kneaded her brow, trying to decide whether to leave the arrow in or yank it out. Perhaps she should leave it for Simon to extract...Simon...The room spun furiously as her blood drained to her feet, and she gulped back a strangled sob. *My God*, she silently pleaded, *where is Simon?! Is he alive, is Owain, are the children?!* Maura's eyes flew open as she smelled smoke. It danced in the air and clogged her nose. She gagged into her palm and, from the corner of her eye, spotted Henry surging for the door. Too late, she flew after him and collided with the slammed barrier. Ramming it with her shoulder accomplished little, so she beat at the wood and screamed, "Henry! Come back! You'll be killed. Henry!"

His shouts drowned her entreaty. He stood on the top stair, his back forcing the door shut and his arms stretched wide in supplication. "Stop!" he bellowed in the direction of the assault. "Bernard, stop this insanity! We'll all be slaughtered, you flaming idiot! God's blood! Stop this madness!"

Henry's wail, violent and searing, rattled the wood. Maura kicked open the door and gasped at the ghastly sight of his crumpled body, stuck with a flaming arrow! She groped for the back of his collar, tautened her grip, and yanked back mightily. He barely budged, and she yelled, "Help me! Rhys, Taredd, help me save Henry!"

In a flash, they were by her side. Dodging arrows, the three heaved Henry inside, where Rhys ripped a tapestry from the rafters and used it to smother Henry's blazing arm. Henry writhed and groaned in terrible agony, while Maura carefully peeled the scorched remains of his tunic and shirt from his blistering skin. She sighed with relief, noting that the arrow had not pierced his skin. "Rhys," she called softly to avert panic, "It's but a burn. Please carry him to a mat and blanket him. I'll fetch soaked towels." Rhys obliged and marveled at her calm control. He stayed by Henry, listening to his muttered madness and, ashamedly, took in the surrounding bedlam—the women flitting between moaning soldiers, smoke seeping from the thatch in the roof, soldiers rapidly volleying a scant supply of arrows. He should have been more vigilant, more suspicious, and taken seriously the warnings of Sulien, Simon, Owain! If lives were lost on account of his foolish games, he'd never forgive himself...never! Maura rejoined them, armed with milk-dampened towels. She knelt, stroked Henry's brow, and soothed, "I'll wrap your arm, and I want you to drink all of this mead. It will help ease your pain."

Rhys accepted the passed cup, supported Henry's head, and touched the rim to his lips. Henry gulped hungrily, emptying the sweet contents in seconds. Fascinated, Rhys watched Henry's fevered eyes lock on Maura's face, as she tenderly bandaged his burn. Henry's good arm rose deliberately to the side of Maura's face and his rigid fingers strangled a handful of her hair. He fiercely yanked her face to his and shrilled, "Stay with me, Maura! Don't let me die! I need you, must have you! Don't leave me!"

The pain he inflicted thrust her backwards, and she whimpered and strained for freedom. Rhys broke Henry's hold with a sound strike to his forearm, shoved Maura aside, and quickly restrained the FitzRoy. She shook from her shock, and strove to tame the frenzy swelling within her as she quavered, "I...I won't leave you, Henry, but others need tending as well. Others need tending."

Maura reached out to Rhys, her eyes tearing in thanks, and Rhys cringed to her distress. Because of him her husband could very well be lying dead on a mountain road...strictly because of him. He dropped his guilty gaze to his lap and, as Henry's thrashing began to subside, Rhys whispered to Maura, "I must go soon. I'll take Taredd and rally my troops camped outside the village, if any are left alive. I'll leave you ten soldiers and Marc will stay." He glanced warily at the hovering smoke and guessed, "The thatch is too damp to burn, but the smoke may prove treacherous. You'll breathe easier if you mask your mouth with a wet towel. I will not return till the Normans are routed, but then again, I may not return at all. I trust you to handle matters here in your usual steadfast way, and I am forever in debt to your loyalty...my Lady." Rhys reached for her hand and kissed it. Her fingers touched his scraggly cheek as he stood, puffed out his chest, and began booming orders.

*****

Simon reined Noir at the hill's crest and searched for Owain. The Welshman had gained a good amount of ground and his swift advance up the side of the hill pleased Simon, for he had hoped for a decent challenge from Owain. The boys had quit the race, which pleased Simon as well, and his joyous grunt of encouragement sent Noir bounding down the peak.

Fury drove Owain and Ivo up the hill. Owain kicked at the stallion's flanks and, without slowing his fierce pace, Ivo twisted his head to chomp at Owain's leg. Owain wondered how long the beast would allow him his tenuous seat. He had to win this race! He had to humiliate the Norman bastard, and prove to Rhys that his darling boy Simon wasn't worthy of licking his boots! Then he would deal with that pompous whelp—Henry. At the crest, Ivo abruptly stopped, catapulting Owain forward over his neck. While in flight, Owain's one hand caught an ear, the other a fistful of mane. His legs hugged Ivo's neck, and he dangled beneath the horse's drooling lips, precariously close to the ledge of the precipice, pondering his next move. He knew if he let go the horse would bolt, so he began swinging his body from side to side, finally mustering enough momentum to hook one knee over the steed's withers. Then he pulled, pushed, and squirmed himself back astride the grey, screamed more curses, and kicked. Ivo again balked. Owain had raised his palm to slap Ivo's rump when he noticed the horse's ears were pricked straight up, not flat as in anger. Alerted, he pricked up his own ears, but heard nothing but the soft sigh of the wind and ruffling leaves. He sighed and figured the prig of a doctor would about now be clambering the next hill. Glancing that way, he beheld Simon thundering along. Simon spied Owain as well and waved. The gesture boiled Owain's insides, making him sputter and hiss, "I...I...somehow...I will catch and beat the bleeding bastard!" His grumbling magically spurred Ivo forward at such a tremendous speed that Owain had to grab hold again, and he began muttering prayers for his own safety and for the race to end...soon.

Gruffydd restrained the wriggling, whining pup, and whispered harshly, "Hush! They'll hear us!" He peeked through the brambles that hid him, Cynan, and the pup. He saw nothing, but heard much—shouts and ominous sounds beyond the wall—that told him something terrible was happening. Riding back to the village, they had seen the flaming arrows, the smoke, the burning huts, and they had abandoned their ponies and scrambled behind the bramble bushes that braced the outer wall of the commote. His mam had told him, if he saw anything strange, especially since the Normans were visiting, to hide and wait for a villager to rescue them. And he had done as told, but he still felt so scared, so helpless. His heart's pounding ached his chest, and he swiped irritably at tears as he wrestled with the pup and patted Cynan's shoulder, who was sobbing because he'd seen his home ablaze. He wanted to run into the village to save Cynan's mam, to find his own mam! Then deep within his mind, he heard a chant; it grew ever louder, and he quietly recited the saving verse to Cynan, "If we're to see our mams and friends again, we must stay strong, and hide, and wait."

As Noir puffed up the second, steeper hill, Simon glanced across the ravine, and noticed his wave had more than doubled Ivo's speed. He'd meant the gesture in fun,

209

but he surmised Owain had most likely taken it as an insult. *He is such an odd, infuriating fellow*, thought Simon, *but Maura likes him, so he must have a bit of goodness in him somewhere*. Owain and Ivo disappeared behind a dense grove of trees, and Simon turned his head to whisper encouragement to Noir. As they neared the peak, Simon looked once more for his rival, yet the only creature to emerge from the grove was Ivo. Simon halted Noir and peered the long distance, expecting to see the comical sight of Owain racing after Henry's horse. But Ivo continued trotting along the path alone. Sudden fear and apprehension fluttered Simon's heart. He started back down the road at a full gallop, hoping he'd find Owain stuck in a bog, flailing and blaring curses.

From nowhere came a bolt of death. Noir's knees crumpled beneath him, hurling him forward to the ground. Simon dove for his life and hit the dirt at a roll. The great black stallion somersaulted once, then lay flat and twitching. Simon's tumbling ended soundly against a tree trunk. He leapt to his feet and ran back to the steed, but the arrow stuck in Noir's neck made him freeze and drop again to the ground. Another volley of darts punctured the horse's girth and legs and pierced the surrounding ground. Simon slithered on his belly off the road and under a dense growth of thistle. He coiled in a tight ball as another flock of arrows descended and sheared leaves from the bush by his side. He cried out from shock and surprise, then struggled to think rationally. Whoever attacked fired their weapons from atop the facing hill. A thick amount of growth hugged the road, continued over the ledge, and infested the ravine between the hills. Keeping well covered, Simon dragged himself to the ledge and waited for the next assault. The darts hit perilously close, and he was glad, for he swiftly snatched up an arrow, held it as though it had struck his chest, and let himself fall the ten or so feet into the ravine. He tossed the arrow as he bounced off a cushioning bush, and sank into a bog of sucking mud. A low branch kept him from sinking deeper. He sucked a breath and fought his panic. *Will they come to find me and make certain of my death?!* If the Normans had also attacked the village, Rhys' troops would certainly arrive soon to rescue Owain, and hopefully himself as well. The time arrived and passed for another volley, yet no arrows fell. Simon let out his breath, and used the limb to extricate himself from the swamp that had swallowed the entire lower half of his body. He scuttled on his hands and knees through ferns, reeds, and leafy mold, frequently glancing upward to determine his bearings. The ledge bracing the opposite road was far less steep; he easily scaled the slippery rock and raced to the nearest grove. There he found Owain, sprawled and still. Arrows jutted obscenely from his shoulder and thigh and, as Simon crouched to check for more damage, he noticed one had broken off and was lodged deeply in his back. Owain's chest rose and fell ever so faintly; blood drenched his breeches and continued to pump readily from the wound in his thigh. Simon forced still his shaky hands and ripped Owain's trousers to view the puncture and make a bandage. He didn't dare remove the weapon, for besides causing the bleeding, it also held back a good portion of it. Simon tore away a thin, long piece of Owain's trousers, tied a tourniquet round his thigh, and worried, *Can we safely wait for a rescue, or should I try carrying Owain back to the commote?* While caught in his frantic musing, he didn't notice Owain's eyes—bulged wide, fierce, and glaring. Simon also failed to see the Welshman's hands surge up from his sides, but he felt them capture his throat and squeeze. Simon gasped horrible breaths and threw himself backward, thrashing and swinging as he hit the ground. Owain flew with him, his grip not in the least bit deterred. Simon raked and pinched at Owain's fingers, beat at his head, kneed his groin, but his gyrations were in vain. Owain's grip only strengthened and dug deeper. Simon's face colored purple, his gasps shortened, his eyes closed, and his fight died.

As Owain's blood drained away, so did his vengeance. His rigid fingers slid from his enemy's neck and, dazed and confused, he watched Simon topple lifelessly to the dirt. He looked away from the gruesome sight and noticed—the tourniquet. The jolting realization that he had just murdered the one man who could have saved his life ignited his guilt and panic. He wailed his misery to the heavens and fought futilely to rouse Simon, shaking him and slapping his face. Suddenly, as if in punishment, a piercing pain attacked Owain, arched his body, and dropped him to Simon's side. The clouds swirling high above blackened along with his sight and, as his consciousness dimmed, he managed one final thought—*What a damned fool I've been!*

*****

CHAPTER THIRTEEN - SHATTERINGS

𝕸aura cautiously approached Gael, who was standing by the mead keg, her anguish directed at the bolted door. Gael's rigid fingers strangled a full cup of mead so, not to startle, Maura whispered carefully, "Gael."

Gael slowly turned toward her friend and answered with a flat, "Yes."

"Do you think you could help me?"

"Help you what?"

"I don't know when Simon will return and I feel it would be best to extract the arrow head from..." She searched the floor, found her intended patient, then pointed. "...his shoulder."

With a vague nod, Gael followed Maura. They knelt on either side of the unconscious man, and Maura relieved Gael of her cup of mead. Over her lap she unrolled a square of linen that held several needles and a crop of suturing thread.

"Where did you get those?" asked Gael.

"Raythyen found them. Sulien keeps a supply at the llys for emergencies."

"And what will you cut him with?"

"This." Maura extracted a dagger from the taut cuff of her chemise.

"An interesting spot to keep a knife," remarked Gael.

"No one knows I have it...till I need it," said Maura.

While Maura used a damp towel to swab away encrusted blood, Gael seemingly knew her thought. "Simon might *not* return, Maura."

"I choose to believe he will, as well as Gruffydd, Cynan, Owain, and the pup."

"How can you be so optimistic?" Gael wondered.

"Someone has to be. Could you please thread the needle?"

Gael squinted to perform her task and inquired, "Where's Rhys gone?"

"He's rallying his troops on the outskirts of the commote."

"Then why don't the arrows stop?" Gael asked in a strained voice.

"Because he's only just left. Surely the commote has seen trouble such as this before."

"Once...a few years back. I was away at the time. You've obviously seen this sort of trouble before."

"Yes," said Maura, "...several times. One of the many unfortunate consequences of being too close to royalty."

"And a member of your *too* close royalty lies three mats down," noted Gael.

"Yes, but we need not mention him just now." Maura touched the tip of the dagger to the side of the arrow head and pressed a clean cut down to the depths of the wound. The soldier never stirred.

"How do you know how to do this?"

"I've seen Simon do this countless times."

Gael watched in wonder as Maura eased out the knife and performed a similar cut on the opposite side of the head, then she wiggled the blade at the top and bottom of the slice, while jiggling the stick. In little time, the stone emerged. They both exhaled relief; Maura pressed the towel to their patient's shoulder to help staunch the blood, and Gael passed her the threaded needle.

"I'm impressed, Maura."

Maura shrugged, and strove to lighten the mood. "I'd like to thank you again for allowing Simon and me the opportunity to talk last evening."

Gael snorted, "You never talked."

Maura pinched the skin together and spoke her words as carefully as she placed her stitches. "Of course...we talked."

"When?"

"Before, during...between...and after."

"You never slept?"

"No," Maura answered sheepishly.

"What did you talk about?"

"Everything...and nothing."

"About me and Marc?"

"We didn't know about you and Marc till today. I'm sorry for what I asked before." Gael shook her head in confusion, and Maura reminded, "About when you'd become fond of Marc."

"I'd forgotten."

"I haven't," said Maura. "It's not my place to preach to you or anyone."

"You weren't preaching...You were concerned for your brother. I consider Simon my brother. When Nesta accused him of adultery, I thought of murdering her."

"But Gael...you are nothing like Nesta."

"Thank the Lord."

"I would love to see you and Marc become closer. But—"

Maura stopped to knot her handiwork and Gael, inhaling deeply, finished for her, "Since I will marry in three months' time, and your brother, being the moral man he is—and that is not meant as a criticism—would never agree to committing adultery, a decision to become closer would most likely prove disastrous. Is that what you were going to say?"

Maura glanced up and said weakly, "Something very similar to that, yes."

"In this instance, I hate to agree with you...but I must."

"And Marc?" asked Maura.

"He also agrees with you."

Gael's brimming tears made Maura want to cry as well, but she held back, and said, "I'll fetch a fresh bandage."

Gael rose first, swiping self-consciously at her escaping tears, and gently admonished, "No...You've performed enough heroics for one day. You need rest, for once this baby comes, you won't rest properly for months."

Maura did not argue and her small grateful grin followed Gael as she ambled wearily away.

Laboriously the day wore on; outside grew dusky, the sounds of thudding arrows too slowly dwindled, and the smoke at last scattered. Soldiers risked abandoning their posts to seek out drink and food and a moment of well-deserved rest. Yet the women's work was far from finished. A new and much larger group of wounded arrived, newly maimed by an assault on Bernard's archers. The least injured soldiers bragged of Rhys' relentless and brutal onslaught, routing the Normans north and chasing them forever from Deheubarth. Marc recognized a few key words spoken by the Welsh sentries; listening, he worriedly surveyed the medical catastrophe strewn over the floor before him and decided, since the Normans were escaping north, it was probably safe for him to travel east to find and fetch Simon. He located Maura, involved in a hectic search for more suturing thread, and announced, "Maura...I'm going for Simon and Owain and the boys."

"It's not safe for you to go!" worried Maura.

"I believe it is, at least for a short while."

"You won't go alone!"

"Whom do you suggest I take?"

213

The name of the finest candidate came to her quickly. "Hywel. I saw him at the mead keg, having a drink before he needs to leave again. We'll catch him," she said as they hastened for the door. Maura waved wildly and yelled, "Hywel!"

Hywel paused before the closed door, and searched the room for his crier. When he noticed Maura and Marc headed his way, his expectant look soured and he grumbled, "What is it, Maura? I've got to get back to Rhys. There will be more wounded and I will need to haul them back here and to the infirmary. I can't stay to help with their nursing."

"I'm not asking you for that," she answered as sternly. "We need you to help find Simon and Owain. The troops need Owain, and the wounded need Simon. Will you go with Marc?"

His jowly face pinched with indecision before sputtering, "I...I suppose I will go. But we must make haste. Bernard's men may return."

"And please, Hywel," implored Maura, "speak in English to Marc!"

With a curt nod, Hywel left the llys. Maura gave Marc a kiss for luck, and hustled him out behind Hywel's massive figure. Peeking through a knot hole in the door, she muttered a short prayer for their mission's success, and watched them gallop away on Welsh ponies.

*****

Gruffydd had garnered the courage to squirm on his belly along the wall to the gate. Rhys and someone Gruffydd didn't know had left a long while past. Some had ridden in and out with bodies draped on their mounts, yet no one had noticed Gruffydd's screams and waves. And so he had waited over the long hours, and as dark fell he was rapidly losing hope. He glanced back at the bramble bush where Cynan and the pup waited patiently, well at least Cynan was cooperating. Gruffydd lay his ear to the ground and prayed. Almost imperceptibly his prayer was answered—hoof beats approached, rumbling the ground, and driving the boy to his feet. With no thought to his own safety, Gruffydd dashed out to the center of the road, leapt about, flapped his arms, and screamed, "Stop! Please stop and save us!"

Marc and Hywel barely managed to rein their ponies before trampling the boy. They flew off their steeds; Marc caught Gruffydd in a smothering hug and the boy cried out in anguish, "We were riding back and saw the arrows and the fires. We hid out here and waited, but no one stopped for us!"

Cynan joined their hug, wailing in Welsh, "My hut's burned down! Where's my mam? Where are my brother and sister?"

Hywel gruffly answered, "They're safe at the llys, which is where you should be, not chasing nonsense." He spoke to Marc, "I'll take them back. You ride on and take the mutt with you. If need be, he'll help sniff them out."

Marc stood to mount, but the boys still hung on him, clutching at his tunic, whining their fear. He knelt again to assure, "I'll return shortly," and gently to Cynan, stressed, "Paid a becso, Cynan."

Gruffydd immediately started to translate, then realized Marc had spoken 'Don't worry, Cynan' in Welsh! He beamed in awe, then emphasized to Cynan, "He's right, Cynan. We'll go with Hywel. Marc will soon bring home Simon and Owain."

Hywel hoisted the boys up onto his saddle, and lurched up behind them. Marc shouted at Pup to "Stay!" Once the boys were safely away, he muttered, "Come. We'll find Simon and Owain," and whistled. The dog scurried to catch his gallop.

Gael was bandaging a cut when a great clamor sounded at the door. Hywel barged his way inside, a boy tucked under each arm. The gauze Gael was wrapping unraveled as she shot up and barreled her way between the loitering troops, crying "Gruffydd! Cynan!"

214

Olwen heard her cry and hurried as fast as her condition would allow to the door where a joyous and tearful reunion ensued. "I did what you told me to do, Mam," sobbed Gruffydd, crushed in Gael's embrace. "I hid and waited. Rhys didn't see me, but Marc did. He's gone to get Simon..." He lifted his head from her breast and checked for her response to his finish, "...and Owain."

But nothing could mar her smile, nor quell her tears. They gushed in torrents, spattering Gruffydd's hair as he surged back into her hug and heard her reply, "And he will find them and bring them home to us."

Maura looked on, relieved and delighted to see the boys safe and well, yet she lost her grin as visions of Simon's and Owain's bodies, sprawled and pierced, flashed before her eyes. She forced her concentration to the injury at hand, and suddenly was overwhelmed by nausea and heavy exhaustion. Maura knew if she could rest a short while, she'd surely find the vigor to continue nursing the soldiers and hopefully...her husband as well. Angharad, a willowy, black-haired woman, with milky pale skin, knelt nearby, cleansing a leg wound. Maura tapped her shoulder and softly requested, "Angharad...after you've finished there, could you wrap this man's brow? It's not a deep cut."

Angharad owed Maura and Simon much for helping, and not condemning her in times of need. Maura's pallid countenance and bleary eyes worried her; she pointed to the opposite end of the hall. "There's a spot in the far corner where you can lie awhile. I'll help Gael and your patients. And when you wake, Simon will be here."

Maura nodded her thanks, and forced her complaining body up and across the hall to the corner. Not far away lay a line of dead, their faces shrouded by blankets. She shuddered with grief, and sank down upon the crisp rushes, her palms pressed to her eyes, blocking the horrors. Sleep rushed to rescue her from her worries, yet before she could fully succumb, a frantic squall startled her awake. "Get your filthy fingers off me, you mangy bitch. I'll have Maura and no one else! Maura! Where've you gone? Don't desert me. Maura!" Maura struggled to sit, and rose shakily to attend to...Henry.

*****

Marc stared mournfully down at his dead stallion. Panic swelled his chest, shortened his breath, and drove his hands to his head. *Where is Simon?! Has he been kidnapped? Has Owain?!* The pup stopped sniffing the carcass and focused instead on the ground around. His nose followed an invisible wiggly path leading to the bushes hugging the road. He stopped at the ledge, raised his muzzle, and howled into the starless, gray night. His lament echoed off the rock walls and told Marc that Simon was near, perhaps in the ravine, though with total dark rapidly approaching, finding him would be near to impossible. And then the pup sprang from the ledge, and dove the long distance into the ravine, disappearing beneath the dense greenery. Marc started to scramble after him, yet wisely changed his mind; he'd wait instead for the dog's signal. And he hadn't waited long before he again heard the pup's howl. This time, however, his tone was cheerier and he was no longer in the ravine, but on the road opposite. Marc jumped on his pony and sped back around the sharp curve of the road.

Pup! The damned dog is licking my face! I hate the dog licking my face! Simon shoved Pup away and jerked up from the ground, wide-eyed and gasping from the agony that tortured his throat. He heard approaching boot steps and scrambled to hide, snatching up the dog with one hand, and yanking Owain along with the other.

Marc spotted the commotion and raced forward, yelling, "Simon! Simon! It's Marc. Don't move!" Simon's elation at being alive thrust Simon to his feet. He bolted for Marc, but Owain's foot tripped his flight, and he crashed once more to the ground. He beat and kicked at the dirt, and moaned in hoarse exasperation. He was promptly answered by Marc. "Give me your arm. I'll help you." Simon sat and grabbed his brother in a desperate clutch. Marc squeezed back and asked, "Are you hurt?" Simon hardly wagged his head, and Marc, alarmed by his frenzied silence, pulled back a moment to check. Even in the dark, Marc could clearly make out the black bruising banding Simon's neck. He glanced briefly down at Owain, counted two jutting sticks, then snapped back to Simon in disbelief. "God's breath, what did he try to do to you?!"

Simon shook his head again and attempted to speak, yet all he could manage were squeaks. He ceased trying and crawled to Owain. Miraculously he touched warmth on Owain's skin, and felt a sound pulse reverberating from his chest. He noticed the tourniquet still tied, and waved vigorously at Marc to come nearer. In a raspy and incredulous whisper, he stammered, "I...I don't know how, but he...he's still alive. We must ge...get him to the infirmary...quickly!"

Hoof beats sounded; Simon tensed and Marc calmed, "It's only Hywel. He's come to help."

"What's happened?" croaked Simon, as he hooked his arms carefully under Owain's.

"Bernard didn't care much for losing the games," sneered Hywel.

Marc braced his arms under Owain's knees and clarified, "The Normans attacked soon after the race began."

Simon and Marc guardedly lifted Owain, and Simon grunted his concern, "The boys?"

Hywel led his pony closer and grunted back, "Are fine, and in the llys."

"Maura...Gael?"

"Fine as well," said Marc. "A makeshift infirmary has been set up at the llys. Maura has been handily directing the nursing, but she very much would like to have you there."

"Mind the wound in his back," stressed Simon. As he helped Marc hoist Owain up into Hywel's waiting arms, Simon heard something drop. He squatted, peered, and skimmed the ground near his feet. His grasp took up what appeared to be a fat stick. Feeling further, Simon discovered it to be hollow, and carved with regularly spaced holes. Rather than toss it, he stuck it in the pouch dangling from his belt, and swung up into Marc's pony's saddle. He twisted to Hywel, and asked, "How many are wounded?"

Hywel held Owain as tenderly as if he held a baby, a sight much in contrast to his fractious reply, "Too many. No more questions...I must get back to Rhys!"

Simon pressed further, "Is the village secure?"

"Yes," said Marc, mounting behind him.

"Then..." Simon took a moment to cough, and forced his wavering voice louder, "Hywel, take Owain to the llys and have Maura prepare him for surgery. Marc and I will stop at our hut to fetch more supplies."

"Don't dally," was Hywel's only reply as he jerked his pony round and vanished into the dark. Marc's shrill whistle made Simon jump and their pony bound forward; Pup yipped merrily, sprinting behind and snapping at the pony's feet.

Simon and Marc spilled breathlessly inside the cottage and briskly began gathering and depositing into Simon's shoulder satchel, thread, bandage material, poultices, salves, and lotions. They didn't notice John, sitting before his closed book, staring anxiously. He drew gasps from each by asking, "Where's Lord Henry?"

When his heart had slowed a bit, Marc said, "He's at the llys, suffering from a burn."

His answer received a concerned glance from Simon, and a whine from John, "Is he hurt badly?"

"Not too," said Marc, "but he'll do better with your company."

Simon rested leery eyes on the curious young man. "You don't know what's happened?"

"No," John innocently returned. "I've been here all the day reading, and wondered why no one had returned."

Suspiciously, Marc wondered, "And you didn't think to look for your Lord?"

"No...I did feed the beasts."

Marc and Simon exchanged baffled looks, then shrugged and continued their task. With the bag bulged to capacity, Simon darted into the bedchamber and returned cleanly dressed. "You take John on the pony," he directed to Marc, "I'll ride E'dain and..." He searched the floor and spotted Pup, sniffing round his bowl. Simon took him gently in his arms and placed a firm kiss on the top of his head. "Hence forth, I grant you permission to slobber my face anytime you please, but for now you must stay here where it's safe." He swiftly ladled some congealed cold stew from the cauldron and plopped it into the mutt's bowl. He added water from the pitcher to a second bowl, swung the bag over his shoulder and called out, "We'll go."

*****

"Why did you leave me?" demanded Henry, securing Maura's hands.

"You were sleeping, and there are many who are more needy," she answered. "What is it you want?"

"You..."

Maura ignored his nonsense. "Your injury is not serious." Yet as she spoke, she noticed his touch did seem overly warm, and his brow blazed hotter. "You've caught a fever, but I don't think it was caused by your burn."

"Will I die?" he whined.

"No...Simon knows many recipes for treating fevers."

"Simon's dead!"

"Henry!" Appalled, she wrenched from his hold. "How can you say such a thing to me? Hywel and Marc have gone to fetch Simon and Owain. They found the boys, they will find the men!"

And now he snubbed her assertion to plead, "The cool towels you used before, please use them again. I'm so hot! Please, Maura, I can stand only your touch. Don't allow those other bitches near me, *please!*"

"Henry, if you don't stop your slandering," she hotly warned, "no one will tend you! I'll bring the towels. You stay quiet and behave!"

Henry opened his eyes as a heavenly coolness wrapped his shoulder. He intently studied his goddess, hovering so near he could taste her sweet scent, and he reached to stroke her silken cheek. Her answering gaze was seductive and yielding, and he felt certain she craved him as terribly as he craved her. *Soon...very soon*, he convinced himself, *she'll profess her passion...soon.* A strident plea shattered his fantasy.

"Help! I need help!"

Maura snapped her attention to Hywel, who juggled a body and battled with the door. She promptly abandoned Henry and rushed to help him. Seeing he didn't carry Simon, her control cracked. "Where's Simon?!" she cried, erupting with sobs. "Where have you left him?! He's dead...You've left him because he's dead!"

"No!" retorted Hywel. Two nearby soldiers carefully took Owain from Hywel, while he carped on, "Your man's perfectly well, which makes me wonder why he didn't come here earlier for aid. If he had, Owain wouldn't be so poorly."

"Where is he?!" she cried again.

"Gone with your brother for supplies," he groused back. "He'd best arrive shortly. He said for you to prepare Owain for cutting." He left with a huff, and she was glad, but her anger quickly ebbed at the piteous sight of Owain. *Oh my Lord*, she silently prayed

217

and sank to her knees by his side, *please give us the strength and knowledge to heal him.*

A fierce grip on her shoulder flung her backwards, and Henry's scream blared in her face, "Damn you fickle whore! No woman deserts me, not for some stinking Welsh turd."

She squirmed and ranted, "Let me go, Henry!" His grip on the base of her neck bit deeper, and she begged, "Get him off me, please! Someone help!"

The same soldiers who'd taken Owain wrested Henry off her back. He swung punches and kicked at them, screamed gibberish and spat curses. A swift blow to his jaw soundly hushed his fit, and the sentries tossed him senseless back upon his mat.

Maura crushed her palms to her temples and rocked to and fro, fighting back her nausea and the scream that clawed menacingly at her throat. She felt a soft pat on the top of her head and looked up to see Gruffydd. Cracking a cautious smile, he offered her a cup of steaming mead and the advice, "Maybe you should drink this before you tend to Owain."

She grinned wanly, whispered a heartfelt, "Thank you," and accepted his gift.

"I'd stay to help, but I have more mead to pass out."

"You have helped, immensely, Gruffydd," she encouraged with a kiss to his hand. "Now go and pass out your mead. Simon will soon be here."

And suddenly he *was* there, plucking her up from the floor, squeezing her breath away, and murmuring, "God's breath, woman, I've missed you!" She hung in his taut clutch, whimpering endearments, and kissing his mouth and every place else she could reach. His lips avidly returned her fervor, but gradually the arduous chore awaiting them seeped through their bliss. They eased apart and Simon swept a fleeting glance over the room. "You've worked wonders here!" he marveled.

"Not alone," she excused, "...and there's much left for us to do."

"Tell me."

"Extractions, fractures, sprains, gashes. Owain seems the worst."

"I'll fetch what I need. I believe it's best if you assist me, Maura, for you are the only one of the village he takes kindly to."

Maura nodded and watched him weave away through the crowd. She knelt, and cringed at the vast amount of blood that drenched Owain's breeches. How could he still be alive? But then the Welsh were hardy stock and Owain probably kept breathing just to spite the Normans. All his wounds afflicted the same side of his body, so he'd been lain on his other side. She searched his face for twitches of consciousness, yet found none, and mused how peaceful he looked this way...almost gentle. His mussed chestnut locks hung down, obscuring his eyes, and his closely cropped beard was dusted with pale dirt, making him appear older. She was astonished to glimpse a hint of color rouging his cheeks. Simon reappeared balancing implements and a candle; she freed him of the least necessary items, and began tenderly swabbing the areas around Owain's wounds.

"He looks amazingly well...considering," commented Maura.

"I agree," said Simon, "but then the Welsh are hardy folk."

She grinned his way. "I was thinking that as well."

"We've been known to think alike...occasionally."

His quip made her smile again, then her tone turned grim, "Tell me what happened, Simon."

"We were racing, I looked back and saw Ivo trotting on his own. I was riding back to see to Owain, when the arrows fell and killed Noir. I escaped them by leaping into a ravine. When all was quiet, I climbed back on the road, where I found Owain—like this." As he told his grisly tale, he gently shifted Owain to his back and placed a pillow directly below his back injury to keep it clear of the floor. Maura took up the candle and held it over the thigh wound. She almost dropped the taper when an upward glance showed the bruising on Simon's neck.

She reached out tentatively, stammering, "Si...Simon, what..."

"He tried to strangle me, and came too damn close to succeeding," Simon uttered as he sliced into Owain's flesh.

Maura paled and sat back on her heels. She strove to still the trembling candle and worried, what further chaos would erupt when this rabid creature woke.

Simon cut, extracted, and stitched; Maura mopped and bandaged, and kept up a mild, soothing conversation of what had happened at the llys and what yet needed to be accomplished. Gruffydd and Gael ventured near to watch awhile, and present Simon with a hug and a cup of mead to help stave off his coughing spells.

"Henry's waking, Maura," Gael said in a portentous tone.

"I can't come to him now."

Simon paused his stitching to demand, "What's he done?"

"Nothing, Simon," Maura swiftly dismissed.

Gael grinned snidely, "I'll see to him, Maura...and if he dares give me trouble, I'll set Marc on him."

They grinned with her, but Gael's expression darkened as she gazed upon Owain, and she asked Simon with scant emotion, "Will he live?"

Simon didn't have an answer for her, so he shrugged and stitched on. Henry roared for Maura; Gael humphed in annoyance, took Gruffydd's hand, and left to deal with the pampered Prince.

Owain woke on his belly; immediately, he arched up off the floor, but his move provoked an agony that dropped him flat and wrenched from him a howl brimming with misery. Simon shouted for a soldier, who knelt at Owain's head and restrained his arms. Maura petted his hair, all the while cooing, "Owain...it's Maura. You're safe and in the llys. All the arrows have been removed, but you've lost a good deal of blood. You must remain still..."

"Your...your hus...band...Your husband..." he rasped.

"He's here as well, stitching you."

The shock blanching Owain's face shot shivers up Maura's spine. He reared up again, squalling, "Get him off me!" His attempted flip was stalled by Simon and two other sentries who sat on his good side to keep him still. He groaned hate and anguish, pummeled the rushes and writhed, trying to unseat Simon. Sulien settled heavily on his lower legs and Owain gradually lost his battle.

His curses, though, continued to rustle the rushes, and rumbled louder to Simon's goading, "I fear we'll be stuck here together for quite a while longer but, believe me Owain, I'm as eager to escape you as you are to escape me."

"Bleeding bastard!" howled Owain.

"You're the one who's doing all the bleeding, Sir, but you are correct with your other assertion—my parents never married."

Maura scolded, aghast, "Simon!"

Simon burst an indignant laugh. "I refuse to be pleasant to the wretch who tried to murder me."

"After you tried to murder me!" countered Owain.

"Yes, I always tie tourniquets round the legs of those I intend to kill. It provides so much more of a challenge."

Owain bucked and wailed, "You damn pig! Get away!"

"And let you die?" gritted Simon. "...No, I have far too much left to say."

"Simon, stop!" berated Maura.

219

Simon raved back, "No I won't stop! I'm sick of his railing and his bigotry. He offends me, you, and my friends, and I admit that I'm enjoying his suffering. I don't mean his pain. What hurts him more is the excruciating fact that he must rely on *me*, the one he hates most of all to save his life!"

Neither Owain nor Maura dared protest Simon's haranguing; she sat stunned, watching Owain's twitching lessen and finally cease. Then she turned her wary attention to her husband. If Simon still felt rage, it wasn't evident in his deft tacking. His fingers worked with a graceful calm, yet his expression held a lost, bemused look. And she didn't know what to feel for Owain—pity, concern, disgust? He had almost robbed her of her closest companion and one true passion. Was Owain's assault on Simon an honest mistake, or a premeditated strike? And if the latter, why did he hate Simon so? But her mind and body were too weary to conjure any answers to such a puzzle. She felt Simon's thumb brush across her jaw; his other four fingers cupped and slightly raised her chin, and he spoke adoringly, "I'm sorry you had to hear that, but he almost took me from you and, at this point in time, I loathe him for it. Perhaps later, I'll see and feel things differently. You, my love, are clearly exhausted. I'll finish here, then recruit Marc and Gael to keep everyone, including Henry, comforted while you rest."

Maura couldn't argue; she received his kiss, laced her fingers through his hair, then crawled back to the corner to attempt sleep again. And successful she was, for when next she awoke, the gray sheen of dawn seeped through cracks in the shutters illuminating a scene of serene brutality. All crowding the llys, save Gael, Simon, and Marc, lay still either in death or slumber.

Gael's question, "Would you like some?" woke Maura further. She struggled to sit up, smiled at Gruffydd snoozing upon his mother's lap, and peeked into Gael's bowl. The gruel sticking to its sides and base appeared too rigid to be appetizing.

Maura wagged her head and began instinctively re-weaving her mussed plaits. "Have you slept?" she mumbled.

"Amazingly, yes," said Gael, petting her son's hair. She trailed Maura's narrow gaze over to Simon and Marc, slouched and facing each other over a patient, and mentioned, "They've worked the entire night through. It appears the worst is over. There have been no new wounded since midnight, and the arrows have stopped...You've gone quite gray."

Maura turned a quizzical look, then switched worries. "How has Henry behaved?"

"Terribly, but his fever's kept him still. And his man is taking care of his needs."

"And...Owain?"

"I was near his side when he woke, round mid-night," said Gael. "He wasn't pleased with my presence, but his pain hushed his complaining. Simon stopped by and a most interesting exchange occurred. They glared at each other for the longest while, then Owain closed his eyes and moaned the saddest moan. When he reopened his eyes, Simon supported his head, and held a draught to his lips. I thought Owain would refuse, bat it away, or hurl it at Simon, but Maura...he gulped down every drop, and afterward actually looked grateful. They never spoke, though I sensed a peace settle between them. Then again, I could be mistaken."

"Did Simon tell you what happened?"

"No, Marc did. If I were Simon, I'd let Owain rot."

"Gael..." Maura chided at her crassness. "We've yet to hear Owain's version of their encounter."

"Don't you mean his lies?" sniped Gael.

"Why are you so bitter?" Maura sharply returned. "You don't have to marry the man."

Gael refused her a reply, and settled back with Gruffydd. Weary of the hatred, Maura left the corner to take Marc's place so he could rest. On her way across the room, she crouched beside Owain and stroked his brow, feeling for fever. Her touch opened his eyes; their meanness had vanished, replaced by a needy innocence. She knelt and lowered her ear to hear his whisper, "My pipe...my pipe's missing."

"I don't understand, Owain...Your pipe?"

"My whistle. You heard me play it the other evening."

She remembered and smiled, "Yes...I don't know where it is, but I'll ask Simon."

"No...don't bother him. I probably lost it in the scuffle."

"Do you want for something else, mead, or water? Can it be too soon to hope you're hungry?"

"Is there more of your husband's potion?"

"I'll go look." She rose, tip-toed her way to the trestle table and sniffed at several bowls sitting in a row. Their odors pungently told their properties; she ladled a cupful from the middle bowl, and returned to Owain. He wordlessly accepted her support and downed the drink. As she fussed with his blanket, she chanced asking, "I believed you liked me, Sir, or at least tolerated my presence?"

Suspiciously, he sputtered, "I...I do."

"Then tell me why you tried to kill my husband. I believe you know I *am* quite fond of him."

So, Owain surmised, her game was to pry from him his rendition of the tale, and he wasn't certain why, but he quickly obliged. "When I first woke, after the arrows struck, I felt horrible pain and saw your man kneeling over me, making my pain worse. I reacted as anyone would—I attacked my attacker."

"But Owain...Simon has never given you cause to think him your enemy! Despite your pain you must have considered during your struggle that he might be trying to help you. After all, he couldn't have shot the arrows."

He wanted to argue with her—to say he wasn't convinced that Simon hadn't shot him, or been involved in some way in Bernard's ambush, and that all Normans were his enemies. Yet she was Norman, and clearly not his enemy. The confusion he felt was immense and steeply hiked his hurt and guilt.

She sensed his pain and trouble and knew he wasn't prepared to agree with her...yet. Simon obviously intended to heal Owain, whether or not he wanted to be healed, and would soon prove himself blameless. Owain seemed close to sleep, and she whispered, "I'll leave you now. If you need for anything, Simon and I will be near enough to hear."

He forced his eyes wide and reached out, yet stopped his hand before contacting her skin. "Do...don't go," he pleaded. "I'd like to talk."

Never before had Owain wanted to talk. She couldn't refuse his rare show of civility. "If you wish."

He stuttered through his first few clumsy attempts, then organized his thoughts. "The past evening at your husband's feast...Outside...I heard what you spoke of...with Rhys." His last words trembled, "Your family's murder."

"Yes," she acknowledged.

"I've thought on your question. My family hails from the north, the island of Mon. Sixteen or seventeen years past we were driven south by the Normans' raids."

Maura's eyes grew round with intrigue. "Do you know of my parents?"

"No...I don't recall many details. I do know that dozens of commotes were razed, and most of the Welsh inhabiting them were slaughtered...and that no Norman barons suffered the same fate."

"What are you saying?"

221

"I'm saying your father was no Norman baron, not on the north border, not seventeen years past."

"Then Rhys must have been correct," decided Maura. "My father was a seneschal, or a sheriff, someone of importance, otherwise I would never have been accepted as a possible wife to King William's son."

"There were very few Norman casualties," said Owain, "and why would any Norman risk having young children present during the raids?"

"Simon wonders that as well," said she.

"He's right to."

Maura wasn't prepared to accept Lord Robert's story of murder in Cornwall over Rose's Welsh border tale, so she cleverly switched the burden of their conversation to Owain, "Is your family still living close by?"

"My family's dead," he said with coarse bluntness.

"I...I'm sorry," she sputtered ruefully, and wondered if their deaths were the reason for his ire and bigotry. "Did they die recently?" she carefully prompted.

"They've been gone ten years."

"How did they die?"

She wasn't surprised to hear, "Butchered by Normans."

"How did you escape?"

"I wasn't home at the time," said he. "I had run off, angry."

"Angry with whom?"

"My betrothed."

Maura almost choked on her shock. It was terribly hard imagining Owain voluntarily betrothed to anyone. He seemed not to mind her prodding; in fact, his restive gaze oddly encouraged it, so she delved further, "Why angry?"

"She'd decided not to marry me. She preferred a Norman's bed to mine."

"Did you love her?"

"I barely knew her. But she insulted me, so I hated her."

"Did she go to the Norman?"

"She died with my family."

Maura expected him to add—*and her's was a just punishment*—but he didn't, and she asked on, "How old were you when they died?"

"Twenty."

"Were you an only child?"

His voice cracked to tell, "There were five of us. Three boys, two girls. I was the eldest, and had been living with Rhys for five years training to be his soldier."

"Had your father also served Rhys?"

"In a way."

Maura spotted his blush, but that didn't stall her question, "In what way?"

"As his Ovate."

Again his Welsh eluded her. "I don't understand ovate?"

Owain roughly explained, "He predicted and guided Rhys' future."

She couldn't mask her wonderment, and asked skeptically, "And was he successful in his trade?"

Owain spoke as if slighted, "Most times."

"I apologize, Owain. It's just I've never heard of such a thing."

"In Welsh society, the Ovate is second only to the Prince. It's said I've inherited his vision," Owain stated almost proudly.

"Do you truly believe you have?"

"I pray not...for it would be a heavy burden. Don't you agree?"

"Yes...I suppose it would be." She forced an awkward grin. "I shouldn't have kept you talking for so long. How's your pain?"

"Simon's draught works well."

For the first time, he'd spoken Simon's Christian name in a casual manner. Maura smiled fully, and suggested, "You should try to rest more."

"I can't do much else," he groused, then haltingly asked, "What are the marks on Simon's back?"

She wondered how he'd seen Simon's scars, but then remembered they had raced bareback. "His father had him flogged less than a year past."

"Why?"

"Simon refused to swear him homage."

"And did his father deserve his homage?"

"Not at that moment...no. And now, Sir," she said, "I thank you for your knowledge of the Norman barons of the north, and I am sorry for the horrors that befell your family."

"The same befell yours."

"So," she asked, "do I dare propose that we have enough in common to risk becoming friends?"

He arched one slim brow, which she took to mean yes. She fussed again with his blanket and took up his cup, adding mildly, "Perhaps soon, it will be safe to move you to the infirmary. The cots are far softer and you'd feel more at ease with Sulien. He's helping here and at the—"

"I'd prefer staying here," he interjected. She cocked her head in question, and he blurted, "I don't want to be too close to God..." Maura was about to beg an explanation, when he provided, "...till I have Simon's and your forgiveness."

With an uncertain nod, she stood to go, then a flash of insight propelled her to ask one more question, "Owain, was perchance your betrothed yellow-haired and Saxon?"

"Yes," he easily answered, "but how could you know that?"

"Only a guess," Maura replied, as she left him.

*****

Simon accepted the passed brace from Marc and asked "How did it feel, lobbing arrows at Normans?"

"I wasn't shooting at Normans, Simon. I was warding off a threat to my friends and family. I'd rather help you, though. Doctoring seems much more productive."

"I'd much prefer you helping me as well, and...I believe we're almost done."

"Two left," said Marc.

"And five dead," Simon sadly finished.

"Not from your intervention," reminded Marc.

"I know. But this horror didn't have to be."

"Rhys realizes that and I sensed his guilt."

Maura crawled near, rested her arm round Marc's shoulders, and encouraged with a kiss. "You need sleep. I'll help Simon."

Marc didn't like her paleness; he figured its cause was the dull light. He accepted her offer and asked, "Where's Gael?"

"In the far corner with Gruffydd."

Marc received an emphatic, "I'm obliged to you, Marc!" from Simon, as he headed for the corner. Maura reached to squeeze Simon's outstretched hand; he kissed her fingers, and admonished, "You haven't eaten, have you?"

"No..."

"And not last evening either?"

"There wasn't time."

"Well there is now," he said firmly. "Go fetch yourself some gruel. All that's needed here is wrapping his brace, which I believe I can handle adequately on my own."

They kissed and she left him, amazed that he still had some humor left after his onerous night. And as she munched on her tasteless fare, she swept her hooded gaze over the floor. Dozens of wounded crowded every bit of its space, and most had been cared for by Simon. Her immense pride in his skill and accomplishment swelled her heart with love, and her eyes with heavy tears. They dribbled down her cheeks, blending with her gruel. Maura forced herself to swallow three spoonfuls, then her nausea returned with force. She abandoned her meal to return to Simon, and sat beside and not opposite him, so they could touch as they worked. His first question was not surprising, "So, what did he have to say?"

She barely smiled. "Quite a lot, actually. Listening to him, I felt he regrets what he did to you and longs for your forgiveness."

"Was your interpretation only a feeling, or did he say as much?"

"He said as much, Simon."

Simon stopped his work to stare away a moment, then wondered more. "Has he a fever?"

"No, and I don't believe he'll get one. I see him up and about in a few days' time."

"Unfortunately," grumbled Simon, "so do I."

"Perhaps you should try to talk with him."

"Do I *have* to?" he griped.

"No...But if you do, you may discover a great deal about him, and I dare say much about yourself as well."

"I may...if I ever have a free moment."

Maura promised, "I'll arrange for you to have several."

"I thought you might." They rubbed cheeks and worked on, Maura relating most of Owain's other astounding revelations. Once Simon's last patient had been doctored, Maura took over administering to the recuperating, and waved Simon in Owain's direction. He obeyed, carrying bandages as an excuse and feeling ridiculously tongue-tied and exasperated. Finally, he knelt and off-handedly inquired, "How's your pain?" Owain only shrugged, and Simon pressed, "You must know if you hurt?"

"My pain is tolerable," muttered Owain.

"Fine. I will check your wounds."

"You needn't."

"No I needn't," Simon snidely agreed, "yet they may become infected."

"Which would make you quite pleased," parried Owain.

Simon's jaw fell slack, and he scorned, "What *is* your problem, Sir? You've more than proven your hatred, your strength, and your stubborn meanness, and now what I believe I'm hearing is you'd rather die than have me treat you. Well I'm rapidly approaching the point where I will happily honor your stupidity."

Simon whirled to leave; Owain caught his arm and hoarsely despaired, "Don't let me die!"

Simon puffed up to hurl more scourge, yet instead exhaled, "I...I won't let you die." Owain held still while Simon assessed his wounds, bandaged them again, and diagnosed, "You have very thick muscles, Sir, and, luckily for you, each arrow penetrated only the sinew and ventured no further. I see little inflammation, and I don't expect any more, if you cooperate and give your body the rest and time it needs to heal." Owain grunted in response, and Simon slyly asked, "Maura says you don't care to move to the infirmary."

"Did she say why?" Owain cautiously asked.

224

"Yes..."

Owain blurted, "I've lost my pipe. I had it with me on the race, but now it's gone."

Confused by Owain's rapid broach of topics, Simon closed his eyes a moment, then recalled the stick he had retrieved from the ground. "Are you speaking of this?" he wondered brightly, rummaging through his belt pouch, and producing the flute.

Simon had never seen Owain smile, let alone beam, but he beamed now, and was about to grab the pipe from Simon's clutch when he stopped his rudeness just short of Simon's hand. "May I have it back?" he meekly asked.

"If you make me one promise."

Owain turned glum again. "Promise you what?"

"That you'll play something soothing for the injured."

Ashamedly, Owain averted and softened his glare, then spread his palm in assent. Simon returned Owain's prized object, and gathered up his bandages to leave.

He paused to Owain's whispered wish, "Simon, stay a while."

"I have others waiting."

"You must tell me..."

"What?"

"Is...is it safe for me to go to the infirmary?"

Simon grinned knowingly. "I'm certain you'll be quite comfortable there, but you won't go till you've played a few healing tunes."

Owain nodded, and blew dirt from his pipe.

Simon had walked only a few steps before Owain's next peculiar comment stopped him. "You need to toss out your cousin and his pack of scoundrels...very soon."

"He's feverish and can't travel," Simon argued and defended, "And I don't believe that he had any foreknowledge of this catastrophe or that he encouraged Bernard—"

"You aren't listening," chided Owain. "I said—toss him and his men out—soon."

Simon winced with puzzlement and irritation, and he was about to protest more, when Owain pressed his pipe to his lips, and began blowing a tenderly haunting melody.

*****

Gruffydd crawled upon Marc's lap, and promptly fell back to sleep, causing Marc to rearrange himself and whisper, "Simon's seen to everyone."

"And what's his diagnosis?" Gael whispered back.

"That all now alive will stay alive."

With a relieved sigh, she took Marc's hand and spoke with a quiet passion, "The village owes you dearly, Sir. There will be no need to hold a session on whether or not to accept you for, in the weeks to come, I see you receiving their abundant gratitude and approval."

"No one need do anything special for me," excused Marc. "Besides, I feel I have lived here for ages and maybe I have—in my dreams." Marc brushed an escaped lock of pale hair from her eye. He remembered Taredd being present the night before and asked, "Where's your betrothed gone to?"

"With Rhys, I suppose. He's not said a word to me about my decision to wed him. Maybe he doesn't know."

"I think he does," said Marc.

"Why?"

"The evil way he looks at me."

She crushed his fingers between hers and flared, "He has no cause to be jealous! I'm not yet his property!"

Marc interpreted her comment as encouragement, and murmuring, "We could give him cause," leant further down to kiss, but Gael's focus was not fixed on him. She glared at Owain, peacefully playing his pipe. And he noticed something other than pure ire sparking her eyes, exactly what he couldn't determine.

*****

Days passed and gradually the injured regained their health and strength, and emptied the llys to join in rebuilding the village. Simon's doctoring at last slackened, and he divided his time between the construction, and returning both the llys and the infirmary to their normally placid states. Henry stubbornly held to his spot on the floor, and was one of the last of the wounded to vacate the llys. He had become disturbingly withdrawn, and spent the majority of his idle time lounging about, watching others work, and screeching obscenities at his men, especially John, who suffered his abuse with surprisingly calmness. Simon wasn't certain, for Henry repeatedly shunned his attempts to examine him or his wound, but he thought he still spotted a fever glazing Henry's eyes. He hoped this was the cause of his cousin's egregious behavior. It was, of course, highly possible that his moodiness was the result of some inadvertent offense committed by Simon or Maura. Simon never received an answer to his repeated shows of concern. Henry absolutely refused to speak to him, and his volatile manner was escalating.

What perturbed Maura most were Henry's unrelenting leers. She knew he was angry with her for not groveling to meet his every need, but then his wrath seemed equally directed amongst the entire commote, and no one had a notion why. In her estimation he owed the village and particularly Rhys much for saving his life. Her nausea still plagued her, making it difficult for her to eat, and thus she felt weakened and overly weary. She hadn't burdened Simon with her minor malady, for he was far too engrossed with the welfare of the village, as he should be.

Once he could stand, Owain mysteriously stole away, no one knew where. His disappearance affected Simon and Maura in a fretful way, and incensed Gael. Henry rattled and cursed incessantly about Owain stealing his horse, and swore to avenge his loss when and if Owain returned. And Simon reflected often on Owain's portent regarding Henry, and seriously began to consider taking his advice.

After burying his horse, Marc kept himself perpetually busy, relishing the opportunity to be useful, as well as his time with Gael and Gruffydd. He returned to the cottage daily to care for the beasts, and had freed the pup, who consequently reveled in making misery for the builders, and every beast grazing upon the common.

The Sabbath arrived, bright and balmy, yet Rhys had still not returned. A special mass was held in honor of the dead and everyone who had donated time and energy to remedy the disaster. After the service, Simon and Maura decided to return home, as did Gael and Gruffydd. Marc volunteered to help Olwen move into her newly raised cottage. And Henry figured the village only endured his abuse out of respect for Simon and Maura, so he thought it wise to follow them to their cottage. He strolled a few feet behind the couple, stormily watching the mutt's yipping and squirming, and Simon and Maura's unabashed and sickening displays of affection. Their arms cinched each other's waists as they ambled along; they cooed and murmured, grinned sweetly, and occasionally kissed and laughed. Their felicity repulsed him, as did the disgusting treatment they'd shown him over the past week. Well their disrespect would not last much longer, for the time loomed near for his departure. Dizziness struck him, wavering his steps, and his shoulder pain raged. He paused a moment to regain his sight and stance, then plodded on, forcing his eyes away from their cursed cuddling.

The cottage smelled musty and required straightening and airing, new rushes, and a cooking fire. Simon set about storing the foodstuffs received from Sulien, while Maura tidied up and laid a fire. John resumed his reading at the table and the guards promptly plopped themselves down in their usual spots of leisure; Geoffrey broke open the ale

226

keg and they began heartily imbibing the bitter liquor. Henry sat upon Simon's physician table, fuming at the sight of his cousins' flitting. "Don't you ever stop?!" he blared at Maura.

Maura did stop and turned a simmering glare on him, yet her answer she delivered politely, "There's a lot that needs doing, Henry." She noticed the honey pot peeking out from behind his back. "Could you please pass me the honey?" she asked. "I'm going—"

"Get it yourself, you lazy sow," he snarled.

Maura's patience died, and she couldn't stop her pent up rage from lashing out. "You stinking wretch! You get your backside off Simon's table and help us now, or you'll be spending the night in the stable with the other pigs!"

The guards rose to her tirade, and Simon flew in from the bedchamber demanding, "Henry! What did you say?!"

"I called her..." Henry's lips twisted fiercely, "...a lazy sow...and..." He heaved the honey pot at the door, shattering it into dozens of stabbing shards. "If she wants the blasted honey, she can lick it off the damn door!"

Maura stared aghast at the dripping door, then at Henry still puffed up with repulsion, and lastly at Simon whose blazing eyes spit hate. She waited tensely for the eruption that had been forever festering, yet the only racket that arose came from the pup who barked crazily, scratched, and lapped at the door.

Stunningly calm, Simon turned and wove gracefully between the sentries to the corner of the room. He bent to pluck up Henry's satchel, then as carefully retraced his steps. With an outthrust arm, he ordered Henry, "Take this and your men, and leave here...Now!"

*****

In the village, Gael tidied her hut and grew irritated with her chattering son's imminent plans, "I'm needed at Cynan's to help set up—"

"Only after you've finished your chores here," interrupted Gael.

"Chores?" whined Gruffydd.

"Yes...This past week has left me exhausted. I require your help as do your beasts. They need grooming, feeding, and exercising."

Gruffydd swept a swift and irked glare about the tiny room and loudly complained, "Ill tend to my beasts, but there's little to fix in here."

Gael stopped her work, massaged her temples, and gritted, "I won't stand an argument, Gruffydd. I need you here with me!"

Studying his mother, Gruffydd gently probed, "Mam, something's wrong. Please tell me what."

Gael seemed to shrink at his astute observation, then she partly smiled and gestured him closer. He knelt upon the pelts at her feet and beckoned her down by him with a finger. Her somber, loving gaze lingered too long and Gruffydd grew restive with worry. "Have I done something to make you angry?"

"No...no," Gael cooed, combing her fingers through his wavy locks. "It's nothing that you've done. It's about a decision that I've recently made and that you need to hear." Her tone turned listless. "Come Christmas, I'm to wed."

Gruffydd's face creased with confusion, then lit with hope as he burst, "Wed!"

Gael sadly nodded and Gruffydd's shock sweetened to elation as the face of the most favorable prospect for a stepfather came clear in his mind. "Marc!" he cried. "You're to marry Marc! Oh, Mam!" He popped up from the floor, yanked her with him, hugged her waist and spun her round and round. "I prayed this would happen," he gabbled. "I prayed so hard and when I saw you and Marc kiss like Simon and Maura do, I knew you'd tell me! But I didn't think you'd say it so soon."

"Gruffydd stop!" Her brusque command slowed their spinning and her blunt response, "I'll not marry Marc," killed his gaiety.

He paled and stuttered, "Bu...but...of course it's Marc. Who else could there be but Marc? He slept here with us, with you, so you must love him, and I—"

"Gruffydd..." She gripped his shoulders and knelt before him to say carefully, "Please understand, I don't know Marc well enough to love him. I am fond of—"

"*I* love him! It has to be Marc!"

"Marc," she impressed, "is a Norman, and as the Pennaeth's widow I would never be allowed to wed a Norman."

Gruffydd blubbered, "Marc fought the Normans to save our commote. He rescued me and Cynan, Simon and Owain!"

"I know the good he's done and if matters were different, I would consider—"

"Who...who will be my tad?" Gruffydd starkly interrupted.

"No one can take your tad's place," consoled Gael. "My new husband will serve as guardian and model for you—"

"Who will it be?"

"He's called Taredd and he is a soldier and advisor to Rhys."

"I don't know a Taredd," he said with reserve.

"I've spoken but a very few words to him myself."

"You don't know him either!" Gruffydd railed in horror.

"It's not unusual in an arranged marriage," said Gael. "I scarcely knew your tad when we were wed."

"This Taredd could be evil!" shrilled the boy. "He might hurt you or me or my beasts."

"Rhys assured me that Taredd is a fine man."

"You can't know that for certain! Please Mam, don't do this. Please tell Rhys and Taredd no! Tell them you'd rather stay a widow. I don't want a stranger living here."

"Taredd is to be the new Pennaeth and we will move back to the llys."

Gruffydd fought, "No, I won't leave here! My beasts are here, my carvings!"

"I can't tell Taredd or Rhys no! If I do I'll lose—"

Gruffydd cut short the dire truth by bolting from her hold and out the door. Gael didn't bother chasing him, for she knew he was escaping to Marc, which she was wanting to do as well. "Gruffydd come back," she rasped futilely to the swinging door. "I have to tell you why...why it seems I'm deliberately making your life so very miserable."

*****

Henry wriggled with disquiet, and sat up tall to proclaim, "I have every intention of leaving, as soon as you wish, with one...no, two stipulations."

"What...stipulations?" grumbled Simon.

"You and your sweet lady will be leaving with me."

Maura stood dumbly in the center of the room, her incredulous stare darting between Henry and Simon, Henry's guards and John. The pup barked on and Simon's temper finally blew, "If you truly believe either one of us would voluntarily accompany you anywhere—you are horribly demented!"

"I didn't mention voluntarily, did I?" Henry smugly corrected and, while he bragged further, his men rose in unison, their fingers wrapped threateningly round their sword's hilts. "And I resent the term demented. On the contrary, I am shrewdly gathering the finest minds and bodies to help guide and prepare me for my role as King."

Maura prayed Henry's threat was a bluff as she stuttered, "You...you're intending on kidnapping us?"

228

Henry winked. "Only if you resist, and you, my lusty lady, can't honestly resist me much longer, can you?"

Simon shouted, "Maura, get yourself inside the bedchamber and secure the door. Hurry!"

The urgency straining his voice and expression stifled any argument she may have considered. Yet as she moved to obey, Henry's men stepped forward ominously. She hesitated; Simon glanced anxiously at the dagger stuck in its sheath by the door and yelled, "Let her go!" He returned his narrow glare to his cousin, and fumbled frantically to conjure a peaceful solution to this insanity. Was Henry suffering from brain fever or had he, as had his brothers, at last rotted to a monster?

Henry spouted, "Yes, go to the bedchamber Maura, and while there, gather what you'll need for a rather lengthy journey." She vanished so swiftly that Henry missed the opportunity to fondle her and ruffle Simon further. For what mode of retaliation could the traitor chance when seven burly bulls stood handily by, ready to hack off whatever body part Simon used to stop him.

Henry nonetheless was enjoying himself thoroughly; the power he had achieved was dizzying and he was about to embark on a description of Simon's responsibilities as chief advisor when his cousin's unwavering growl intruded, "Send your guards outside, Henry. Our dispute concerns only you and me and we will settle it with no help from others."

"No..." Henry refused in a pout. "I want them to stay."

"Why?" Simon taunted, "What frightens you?"

"Not you," snorted Henry.

"Maura?" said Simon.

"Never..."

"Then order them outside...John as well."

Henry's face twitched with dread as he hopped from his perch, waved limply in the air, and ordered, "Wait for me outside...and prepare the steeds to depart." Curiously, he then turned his back on Simon and seemed to be intently scrutinizing his medical supplies. When the last sentry had exited, Henry grabbed up a weighty jar of ointment, whipped round and hurled the crockery at Simon. Simon ducked; the missile missed his skull by a hair and, before he could fully recover his balance, Henry launched another jar and another and another, reveling in the sounds and sights of destruction. Simon dodged his way closer and, when near enough, lunged to stop Henry. But Henry's pitching arm flailed wildly and walloped Simon with a force that reeled him backwards and laid him flat across the larger trestle table.

Maura beat at the door, wailing for Simon. He rolled off the table, dropped soundly on his feet and roared back, "Stay where you are, Maura! I'm fine and Henry will very soon be gone!"

The ferocity of Simon's assurance rocked Henry's guile. In their entire history as friends and cousins, Henry had never struck Simon. And there was a brilliant reason why he had not attempted such a blunder—Simon could easily murder him, bare handed. There were no more jars to hurl, no guards to protect him, and Henry suddenly felt so tired; too tired to scream for mercy or move away from Simon's fist. He heard a sickening crack and screamed from the blood gushing from his nostrils and mouth. He choked and spat, as his blurring sight noted the blow had catapulted him the entire length of the room. He lay sprawled up against the door in a puddle of honey. Simon loomed above, brandishing a dagger and a savage look. He reached over Henry's head and unlatched the door, tumbling Henry backwards down the few steps to the ground. Henry had never known such humiliation—his men sniggered at his bloody defeat; even John grinned! He flipped to his belly, struggled and snarled his way back inside.

Wielding a fist, he gurgled, "Don't...don't believe you've beaten me, you pumped up, gutless, milk-sop! You've only knocked me down and I'll rise again and when I do, I'll crush everything you own and love, and leave you with nothing. For that's what you are and always will be—nothing!" He managed to climb to his knees, flailed, and shrilled, "Never let down your guard, never feel safe! Heed what I say—"

Simon was sick of suffering Henry's banality and promptly kicked his cousin outside. He slammed and latched the door, and hastened to free Maura. "Henry's gone, Maura," he soothed. "Move the—" Just then a new and paralyzing fear shook Simon—smoke clogged his nostrils and clouded the air. "No, Maura!" he yelled. "Stay...keep the trunk where it is and latch the shutters. Don't leave this room till I come to get you! Don't leave!"

As Maura sniffed the smoke, panic gripped her, lurching the baby and tightening her belly, as had happened too many times since arriving home. She sank stiffly down on the bed and prayed loudly and frantically for protection.

Simon raced from the cottage to save his burning barn. The terrified beasts charged from the structure, almost trampling him in their frenzy. He snatched up a pail and tore through the wild flowers in the direction of the path, slowing as he recognized Henry's red tunic and coal black hair disappear off the plateau. Simon waited as long as he dared and, once convinced the Prince was truly gone, he ran for the trough and water.

*****

On her search for Marc and Gruffydd, Gael scuttled along the main road leading to the llys. A sideways glimpse of Hywel's ramshackle hut revealed a most peculiar sight. Owain emerged gingerly from the entrance and stopped short at her gawking. "Where have you been?" she curtly greeted.

"Here," he tersely replied and tried vainly to hide his limp as he approached his pony.

Gael continued her interrogation, "Why Hywel's?"

With obvious effort, Owain managed to lift his foot to the stirrup and grunted, "He's my uncle," as he straddled his mount.

Gael's jaw dropped open. "Truly?"

"Truly," he emphasized with irritation. "I've just seen your son in some great hurry, heading south."

Gael searched for the cathedral, gained her bearings and realized she was traveling north.

Owain guided his pony to Gael's side and added, "He looked upset."

"He is," she admitted.

"Why?"

She felt he needn't know, yet answered anyway, "I've told him about Taredd."

"Then I can understand his upset."

"You don't care for Taredd?"

"I don't think of him much, though I am quite content with your choice of a husband."

"As am I," she heartily agreed.

He simpered and spurred his pony to a walk; Gael straggled alongside, and asked, "Should you be riding?"

"I'm fully healed."

"I don't see how you could be...considering—"

He cocked his chin in wait for her finish, but she only wagged her head, and strolled on. He eased his gruffness and offered the truth, "Rhys won't likely allow me to soldier, so I'm off to the hills to heal more and rebuild a house."

"Will you be leaving permanently?" she asked with a hint of hope.

"I might be."

"Then who will I rail at?"

"Your new husband, perhaps," he returned with a smirk.

She sneered in response, then frowned as she watched him trot away.

*****

Maura heard Simon's footsteps, lurched from the bed, and wrestled the trunk slightly away from the door. Yet a weight much mightier than Simon's drove the door open and in barged a guard and Henry, his face bruised and bloodied. Maura flew for the window. The sentry barred her escape, and Henry caught and wrenched her arm to her back. "You're coming with me," he gritted.

"No!" Maura wailed and tried to thrash free but the tightening in her belly intensified. She immediately ceased resisting and battled with words, "You steal me and Simon will catch us! He'll kill you, Henry. And if he can't, Rhys and his soldiers will. You know I speak the truth!"

The slack in Henry's grip told Maura that Simon was still alive, or Henry wouldn't be rethinking his game, and Simon would soon come and stop Henry from any atrocity he might commit! He'd soon come!

Henry's treachery faltered; her warning was true. He surely would be murdered and, as violently as he craved her, the bitch wasn't worth his life. Yet then again, the fear sparking her eyes excited him, and Simon was presently occupied with saving his pets, and hadn't noticed Henry skulk back on foot to the cottage. One guard kept a hidden watch on the barn and the one accompanying Henry could help restrain Maura if necessary. He whirled her around, his hands still clamping hers at her back as he buried his face in her hair and drank in her heady scent; his lips tasted the sweetness of her neck and found her resisting lips. She moaned her misery and tripped on scattered books as he staggered her backwards. Henry easily caught her fall, dragged her up, and flung her against the wall. Her arms he clasped above her head, and his weight firmly thrust her to the wood.

Fighting was useless, his strength was too great; words were futile for she could only utter groans! Yet she refused to submit to this devil! His mouth crushed hers, the rancid taste of stale blood cramped her belly and bile crept up her throat. She jerked her mouth away to gag, and felt his hold strengthen.

His need for her swelled him so, he hurt. Henry felt safe releasing one of his hands. He was certain she wouldn't stage much of a fight, for he knew how hotly she desired him, and she'd do nothing to jeopardize her child. But he'd not be a kind lover; he'd take her viciously, rip into her till she screamed out in misery; punish her for denying him the love he deserved from her, from all women! And only after her vanquishing would he turn her pain to pleasure and she'd cry out again as she did for Simon, only this time she wouldn't be pretending.

Beneath Maura's chemise, his fingers groped, pinched, and scratched their way up and between her legs. She twisted in his hold, while his fingers fumbled further, and groaned to the feel of his naked flesh stabbing at hers. "Why?" she sobbed and struggled. "Why hurt me, Henry?"

"Because it seems you're the only one here I *can* hurt." He looked to his guard, and Maura saw a flash of silver leap the space between them. "I intend to destroy or procure all that is his," Henry gloated on, "and will start with his most prized possession."

"You swore you loved me! Loved him!"

"I lied," he hissed and his lips smothered hers again; her attempt to lurch away was promptly staunched by the sting of cold metal on her bare belly.

231

Maura swooned and sagged lower to the daunting realization—to have her, he'd gladly murder her child! The tightening struck again, more intense, more painful! She couldn't fight him; she must save her child!

Henry briefly lifted his face from hers to study and revel in her turmoil—her clenched eyes gushed tears; her lips, bitten and cracked, whimpered piteously; and her every muscle tensed in wait for his assault.

The burning in Henry's shoulder flared, and the room whirled madly round him as his whole being wilted. He fought to enter her but couldn't, and his torment rattled the walls, "Witch! What have you done to me?!" His rage frothed his lips, tripped his speech, "Wi...wi...witch and whore! I'll kill you and that putrid deformity you carry. I'll kill you all!"

Maura cringed for the beating sure to come, but Henry's hand returned to strangle her wrists, confusing and scaring her more. Then came a stabbing pain in her belly. She screamed, believing it the knife, yet it couldn't be, for both his hands held hers! It struck again harder, vanquishing any strength she had left, and stealing her sight.

He lowered his knee from her belly and let go of her hands. She slumped heavily to the rushes and he dropped from dizziness and exhaustion to her side. He groped for the abandoned dagger, but his hands shook so violently, he only pushed it further away. A glint emanating from her hand caught his fevered eye. He wrenched her finger, tugged and yanked off her ring. She half woke to his crime, and surged up to stop him. He won their wrestling and, with his prize locked snugly in his fist, shoved her back to the rushes. He stumbled into the main room, and was greeted with a piercing bite to his ankle. He kicked the pup loose and hissed to his man, "Silence him." The guard ran the dog through with his sword and, as if donning a medal, wiped the blood on his tunic.

Simon jumped and gasped to a nudge on his shoulder. He dropped the pail and whirled round to see the FitzRoy's guard Guy dash from the tumbling barn. Someone else sped by, squalling orders, and after him came Henry. He paused a glaring moment, his regal stature framed by the skeletal remains of the doorway, the loathing in his eyes as searing as the dripping flames. Frozen in shock, Simon wiped unbelievingly at his burning, stinging eyes, looked again and found Henry gone. Then his most heinous nightmare jolted him out of the inferno and into the hut. Simon tripped over the pup's carcass and crashed into the bedchamber door, splitting and flinging it wide. He vaulted the trunk and scrambled over the bed, crying out, "Maura...My God, Maura!" She lay unmoving beneath the window, coiled in a tight ball, her eyes staring vacantly at nothing. He fell to his knees, his hands trembling and hovering, afraid to touch, to hurt, and his voice quavered almost unintelligibly, "What...what's happened? What's he done to you?! We...we must get you off the floor. *Please* Maura, speak to me!" He gently raised her arms, but she screamed with such agony that he shrilled in panic, "Please...please help me! Tell me how he's hurt you. Talk to me, tell me!"

Simon brushed her tangled hair from her face and held his ear to her lips to hear her whimper, "I'm afraid to move...the pain."

His cheek cooled her damp brow and their tears mingled as he struggled in a murmur, "Don't move, I'll lift you."

"No...Simon! I'm afraid."

"I know, my love, as am I. Let me help you." He gathered her up and effortlessly raised her to the bed. Her tortured and constant moaning spiked his alarm, and he pleaded, "Stretch out, Maura. I'll see why you hurt so."

"No!" she cried in terror. "Please, don't look, don't touch! Stay here by my head, stay with me here."

"I won't look," he quickly acquiesced, "I'll stay...I'll stay." By barely moving, he blanketed her and, resting her head in his lap, he stroked her hair and soothed with endearments. All the while guilt battered his soul as his mind raced with the dreaded possibilities of what might have occurred, and what would surely happen if help didn't soon arrive. There was no medicine to heal, no ale to calm; Henry had made certain of that. And no one would be coming, not even Marc. He began to feel a rhythmic pressure in her clutch, and knew if nothing was done the child would be born dead, and perhaps take Maura with her. His desperate prayer begged, *My God, send someone to help and spare us from Henry's treachery! Please!* For Simon knew Henry would surely return to finish his dirty deeds and bring the other devils along to join in his game.

Owain's pony Ceffyl trudged beyond the commote's gate, her rider muttering again his speech of atonement and thanks. Owain reckoned he would get it wrong, he always did, but hopefully Maura and Simon wouldn't mind. And he supposed Simon would argue with him over his planned trip to the hills, yet whatever he said, Owain aimed to go. From nowhere, a rush of horses thundered by, spooking both Owain and his pony. He fought and wrestled the reins to stop his mare's circling, and squinted through the dust the rude ones had rousted. It was, not surprisingly, the FitzRoy's troop. "Pigs," he grunted, then, guiding his mount up the path to the doctor's cottage, he quickly spied the smoke; his heart leapt to his throat as he spurred his mount to a full gallop. Nearing the fiery shell of a building, Ceffyl balked. Owain jumped from the saddle and sprinted the rest of the way to the cottage. Stealthily, he crept inside and first beheld the dead dog. A glut of emotions seized and staggered him outside as the horror of his family's demise ravaged his mind—his father and brothers castrated, their limbs cleaved and strewn; his mother, sisters, and betrothed raped and brutalized; their home ablaze, beasts slaughtered and scattered! He couldn't go inside, couldn't see it all again! He stayed stuck to the hut's wall, furiously wrestling doubts and fears, and then the unlikely notion that Simon and Maura might still be alive struck and drove him back inside. At Owain's abrupt arrival, Simon bolted up from the bed, flourishing his dagger. Owain shielded his head and screamed, "Stop! It's Owain, not Henry! It's Owain!"

Simon almost dropped in relief. Owain caught his slump, glimpsed Maura lying too still on the bed, and sputtered with dread, "Wha...what's happened?"

"I don't really know. We need your help."

"Anything," answered Owain.

Simon struggled to speak calmly, "Please Owain, hurry to the cathedral and have Sulien fetch his most potent wine. Bring him here...and Gael and Marc, if you can find them. Hurry!"

"But Maura...what—"

"There's little time...*Please*, Owain, go!"

Owain asked nothing more and whisked himself away to the church.

At the entrance to the llys, Gael was conversing with Sulien and Rhys, who'd just returned to the commote, when she heard racing hoof beats. All three jerked to the commotion, Rhys fretting, "Please Lord, not another attack."

"It's Owain," tensely returned Gael, "and something's not right."

They hastened past the fence, and met his stop. "Sulien," he breathlessly shouted, "fetch your strongest wine—two, three flagons." He spotted Rhys' pony. "Rhys, ride him to the doctor's...and be quick. I fear something terrible has happened. Gael, come with me."

Her blood drained to her feet at his harrowed expression. She felt she would faint and swiped out for Owain's hand, which he provided and swung her up and behind him in his saddle. They bounded away, their winged speed forcing her to hug his waist and bury her face in the folds of his tunic. And thus secured, she prayed.

Simon knelt by the bed and tenuously promised, "Owain will bring wine, Maura. Wine will stop your pains. Gael is coming and Sulien."

Maura struggled, "Hen...Henry? Where is Henry?"

"He's gone and will die if he dares return."

She nodded and tried valiantly to caress his face, but her hand fell limply to the bed. Simon ardently caught it up, pressed her palm to his lips, and choked on his tears.

All at once there were loud flurried voices and heavy footsteps. Owain and Gael appeared, moving and speaking too rapidly. Simon strove to understand them, but both spoke at the same time. Sulien and Rhys soon followed, crowding the bedchamber, adding to the chaos. Then Sulien passed Simon the wine, and the fog of confusion cloaking his mind lifted. He clambered onto the bed, and carefully raised Maura's head to drink. Simon felt her faint resistance, and fleetingly recalled another terrible time she'd been forced to drink. He paused and comforted, "It's Simon, Maura. Open your eyes and see me. I will stop your pain, not cause you more. Believe it's me and drink the wine."

Gael and Owain stood by, their shocked expressions turning hopeful as Maura eagerly drank the wine. After half a flagon disappeared, Maura fell into a welcome stupor, and Gael stepped cautiously forward to suggest, "Simon...Owain will take you in the other room for only a short while. I'll see to Maura."

"No!" Simon stiffened and railed, "I won't go!"

Owain watched in wonder as Gael came close, wrapped her fingers round Simon's arms and murmured, "If you see something you're not wanting to see, I fear your reaction might stress her further. Please Simon, only for a short while. Owain..."

Owain cupped Simon's elbow and urged him out to the main chamber. They were quickly joined by Rhys and Sulien, who carried the pup outside. Simon glared vigilantly out the window toward the path as if expecting to see Henry charging back to torture them further. He mumbled to himself and Owain moved close enough to hear his madness, "He'll return with Odo, Rufus, Will. I'll fail her again and they'll steal her from me. I always fail her..." Owain waited for more, but Simon only hung his head and was starkly silent.

Rhys beckoned Owain to his side and whispered, "What's he said?"

"Very little," offered Owain. "He thinks the Norman Prince will return and steal away Maura. Henry couldn't have run far. I could chase him, and fetch him back."

"No," Rhys soundly protested. "I won't have the wrath of the entire Norman Dynasty upon my head."

"But Rhys," Owain fiercely argued, "he's wounded the lady and must be punished!"

"My concern is strictly political. I trust the lady will heal, she seems quite resilient. And I will grant Maura and Simon and their child protection."

Owain glowered at his Prince's coldness, then snapped his head to the sound of the bedchamber door opening.

Simon pushed past them and drew Gael inside to speak privately. She clasped both his hands and encouraged, "There is some blood, but no dampness. I believe her pains have started from a wicked bruise on her belly. With more wine, forcing her still, and the grace of God, we'll keep that child inside her till Christmas." He fell into her hug and, with a grateful kiss, slipped back to Maura.

Maura's eyes fluttered open to his ruffling her pillow, and she strained, "I love you, Simon...You mustn't blame yourself. You didn't know he'd come back."

He could only concede a quavered, "And I *love* you," as he eased her head back upon his lap, and offered more wine.

Gael sank down upon the trunk, fitful that her optimistic diagnosis was a mistake, but then something Maura had said not long past returned to still her upset, 'Someone has to be optimistic...'

Owain hovered above her, wanting an assessment she supposed, yet uncannily he asked instead, "What didn't you tell him?"

Again she questioned confessing to him, but her doubt didn't stop her broken whisper, "I...I believe she's been raped." She grew frightened at Owain's heaving chest, the intense flaring of his eyes, the scarlet flush of his skin.

Yet as quickly as Owain's ire swelled, it sputtered away to Sulien's solemn request, "Simon, we'll kneel and pray for the lives of your wife and child."

Simon rested the empty flagon upon the table, shifted Maura's head back to the pillow, and joined the others on the rushes.

As Owain crossed himself and watched Simon stroke Maura's hair and recite Sulien's prayers, he heard deep inside his mind his own prayer drown out the Bishop's—*Lord, don't punish this sweet Lady! For she's done only good, caring for us, loving her family. If you need punish someone let it be me, for I've done these gentle people great harm. And if you spare her and her child, I swear to change my ways and protect them—and Simon as well—from any tragedy. Please Lord...heed my prayer.* He glanced back to the bed and witnessed Simon place a kiss with excruciating tenderness upon Maura's cheek. Emotions again threatened to drown Owain, and he wanted to run away and hide, for he dare not let anyone, especially Gael, catch him weeping! As if he'd heard his concern, Simon turned toward Owain, the devastation in his eyes offering him thanks and begging him to stay. Owain humbly obeyed.

*****

235

CHAPTER FOURTEEN - AND THEN THERE WAS WILL

Urgent knocking disrupted Will's glorious dream of slavish women and untold riches. William, called Will for clarity and legitimate son of Robert, Count of Mortain and Earl of Cornwall, struggled out from under silk bedsheets and, with a grunted effort, sat up in his massive, ornately carved bed. The muted brightness of midday made him squint, and he winced to the continued hammering. "Blast your pounding, Ralf!" he roared. "Get yourself inside, but only if it's important, and if it's not I'll—" A quick glance upward stopped his threat; his pale blue eyes bulged to the sight of not his squire, but an unfamiliar, tallish woman, standing at the foot of his bed, arms clasped firmly at her breast, and her stern, though not unattractive face twisted in a ferocious scowl. He raised his sheet modestly to his naked chest, patted his coal-black, closely-cropped curls, and uttered, "Madam...Is there something I can assist you with?"

"There is indeed," she spat, her black eyes afire. "I've word from my brother."

"And your brother is?"

"Hugh of Ryedale...The name should be familiar to you."

"It is...very much so. And what was his word?"

"He wants his wife."

"Yes...I expect he does. Has he arrived home?"

"Not as yet...But he's due to arrive shortly."

Will needed time to invent an excuse and, with this harridan hovering so close, he couldn't think clearly, so with effusive politeness and a forced smile, he suggested, "My dear Lady, would you be so kind as to leave me to wash and dress. My squire..." He shouted at the door, "Ralf!" then quickly softened his tone, "will escort you to the great hall where a lavish meal will be set out for you, and I will strive to join you there— swiftly."

She failed to move, and a tapping of her foot had joined her fierce posturing. Will took on his most cloying look, and gradually the woman disengaged her arms, relaxed her scowl, and conceded, "As you wish, my Lord. But I will not leave this manor—my *brother's manor*—till you turn over his wife or I have a written pledge from you that Hugh's betrothal contract will be honored. If not, my Lord, you will be seeking other lodgings." She spun on her heels and flounced away, her graceful chin cocked and up-turned nose tilted slightly to the ceiling.

Will waited till the door slammed shut, kicked away his bedsheets, and grumbled himself up and to the window. There, he flung wide the shutters and snarled at the incessant veil of rain that greeted him. He'd been considering leaving Helmsley Manor for the whole month of October in Yorkshire had proven horribly oppressive. No matter how luxuriantly he furnished his new acquisition a perpetual gloom still lurked. And now this trouble. He'd hoped Hugh would have dutifully perished in the wars, but it seemed Will's luck had failed him again, and the dolt of a soldier would presently be a returning hero, and expecting his prize of a wife. Will rubbed sorely at his shoulder, cringed at the ache that answered, and snorted at the word—prize. A more accurate label would be punishment. And where was Hugh's wife? Will loathed the notion of trudging the entire island of Britain searching for the bitch. Perhaps there was some member of his ill-bred tribe who could relate her whereabouts and, of course, the bastard's as well. For this cursed disarray was all Simon's doing. If only he'd stayed away, like all bastards should. Lately he'd heard Almodis had delivered a healthy boy, and returned to his father, and his father was once again sweet on Simon, the results of which could be catastrophic. From inside his mind, the Norman hierarchical custom mocked him—first sons receive their father's Normandy holdings, subsequent sons receive English holdings. But not dead subsequent sons, he answered, and that's what Simon and his new brother would be—very soon. And then he'd eliminate his father's wife to ensure no other leeches were begotten, and perhaps others would need to be vanquished as well, for he'd have no contenders to his inheritance—he'd have Normandy; he'd have England; he'd have it all!

Maura's attack to his body had depleted his strength and his youth, and he abhorred her. Once he'd made her a widow and she was back within his grip, he'd torment her perpetually, make her suffer for the months he'd been forced to remain bedridden, barely clinging to life. *Yes*, Will determined, reaching out to disrupt the torrent of rain, *Somehow, I'll garner the guile and the resources to begin implementing my plot.* He'd thought hard and long on his ingenious ploy guaranteed to prove his superiority to all the feckless fools that made up his family, and especially designed to rid him forever of the fair-haired feculent pustule that was his brother—Simon.

Joanna sat at the dais, impatiently drumming her spoon on the table top while awaiting her host. She huffed discontent and, balancing her chin in her palm, snidely surveyed the opulence surrounding her. A hearth contained in a side wall caught her gawk. She'd never beheld such splendor; a cloth of crisp, ivory linen draped the raised table; silver utensils flanked her trencher; her goblet, silver as well, shone back her reflection, prompting her to tuck escaped tendrils of peppered black hair back beneath her veil. There were no coarse rushes blanketing the planked floor. Rather, thin reed-woven mats, some dyed the most fetching colors, served as carpets, and tapestries, huge and thick, dangled from buttressed stone walls, their exquisite artwork calming. Lord William had indeed worked miracles on this rubble, for that's what Helmsley Manor had decayed to before the blending of their families. But something seemed tainted about the arrangement; particularly the bride's absence from the nuptials, and when Hugh had visited home a few months past, Lord William had been too ill for an audience. And then Hugh was called back to Normandy and Joanna's promised freedom had been postponed once again. But no more, she concluded, stabbing at her slab of beef. Either Lord William produced this elusive sister-in-law, or Joanna would insist that *she* remain here and he move into their dreary, drafty manor house and wait endlessly upon her infirmed father and pesty niece. Yes...she decided with a satisfied grin, she could become most comfortable...here.

She snapped to alertness at Lord William's regal presence paused in the doorway. He whispered something to his squire, who appeared an exact miniature of his Liege, and glided majestically the distance to the dais. His squire arrived an instant before, yanked out the bulky center chair, waited for Will to sit, then draped a silk serviette over his liege's lap, filled his wine goblet, and stepped back a foot, standing tense and ready to serve more. Will held his goblet in a saluting gesture, and addressed Joanna, "My Lady, I apologize for the delay. I pray my servants have adequately seen to your comfort."

Joanna raised her cup in the same manner. "Quite adequately, my Lord." For a lengthy and intense moment, each scrutinized the other, appraising and assessing. As if some silent compromise had been met, they set their cups in unison upon the table, and relaxed into their chairs.

"You needn't bother with 'my Lord'," noted Will, "...Will should do nicely, after all we're practically related."

"Agreed...Will. I am Joanna."

"A lovely name for a lovely woman."

"I don't believe or need your compliments, Will."

An excellent judge of character, Will sensed this woman's nature to be as acerbically blunt as his, and he relented, "No...I don't suppose you do, though I speak the truth. You want your sister-in-law."

"That's why I've come."

"Is it truly?" Will replied with a suspect grin.

"And what are you implying?"

"I'm implying that you were itching to inspect my abode and, if you found it to your liking, you'd accuse me of reneging on my pledge to your brother, and attempt to snatch it back for yourself."

Joanna swelled up to rally her defense, but instead her anger drained away as she said, "You read me well, Will."

He broke a smug smirk. "As I'm certain you do me."

"Where is my sister-in-law?"

There was no reason to lie, and Will confessed, "I don't really know and, up till your unheralded arrival, I hadn't cared. But I did promise to produce her and I will..." He paused to calculate, then blurted, "Within the twelve days of Christmas."

"My brother doesn't care for waiting, and he's met his wife so you won't fool anyone with an impostor."

"Be assured, my Lady Joanna, I crave Maura's return as eagerly as does Hugh. There will be no impostor. Hugh has waited this long, he will wait longer."

"He may, but I won't."

Will turned a leery ice blue eye on Joanna. "Why your hurry?"

"I want my freedom."

"Freedom from what or whom?"

"I've been forced to care for my infirm father my entire life, Sir, and for the past six years for my niece as well. I am tired of duty."

"And in years your entire life has been?"

"Forty."

Will shook with disbelief. "Surely, you've entertained some distraction—"

"I'm the youngest daughter, Sir, which is equivalent to slave. My other three sisters have been meted out as teacher, wet-nurse, and nun but, alas, I lost my chance to escape."

"And escape you'd like to do."

"Precisely."

"Your freedom depends on Maura's return?"

"Promptly upon her arrival, I will relinquish all my chores to the Lady."

"And then your intentions?"

Joanna's intense gaze left Helmsley and journeyed to her dreams. "Travel perhaps, or build myself a modest home on my family's new hide in Cornwall, and spend my remaining days doing nothing but what I like."

Will enjoyed the Lady's candor and found himself prompting for more, "What do you like to do?"

"I like meeting and talking to people, exciting people, people who've lived adventurous lives. I enjoy reading."

"You read?"

"Yes...Latin, French, Greek, English."

"And write?"

"I've been complimented on my script."

"Don't you desire marriage, children?"

"Not in the least. Besides I'm well past my prime."

"I beg to differ, Joanna. Your prime may be just beginning."

238

"Explain, Sir," she asked with suspicious tone and eye.

"If I honor my pledge and deliver Maura to your brother by the date promised, would you consider becoming a member of my household?"

"I won't become your slave," she stated adamantly.

"That wasn't my proposal, Joanna. You presumably are expert at running a household—"

"I won't be chambermaid."

"God's breath, woman, let me speak," he ruffled. "I don't want a chambermaid, I want a steward."

"Women aren't stewards, Sir."

"And why not? I've never seen that commandment carved in stone. I've gone through four since I moved here six month's past. A batch of simpletons they were. I'm not well, and being forced to make trivial decisions and scream at servants has injured my health further."

"I'd like to retire to leisure."

"No, you don't," he scoffed. "In a week's time, you'd find yourself bored and fidgeting for something to do. I'll give you something to do, and it won't be toil, it will be enjoyable. I feel a strong connection between us—"

"I won't be your whore."

He couldn't help a guffaw. "That, Joanna, was definitely not my thought. I've fairly renounced women. All the ones I've wasted the better part of my life on have caused me nothing but adversity and torment. At present, I sleep chaste and alone."

His solemn look and astounding revelation piqued Joanna. She took a sip of wine and a lengthy moment to scrutinize again her odd host. Despite his attempts to brighten his appearance—his long and crimson tunic, his silk shirt with embroidered collar and cuffs—his skin still owned a gray pallor, his cheeks were hollowed, and his light eyes shone dull. He didn't seem to have the vigor to lie. What he proposed was compelling and tempting—to direct the household of a vassal to the King, a close relative to the same; never to be hungry, dirty, tired, or discouraged again; to order and not be ordered. But none of this would come to fruition if Will failed to find Hugh's wife, and she hotly reassessed, "Are you certain you will find her?"

"Her meaning Maura?"

"I didn't know her name."

"I *will* find her...and tell me this. Are you fond of your brother?"

"Not overly."

"Excellent!" Will exclaimed. "For the wife we've chosen for him is a shrew, a witch, a harpy..."

"You needn't keep on," wickedly laughed Joanna. "He will be harried?"

"I pray so."

"Then so do I."

"We have much in common."

"That we do."

Will smugly resolved, "Then we'll join our strengths and our minds, and achieve greatness and wealth."

"And revenge," added Joanna with a triumphant snort.

"Mostly revenge," clarified Will.

Joanna swept a long, now admiring gaze over her liege and discerned, "My Lord Will, you are a marked peaked. Are you not well?"

"It's *her* doing," Will growled. "The bitch stabbed me eight months past. I've yet to recover completely."

"Then may I be free to offer you medical advice as well?"

239

"Please do...I've been bled till I'm nothing but skin and bones and—"

"Oh no, that won't do," she kindly interrupted. "You most likely need more blood, not less. In Ryedale, we are fortunate to own an admirable leech."

"I won't have a Saxon touching me."

"I know not her family. She lives alone and speaks French and English fluently. She cares for my father, who's past seventy years now. Her tonics keep me feeling quite bonny. Perhaps you could make a visit to her hut."

"Why are you trying to poison me before you've started your new position?" wrangled Will.

"Why are you naturally suspicious?" she countered.

"One must be to survive," he answered with petulance.

"Well, if you aim to survive, I suggest we go and see the leech. While we are so near my brother's manor, you can take the opportunity to meet with my father and obtain his permission for me to leave his household and join yours."

"Does this have to be so formal?" griped Will.

"To keep peace and respect between our families, indeed it does."

"He'll want payment?"

"I suspect as much."

Will struck a crooked grin and asked, "How much do you believe you're worth?"

Joanna laughed and returned, "If you promise him another hide of land in Cornwall, he'd release me in an instant."

"Not much then?"

"Not in his estimation."

"Well, if you show promise in your position as steward, and help make my holdings, slim as they be, profitable, you will be worth untold wealth to me."

"I will strive to succeed, my Lord."

"I appreciate your determination, my Lady."

They clasped hands to seal their agreement, saluted their partnership with a gulp of claret and a clicking of glasses, then indulged themselves of the succulent repast.

*****

Will ambled about the minuscule cottage perusing the many hanging clutches of herbs. He inhaled deeply. A look of ecstasy followed, and he murmured to himself, "How heavenly."

"What did you say, my Lord?" spouted Joanna, pausing in her discourse with a middle-aged, shrouded woman.

"I told you not to call me 'Lord'. And...the smell of this place brings back the most glorious memories."

"Of?" asked Joanna.

"My grandmother Mabel's solar."

"Was she a healer?"

"Hardly," laughed Will. "She dabbled in poison, quite expertly I might add."

Joanna promptly left the leech and with two wide eyes and broad steps arrived at Will's side excitedly to press, "Tell me more!"

He shrugged and shivered. "Not here...Let's get this done. I'm chilled to the bone by this blasted rain, and I want to go home."

"But we still must visit my father."

"Yes, I know, I know," he answered irritably. "I pray my purchase won't take long?"

"My father is a man of few words," assured Joanna.

"Good. Now hurry."

Joanna used the coins Will had advanced her to buy a batch of herbs and recipes, and hastened after him out the door and into the deluge. Knowing Joanna well, the villagers stopped to gawk at her foppishly clad companion. Will didn't seemed to notice, but Joanna did; she struck a haughty pose and purposely guided her mare closer to her Lord's.

As they approached the meager manor home, Will remembered with distaste his last visit here. His father, intent on ending Maura's betrothal to Hugh, came desperately seeking an impediment in order to free her for Rufus. He smiled, remembering his father's ludicrous claims: the writ hadn't been dated—it had; Robert had been plied with drink and forced to sign the writ—he hadn't; and the most ridiculous of all, Maura was not a virgin—which was true, but excepting the few hags locked away forever in a convent, there weren't many twenty-two year old virgins left. Despite Robert's attempts to end Hugh's contract, Rufus' betrothal had been the one annulled. Then Simon had somehow finagled a pact with his soul-mate the King to punish Robert for his chicanery, and King William had ended the Ryedale marriage and granted the bitch to Simon. But Will had been shrewder, duping Hugh into believing the contract was still intact and his bride-to-be had been forced to travel to her guardian's home to nurse Rose's serious fictitious illness. A servant had stood in for Maura at the altar, and the wedding had been completed as arranged. Yet the shoulder wound Maura had thrust upon Will raged full force that day, and he had collapsed and woken a week later, too near death. When he would meet her again, and the much anticipated reunion would occur mighty soon, she'd pay dearly for the torment she caused him—dearly!

"Will...Will?" called Joanna. "Are you well?"

"What?" Will shook from fantasies of revenge and, with difficulty, focused on his steward's fretful expression.

"Do you need help dismounting?"

Will glanced around and was astounded to find himself inside a deserted, shabby, and smelly stable. He hadn't recalled entering the bailey.

"Do you require help, Will?" Joanna asked concernedly.

"No...of course not," Will dully replied. Slipping wearily from his saddle, he quickly grasped and linked her arm with his. "Only please, we'll make this quick."

The damp, dark, wooden manor boasted one hall blanketed with fragrant rushes and partitioned with worn tapestries. A single trestle table sat empty before a cold hearth, puddled with rain dripping from a vent in the thatched roof.

"Father!" Joanna called out, sweeping across the rushes, past the trestle table, and leaning to search out the open postern door. "Father, I'm home!"

A feeble voice drifted from behind a tapestry, "We're here, daughter."

Will gestured his guards to wait by the door, and gingerly followed Joanna behind the thick cloth. Aubrey, Joanna's aged father, cloaked in a long tunic and a blanket to discourage the chill, sat upon a padded chair. His large vibrant brown eyes shone with a youthful intensity, and his yellow saggy skin crinkled from his smile as he beheld the obviously wealthy gentleman at Joanna's side. Perched atop his lap sat a comely girl child, aged six years. Two golden brown plaits reached to her waist; her eyes, identical to her grandfather's, grew large with wonder, and she wiggled off Aubrey's lap and sprightly asked, "Who are you?"

"Emma!" Joanna admonished, then to Will she excused, "I've never been able to teach the child manners."

"Why..." spoke up Aubrey, "I was about to ask the same—who are you? I am Aubrey of Ryedale, Joanna's father. I'd stand, Sir, but my bones pain me."

"You needn't," said Will.

241

Will's austere glance Joanna's way began her introduction, "Father and...Emma, this is Lord William FitzRobert, our Liege's son. Bow, Emma," ordered Joanna, and Emma, though she didn't truly know why she should, did so dramatically.

Aubrey held out his hand, received Will's in return, then asked, askance, "We've been wondering what had become of you."

"I've been close by, Sir. I reside at Helmsley."

"Yes...but very reclusively. My son attempted to contact you many times during his last sojourn here, and was always disappointed."

"Lord William has been ill, Father," defended Joanna.

"I'm here now, Sir," cut in Will, "and have heard from your fine daughter that Hugh is to return shortly and will be wanting his wife."

"I'm certain he will insist upon her delivery."

"And he shall not be disappointed more, for I intend to travel to her guardian's home and personally escort the Lady Maura to your home. She will arrive within the twelve days of Christmas."

"If she doesn't arrive," cautioned Aubrey, "my son and I will have to place a formal objection with the King. I believe he is your cousin?"

"He is, Sir. And your objection will state?"

"That if she is not presented, we intend to keep the entire dowry, and deprive you of your gifted land grants, and that, my Lord, includes Helmsley."

Will swallowed noisily, then assured, "She will come, Sir. Believe my pledge."

"I would love to," said Aubrey. "She was complimented highly by your brother Simon, and I long to meet the Lady as does Emma."

Will cringed a little to the mention of his sibling; in contrast, Emma brightened to the name and the memory. "Simon...Simon is your brother?"

"Yes," Will replied with disdain.

"Has he come with you, my Lord?" she asked with a happy jump. "Please say he's come!"

"Unfortunately," said Will with a sardonic grin, "he's not with me just now."

"Simon and Emma struck up quite a friendship when he visited last..." Aubrey took a moment to remember, then uttered, "I believe it was last November. He also managed some superb mediating in Pickering. If you should see Simon, would you inform him that we would very much appreciate his company here again. Wouldn't we, Emma?"

"Oh yes!" she gushed. "He was so handsome, and told me the most wonderful stories, and let me ride his horse around the bailey three times, and promised he'd come back...someday." She turned suddenly solemn. "I've been hoping it would be soon."

"And I've grown quite weary of hearing about this *Simon*," intruded Joanna. "Father, Lord William has come to you with an urgent request."

"Speak, my Lord," stated Aubrey. "What is it you wish?"

"I wish..." Will hesitated as he found his throat painfully dry again. He gulped and croaked, "...for your daughter."

"In marriage?!" asked Aubrey, shocked.

Will coughed through his entreaty, "No...I've need of a seneschal and she...she seems to possess the qualities re...required and more. I...I've had bad luck with my appointments, and mean to...to try something different."

Aubrey shifted uncomfortably to Will's trouble, and waved him toward the modest bed that sat close by. "I think you should sit, my Lord. And would you care for some wine?"

"No, Sir," Will announced with a clear voice. "I don't have the time for sitting, drinking, or chatting. I must return to Helmsley and prepare for my journey west. I am prepared to compensate you handsomely for Joanna's absence."

"The child requires a great deal of attention that I can't always provide," said Aubrey. "I don't see how I can—"

"Father," said Joanna abruptly. "You brought in that woman from the village last time I was away. She should manage just fine till Maura arrives."

Aubrey swiftly retorted, "And she is overly strict and harsh, not that you ever have a kind word for the child!"

Emma knew they were arguing over her and she hated it. But she hated the woman from the village worse than she did Joanna, and asked with a humble whine, "Joanna, please stay till my new mother comes."

"No!" Joanna railed back. "This is my opportunity to achieve greatness, and I won't let it slip away because of some simpering little snipe of a—"

"Joanna!" roared Aubrey. "Enough!" His flaring eyes dropped to his lap, his gnarled fingers massaged his brow and dragged through his wispy white locks. Finally, he lifted a defeated expression, and resolved, "Perhaps with your handsome compensation, my Lord, I will be able to hire someone more suitable to my grandchild's disposition. The child is in dire need of warmth. Hugh is due back within the week and can assist me. Go Joanna, do what you like. Perhaps being away from here will make you a nicer person."

"Does 50 marks seem a fair price, Sir?" spouted Will.

"Fair enough," agreed Aubrey.

"I don't carry that amount of money on my person. I have twenty here..." Will untied and passed his belt pouch to Aubrey. "My squire Ralf will deliver the remainder later this evening." Will struck a forced smile, and added with stiff politeness, "After I've brought you Maura and am reestablished in my home at Helmsley, you must come and visit."

With little enthusiasm, Aubrey nodded. He disliked this man as much as he had disliked his father, Lord Robert. Slimy tricksters they both were, and highly skilled at their craft. Well, he could gladly have Joanna. Aubrey was weary of her tirades and harangues, her verbal abuse and constant discontent. Maybe a liaison with this man would make her happier. He longed for Maura's arrival and clearly remembered Simon's assurance that she would make an excellent, caring mother. He wouldn't have his granddaughter's sweetness blighted by any more cold-hearted harpies! And what of this Simon? Though he'd only stayed a short while, he'd made a grand impression. It seemed astonishing the two men were related, but then Simon had mentioned he and his father didn't speak, that he'd come on the King's account and not his immediate family's. Simon had willingly destroyed his father's sneaky plans to ignore the contract with Hugh in favor of a betrothal with the King's son. And so, Aubrey rightly deduced, Will's spiteful remark, 'Unfortunately, he's not with me now,' made perfect sense. The family was at war. Aubrey struck a wry grin and taunted, "Where is your brother?"

"I don't know, Sir, nor do I care."

"And why not?"

Will replied snidely, "He is not a legitimate member of our household and doesn't deserve a thought."

"Pity, I quite liked him," smiled Aubrey. "He seemed to know the Lady Maura...well."

"They grew up together, Grandfather," Emma piped in. "He told me all about her in his stories."

Feeling extremely uncomfortable around the brat and her overly inquisitive grandfather, Will announced, "Yes, that they did. Now as I said before, I have little time for chatter." He turned to find Joanna gone. "Joanna?" he called out and darted from behind the tapestry to find her.

She appeared breathless with excitement and carrying a stuffed ragged satchel. "I needed to collect a few things, but I'm ready Will...I'm far beyond ready."

"If what you've collected matches what you're wearing now," he grimly commented, "please leave it behind. I'll ensure you're fittingly dressed to flatter my court."

Joanna glanced a frown down at her worn unbleached tunic, and gratefully tossed her bag.

Will grimaced and dipped back under the curtain to conclude, "We'll take our leave, Sir." He extended his hand and praised on, "I'm delighted you've agreed to part with your daughter. I shall personally see to her safety and comfort."

Aubrey received his clasp and squeezed harder to emphasize, "And if you don't, I'm certain she will return here to complain. If you care to remain our neighbor, my Lord, I expect to see your squire this evening, and you again during Christmastide with the Lady Maura."

"You definitely will, Sir," Will affirmed, extricating his hand and gracefully bowing.

Emma skipped at his heels as he swept his way to the main door, beseeching, "May I ride on your horse, my Lord?"

"No!" he barked and slapped away her reaching hand. He brusquely cupped Joanna's elbow and hurried out the door and away, muttering to his steward as they rode from the bailey, "I thank God each and every day that I'm still and will always remain a bachelor."

Emma stood pouting in the hall. Aubrey shuffled over, patted her shoulders, and soothed, "Don't waste your sadness on them, little one. When the Lady Maura arrives, I'm certain all will change for the better. You must believe that. Now come, we'll finish our stories." Emma's smile returned as she took Aubrey's hand and wandered with him back to their chair.

As Will rode through the heckling rain, he felt the dreaded chill spreading over his limbs, weakening his mind and his heart. It seemed any exertion caused him to become ill again and, alas, no cure could be found. "Joanna," he asked in a quaver, "do you truly believe those leaves you bought can make me well?"

"I pray so, my Lord. Will...you promised me the tale of your Grandmother."

"When I'm warmer, I'll tell you all." His eyes livened with malice as he added low and gritty, "But there is one important facet of the tale you must hear now and always remember. Mabel granted me her recipe book. I've memorized the lot of them, and you'd be amazed at the terrors they can wreak. In my household, tragedy comes to those who flirt with disloyalty—tragedy. Do I make myself clear, my Lady?"

"Blatantly," answered Joanna, her guile rivaling his.

"Good...Now that my position is known, I confess to being quite pleased to have you do my bidding...Joanna."

*****

Demons ripped and chomped at Henry's shoulder, the fires of Hell burned his gut and boiled his blood. He bolted up in bed and screamed, "My God, have mercy! My fever made me hurt her. Please, spare me your scourge...spare me!" He slumped back upon the bed, lolled and moaned more misery, then fluttered his eyelids open to a sympathetic touch and a pale, gaunt face. "John..." he rasped, seizing his butler's tunic with balled fists, and yanking him near, "save me, don't let me die! I know I should die for my sin...but I must live long enough to beg her forgiveness." Despair tripped his entreaty, "Hel...help me. *Please* help!"

"I'm helping as well as I can, my Lord," strained John. "You should have told Simon of your affliction. He would have healed you."

244

The flush of his fever drained away, leaving Henry's face ghastly white. "Simon..." He swallowed dryly and released John's tunic. "If God doesn't get me...Simon will. Is he here?!" he wailed. John's thoughtful silence made him gasp, "He is here!" and lurch his way into the corner of the canopied bed, trying vainly to burrow beneath the meager bed clothes.

"He's not here, my Lord," John appeased and wrung water from a soaked linen towel. "He'll not leave his wounded wife to find you."

John's assurance didn't diminish the terror glazing Henry's eyes, and the FitzRoy shakily ordered, "More guards...I'll have more guards posted at my door!"

"There are far too many posted already. No one can get in or out."

"Am I in prison?"

"No...You are visiting Lord Hugh's castle on the north border of Wales."

"I don't remember—"

"It took us an immensely long period of time to arrive at Lord Hugh's home. You collapsed three weeks past, and rode the remainder of your journey unconscious in a cart."

"Will I die?"

"I don't believe so, but you have suffered horrendous dreams." John arched his brow. "And they were most revealing."

Henry quickly regained his senses. He shifted closer, snatched away the cloth to mop his beaded brow, and warily blurted, "What, what did you hear?"

John didn't say; instead he scolded, "Why did you go back and hurt Maura? Why did you attack Simon? They housed you, nursed you, were kind to you—"

"Kind..." Henry scoffed.

"Yes, kind! And too indulgent."

"Mind your tongue you cretin or I'll heave you in a pile of dung—"

"Enough..." John sat up tall, shook his hair back, and staunchly announced, "You won't heave me anywhere, my Lord. I'm all you have left, for your guards hold you little loyalty. Four of them are right now considering defecting to Lord Hugh's service. It seems he feeds his sentries better, and he lives a most debauched life, and welcomes all sorts of depravities at his court."

"I'm debauched as well," limply defended Henry.

"I won't argue *that* fact, my Lord. But compared to Lord Hugh, you appear an angel. Now, if you're able, tell the truth—why did you hurt your cousins?"

Henry spit out, "They ignored me!"

"It is impossible to ignore you, my Lord."

"I hurt them because they...because she—"

John promptly provided, "Because she is not and never has been your lover and you can't stand Simon having something that you don't have. It is also incomprehensible to you that there is any woman on this earth who doesn't desire you! And I thank God you weren't able to violate her. You're guilty of jealousy...sickening jealousy. Your sin is envy..."

Henry stared aghast at John; in time, he shut his hung jaw, swabbed his brow once more, took a long swig from a wine tankard setting on a table by the bed, and sputtered, "You...you filthy, stinking, snotty nose rat. How dare you—"

"I'll remind you once again, my Lord, snotty or no, I'm all you have left. And I have learned that when you have no defense, you spew insults instead. Now I suggest you lie back down, and if I can forge my way through your contingent outside, I will bring you more broth."

Henry kept his eyes wide as he shrank down upon the bed and let John blanket him. He considered complaining about the broth, but thought better of it, and asked faintly, "Does anyone else know?"

"Know what, my Lord?"

"That I didn't succeed with my treachery against Maura?"

"The correct word is 'rape' and I don't believe so."

Henry squirmed beneath his coverlet, and carefully inquired, "You wouldn't tattle such a thing, would you?"

"I truly hadn't thought of it."

"That's wise." Henry tried but failed to sound stringent, "I don't think you have cause to be so sanctimonious. You went back to their cottage as well, and after I'd ordered you to stay away."

"I returned with Guy to warn Simon."

Henry half sat and railed, "You willfully betrayed me!"

"Yes...and I'd gladly do so again."

"If I disgust you so," returned Henry, "why do you stay with me?"

"My conscience has been deliberating that quandary for a full week, and has resolved that I have a peculiar need to serve someone such as yourself, my Lord, as you, in turn, have a dire need to be served by someone such as me. Now rest...I'll bring the broth."

Henry lay still and warily watched John stride away. The burning in his shoulder and belly raged, making him groan bitterly. He was certain he'd suffer God's wrath for eternity if he didn't soon make his confession. Perhaps Hugh would kindly lend him his priest, but as John's observation of Hugh's household had been astutely correct, Hugh most likely didn't keep a priest, or, if he did, the cleric was probably as dissolute as he. He couldn't return to Menevia and beg forgiveness; no one would or should believe him, and he'd promptly be relieved of his head or some other vital appendage. And he'd never see, talk, or joke with Simon again. Remorse smothered Henry like a ponderous black cloud, rendering him pitiful; tears gushed from his eyes as he yearned for an earlier time, a time of innocence and hope, when he'd been certain of his father's love. He longed for Rouen, and his mother's solar with the hearth cozily blazing, where he was always welcome to cry, complain, laugh...She had loved him, yet deserted him in death when he most needed her. Everyone he had loved had deserted him, everyone but...John. Yes, John would take him home, love and care for him, just as Simon had, no better—for John knew and accepted his station in life, while Simon could never reconcile himself to his baseness. And perhaps, thought Henry, sighing miserably, he could visit Cecily...for she wouldn't judge or condemn him, she'd only soothe. Yet...something horrid lingered that he couldn't quite ignore. When he was with Maura, the look on her face of total fear and helplessness—that look had somehow pleased and thrilled him. God knew this and would therefore never forgive him, but then again, did Henry really care?

John stared down into the bubbling, odiferous liquid and saw boiling there his emotions, his life, his soul. He was under strict instructions to return to Bayeux by the end of November. They'd been at Lord Hugh's far too long, and if the FitzRoy kept insisting he was dying, they would likely be late and he shuddered at the consequences of such a blunder. He ladled broth into a bowl, took up a spoon, and started to leave, but he stopped momentarily in the doorway to reflect on their final hours at Menevia. Indeed, Henry was irritating, spoiled, rude, coarse; he could conjure up reproofs indefinitely, yet at Simon's cottage, John had witnessed for the first time his Lord's true maleficence. But why was his behavior so astonishing? Wasn't he kin to the most ruthless tribe ever to conquer and inhabit Britain and the Continent? The Normans flourished their brutality with pride, and Henry had shown shame that he hadn't fully vilified his victim. His nightmares, though, had been full of effusive pleas for forgiveness and regret. Was Henry's soul salvageable? In time, John supposed he'd gain the answer to that puzzle, and the countless others that plagued him. His past two months with Henry had been a maelstrom of adventures the likes of which he'd never dreamt of encountering. A small part of him craved more excitement, but a larger part craved instead the tranquility of Bayeux, his books, his fellow clerks, and his writings. All he need do to get back was to convince Henry he was fit to travel, which he was, yet it was so difficult convincing the FitzRoy of anything. A mental reminder that he must return by the close of November strengthened John's resolve, and propelled him out of the doorway and along the tunneled passageway to his Liege's chamber.

*****

"Mate!" exclaimed Almodis, clapping her hands gleefully together over the chess board.

Across from her Robert raised irritated eyes and snapped, "You cheated."

"I did not!" returned Almodis as adamantly.

"You did something with my foot awhile back. Distracted me."

"So you noticed. I was beginning to think you were totally numb." Almodis gathered her pieces and resolutely decided, "We'll play again."

"Oh no we won't. It's all too depressing."

"But you may triumph this time."

"After five losses, it seems unlikely," said Robert.

"What shall we play for this round?"

"You've won my pillow, my side of the bed, my fur cloak, my favorite goblet, and lastly my steed. What more is there, Almodis?"

"How about..." Almodis tapped her pursed lips, and enticed, "The clothes you wear presently."

"Don't be vulgar."

"I believed you were beginning to appreciate my vulgarities, Husband."

"Not here, not now."

Almodis leant over the table, caressed his chin, and lifted his weary eyes to hers. "What is it, Robert? You've been unnecessarily testy all evening."

He readily and loudly confessed, "I want to return to Mortain!"

"As do I, my Lord."

"This place stinks of Will."

"I agree."

"And..."

"Yes?" Almodis prodded.

Robert lowered his voice as in secret. "Odo unnerves me. It seemed simple enough convincing him to leave England. But he insists on making innumerable stops along the way to meet with 'old friends'. And with the countless friends he's discovered on our journey, we'll never reach the coast."

"He's not seen his 'friends' for years, my Lord," said Almodis. "It's understandable that he wishes to renew his acquaintances."

Robert turned a dubious eye on his comely wife. "That's the first congenial statement I've heard you speak of my brother."

"The only purpose of my congeniality is to quell your uneasiness, Robert."

"I don't think he's renewing friendships. I believe he's collecting allies."

Piqued, Almodis sat taller and pried, "Why?"

"I don't know." Robert's fist struck the table with frustration, rocking the chess pieces as he rapidly complained, "He confides nothing, and he knows his silence infuriates me. This past week at Berkhamstead, he's done no visiting, only kept to his chamber, writing, reading, looking secretive."

"Why don't you demand we depart?" offered Almodis, cloaking his fist with her palm.

"I've raised that notion several times, and he begs to stay awhile longer, for he craves the luxury Will has provided here."

"Well I won't fault him there either," remarked Almodis. Her fingers crept up his starched linen sleeve and came to rest on the shoulder of his gray woolen tunic as she suggested, "If I weren't so wary of Will arriving, and determined to return Odo to Normandy, I'd suggest you make this location your principle residence in England."

"What's wrong with my other castles in England?" asked Robert, a touch wounded.

"They're putrid pits, Robert." To his flinch, she unconvincingly acquiesced, "Not that it especially matters...to me."

Yet Robert fired back, "And pertaining to my foul mood, you my Lady are not faultless—"

"What have I done but beaten you at chess?!" she interjected as hotly.

"You drive me mad with your squabbling."

"With you?"

"No, with Odo."

She feigned innocence, "He sparks the jousts, my Lord."

"Perhaps," he barked, "then you gladly heap on the fuel."

"Oh Robert, you exaggerate."

"Don't call me Robert!"

"I beg your pardon...*my Lord*, you greatly exaggerate."

"I don't!"

"You do!"

"My dear brother, Robert...my gracious Lady, Almodis..." The rich resonant, slightly devious voice drifted to the dais, silencing the squabble. The couple snapped their heads to see Odo, standing half in, half out of the shadowed doorway. "I pray," he continued meekly, "that I'm not interrupting some love making in process."

Robert stood, Almodis remained seated and absently fiddled with a bishop as Robert firmly answered, "No of course not." He shot Almodis a cautionary look, exhaled loudly, and offered, "Please join us, Brother.

"How considerate, Robert. The late meal was unduly heavy. I was unable to sleep, and craved your solacing company." Odo pretended infirmity as, shrouded in his sleeping robes, he shuffled to the dais. "Have you wine left?" he asked, sitting stiffly.

"Yes, there should be two or three fingerfuls left in the carafe," said Robert.

"Oh," noticed Odo, draining the claret into a nearby cup. "I see you've been gaming. How kind of you Robert to encourage your wife's training in social niceties."

"It's he who needs the training," Almodis readily sniped. "I've trounced him five matches in a row."

With a condescending look, Odo contested, "His soft heart allowed you to believe you excelled."

"I won fairly!"

"Women don't own the intelligence to win at anything...my Lady."

"Why you niggling, pumped-up viper!" she flamed, then challenged, "Care for a game? I'll have you vanquished in ten moves."

"Almodis, leave here now," insisted Robert.

"No! And you demand he apologize to me!"

"It was you who did the slandering," corrected Robert stringently. "I won't argue with you more. I want you gone...now. We'll speak of this episode later."

248

"But I—"

Robert dropped his glare to the table and Almodis promptly quit her tantrum. If she didn't, he'd fail to visit her later, and over the past two months she'd come to expect and even anticipate their nightly encounters. She stumbled through her parting speech, "I...I suppose there is something that needs doing concerning our son. And I hope, my Lord, that we will be able to discuss this episode to both our satisfaction...later. My Lords." With a pert bow, she swept not far away into Robert's bedchamber.

At the sound of the clicking door, Odo sneered, "How can you suffer that witch near?"

Robert pointed accusingly at his brother. "I warn you, Odo, don't keep on with this."

"This what?" Odo parried.

"Don't you beg innocence with me. Haranguing my wife!"

"It was quite clear," said Odo, "as you stated, who began this tiff."

Robert fumed, "I don't care who began what, I command it to cease! We'll leave on the morrow and part company at Barfleur."

"Where will you go, Brother?"

"Where I can find peace...To Mortain."

"You'll never find peace saddled with her, Robert," Odo portended. "She's as bad as they come, quite likely plotting your demise, and mine as well, rutting with your steward—"

"Enough of your lies," Robert hurled back.

"Are they lies, Robert? I didn't invent her scurrilous reputation, she accomplished that all on her own. And she owns the beauty and wiles to make you believe anything...But take my heed, there is no woman alive who can be trusted, for every one of them is the Devil's whore. And your bitch holds a most exalted position with Satan. Banish her before she sucks out your soul—"

Robert stood and opened his mouth to rage, but the door's creaking and muted voices postponed his tirade. His jaw dropped lower, shoulders tensed higher, and color rouged redder as he beheld Will.

Will sported the same gape, and sputtered, "God...God's teeth, Father! What are you doing here?! We made a pact...I'm to reside in England and you're to keep yourself on the Continent. Why—" The gentleman sitting to the side of his father faltered his gnashing, "Un...Uncle O...Odo!" Will's paleness vanished, and was replaced with a divine radiance. He thrust his arms out, and loped forward catching his uncle in an abundant hug.

Odo returned his exuberance, "Oh, how I've missed you, lad!" He stepped back and worriedly took in Will's frail countenance. "What's befallen you? You've aged decades since I was locked away."

"It's not important. What is important is that you're here, obviously well and free! My constant prayer has finally been granted. Surely you'll stay awhile."

"I would love to...but, alas, your father is playing my jailer and insists upon my return to Normandy. He just issued his decree that we leave on the morrow." He faked a hug to disclose, "He's afraid I'll find and remove his bastard."

"How curious," whispered Will, "that's exactly what I'm wanting to do."

"I've always suspected our minds were brilliantly attuned," said Odo. "Let's leave this crusty old fart and discuss the matter of Robert's mistake at length in my chamber at the far end of the hall."

"Granted, but let me pacify him first."

Odo glanced beyond Will's shoulder and was astonished to see Joanna, standing starkly in the center of the hall. "Who's that?" he asked in a perturbed voice. "You haven't gone and sullied yourself with marriage, have you?"

"No...nothing so horrifying as that. That, Uncle, is Joanna. She is my steward, and has more than proven her worth these past two months."

Odo, a lewd twinkle in his eye, asked, "Proved it how?"

"Not intimately, politically. She runs my household with fierce perfection, and sees over my health, which has improved greatly since I found her. I'm certain our present mission will intrigue you."

Odo's gleaming eyes admitted his delight, and he jerked toward Robert and announced, "I thank you Brother, for the wine and lulling discourse. I do believe I can now sleep without further bother and will take my leave."

"Remember Odo," glared Robert, "we leave tomorrow."

"How can I forget?"

With Odo gone, Will grew snide and suspicious. "Are you here alone, Father?" Robert didn't grace Will a reply; instead he started to sit but hesitated to Will's caution, "For your family's safety, I think it wise you *do* leave tomorrow, for you are fairly outranked here, in intelligence, and definitely ruthlessness."

"But not in manpower," Robert stoically parried.

"N...no..." Will conceded with a struggle, "not in manpower."

*****

Will almost skipped to Odo's chamber. Miraculously his luck had returned in the form of the black-hearted Bishop of Bayeux. There was no horror Odo wouldn't perform...for a price, or in this case—when their ambitions were so closely matched—for nothing more than the exaltation of ridding the world of a wretchedly virtuous bastard. He tapped excitedly on the door and it swung open exposing a lavish bedchamber, boasting tapestries, gold candlesticks, a walled hearth, wooden tub, and a most sumptuous quilted feather bed. He paused, touched a spot on his head and squeamishly remembered this chamber was the one Maura had inhabited on her last and only sojourn here. "Odo!" he called out, swaggering inside. He stopped at the peculiar sight of his uncle, stretched out long on the bed, hands clasped at his chest, and eyes fixed on the canopy. He appeared laid out for burial. "Odo!" he exclaimed, striding forward. "Are you ill?"

Odo's body stayed still, while he turned only his stare, and uttered with a wicked grin, "Heavens no. I was only anticipating..."

Will's zeal burst forth, "What?! Tell me what!" as he grabbed up a padded chair and set it swiftly by the bed and himself in its seat.

"The wonders we can work...together. I've purposely kept Robert here seven laborious days, praying you'd appear. And I should receive a sainthood for my patience, for your father has become exceedingly dull." He sat to his concern, "What's happened to him, Will? He was once so vibrant, so malleable. Now we seem to have nothing in common, and he's taken to retorts."

"His woman has ruined him," said Will, "as did the first, and second."

"I agree, and this one is the worst. The others knew their place and kept away, but the Lady Almodis revels in rudeness. She's always there at his side, sporting a waggish smirk, stinking like a brothel. Her every move is polished, seductive, and indignant. I loathe her."

"As do I, my Grace...and her brat."

"The grub is not Robert's," said Odo, clasping his hands together and squeezing them between his knees. "It couldn't be at his advanced age. And she's romped with so

250

many. Who knows whose mongrel will inherit this fine abode, and all the others in England?"

Will hiked the suspense. "I have a theory concerning the child's paternity that reeks of incest, Uncle...I'm certain you'll love to hear it."

"Have you now...?"

"It's Simon's bastard, conceived last year on a journey from here to Gloucester for Christmas Court. He'd played the hero, rescued her from some rabid dogs or cats, I can't remember. We sojourned the night in an abbey. He invited her to his chamber to tend her wounds, and once there, he proceeded with his doctoring, and much more."

Odo performed some quick calculating and surmised with a frown, "Will...the child was born in May...which means he was conceived in September, not December. A promising case for condemnation, but your father has sired six children and, despite his dullness, he does know the length of a pregnancy. Did they truly copulate...Simon and Almodis?"

Will picked at lint on his tunic, and wriggled uneasily to his lie, "I didn't actually see the momentous event, yet after that night, she became besotted, to say the least, always rallying to his defense, shamelessly flirting."

"Fascinating...So we have treason." Odo twiddled his thumbs and hoped, "What else can we concoct against her?"

Will scooted to the fore of his chair and rapidly provided, "Plotting my demise, and father's and perhaps yours as well with the Saxon harlot Edith. My spies finally caught up with Almodis shortly before she returned to Father. And they discovered her hiding out in Edith's cottage, accompanied by her most recent lover."

"That must have been immediately after I detained Edith."

"Detained?" puzzled Will.

"I needed information only she could provide."

"Simon's whereabouts?"

"Precisely."

"Did she say?"

"No..." Odo sadly admitted. "I had to resort to burning away the soles of her feet, yet she betrayed nothing."

"How grisly, Uncle."

"Martyrs relish torture, and Edith has always aspired to martyrdom. She no doubt enjoyed it.

Disappointed, Will huffed, "So you don't know where he is either?"

"Not as yet, but I will, perhaps as soon as the close of this month."

"How?"

"A spy..." Odo's effusive evil thrust him to his feet and he paced almost a dance round Will's chair. "I've ingeniously placed him in the service of Henry FitzRoy. Surely you know how tight Henry and Simon are, I always suspected buggery. Henry was at Rouen when I was released, and left almost immediately, his destination secret to most, but not me. He was off to warn his lover of my freedom and intentions. My man is due back in Bayeux by the thirtieth of November. I will swiftly locate Robert's runt, charge and try him, then dispense his punishment. Would you consider aiding my crusade?"

"Oh, my dearest Uncle!" Will extolled, and knelt on his chair, facing Odo. "I've wished for nothing but his prosecution for the past twenty-five years. But what of Henry, won't his loyalty to Simon prove troublesome?"

"Henry's easily squashed."

"Marvelous," laughed Will. "...And I have another vital mission that requires locating Simon."

"And what's that?"

"I want his wife."

"His wife?! Who in God's domain would consent to marrying *him*?"

"Maura..." hissed Will.

The name rocked Odo's mastery, he shuddered once, and sputtered aghast, "Ma...Maura? Robert's ward?"

"Yes...Simon and she were fornicating after you were confined."

"But she was slated to marry a Montgomery."

Will slumped back into his chair, and imparted with glee, "Simon had impregnated her! I tattled to Grandfather Roger, and despite my success in aborting the monster, Roger nonetheless annulled the union. She's been betrothed a number of times since, once to Rufus. Presently she's wed to Simon and also to a poor sod of a soldier from Ryedale—though she doesn't know of her second husband yet. I must present her to him during the twelve days of Christmas or he'll steal back my new home, Helmsley Manor..."

Odo's mind spun with Will's yammering and he implored, "Will, please take heed of my age. What in Heaven's name are you talking about?"

Will almost spit, "Forget the details, Uncle, just know I need her—alive and him—dead."

"If you help me achieve your second goal, I vow to assist you with your first."

"Bless you Uncle, but I'm concerned with the time. Are you certain your spy will meet you when you arrive in Bayeux?"

"If he's smart he will, and he's capable of being very smart," confirmed Odo. "There should be no problem."

"Then I shall wait for you here. And if you don't arrive by the second week of December, I shall have to take matters into my own hands."

A look of disdain followed Will's distrust, and Odo sneered, "And fail as usual."

"Not this time, Uncle!" rallied Will. "Simon will be vanquished, Maura captured, the Lady Almodis banished, and the child disinherited, all by the end of January."

"Grand plans, Will."

"Nothing too grand for me."

"I will return by the second week of December," pledged Odo, "maybe sooner. If my man does not relate Simon's location, then we will venture another visit to the Lady Edith."

"More coercion?" asked Will.

"No...to sow rumors. If perchance she happens to hear that you or I have discovered his hiding place and are advancing, she undoubtedly will run to save him, and in turn guide us directly to his door."

"Amazing is your mind, Uncle," Will breathlessly complimented.

"I know, and I'm much loving using it again. Now leave me, lad." Odo clambered back into bed, and kicked and wrestled with the quilt. "I must get a full night's sleep, for suffering your father and his whore is a wearying business. Do you sleep with your steward?" he asked off-handedly.

"No...I sleep alone."

"As you should," lectured Odo. "Fornication dulls the wit and withers the soul."

"Yes, Uncle...certainly my history with the opposite sex supports that fact."

"Always remember, lad, the fastest route to Heaven is by keeping yourself pure."

"By pure you undoubtedly mean—only in the genital sense."

Odo grunted, and rolled away, seemingly deaf to Will's snickering.

*****

252

While her Liege was closeted with his uncle, Joanna took time for a well-deserved respite and toured the magnificent mansion. Berkhamstead rivaled Helmsley in luxuriance and wealth. How the villagers must have suffered for the cost of Will's comfort! But what did she care, now that she too was wealthy. And how honored she felt to be in the presence of such remarkable men, the late King's brothers! Her knees wobbled a little at the thought, and what most intrigued her were their glances, stealthy, scheming, cunning. Something nasty was afoot, something she was soon to discover, for over the past two months she had managed most shrewdly to capture Will's complete trust. As she rambled back to her chamber, she passed by the great hall, its door ajar, and saw Lord Robert slumped in his seat, his palm supporting his brow, looking vexed. What was he thinking...plotting? These people fascinated Joanna; their lives seemed an endless series of stunning ploys each designed to rid themselves of each other. Were they only playing, or deadly serious? Well, she exuberantly decided, as she entered a chamber she was certain resembled Heaven, she'd presently find out.

*****

Robert could think no more; he stood shakily, and dragged himself to his bedchamber. He nodded to Thomas and Benjamin, both reposing awake on their pallets by the door, and muttered to Benjamin, "I need you alert the entire night." Benjamin wordlessly obeyed and stood to stave off his sleepiness. Robert entered his chamber. Only one candle flickered on a table by Almodis' side of their bed. He tip-toed to her side and felt his heart lurch to the touching sight of her and Adam curled up together in a gentle sleep. He reached to stroke the child's cheek and his mother's hair, and by accident woke her. She lifted her head and turned a puzzled look which quickly grew worried. "Robert? What's upset you? What's Odo done or said now?"

"It's not Odo. It's Will...he arrived directly after you left."

At the harrowing news, her head dropped and lolled on the pillow. She let out a strained and desperate moan, and clutched her child closer. Robert sat, his hands hovering, wanting but not knowing how to soothe, but then she stretched a needy hand out to him...Their fingers mingled a moment, then clenched tightly together.

*****

CHAPTER FIFTEEN - FAMILY

The vessel lurched sharply as Almodis accepted her thickly bundled son from his nurse, Estrith. "My Lady," worried Estrith. "Perhaps we should keep the boy down here. The air above might be too crisp."

"Nonsense," argued Almodis, wrapped snugly in furs herself. "It's stifling down here. Both he and I crave clean air...and his father."

"Yes, my Lady. But don't stay up too long."

"We won't...And thank you again, Estrith, for deciding to travel with us to Mortain."

"I must confess, I am very excited, my Lady, for I've never been out of Dunheved."

"Well Normandy doesn't appear much different from England, but Mortain is as magnificent as Berkhamstead, and larger."

"Truly, my Lady?"

"Truly."

"When will we arrive?"

"We're to dock at Barfleur by dusk, travel one day to Bayeux, then further on a day to Mortain."

"Will we leave the Bishop in Bayeux?"

Almodis' eyes twinkled to her twitter, "Oh yes...and how I've anticipated that joyous event."

Estrith giggled in a whisper, "As have I."

Almodis emerged on deck, squinting from a harsh sun. She wiped a stinging tear, shivered in the brusque wind, and searched for Robert. She spotted him planted in the center of the oarsmen, one arm hugging a mast, and his stare focused on something she couldn't see. She craned her neck, shifted her gaze to the stem and spied Odo. He hung perilously far over the railing. She hoped he was puking, or that one of the gaggle of gulls circling above his head would shit on him. Sporting a snide grin, Almodis found her balance and trod carefully to Robert's side. "What's his trouble?" she asked, breaking Robert's trance.

"He's sick," he answered concernedly.

"Poor soul," she offered with sarcasm.

Robert turned an irked look to her shrug of innocence. Then his eyes softened to Adam's mewling. "Should he be up here? With this wind?"

"He specifically asked for you," she beamed and passed the son to his father. A warmness engulfed her as she watched them together. Slightly less than two months past, she never would have imagined Robert exposing such a tenderness for the child and herself. The whole night before at Berkhamstead they had lain together, talking and quibbling about trivial matters and playing with the boy, trying desperately to distract themselves from the very real likelihood of being murdered in their bed. And she'd felt fonder of him than ever before, and amazed at how more similar they became with each day. "Why did Will leave, Robert?" she asked impulsively.

He stopped his cooing to say, "I don't know, Almodis. He was traveling with only a small contingent of guards. Definitely not an adequate defense against my horde of soldiers."

"He not follow us, will he?"

"No...He's allied with Rufus. Curthose knows that folly, and would no doubt arrest him, probably before he'd disembarked his ship."

"The servants told Estrith that he spoke a long while with Odo."

"They've always been friendly," Robert excused, "and hadn't spoken in many years. It's natural they wanted to reminisce."

"I pray it was only that."

"Try not to fret so." His concern left her and traveled again to his brother still slumped over the stem. "I must try to help him."

"No...You stay with Adam. I'll see to the Bishop."

"Almodis...Promise me, no squabbling."

"I will be sickening sweet, my Husband."

"He doesn't need more sickening."

At his smile, she snorted a laugh, and crept cautiously forward, colliding every foot or so with a straining oarsman. She struggled up the steps and, with a firm grip on the railing, reached out and touched Odo's shoulder. He whirled round, purple with rage, struck away her arm, and spewed saliva and curses, "Get your filthy claws off me you bitch of a she-goat!" She gasped and shrank from his fit, which abruptly ended as he jerked away to wipe his mouth with his sleeve. And when he looked back, his pale sky-blue eyes begged forgiveness, his snarl eased to an affectionate grin, and his posturing slumped submissive. A paralyzing shudder jolted her as his hand rested on and slightly depressed her shoulder. "I heartily apologize for my distemper, my Lady, but I've been indisposed and—"

"There's no...no need," she stuttered, not a little frightened.

Almodis ducked from his touch, stumbled back two paces, and paused her awkward exit to his entreaty, "Don't go, Madam. I'm in desperate need of something more pleasing to gaze upon than these blasted waves, and we must talk."

"About?"

"Will."

Piqued, she chose to stay, and asked with a noticeable tremor, "What about Will?"

"He spoke much treachery last evening. He's not overly fond of you or the child."

"I'm well aware of his feelings, my Lord, and wholeheartedly return them. Perhaps your belly will fare better down stairs."

Almodis turned to go, but Odo stopped her with the queer assurance, "My nephew amuses me with his bragging, but my loyalty lies solely with my brother, your husband. No one will harm Adam, or yourself, Madam, for I have well learned of Robert's devotion to you." Almodis nodded warily, yet her attempt to leave was again spoiled by Odo's accusatory comment, "If indeed the child *is* Robert's. Is he, my Lady?"

His leery eye lurched her belly worse than the boat's rocking, but she gathered herself tall to reply, "Of course he's Robert's. Who else would be his father?"

"A nephew of mine?"

Thinking he meant Will, she returned in offense, "I don't appreciate what you're implying, Sir."

His expression was snide, condemning. "Will informed me of your tumble with Simon."

"Simon!" She threw back her head and laughed wildly into the wind. "And I thought you were being serious."

"Frighteningly serious, Madam. You do care for the bastard."

"Of course I do. He is, after all, a most remarkable, giving and gracious man. And as you ensure my safety, Odo, I in turn ensure Simon's." Her tone turned forbidding, "You won't get to him. Robert and I will make certain of that."

"We shall see, my Lady. We shall see—"

She watched with satisfaction his face color green. He flopped himself again over the railing, heaving wretchedly and, as the ship lurched, she found herself hoping he'd somersault completely over the railing. But he didn't, and his retching began to infect her. She left and stumbled back to Robert, who was totally immersed in a conversation with his boy, and interrupted queasily, "Robert, I must take myself downstairs. Do you wish to keep Adam with you?"

"Not up here. The air is too chilled. We'll all go down."

She clung to his arm the whole of their journey. Once below they gave custody of the child to Estrith, and found a quiet, dry and fairly warm spot at a corner table to talk. Thomas poured them both a cup of hot mead, then left dutifully to Robert's waved dismissal. Privacy allowed them to cuddle for more warmth, and Robert worried, "Almodis, you're mighty peaked. Perhaps you shouldn't have bothered with Odo."

"No...it's these cursed jaunts cross the channel. Each time I travel, the waves seem purposely riled by the fact I'm disrupting their tranquility. Robert..." She snuggled nearer and humbly asked, "When we land at Barfleur, may we part company with the Bishop there, and travel directly to Mortain?"

"What's he said?" Robert abruptly demanded.

She waited a moment, mentally floundering whether to skirt the issue or approach it directly. She decided direct was best. "He inferred Adam is Simon's child."

"He what?!" Robert asked, aghast.

"I was shocked as well, my Lord, then I began to realize his ruse. Will wants to deprive the world of Simon as intensely as does Odo, but Will's scheme also includes me and the child. Odo claimed his sole loyalty is to you. If Will has convinced him that Adam is Simon's, then Odo is bound by chivalry to dispose of anyone caught in treason against you—namely me, Simon, and Adam."

Robert mentioned askance, "Awhile back I also had doubts about the child's paternity."

To which Almodis speedily and with passion acknowledged, "I've never admitted to complete fidelity during our marriage, and now regret my sins, and have confessed them to our priest. I swear the child is yours and I do pledge single heartedness to you, my Husband...forever more."

Six months past he would never have believed her overly formal profession of fidelity. Yet since she'd returned, and he'd honored his pledge to be kinder, more attentive, and protective, she'd been transformed from a flighty, arrogant, angry stranger to a caring, though sharp-tongued, almost contented partner. And as he pondered further their short, tremulous marriage, he noted that she may have withheld secrets from him, but she'd never purposely lied. And as in the case of Maura, Simon and Alan, if an untruth had ever escaped her lips, it was spoken to protect someone other than herself.

The intensity in her gaze sharpened, and worry plagued her voice, "Robert speak to me. Surely you don't believe—"

"Why Simon?" he blurted. "Why state something so ludicrous?"

Her guilty gaze slipped to the table top and she hesitantly divulged, "Will no doubt related to Odo the tale of our trip last December from Berkhamstead to Gloucester for Christmas Court. I've not told you?"

Suspiciously, he replied, "You neglected to relate any of that episode, my Lady."

She traced the rim of her cup, blew away steam, and braced for his eruption. "Well then, you'll hear it all...my Lord. One late afternoon on the road to Gloucester, the weather turned snowy and it was nearing dark. Will refused Simon's suggestion to find shelter. We heard the hungry calls of wolves, but Will would not be dissuaded. My party of women traveled at the rear of the entourage with little protection. A pack of wolves chose us for their dinner, quickly separated us from the others, and began circling and salivating. I screamed for help and who should valiantly appear, not your dark son, my Lord, but your golden one. He risked his life to save mine. Later that evening at an Abbey, he invited me to his chamber to tend..." She paused, paled and faltered, "my...my wounds."

Robert severely pressed, "You swore to tell me all, Almodis."

True anguish strained her reply, "What I did, I didn't do to offend you, my Lord! I barely knew you, and didn't much like what I'd met. I was lonely and bored and faced with a highly pretty young man, graced with the most gentle hands, and tender manner. I...I offered my body in return for his doctoring."

She waited for the explosion that didn't come. Instead, Robert dropped his disappointment to his lap, stiffened, and muttered, "And?"

"Your son very politely rebuffed me," she replied admiringly. "He begged instead for my friendship, which I readily agreed to, and each time I saw or spoke to him after, my affection grew and flourished, for Robert, he is an extraordinarily fine man, who not only deserves your protection but your complete allegiance and love."

"He once owned those and more," he whispered.

But she didn't hear and continued her praise, her expression wistful, "He was present at Adam's birth and helped me through my pains, and made known his wish that this sibling would come to know and care for him. Robert...Simon's bastardy is not his doing, yet he has suffered innumerable travesties as a result. Your brother William shared the same shame and, perhaps because of it, loved your son as his own—no, far better than his own. You must see beyond Will and Odo's bigotry, hate and lies, remember how greatly you once loved Simon, and his mother. He and Maura no longer have the King's protection, and they must have yours."

Robert turned a vague face to Almodis and asked, "He told you no?"

"He told me no..."

He stared off to somewhere, she supposed sorting out all else she had flagrantly revealed. Finally, his wondering gaze again met hers. "And how do you know of my past with Edith?"

The truth proved easier now and she blurted, "She told me. While staying with Rose, I rightly became Edith's staunch ally. And I saw the results of the punishment Odo inflicted upon her. She deserves your loyalty as well, my Lord, for she indulged you with hers for many, many years. How can you care for Odo, my Lord? He's hurt and destroyed so many...including yourself."

"He is my brother."

"Love for a sibling is not an edict, Robert."

"I always felt...pity for him."

Almodis incredulously spat, "Pity?"

"Yes...pity. When we were younger, our lives were always in peril. William became Duke at seven, and had to be constantly protected from assassination by my father, mother, and uncles. Two of my uncles were struck down dead, only feet from William's pallet! The attacks strengthened William, but weakened Odo. He suffered horrible nightmares, was forever hiding, and seeking out comfort from me. Odo claimed all my parents' care and devotion went to William, which wasn't true, my parents loved all of us equally. But as the years became calmer, Odo withdrew all affection from our father, whom he always considered a coward."

"Was he?"

"No...After years of fighting to keep his step-son alive, he preferred to live the remainder of his years peacefully. And for that Odo abhorred him. Our mother Herleve was a saint. Odo never forgave her for her liaison with Duke Robert, or giving birth to William and Adelaide, William's true sister. He never hesitated to scream 'whore' in her face, and when he grew big enough he began beating her. By then, Father had died, and William had moved to Rouen. The onerous job of protecting Mother fell to me. I cherished her, as did William, and she worked very hard to teach us how to care, and to love, but Odo taught us to hate better. After Mother died, I reluctantly went to live with Odo and William at Rouen."

"Why reluctantly?"

"I suppose I inherited my father's need for calm. I reckoned there would be nothing but chaos awaiting me at Rouen. And I was correct. Odo could never understand why William was Duke and we were only Counts. Even after William made him a Bishop, which wasn't due to any religious calling Odo may have received, but simply to pacify, Odo's jealously continued. It eased a bit after the Conquest, when William regularly left Odo to rule in his absence. Yet even in those instances, Odo fought savagely with the Queen. Yet Matilda owned the stronger constitution, and was always victorious. Then he'd run to me to rage and cry, beg solace and understanding."

"Which you devotedly provided."

"He had only me, Almodis," Robert stressed, "no wife, no children, no true home. Only me!"

"Well, I do believe he aims for you to have only him again. Please my Lord, his anger frightens me. May we travel directly to Mortain?"

"I suppose that can be arranged."

"I'm grateful to you Robert...for not condemning me for my indiscretions."

"It seems rather ridiculous punishing you now that we're friends."

"I must tend to Adam," she declared, smiling, standing and fidgeting with her cloak. "It's well past his feeding time."

"Almodis..." Robert asked with a vague reach. "Did Simon refuse you out of loyalty to me?"

"Oh no, Robert," she scoffed. "He refused me, I suppose, on moral grounds and also, I'm certain, out of loyalty for his beloved Maura."

*****

Henry stared trance-like at the snow sifting weightlessly through an icy mist, and shivered from weakness and dismay. He and John had parted company at Boulogne, and how he missed his butler! Henry not only credited John with his healing, but also for not badgering him about his many misdeeds. He could have done so, and been justified in his condemnation, yet instead, over their long, often tedious journey, John had striven to distract and cheer. Henry admitted that John's discourse most times proved horrendously boring, yet there was a glibness about him that was appealing. And he never felt inconsequential to John as he had with Simon, and John was every bit as learned as Simon, at least in what one could learn from books. Yet the hole in his heart still bled for Simon, and his belly knotted to the heinous prospect that he had, in fact, killed Maura and the baby. The reins slipped from his hands as he slumped with remorse and nausea. His mount faltered and waited patiently for his master's directions. Henry slowly regained his posture, kicked his steed forward, and vowed eternal penitence for his crime. But as of yet, he had failed to convince himself that an audience with the wronged parties was essential for his complete absolution; that notion still held the high probability of execution—his execution.

He had much to accomplish over this final week of November. A side trip to Abbeville; a short sojourn at Rouen to appease his brother, Curthose, and withdraw revenue; on to Caen to seek condolence from his sister, Cecily; to Bayeux to purchase John from Odo; then to where else? He had no home, no friends or relatives who were able or willing to keep him. Perhaps he could purchase a hide or two from Curthose, where he could set up his own headquarters, and begin devising his ingenious scheme to someday become King. A memory brought back his dolor, a memory from when he and Maura had journeyed to Normandy and his father to seek Simon's release from Uncle

Robert. Henry had bragged to her of his plans and she had off-handedly asked, 'And when do you expect to become King?' He hadn't an answer for her then and, at present, wasn't any closer to establishing the date of his coronation. He'd hoped his brothers would have begun immediately chomping at each other's shores but, alas, they were behaving like saintly sweet and ingratiating monarchs. He had lacked the constitution and gall to visit Rufus on his journey from Wales—which probably was wise, for he knew Curthose kept spies at Rufus' court. Henry had been a bit surprised that Curthose's punishment for his last foray with Rufus hadn't been promptly dispensed upon him when he'd debarked at Boulogne. Henry glanced up and spied Guy through the veil of ice crystals. Guy—his only guard who owned a conscience. John had confessed that Guy had accompanied him back to Simon's barn to warn him of Henry's return and intended treachery upon Maura. After that revelation, Henry had kept Guy and tossed the rest of the scum; they hadn't seemed too devastated with their transfer to Lord Hugh's service. *To Hell with them all*, Henry growled to himself, then shouted to Guy, "Guy, how much longer? I can't abide this wretched cold."

"We're directly outside the village wall, my Lord. You'll soon be dry, warm, and fed."

Henry nodded from relief, then felt an icy uneasiness creep quicker than the cold up his spine. He wanted desperately to retreat and find other lodgings in some other town. But a tenacious force spurred him onward, past the stone gates, along the high street lined with trussed market stalls and ramshackle huts, beyond the common to the river. Standing directly before the bridge that crossed the Somme sat a modest house, its torches blazing brightly through a smoky haze, beckoning him to its warmth and comfort, and ultimately perhaps its danger as well. Inside dwelled the person he'd resolved to visit and make peace with, and hopefully receive a bit of sympathy from— his former mistress, Sybil.

The proprietor, Ralph, stared dubiously at Henry and excused, "I don't believe your request wise, my Lord."

Henry forced his voice sterner, "I'll see her now."

"After what occurred with your last visit, I don't see how I can agree."

"Ralph, I don't mean to hurt her. I want to see how she's faring. *Please*...I'll stay only a short while."

With a tenuous nod, Ralph acquiesced, "As you wish...But I won't force her to see you."

"No...don't. Only if she wishes..."

Ralph left to fetch Sybil, and Henry fidgeted with fear and foundered for the correct words. What if her brute of a husband was lurking about, waiting to pounce? And after their last escapade, she'd most likely cheer the lug on, and he cursed to himself, *God's teeth, why did I come here and why can't I stop punishing myself?*

"Henry..." The sweet voice rescued him from his quandary, and he turned a well-practiced look of simpering innocence on his raven-haired lover. Her immediate response was to look away and light her darting dark eyes upon everything in the room but Henry. Soon enough, they mawkishly settled on him, and she noticed how thin he'd become, his pale coloring, and darkened smudged eyes. Her heart lurched to his shamed expression; his heart melted to her buxom beauty, the fullness of her tunic could not disguise the rich curves of her breasts and hips. Her hair, so black it shone blue, dangled in two fat plaits past her waist and, as her marital state dictated, was covered round her lovely pink and ivory face by a wimple. She hugged herself from his scrutiny and cautioned, "Henry, Herbert's away but not far. He'll come home soon. You can't stay...Last time, after you left, he beat me. I almost lost the child. You can't stay."

The child, she'd been with child, his child, and now was svelte again! Hope lit his eyes. "So you've had it?"

"Yes..."

"And?"

"A boy...We call him William."

"May I see him?"

"I don't know, Henry. If Herbert catches us—"

"He won't. You can't deny me one look."

She haltingly waved him along to a back chamber, crowded with a cradle, and mats sprawled with two small sleeping children, the larger not more than four years old. Sybil bundled up the infant from the crib and said, "I'll bring him to the main room. I don't want to wake the others."

"Would you give me a moment?" asked Henry.

Sybil cast him a puzzled look, for he'd never asked to see the children before. The torches from the main room threw a tall pillar of light into the room. He knelt and inspected each young one; the eldest, a girl called Sybil, sported a cherubic look and thick shock of black hair. Her brother Rainald, two years younger and black-haired as well, lay nearby, tangled in pelts and dreams. Henry felt his sadness erupt and brim his eyes with nettlesome tears; this tendency toward the maudlin was becoming quite irritating, but he couldn't seem to temper it. He reached to touch the warm, rouged cheeks of his offspring, and stood to join Sybil in the main room.

The baby was dark as well, and plump, squeaky, and flailing. "Would you care to hold him?" asked Sybil, amazed by Henry's drastic emotional turnabout.

"No..." He awkwardly answered and tentatively offered William a finger, which he instantly caught and stuck in his mouth. Henry broke a smile, as did Sybil, and when their happy gazes mingled, each battled an overwhelming urge to clasp hold of the other and never let go. Yet, somehow, they managed to hold back. Henry swiped ashamedly at a dribbling tear, then sniffled, "You said Herbert beat you. Why?"

"Henry," she answered incredulously. "It was his right. After all we almost committed adultery at his feet!"

"Oh yes, now I remember. Still, that's no excuse to risk the life of a...child." His harrowed gaze drew inward.

"What is it Henry? What's happened to you? You look awful."

"No...nothing. I've only come to see how you're faring and if you need of anything."

"That's kind of you, but Herbert and Father have built another ale-house on the north of town, and Herbert will be proprietor there. We're to move shortly. I'm glad you came. Every time you go, I fear you'll forget me."

He gently stroked an escaped lock of her hair back to its proper place, traced her red ripe lips with his fingers, and sadly sighed, "No...I won't ever forget you."

"And the children...You'll remember the children if you should ever become...King?"

"They are mine?"

"All of them. Can't you tell?"

He only nodded, and found it painfully difficult to pry himself away from this luscious woman who had, since they both were barely sixteen, selflessly provided him with caring and physical warmth. His gaze hardened as he turned to go and coldly realized—he'd no doubt find another; there were plenty of willing wenches about and he still possessed his youth, his fairness, and the allure of riches. Henry found Guy awaiting him outside, and answered his concerned expression with the directions, "I can't stay here. We'll go to some other house...some place full of strangers." The cold attacked, rendering him miserable, and he had a sudden urge to barge back into the house, sweep up Sybil, lock her away in their chamber, and take back her warmth again and again. Yet as he mounted, he knew he couldn't do such a thing, not that she wouldn't be willing, and he'd only need pay several of the burly soldiers inside to restrain Herbert. Henry's problem lay with the part of his body that would most enjoy such an adventure...His simply was no longer functional.

*****

Abrupt knocking woke John from a sleep crazed by bishops and demons. He hid beneath his paltry blanket, praying he still dreamt and would soon awake far from Bayeux. Yet the dark of his sanctuary failed to mute the insistent rapping and he tossed back the coverlet and yelled to the squalling of his name, "I'm awake...and will join the Bishop in the great hall...shortly.

He pulled on wrinkled, though presentable clothing and gasped as he splashed frigid water on his face. The shock jolted him into a panic. What was he going to say?! Would he lie? Could he lie?! If Henry were here, he'd conjure them a way out of this. Yet he could never confess his espionage to Henry. If he did, Henry wouldn't come take him from this place...a place that once offered blissful serenity, and now promised only imminent terror. *I'll lie*, John decided as he palmed back his damp hair, anxiously straightened his tunic, and shot out his chamber door and down the tortuous passageway and curling staircase leading to the hall.

Odo sat on his throne centering the dais, impeccably robed and combed, his skin shiny and rouged from too much scrubbing, a golden goblet of wine snug in his jeweled clutch. His placid smile couldn't mask the sinister glint in his eyes. He pulled himself erect at the sight of his clerk, obviously jittery and partly obscured by the shadows. "Come forward, John. There's absolutely nothing to fear. I'm immensely pleased you've returned in time for my visiting."

"Won't you be staying, my Lord?" John squeaked, propelling himself into the glow of the blazing hearth, and bowing lowly.

"You know I won't be. And did you enjoy your adventures with Henry?"

Odo's attempts at sounding genuinely interested in one's doings always emerged pretentious and sneering. John stayed on one knee, his eyes focused on the rushes, and carefully explained, "I'm not certain enjoy is the correct term, your Grace. Henry made me his butler, and I have earned his trust and allegiance. If I may add, your Grace, he's presently journeying here to ask you to release me into his permanent service, and I'm hoping you'll see the sense in such—"

"Get up, John. You are such a whey-faced, maggoty worm."

John rose shakily and stretched his lips into a gawky grin.

Odo eyed his clerk skeptically, delicately sipped wine and replied, "I may consider the FitzRoy's request if in turn you are prepared to honor *my* request. You *are* ready to do so, aren't you?

"What request is that, your Grace?"

"Don't toy with me, you dunce!" flared Odo. "I'll have Simon's whereabouts and I'll have them now!"

John burbled, "We...we never visited Simon. Henry mentioned him once or twice, but never in a friendly manner. There had been some disagreement over Simon's wife...It seems Henry coveted her, and they'd argued. We stayed awhile with King William, and traveled to Hugh of Avranche's fief on the north border of Wales to discuss the status of Henry's mother's property. That was the extent of our trip, your Grace, I swear."

261

"Enough..." growled Odo. "You don't lie well...You don't do anything well. I'll ask again politely and then..." Odo tapped his cheek and from two blackened corners of the hall emerged four monstrous, glowering guards.

John struggled forward, arms and hands spread in submission, voice heightened with despair. *"Why*, your Grace, why hurt Simon?"

"Why does everyone assume I aim to hurt him? I only want to speak to him, discuss my imprisonment and his role in the debacle. So many question his capacity for evil-doing and I long to discover the truth. And I miss him..." Odo gushed with distaste, "He was always such an intriguing mongrel."

John gripped the edge of the dais, and stared blankly at his Liege. He had never argued with, slandered, disobeyed, interrupted, or spoken to his Lord without permission. Yet now a voice shouted out loudly from deep inside his mind and his soul, a persistent voice that bade him not betray Odo's nephew. It cried out that Simon and Maura had already suffered immeasurably from their family's insults, and that Odo no doubt intended to inflict upon them the vilest assault of all. No...They'd been good to him, fed and sheltered him, made him feel special. And absolutely no one excepting his good mother, bless her soul, had ever purposefully been nice to him before.

"John, you know excruciatingly well that I am not a patient man and I'm shocked by your obstreperous behavior. Perhaps Henry was not the best choice of a traveling partner for you, for it seems he's taught you spitefulness, disloyalty, and deceit. I don't think you should keep company with him further."

"But my Lord...Henry needs me! He's forgetful, reckless, and needs caring and guidance. He likes me...And his *butler*, surely my ascent to such a position should make you proud—"

"Proud...that you're to become his purveyor of women, for to Henry that's all a butler is. And to do his bidding all you need be is alive and depraved." As Odo rose, so did his color and rage; his knotted fist beat the air in time with his tirade, "No I am not proud! I'm disgusted by your obstinacy, but mostly I'm repulsed by you, you sniveling weasel! I gave you the gift of my home, my precious time, and my instruction, and now you dare defy me!"

All the sentries strode one ominous step forward. John wilted and doubted his resolve, but the voice from inside stressed louder—*Don't say, never say!* "I...I don't know where Simon is," he shrilled. "I swear I don't know—" A fist struck John's belly with a force that launched him through the air. He landed crunched and dazed, dangerously near the blazing hearth. John gasped horribly and rasped, "No, your Grace!" He rolled to his hands and knees and scuttled forward for mercy. *"Please*, I beseech you—" A boot tip caught his jaw and slammed his head against a stone circling the pit. He smelled the stench of sizzled hair.

The room and the sentries spun nearer, Odo loomed larger; John's tunic ripped to a treacherous grip, while another fist pounded his eye. As he swooned he heard more kicking, more punching; his body jerked in spasms to the pernicious onslaught, spewed blood and vomit, and then there came a tenuous pause in the violence and an eerily calm voice that filled his dulled mind with extreme horror. "Just the name of the town...or city...and country. That's all I require, and then you may join Henry if indeed he comes for you, which I doubt. Otherwise, you can expect this sort of admonishment each day for the remainder of your pitiful life, however short it might be. Now tell me John...where is he?"

The light in the room shivered as John strained to focus on his nemesis, but Odo's complacent features blurred as did John's answer, "Me...Me..."

Odo knelt to hear better and lay a gentle touch on John's sweat soaked brow. "Again, John...more slowly. Confess where."

John risked resistance one last time, "I don't know——" But the glaring flash of a dagger's blade stung his wounded eye and before it closed, he sputtered, "Me...Menevia, Wales."

With an unnatural slowness Odo removed his palm, and lifted clenched hands and moist and grateful eyes to the ceiling. "My thanks go not to this miserable wretch," he extolled, "but to you my venerable Lord...You led him to the fiend and convinced him in time of your will and inescapable wrath. Help John to be a more obedient servant and allow him the temerity to resist the temptations that undoubtedly will accompany his new situation..." Odo stood and his look of sublime adoration uglied to disgust. "Lock the bastard in his room and provide him only water for two full days. And make certain no one bothers me more this night, for I must sleep undisturbed. We depart at dawn for Berkhamstead to collect Will, then journey to the Montgomery's fief on the border of Wales. There we will garner Roger's assistance, and then we'll undertake our pilgrimage to..." The bliss returned, its effect dizzying; Odo clutched his nearest man's shoulder and zealously breathed, "Menevia."

*****

Bad luck had visited Henry once again, this time in the form of his grossly pregnant and formidable sister, Adela, Countess of Blois. He'd journeyed from Abbeville to Rouen anticipating a raucous rendezvous with his brother Curthose but, alas, he was off debauching with his comrade of ill-repute, King Philip. Henry extracted money from the coffers, and left Curthose a detailed letter stating his desire to purchase a fief or two and the title, Count. He also wrote that he'd be visiting Cecily for several days, travel to Bayeux to pick up his butler, then return to Rouen, hopefully to find Curthose in residence. And he'd been just about to leave for Caen when Adela arrived and suggested rather stringently that he stay and comfort her, for she and her husband Stephen had suffered another spat. A marriage mediator Henry wasn't, but considering this trial as part of his penance, he'd politely listened to her woes, and listened, and listened. When finally, he'd worked up the courage to announce his plans to visit Cecily, Adela adamantly stated her decision to do the same. So here they were, slogging through mud and slush and snow, and she talked incessantly, never stopping even when she ate. Henry reckoned she continued yammering in her sleep, and that's why Stephen had run off with Curthose. His neck ached from nodding, and his cheek stung from her slaps, for a number of times, he'd rudely fallen asleep while she was mid-sentence. More than once, he'd considered leaving Adela and visiting Cecily after he'd bought John, but his soul was in immediate need of Cecily's counsel; his depression had deepened and guilt clogged and tangled his mind, threatening his sanity. He rarely slept, his appetite had dwindled. He had to find a way to absolve himself from this torture! Cecily would help him, she had to help him, there was no one else, no one!

"Henry!" Adela's shout jarred him from his anguish, "Did you hear what I said?"

"Yes..." he sighed.

"Then why didn't you answer?"

"I'm tired Adela, too tired to talk."

"Are you ill? You look ill."

"I don't know," said Henry. He glanced ahead and noticed the spires of St. Stephen's, jutting ghostly through the frigid fog. "Adela," he said feebly, "Caen is near. Please, could we possibly ride the next mile in silence. It's not that I don't welcome your discourse. My head pains me terribly."

Adela's choleric expression pinched with concern. "Of course, Henry. Why didn't you ask before? Cecily's house employs the most competent physician. He's seen successfully to my complaints and I'm certain will brew you something to ease your discomfort. Cecily herself is quite proficient with herbal tonics and just conversing with

263

her seems to tame my tempers. But then when we were younger and all at Rouen, she always played the mother, didn't she? It's a cursed shame she was robbed of the opportunity to become one herself, and I blame Mother entirely for that atrocity..."

Her rambling faded from Henry's ears only to be overtaken by a deafening pounding; he cringed, quietly moaned, and began seriously to question if he would survive the next mile.

*****

"Madam..." The young veiled novice bowed to Cecily, who seemed surprised at the intrusion. The house of the Holy Trinity rarely entertained visitors at supper time.

The excitement glimmering the girl's eyes promptly set Cecily on her feet, and she asked pointedly, "What is it, Sister?" patting her lips with her serviette.

"A man and woman claiming to be your brother and sister await you at the door, Madam."

"At the door?" Cecily asked with strict curiosity as she nodded to the other Sisters, and hurried the girl and herself out of the refectory. "Haven't you let them in?"

"Yes...But you've always said to come and fetch you when I didn't recognize—"

"Fine...fine," she interjected and glanced forward to see her huge, flaxen-haired sister barreling towards her.

To Adela's effusive cry, "Cecily!" the Abbess paused and lay one hand upon her chest to still her apprehension.

Then she beamed a convincing smile, and gushed as she disappeared into Adela's tackling embrace, "Adela! My, what a pleasure to see you...so well!" Clamped tightly to Adela's cumbersome figure, she realized warily, "And so near due!"

They both stepped back and narrowly appraised each other. The striking contrasts in their coloring and figures made it difficult to believe they were indeed family; Adela, big-boned, mannish, and blowsy, and Cecily, brown haired, pretty and petite. Both seemed pleased with what they saw and hugged again, this time more gently. Cecily giggled nervously, "You aren't intending on giving birth to that child here, are you Sister?"

"No...He's not due to arrive for a full month and none of my children dare come till I'm ready for them."

"You expect another boy?"

"Of course, what else?" Adela answered in all seriousness.

"I hear a brother has come with you. Is it Curthose?"

Adela eagerly tugged Cecily towards the door. "No....he's taken Stephen off somewhere, and I'm irked at them both." She added with a touch of mystery, "Henry's here with me and he's been acting most peculiar. I figure he's done something despicable and has come to beg for forgiveness."

Cecily worriedly dismissed, "Surely not despicable."

"I've never seen him this vexed."

"Well...we'll soon find out, won't we," obliged Cecily as she resolutely strode to her younger brother, slouched up against the door looking terribly lost and chastened. "Henry!" she gushed with outstretched arms. "How kind of you to come. I've missed you and after our last visit, I must admit to fretting quite a bit—" His frail countenance alarmed her and cut short her greeting. He slumped into her embrace, trembling and needy, and she shouted over her shoulder for assistance. "Sister! Please fetch our most potent wine, and warm stew and bread." She eased slightly away, pressed her palm to his very cold cheek, and gently urged, "Come Henry, we'll go to my chamber to rest and talk."

He barely nodded and steadfastly kept snug to her side as they silently walked the halls. Adela followed, sulky at being shunned. Their torpid journey allowed the wine and stew to arrive before them, and when at last they'd reached the chamber, Cecily ushered Henry inside and, to her sister, suggested kindly, "Adela, perhaps it's best if you waited next door for only a short while. Sister will see to your comfort."

"I'll come in as well," Adela answered defiantly.

"I don't want her here," cut in Henry, "not till I tell *you* what's happened."

Cecily took Adela's hand, her large, doe-like eyes pleading, "Only a short while, Adela, please."

Adela's slate gray, squinty eyes flared in response as she jerked from Cecily's touch, spun on her heels, and flounced away in a waddle. But her stormy pace halted to the sound of the clicking latch. On tip-toe she slunk back, planted herself shamelessly before the door, yanked off her wimple, and stuck her ear to the keyhole.

"Drink the wine quickly, it will warm you. You're so thin, Henry! Have you been ill?"

"I'm still recovering from a mean fever," he answered. "My butler had been caring for me, but he had some business to attend to in Bayeux."

"Well you'll stay here with me till you're fully well. But it's not only your illness that's dulled your color. Confess what else."

"I...I will," he replied unsteadily. "When I'm done eating." He sat on her bed and humbly accepted the stew; after tasting a spoonful he rapidly slopped up the rest, and wondered between slurps, "How have you fared?"

"Nothing changes here, Henry. I'm fit and content. I've been put in charge of the new novices and some have proven fairly troublesome, but eventually they will learn our rituals and do well in their vocation. Normandy seems quiet, and England the same. Could it be that Curthose and Rufus have at last become comrades?"

"Nothing as smarmy as that," quipped Henry, swabbing the last bit of gravy from his bowl with a hunk of bread. He stuffed the whole hunk in his mouth, and mumbled. "Their friendly...pre...tense will end soon enough. They won't fight in winter...Perhaps at Easter their hatred will be resurrected."

"Henry what a clever tongue you have...Has Curthose asked you to serve as advisor?"

"No...That coveted position has been gifted jointly to Odo and Robert, but I suspect Uncle Robert has more pressing matters to attend to."

"Yes, I've heard we have a new cousin."

"A new what?!" asked Henry, agape.

"Robert's wife Almodis gave birth recently in England and they are returning to Mortain. Denise happened by and mentioned the news rather mordantly."

Henry's confusion soared, "Denise?"

"Your cousin Denise, Robert's eldest daughter."

Henry shook his head in exasperation and scorned, "Damn our family. Why does it have to be so large?"

"Nature takes its course, Henry."

"A bit too liberally at times. And what sex did Almodis deliver?"

"A boy...He's called Adam."

"Amazing," said Henry with scant emotion. "Will must be livid." His attention wandered to the tiled circular hearth centering and warming the chamber.

The flames dancing in his eyes did little to brighten his expression and Cecily asked, "Would you like more stew, or wine?" Henry shook his head and eased himself down upon the floor, taking several pillows with him. He offered the empty bowl and a pillow to Cecily. She smiled in thanks, gathered up her robes, and sank down beside him, deciding, "Now you'll say what troubles you."

On the verge of dozing, Adela piqued when the words she had been so patiently awaiting filtered through the key hole. She flattened her ear to the cold iron, and smirked in anticipation.

"When I was here before...at Father's funeral...I may have mentioned a woman I care for...deeply."

Cecily guessed there was a reason Henry hadn't mentioned Maura's name, and knowingly replied, "Yes, you did. And that you'd see her soon. Have you?"

"Yes, and her husband as well."

Adela's eyes glittered with glee. Henry's affairs made for such stimulating story telling.

"And are they well?" Cecily asked in wary suspense.

Henry shrank a bit and barely replied, "She's pregnant."

"How wonderful," sighed Cecily in ecstatic relief. "I'd heard rumors, again from Denise, quite a while back that the first child they'd conceived had died under suspicious circumstances."

For a long moment, she thought Henry would faint, then in a strangled effort, he managed, "Their...their first child?"

"Yes, Denise never offered details, but the tragedy occurred directly after Odo had been imprisoned. The child was an obstacle to a profitable marriage, I believe with the Montgomerys, and the obstacle was forcibly removed, along with its father. Henry..." Cecily limply confessed, "At times, our family's doings repulse me and I'm glad to be here...protected."

Henry scrambled to his feet, grabbed hold of the bedpost for support and spurted, "I think I should go."

"Go where?"

"Back to Wales."

Cecily's reply shuddered with dread, "Wh...Why? What have you done?"

"I can't say," he whined. "I don't know for certain, and I must know. Not knowing eats at my soul."

"What have you done, Henry?!" She grabbed hold and shook his shoulders.

"I was sick...my fever made me do something horrible."

"To whom, Henry?"

"Why didn't he tell me?!"

Terror shrilled her voice. "Who tell you what?!"

"Simon...He should have told me about the other...baby. He's always told me everything."

The mention of Simon lifted Adela to her knees and a creeping uneasiness began to sour her fun.

"The loss of a child is a very personal sorrow, Henry," quavered Cecily, desperately trying to calm.

"But what I might have done...There could be nothing worse."

Panic gripped her again, her heart felt about to erupt. "You're scaring me Henry. What do you mean 'might have done'?"

Henry slid down the post and sagged back into the rushes; his chest heaved and lips pouted, as he focused his shame on his fingers fiddling with the grass and trepidly began, "There was a battle...Bernard attacked the village and me. My shoulder was burned...She nursed me, but my fever stayed and worsened. It made my thoughts crazy. I believed everyone hated me and wanted me harmed. I fought with him, I can't remember why. He quickly humbled me, and I left...But I stopped at the base of the hill and snuck back on foot. My men had set fire to their stables. I hadn't ordered it, but I felt glad they had, and my meanness grew." His eyes gorged with guilt, met and held hers as he shrilled, "I couldn't stop myself, Cecily, I couldn't! I wanted her, I've always wanted her, but she kept spurning me! I tried to kidnap her, something she said changed my mind, I don't recall what...And then I—" Cecily did not move closer to console. The horror brewing in her imagination widened the space between them. His cry to the heavens, "My God what have I done!" shot her to her feet and his anguished look bore through her, begging deliverance, and twisting her belly. "When I think back, it's someone else with her, not me. It couldn't have been me. I loved her...loved her!"

Shock made her stutter, "How did you...hurt Maura, Henry?"

"I...I tried to rape her, but couldn't." In an instant, his shame flashed to rage. "I blamed her for my failure, wanted to kill her and the baby and everything Simon's ever loved! I would have stabbed her, but I lost my dagger in the rushes. I rammed my knee into her belly...twice I think. She dropped and didn't get up. Then I ran."

Each evil he confessed drove Cecily one step further across the chamber. This mad criminal sitting on her floor couldn't be her little brother, Henry...Curthose, maybe, Rufus, definitely, but never Henry! He'd been her last hope, the clever one, the gentle and caring one whose heart hadn't yet rotted. Yet clearly he'd become just as monstrously repellent and befouled as his brothers. She hung her head and with a trembling and tear-filled voice, ordered, "You'll leave here now."

"No!" he wildly protested, scrambling her way. "You'll help me, you have to help me! The guilt is killing me. God's forsaken me!"

"As he should," Cecily sternly decided, "as we all should."

At her feet, he crushed the hem of her robe in his fists and cried, "No! Tell me what to do. Tell me how to save myself!"

"You selfish fiend," she scourged and spat, "Save yourself?! What about the sweet lady you left lying, maybe dead, in the rushes, the good husband you left a childless widower? Who saves them?!" She jerked her skirt from his grip and railed, "Get yourself from this house! It's defiled by your presence. Get out now!"

Suddenly, something yanked him weightlessly up from the floor. Dagger-like nails sliced at his eyes, face, and neck. He screamed and cowered from the savage assault, and gaped terrified at Adela, swelled up purple; too enraged to speak, she spewed rabid foam from her howling lips, while viciously pummeling, kicking, raking.

The cramped chamber offered Henry no refuge from Adela's rage, but he was far past caring, and welcomed the abuse. Adela delivered one last sound kick to Henry's backside, propelling him out the door, before her wrath crumpled to hysterical sobs. And as he lay defeated, throbbing with pain and self-pity, he heard drifting from the chamber Adela's muffled wailings, and Cecily's gushes of sympathy—the sympathy rightly due him.

*****

Henry heard God snickering at him as he straggled with a limp down the central aisle of Bayeux Cathedral. There seemed to be no one about on this dripping despondent day except a preponderance of garish icons, glaring and condemning. He'd considered confessing to Odo, but instead of receiving penance, he'd more likely received lavish praise and the prospect of sainthood. *Where is Odo?* wondered Henry, suddenly suspicious. And what would Adela do with the damning evidence he'd so stupidly provided her? She was apt to declare a war against him for the honor of her adopted cousin, with whom she had once been very close. She'd waged many wars for far trivial causes, and was not easily squelched. Well, he really didn't have the time or vigor for worry. He must find John, return to Rouen and buy himself a barrow in the farthest corner of Normandy, where no one could find him and he could find some peace. He slipped onto a pew and cradled his splitting head in his palms, relishing the

267

quiet, which was promptly disturbed by the touch of a hand and a young voice, "Can I be of some help, my Lord?"

Henry looked up into the pimpled face of a young page, and dully answered, "Is the Bishop about?"

"No, my Lord. But you may speak to his seneschal."

"Actually, I've come to see a lad named John. Perhaps you know his whereabouts."

"John, the clerk?"

"Yes, I believe that's his title. If you would lead me to his chamber, I would be most—"

"I don't think I can do that, my Lord."

Henry stood to the refusal. "And what stops you?"

"The Bishop's orders."

"Piss on the Bishop's orders," he flared. "I aim to rescue John from this putrid Hell hole, and you will be amply rewarded for your bravery if you give aid to my cause."

"Pardon, my Lord?" the boy calmly implored.

"Help me and I'll give you money."

"Oh!" The page beamed and excitedly beckoned. "Yes, my Lord. Follow me."

Henry waved Guy forward and, when they arrived at the chamber's door, Henry rapped briskly and called, "John...John, wake up! It's sinful to sleep this late. It's Henry, I've come to buy you, but instead, since Odo's away, I'll kidnap you for free. Come and open the door. John?"

There was no answer and Henry worriedly asked the page, "Why doesn't he answer?"

"I don't know my, Lord."

Henry futilely rattled the latch, banged on the door, and railed, "Why is it locked?"

"The Bishop's orders, my Lord."

"Damn you and your insipid answers. Fetch the key, immediately."

"I'll try, my Lord, but the Bishop said to keep him locked away for—"

"Fetch the blasted key!"

The boy bowed repeatedly as he scurried backwards down the corridor.

"Kick it in Guy!" Henry commanded.

"I can't break iron, my Lord."

"What bleeding good are you then? I should have booted you out with the rest of the slime. You can't even keep a pregnant woman off me, you feckless turd." Henry scratched irritably at the nail bites, some already festering, and fumed, "John! Answer me, you worm! If you don't I swear I'll leave you here to rot." He thought he heard a mumbled moan inside, and from the corner of his wary eye spied the page rapidly approaching followed by a rotund, white-haired man, shrouded in priests' robes. Henry didn't wait for a greeting, but flourished his dagger and yanked Guy forward, gesturing awkwardly for his cooperation. Guy's long sword emerged from its sheath, its menace blinding.

The page dropped to the floor and the priest retreated two broad steps, and groveled, "My...my Lord, might you be Henry FitzRoy?"

"I am," Henry replied prestigiously.

"Then, my Lord. There is no need for this fuss. Bishop Odo gave explicit directions that his man, John, is to be given to you upon your arrival."

"Then why the locked door?" asked Henry, motioning to Guy for calm.

"John's had a punishment to endure," replied the priest.

"Punishment?" Henry snorted. "God's breath, for what? I suspect he's never even belched without permission."

The priest fumbled for the correct key, then wrestled with the lock, trembling his answer, "Impudence, disobedience, and disrespect."

The door at last swung open and an overpowering stench sent the three men reeling. "Bleeding Jesus!" gasped Henry, through parted fingers. "What ...what's happened? Has he died?!" He refused to enter and furiously waved the priest into the room to root out the problem.

His mission was quick; he lurched back out the door and announced, "He's been badly beaten, and he's been sick, and unable to fend for himself. My Lord, I—"

"Fetch servants, water for washing, clothing!" bellowed Henry. "Damn you, get him out of that filth! When he's presentable, call for me. I'll wait in Odo's hall. Get to it, man!"

The priest bustled away down the hall, swatting at the page in punishment for his own razing. Terrible dread struck Henry as his mind swam with too many whys. Why would Odo have John beaten? And why wasn't Odo here? Why had John been so freely given to him, before and now? On his uncertain trek to the hall, the ache in his head returned with a vengeance, its ferocity hammering his skull. Henry wavered; Guy instantly spotted his difficulty, supported his elbow and his weight, and assured, "Wine...wine will set you right, my Lord."

Henry's third cup of claret began to deliver the numbing effect he'd been promised, yet still the dread lingered. He didn't really want to see John, didn't want any answers, didn't want the responsibility of responding to yet another crisis. Perhaps if he just slunk away no one would know—

"My Lord!"

The shrill greeting disrupted his cowardice and he nodded to the page and heard, "John is awake and prepared to see you now."

Henry groaned, "I will join him presently." Along the passageway to his butler's new chamber, Henry took on a sluggish, solemn gait, as if he were approaching his own execution.

He hesitated before the closed door and Guy offered, "I'll enter first if you please, my Lord."

"No...you wait here. Are the horses prepared to depart?"

"Yes, my Lord."

"If he's able, I want to remove John from this pit immediately." Guy nodded and stood guard, while Henry gingerly entered. What he beheld made him stop short, and loudly suck a shocked breath. John lay barely conscious upon a skinny cot, his face mottled by bruises. "My God," Henry quaked, "what's he done to you?"

John carefully licked his swollen, cracked and bloodied lips, and achingly whispered, "I deserved it." Henry moved closer, mentally counting the bruises, and wincing at their severity. John's good eye squinted curiously at Henry's sores and croaked, "What's happened to you?"

"My sister...Adela," jested Henry, "has these murderous spells, mostly when I'm around." Henry shook from his joke, yanked a chair near, and sat to ask, "Can you walk?"

"I believe so," rasped John. "I don't think they fractured anything. May I have some more water?"

"Of course." Henry held a cup to John's lips, waited till he'd emptied it, then set it aside. "Who are *they*?"

"Odo's guards."

"Where is he now?"

John swooned; Henry tensed and his voice panicked as the obvious at last loomed. "My God, man, what did you tell him?!"

269

John only moaned in response. Henry seized John's shirt, jerked him close and raged, "You'll tell me, now! What business did you have with Odo, you stinking spy? He sent you with me purposely to find Simon, didn't he? Didn't he?!" John's shirt ripped from Henry's ferocity, then as quickly as it swelled, his anger ebbed, and his tone turned frantic, "Did you tell him?! You couldn't have, you swore your loyalty, your honor...You couldn't have betrayed me! Please say you didn't, *please*!"

"I had to say," John blubbered, "...I had to."

"Because they beat you? Are you aware what he intends for Simon?!"

"I couldn't deny him!" John defended. "He took me in, cared for me after my mother died, taught me!"

Henry's grief paused a moment to ponder John's curious defense. He knew, as did everyone, that Odo believed poverty to be God's punishment to those less worthy, and always refused entreaties from the poor and struggling, especially orphans, whom he considered the spawn of fornicators, deserving of their lot. "Why? Why would he take you in? He's never taken in another! Why you?!"

John shut his good eye and, before answering, wrestled furiously with his reply. But why keep the secret longer, what did it matter, there was never any love to be lost, only duty...only duty.

"Why you?!" Henry insisted meaner.

"Because he is my father."

Henry mind swirled to the words, and his lips tripped in disbelief, "Who...who is your father?"

"Odo...The Bishop Odo is my father, you are my cousin, and I've betrayed you. You who have shown me more affection in three months than my father has in eight years. I've earned my beating, and your desertion and—"

"Shut you gob!" demanded Henry.

John promptly obeyed and, willingly, awaited more abuse. But it didn't come. Instead, Henry paced, his mind still reeling from the astounding revelation. He stopped and hurled his crass question, "How many more slugs like you did he spawn?!"

"I don't know, but I've heard rumors of siblings."

Henry threw up his hands in exasperation. "No...no...I've changed my mind, I don't want to know. I don't know why I'm surprised. Nothing ignoble carried out by our family should shock me." He sat again and, twitchy with indecision, beseeched, "What you need tell me are Odo's plans, for I have to stop him."

"You can't stop him," John dully replied.

"With help I can."

"Whose help? Everyone hates Simon, even you."

"I won't have the sin of Simon's murder smudging my soul," returned Henry. "It's blackened enough already. Tell me what happened."

John carefully obliged, "When he enlisted my help, he told me how he'd overheard you talking to Uncle Robert about Simon, and you promised to inform Simon of Father's release. Father believed you would leave directly and warn Simon, so he decided you needed a riding partner."

"I didn't want you with me, but that glib tongue of yours won me over. You scheming pig!"

"Father said Simon had willfully lied to King William just to get Father imprisoned, so that he...Simon, could take his place in William's heart and his court. He told me tales, horrendous tales, of the torture he endured in prison."

"Torture?!" Henry scoffed in a guffaw. "He never missed a meal, or a bath, was served the best claret, continually entertained visitors, including myself, slept on a thick down bed, cushioned with pelts, employed five servants...Torture...Wouldn't we all love to endure that sort of torture? Didn't you ever visit him?"

"He forbade it. He thought I might raise suspicions. But he did pen me letters, very detailed letters, some even sounding kind."

"Get up!" commanded Henry.

"But my Lord, I don't know if I can."

"You can if you want to continue living. Guy!" Henry shouted and the guard instantly appeared.

"Help me hoist this slug out of bed. We're going."

"Going where?" croaked John.

Guy rounded the bed and clasped one arm, Henry clamped the other, and they lifted John, howling in protest, from his cot. "Walk!" shouted Henry, "Walk, you flaming fart!" John shuffled a few feet with their assistance, then shoved them away, and lumbered drunkenly about the minuscule chamber. Once his footing turned more assured, Henry resolutely determined, "We'll go directly to Mortain and have a chat with Uncle Robert, hopefully receive his blessing, his troops and, if we're tremendously lucky, his presence as well. Then we'll return to Wales."

"How can you go back there? Simon will murder you, or Marc will, or Maura."

"I didn't say where in Wales I'd go, did I? I plan to visit Dinefwr and alert Prince Rhys to Odo's treachery, and have him go save Simon."

"The coward's way."

"Yes indeed, Cousin," concurred Henry, "for that's the way *we* know best."

*****

271

CHAPTER SIXTEEN - A FRAGILE JOY

𝕬𝖘 Almodis soaked in her leather-cushioned tub, she drank in the scented steam and contemplated her wrinkled toes and her near-perfect existence. *What wonderful thing have I done to deserve residing in this palatial estate, being mother to the most handsome, whimsical, and brilliant boy ever born, and wife to a fitting and powerful husband?* Perhaps, the answer was she'd suffered enough and, at last, was due her rightful compensation. She tingled with anticipation, thinking on the next evening's celebrations—Feast of the Immaculate Conception, start of Christmas Court, and the return of Mortain's Liege. She was at her pinnacle when entertaining; expert at choosing menus, wine, guests, music, dances. And no woman, even one half her age, could turn a man's head with quite the same allure as she. Almodis smiled as she recalled Christmas Court at Gloucester one year past. There had been a woman present who had proven to be a worthy competitor—Maura. All the pretty boys, including Almodis' lover of the moment, Will, had tripped over each other in their clumsy pursuit of the intelligent, striking, though also seemingly innocent lady. And Almodis had despised her, even plotted her undoing. But then came the most shocking upset of all, for soon after, they had become the closest of confidants. And now Almodis missed Maura more than she was comfortable admitting; she longed to hear of her provincial life in Wales, her passionate marriage and, also, Almodis prayed, her pregnancy. "God..." she mumbled to her toes, "I know we don't speak often, yet I'm thankful for your many blessings and also beg of you to make certain of Maura's happiness, for I'm sure you'll agree that no one on your earth deserves to know joy more than she."

The door clicking shut disturbed her piety. She turned a tight gasp on her husband. He appeared guilty at having startled her. "I'm sorry. I...I didn't know," Robert stuttered. "I'll leave you to your privacy."

"No," she swiftly argued. "Please, Robert, stay awhile." With a cautious nod, he skirted past the tub and crouched by the cradle. Almodis looked on, a mawkish smile on her lips, while he fussed with Adam's blanket and pet his coal-black hair. "Is it very late?" she asked, unbinding her plaits.

"No...not too. I've just finished my court."

"And what austere judgments did you deliver?" she asked with a hint of sarcasm.

"I pardoned them all."

"You what?!" she exclaimed, sloshing water over the side of the tub.

"They've done nothing that deserves punishment," defended Robert, "only stolen a few eggs, cursed in public, exhibited excessive drunkenness, and they seemed genuinely repentant."

"How gracious of you, Robert," she said sincerely. "Are they to attend our festivities tomorrow evening?"

"The villagers would never dare ignore their Liege's feast."

He spoke with a slight sharpness to his voice and, despite the generosity he'd shown to his subjects, Almodis sensed a coolness in her presence. It was that damned Bishop's fault, she decided. Odo's insistent harangues concerning the evils of physical pleasure between married couples frustrated their intimate relations. If only Robert would realize the absurdity of his brother's sermons—they were married legally and spiritually, and as such were allowed the luxury of pleasuring each other. Why else would God have gifted them with such sensitive parts! She'd striven hard to rid Robert of his inhibitions, and had achieved some progress, though not nearly enough. She squirmed in the tepid water and grudgingly acknowledged that Robert's resistance might not be entirely

Odo's doing. She guessed Edith played a stellar role in his rigidness. Perhaps he believed lying with her showed Edith disloyalty. Almodis knew she'd never fully snuff the flame that still flared for his long-time lover. She didn't care to, but Hell, Edith had found and enjoyed a new partner. It was far past time Robert did the same. Her resolve thrust her to her feet, and as water bubbled over her oiled olive skin and dribbled to puddles at the tub's base, she demanded sultrily, "Robert, come close."

He averted his awed gaze to the boy, and stuttered, "I...I don't think so, Almodis. I'm tired and tomorrow threatens to be as hectic as today."

"Husband, I'm cold. I need my robe...and your touch. You wouldn't deny your wife's simple needs...would you?"

'Simple needs', Robert repeated to himself with a weary sigh. There was absolutely nothing simple about the Lady Almodis, or her needs. Needs that he'd come to anticipate, and think on endlessly, and worry that he was incapable of fulfilling. He frankly admitted that she frightened him, and he hated the fear. He longed to experience the same joy she felt when they came together, laugh as she so often did, show to her the honesty she freely showed him, if sometimes brutally. Yet no matter how hard he tried, the ice that chilled his veins refused to melt.

During Robert's musing, Almodis had left the tub and now stood before him, with no robe to cloak her charms. She sank down by his side and draped pelts over her lap. Then she reached to touch, yet stopped, her hand hovering, and spoke as if wounded, "Sometimes I wonder if I repulse you."

"No," he speedily assured. "Never think that."

"Then could the trouble be that...I'm too bold?"

He only shook his head and hadn't yet looked at her. She felt dreadfully confused. Before, if a man had spurned her, and very few had, she would instantly seek out another. Only this time, she didn't want another...and that prospect in itself was odd— odd and compelling. "Robert, is there anything about me you *do* like?"

He slowly turned and her riveting eyes, dark pools of bewilderment, easily captured his. "There...there are many things I like about you," he affirmed, looking away again and dragging his fingers awkwardly across his pate.

She waited; he said no more. She grew impatient, lifted herself up an inch and dropped down hard on the bed, ruffling his silence. "Robert, I'd like you to look at me and tell me what those things are."

"Why?"

"Because I'd like to feel appreciated."

"You are appreciated," he returned sternly. "There, I've said it."

"Look at me, Robert!"

He did, warily, then dropped his eyes to his lap and said, "I wish you to cover yourself."

"I have."

"Your whole self."

"No you don't. You love to look at my breasts. You told me once, so that's one, no two things—"

His skin reddened and fists clenched as he gritted, "Stop, Almodis."

"No," she pertly complained. "Why should I stop trying to be closer to you?"

"You try too hard."

"I don't understand 'too hard'. Are you saying I'm too brazen?"

"Not brazen," corrected Robert. "Flagrant better states it. You uncover too much, are never subtle, don't know when to be silent—"

"Then how do you wish me to be," she smugly intruded, "...like Edith?"

"Don't you dare mention her name!" he flared. "Especially not now!"

She softened to explain, "Robert, I don't mind if you still love her, I prefer it—"

He grew more rigid. "I said no more, Almodis. I demand you stop!"

"She is my friend," she babbled on, "and as such I don't feel jealous."

"Almodis!" His anger drove him to his feet, and he stated with forced calm, "It is clear that no matter what I ask of you, you refuse to obey. I will take my leave."

"No!" she cried out, grabbing a handful of his tunic's skirt. "Robert, don't leave! I regret my persistence and my flagrancy, and I will cover my breasts, if only you'll stay!"

Their wrangling woke the child. Adam scrunched his face into an enormous pout, then, beating at the sky, let out an enormous wail. They both rushed to help him. Almodis floundered into her robe, and Robert gathered up Adam, and held him away from Almodis' reach, suggesting with a grimace, "Get yourself dressed...I'll settle the boy."

Her madness and frustration flared; now he was accusing her of being an inept mother! "Let me have him, Robert! He is my son!"

"And as you so fervently claim, mine as well!" he parried. "You are not in a proper state to calm the child."

"How dare you!" she shrilled as she jerked her robe snug to her body and fiercely cinched it with a braided cord. "He's hungry...and *that* you can do nothing about."

"No he's not, he's just eaten. Go! You're only upsetting him further with your fussing. Go and walk off your temper."

Almodis' blood boiled again at his dismissing manner and wave. He spun away and paced, jiggling the boy, murmuring and soothing. She stood heaving and hissing, wanting to lob something, kick the rushes, rip the curtains from the bed. Her hands flew to her head as she surrendered to her rage and her Lord. She stormed from the chamber and stomped from one hallway to the next, unable to stop, too flustered to see reason; pages, squires, guards, and servants halted their tasks to dodge and gawk at their fascinating Lady, whose every word and gesture sent tongues aclucking. She escaped to the battlements, where the dark and cold slowed her rabid pace; she leant against the cut stone and gulped in breaths; her nails dug into ice that lined the crevasses, and her moist eyes searched the star cluttered sky. Perhaps her life wasn't as near perfect as she believed. But why? Because they'd argued? They were both easily agitated, as was their son. She recalled Robert's criticism, 'You try too hard.' But if she didn't try too hard, no one would listen to her, look at her, or talk to her! She had always received attention by being flagrant, that was her way. But it wasn't his way. She began to lose feeling in her bare toes, and decided to return inside and go—where?! She couldn't return to their chamber, not yet, she was still too harried. So she ambled aimlessly, or what she thought was aimlessly, till she found herself standing before Estrith's door, her fist raised to knock.

Estrith answered the light rapping, and asked with a tinge of panic, "My Lady?! Is something amiss? Do you need anything? Is there something wrong with Adam?!"

Finally, Almodis replied, "May I come in?"

"Of course, my Lady," Estrith said, holding open the door, and waving invitingly. "Please sit. Would you care for some honeyed milk or a cake?"

"No..." Almodis answered briskly as she sat on the meager bed and hugged her robe tighter to quell her discomfort. It helped a bit, and she stressed, "Don't let me stop your snack."

Estrith strove not to appear too inquisitive; subtlety worked best with the Lady Almodis. "Have you need of me, my Lady?"

"I'm not certain...Perhaps. I was strolling and the rushes stung my feet. I needed to sit and your room was near. Actually, the child woke and was fussing...Robert...I mean

Lord Robert is settling him and I decided to...Hell, Estrith!" Almodis shot up from the bed and barreled her way about the minuscule chamber, flailing, and grousing, "We fought and I left our chamber to walk off my rage!"

"And is it gone, my Lady?" Estrith gently wondered.

"Not entirely...I don't understand him, he can be so kind one moment, then fierce as a boar the next."

Estrith thought yet dared not speak, *Just like you.*

"I am fond of Robert," Almodis grumbled on, "I mean Lord Robert. He is generous to me and the child, and oft times affectionate, yet other times he blatantly ignores my wants, and acts cruel and domineering. And he's that way precisely when I'm feeling most giving."

"Most giving, my Lady?"

"As a wife should be to her husband."

"Oh, I see, my Lady."

Almodis sat heavily, sulked, and asked, "What am I doing wrong, Estrith?"

"I've never been married, my Lady, so I don't know if my advice would be fitting."

"Surely you must have coupled with a man or two?"

Estrith blushed apple red, wrung her hands, and stammered, "I've kept company with very few men, but I'm—"

"Then you're capable of guiding me," Almodis abruptly discerned. "You've also known Lord Robert longer than I have, and knew him when he resided with Edith. How was she when around him?"

"Of course," Estrith answered clumsily, "I never was privy to their...intimate moments, but they spent much time together, umh, doing other things as well."

"What other things are there?"

"Riding, hawking, visiting other vassals, outings with the children. They were the dearest of friends, as well as lovers. She was highly respected by every member of Lord Robert's household. Edith is tremendously strong-willed, and yet she knows when to yield."

"Yield?" puzzled Almodis.

"Yes, compromise. It seems to me that when around Edith, Robert, I mean Lord Robert, always felt...appreciated."

"Appreciated..." Almodis repeated pointedly. "He still loves her, Estrith."

"And always will."

"Not that I mind," Almodis was quick to clarify. "Yet I would like to improve my times with my husband. I'm weary of our disagreements."

"As is he. It's quite clear he's immensely fond of you, my Lady."

"Is he truly?" strained Almodis.

"I wouldn't lie to you."

"No you wouldn't," Almodis limply conceded.

"Don't order him to be with you," encouraged Estrith. "Let him come to *you*, tell you *his* wants. Be interested in him in different ways, include him in the business you conduct with the household, make it known you value his opinion. Tell him how grateful you are that he is a loving father. If you can gain his respect and trust, then he'll never believe any of the Bishop's or Lord William's lies or anyone else's lies about you."

"He trusted Edith, yet banished her nonetheless," reminded Almodis mordantly.

"At that time, for reasons none of us could understand, his brother's influence was all-powerful, as was his son's. But the guilt Robert suffers over that terrible time will keep them from ever stealing his soul again...I'll walk you to your chamber, my Lady, and take the child back here with me. You need time together, alone."

Almodis gently pried Adam from Robert's sleepy clutch and passed the dozing child to Estrith. She placed a kiss on his brow, whispered to Estrith an effusive, "I'm grateful," and watched with deep affection her servant and Adam leave. Then she looked to her husband; the creases between his brows were thick with worry and, she hoped, remorse. He moaned and shifted to his side. Slipping off his boots, Almodis blanketed him, then circled round to her side of the bed. She was about to remove her robe, but thought again—if he woke later, needy for her touch, she'd allow him to remove it.

*****

With a resounding thwack, the flat of the sword slammed against Simon's back. He crashed to the dirt on his belly and a quick flip revealed his rival poised to pounce. His knees jerked to his chin and feet rammed the soldier's chest, catapulting him into the air. The man hit the ground with a sickening crunch, and lay there awhile dazed. Simon flew up, hissing spit and wrath, his sword brandished, his posture steeled and deadly. His next contender struck. The vicious clashing of their swords shot sparks into the gray morn, and their groans and howls ruffled the beasts in their stalls. The downed sentry sprang back upon his feet and, fully restored, attacked again. A sharp kick to the belly of Simon's present battler distracted him while Simon launched into his next more arduous assault. After several dodged whacks, their swords stuck and scraped together, their bodies strained and shoved, their feet dug at the ground as they grunted and cursed in their savage quest to conquer. Simon sensed a surge in his rival's strength, and nimbly sprang sideways. The man lurched forward, stumbling to his defeat in the dirt. Simon loped a few feet ahead, then whirled and braced for a double onslaught. But in their frenzy to strike, his contenders collided and sent each other reeling. Once they'd regained their footing, their madness flamed hotter and they charged for Simon like raving bulls. Their advance injured Simon well before their weapons struck; a light-headed fatigue weakened his body and his mind. His sword fell heavily to his side as he sank to one knee and hung his head in surrender. He felt their looming heat, heard their heaving breaths; he lifted meek eyes to their mean ones and sighed, "I'm dead."

He raised his arms; they clasped a hand each and hoisted him up. Marc's arm circled and hugged his shoulders, and his gushed praise broke through his mask of anger, "That was magnificent, Simon! Especially the part where you sent Owain tripping into the dirt."

"Not magnificent enough," Owain darkly remarked, turning a glared smirk on Marc.

Marc swiftly checked Simon's response, which was a shrug and a faint, "He's correct." Simon wiped mud off his cheek with his sleeve, dragged his fingers through his sweat-dampened hair, and trudged dejectedly for the cottage.

"Why did you have to say it *that* way?" Marc grumbled lowly to Owain.

"How would you have me say it?" Owain answered as petulantly. "I won't lie to him."

"He needs encouragement as well as criticism."

"You handle the encouragement part just fine."

Marc snorted in exasperation, "I'll tend to the beasts. Are you planning to fish with us?"

"Fish?" asked Owain, slightly surprised.

"Yes, I mentioned it to you last evening, and you grunted. I don't know yet what your grunts mean."

"I suppose I'll go. Do you plan to take the coracle?" Owain asked with some trepidation.

"That's what they're used for."

"They are way too tiny, their circle shape makes no sense, and the wind could quickly blow them out to sea. They are far too dangerous. Who else is going?"

"Gruffydd, Cynan and Nia."

"What if they make trouble, being children and all?"

"They won't," said Marc irritably. "Are you going or not?"

"Ye...yes, I'll go. You might need help."

Marc wagged his head, caught up a pail by the door, and headed for the newly constructed and much larger stables. Owain watched till he'd disappeared, then dropped his uneasy gaze to Simon, slumped upon the doorstep, hands supporting his heavy head. Owain considered his earlier comment, and really didn't understand Marc's upset. He didn't believe in coddling, yet a tinge of regret tightened his chest, and he sagged down beside Simon, and muttered, "You worry too much."

Simon briefly looked up and snorted, "Do I?"

"Yes...If you're properly prepared, there's no need for worry."

"And am I properly prepared?" asked Simon.

Owain gracefully skirted the question, and answered instead, "Worry interferes with the joy of life."

Simon settled a perplexed gaze on Owain, and was about to blurt a sarcastic retort when he sighed a smile and mumbled, "And you're correct again. Will you go to the llys?"

"No...Marc wants me to go fishing."

Simon shuddered at the thought. "In this weather?"

"Why not? The water is smooth. The children are coming along, and he might need help."

"But it's so cold," whined Simon, chafing his hands and arms.

"No it isn't."

Simon knew better than to argue with Owain, for Owain loved arguing, and if Simon obliged him, they'd probably still be bickering come nightfall. Instead, he suggested with a wry grin, "Then...enjoy yourselves."

Owain nodded uncertainly and asked as Simon rose, "And what will you do?"

"Finish chores and entertain my wife."

"Your Lady owns great patience."

"That she does." Simon crossed his arms and, with a satisfied smirk, assessed, "Have you noticed, Owain, that we agree far more often these days?"

Owain returned his smirk. "I've noticed, and I am pleased."

"And we are also pleased," Simon stated indulgently, "and most grateful for your presence and care."

Simon detected a blush and an embarrassed quaver in Owain's reply, "I'll go to Marc now."

Simon nodded and ventured inside, where the warmth of the crackling fire and the fragrant scent of perfumed rushes and spices greeted him. He didn't go directly to the sleeping chamber, but stopped and sat at his table to brew up a tonic. He pried his bleary eyes wide and surveyed the many strewn clay jars and snatches of dried herbs. Quickly, he found his vial of mistletoe powder, poured oak beer into a cauldron, added two taps of powder, and two spoonfuls of honey, then left his seat to hook the pot's handle to a chain dangling over the central hearth. Simon sank down by its heat, waiting and reflecting over his hectic morning. It seemed forever had passed since dawn when he'd begun his doctoring rounds. Coughs, nausea, headaches, hemorrhage; he'd never known so many in the village ill, and felt fortunate he hadn't succumbed himself, for he needed to stay well and strong and alert...in case. Owain's wise words, 'If you're properly prepared, there's no need for worry', came to mind and Simon's frustration

277

swelled. He struggled so hard, yet achieved so little! And, he pondered with a long, quivering sigh, *What exactly am I preparing myself for—an assault, a kidnapping? From Henry, Odo, Will? Or perhaps all three will combine resources and manpower, and attack together. If so, what chance do we have for survival? Absolutely none*, he decided as he ladled the steaming beer into a tankard. His thoughts scattered and his aches brought to mind this morning's grueling practice. For a full two months, each day had included 'the squabbles' as Simon had taken to calling the mock battles. Then again, there was nothing mock about them, save the fact they hadn't yet run each other through. Most times, his rivals were played with expert vivacity by Owain and Marc, yet quite a few village men, and a number of capable women as well, had zealously joined in the frays. He prayed the exhaustive efforts were helping, for with all his other obligations, he grew wearier each day. If only he slept better. None of his potions though seemed able to cure his insomnia, and again Owain's astute comment, 'You worry too much,' echoed, causing Simon to admit its truth. *Yet how can I not worry? Be prepared? Prepared for what, from whom?* The circular wrangling pained his head and a rustling lurched his heart. He gasped upward into Owain's severe stare. "I wish you wouldn't do that," complained Simon, rising with effort.

"Do what?" asked Owain.

"Scare me. I thought you were helping Marc."

"He doesn't need any. What are you doing?" Owain leant over the cauldron and headily drank in the odoriferous steam.

"Warming Maura's tonic."

"My father brewed us the same each morning I was at home," said Owain.

"Oak beer? Truly?" Simon asked, amazed.

Owain nodded, and Simon ventured further, "How did he know the recipe? I was told the knowledge was sacred."

"It is...sacred," Owain said with mystery.

Simon waited but Owain offered no more, so he prodded, "So how did he acquire the knowledge?"

"Maura must have told you of my father's vocation."

"Yes...Seer to the Prince."

"He claimed to draw his power from our ancestors. He was a direct descendant of a Druid priestess."

"Was he?" Simon's eyes bulged and he begged, "Tell me more."

"Your lotions, tonics, and salves are all derived from ancient Druidic medicines," obliged Owain.

"I never knew. At Myddfai it was never said."

"Because the physicians there are loathe to admit their practice is *heathen sorcery*." Owain laughed sharply, and stoked Simon's curiosity further with the taunt, "Father also kept an altar in the oaks. It's still there...if needed. If you like, I'll show it to you when we visit my family's home." Owain left as noiselessly as he arrived. At times, Simon imagined him a forest elf who appeared and disappeared in a puff of smoke. After that terrible night two months past, Owain had abruptly moved in with them, pledging his eternal loyalty. They'd never disputed his guardianship; on the contrary, they'd heartily welcomed him, his wisdom, his strength, and his exceedingly odd ways. He was a puzzle of contradictions, shy and brash, garrulous and mute, passionate and aloof. Simon considered with affection what an integral part of their family he'd swiftly become, and sorting out the mystery of his many selves had taken on the enjoyment and intrigue of a game. And since he'd come to stay, he'd been appointed by Rhys and Sulien to serve as Pennaeth till Taredd's induction. After a fortnight of flailing, fuming, and curses, Owain had settled with tremulous aplomb into his temporary position, and now met regularly with the villagers to hear and attend to their complaints and troubles. Their disaffection for him had grudgingly waned over time, to the astonishing extent that some neighbors actually sought out his counsel—voluntarily.

Simon nudged the bedchamber door open and saw Maura still asleep, her posture coiled and tense, her expression careworn. His heart cracked to her distress, and he marveled at how adept she was at hiding her worries when awake. As he placed the tonic on the table beside the bed, he wondered what she dreamt, and shuddered to the memory of the weeks directly following Henry's attack. That terrible time had been fraught with horrific nightmares, both waking and sleeping, that not only threatened Maura's sanity, but her life, and that of their child's as well. After a month had passed, her mind grew calmer, as did the child; her fretting eased somewhat; and she'd readily reconciled herself to a state of prolonged inactivity. She spoke little about the incident, only that Henry had not succeeded with the true intent of his treachery. Yet Simon was certain that if Henry had succeeded in raping and murdering Maura, he couldn't have tortured her more.

Simon's craving for revenge ripped at his gut and weakened his knees. He strove to force it from his thoughts, but it never left completely, and its lurking burned. He needed her succoring embrace, her sweet assurance that all would be well, yet he couldn't wake her so selfishly. A tumbling movement on the floor by the bed stole his attention. A tiny fuzzy ball of black romped from behind the hanging quilt, stalking some imaginary foe. Following their bold leader came her three siblings, one orange, one white, and one a jumble of the other's colors. He smiled at the kittens, and remembered fondly when Owain had gifted them with the feline family. He'd claimed his Uncle Hywel was set on drowning the lot, and since they'd recently lost Pup, perhaps the kittens could help fill the void. Overfill the void better described the cats' antics; their mischief and affection had more than cheered their home and hearts. The orange one, christened Clyde by Maura, discovered the tip of Maura's braid and swiped at it furiously, finally catching hold and swinging. Simon tip-toed in a hurry over to the bed to stop Clyde before he woke Maura, but his flurried advance scattered the four. On hands and knees he scuttled about, trying futilely to collect the pride and deposit them outside.

Maura woke to the perplexing sight of a familiar backside. She pushed up slightly, and glanced down at her husband frantically pleading with the kittens to cooperate. She laughed an astonished laugh. "Simon, what are you doing?"

Without moving, Simon answered distractedly, "I'm trying to stop them from waking—" He sat back on his heels, and finished with an embarrassed smirk, "—you."

"That was very considerate," she praised, reaching out for him. He struggled up and helped her sit by plumping pillows behind her back, then sat himself and partook of a sweet good-morning kiss. "You look tired and cold," she observed. "Come join me?" Maura lifted the blanket enticingly. Simon stripped off his tunic, swatted dried mud from his braies, and hopped out of his boots. He clambered into the bed and, while he shifted and molded to her warmth, she wondered aloud, "And how did the squabbles go this morning?" Simon only shrugged and Maura worried, "Was it *that* bad?"

"They killed me...*three* times," muttered Simon with exasperation. "I don't know why I bother, it doesn't help, it only hurts." He rested his head upon her shoulder, and spread his palm over her belly. The child's stirrings lightened his upset, making him sigh through a thin smile and nestle nearer.

Maura thought it best not to press the battle issue further; instead, she rolled to her side and wrapped Simon in a sympathetic and taut hug, laced her fingers through his hair, and murmured, "I love this time best. When all the others are away and the three of us are here, wrapped cozily—together."

"Seven of us," Simon added, noticing an assault on their toes.

"Whatever...it's so special and..."

She quavered her last word; he knew her anguish and, easing slightly away, strove to cheer, "Maura...last night, I did some calculating, and discovered we've only three weeks left till Christmas!"

"Yes...and..." she prompted, arching an inquisitive brow.

"Well, considering the child's robust size and that she's due to appear around Christmas, I don't see why you can't...if you promise to take care—"

Maura didn't wait for his finish, she grabbed him in a suffocating hold, and burbled, "Oh Simon! I can get up! Are you saying I can get up and walk and run and—"

"Not run, not yet, and walk only short distances. I'm so sorry how you've suffered."

Suffered?" she scoffed. "Hardly...I've been sung to, read to, cooked for, entertained endlessly by our friends and our daughter, and loved so intensely by...you."

He swallowed his woe and beamed at the euphoria that now glittered her eyes and flushed her skin. A blissful moment lingered as she warmed his cheek with her palm and he fingered the two rings dangling from a chain round her neck—the Welsh band and his wedding band. A touch to his ring faltered his smile; she closed her hand over his, and begged, "Don't you dare think of him, don't let Henry ruin this moment, Simon. He will never again ruin a single moment of ours."

He nodded in assent, and found her embrace again. Exhaustion dragged him back to the pillows, and she joined him there, petting and encouraging, "Sleep now, my love. And when you wake, we'll walk together, as far as you deem safe...we'll walk."

Her words, soft as a lullaby, soothed his mind and he mumbled, "We'll be needing a name soon."

As he drifted off he wondered at the swiftness of her reply, "Elyn...We'll name her Elyn."

And she wondered as well. Where had the name come from? She knew no one named Elyn. But it didn't seem important, not when at last she was free to rejoin the world of the walking. Bliss drew bumps to her skin as she plotted their stroll. First to the beach to surprise Marc, Owain, and the children; then to the village to visit Sulien and Raythyen, Olwen and the baby. The baby...Maura smiled as Olwen's newest son appeared to her, plump, red-haired and cheeked, always smiling. He had been the one sparkle of brightness on the day of her tragedy. Marc and Gruffydd had been assisting Olwen in her move to her new cottage, when the baby, Morgan, decided to disrupt the proceedings. Marc had delivered the boy with Gruffydd and Olwen's helpful suggestions and, since that day, Olwen and Marc had taken to spending a good portion of their days together. And Maura hoped that in time, Olwen would replace Gael in his thoughts, and his heart as well, for when Gael came to call, which was rare, Maura sensed the smoldering of neglected desires. Neither had spoken much of their frustrations. Gael had taken to avoiding Owain as if he carried some contagion and, in turn, avoided them as well. Maura missed her sorely, but it seemed unfair to insist Owain leave simply so Gael could visit. To Maura, Gael's behavior verged on childish, and she desperately wanted to know the true cause of her peculiar remoteness. She'd left for Dinefwr a week past to wed Taredd, and now that Maura could walk, she decided to descend upon the llys as soon as Gael and Taredd were settled, take Gael off away from any distractions, discover the source of her troubles...and strive somehow to help.

Simon shifted nearer and Maura gazed plaintively upon his pristine expression. How desperately she loved him, and she was immensely thankful for his seemingly endless energy and devotion. He'd readily seen to all her needs and also to the villagers' health, but tended to the villagers early so he could be by her side all the while she was awake.

They'd grown closer since the fateful incident, something she'd not believed possible. And lately, his crippling guilt appeared to be easing somewhat. He smiled more, even laughed at times, yet his frequent brooding over their tenuous future continued to intrude on his sleep, his appetite, and his normally determined will. Perhaps now that she could stop being an invalid, his fretting would cease completely. And Henry—the wounds he'd inflicted still festered and would likely never fully mend. When flashes of his assault flickered, the face was different, for her heart could not wholly accept the fact that her staunch friend and cousin, who'd pledged eternal love and homage, had so vilely assaulted her. She shoved the memories, the sadness, and the worry from her mind, and focused again on her imminent deliverance from the bed, and also on the tiny black whiskered face staring at her from behind a wrinkle in the cover. She teasingly tickled her fingers over the quilt and Rose pounced, making Maura laugh and tickle more. As Maura stroked the kitten's blue-black belly and felt her vibrate with happiness, she thought of the cat's namesake, and felt a stabbing pang of yearning for her guardian's loving and vigilant presence.

*****

Owain glanced nervously up into a bland colored sky, dense with clouds going nowhere. He shivered and silently agreed with Simon—it was far too cold to be fishing. But the weather seemed to be having no debilitating effect on Marc or the children, who hung precariously over the edge of the woven cup of a boat. He shifted and peered with distaste into a pail, half filled with fish carcasses, then surreptitiously at Marc's handiwork. Marc cut a cord several feet long from a ball of hemp, then from a small cloth bag, he extracted a chicken feather. Deftly, he tied the feather to the string and the string to a stick, then passed the rod to Cynan. Cynan in turn stuck the feathered end into the water. Marc nonchalantly passed Owain a cord and a feather, and asked, "Could you make Gruffydd a new one?" Owain clumsily attempted to mimic what he'd just studied, except the cord kept slipping off the feather and, frustrated, he mumbled a curse. He sensed Marc's questioning gaze, and flushed a bit at his awkwardness. Marc reached out and kindly offered, "Here let me."

"No..." Owain flinched back and insisted. "I'll get it, my fingers are stiff from cold, that's all."

Marc nodded and swiftly strung a new rod for Nia, who accepted it with gushing enthusiasm. He noticed Owain still struggling with his feather and smiled as he realized, "You've never done this before, have you?"

Owain opened his mouth to argue, but shut it a moment to reconsider. Finally, he blurted, "And what's wrong with that?"

"Nothing...it's just that I thought with you living so near the sea, fishing would be something you knew a lot about."

"I've never lived near the sea. Well, I have since Rhys insisted I watch over Mynyw, but that wasn't my choice. You know I lived in the hills, you helped me build the house back up. We kept cattle."

Marc snorted and asked with a teasing air, "And what else have you never done?"

Owain dropped his eyes to the crinkled feather in his opening fist, and swiftly returned, "The same as you, I reckon."

Marc lowered his eyes as well, and cringed to the discomforting sensation which he experienced too often in Owain's presence, that somehow Owain knew exactly what he was thinking, feeling, and hiding. How could this man, ten years his senior, who'd lived such a varied and tumultuous life, be as innocent as he? He raised his guarded gaze, expecting a mocking look in return, and was relieved to find instead kindness and understanding in Owain's expression.

281

"Gael and Taredd are due to arrive any time now," said Owain, switching thoughts with a small grin.

"How do you know?" asked Marc.

"A messenger from Dinefwr arrived late last evening."

"Have you told Gruffydd?"

"Yes."

"What do you know of Taredd?"

"Not a lot, no one does."

"Doesn't Rhys?" asked Marc.

"I hope so. I don't trust Taredd."

"You don't trust many."

"It's safest that way," returned Owain.

Marc shrugged and took on a somber guise as he tied Gruffydd's rod. A shrill squeal made them both look up. "Nia's caught another one!" exclaimed Gruffydd. "A big one!"

She jerked her rod backward and the fish flew inside the boat, and flopped about till Marc thudded it hard with his fist. "That was wonderful, Nia!" he praised. "See if you can get us a bigger one."

Nia beamed with excitement, accepted another feather from Marc, tied it swiftly to her cord, and flung the string back into the water. Gruffydd flashed her a winning smile, and Cynan grumbled lowly to Gruffydd, "Why did *she* have to come?"

"Because she's my friend."

"I thought *I* was your friend."

"I can have more than one, can't I?"

"Yes...but not her."

"And why not?"

"She's a girl *and* my sister."

"So..." argued Gruffydd. "She can do anything you can do...most times better. She doesn't whine as much as you, and with your new brother here, she's probably feeling outnumbered. She can come with me anywhere. And if you don't like it, maybe you should stay home."

"Maybe I will!" flared Cynan.

"Good!" fired back Gruffydd.

Marc intervened, "What's wrong?"

"Cynan doesn't want Nia here," said Gruffydd.

Nia didn't seem to notice she had become a topic of contention. Her rapt attention was focused only on the sea and anything squirming within.

"Nia is welcome with us anytime, Cynan," said Marc mildly.

"See...I told you," snipped Gruffydd.

Cynan huffed in contempt and fiercely jiggled his rod, hoping to entice anything under the surface.

Owain looked in question to Marc, who quietly explained, "Cynan's often upset since Morgan arrived. I'm not certain why. His mother works hard to spend time with all her children. I know it sounds strange, but sometimes I feel he sees me as some sort of a rival. Olwen doesn't speak much of her late husband. Do you know what happened to him?"

Owain with a smirk provided, "He drank too much mead one moonless night and wandered off a cliff."

"Truly?"

"That's what is said," replied Owain. "The villagers say he was a selfish, lazy scoundrel, who practically kept Olwen a prisoner, and that since his long dive, she's never been happier."

"When did this happen?" asked Marc.

"Directly before Simon and Maura arrived. You care for Olwen?"

"Of course I do."

"I mean more than most."

Owain's abbreviated speech was often difficult to fathom and Marc wondered, "What?"

Owain grew impatient and blurted, "You are fond of her."

"Oh...Yes."

"But there's still Gael."

"Yes there's still Gael," Marc sadly conceded.

"And you won't attempt to interfere?" asked Owain, arching an eyebrow.

"No...not at all."

Owain hesitated his tribute, "She...she would have done well with you."

"Thank you, Owain," Marc answered with a tinge of astonishment. "I only wish she could have had the chance to pick me. And who are you fond of?"

"No one," Owain assuredly answered.

"Maura said you almost married."

"Almost. That was long past."

"And since then?"

"I've kept myself away from...people."

Marc stated dubiously, "You've been a commander of a huge army, and lived with a Prince who has a large household. How could you keep away from people?"

"It's simple. You don't let anyone know you're around, if they haven't a need to know. And when I was at Dinefwr or here at Mynyw, my mind was elsewhere."

"Where?"

Marc noticed a dreaminess in Owain's gaze as he reflected, "All sorts of places...Places I remember from my childhood, places I long to go to but have never been. And I've wasted too much time being angry...mostly at myself."

"For what?"

"My family's death."

"From what you've told me of that time," recalled Marc, "it couldn't have been your fault."

Owain couldn't mask his upset; it strained his face and his words, "But I left them...just because I was angry, I left them! If I'd stayed, I might have been able to help fight off...well at least I would have died with them. I've never understood why I was spared."

"Obviously," offered Marc, "God chose you to live, to carry on your family's pride, and make a family for yourself."

"A family? No...never."

"Why not?"

"I can't take that chance."

"What chance?"

"Of losing who I love, not again."

Marc couldn't conjure any advice for Owain's dilemma. He felt as torn himself, torn over his fondness for Gael, his budding affection for Olwen, his worry for his sister and his brother, and their child. He sighed with exasperation and fumbled with another feather.

Owain vaguely watched Marc's fingers while pondering this curious man sitting cross-legged opposite him, whom he'd come to know and respect as his friend and confessor. It was too easy to talk to Marc. Especially when Owain considered that during his long career as a soldier, he'd been trained to despise every bit of him; that as a Norman he had no heart, no soul, no conscience; that he knew only how to kill, efficiently, Saxons and Welsh and anyone else who wasn't of his privileged tribe. Owain prided himself on being an astute judge of character, a gift he'd inherited from his father. And always before, he'd been close to correct in his assumptions, but with this family he'd been horribly and dangerously wrong. And now he wondered whom else he might have misjudged. He shook from his doubts, and spoke brightly, "Your sister and Simon..."

"Yes?" prodded Marc.

"They've known each other awhile."

"A long while...over seventeen years now."

Owain's jaw dropped wide, then shut to echo incredulously, "Seventeen years?!"

"Maura and I were orphans in Simon's father's household. The three of us were separated at different times, but our bond stayed strong, and their's eventually grew to love. Did they tell you of their last separation?"

"No."

"I wasn't there and have only recently heard the tale myself. Five years past, they were forced apart, and their child Maura was carrying was murdered."

Owain swelled up huge to demand, "Who was responsible?!"

"Simon's father, Lord Robert, and Robert's legitimate son, Will. I suppose others had a hand in the tragedy, but I don't know who. Their union still threatens some members of our family...and that's what worries Simon and me, and no doubt Maura as well, that they'll discover where they are, and come to separate them...again."

"Who will come?"

"We don't know for certain," regretted Marc. "Not his father...Lord Robert has softened and acknowledges their marriage. But Robert's brother Odo was recently released from prison and—"

"Odo?" Owain's eyes smoldered with dark remembrance.

"Yes..."

"The late King's brother?"

"Yes."

"And a Bishop?"

"Yes, why?"

"I remember his name and the tale. After our commote in the north was threatened and we moved here, my mother told me of a Bishop, brother to the King, who'd come to north Wales on the ruse of a pilgrimage, and instead slaughtered dozens—men, women, children—he wasn't particular."

"We speak of the same man," said Marc. "He blames Simon entirely for his imprisonment, and I'm sure he now seeks revenge. Simon's half-brother, Will, is afraid of the bond between Simon and their father Robert. He wants any contender to his inheritance dead. So he may be the one to expect. And then there's Henry..."

Owain's revenge intruded, "I'll personally murder him before he steps one foot in this village!"

"Of that I've no doubt, for I'll be beside you, slicing him up as well. But, Owain, Henry has the resources to buy an army and thus make himself invincible. If he's intent on taking Maura for himself, he'll be back to get her and this time he'll make sure he succeeds."

"You hold little hope for their future, then?"

"I don't know what to think, neither does Simon or Maura. I suppose we should just concentrate on getting this child safely born."

A helpful notion flashed in Owain's mind. "My home! After the child comes, they'll hide in my home. You know how well hidden it is. No one but the villagers will know their location, and they'd never betray your family to anyone."

Marc gently corrected, "You mean our family, don't you?"

Owain beamed so that most of his teeth showed, then dropped his blush to his feather and began again his fidgeting.

Gruffydd's yell rocked the boat and its inhabitants, "Look! Marc, Owain, look to the shore!"

They knelt to see better. Two people, a man and a woman, one blond, one red-haired, stood on the sand waving. "It couldn't be!" exclaimed Marc.

"Is he mad?!" cried Owain. "Is she?!"

"No...not mad," figured Marc. "Maybe...maybe it's time for Maura to have this baby! Gruffydd, Cynan, Nia, pull in your rods. We're finished with fishing for this day. Take an oar, Owain. Let's hurry!"

Maura stopped waving to hang heavily on Simon's arm. Her other arm wrapped her belly and Simon fretted, "What is it, Maura?"

"Nothing...I think...I'm not use to being upright with this child. She's grown quite a bit...and my balance isn't what it was."

"You're not tired?"

"No...not at all." Excitement laced its way through her burbling, "I'd like to spend the remainder of the day walking and visiting in the commote, then cook the supper and see to the beasts, and then if we don't fall directly asleep, perhaps we can go off somewhere, so we won't bother anyone, perhaps the stable and love with the abandon we used to know before..."

Simon laughed and warned, "We'll see...You mustn't rush everything or you'll find yourself a prisoner to the bed again."

"I wouldn't mind so much if you were a prisoner with me."

"Yes you would."

"I suppose you're right. But I can be up more, when we get home, can't I, Simon?"

"As long as you don't tire yourself."

"I won't. It looks as though they're headed back. I guess we surprised them."

"More likely panicked them," said Simon.

Their fingers wove tightly together, and their lips and cheeks nuzzled as Maura murmured, "I so missed standing beside you."

"Me too," whispered Simon.

A wave of frigid water soaked through their soft boots, and nipped at their toes, making them leap back with exclamations. The boat stuck on the sand and its sailors spilled out. Owain and Marc rushed for Simon and Maura, while Nia and Cynan dragged the boat further onto shore, and Gruffydd grabbed the pail and raced after Owain and Marc. Marc was first to greet the couple, breathlessly yelling, "Maura! Simon! Is...is it time?!"

"Time for what?" she calmly responded.

"The baby!" croaked Owain.

"Oh!" She laughed and looked to Simon. "I don't think so, do you Simon?"

"I pray not."

"Then why are you up?" asked Gruffydd.

"I got tired of feeling jealous of all the fun everyone else was having."

"But...is it safe?" fretted Owain.

"We believe so," said Simon. "And how was the fishing?"

285

Gruffydd victoriously wielded the pail. "It's practically full! Nia caught the most."

"Good for you, Nia!" praised Simon, ruffling her hair as she hugged his waist.

"We'll cook a celebratory supper this night!" Maura joyously declared. "But first, who would like to join our walk to the commote?"

All exuberantly agreed. They pulled the coracle up into the grass and trod lightly from the beach and onto the path that bypassed the plateau and led directly to the one road entering the village. Marc took the pail from Gruffydd, who dashed after the other children to play a chasing game. "My mam's due home," he cried over his shoulder. "Maybe she'll be there!"

Maura looked expectantly to Marc. "Will she be?"

"I've heard nothing...It's Owain who knows."

"Owain?"

"She may," Owain muttered.

"Well *I* hope it's true." Maura wondered at both men's nebulous expressions.

Only Simon seemed to share her cheer as he spouted, "As do I. I've missed the Lady Gael greatly. Owain," Simon asked, "how do you feel Taredd will fare with the villagers?"

"Not well...in the beginning. They're a suspicious lot."

"And as a father," Maura added. "Will he treat Gruffydd kindly?"

"I don't know Taredd well enough to predict. But I wouldn't worry about the lad. He'll never need for a father."

Maura thought on the veracity of Owain's reply. All the men she walked with Gruffydd idolized, and rightly so.

The adults continued their animated chatter into town. Gruffydd broke from his friends and sprinted ahead to his cottage. He emerged shortly sporting a long frown. "It's still empty...Are you sure they said soon, Owain?"

Owain joined Gruffydd at the hut's gate. "The weather may have slowed them. We'll fill the time by moving your beasts to the llys' stables."

Gruffydd brightened and soberly suggested, "Yes...and move my carvings as well, but some are easily broken, so we need to go slow."

As Maura, Simon, and Marc watched the two disappear into the hut, each admitted privately, Marc more cautiously than the others, that Gael may have made a terrible mistake in her choice of a husband. Yet they were also certain that Gael, no matter the dire consequences, would not easily admit to such an error.

They walked on toward Olwen's hut, Nia and Cynan following hand-in-hand. Villagers on the way looked twice at the startling sight of Maura happy and snug between Simon and Marc. They hastened to join their stroll, welcoming her with hugs and congratulations. And as Maura reveled in their warm affection she at last felt— belonging.

*****

Almodis swooned to moist kisses creeping their way down her neck; she stirred and quivered as Robert's grip firmed round her hips, easing her robe away and drawing her nearer. The heat of their skin melding and his deft stroking never failed to rouse her fully, and she felt her desire flare to his breathy confession, "I like how you sting me, with touch and tongue, the envious stares I get when you're at my arm, that no one can predict what you'll say or do...and you make me, ancient as I am, feel young and wanted. I like how you can seduce me with merely a glance, a word, a sweep of your skirt, and that you're far more intelligent and infinitely more exciting than anyone else I'm presently surrounded by. I love how you dote on our child, and sometimes on me. I'm sorry for our fight. May we be friends again?"

"Oh...yes..." she sighed with ecstasy and welcomed his body over hers, pressing her into the down, searching, searing. Her thighs parted and hips rose to accept him inside her belly, while the rest of her encircled him; legs locking him astride, hands kneading the long taut muscles of his back, roaming lower to cup his flanks and urge him deeper. They moved together in a lengthy, slow and sumptuous dance. She stayed pliant and let him determine where their passion would take them. He wouldn't be hurried, and for that, she was thankful and also for his astounding endurance. He spoke little during their unions, so she kept silent as well, till her pleasure peaked and she couldn't quiet her moan.

It was rare that they looked on each other, for their intimacies usually occurred during the darkest part of night. The light of early morn snuck its way between the closed shutters, illuminating the beauty of their oneness. And when their eyes met, the pale, piercing intensity of his gaze humbled her, creating an odd and wondrous sensation that fluttered her heart and swept her tighter in his clutch.

His shuddering done, he kept her close, playing awkwardly with her mussed hair. He dreaded the slim, appeasing smile that always preceded her pulling away and prayed it wouldn't happen, that she'd stay near, for this time she'd seemed somehow different, less insistent, less selfish.

Nestled in his hold, Almodis waited for the cold emptiness to attack, pry her from his grip, and turn her to ice. Yet seeing him this way, his gaze so sincere, so needy, and she was certain that he saw only her—not someone else he'd rather lie with—only her, she stayed in his clutch. She reached to stroke his cheek; he swiftly responded to her tender gesture by guiding her face to his. Their lips gently joined, not in a manner to stir more passion, but perhaps, they both hoped, to sow a little love. Radiant with warmth, Almodis broke their kiss just an instant to murmur, "And what I like best about you, my most gracious Lord, is—I needn't pretend I care for you."

A while later, she lay propped up on an elbow, and watched admiringly as he sluggishly dressed. "And what shall we do today?" she asked with an enthused lightness.

"I thought you had further preparations to tend to for the feast."

"Everything is mostly done. I'll oversee the cooking, but not till later. If the weather is conciliatory, why don't we take a stroll with Adam and Estrith through the village?"

"Why would we want to do that?" he asked, a tad suspicious.

"For no specific reason...Perhaps we'll spread a bit of cheer, and I'll show such pride at having you on my arm."

He beamed, then tensed and focused on a rumbling at the door. Almodis jerked to the commotion and snatched up her robe, covering herself an instant before the door flung wide, and in barged Adela, rouged and raving, "Let me in, you sniveling pukes!"

Benjamin tumbled in at her heels, swiping out in vain to slow her advance. Robert gestured for both of them to halt, and Benjamin sank to one knee and blubbered, "Forgive me, my Lord. I tried to keep her out."

"Uncle, banish this grub!" Adela hurled a sneer at Benjamin, then her disgust shifted to Almodis. Her cheeks colored darker as she gasped and loudly admonished, "Uncle Robert...I'm shocked! How could you, at your age and with your wife recently delivered, bring this shameless tramp into your bed? I'll find your lady, and alert her at once to your foulness and perversity—"

"Adela...quiet!" commanded Robert. "Benjamin go and find Adam. I expect he's hungry." Benjamin hesitantly obeyed. Almodis lay back, exuding smugness, as Robert clumsily muttered, "A...Adela, may I present, my wife, the Lady Almodis. Almodis, this is my niece, Adela, Countess of Blois."

Almodis reached out a limp hand and breathed, "I couldn't be more charmed..."

Adela tried but couldn't quiet her embarrassment. "I'm so sorry, Uncle...Almodis. I thought...I didn't realize." Finally, her stuttering ended, and she pulled her huge self taller and stringently relayed, "I'm charmed as well, my Lady, but I must delay our introduction to speak alone with your husband. It is a matter of utmost importance, Uncle."

"I keep nothing from my wife, Adela," said Robert. "Speak freely."

"No," Adela countered. "On account of the delicacy of the subject, I must insist on privacy. You needn't rise Almodis...We can speak elsewhere, Uncle."

Robert looked to Almodis, received a smile, a shrug, and the whispered assurance, "We can stroll later, Robert. Go pacify her before she ruptures something." He yielded to her wisdom, and waved Adela toward the door.

There, they were met by Estrith and the boy. Adela turned painfully mushy, effusing compliments, which made Robert bristle, "Adela, you can play with Adam later. You mentioned the matter was of utmost importance."

"That it is, my Lord," she conceded with a humph. "Indeed it is!"

*****

CHAPTER SEVENTEEN - COMPLICATIONS

"𝕹ow that you have me *alone*...Adela, please explain your rude and obnoxious behavior!" Robert stood indignantly erect at the center of the dais, supported on rigid arms, and sporting an incensed expression.

"Un...Uncle Robert," Adela gibbered from her spot opposite, "surely you don't believe I purposely slandered your good wife...It's just rather late still to be abed, so I supposed you were indulging in some sort of sordid rendezvous."

"I wasn't and never have indulged in any sort of sordid rendezvous."

"I beg to disagree, my Lord. You dallied with that Saxon whore for—"

"Adela!" Robert's fist pounded the table, and his bellow ruffled the rafter birds from their nests. "If you dare utter one more word criticizing my private affairs, you will find yourself locked outside these castle walls forever. My patience wears thin, my Lady, so speak only on the matter you alluded to in my chamber, and be brief."

"Brief..." Adela shrank before her uncle's ire, yet as she mentally gathered the facts to be presented regarding Henry and Maura, her wrath again ballooned her already formidable figure. "It's about Henry!" she spat. "Henry and Maura!"

"Henry...your brother, and Maura...my ward?"

"Yes..." She paused and feigned feebleness. "Uncle, may I sit and have some wine? I'm afraid my upset concerning my brother's doings will injure my health and that of my child."

Robert's posture and eyes softened as he swung his arm toward the seat flanking his own. He clapped and barked, "Thomas!"

The boy sprinted from the direction of the Lord's chamber and, before he could bow or ask for instructions, Robert muttered, "Bring wine and a pillow for the Lady."

Thomas completed his bow and disappeared to return quickly, juggling a tankard, two cups, and a pillow stuck up under his arm. Robert extracted the items from Thomas' fumbling rasp, set the pillow on the chair, and supported Adela's elbow as she sank into it with a look of sublime relief. Robert perched himself on the edge of his seat, passed her a cup of wine, and assured, "My physician is available if you're in need of his services." Then he added trepidly, "How soon is the child due?"

Adela shrugged. "Don't you worry yourself about this child, Uncle. He won't arrive till I command him to. And I do apologize for my earlier comment. At times I can't control my disgust for the Saxon branch of your family."

"You've made your disgust for my son, Simon, and his mother adequately clear, Adela."

She imbibed her entire goblet of wine in three gulps, thrust out her cup for refilling, and sighed, "Yes...I'm feeling much fortified. And you, Uncle, may I say that you are looking quite fit? Marriage obviously has been kind to you."

"Thank you, Adela," he interrupted stiffly, cringing at her leer. He hated people who spewed incessant drivel just to listen to themselves. And Adela was champion of the long-winded, always gushing false compliments, derision, and mock rage. Yet she had mentioned Maura, and he needed to know why. "Adela, you spoke of Maura. Do you know where she is?"

"He didn't confess her location."

"He meaning Henry?" asked Robert.

"Yes." She threw back more wine, the effect of which exaggerated her gestures and emboldened her tongue. "That putrid slime of a rake. I'm surprised that he hasn't decayed from the thousands of diseased whores he's rutted with, and he has the audacity to act the innocent babe, never responsible for his crimes—"

"Crimes?! What crimes?"

"Besides polluting the honorable essence of our family, his crimes against Maura," she emphasized, surprised he hadn't comprehended her every word.

"What crimes against Maura?!" demanded Robert with an impatient glare.

"Assault, attempted rape, and kidnapping."

He shot up and repeated aghast, "Rape?!" then stuttered, "Sure...surely you heard wrong. When and where did he confess this?"

"At Caen, in Cecily's cell. I was listening outside the keyhole."

"Then you can't be certain," Robert swiftly contested.

"Oh yes, I am *very* certain, Uncle, for, after I'd kicked him out of her chamber, Cecily confirmed every sin that he blabbed, or better put—boasted to. She banished him forever from her house, as I will do, and you should as well."

"My ward allegedly married Simon," Robert stated pensively, trying desperately to temper his rising upset. "I don't know where they are hiding, but I'm positive it is not in Normandy. How could Henry—"

"He visited them," she cut in, "...wherever...and he did spout something about Maura and her mongrel being content." Adela paused for effect, then added with an accusing air, "He also mentioned her pregnancy."

Robert's head swam with confusion and dread. Dizziness dropped him back into his seat, and his head into his hands. When at last he looked up he spoke deliberately, praying his niece would follow his example, "At Caen, you overheard Henry's closeted confession to your sister that he had assaulted, and attempted to rape and kidnap my former ward and now pregnant daughter-in-law, Maura."

Her confident speech wilted to a slur, "That is pre...pre...cise...Oh Hell, yes that's what he said!"

"Where is Henry now?"

"I...I don't know, but my spies are afoot, and have been instructed to return any knowledge of his whereabouts, or better—Henry himself...here. Uncle, you are no doubt aware of the punishment for the crime of rape."

"You said attempted rape," Robert limply defended.

"What's the difference?" she scoffed in a huff. "Maura was still violated, and she is, well once was, my dearest friend. I'll never understand how she could have chosen to be with that slatternly half-breed you begot—"

Robert pressed his palms together and almost whined, "Adela, *please*! Are you actually suggesting that I exact the punishment of castration on your brother?"

"Who better to exact it? You *are* Maura's Liege."

"Was her Liege," he clarified.

"Uncle Robert..." Adela condescended, "if you get weak-kneed about this matter, I will have to raise up my army and avenge Maura's virtue on my own, and in my present condition that will prove to be a horrendous undertaking."

After a bracing gulp of claret, Robert stressed, "I won't promise you his genitals, not till I've spoken to him myself. Then, and only then, will I make judgment."

But Adela knew the exact remark to nudge him into action, "He believes he may have hurt or killed the child she carries."

Wine misted the air and dribbled down his chin as he spat, "You find him and drag him before me, and I will uncover the truth!" His temper ebbed as he wiped his chin and curiously regarded the claret left in the bottom of his cup. "When I last saw Henry and Maura together, he acted quite sweet to her...It was clear they were close. I find it difficult to believe that he would do something so vile."

"Henry's not above vile," sneered Adela. "He's sunk far, far below it. I really can't conjure up a word that accurately describes his foulness. And to think he's constantly spawning new monsters whenever he beds down with another—well...the thought makes me want to vomit. My men will find him and they'll bring him here. If you will allow me the comfort of your home till the scum arrives—"

"Of course, of course. Almodis will enjoy your presence." He noticed her eyelids drooping and her head tilting toward the table, and supposed he should suggest that she rest. Before he dismissed her, though, he had to make one final request. "Adela swear that you will not mention any details of our discourse with my Lady. Swear to this!"

"Why, Uncle?" she mumbled.

"Because she is extremely fond of Maura and Simon, and if she hears that either has been purposely harmed...I can't predict her reaction, only that it is sure to be explosive. I will tell her at the proper time and place. Swear you'll keep silent!"

His intensity humbled her and she staunchly agreed, "I swear, Uncle. I swear."

"Then please follow Thomas." Robert clapped and the boy popped up from his seat by the leg of Robert's chair. "He will take you to a suitable chamber where you can rest. We plan a feast for this night, and you are welcome to join us." Robert assisted Adela up, and for a tense moment, he wasn't convinced that Thomas could support the Lady should she lose her step. Yet though he wobbled a bit, Thomas stood strong under her grip and guided her across the hall and out the doors. All the while Adela never ceased her prattling.

The instant Robert was certain Adela was gone, he strode with great urgency to his stables, saddled his steed on his own, and took off in a rousing gallop to anywhere.

*****

"I can't..." shuddered Simon, peering with trepidation into the frigid waters of the communal washing tub, standing at the rear of the llys.

"You have to," returned Owain in a bolder and somewhat accusatory tone. "You stink."

"Well so do you!" Simon shot back. "And your body's used to this sort of shock. Mine's not and, well, I might freeze to the point of things breaking off, and the things that might break off, I'm mighty fond of...I won't...I can't...*Please* don't make me!"

"It's our own fault."

"No it isn't, it's your uncle's fault!" retorted Simon. "He's certainly a sadistic thug."

"What does that mean?"

"He takes great delight in torturing innocent people and small animals."

"That he does. Come," sighed Owain, peeling off his soiled tunic and breeches. "Let's get this done."

To Simon's urging, "You go first," Owain cast a surreptitious eye round the tight circle of lit torches that illuminated the tub, and satisfied that Simon and Hywel were the only humans near, he vaulted the wall. His shrill howl of agony rumbled the still of the early evening. Dogs yowled in sympathy and Simon bolted; but he couldn't run far. At the ominous sight of Hywel's huge boots, he stopped short, and raised humble eyes and a filthy face to plead, "Please, Hywel...torture me some other way!"

Hywel pointed rigidly at the tub and grunted, "In...now!"

Simon swallowed, wilted in surrender, and dragged himself back to the tub. Owain looked bluish, and failed to convince through chattering teeth, "It gets warmer the longer you're in." Simon cringed as he disrobed, snatched up a hunk of soap, swung one leg over the wall, and paused to Owain's off-handed comment, "The last time I did this...not wash...but wash in a communal tub, it was at Dinefwr. Someone spied on me."

And Simon foolishly remarked, "I know, she told me."

Simon felt heat rise from the water as Owain rose up, his fury swelling huge waves that slapped over Simon's skin and cascaded over the wall. He howled his shock and leapt backwards to Owain's thundered, "She what?!"

"Now, Owain...calm yourself...I don't mean to imply that we gossiped about your..."

Simon wisely shut his mouth and retreated further as Owain scrambled over the wall, his expression and command murderous, "You'll tell me what she said!"

"I can't tell you that! It's a secret."

"Not for long!" cried Owain. His feet hit the ground at a run.

Simon sprinted for his life, squalling to Hywel, "Save me!"

Hywel shook his head in exasperation, and followed at a trot, grumbling, "They won't get free that easily."

Maura left the llys, descended four steps, and plopped her cumbersome self down by Gruffydd. She followed his intense stare down the road and offered, "Gruffydd, it's getting too dark to see. Why don't you come inside where it's warmer? She will come and watching is not going to make it happen any faster."

"I know," he sadly sighed.

She sensed there was more than his mother's lateness upsetting him. "What else troubles you? Is it Taredd?"

"No...not really," he answered vaguely. "It's Cynan. He seems different...mad, most times at me. I don't know why."

"Have you asked him?"

"He says there's nothing wrong. He's mean to Marc and that makes me mad. Why can't he see how lucky he is?"

"Lucky how?"

"To have Marc courting his mam. I'd do anything to have—" He stopped and his expression sagged lower.

Maura nodded knowingly. "Marc will always be near for you *and* your mam. Of that you can be certain." Her arm circled his shoulders, and with a quick hug, she strove to cheer. "What fun we had after arriving here."

Gruffydd broke a full smile, and asked secretly, "Who threw the fish that hit Hywel?"

"Marc did."

"I thought so...but why didn't Hywel punish him?"

"He didn't see him throw it, and Marc has always had the talent to act the innocent. Hywel only caught Simon and Owain fish-handed."

"You had one too."

"I don't think he can pick me up."

Gruffydd laughed at Maura's answer and also at the buoyant memory of Hywel, with Simon held captive across one of his shoulders and Owain slung across the other, striding to and dumping them in a mountain of manure. He then forked more over them till they were completely buried in the stinking muck.

Maura snapped in alertness to what she thought was a scream emanating from up the road, toward the cliffs. She heard nothing more and tempted with a shiver, "If you come inside, I'll play dice with you."

Gruffydd beamed and stood. "Yes...And I'll beat you this time...Then we can go and make fun of Simon and Owain, they hate that...And Maura, now that you're up, could we start shooting arrows again?"

"I don't see why not," she answered with profound affection.

Simon felt Owain's breath on his neck and knew death was imminent. But instead of hands on his throat, Simon heard Owain's panted warning, "He's gaining on us. Run back to the tub. We're safe in there...He hates cold!"

Both increased their speed as they circled round the back of the village, luring dogs from their shelters and gawkers out of their huts, yelping and roaring with laughter at the outrageous sight of a puffing giant in deadly pursuit of two naked runners.

Gael guided her horse through the gate to Mynyw's commote and sighed a weary yet happy sigh. Home at last, to see her son, her friends, and...others, and begin her new existence—well not entirely new—as wife of the Pennaeth. But where was her husband? Perhaps he was waiting for her at the llys? The idea didn't help dispel the ambivalence she felt for Taredd. She looked ahead to Rhys; his slumped posture belied exhaustion, for they'd traveled the entire day with only one respite. And she glanced backward to her sister, Ella, looking as lost and flighty as when they'd started their journey, and still carrying on her odd chattering that was meant for no one and had little meaning.

The horses leading the troop shied to a sharp yell and a rumbling disturbance by the side of the road. Simon and Owain, never breaking their frantic pace, dashed dangerously close to the beasts and across the road, with Hywel bustling behind.

Rhys stuttered aghast, "What in the Gods'—Stop! I command you to—" But he commanded no one; the wild ones had vanished. Gael spurred her steed to Rhys' side, and smiled at his grousing, "Who were they?! I'll have them cuffed for impudence, endangering their ruler, and...exposure...and—"

"Owain, and Simon, and Hywel, Owain's uncle," Gael intruded with a mysterious smirk.

"How can you know that?" pressed Rhys. "It's too dark to see faces."

"I didn't need to see faces," teased Gael. She rode on, leaving Rhys to ponder her curious observation.

A few feet from the tub, Owain risked a dive, praying vehemently he'd clear the wall. Simon followed his example and as they splashed, their combined wails roused the Prince's party's concern, prompting them to canter the remaining distance to the llys.

The shock of cold, and Hywel's ferocious yet futile swiping brought Simon and Owain to hysterics. They taunted and splashed their adversary, till Owain grew glumly silent. Simon stopped his hooting and asked, "Owain what's wrong?"

"I just thought...eventually, we'll have to get out." The dreadful notion and Hywel's evil snicker quieted Simon as well; with furrowed brow, he searched absently beneath the water's surface for the soap, and once he'd caught it, began scrubbing. Owain, wide-eyed and trembling, waited for the soap while watching his uncle lumber into the llys. In a quaver, he hoped, "Can we kill Marc when we get out?"

"His death is clearly warranted," mumbled Simon through bubbles.

Gael was first to enter the llys, but no one inside seemed to notice. All were keenly engaged in chores aimed at readying the llys for the wedding party's arrival. The heavenly aroma of baking fish and bread teased Gael's belly, and the sight of a woman, her back to Gael, and her long plaits resembling Maura's, quickened her heart. The woman didn't look pregnant, not from behind, and Gael lunged forward, crying out, "Maura, is it you?!"

Maura spun with a gasp; her shock quickly glowed to joy and her delighted cry, "Gael!" turned everyone's heads.

Gruffydd beat all to her hug. Gael knelt to firm their grip; tears tumbled from their eyes, and they were ecstatically quiet. Finally, they parted slightly and Gael sniffed, "I've missed you so."

"And I've missed you," Gruffydd said, swabbing his damp cheeks with his sleeve.

"Have you behaved yourself?" she asked.

"I think so..." he peered shyly beyond her shoulder for Taredd. He noticed only Rhys climbing the stairs, and at his rear came someone familiar and friendly. "Aunt Ella!" he burst to his mam. "Aunt Ella's come!"

"Yes...and she's eager to give you a hug. Go and greet her." Gruffydd hurried to obey, and Gael rose and gladly stepped into Maura's embrace, exclaiming, "You're up, still pregnant, and looking radiant! I suppose this means your physician has given his permission for this child to be born."

"He has!" beamed Maura. They parted and clutched hands a long comfortable moment, sharing warm smiles, then Maura spouted, "Where's your husband?"

"I'm wondering that myself," snorted Gael, then she linked her arm in Maura's, led her away from the door, and dismissed her question with excited chatter. "Who's cooking? Raythyen I hope. I'm famished and haven't eaten since mid-morning. Have there been many disasters since I've been gone? It seems hundreds of years doesn't it?"

Rhys brushed past them, fretting loudly, "What mayhem is going on outside?! We heard the screams as we approached."

"It's only Simon and Owain playing in the tub," Maura said.

Rhys looked muddled, wagged his head, and vigorously repeated, "Owain playing? Never! I must witness this for myself." He paused, peered quizzically at Maura, and noticed, "You're up. I'm pleased," and to Gael, remarked askance, "And so...you were correct in your identification. You'll tell me later how you knew."

Gael looked smug; Maura just looked bewildered, and as Gael swung her round to meet her sister, Maura felt more so, for she did not recognize the near skeletal, unkempt creature standing before them as Gael's sister.

"Ella...Mam, can I go with Rhys?" Gruffydd pleaded, jiggling Ella's hand in anticipation.

Gael easily answered, "Yes...But don't get wet, and if they're cursing, don't listen."

"I won't!" he promised and darted off.

"Maura...you remember Ella?"

"Of course, I remember." Maura smiled and stepped forward, her hand extended.

Ella retreated a step and Gael spoke to her, softly and precisely as if she were younger than Gruffydd. "It's only Maura. You may take her hand."

Ella swept a tightly coiled lock of chestnut hair from her dull green eyes; she raised an expression, ashen and leery, and limply took Maura's hand.

"It's wonderful you could visit your sister and our village," said Maura.

"She's not visiting," Gael interceded. "She's here permanently, but I'll tell you why later."

As if scalded, Ella jerked from Maura's touch, slouched, and hid again beneath her hair.

"I'll be with you shortly, Maura," said Gael as she steered her sister to a nearby bench, and whispered briefly. After receiving a half nod, Gael returned warily to Maura's side. "I don't know what to do with her."

"What's happened?" worried Maura. "I remember her being so lively, not always happy, but very talkative."

"Rhys sent her here out of concern, not as punishment. Everyone believed her gone, but she wandered into the llys at Dinefwr late one night, disheveled and starving, and since that time she's become like a recluse, not carrying out her tasks, refusing to eat. Rhys fears that while she's in this strange state, some of his unscrupulous soldiers may try to take advantage of her. I'm hoping Simon will be able to find out what's wrong...I'm mostly afraid she's been hurt, but I found no visible bruises. There still might be damage inside. Gruffydd has always had a livening effect on Ella. Maybe he can return her to us, or at least get her to confess what's happened."

"Simon...and the rest of us will do all we can to help her."

"I'm grateful, Maura, but I'm also dying to know, when did you finally leave your bed?"

"Just this morning."

"And you're feeling?"

"Wonderfully well." Maura ran her hands lovingly over her belly and gushed on, "and she's been so quiet and still..." Her puzzled look returned and she interrupted herself to ask, "Gael, what's happened to your husband? You *did* marry?"

Gael sank with a loud sigh of exhaustion onto a nearby chair, cast a furtive glance at her sister, then turned back to answer, "Yes, and we were part-way through the feast when a messenger arrived to say that there's trouble with the three brothers who rule Powys erupting on the north-east border of Dehuebarth and Powys. Despite Rhys' objections, Taredd volunteered to go and see to the problem. He promised to return quickly, but after three days of waiting, I decided I couldn't be away from Gruffydd any longer. Rhys agreed and sent word north to Taredd to meet us here and also, if possible, to bring one of the brothers with him for mediation. I expect since you're up, he'll be discussing the matter with you."

"For my intervention?"

"Indeed."

"Oh...I don't know," said Maura. "I don't think Simon would approve, not after what happened last time."

"And I wouldn't blame him."

"But the Powys brothers aren't Norman."

"That's no guarantee they'll act civilized, Maura. I'm certain Simon will allow *you* the final decision."

"Speaking of Simon," said Maura, searching the room. "I wonder what's happened to him and Owain. I hope they're not still in that tub. They'll be frozen stiff."

"Where's Marc?" Gael asked distractedly.

"He's gone to fetch them clean clothing."

"Why was Hywel chasing them?"

"It's a long and very silly story," warned Maura.

Gael glimpsed her sister seemingly happy, talking to her fingers, and implored, "Then please tell me every bit of it...I desperately need to laugh."

While Rhys railed interminably about behavior not befitting members of his commote and army, Simon and Owain stood outside the tub, chastened and miserable, waiting for clothes. Gruffydd crouched bug-eyed nearby, astonished that grown men were being scolded. Marc arrived and, noting Simon and Owain's snarling, approached charily. Owain, intent on pitching Marc into the tub, lunged to rip the garments out of his arms, then spotted his whistle resting neatly atop a shirt. He paused, glared, and gritted, "I can't kill him, he's brought my whistle."

And to Simon's chagrin, he noticed Marc had chosen his favorite suit of clothing, and added with a wicked smirk, "He always knows the exact nicety to perform to melt his executioners' hearts. That's the only reason he still lives."

Marc pulled a simper, turned on his heels, and strode smoothly away.

"I'll get him later," Simon gloated to Owain. "He'll not know when or where."

"You'll bungle it."

"I appreciate your support," griped Simon.

"You always bungle your revenge," stressed Owain. "When you're about to strike, you start laughing..."

They bickered incessantly while dressing, and kept on till they encountered Hywel blocking the rear door to the llys. As if rehearsed, they both slumped in humble postures and Simon declared dutifully, "We suffered sufficiently, Hywel."

Owain added, "And will never throw fish again."

"Particularly when you are around," finished Simon.

A satisfied grin took Hywel away and, following him up the stairs, Owain nudged Simon. "Well?"

"Well what?"

"What did she say about me?"

"I swore I wouldn't tell. If it's so damned important, ask her yourself."

"I couldn't," Owain answered, appalled.

"Why not?"

"She might say something I don't like."

"That's something you need to become accustomed to," Simon advised and hurried inside.

Recognizing Gael's voice, Owain hesitated near the door. He didn't want to see her; he never knew what to say to her. It was clear she still hated him. He didn't dislike her anymore and had tried to act kindly, but she hadn't or didn't want to notice his changing. Recalling the episode outside the tub at Dinefwr had upturned all the shame, and uncertainty, and he considered retreating to Simon and Maura's cottage. Instead, he fought for and mustered the guile to straighten and glide into the main hall of the llys. Simon, Marc, Maura, and Gael were gathered in a taut circle, hugging and laughing. He envied their easy way and wondered if he'd ever feel confident enough to act the same. His restive gaze lit upon a thin and wispy waif sitting alone across the room. He studied her a thoughtful moment. His expression briefly lit with recognition—Gael's sister; then darkened with a not so pleasant memory—she'd obviously been found, but under what circumstances? She looked so sickly that the suspicion he'd once held for her softened to pity, and he started toward her with no thought as to what to say. She cried out at his advance and leapt up, tipping her chair in her frenzy. Owain froze; Gael's sharp gesture held everyone at bay, and she rushed with Gruffydd to her sister's aid. Ella whined gibberish, batted away helping hands, moaned, and tugged at her hair. Gael shot Owain a murderous look; he bristled in return and hurried to the others for an explanation.

Maura steered him away and calmly addressed his fluster, "It's nothing you've done, Owain. Ella believed I was her enemy as well. Gael fears she's been hurt, but she can't get her to confess how."

"Gael blames me," blurted Owain.

"No she doesn't."

"She does, with her eyes."

"Gael's tired and worried. Ella's been placed in her care, and she's feeling protective."

"I wouldn't have hurt her. I wanted to help."

"I know you did." Maura shared his frustration. "I too wonder why Gael acts so hateful to you."

Owain's hurt flared, then faded with his voice, "I've tried to change."

"And succeeded...When she's alone, I'll take her aside and discover the trouble."

"You needn't bother," he said curtly and huffed himself down upon the rushes. Simon had joined Gael and Gruffydd, and they were making slow but steady progress calming Ella. Marc stayed where he was, and Maura sank to her knees by Owain, watching the group intently. In turn, Owain watched her. He realized his complaint trivial, yet she had taken time to console and encourage, and he was thankful. "Maura," he said more gently. She turned and her pinched expression eased to his grin and memory, "Remember when we first talked?"

"Yes..." she answered with a wistful air, "the morning after we'd arrived in Mynyw, on the cliffs. You wanted so much to hate me."

"And you should have hated me."

"But I knew even then you were bluffing."

"How?"

"A kindness in your eyes told me your anger wasn't meant for me, or Simon, or...Gael. But it took a long while convincing you of that."

"Far too long. How's that child?"

"Very content."

"My sister was pregnant, as far along as you when—"

Despite his hesitation, Maura knew he longed to reminisce, so she prompted, "Tell me about her."

"She...Gwen, was a year younger than me, and when we were home together, our hearts and minds always seemed in harmony. She wed, and shortly after I went to live permanently with Rhys. I missed her. She'd returned home for my wedding..." His voice broke and eyes moistened, and Maura figured what he couldn't bring himself to say. He focused on his fingers, tangled tightly together on his lap, and whispered woefully, "She was special. You remind me of her..."

Maura rested a warm touch to his shoulder. "Thank you, Owain, for sharing—"

"Maura," Gael cut in brusquely.

Maura jerked her eyes up, and beheld an expression stark with distrust. Gael's lips stretched to a stiff grin and she too politely asked, "I need to take Ella to my hut. She won't have any men near and I was wondering if you'd come with us."

"Of course," Maura said. Owain stood to help hoist Maura up, and smiled shyly as she patted his hand and waddled over to Simon. "I'll be back very soon," she vowed with a kiss to his still cold lips, and lured, "You'll be needing some heating up later—"

At the command, "Maura, come!" they winced apart. Maura obediently followed Gael, Simon joined Owain on the floor, and Marc went to fetch food.

*****

A brittle silence accompanied them as Gael briskly tugged her sister along the road rutted with icy mud; Gruffydd trailed at a trot and Maura struggled to keep pace behind him. Once inside the hut, Gruffydd swiftly found a flint to spark the fire, and extracted a flaming rush to light the few remaining candles. As the near empty room brightened, Gael's eyes bulged wide with shock, and she gasped, "Where have my things gone?!"

Maura replied with an edgy calm, "Gruffydd and Owain spent the afternoon moving your belongings to the llys."

"He touched my things!" Gael fumed. "He had no right!"

"Gael...he was only helping," said Maura.

It was painfully clear that Gruffydd didn't and couldn't comprehend his mother's upset as he added in a cautious voice, "We left the pelts in case someone needed to stay here. We even moved all my beasts."

Ella stood by, still and rigid, quietly giggling.

Gael's crazed eyes darted off her, leapt from Maura's disquiet to Gruffydd's guarded expression, and lastly lit on the cleared space where her trunk had once sat. Her fingers dug into her brow, supporting her wagging head, and she burst, "I can't stay here! I can't..."

The door slammed behind her bolting figure, and Gruffydd lurched to chase. Maura restrained him with some difficulty, and repeatedly assured, "Gruffydd, she'll be fine...She needs time alone, and she'll be back. We need to get your aunt settled, then we'll wait here for your mam, together."

Gruffydd wiped away tears of confusion and, gripping Maura's clutch, followed to help. She marveled at his nurturing way; he spoke to his aunt as if she were a helpless younger sibling. Ella readily responded to his tender suggestions to drink the little ale left in the keg, and eat the remaining hunks of bread and cheese. Something about Ella's vacant manner haunted Maura; she vividly recalled a time when she too had shunned the world in order to save her sanity, and ached to think what tragedy might have befallen this once lovely and winsome child.

*****

Marc passed Simon and Owain trenchers steeped with broiled fish and sauce, and received grateful nods as he sat with them, and attended to their serious discourse. "Have you any idea what might have happened to Ella?" Simon asked Owain. Fascinated, Simon studied Owain's suspended silence; his hands cupped his bearded chin, his moss brown eyes glared narrowly at the fire, and a thin veil of moisture coated his skin. Simon could almost hear the workings of his mind. When in this trance-like state, Owain possessed an unearthly ability to solve the most baffling of mysteries.

Simon hoped Owain's gift would triumph this time as well, and expectantly heard him mutter, "Last I was at Dinefwr, Rhys ordered me to question Ella about her doings with the Normans. Rhys' spies had uncovered Ella's affection for a squire residing with the Montgomerys. Then she'd gone missing, and Rhys feared she was being exploited for information and being paid for her treason."

Piqued at his former Lord's name, Marc moved in closer and became as intent as Simon.

"I wasn't at Dinefwr when she returned," said Owain. "I was here, playing nursemaid for the Princess Nesta. But a few of Rhys' more reliable men told me Ella had been abandoned by her lover and the Normans. I was surprised, for I'd heard they execute spies no longer useful."

He looked to Simon for agreement, and Simon duly commented, "Ruthlessness is not exclusively a Norman trait."

Owain shrugged and continued, "I thought it queer the Montgomerys let her go unharmed, and reckoned that she didn't realize she'd done anything wrong, or that she knew nothing important to tell them. But Rhys' wife, Gwladys, may have demanded Rhys send Ella back to her father in Shrewsbury. She'd been harping that demand for months."

Simon's chin fell slack and he echoed, "Her father...Gael's mentioned him once or twice, and never in a kind way. Wasn't he being paid by Rhys for Ella's services?"

"Yes, and Rhys' commitment to keep her also included a promise to find her a rich husband."

"The same as he'd done for Gael?" asked Marc.

"Yes..."

"So what do you believe happened next?" pried Simon.

Owain spoke in a troubled voice as if he'd personally witnessed the entire tragedy, "Her father punished her for denying him wealth, and banished her. She returned to Dinefwr, barely surviving the trip, and may have been abused by the many corrupt leeches who live off Rhys' generosity. Rhys discovered their crimes and sent Ella here, to recuperate safely with her sister who cares for her."

"How do you know all this?" asked Marc, shifting in amazement.

Owain shrugged and stressed, "I don't. But I know too well everyone in Rhys' household, the goodness and evil they are capable of committing, and I know for a fact

Ella spent time with the Montgomerys. With that evidence, I've conjured a notion, and that's all."

"A damned remarkable notion," rumbled Rhys from behind a tapestry. He loomed largely into view and concurred, "I shudder to think what sentence her father dealt her, but whatever, her mind was damaged as a result, and I did catch a very few of my men abusing her...I had them whipped and banished. In regard to her treason, we don't believe she was capable of betraying any crucial secrets concerning my army."

"If you truly believed that..." Simon scorned, "how could you send her to her father! Surely Gael told you of his treachery."

"It was my wife who made the decision," excused Rhys. "She has precedence over the running of our household, the servant's affairs and such. It was not my place to intervene."

"Yet now," said Simon, "it's your place to repair the damage."

"Yes..." Rhys answered ashamedly. "And what would you have done differently?"

"I would have argued with your *Lady* wife."

"That, my lad, is not such a simple task."

"What if Ella told the Montgomerys about Simon, or about me?" intruded Marc.

"Why would she?" said Simon. "She doesn't know my background or that you're here."

"Are you certain, Simon?" questioned Owain. "She was Nesta's servant, and Nesta has made a deliberate effort to learn everything about you, and she brags about your imagined doings to anyone who'll listen, including Ella."

"And so the Montgomerys may be after me as well," Simon stated sourly. "What a comforting thought. God's blood, please let's discuss something not so depressing...Where's Taredd?"

"Due here soon," answered Rhys, after a swig of mead. "He's bringing a Powys brother."

"A who?" wondered Marc.

"One of the three Princes who rule Powys. They've been encroaching on my territory. Taredd volunteered to seek out and remedy the problem. He's been instructed to return with a brother for mediation." Rhys directed his plan to Simon, "I'll be wanting Maura to intervene."

Simon stood to object. "No. I can't allow it." He almost whined, "She's only just gotten out of bed, and with what occurred last time...No. I won't allow it, and she will agree."

"That's pompously presumptuous of you," Rhys snorted in Simon's face. "She might want to help."

"She'll help some other way."

Owain stood to their smoldering and offered, "I'll do it."

Rhys gaped and burst a full-throated guffaw. "You! A mediator! With you in charge, a simple disagreement would surely erupt into total war."

"Don't laugh *too* loud, Rhys," defended Simon. "We've been instructing Owain."

"Teaching him what," Rhys mocked, "how to act like a ruddy fool, and shame himself, and my army, and my name by parading about—"

"The art of mediation," finished Marc.

Suddenly Rhys grew serious. "Truly?"

"Yes," said Owain.

"And have you learned anything useful?" Rhys said with a dubious flair.

"I feel so," answered Owain.

"Simon," said Rhys, "I'll have your impression."

"I believe Owain will do himself, your army, and your name proud...as mediator."

Rhys sought one more review. "Marc, do you agree?"

"Absolutely."

"Well then, Owain, that sort of praise warrants at least an attempt at peacemaking."

Owain beamed to his Lord's confidence, then instantly sobered as Rhys asked, "Are there any judgments to dispense, other than the one meant for the two of you?"

Owain meekly wagged his head and, with Simon, heaved a heavy sigh of relief as Rhys threw back the rest of his mead, belched, and wandered away.

"And so," digressed Simon, "what's to be done about Ella?"

"Can you suggest some curing herbs?" wondered Marc.

"I know little about illnesses of the mind."

"Perhaps being with loved ones will be cure enough," offered Owain.

Simon scrunched up his face in thought, then nodded. "Perhaps you're correct again, Owain."

*****

"You didn't run far," said Maura as she emerged from the cottage and beheld Gael propped up against the front wall of her cottage, staring vacantly at the slip of moon veiled by thickening clouds.

Gael forced a grin. "I didn't have anywhere better to go. I'm tired of praying, and sick of Rhys' pawing attempts at seduction. I wanted to be somewhere familiar, but even my home has changed...I want to be near my son, and he's obviously more skilled at soothing my sister than I am. Oh Maura, I'm sorry for my outburst, I feel so muddled, so useless. This past week was near to a nightmare. My husband took the first offered opportunity to escape me, Nesta's nagging was unbearable, and Gwladys was hateful. I'm so thankful to be home, yet all I can show is anger."

"We've missed you terribly," bolstered Maura.

"And I've missed you."

"I was thinking just this morning," said Maura, "how rarely you come to visit, and wondered why. I was powerless to change things before, but I'm not now and I'm needing to know. Have we done something to offend—"

"Oh no," Gael explicitly replied. "It's nothing you, or Simon, or Marc has done...I'm ashamed at my absence, and I could spout a thousand excuses, but none would be true."

"It's Owain, isn't it?" Gael's sudden silence confirmed Maura's suspicion, and she prodded, "Why did you scorn him when he was wanting to help your sister?"

"He wasn't wanting to help," scoffed Gael.

"He was."

Gael instantly flared, "I won't let him near her, not when I suspect him to be one of the vile pigs who abused—"

"What do you mean by 'abused'?"

"Beaten, raped, seduced, Rhys wasn't specific."

"Owain couldn't have hurt your sister."

"And what makes you so certain?" Gael returned snidely.

"Because what you accuse is entirely ludicrous. He's been nowhere but here for the last two full months, and I know him well enough to insist he's not capable of—"

"As well as you knew your cousin?"

Maura reeled from the barb, and rallied her cause, "I've spent more time with Owain than I've ever spent with Henry...I'm supposing you speak of Henry. Owain owns my complete trust and friendship—"

"And does your husband know of this trust and friendship?"

Maura couldn't believe Gael's insinuations. She quaked from rage and hurt, yet forced still her heart and her tone to parry, "Simon knew, for he was always there with

300

us...You won't get him, or Marc, or your son, or the village to agree with your hate, for Owain's become dear to us all. I'll go now."

Maura turned and had strode only three steps away when Gael's wailed anguish, "Maura...don't go, *please* don't go!" stalled her exit and anger.

She returned in fewer steps and watched, alarmed, as Gael slipped down the wall, her hands hiding what Maura guessed were copious tears. With effort, Maura crouched near to assure firmly, "Gael...Ella will trust again, it will take time but she will trust again, and so will you. Gruffydd knows well how to treat her, and we will do what we can to help both of you. Your husband will return—"

Gael lifted a harrowed expression to plead, "You don't think he's run from me?"

"Of course not...We only pray he's worthy of you."

Gael dabbed her drenched cheeks with her skirt and sniffed, "I wanted so much to come home, but then in the llys...when I noticed Owain heading for Ella, the ache and the rage returned."

Maura's confusion soared. "What ache? Why rage?!"

"I don't know!" Gael raved. "And not knowing makes the hurt worse. Before Henry, there was a reason for the rage—we yelled and spit at each other, avoided each other, yet when our battling stopped, I couldn't remember why it had happened...What reason did we have for hating each other?! It somehow felt right to hate him and now...I'm scared not to. I need to find the reason again Maura, but I can't. Help me find it?"

"I won't do that. If you can't remember the reason, then there is no reason. Come..." Maura gingerly took her hand. "We'll check to see that Gruffydd and Ella are settled, then go back to the llys for some much needed cheer."

Gael pulled back. "I don't like how I feel when I'm around Owain."

"Will you shun *our* company simply because of a vague discomfort?"

"No..."

"Perhaps if you speak to him nicely, the hurt will leave." Gael's doubtful expression took her to her feet. She helped haul Maura up and shrugged to her suggestion, "And shouldn't we be concentrating instead on your husband? How was he at the ceremony, attentive?"

"Fidgety," Gael offered bluntly.

"Maybe he's shy...Shy is nice."

"Maura you're doing it again."

"Doing what?"

"Making saints out of devils."

Maura smirked and teased, "Surely Taredd's not a devil...and," she added with a wink, "hopefully not a saint either."

Gael peeked in the door and clarified in a whisper, "I was speaking in a general sense." Satisfied that the young ones slept soundly, the women started back to the llys, Gael continuing her complaint, "Not everyone is salvageable. And if you truly believe that Owain is deserving of my respect and kindness, why was he so hateful to me before?"

"I believe I know the answer to just that question," Maura readily replied. "He was spurned by his betrothed. She was blond and Saxon, and somehow, he thought of you as her."

"Betrothed?" Gael echoed incredulously. "Owain? No, I can't imagine...What happened to her?"

Maura seemed hesitant to divulge the grim tale, but after a bracing breath, she spilled, "About ten years past, she and his family were murdered by Normans."

The startling statement bulged Gael's eyes and slowed her gait. She swallowed noisily and said in a quaver, "How...how horrible. I didn't know...Why didn't you tell me?"

"You haven't been around much to tell you anything. And I didn't know if Owain wanted me to say. In this instance, I don't think he'll mind."

"And that's also why he despised you and Simon and Marc," Gael concluded.

"Yes, but he regrets his mistake, with us and with you."

Gael couldn't believe Maura's confession. "He told you this...about me?"

"Yes."

Gael was quietly thoughtful the remainder of their journey, and her posture, weighted by far too many complications, sagged low.

*****

The men stood in respect as the women entered. Maura's affable grin told them all was well, at least for the moment. Many more villagers had gathered, providing food and mead and brimming the room with cheer. Exuberantly, they expressed ribald greetings for the bride. In response, she blushed crimson and sought out a darkened corner to hide. Her barrow was promptly brightened by an oil lamp and her closest friends' smiles. Owain sat, not too close, fiddling with his whistle and unobtrusively listening.

"Where's Ella?" asked Simon, offering Gael and Maura their suppers.

"Sleeping peacefully," sighed Gael.

"Good."

"She looks very young," remarked Marc as he presented them mead.

"She's only just turned seventeen," said Gael.

"Are there other siblings in your family?" asked Maura.

"No. There were three born between us, but they died young." Gael immediately regretted her sad comment, and swiftly returned, "The villagers seem healthy and chipper. I hope their high spirits continue when Taredd arrives." She cast a furtive glance to Owain, who seemed kingdoms away. Of all who surrounded her, only he had personal knowledge of her husband; knowledge she was desperate to discover, yet far too shy to request. A shouted call of Owain's name set him on his feet and he hurried to the group of musicians arranging themselves on bales of straw.

"There's to be dancing!" exclaimed Maura.

Gael grunted and Marc returned, "I have to fetch Olwen soon. Before I go, would you agree to a twirl?"

She gazed at his expectant guise and felt a stab of hurt so severe it momentarily shook her breath; she achingly recalled their first dance, the shared sweetness that swiftly had grown between them, then just as quickly crumbled, never to disappear completely. Such a wondrous opportunity for caring stolen away by a mark on a contract based on nothing but propriety. "I...I would..." she stumbled, not catching a wayward tear, "would be honored to twirl with you, Sir."

They rose and moved upon the rushes with a mesmerizing grace. Simon and Maura eagerly joined their fun, as did most of the others. The tempo and gaiety heightened; they hooted, skipped, dipped, and swirled, mixing steps and partners, creating a glorious oneness. Rhys couldn't help but notice the rapport, and briefly prayed that the inclusion of a stranger as Pennaeth wouldn't rock the peace. He studied individuals—Gael radiant in the arms of her besotted knight; Maura and Simon exuding elation and passion; and bewilderment tangled his mind and creased his brow as he spotted a highly animated Owain, blowing gleefully on his whistle, delighting in his concert. Obviously, he'd never truly known this once gruff, intensely private man, and marveled at his transformation. He'd received excellent reviews of Owain's performance as Pennaeth, and was hesitant to force him back into a military role. Maybe there was something else he could do. What was discussed previously jolted his mind, and again he cringed at the farcical notion—Owain the mediator?

Simon whispered in Maura's ear; she beamed at his suggestion and, with a kiss, left his arms. She boldly approached the band, caught Owain's eye, and beckoned with crooked finger and wry grin. He paused mid note, and took on an attentive expression that swiftly turned wary. "Oh no," he said, "not me...It's been too long of a time, and I was never—"

"Nonsense," she laughingly assured. "I'll reteach you. It's not difficult and quite a lot of fun. Please come."

Her imploring look and indulgent reach temporarily hushed his argument and he grudgingly followed her grip to the far edge of the open expanse of floor. "I really don't think this is a good idea," he countered again.

To which she shrewdly parried, "If your lips and fingers have rhythm, then your feet must as well. Take my hands."

He clasped her hands, drew a full steadying breath, then rasped, "Now...now what?"

"Listen to the music, and hear the rhythm." They both did so, their heads cocked, and their bodies bobbing in unison. His rigid posture eased just enough for her to steer him sideways. "Now...walk three steps this way." He mimicked; she encouraged, "Fine, very nice. Now kick..." She cringed to the nick on her shin and chided, "Not me, Owain, to the side."

"Oh, I'm sorry," he atoned.

She laughed at his pout. "It's all right...really. And expected. We'll wait for the music and go the other way."

He agreed with an energetic nod, and they bounced up and down awhile, then proceeded, with much success, in the opposite direction. After a few more kicks, and as many rousing compliments, Owain became quite jaunty. "I do like this! Teach me another."

"One more, then we'll find you a real partner."

Owain froze mid-step, practically choking, "A...a what?"

"A partner."

"I...I don't think so," He shrank and mumbled, "I'll keep dancing with you."

"Dancing with me is like dancing with a sister. I make an adequate teacher, but there's absolutely no reason to impress me."

"Impress?"

"Yes, impress. I expect there are a good number of women here tonight who wouldn't mind an impression of you." His stark look of dread tickled her. "Believe me, Owain, you will survive. This second one is slightly more difficult, though nothing you can't tackle. Shall we?"

"I suppose..." he answered with great hesitancy.

"I don't believe what I'm seeing," said Gael, aghast. She twisted in Simon's hold and craned her neck to see the odd couple more clearly. "Owain dancing and smiling while he's doing it...It's simply amazing what you've done with him."

"No, not what we've done...He only needed permission to enjoy himself."

"And you gave it."

"Not only us...The village also played a huge part in his blooming. Now that Taredd's due to arrive, it's almost a shame—" Remembering who he held in his arms, Simon paused his opinion, and artfully switched topics, "So...how fares Ella?"

"As I told you, she's sleeping peacefully, as is Gruffydd. Finish your thought, Simon—now that Taredd's due to arrive...what?"

"It's...it's just that the village doesn't bestow trust easily. Owain has rightfully earned their loyalty. I pray Taredd proves himself as worthy." Gael shrugged and Simon carefully delved, "How many words did you speak to Taredd before he left Dinefwr?"

She smiled wanly, "Not enough to make a sentence."

"Gael, have you considered the possibility that your union could very well turn out to be quite successful?"

She didn't share his adamancy and mumbled, "Successful how?"

"God's blood, I don't know. I'm trying to get you to smile, but I'm failing miserably."

"No..." Gael managed a small grin. "And I do appreciate your effort." Marc's leaving diverted Gael's attention. She grew more somber, and Simon stopped their dance and urged her into a quiet corner. There they sat and she eagerly confessed, "I don't want Taredd to come here tonight, Simon, or any other night."

"What frightens you?"

"I don't want to be with a man I don't know. I want and need time for dancing, walking, courting."

"So take the time," Simon simply answered.

"What if he doesn't agree to waiting?"

"If you are to be together for eternity, compromise is vital."

"And if he doesn't like compromise and insists—"

"You inform Rhys and he annuls the union."

"He wouldn't," returned Gael.

"I've seen him annul marriages for a great deal less...When I was treating him awhile back, he dissolved a union strictly on the wife's complaint of her husband's fetid breath."

"You're jesting!" Gael replied, astonished.

"No...I was just as shocked as you are now, for once a Norman woman is wed, usually against her will and to a stranger, the Norman church promptly strips away all her rights. Her husband is allowed and encouraged his indiscretions, where the wife is held to a strict set of ridiculously prudent rulings and punished severely if she chooses to ignore them."

"So you're saying I should feel fortunate?"

"Not exactly fortunate, maybe not so stuck says it better."

In a strained voice, Gael spilled her quandary, "A part of me wants this marriage to work, wants it to be all my first marriage was, and also what it wasn't. But I'm not certain I know how...to enjoy...Simon, what is it about Maura that makes you want to paw and slobber over her all the time?"

He flushed and laughed an embarrassed laugh. "Gael I'm no expert—"

She countered with emphasis, "To me you are, as is she...And I aim to ask her the same when I'm done with you."

Simon paused to explore that glorious facet of their life he rarely felt a need to inspect. "What...what we share physically is not something one can pretend or force. It definitely takes time to achieve our sort of closeness. I honestly believe we were fated to be together. We know one another almost as well as we know ourselves, actually...at times better." Frustrated, he asked, "Am I making any sense at all?"

"I think so...but you've not come close to answering my question. What about Maura is so damned attractive to you?"

"That, Gael, is private."

She rolled her eyes and exasperated, "I don't want details...I want an idea, something to look for, hope for, think about."

"Oh...is that all? Well then..." He searched, then feasted adoring eyes on his lady love. She and Owain whirled crazily till both broke from their clutch, and doubled over in hysterics, plopped onto a bench.

Gael grew impatient, and off-handedly wondered, "Doesn't it bother you...her with him?"

"Why would it?" he said, dreamlike, never breaking his trance.

"I suppose I don't know him well enough to trust."

"You will...someday soon, we hope." Gael puzzled to his queer answer and especially his finish, "And after all, I suggested she teach him. As yet, she's the only woman *he* trusts." He soon captured Maura's eye, and as if speaking intimately to her, whispered in exaltation, "I cherish her wholly, and relish how and where she touches and kisses me, what she says, how and when she says it. She delights me as I delight her, never holding back, never bargaining or wasting something so precious...as our love. I can't imagine being without her."

Gael wilted to his eloquence and, following his soppy stare, saw, not surprisingly, Maura mirroring the same expression, except her impassioned review was spoken for Owain's benefit. "Why I like him?" she echoed, blissful in Simon's alluring gaze. "Why do you need to know?"

"No specific reason," he stated with interest. "It might prove useful in the future..."

Maura smiled knowingly and, without hesitation, vehemently obliged, "He's a most generous lover and infinitely affectionate, but I suppose you've noticed that. We enjoy each other equally and he's totally honest in his love, which makes me always crave his scent, his touch, his lips...And I do so thrill in giving him pleasure..." No longer able to contain their ardor, they rose enraptured and almost floated to the center of the dancers, finally to meet in a gasping and abundant clutch.

Owain smiled and wagged his head in exasperation. He struggled up, dusted off his breeches and ambled over to the band. After retrieving his whistle, he and the band launched into a heart-racing jig. While all around, bounders leapt, hooted, and kicked up their heels to the raucous tune, Maura and Simon simply kissed and swayed. Gael scrutinized Owain as intensely as she'd done at Dinefwr. She was convinced he was an entirely different person, perhaps a twin, and the crude, loathsome turd who'd continually vexed her had departed. Everything rough about him had softened; his once swarthy skin now held a rouged glow; his piercing glare was now wide with joy; his crusty leather armor had been replaced by a loosely woven wool tunic dyed the earthy, sumptuous hue of the forest; his beard and hair were snipped shorter, the auburn waves loose and flattering. He was almost handsome, she considered as she rose and wrapped her cloak to leave. She wanted to thank Simon for his exquisite profession of desire, but, surveying the crowd on tip-toe, she found the couple gone. His awe-inspiring salute had more than succeeded in stirring her imagination, swelling her hopes. Yet, she remained certain of only one sobering thought—after a full week of marriage, this night, as on the seven others, she would occupy her pallet alone.

*****

CHAPTER EIGHTEEN - A QUANDARY CALLED HENRY

𝕽𝕺𝕭𝕰𝕽𝕿 loped down the center aisle of an unfamiliar chapel housed within a stone vestry, nestled in a dense wood many miles from Mortain. He twisted every which way, his anguished eyes searching for a priest, or a lower member of the clergy, or in desperation, even a layman could perform the needed chore! Someone, anyone must advise him on this curious, most debilitating of quandaries—what to do about Henry?

He spied a vested, squat, elderly gentleman neatening the altar in the sacristy, and hurried his way, waving and calling out deliberately, "Sir...might you be a priest?"

The fellow snapped to alertness, astounded and not a little frightened to see an obviously privileged man, well-armed and approaching frenziedly. He grabbed hold of the edge of the altar and kept to its rear, stuttering his guarded greeting, "I...I am...And who might you be...Sir?"

"It matters not...I'd rather you not know. I require only a bit of your time and patience...for my confession."

"Confession?" repeated the Priest with arched brow. "You seem a tad hasty. Are you in imminent danger of death?"

"No...no. At least I pray it not so. My soul may be, and I'm terribly muddled. I need immediate guidance, for shortly I will be obliged to pass judgment, and I don't believe that I can muster the moral courage to do so...without your help."

"Why me? By the look of you, I expect you keep a priest, and are able to compensate him adequately."

"I do...but he's very ancient, and knows nothing about what I need to speak of...and...the shock would most likely kill him. Then I'd have his death on my conscience as well, and—"

"Sir...you needn't rave more. I will see you and hear your confession. And advise you as I'm able."

In a rare show of zeal, Robert extolled, "I am grateful, your Grace...eternally grateful!"

"Come to my solar...There we will be undisturbed, and warmer."

Robert, jittery as a child, grinned in submission and followed the Cleric.

*****

Almodis' insides tingled to her resplendent reflection in her looking glass. She inched nearer and peered intently at herself, alert for flaws, blemishes, hair askew, or wrinkles in her coif or gown. Seeing none, she beamed with satisfaction, then tapped her bottom lip, her black eyes flicking mischief. This was the part of her primping she relished the most; bringing her hands together, she called out coyly, "Benjamin...you may enter."

Instantly the door flung wide and in bounced her husband's guard, his hands clasped tightly to his back to hide their fidgeting, his color high and darkening, his eyes love-sick. She turned with drama, letting her skirt flare, and her eyes flirt. Her hands sensuously skimmed her bodice, then gripped and rested on her hips.

His Lady's elegance dizzied Benjamin; his knees knocked, palms moistened, mouth grew parched, and as always he rasped his ritual greeting, "You...you have need of me...my Lady?"

"Indeed I do," she trifled with a wink. "I request a critique of my appearance, Sir."

Benjamin gulped and gaped, starting his scrutiny at her veil, held tight by a gold circlet that highlighted yet didn't conceal her lush brunette locks, loosely braided and framing, in his estimation, the perfection of beauty—Her eyes were large, almond orbs of desire; her lips, slightly parted, were red and wet; her swan-like neck led to the most exquisitely winsome figure, the taut curves obvious beneath a thin layer of plum colored silk. She wore no jewels, none were needed, and might even detract from her loveliness. Benjamin offered silent and impassioned thanks to God for the honor of simply glimpsing this impeccable image of womanhood. He shrank a bit and sighed, "My gracious Lady...your fairness is, without question, unequaled in this land as well as all others and also Heaven above."

He sang the same awkward praise every time she asked, and she never wearied of hearing his glorification, or observing his painstaking performance of love. She kissed her finger, swept across the room and touched lightly its tip to his lips. If she didn't leave soon, he'd surely faint, so to her breathy remark, "I'm grateful, and anticipate our next meeting," she glided away. Benjamin stayed stuck to his spot, remaining transfixed on the swinging door, and whispering his appreciation to the Lady for allowing him a role in their innocent, yet nonetheless tantalizing fantasy.

Almodis interrupted Estrith's journey to her chamber with a demand edged with bother and also a touch of concern. "And where is my husband, Estrith?"

"I know not, my Lady...No one's seen him since mid-morning. And Thomas is about, so where he's gone, he's gone alone."

Almodis gathered Adam in her arms, and while rearranging his ivory silk wrap, straightening his coal black curls, and wiping a smudge of gruel from his mouth, muttered over his fussing, "It must have been something his niece reported. She seems purposely to be avoiding *me*. He'd best return soon, although I propose that the visitors cannot be kept waiting longer. They're liable to drink themselves to a riotous frenzy before they should." Almodis eyed her servant's blandly dyed, embroidered tunic and wrapped wimple with vague admiration, and commented, "You look...very nice, Estrith."

"Thank you, my Lady." Estrith performed her perfunctory bow and acknowledged, "And you look lovely."

"I know," Almodis answered with a sly wink. "Benjamin told me." They both chuckled and traded quips and gossip on their journey to the great hall, Adam wide-eyed and squirming with fascination and fatigue.

The guards flanking the hall's doors spotted their advance. Bowing low, they grasped handles and in unison dragged apart the groaning apertures. One loudly announced to the boisterous, bustling crowd inside, "My Lords and Ladies...Please may we have silence for the Countess of Mortain—our Lady Almodis and our Liege's son...Adam FitzRobert."

An abrupt hush descended as those attending turned awed expressions upon their Lady. Babe in arms, she strode with proud determination down a path swiftly parted, nodding and smiling sweetly to one side, then the other. Almodis' sharp eye spied a number of familiar faces, namely Emma, Robert's middle daughter, Countess of Toulouse, and readily deduced by the huge, garish grin she wore that she was in need of something, probably money. She also beheld Robert Guiscard, a military companion of Robert's and conqueror of Sicily, appearing predictably haughty; and Arthur, Robert's chief butler at Mortain, fluffed up in silk and glitter and looking terribly discomfited. She cleared her throat to halt her snicker and fluidly rounded the dais, content that the servants had lain the linen, utensils, goblets, washing bowls, and candelabras exactly as she had directed. Estrith, at Almodis' elbow, reached for the child, who in delight, giggled and burbled to the excitement. Almodis tickled under his chin, murmured a sweetness, and then bestowed an indulgent smile on her subjects. "My most welcome and gracious guests," she began, her arms wide and engaging, "my Lord and I are honored that you have chosen to share in our homecoming celebration. Lord Robert, unfortunately, has been detained, yet I pray he will join our revel shortly. So, please sit, eat heartily, drink with vigor, and enjoy our hospitality." Almodis started to sit, then remembered with an embarrassed grin, "I believe that I've neglected to introduce the newest member of our family, our dear son...Adam." She motioned to the boy, whose brilliant smile mirrored his mother's. Estrith hoisted him higher so all could see.

After a combined chorus of "aaahhhs", a rousing cheer arose that paled Adam's cheeks and rouged Almodis'. She sat to soothe his fright, and the ranking Lords and Ladies clambered the one stair to occupy their lofty spots at the dais. Almodis waited till everyone had settled, then nodded to a servant lad, who clapped in response and ushered in a trail of servants, brandishing silver platters steeped with steaming fish and fowl, mounds of bread, dried and decorated fruits, custards, sauces, and spices. They served the dais first, then skirted the many trestle tables below the salt to accommodate the less illustrious guests. Almodis engaged in sprightly chatter with her tablemates, and wasn't the least surprised when Emma purposely snubbed her and Adam. She glanced frequently at the empty seat beside her, and longed for Robert's stern though yielding presence, for she so cherished their dinner banter. Worry began to cramp her belly, and over the expanse of the hall, she swept a quick furtive search for Adela. The Countess was nowhere to be seen.

*****

"It's past dark," complained Robert, perched attentively on the edge of a padded chair, one of only two that furnished the Priest's tiny chamber. "You've been long in your pondering...I've a feast I must attend."

The Cleric never took his eyes from the shrinking flames of his meager hearth while disclosing, "One does not hurry God, my Lord. What you've told me is not only horrendously evil, and with your present quandary, near impossible to address."

"How impossible?" contested Robert hotly. "God is all-forgiving!"

"No...you've heard wrong. He is indeed all-forgiving to those who deserve forgiveness. The cruelties you subjected your family to, if performed by someone of a lower status, would be cause for instant excommunication. God may overlook atrocities committed in the context of war, but not executed in the bosom of one's family."

"Would the legal status of the family enter into God's assumption of guilt?" asked Robert.

The Priest took on an incredulous air, "Are you implying that if the persons you offended are not tied legitimately to you, that somehow they deserved the indignities you inflicted?"

"No...of course not...I don't know," Robert sputtered. "She wasn't mine...She's always made me uneasy, and...and seemed to work questionable powers over my family."

Piqued, the Cleric pulled himself taller. "What sort of powers?"

"The ability to bend others to her will...especially my son. She weakened him."

"Your son loves her!" the Priest forcefully returned. "Surely that is the greatest power one can possess. Love strengthens, not weakens."

"Not love...It was more insidious, something akin to an obsession."

"My Lord, from what you've described, your son and ward have undergone tremendously perilous obstacles simply to remain together. There is no question in my mind and heart that their love is indeed true, pure, and enviable."

"So...are you saying I can expect no deliverance for my folly?"

The Priest wagged his head forlornly. "*Folly*...What an interesting word to describe your crimes. I will attempt to sum up all you have related to ensure I have a clear understanding of your confession, and that I've not neglected any pertinent facts. A girl child, whom you saved from death at the hands of Welsh invaders, became your ward.

308

You intended to use her in marriage to improve your wealth and status, and had arranged a profitable alliance with the Montgomerys. At the time of the betrothal, you found trouble with your bastard son, some sort of perceived treason against your brother, that you've since come to discover was false. You returned to your residence in England, passed the judgment of disinheritance upon your son, and intended to rid yourself of his mother as well."

"I believed she had encouraged my son's treachery!" interjected Robert. "She's always hated my brother."

"Your brother being?"

"I'd rather not say."

Almost offended, the Cleric obliged, "As you wish...Now, may I continue?"

Robert gestured limply and the Priest rattled on, "It was on the night of this judgment that you uncovered the relationship between your ward and son. Your son caught you striking his mother, struck you unconscious, and barely escaped your guards and death. Your fury you then turned on your mistress, banishing her. What occurred next is difficult for me to fathom or repeat...You set your guards on your pregnant ward to kill the child, *your* grandchild, and they beat her near to death. They were successful, and you had her taken to a nearby abbey for her to heal. The Montgomerys found out about the pregnancy and broke the betrothal. Thanks to God, she did heal, at least physically. I'll pause here to ask you again, and pray you see clear to answering—my Lord, during that catastrophic evening and morning, did your soul ever once question your barbarity?"

Robert retreated to a sort of stupor, his face a stone mask, and the Priest decided he'd get no explanation. Yet just as he opened his mouth to question more, Robert wrung and strangled his hands and relayed in a shamed whisper, "My eldest son, William, was with me that night and morn. He encouraged and spurred on my wrath, and at times I felt near to deranged." His whisper heightened and cracked with remorse, "I couldn't stop the carnage...There was too much hate, too much pain, I had to strike out at someone. She was the only one left to punish!"

"And where is *your* William, and why isn't he confessing as well?"

"He has no soul to save, your Grace."

"I see...Well, despite your attempts to correct the supposed wrongs done to you by your ward, in the end, your bastard son won her fairly."

"They had no fight from me," Robert rigidly defended. "I let them go...I was weary of the hatred. I once loved Simon and—"

The Priest finished his emotion, "And still do, or your conscience would not be in such turmoil. And now you've heard the distressing news that your nephew attempted to kidnap, rape, and murder your ward. You've been instructed to pass sentence for his 'folly' that too closely resembles your own, and you're wanting advice. The answer is simple, my Lord. Yet before I proclaim it, I'm wondering, why your hesitation to avenge your ward's honor? Do you still blame her for denying you wealth?"

"No," Robert answered easily, then hesitated before stating, "but she may possess evidence that if revealed could ultimately destroy what little connection my family still holds."

"So the culprit again is greed."

"No...No...not entirely. I'm old, I crave peace for the very short while I have left on this earth, especially with my family, for I have a new son to provide for, and I care for my wife and my brother."

"You believe that if you ignore your ward and her troubles, you will achieve this peace."

"At least my family will still speak to me."

"Perhaps some of them don't deserve your discourse."

Robert spoke curtly, "I don't care for an opinion of the rest of my family. Now please, I'll have your guidance."

The Priest stood to lord over Robert. He wielded a damning finger, scowled, and lectured, "What you must do is this—pass harsh judgment on your nephew, the perpetrator of the despicable crimes against your ward. And for your remaining days, you shall make amends to God through charitable work and protecting your family so that they receive no further hardship! You reinstate your bastard as a legitimate member of your family, and ensure your connection to your new son is not spoiled by avarice. You will plead forgiveness from your former mistress, and your ward, her late child, and the one she presently carries, though I doubt they will grant it to you. And every single day you still breathe, you beg for God's absolution. Do nothing more to rile Him! Perhaps when you've achieved these penances, you may have a chance, however slim, of spending an eternity of peace in Heaven."

"There is no guarantee?"

"*You* are the guarantee, Sir. There is good still in you, my Lord, though it's been bruised and buried. With care and prayers, it might heal and sprout again." The Priest noticed a sulk. "I see you're not overly pleased with my summation or conclusion."

"I'm irked by the fact that I had a suspicion of your conclusions before I sought you out."

"Then you feel your time here has been wasted?"

Robert shrugged and shrewdly surmised, "Not at all. Hearing my thoughts restated by someone such as yourself inspires me not only to ponder my deliverance, but also to act on it. I am grateful, your Grace, for your assistance and patience." Robert swept a critical eye over the decaying walls and roof of the parish, and decided with scant emotion, "I'll send workmen to patch up your chapel...Will tomorrow do?"

The Priest appeared humbly surprised. "No time is too soon, my Lord..."

"Robert."

The Priest pondered the name a while, then the shocking revelation tripped from his lips, "You are Robert...Count of Mortain?"

"The same, your Grace." Robert stood, straightened his tunic, and self-consciously fingered the brooch clasping his mantle. He seemed poised to say something more, then a fleeting glance and jerk of a nod whisked him away. The Priest waved the sign of the cross in his direction, shuddered, and scooted his seat nearer the fire.

*****

The trenchers and platters gone, Almodis sipped wine, drummed the table, and tapped her foot along with the lively tune being performed by a group of musicians who were clustered in a small gallery jutting from the back wall of the hall. The trestle tables below the salt had been stacked away and the floor swept clear for dancing, and romping dancers her guests were proving to be. She delighted to the tremble of the floor, the rock of the dais, and the felicity pulsating throughout the room. Somehow, despite the din, her son had fallen asleep. Estrith had taken him away, and the Lady saddened to her servant's leaving, for Almodis considered the nurse the only attendee worth speaking to; all the others had proved excruciatingly dull. There was a lull in the music, and Almodis shifted her attention to the embroidery decorating the table linen. Her finger traced the delicately sewn rose pattern, and she remembered with distaste a time very long past when she had been forced to perform the tedious task endlessly.

Fingers covered hers, stopping her tracing—long, bronzed, and graceful fingers with impeccably polished nails. Her curiosity climbed the arm attached, dressed in royal blue, and came to rest upon an astonishingly comely face, black-haired and bearded, owning large captivating brown eyes, and the sweetest most enthralling smile. His

310

fingers tightened to hers and he easily drew her up and close to say, his voice soft as a song, "My lovely Lady, you appear bored."

Her first attempt to answer emerged as a squeak; she cleared her throat to reply, "I am rather, my..." She swiftly rated the style, material, and cut of his costume, and finished, "my Lord."

"I've been watching your fingers, your feet, and the other most attractive parts of you, and concluded you wish to dance. But alas, all the men gathered here are witless fools for neglecting your desires. In contrast, *I*, my Lady, am no fool. Would you do me the honor?"

He seemed familiar, but she couldn't place where they'd met before, or why. He appeared young, perhaps not yet twenty, but held an air of maturity and fine breeding. "Before I agree, I'll have your name."

With a mysterious smirk, he challenged, "You know of me, my Lady, and we have met, though long ago. Our game will be that you ask me questions that require only yes or no as an answer, and you attempt to guess my identity by the end of our jig."

"And what is my prize if I succeed?"

"The same as if you fail."

"I am intrigued, and accept your challenge, my Lord."

"Then...shall we?" He wove his arm in hers, and smoothly guided her from the dais to the floor. The throng parted for the handsome couple, and to a sweeping wave of the stranger's arm, the band commenced playing a tune, spirited enough for prancing, yet slow enough for talk. "Ask away..." he prompted.

"Are you a relative?"

"Yes."

"By blood?"

"No."

"Then you are kin to my husband."

"Yes."

"There are so many of you, yet by your looks I take you to be from the wealthy branch."

"Pardon?"

"You are rich?"

"Very."

"Are you titled?"

"Yes."

"Married?"

"No."

"Earl?"

"No."

"Count?"

"Yes."

"Then you reside in Normandy?"

"Yes."

"The dance is done," stated Almodis, "and I have failed, so confess your name, Lord Count, and your relation to my husband."

"I don't know if I want to," teased the stranger. "It's so alluring remaining an enigma."

"If you don't confess," she countered, "I won't dance with you further."

"I don't believe you...for you want to know your prize."

Almodis grew weary of his flippancy; her craving for Robert flared. The man sensed her fading interest, and rivaled, "Where is your husband, my Lady?"

"I know not...and his absence is disconcerting, and fastly becoming worrisome. I really must speak with his guards, seneschal, and butler and direct them to start a search. I enjoyed our dance, my Lord, and will—"

With slight pressure, he urged her back in his hold and, dripping charm, argued, "One more dance and I'll reveal everything about myself, only...somewhere quieter, more private...and you'll reveal everything about yourself."

"No!" she insisted firmly. "I'm not interested." Irritated, she attempted to jerk her hand from his, yet a silver band gracing his little finger captured her attention. She drew his hand close to her face. He hoped she would kiss it. She studied the ring instead, and, in shock, loudly determined, "Why have you Maura's wedding band?!"

Her astute discovery rendered him ashen and speechless, then he fumbled his reply, "Maura? Who is this Maura? The ring belongs to me...It is a token of love given me by—"

"Liar!" she hurled back. "Her band was unique! The silver was purposely dented and not smoothly finished. She never would have parted with her ring voluntarily. Why and how did you steal it?!"

"My Lady...surely you can't condemn me on such flimsy evidence. I know not this Maura, nor did I steal her ring, or do her harm. I was invited by your husband to attend this soiree, and—"

"Your lies condemn you, Sir! I drew up the invitations, not my husband."

"Henry!" The bellow thundered through the hall, sending most of the revelers scuttling from the forbidding sight of Adela's crazed figure barreling toward the center of the floor.

Henry's eyes practically popped out of his skull; squalling, "Save me!" he grabbed Almodis' waist from behind and brandished her like a shield. He inched backward, sputtering, "She...she aims to do me grievous harm, my Lady! Help me escape, and I will be eternally in your debt."

Almodis' heel cracked Henry's knee, spilling him to the floor. While he scrambled for his footing, Adela gained momentum. She shoved Almodis from her path and aimed a hearty blow at her brother's jaw. Henry barely dodged her fist and dashed for the kitchen entrance.

Almodis regained her balance and majesty, and shouted, "Guards, block the exits!" They bounded to her command.

Trapped, Henry darted one way, then another. He twisted and moaned in panic, "Let me go! I've done nothing! Don't let her at me!" His desperation drove him to the dais. He leapt upon the table, and scattered candles and goblets in a breathtaking attempt to reach the postern door. He vaulted a ducking lady, landed with remarkable finesse on one foot, and sprinted his final dash for freedom. But, alas, he failed to glance up in time to avoid colliding with his stolidly braced Uncle Robert. Henry reeled from the impact; Robert didn't budge. Henry flung himself at Robert's feet. "Save me, Uncle Robert!" he beseeched. "Adela's gone mad and wants my head!"

Robert retreated a foot and remarked with absolute calm, "Actually, she mentioned another part of your anatomy, but whatever...Guards," he loudly proclaimed, "shackle this scoundrel and lock him in the buttery!"

Henry seized hold and clambered up Robert's tunic, shock and disbelief spewing from his lips, "No...No...You can't do this! I've done nothing! What are her lies? She hates me, wants me dead. Her pregnancy makes her hysterical. Hear me out, Uncle Robert. You can't imprison me till you've heard me out!"

Fear propelled Almodis in the direction of the ruckus, her arms hugging her waist, her eyes clouded with dread. Drawing near, she at first whispered, "What has he done, Robert?" The fierceness in her husband's eyes swelled her panic, and shrilled her cry,

"What haven't you told me?! Why does he have Maura's ring? What has he done to her?!"

Benjamin batted at Henry's grip, freeing his Lord, and Robert's sharp gesture and shout, "Take him!" sent his other guards pouncing.

Henry writhed and bucked as they hauled him away; his demented howling rumbled the walls, "I'll see you disemboweled, you putrid old snake, and your bitch and boy! Sister...I'll torch your castle and murder your runts. I swear I'll kill you all! John! John, where've you gone, you stinking coward? John!"

Adela elbowed her way through the throng, now packed tensely round the dais. "Well...you came extremely close to botching that capture, Uncle," she bellowed. "Your good wife failed to alert me that Henry was in fact attending your feast. If I'd known, we would have apprehended him before he'd entered the hall. She seemed more intent on seducing my most *charming* sibling."

Almodis turned a ferocious gape on Adela and countered as vehemently, "I didn't know his identity! And I certainly didn't invite him here, nor did I have any intent of seducing him! How dare you accuse me, you pumped up prig!"

"We all know of your scandalous reputation, my very fickle lady," Adela sneered back, "and I personally witnessed your overly polite tete-a-tete while you danced with my brother."

Almodis ruffled to rave more, yet instead she shrewdly swallowed her insult. There was absolutely no sane reason to risk her status and waste precious time wrangling with this wild-eyed witch. She snatched up Robert's hand and yanked him toward their bedchamber. He followed tamely and suggested over his shoulder, "Adela, eat something. Calm yourself with wine. I'll call for you when we're done talking."

The door bolted. Almodis whirled, flailed, and burst a mix of rage and fear, "Where have you been?! I've been mad with worry. And now this! What haven't you told me? What has he done?!"

Robert, his guise that of a child about to be whipped, sagged upon their bed and confessed in a rattling sigh, "I had to get away, to think..."

"Think of what?!" Almodis demanded, storming closer.

"What to do about Henry."

"Then you knew he'd done something wrong, but didn't feel the need to inform me."

"I had no idea he'd show up here this night. I'd planned to inform you."

"When?!" she cried.

"After the feast?" he weakly guessed.

"Well I decree the feast done! Now tell me everything. Why does he have Maura's ring?!"

"I didn't know he did...but the fact that he does have it supports Adela's claims."

"What claims?!" She waited too long for an answer, then cursed, "Damn you! I refuse to prod each and every morbid detail out of you Robert. You'll say all this very instant, with no interruptions!"

Robert nodded in weary assent, and quavered, "Adela claims she heard Henry confess to their sister, the Abbess Cecily, that he assaulted and attempted to kidnap and rape Maura."

Robert watched his normally intrepid wife shudder violently and clasp her hands over her face to hide her trauma. Then just as quickly, her quaking stopped and her hands fell away to reveal a stark and tenacious expression. "Do you believe her accusations?"

"I don't know what or whom to believe. The last time I saw Maura and Henry together, they seemed friendly."

313

"And to me," added Almodis, "she spoke sweetly of him...once."

"Yet he has her ring," said Robert.

"And claimed not to know her," said Almodis. "Something is very wrong. We must go and speak to him."

Hesitantly he caught her hand, then assuredly firmed his hold. "There's more, Almodis. If Simon and Maura have confided fully to Henry of their past, and we discover he has indeed violated Maura, he will contest any decision I make concerning his punishment."

He expected a 'why' and was amazed and more than a little daunted when she sat by him and returned in frustration, "Yes, and he'd have just cause."

"You..." He gulped dryly and sputtered, "You...you know what I've done?"

"I've heard only pieces of the tragedy, but I've managed to fit the whole sordid puzzle together."

"Heard from whom?"

"Those most intimately involved—Maura, Edith, Rose...not Simon."

His eyes grew moist and rounder. "You knew about my crimes...yet still decided to return to me?"

"Few of us are saints, Robert," she appeased. "And I can't claim to have lived an exemplary life myself. At first my returning was based strictly on protecting Edith's family, including Simon and Maura. Now that I know you better, I've come to see my decision to remain has been most beneficial to us both." The stiffness left her voice and body. "You are not entirely to blame for that terrible time. Will was with you and, no doubt, pressured you. I too have fallen prey to his scurrilous spells, and know how easily he can turn an angel into a fiend. You know of my time with him?"

He barely nodded.

"And despite that knowledge, you've chosen to keep me with you, protect me, and care for me." Eyes downcast, their faces almost touched. She felt him tremble to her nearness, her caress of his cheek, her tender soothing, "In the night, I hear and ache to your cries for redemption. Your guilt for the past pervades everything you do and say. I won't judge or punish you, Robert, for I'm no better. Perhaps that's why I feel so close to you. We'll go together and talk to Henry, and pray he's not done Maura harm, but if he has, he will be duly punished—by *my* edict."

Tears stained the palm she removed from his cheek. She wiped away two of her own, stood, and urged him up with a needy reach. Their fingers knitted together and at the door, Robert mentioned humbly, "I've met with a priest this day, not ours, one more capable, and he had advised me on how to achieve forgiveness. What he proposed may prove difficult, and I will need your help."

Her grip firmed as she resolved, "And you shall have it, my Lord. We'll check on Adam, then meet with Henry."

"Yes...I've missed our son." He thought a moment, then added, "And we need to take a blanket for your shoulders...There's a wicked chill in the buttery."

Lord, Lady, and Countess marched onward to Henry's interrogation, Benjamin leading the resolute parade, Thomas following. No one noticed the tall, gawky, shrouded fellow skulking behind. Deep in the moldy, dank bowels of the castle, Henry rattled his iron cuff, and spat and salivated like a rabid dog. His amply armored keepers took little notice of his screamed slurs and obscenities, but shifted their stance to a broad band of light flooding in from the opening door. Henry paused his ravings, wiped foam from his mouth and beard, and slouched into a meek posture for his accusers' arrival. Benjamin stuck their torch into the iron girding bracing the wall, and retreated to his Lord's side. Robert lacked expression as he strode boldly to within a foot of his nephew and demanded, "You'll tell me how you've harmed Maura."

Henry puffed up to parry, "Where's John?"

Fuddled, Robert looked about, then questioned irritably, "Who is this John?"

"My butler John. He arrived with me. We have the most critical news to relate to you, my Lord Robert, concerning your son and your ward."

"Stop purposely confusing me, Henry, and confess what you've done to Maura."

Henry spotted Adela, heaving her corpulence, and nearby, the biting glare of his uncle's most exquisite lady. Suddenly wary, he swallowed and, desperate for moisture, cracked, "Please, my Lord, I'm parched and in need of water or, if you could be so generous, a sip of wine. My voice grows thin and will surely vanish completely if you'll not—"

"Quiet!" scolded Robert. "I'm sick of your pretentious blather. You'll answer me now, or I shall set your sister on you."

"Wait!" gasped Henry. "It's not like you to be so hasty, Uncle. I need a moment to recall...Ye...yes...Directly after Father's funeral I visited your bastard and his lady wife simply to relay your warning concerning Odo's release. As always, I enjoyed their company, then returned promptly to Normandy."

Robert questioned, askance, "And how fare my son and ward?"

"They fare extremely well, my Lord. They are ecstatic in their union, and joyously anticipate the imminent birth of their child, *your* grandchild."

Despite Adela's deafening cry, "He stinks with lies, my Lord!" relief engulfed Almodis. She swooned with happiness, then the peculiar discovery of the ring returned to fuddle her.

She pulled herself taller and nudged Robert. "Ask him about the ring."

"My wife claims you wear Maura's wedding ring. If she is, as you say, ecstatic in her union with my son, why did she give you her ring?"

"Your lovely wife is mistaken, Uncle. I wear no ring." Almodis pushed by Robert, grabbed up Henry's free hand, and found it bare. "Perhaps," Henry wryly suggested, "...your lady imbibed a bit too much claret and imagined—"

She slapped his insolent grin; he swung to counterstrike, but froze as the sting of Robert's dagger tip nipped his throat. "Why are you trying to die, Henry?" Robert gritted. "Are you deserving of execution? Did you kill Maura and her child?"

Robert's dreadful accusation unleashed Almodis' greatest and as yet unspoken fear. She lurched from Henry's side, yanked the torch off the wall, and frenziedly began a crawling search of the buttery's puddled and moldy floor. Her sudden strangeness distracted Henry and, for once, she was glad for his silence. It wasn't long before she located the shining contested object. Almodis scrambled up and, after inhaling a long, steadying breath, proclaimed, "I found it! He only tossed it aside. My Lord, I beg an audience with our prisoner." Robert willingly stepped aside, waved her forward, and straightened her mussed blanket as she wielded the ring and began, "My Lord, not being royal born, I may seem to you a flighty fool. But your impression of me is grossly flawed. I am clearly from a far better stock than you, for I believe and trust in the sacredness of friendship. Maura bragged of your bravery and spoke sweetly of your affection. And all know of Simon's intense, though misguided, respect for you. If you've done either of them the slightest harm, Sir, I have been granted by my Lord Husband the honor, and oh what an honor it will be to castrate you. And if you refuse to speak or choose to continue your blatant lies, you will be whipped till you see the wisdom of the truth. We'll leave you a moment to consider my offer." Almodis and Robert ambled with their servants to a darkened corner.

Henry noticed that Adela had mysteriously departed, and railed to the muttering silhouettes, "What offer?! You'll geld me no matter what I decide!" He got no answer, so, mumbling curses, he slumped against the wall, cradled his splitting skull, and floundered for a saving response. Of course she was no flighty fool, and could no doubt carve out his heart quicker than she could hurl a gob of spit, and surely enjoy it more. He'd tell the truth, then parley swiftly the prospect that they need him alive to help locate and rescue Simon and Maura from Odo and Will's treachery, for—He whispered upward a desperate prayer, "Please Lord, don't let them know where Simon and Maura are hiding. That knowledge alone will save me from these ignorant vipers." Henry squeezed shut his eyes and, as if he heard and was content with God's reply, reopened them and called out, "Uncle Robert and my Lady Almodis, I've made my decision."

They promptly returned and, sharing expectant expressions, spouted, "Yes?" in unison.

"If you'll see to unshackling me, I swear not to attempt escape, and will tell in a warmer and more placid place of the damage I've done to your family. Yet I do repeat there is more to be related, a forthcoming danger to your son and his wife, and a piece of distressing news concerning your brother Odo. I must find my butler, John, for he will confirm all that I tell you is God's truth. Please, my Lord...and Lady. Please say you agree to my humble request!"

Robert looked to Almodis. She rolled her eyes, and he surrendered with a heavy sigh and curse, "God's breath, Henry! Why is everything you do and say so painfully complicated?" He gestured and directed to his guards, "Release and escort him...carefully to my chamber."

Robert and Almodis sat side by side upon their bed looking surly, wan, and drained, separated from Henry by the crackling hearth. He, in contrast, sat at a dining table, vigorously studying the oil swirling the surface of his goblet of claret. He threw back a huge gulp, belched, then remarked, "I don't want your Lady present when I confess to my wrongs, for being a woman, she couldn't possibly understand the temptations forced upon me these past weeks."

"Actually," Robert wearily replied, "I believe she'd understand temptations such as yours far better than I would."

Almodis shot Robert an insulted look, which he hurried to remedy, "I mean being so much younger than I, not that she'd ever act in a manner disrespectful to her station...God's breath, Henry, aren't you ready yet?"

"Have you any sweets?"

"No, get on with it," growled Almodis; she stifled a huge yawn and noted, "The time grows very late, my Lord."

A knock interrupted. Robert uttered, "Come..."

Estrith entered gingerly and spoke lowly to Almodis, "The Lady Adela requests your immediate presence in her chamber."

"For Heaven's sake why? She hates me."

"Not at the moment, my Lady...She has picked this time to deliver her child."

Almodis fumed up from the bed, muttering madly, "No! No, not now. She can't! She's done this on purpose, Robert. Your family delights in driving me mad!"

Robert caught his hanging head in his hands, and exasperated, "God, give me some peace!"

Henry beamed his comment. "How marvelous! Then she won't be bothering us."

"Send someone else, Estrith," implored Almodis. "I don't care to attend—"

"No," intruded Robert. "Go to her, Almodis."

Almodis sat stubbornly and protested, "No...I prefer staying here."

He whispered, "I'll most likely get more out of him with you gone. We always enjoyed a cordial relationship."

"So I've noticed," she acceded with distaste, then gritted, "Hurry this up, Robert." Almodis huffed a hostile glare Henry's way. He waggishly waved, winked, and then cringed to the slam of the door.

"You'll show her more respect, Henry," chided Robert.

Henry shrugged, plopped his boots upon the table, and loftily took in the scant, though refined furnishings of the chamber. "She has definitely improved your decor, Uncle. Your residences used to be so hideously oppressive."

"You were speaking of temptations, Henry. What did you do to Maura?"

"Uncle Robert," Henry digressed, "...I'll never comprehend the charm you and your son—bastard son, exude over women. You've both somehow managed to procure two of the most exquisitely handsome women I've ever encountered, and both your spouses appear quite devoted as well. It's simply amazing, for neither of you is especially attractive or amply endowed...physically, and dull to the extent—"

"Enough, Henry."

"I do apologize, Uncle...but there is something slightly humorous that I must share with you. Did you know that Father originally intended granting Almodis to Simon? Oh, what a lusty pair they would have made. Yet, alas, Simon inexplicably refused him. I don't believe he ever set eyes on the lady, and you got the prize instead. Then again, Simon didn't go without for long, did he?" Suddenly, Henry dropped his feet to the rushes, directed his heated glare to the flames, and became grimly serious, "I wanted Maura. I've wanted her since I met up with her almost a year past at Westminster, when Simon was imprisoned by you. I tried seduction numerous times, and was always spurned. My fantasies of her turned devious and violent. Surely you know of such fantasies, Uncle. While visiting Simon and Maura, I tried to entice them to return to Normandy with me, she to become my lover, and he to advise me on my quest to rule. Stupidly, they refused. I became ill with a fever and, in my deranged state, I attempted to kidnap her. Failing again, I tried rape, but couldn't complete my crime. In my fury, I assaulted her, then raced away. I may have killed her and her child, but I don't believe so. Is that what you've been so eager to hear?"

"Not eager, Henry."

"Why are you so upset, Uncle? *You* never liked her."

Robert stood to leave and blandly stated, "I will relate your confession to my wife, and she will dispense your punishment."

Henry jolted up and stopped Robert with his stringent appeal, "You may relate all you want, but you won't punish me! You need me, Uncle Robert. If your new-found affection for your son and ward is indeed sincere, you need me to take you to where they hide."

"My wife knows where they hide," Robert dismissed.

Panic gripped Henry, squeezing from him more lies, "They moved. I had a terrible time finding them."

"Why did they move?"

"A Norman invasion...They've retreated to a safer location."

"Why should I go there, Henry?"

"Because, your brother has discovered their whereabouts," accounted Henry, "and is at this very moment sallying forth to wreak vengeance upon your son. I'm certain he's employed your legitimate heir to assist him in his mission. And Will won't be still till both Simon and Maura are—"

A rapping came, quieter than the one previous. Henry, furious at the interruption, charged the door, flung it wide, and, beholding John, bellowed, "God's teeth, you stinking maggot, where've you been?!" He seized John's collar, and thrust him inside.

John hit the floor on his knees and groveled, "I'm deeply sorry, my Lord, but when we entered the great hall, you told me to lose myself. I did, and once I managed to find my way back, you were gone. I searched and heard rumors of your disturbance. When the Lord and Lady emerged from their chamber, I followed them unseen to the buttery. I wanted to say something to your credit, but the opportunity never presented itself."

"Shut your gob! This is all your doing! I wish Odo *had* murdered you."

"Who is this, Henry?!" shouted Robert, his agitation spiraling.

"John, my butler." Henry brightened and introduced his cousin as if nothing troubling had recently occurred. "John, I'd like to introduce my reverent Uncle Robert, Count of Mortain and Earl of Cornwall."

John scooted, still on his knees, over to Robert. With hung head, he greeted, "My Lord, it is a divine pleasure at last to make your acquaintance."

"Get up off the floor!" berated Robert. His anger leapt from John back to Henry. "Did you tell Odo Simon's whereabouts, Henry?"

"Of course not!" spouted Henry, astounded that Robert would accuse him of such treachery. "I'd never betray Simon to Odo. John told him."

At this point in Henry's outlandish testimony, Robert seriously considered bolting to his stable, saddling his steed, and escaping back to the solacing chapel with the intention of remaining there forever. The tall, muddled looking boy appeared familiar, and Robert mentioned, askance, "I've seen you before."

"Yes...Odo gave me to Henry at the King's funeral."

"So as Odo's spy, you visited my son as well?"

"Yes, and I very much liked Simon and his Lady, my Lord."

Robert winced at the lad's oddness, then demanded, "When did you give Odo this information?"

"Over a week past," answered John.

"When did you find this out, Henry?"

"A few days later," replied Henry, eyes shining innocence.

Robert strained in confusion, "Then where have you been for the time between? It's but a day's travel between Bayeux and here."

"Oh...Um..." stumbled Henry, "I needed to return to Rouen to meet with Curthose."

"Why?"

"To purchase a title...and a fief or two." He swaggered about and boasted, "I am now Count of Cotentin and Avranchin. Almost as powerful and wealthy as you, Uncle. I've also purchased an elite fighting force to rescue your son."

"A band of mercenaries," Robert grimly corrected.

"They'll do as they're told."

The young men's antics drove Robert to pacing; his gestures sharpened, his tongue spat, "So you took time to do all this purchasing, knowing Odo was well on a week into his pursuit!"

"It takes at least two weeks in favorable weather to get to that God forsaken bog called Wales," excused Henry, "and longer to find—" He scarcely caught his slip. "I almost told you, didn't I? You are a shrewd weasel, Uncle. Before I left Bayeux, I found a moment to script a note to Rufus. He's to watch out for Odo, and distract him awhile."

"Did you mention to Rufus why Odo was to be distracted?"

"Heavens no," chortled Henry. "If Rufus knew, he would exuberantly join their campaign."

"Rufus has no hate for Simon."

"No, but he does lust after his hide. He'd steal him for himself. And that, my Lord, would be for Simon a fate far worse than death."

Robert abruptly halted his storming. He clasped his hands before him, and squeezed shut his eyes for an interminable moment. When at last they reopened, he rambled monotonously, "Henry...you have succeeded in completely confusing me. I've forgotten why I'm holding you, have no idea whose allegiance you hold, what your present plans are, or why you are wasting my time, patience, and sanity. All I do know is that I am extremely tired and I want to go to bed." Robert called out, "Thomas!" He tumbled in the door, and attended to Robert's directions for Henry, "I'll have you secured in a chamber on the floor above and we'll speak more in the morn. Please take your butler with you."

"Uncle Robert!" Henry returned in disbelief, "We can't wait for the morning. We must leave now."

Robert stressed, "Leave for where?"

"I won't tell you that," snorted Henry. "I'll guide the way to your son."

"Has Odo taken a force with him?"

"A medium sized one," answered John.

"And Will most certainly will add his men to the garrison," added Henry.

"If you two know all this, then you must be privy to what exactly Odo plans to do to my son."

John indulgently offered, "He plans only to speak to him, my Lord, about his role in Odo's imprisonment."

"Speak to him!" Henry howled a wretched laugh, then rectified, "He plans to lop off his head and hang it amongst the other countless war trophies he's accumulated."

"Wales..." Robert sighed. "It seems so very far away."

"Will and Odo will surely ally with Roger of Montgomery, then strike with surprise," alerted Henry. "I intend to go directly to the Welsh Prince who protects your son."

His strength dwindling completely, Robert rasped, "Why does he protect Simon?"

"Simon is his physician. I will alert the Prince and have him remove Simon...and Maura to a place of hiding and protection till you can convince Odo to forsake his revenge and go home."

"He's not easily convinced."

"I know that..." scoffed Henry. "Together, we'll conjure a way, we'll pay him off, threaten his lands here, have Rufus bark at him, or better yet have Curthose grant him more power if he remains on the Continent. My men are prepared to leave immediately. What orders should I relay?"

Robert sat down hard on his bed, and soothed his scratchy throat with wine. His voice's resonance swiftly returned, and he loudly decided, "I'll await my wife's return and discuss the matter with her. My squire will provide you our decision as soon as it's made."

"Your wife? Why would you want to upset her unduly, my Lord? Make up an excuse to return to England."

"I don't lie to my wife, Henry. As my help-mate, she is informed and consulted on any matter pertaining to my household or family. She *will* be told. Now, I'm sick of you. Take your man and get out."

"You don't have to act so snippy, Uncle. Come on John, we've much to plan." Henry paused at the door; mischief lit his eyes, and quivered his lips. "Oh, Uncle Robert, I do have another remarkable revelation to burden you with...John here, he's your nephew."

Robert dribbled wine, sputtering, "Wha...what?"

"Your nephew...It seems he was spawned from Odo's wanton seed...as, it is said, were others." He snickered his closing, "We wish you good-night, Uncle."

Robert sat in a sagging, bleary-eyed stupor, his head splitting from the weight of Henry's lies. *Which are lies, and which are truths?* Was it better to believe all than to ignore the one truth that could result in Simon's death? "My God," he loudly prayed, "give me the guidance that eludes me..." He stopped his piety a moment to consider Henry's last blurb—'nephew...Odo's seed...others'. Robert thought back to the relentless admonishments and slurs pressed on him by Odo, starting twenty-nine years past, when he and Edith had first become lovers. And all the while, Odo too had been clumsy—no clumsier, in relations he'd sworn to abstain from, with the gender he'd professed to abhor. Liar! All his family were liars, cheats, and rogues...All but Almodis and Adam, and the Saxons. He found himself grinning at the absurdity of it all, then throwing back the last of the wine, he flopped back upon his bed, and quickly lapsed into a troubled sleep.

Squeezed between a contingent of guards, Henry and John were led up the walled stairway to a meager, minuscule bedchamber. Henry grumbled lowly, "This is a blow to my dignity...I'll kill the ancient toad," as they were bolted inside, and continued his bitter muttering below his breath. John took no notice, disrobed down to his braies and, shivering, crawled beneath a moth eaten blanket. Henry sat on the edge of the straw box that would serve as his bed, and fixed his perturbed stare upon his squirming butler. Yet he wasn't thinking of John, he was pondering his failure to present to Robert a plausible case of the danger affecting Simon and Maura.

John heard Simon's name mumbled and turned a quizzical face to Henry. "What did you say about Simon, my Lord?"

Henry's voice cracked with remorse, "I...I need Simon...here with me, with me always."

"You have me, my Lord."

"You're not good for much though, are you?!" Henry flared.

"Why him, my Lord? Why Simon?"

"Simon loved me, guided me. He knew so much, had been everywhere. He made me look and sound impressive. Robert isn't convinced Simon's in danger...I don't think Robert understood anything I told him. If Simon had been here, he would have insisted I organized my thoughts before I spoke."

"If Simon were here," said John, "there would have been no reason to speak to Robert, or anyone else for that matter."

"But I miss him," Henry sniffled.

"I don't think he misses you, my Lord."

*****

In the llys, Simon lay still upon the only bed, gazing up at dots of candlelight dancing amongst the grasses that thatched the roof. He listened to and relished the disruptions to the tranquil night. A dog yowled somewhere, soft snores rumbled from blackened corners, rushes crunched under shifting pallets, and crickets trilled. This was the peace he constantly craved, and had rarely known elsewhere. He had friends, good and trusting friends, who when needed, never refused to soothe or humor him. His dear adopted brother, whom he feared he'd not see alive again, had miraculously arrived intact and proven himself a continuing source of love and comfort. The village respected him, the Prince relied upon him, his once enemy was now his staunch ally. And the woman he loved with every fiber of his being lay tucked beside him, sleeping sweetly, their child snug between. He felt so serenely blest and wondered why this time, this perfect moment couldn't last forever, never changing, never spoiling...Yet it wouldn't last...couldn't last. An ache of panic lurched within him, quickening his heart. The thudding drowned away the peace of the dog, the snores, the crickets, and Maura's soft breaths. He hated the sound of panic, and twisted toward her for relief. The dim

320

light showed a small crease between her brows, but her posture stayed limp and motionless. Simon rested his cheek upon her hair and wrapped his arms round her waist. He drew her nearer, till her belly touched his, and he felt the child shift to his warmth. Instantly, his panic calmed.

In the cottage, Marc looked up into eyes shining gold from the dwindling hearth light. He tickled Clyde; the sleek orange feline leapt away, to be replaced by his sisters, Rose, Clare, and Grace. He was glad they were bothering him with their climbing and exploring, and also glad to be free of humans this vexing night. Thoughts that sickened and embarrassed plagued him...And doubts that somehow he had failed himself and Gael, that he should have fought harder for her heart and her hand, viciously pestered. His abrupt flip to his side tumbled the kittens, and his muffled, but stark curse, "God's breath!" sent them scuttling away. When he'd walked Olwen to her hut, she'd asked him to stay the night. It seemed a bit rash, since they'd yet to kiss, and he'd awkwardly refused her. He'd seen the hurt his answer evoked, yet wouldn't the hurt have been worse, if he'd stayed and thought of Gael when they loved, for he thought only of Gael in that way...not Olwen. He'd never wanted anything more than he wanted Gael! He ached with longing, and the image of her with Taredd only made the hurt worse—It gnawed at his heart, made him want to strike out, hurl things, scream every curse he knew and those he didn't! But he wouldn't do those things. He'd only lie here, watching the kittens romp, wondering about the morrow, and feeling so very, very miserable.

Gael twisted fitfully on her mat, caught in a strangely enticing dream...Moist warm lips crushed to hers fired her blood, raced her heart, and stirred a vague tickling in her belly and below. She craved more and fumbled beneath her lover's clothing to risk a touch to his fevered skin. He searched much more expertly for her nakedness and discovered it quickly. His fingers played over the tickling and sent it coursing further over the rest of her. She swooned a moan and, locked to his lips and body, gripped him over her...Yelling—a yelling came near, a dark, deep voice cutting through the still of the bright night. Something thudded her lover's back and tore him away. Strong severe arms yanked her up, a rigid hand slapped, knocking her back down. A stick, thickly armed with thorns, pounded her head, shoulders, and her bare legs, bruising and slicing. Words—terrible, hurtful words screamed, "Whore! Slut! Devil's child!" Then laughter, not one but many laughing, sniggering. Dirt hit her face; no, not dirt, dung. She screamed, couldn't stop screaming from the hurt, the unbearable pain! He'd save her, steal her away from this nightmare! She searched and found him not feet away, cackling, his head thrown back, chestnut hair tumbling, mustache and beard cropped short...almost handsome. And his eyes glared accusingly, glinting with triumph...Gael gasped awake and started up from her pallet, quaking with terror, still feeling the shock, the shame, the misery. A lone candle flickered upon her trestle table, illuminating two still lumps nearby. She tried to tame her heart by seeing again her nightmare. It was no fantasy, but a true and heinous memory. She was but a girl, maybe fourteen, her lover, a stranger she'd met only that terrible day. He'd charmed and tempted her, spouting loving lies, touching her just so to make her want more. The man had taken her off alone, assuring that her father knew their destination, and had granted him permission for her hand. She'd liked what they'd done, and knew it was no sin for he'd loved her. He'd sworn so many times that day how beautiful she was, thrilling and alluring. He'd do her no harm.

Her father had found them; his beating broke her bones, her desire, her spirit. And the man—he'd laughed at her torturing. Gael scrutinized her memory of him, and identified a face identical to Owain's. That's where she'd known him before, where her hate had taken root! The man was Owain! She buried her head in her arms and sobbed huge, loud tears of relief. Her anger *was* justified! Owain had defiled her! Yet as her tears swam through his image, they cleansed and disrupted his features, darkened his hair, and crystallized the clue that proclaimed Owain clearly innocent—the man owned gray eyes, not brown.

A barking roused Owain from his light sleep. Miffed, he groped for and tugged his pelt tighter round his shoulders. The llys was colder than the cottage. Nevertheless, he needed to be here, beside Simon and Maura, to protect. He smiled, remembering the time after the dancing. He'd found them behind the tapestry on the bed, Maura asleep, Simon beside her chewing on a piece of straw and brooding. Then when they'd commenced talking, Simon's worry had vanished, and had been replaced by smiles, and soft laughter. Simon was a queer fellow, hard to fathom...admirable, sometimes pompous, but most times humble. His bolstering could make you feel as tall as an oak, yet with nothing but a look, he could swiftly cut you to a twig. Owain recalled feeling like a twig often in Simon's presence, yet that seemed so long past now. Unlike Marc, Simon was quicker to laughter, impulsive, and less rigid. Owain envied his knowledge, the grace of his tongue, his easy manner, and healing skills. And with Simon, he had found fun again. While talking on the bed, Owain had asked Simon to visit his home on the morrow, and Simon had eagerly agreed. Owain was proud of his, no—Marc's and his—accomplishment. The home was once again habitable, and he needed to assure Simon and Maura that, if needed, his home would serve as their sanctuary. Maura had done too much today. He'd warned Simon, and Simon had laughed, suggesting that if he had been bedridden for two months and finally allowed freedom, he would have done too much as well. The thought of the child's birth excited Owain. He'd remembered his siblings being born, the joy that followed their arrival, and the magic of watching and guiding their growing. A sadness followed and was fed by the fact that Taredd would be here soon, and Owain would be obliged to pass on to him the coveted role of Pennaeth. How strange to be sad, when not so long in the past, he'd fought viciously not to have the title, or the woman, or the responsibility. Now looking back, he acknowledged he hadn't done so badly, and the villagers had come to tolerate him. But the woman, well...she most likely would never allow him more than a smile and, curiously, that prospect only made him sadder. Well, he wouldn't have to face her much longer. Rhys was no doubt at this very moment reckoning a future for him, and Owain was about to depart on his annual trek north to visit relatives. And on this journey, along with the tedious visits, he planned to solve a mystery.

Someone's shifting disrupted Owain's musing. He waited, heard nothing more, then thought fondly of the nights in Simon and Maura's cottage. Each evening would unfold in a sort of ritual—They'd all enjoy a warm drink, and engage in spirited talk that gradually turned lazy. After settling on their pallets or bed, Owain would play a sleepy tune on his whistle, and everyone would soon drift off. The closeness of the family filled him with a sense of curious contentment, the same he'd felt with his own clan. Not only did this make him feel wondrous, it also worried him relentlessly.

Shifting sounds disturbed him again and were joined by voices, Simon and Maura's voices—their murmurs were not happy or passionate, but tinged with anguish. He rolled to face the bed, quieted his breath, and listened.

Maura's head lolled. She called out in a half sleep, her whispering pained, "Simon...Simon...don't leave me...*Please* don't leave me."

"Maura..." he called gently, stroking her brow, "wake up. I'm here...Wake up and find me."

She warily fluttered open her eyes and beheld his silhouette hovered over her, haloed by faint candlelight. She was petrified to move, afraid she would jar his image and make real her dream—a portent of death. Her mind and sight sharpened as she shoved up and twisted frantically. This wasn't her home, wasn't her bed! "Where?!

Where are we, Simon?" She clutched at her belly; their child was still with them, and Simon wasn't gone, wasn't hurt.

He urged her carefully back down on the bed, and explained in his most soothing voice, "We're at the llys. You fell asleep and I hadn't the heart to move you. No one minds. Taredd didn't return, and Gael's at her own hut. Why would you fear I'd leave you?"

"My dream..."

"*The* dream?"

"No...and yes. There were the same flames, the same hut, the same man, but this time he struck *you* down."

"You dreamt that version before, less than a year past, the night of Shrove Tuesday...Remember?"

She relaxed to his revelation. "Yes...I remember. Anyone I worry about becomes part of my dream."

"You needn't worry about me, my love. I'm perfectly well, though you...you must take things a little slower tomorrow."

She emphatically replied, "I'm eager and more than ready to have this child, Simon."

He stretched back beside her, and partly agreed, "And I'm also eager, yet perhaps not as ready."

"Why ever not? You'll make the most magnificent father."

"I'm glad you believe so. However, I have some doubts."

"You needn't..." Her grip tensed again. "You'll be by me when she comes?"

He patted her hand to ease her strife and assured, "Of course, I will. Only...I'll let Gael do the helping. I'll most likely be a bit flustered."

"No more than I. I want it to happen now, Simon. I don't want to wait, I'm afraid something will happen—"

"Don't, Maura...don't upset yourself needlessly." His calming had no effect on her fretting; her expression stayed pinched, her posture rigid, her hold strangling. He gathered her close and vowed, "While our destiny remains in *our* power, I will never leave you, and if by someone else's hand we are parted, I will find you as I found you before and will always—"

"But Simon..." she anguished, "my dream...in my dream—"

His finger on her lips and ardent response hushed her misery. "Believe that I will find you, for my love, I absolutely refuse to be without you." His lilting words and warm lips doused most of her fear, yet the fright that insistently burned at her gut still simmered. Any mention of its lingering would only upset him further, and she wouldn't distress—

They both stiffened as new sounds intruded—more dogs barked, horse hooves pounded, brash voices slurred together and cackled. Simon and Owain bolted from their beds. Footfalls encroached on the llys and stomped the stairs. Someone stumbled and crashed against the bolted door, hysterical laughter following.

Rhys' troops were stabled with the beasts, and Rhys himself lay abed in the monastery, leaving only Simon and Owain to defend the llys. Simon carried no weapon; he snatched up and wielded the hooded candle, as Owain cautiously slid his dagger from his sheath. With mincing steps, they snuck to the door. Maura forced herself to sit, hugged securely the pelts, and pressed her panic to the wall. Owain gestured Simon quiet, and demanded, "Who's there?!"

Laughter answered, then a broken, "The...the bride...bridegroom."

"Taredd?" Owain puzzled in a whisper. Simon returned a shrug. Owain gripped the hilt of his knife and, with impeccable care, lifted the bolt. The door burst inward and

Taredd rolled inside, trailed by three staggering, equally intoxicated comrades. Owain kicked at the lump at his feet, snarling, "Get up, you drunken louse!"

Taredd giddily pushed up on his elbows. His head dropped back and, at the sight of Simon looming above, he blanched as he scrambled up from the rushes, swiped the candle from Simon, and charged crazily toward the bed. Simon surged after him and swung his leg in front of Taredd's feet, tripping him, then kicked and crashed Taredd into the wall. The forceful impact of Taredd's skull impacting the timbers at such a quick speed sagged him to a crumpled and senseless heap in the rushes. His friends didn't seem to notice the ruckus. They'd immediately found themselves a soft spot to lounge upon, and one had already commenced snoring.

Owain stomped out the sparks scattered by the tossed candle, and promptly relit it with a rush flamed by the glowing coals. Maura joined Simon and crouched with him to check on Taredd. Their anxious looks eased somewhat when they located his pulse, slightly elevated, but nonetheless thumping healthily. Owain's glare betrayed disgust at his successor; his comment, however, delivered praise, "That was very nice, Simon, but your speed to strike may cause you some trouble."

Simon stood in defense. "He was headed for Maura!"

"I realize that, and I don't question what you've done. It's only—well, you've probably just succeeded in making yourself an enemy of the Pennaeth."

"Maybe," hoped Maura, struggling to rise, "he won't remember, with all the drink he's had..."

"Let's pray so," agreed Owain. "And in the morning, let me take credit for his bruising. He'll believe I kicked him. He hates me."

*****

324

CHAPTER NINETEEN - A BUNDLE OF OATHS

𝔇𝔞𝔴𝔫 barely broke, but its dullness failed to reach the still stark black corridor leading from Adela's bedchamber. Almodis straggled her way along the dank passageway, her hands groping blindly and feet kicking out to intercept any nastiness, human or animal. She muttered curses at whomever should have lit the torches in the hallway, at Henry for acting an inexorable pest, and at his sister for taking such a prolonged and torturous—not for Adela, but for Almodis—length of time to deliver her son. Well, it was done, and Almodis soberly resolved to herself never to utter another word, kind or cruel, to the bellicose Countess. As Almodis tip-toed between Benjamin and Thomas and reached for the latch to her chamber, she whispered a fleeting prayer that Robert had also completed his obligation—the interrogation of the exasperating FitzRoy. Perhaps they could both finally partake of some much needed sleep. She was surprised to find the chamber lightly illuminated and her husband not asleep, but reclining on their bed, feet crossed at the ankles, one hand resting behind his head, the other holding a chalice of wine. Almodis had beheld this odd state of his many a time, his piercing stare stuck on some vague object, his true sight and thoughts far, far away. She didn't want to alarm him, so she approached cautiously. A crunch of a rush startled him from his trance; his austere look gradually softened to her weary, yet immensely fair guise. "Robert..." she chanced, "are you well?"

He set the chalice down by the carafe on the side table; swung his legs to dangle off the side of the massive bed; then, clasping his hands firmly together, answered with light deliberance, "Yes...I am. And how fares Adela?"

Almodis sagged down beside him and sighed heavily. "She's fine...now. She is not a kind woman, Robert. I honestly believed that I had heard and spoken every obscenity there was to speak, yet I was sorely mistaken. Then again, for all her fuss, she's delivered a big and bonny boy."

"His name?"

"Stephen. It's about time she named one for her husband. Are you irked that I didn't name Adam for you?"

"No, not at all. There are far too many Robert's about. Adam suits him fine. Estrith fed him for you."

"I'm glad...for her...consideration," she yawned and stretched out languidly at the foot of the bed, and rested her head on her reaching arm. "Now all I want to do for the entire day is sleep." She nudged his thigh with her foot and hoped, "You'll sleep *with* me?"

"Almodis..." he answered carefully. "There was a decision that needed making, and since you were engaged elsewhere, I considered how I believed you would advise me, and came to a joint decision on my own."

"On how to punish Henry?"

"Yes...and there's more."

"Then he *did* hurt Maura."

"Yes. It took me most of the night to decipher his other ravings, but from them I've discerned that Odo has discovered where Simon and Maura reside, and is at this moment venturing there to seek his revenge."

Almodis pushed sleepily up on her palm, her alarm muffled by exhaustion, "What? How did he find out? Even *I* wouldn't tell you!"

"Henry's butler is the culprit. Odo placed him in Henry's service as a spy. And I've also learned that this spineless young man, named John, is Odo's son, and that there may be others."

Almodis' shock almost toppled her from the bed. She lunged forward to catch Robert's saving grip, and choked, "So...son! By God, Robert, after all the abuse the ogre has spat at you, he's been secretly rutting and spawning tiny ogres all these many years! You must feel an overwhelming sense of vindication. Do you?"

"Actually, I don't know what I feel. However, I do know that I must stop him from tormenting Simon anymore. When I compare what he's made of his son to what my son has made of himself, I can't help but hope that I had some influence on Simon's shaping. Odo has depleted me of much, but he won't rid me of what little pride I still possess. I'll leave this day for Wales, and take half my army along to join with Henry's troops."

"So Henry goes free."

"No...He remains my prisoner, and will guide me to the Welsh Prince who protects Simon and Maura. I pray to arrive in time to hide them till I can succeed in persuading Odo to cease his nonsense and return to Bayeux. Then you and I will deal with Henry."

"I'll come with you!" Almodis' body and voice strained with her plea, "Take me with you! I couldn't bear it if—"

"I can't allow that, Almodis. Will is involved, and you know the treachery he aims for you and Adam."

"I can't stay here, Robert...not so far away. Pevensey—I'll wait for you at Pevensey with Adam! If Will is so intent on murdering Simon, he won't be thinking of us. You may surround us with soldiers a mile thick, but please let me be nearer to you, *please*!"

He couldn't resist her sweetness, and her loyalty which he knew to be trustworthy. "I'll go first. You follow by a week. I will arrange impenetrable protection at Pevensey and will send pages regularly with news of my, I mean our, campaign. Henry still seems to have affectionate ties to Simon."

"Raveled ties. And what of Maura?"

"He wasn't able to complete the rape, and doesn't believe he murdered her or her child."

"I suppose I should be grateful for his inadequacies," spat Almodis. "Please, my Lord, don't let me meet with him. What little control I have will surely falter."

"I'll keep him far from you." He hopped from the bed and appeared quite energized as he strode for the door. "I'll send for servants to complete my packing, then I must eat, and you must as well."

"Robert...wait."

Robert turned to her expression, blatant with such ardent longing he felt his heart near to cracking. Her broken lament barely reached his ears. "I don't want to be without you just now."

He returned swiftly to her side and waved propriety aside to clutch her in his arms, and deliver his solemn oath, "We won't be parted long. I'll see our boy before I go."

She gulped and asked, "How soon will that be?"

"Within the hour," he quavered.

"Then stay with me awhile more."

His resistance ebbed as he melted to the heat of her lips and, with her urging, across the pelts. He'd rarely seen her spill tears, and his threatened to erupt in response to her endearment, "I'll miss you so, as will Adam. And we're so very proud of you."

*****

One hand clutched her arm, the other strangled her skirt, as Maura stood apprehensively over the still senseless Pennaeth and asked, "He will wake won't he, Owain?"

Owain rolled his pallet tight, then secured it with a leather cord. "Of course he will, when the drink's worn off. Don't worry."

Why was he running at me?"

"I've thought on that puzzle half the night...then I remembered. Rumors spreading through the troops at Dinefwr say that your husband keeps for certain two wives here, and maybe more."

"What?!" Maura blurted in amazement. "Me and who else?"

"Gael..." He hoped he hadn't upset her and quickly pacified, "I know it's daft, most of the gossip spewed at Dinefwr is lies. Don't concern yourself—"

"So he thought we'd both be in bed with Simon?"

"I don't know what he thought, but he appeared to be on his way to check."

Maura smiled, then broke into a chuckle. "Wait till Simon hears this."

Relieved, Owain shared her laughter as Simon strolled into the llys, dropped his medicine bag, and wondered with a bemused grin, "What's funny?"

"You tell him," suggested Owain to Maura.

"Gladly. Owain thinks Taredd charged the bed last night expecting to find Gael tucked up between us."

"Why would he think that?" Simon asked with sincere innocence.

Maura coughed to keep from chortling more, then ventured, "According to the gossip at Dinefwr, you keep a harem here."

"Truly?" He beamed and asked Owain, "They believe that of *me*?"

"That's what's whispered."

"Huh," he grunted with satisfaction. "And I thought they hated me."

"Oh they do," assured Owain.

"But that's a compliment, isn't it?" asked Simon. "When it's said of Rhys, all are in awe of his prowess."

"Yes..." answered Owain with hesitation. "However, he's a Prince and they believe, that as such, he deserves lavish attention. You, on the other hand, are considered a whey-faced laggard, a traitor, and a rake, who's at the beck and call of all the women in this village. You are viewed simply as a pretty toy, and a pathetic one at that."

Simon huffed sarcastically. "Why thank you, Owain. You've made me feel so immensely virile."

"You asked..." smirked Owain, hauling up a number of sacks from the floor. He swung them over his shoulders, and strode out of the llys.

Maura rushed to Simon's rescue with outstretched arms, and a look dripping sympathy. "They're only jealous Simon, or they wouldn't bother with the gossip. *I'm* in awe of your prowess."

Simon's beam returned, then vanished as he held her close, and his worry drifted past Maura's shoulder to the spot where Taredd lay. "I should wake Taredd to check for any problems that may have occurred from the blow."

Maura eased their hold. "Surely he didn't hit the wall that hard. Leave him. Owain said he'd wake soon. And I don't want another fight."

"I wouldn't fight him," said Simon.

"I'm not speaking of you...If what Owain said is true, then it will be Taredd who's ripe for battle. Have you eaten?"

"Yes, before I left this morning."

"Then go and help Owain pack," said Maura. "I'll find something other than your lips to munch upon and join you soon. I'm excited about seeing his home. Aren't you?"

"Yes, very much so!"

"Where's Marc?" she wondered

"He's gone to fetch Olwen and the children. Is Gruffydd going with us?"

"Now that Taredd's come, I expect Gael will want him here."

Simon grabbed up a sack and was fuddled by its heaviness. "What *are* we taking with us?"

"We're staying the night, so food stuffs, pallets, and such."

"Oh." He started for the door, then turned to warn, "I don't want to catch you lifting any of these. Promise?"

"I promise," she vowed with a blown kiss, then waddled off to find nourishment.

Simon greeted the brilliant morn with a huge smile, and it returned the favor with a wisp of balmy air and tingling of sun. He flung the bags in the hind of a straw cushioned cart, and shouted cheerily to Owain, who harnessed the horses, "When do we leave?"

"After we've taken care of some important business"

"What's that? Talking with the Powys brothers?"

"No...Taredd couldn't get any of them to visit." Owain tightened the last strap, nonchalantly reached toward the seat of the cart, and when he jerked back around, his glare flashed murderously.

Simon barely caught the hilt of the sword he threw, and dashed three broad steps out from the cart. Braced in a defensive posture, he deftly blocked Owain's first strike, and hollered, "Bleeding Jesus, Owain! I don't want to do this. Not today. I'm tired!"

"So am I!" yelled Owain, slamming two more strikes and driving Simon out onto the common. "A missed day will weaken you."

"I hate this!" howled Simon.

"Show me how much you hate this. Hit me, or do you want me to believe the troop's gossip?"

Simon's explosive response stunned Owain. He was forced to only blocking strikes, and wavered under Simon's ferocious rain of blows. Yet he wouldn't complain. He was pleased when Simon used their practice as more than a game, for it would be no game if and when his true enemies struck. As Owain gathered his guile and bashed back a few hits with equal vigor, a word Simon had used in the night pounded his thoughts—*Power.* In the final battle, whose power would prevail? Owain would fight till eternity to keep his friends' destiny in their hands, and away from the sway of their enemies. But a curious doubt kept interfering with his conviction and focus, and he wondered—*Who exactly are their true enemies*?

Maura wandered out of the llys, a piece of buttered flat bread held to her lips. At the sight of Owain and Simon's squabble, she stopped short and lost her bread to the dirt below. Since they'd started their practice months before, it had always been staged beyond her view. Pride swelled her breast as she beheld her husband and friend's astute capacity for battle. A savage excitement rumbled within her, instantly transporting her to the similar games of their youth. She wanted desperately to grab up a sword and join them.

Owain wanted Simon to beat him fairly, and swiftly conjured a fool-proof method for defeat. He growled and grunted over the clatter of their clash, "Believe me your enemy, Simon! I am Henry and will steal your wife to keep her as my own!" The tremendous spike in Simon's strength made Owain smile and duck to keep his head. He played more and taunted, "Now I'm Will and you've finally caught me alone. Prove to me who's the mightier!" Simon's powerful whack to Owain's shoulder threw him off-balance. He recovered with a somersault, and instantly leapt back from a more intense swipe to his belly. Owain sucked in his gut and gasped at dozens of flecks of fabric sailing in the wake of the slice.

Simon spied Maura watching by the cart. His potency surged, then peaked to Owain's wicked snicker. "I'm your Uncle Odo and will gladly snuff out your life and your entire family's!" In a flash of iron, Owain found himself flat on his back, a boot pressing his belly, and Simon's sword hoisted, the tip aimed directly at Owain's heart. He opened his mouth to pronounce, "I'm dead..." but was struck dumb and rigid with terror as the sword plummeted. His wail, "Simon! No!" rattled the ground, and pierced and pained his ears. It was the only hurt he felt for, when he pried wide his eyes, he gaped at the sword's tip poised not an inch above his heart.

Simon lorded above, dripping sweat and quaking from fear. He tossed his sword, dropped to his knees and, with his hands gripping Owain's shoulders for support, panted, "I'm sorry, Owain...I'm so very sorry." He flopped to Owain's side and lay sprawled and puffing.

Owain rolled to his knees and crept a safe distance away before chancing to rise. As he shakily pulled himself erect, his boomed comment surprised Simon and himself as well, "There's no need for sorry! Yours was my greatest challenge yet!"

Simon barely lifted his head to nod, then sank it back in the cool grass to contemplate his peculiar success and the vivid blue of the sky. Marc's shadow and the cool touch of Maura's palm on his brow interrupted his reflection. Marc offered his hand and hoisted him up to sitting, and Maura's radiance almost blinded him. "And you wondered why you bothered. How gloriously you fought!" she praised.

Owain wandered near and, with a snort, noted to Maura, "All he needed was *you* watching."

"It's my turn now...isn't it?" hoped Marc.

"I'll have a few moments first to revive my *amazing stamina*," croaked Simon, struggling up.

"He's already bragging," laughed Owain. "I'll take you on again up at my cottage."

"And who will you pretend to be next time?"

"I'll think of someone invincible."

Simon snorted back and, after receiving a triumphant kiss from Maura, retrieved his sword for his bout with Marc. "This is the last one for the morning, Marc," he strictly stressed. "And we'll be quick."

Marc grunted and braced himself for combat. They commenced swinging, slowly at first, then very soon their momentum flourished. Simon abandoned the insistency of his first fray, and concentrated more on foot work, and swiftness of response. Marc, as always, proved a relentless contender, allowing no time between strikes for thought, thus forcing his opponent to rely strictly on instinct. And, although few could rally the expertise needed to withstand his assaults, Simon could and did. His plea for expediency was promptly dashed when soldiers scurried en masse out from the stable at the rear of the llys, and jogged alongside Rhys down the lane leading from the cathedral to join in the sport. Olwen, Maura, and the children found themselves a cushioned seat beneath a naked gnarled oak on which to view the rousing show. Maura hungrily accepted the baby from Olwen, and chattered with her excitedly of Simon's victory over Owain. Marc and Simon forsook their squabble, and steeled themselves instead for the Welshmen's furious, good-natured onslaught.

Owain wagged his head to the madness of it all and retreated inside. He crept by Taredd, still sleeping, and pushed beyond the tapestry separating the main hall from the sleeping area. A water bowl and pitcher sat on a table near the bed. He emptied a puddle of water into the bowl and stripped to his breeches. An examination of his tunic revealed a gaping slice gouging the front. He lightheartedly cursed Simon, dipped the ruined garment in the water, then enlisting it as a towel, proceeded to scrub himself free of grime.

Using the back door, Gael gingerly entered the llys. She called out a faint, "Is anyone here?" but received no answer. The room appeared exceptionally neat, far neater than when she lived in it. It must be Raythyen's influence, she decided, as she boldly advanced further. From the corner of her eye, she spotted movement on the floor, and soon discovered her husband shifting and groaning in the rushes. Once he'd found comfort he lapsed into a rattling snore, and she wondered why he'd chosen the floor and not the bed. She gazed at him for an intent while, striving to invoke a tender feeling. Nothing came, so she shrugged, ambled over toward the bed, and brushed aside the tapestry.

Gael's great gasp caused a similar drastic reaction in Owain. His forced breath sprayed the water cupped in his palm unintentionally in her direction. She winced to the shower and his howl, "To the Gods above, woman! You'll make my heart stop!"

"I'm sorry!" she burst as vehemently. "I didn't know you were here. Why didn't you answer my call?"

"What call?" he groused, snatching up his shirt and clutching it modestly to his naked chest.

"When I came in, I asked if anyone was here."

"I didn't hear you." Owain swiftly wriggled into his shirt, scoured his face with his tunic, and palmed back his hair.

All the while Gael watched; a tad too keenly, Owain thought. He glanced over his shoulder, and self-consciously insisted, "What are you gawking at?"

She shook from her stare and vaguely replied, "Nothing..."

Their discomfort with each other was obvious in their darting glances and terse speech.

"That *is* my husband sprawled in the rushes, isn't it?" Gael asked, cracking a wry grin.

"I pray you know who it is."

"Why isn't he on the bed?"

"Maura fell asleep after the dancing," replied Owain. "She and Simon stayed on the bed."

"Oh...Why is he still asleep?"

"He arrived drunk and made a fuss. We had to hurt him to quiet him. It was good you slept elsewhere."

"Who's 'we'?"

"Sorry?"

"We...You mentioned '*we*' hurt him. Who's 'we'?"

"Oh...Simon and I."

"It took the two of you to restrain him?" Gael asked, askance.

"Not really."

Gael didn't dare attempt to question that answer, and muttered, "I suppose he'll be full of questions when he wakes."

Owain nodded stiffly and asked, "Where's your son?"

"With my sister eating."

"How fares your sister?"

"About the same as you saw her last evening."

Owain nodded again, this time with a frown, and chanced a step in her direction to pass. She stepped a broad clumsy stride backward, then as he hurried by, she heard a huge hollering erupt from outside the main door. "What's that?" she blurted.

"Just some nonsense," answered Owain.

330

"Some rather loud nonsense," returned Gael. She strode to the shuttered window and flung it open. "My God!" she exclaimed, and jerked to Owain. "Do you know what's happening out there?!"

"Yes..." he replied mundanely. "Simon and Marc are most likely getting trounced by Rhys' elite command."

Gael looked back outside, and corrected, "No...It's just Marc and Simon and Rhys and someone I don't know."

"What?!" he said with an incredulous shout. He joined her lookout and gaped in awe. "They've made it through the entire army! I don't believe it! I didn't realize *I* was that good."

Why is he so impossibly difficult to understand? Gael grumbled to herself, then demanded in an irked voice, "Good at what? Why aren't you out there helping Simon and Marc?"

"They obviously don't need my help," he returned brusquely. "If you're so concerned, why don't you have a go?"

Gael retorted with a sarcastic guffaw, "Me with a sword?"

His side-long glance caught the twinkle in her eye, and he lauded, "If you aim a sword with the same precision you aim a gob of spit, you'd prove a fearsome challenge."

Gael couldn't stop her laugh; it rumbled out loud and sharp, and stuttered her response, "May...may I take...take that as compliment?"

"Take it as you like," he dismissed, not knowing whether to regret his boldness.

Suddenly tongue-tied, he turned to leave, but his escape was stalled by the light grasp of her fingers on his arm. He forced his expression as bland as possible, yet felt it ease to match her grin, when she spoke kindly, "I'd like to take it as a compliment."

A nod and blush was all the response he could muster as he eased from her touch, and hastened to snatch his cloak from its hook by the door. Halfway out, he twisted back to say, "If Gruffydd would like, he might go with us to my home in the hills."

Gael's hands hugged her waist, soothing the cramp forming. She heard, yet couldn't tame the quaver in her answer. "I'm certain he'd love to, but since Taredd has finally arrived, he should be here."

"What?!" The boy's shrill call rang through the hall, abruptly rousing his step-father, and startling his mother and friend. "What would I love to do?" He ignored the yellow-haired man sitting cross-legged in the rushes, cradling his head, and darted directly to Owain. "What do you want me to do, Owain?" he excitedly asked.

Owain glanced to Gael, received a vague look, and decided frankness was best. "I asked if you'd like to go with us—Simon, Marc, Maura and me, Olwen and her children—to my home in the hills. We'll be staying the night."

"Oh yes!" Gruffydd's exuberance gushed over and spilled to his mother. "I can, can't I, Mam? Owain promised that I could go with him when next he went. Please say yes!"

Gael's fuddle swept from her husband, to Owain, to Gruffydd, and back to her husband. "I don't think so, Gruffydd," she reluctantly answered, gesturing limply toward Taredd. "I'd prefer you spend the day with Taredd and me."

Gruffydd paled to her mention of his new step-father and, as if threatened, clasped himself to Owain's arm. "I'll go with Owain," he abruptly announced. His mam's expression didn't reflect annoyance so, emboldened, he softened and tried once more, "Please say yes!"

"Quiet!" Taredd commanded in a pained bellow. "Throw him out or shut him up!"

Owain, Gruffydd, and Gael cast appalled eyes on the Pennaeth. Gael's gape was quickly drawn back to Owain, visibly swelling and reddening with protective rage. It wouldn't do to have a scuffle here, not when Gruffydd was already showing signs of unease toward Taredd. Gruffydd might bolt for good, and she couldn't have that happen, wouldn't have that happen! Hell, she'd chosen this man strictly because having him would guarantee she kept her son. "Owain," she implored, "please, take him with you, keep him close."

Gruffydd wisely kept silent, yet he dashed to hug his mam, and thanked her with a dazzling smile. He rushed back to Owain, accepted a sack, and scampered outside. Owain held back, surveying the tenuous situation. Taredd's head was once again hidden in his hands, and for the first time, Owain noticed Ella, huddled in her cloak, standing by the back door. To Gael, he cocked his head in Ella's direction, and received a slim smile in response. He felt a terrible puzzle—should he stay or should he go? Was Taredd likely to become violent? Then, considering Gael's tenacious manner, his worry lessened. Sometimes she reminded him of a spirited mare who never could or should be tamed. He looked to her one last time for direction, and sensed she'd been gazing at him all along and had heard every one of his thoughts. He felt his skin sizzle and sighed a mighty sigh when she nodded her excuse, "We'll do fine here, Owain. I thank you. Enjoy your trip."

Content with Gael's blessing, Owain slipped away, and forced his thoughts on the ravaging his Prince was suffering at the hands of his physician. He laughed at the peculiar drama, and the extraordinary cheer he felt at having endured a half-way civil conversation with the Lady Gael. "Simon!" he shouted buoyantly. "Thump him one...for me!"

*****

The cart wobbled along the rutted road with Maura driving. Nia slept, resting her head in Maura's lap, and Simon and Marc dozed in the rear. Olwen had decided, owing to many chores awaiting her at home, to stay back with the baby. The day continued its amiable weather, and Owain rode sans cloak alongside the cart, listening in amusement to Maura's rendition of the morning's melee, which was interrupted regularly by the hooting boys, chasing and racing on their mounts. "Rhys won't truly be upset by his defeat, will he, Owain?" Maura fretted. "He said nothing to Simon, and as you know, Simon will worry about his silence."

"He may not have talked to Simon," said Owain, "but he talked to me. Surprise and admiration describe best what he felt, and also embarrassment."

"Why is everyone so surprised by Simon's victories?"

"Because of what I told you this morning—the gossip."

"Don't they know he trained practically his whole life to be a knight!" she emphasized. "He won't brag to you of this, however I gladly will. He was considered by the ablest of knights and barons to be a matchless warrior—except against Marc."

Owain thought back to the squabbles and realized, that in truth, when Marc and Simon were matched alone, which happened rarely, neither was victor. Simon only lost when attacked by both Owain and Marc. Since Owain believed that Simon, if truly challenged, would be attacked by a mass of men, he had never taken on Simon alone, till that morning. "He's never lost a duel, even against Marc?" he asked.

"Simon taught Marc how to fight. When we were young, Marc never came close to winning, then..."

Owain watched curiously as Maura shifted her gaze inward. Her voice turned dreamy and slightly troubled as she reflected on, "It was almost exactly a year past at Christmas court. Marc had received his knighthood in the morning, and his melee followed. He was allowed to choose his contender, and chose Simon. They'd been separated for years, and as far as I can recall, Simon hadn't swung a sword in ages. They fought for hours, it was grueling, messy, and painful to watch, and would have been a draw if Marc hadn't slipped in the mud. I believe they are entirely equal in ability."

"But," Owain cut in, "if Simon trained to be a knight, why isn't he one, and how did he acquire the knowledge?"

"His Uncle Odo refused him his knighthood, and what knowledge do you mean?"

"Reading, writing, languages."

"Oh...He was also prepared for the priesthood."

"Priesthood?" Owain echoed with surprise. "Well then, I must speak to him about his preparation. Maura, from the little I witnessed this morning, I don't think he need worry anymore about gossip." A glint of mischief gleamed in Owain's eye as he smirked on, "At least regarding his martial skills. It's said you own a talent with a sword."

"By whom?"

"Both your husband and brother. They take great pride in boasting about your achievements."

Maura blushed and scoffed, "I've not practiced in years." She laughed and returned with a wry smile, "Actually, I do much better with a knife and a bow and arrows."

"You'll show me how much better at the cottage," challenged Owain.

"I'd love to!" She burbled further, "I'm excited about Gruffydd's accomplishment. He seems a natural bowman."

"His father was," noted Owain.

"You knew his father?"

"Not as well as I would have liked. I served beneath him my first year as a soldier. Then he retired and became Pennaeth. There have been, and are today, very few persons in Rhys' household and army that I can talk easily with—Rhodri was one. He was a rare soul, gentle and noble. I see Gruffydd to be exactly like him."

"He *is* very special," agreed Maura. "Did you visit Rhodri after he retired to Mynyw?"

"I wanted to but there was never time. He came to Dinefwr regularly to meet with Rhys and sometimes I had the luck to be there. Gael always came with him." He grinned a peculiar grin and noted, "I was at their wedding."

"And was it a happy affair?"

"Seemed so. I stayed out of view."

His pinched look prompted Maura to ask, "What's upset you?"

"Everyone was shocked by his sudden death, especially me. Rhys sent me to Mynyw to investigate. It was a terrible time."

"And what did you discover?" she asked.

"Nothing...But I am convinced he was murdered, most likely by poison."

"But not administered by Gael?"

"No, not by Gael," he readily confirmed. "I never believed that. They always seemed friendly."

"They were. Owain, you said you feel comfortable with only a few of Rhys' household. One of those few wouldn't be Taredd, would it?"

"No," he answered adamantly. "I don't like him, don't trust him, and do my best to avoid him. Tomorrow, we're slated to meet to discuss the status of the village." He suddenly appeared tenuous. "I don't want to do it, and I expect to have to use all the mediation training I received from you lot to survive."

She smiled at his exaggeration and assured, "Always remember, when you feel close to boiling, take a long deep breath."

"A long deep breath," he repeated and, smiling as well, playfully wondered, "Are they going to sleep forever? I thought Simon and I might finish our race."

Maura turned a mawkish glance back on her men, angelic in sleep, then hurled a mocking glare at Owain. "He'd shame you," she touted, "even on E'dain!"

Owain snorted and, with feigned indignance, grunted, "Never!"

*****

Gael shifted discontentedly on a bench and fiddled with the tip of her braid while watching her husband noisily slurp up his midday meal. It's not that he wasn't attractive; he owned an oily sort of bland fairness, with all his features neatly placed; his straw colored hair combed and staying put; his eyes of a vague hue, reflecting whatever color they focused upon; his stature tall and wiry. Yet his prettiness did not excite Gael. Contrarily, it produced a sour feeling in her gut, and with each passing hour, doubts she supposed were normal of a newlywed piled higher. Her attempts at conversation had been met only with nods and grunts, so she'd surrendered to silence and dutifully awaited some interest to emerge from him. It came after he'd thoroughly finished his meal, drained his mead, wiped his mouth, and pushed his bowl and tankard aside. "Why didn't you wait for me last night?" was his perfunctory greeting.

"I did till very late. My son and sister were housed in my former hut, and I felt they needed my presence."

"I needed your presence!" he burst in anger. "I was attacked when I arrived here...Attacked, by the villagers I've come to rule! I needed nursing from my wife, and don't *you* hold that coveted title, Madam?"

"I don't know who else may covet it," she scorned, "but yes, Sir, I am—in title only—your wife. If I had known you'd been hurt, I would have come to your aid, but, alas, no one felt the need to tell me."

"What were you told?"

"Very little."

He pointed accusingly. "Don't lie to me...I heard you and Owain whispering. About what?"

Gael struggled for calm, and squeezed her hands together, paling her knuckles. Lamely, she relayed, "He said you arrived indisposed and as such created a stir that had to be silenced."

"Did he hurt me?"

"He said as much."

"That bleeding bastard!" Taredd flared and leapt up to flail and bark, "Where is he?! If he wants a fight, he'll have a fight. He lost his chance to command this commote. You rejected him and accepted me! You'll not whisper with him again."

"I'll whisper with whomever I choose," Gael snarled back. "And if you must know, I am not overly fond of Owain, but he was kind enough to tell me what had occurred last night, and see to my son when you so rudely banished him. Have you, Sir, any experience with ruling?"

Taken aback by her query, Taredd paused his pacing and pulled himself erect to brag, "I've commanded two armies."

"Two? One with Rhys and one where else?"

"On the border with England. I was raised on the border, and was proclaimed leader of a troop of soldiers at eighteen. I've slaughtered far more Normans than that bastard can ever imagine."

"The bastard being?" Gael asked snidely.

"Owain."

"Oh...Well..." Her fingers splayed over the table and eased her up as she flouted, "I'm highly impressed by your brutality." She then continued in all seriousness. "I'm concerned about your violent past, because this commote is not accustomed to being ruled by anyone. They serve and support the cathedral, and Rhys' household and army when they come to visit or protect, and are a peaceful law-abiding people. Every so often they desire guidance and judgment which you as Pennaeth are obliged to dispense. They require nurturance, not domination, and if you pick the latter as a manner of rule, you will be extricated from this house and this village quicker than even you can ever imagine...*Sir*." She fiddled with her belt and soundly stated, "Now I must see to my sister."

Yet Taredd wasn't done and sniped, "She won't be living here."

"And why not?"

"I won't have madness in my house."

Gael could not disguise the derision in her reply, "This is my house as well and she is not mad, Sir. She is simply confused and, I pray, very soon will be right again. Will you be having my son live someplace else as well?"

"He can stay, if he's quiet. I won't abide him squealing like he did this morning."

"Nine year olds frequently squeal. I expect you'll become accustomed to his exuberance."

"Where is he now?"

"He's gone off with Owain overnight."

"Good. He likes Owain?"

"He does."

"That doesn't bother you?"

"It might have once, but it doesn't now."

Pain caused from his bingeing the night before struck Taredd dumb, and forced him back onto the bench. He supported his splitting head in his palms, cringed, and moaned. Gael lifted his tankard and tried to sound comforting, "I'll fetch you more mead. You're still hurting from last night and—"

He batted the tankard from her grip; she jerked back, aghast, as he lashed out, "I wasn't drunk! He attacked me without cause, or it was that blasted Norman! I want you away...I will be alone in my house!"

"Do you mean permanently away," she asked shakily. "We are married—"

"Get out!" he cried, pounding the table in a tantrum.

"Do I repulse you, Sir?" she unwisely returned.

"Yes...I find you dull looking, your tongue wags too freely, you lack manners, and you are old." His tone turned haughty as he flaunted, "At Dinefwr, I have women, many women weeping at the loss of my attention, beautiful women, who are well schooled in how to respect and attend to a man's needs. You obviously missed your training," he scorned. "But..." He arched a brow in reprieve. "You may not be *too* old to learn your place."

Sickened, Gael croaked, "May I leave, Sir?"

"Please."

"When should I return?"

"Dusk."

Taredd's fuming rejection evoked in Gael a tangle of wrath and relief. She staunchly stood and strode to the rear door. There she paused and glanced back to catch a curious exchange occurring between her husband and their newly appointed servant—Enid. The young woman, tall, chestnut-haired, and in Gael's estimation far too slim, stood at Taredd's side, her back to Gael. They whispered, yet whatever else they shared, Gael couldn't see. Enid had moved from Dinefwr where she had tended to Gwladys on her very few visits each year. Who knew what she got up to the remainder of her time. Gael had a definite hunch as she unmistakably made out a coy giggle. She felt a stab of unbidden jealousy, grabbed up her cloak, and exited the llys. Across the courtyard, she noticed Ella sitting on a bench before the stable, chatting and singing to herself. "Ella!"

Gael called out and was pleased when her sister lifted her eyes in response. "Maura and Simon have asked me to see to their beasts. Would you like to come?"

Ella rose, smiling in assent. Gael considered the temperature, wrapped her cloak round her shoulders, and decided, "We'll walk." Tugging her sister's hand, Gael trod purposefully along the main road which wove its way through the village, past the stone boundary, and up the steep path to the plateau. All the while she carried on a lively, free-flowing conversation with her sister. In truth she spoke mostly to herself about the weather, the competitions of the morning, her talk with Owain, the kittens—anything that would keep her thoughts from the crudities of her husband.

They arrived huffing and puffing at the cottage door and upon opening it were greeted loudly by the furry foursome. The felines wrapped and slunk themselves round the women's' ankles, almost toppling Gael in her quest to find their food bowl. "I'll feed the rascals, you take a look around, Ella." But Ella had crouched to the floor, delirious in the kittens' affection, so Gael hurriedly spooned them a sampling of what remained in the cauldron dangling over the cold coals, and took a look around by herself. She noted little had changed since she'd last visited. Gael couldn't recall when exactly that had been, but what she did vividly remember—the sense of comfort, warmth and tranquility—still prevailed. The main room was neatened, she supposed, by Marc's influence—the medicines arranged on the physician's table by height of their vessels, dried herbs tied tightly and hung in good order, medical volumes impeccably stacked. The fire had been set to light, the rushes underfoot recently cut and sifted with dried lavender, and the trestle table top removed of everything but a crockery pitcher and an oil lamp. Beneath the table were two rolled pallets, one Marc's and the other one, she suspected, belonged to Owain; beside them were stacked and folded pelt blankets. Cooking utensils, a strung ladder climbing to a storage loft, and bulbs of onion and garlic collected in a tower of bowls crowded a back corner. She hugged herself to the inviting and intoxicating ambiance and felt a despairing stab of longing for her friends' gracious, entertaining, and loving company. No doubt, they were experiencing far more fun than she could presently muster. But she'd content herself with memories, scents, and textures, and skirted round her sister to sample more.

Gael entered the bedchamber, which appeared not so tidy, but then Simon and Maura were more relaxed with clutter than was Marc. The bed was rumpled, the quilt slightly askew, and a plethora of letters teetered on the edge of a side table; some had tumbled to the floor. She bent to retrieve one and saw what she knew to be the name 'Rose' scribbled on the fold. While bedridden, Maura had been busily composing a book for her former guardian, relating all the joys and terrors they had encountered while living in Mynyw. Maura had promised to read every word to Gael before passing it over to Rose, whenever that desired event should come to pass. Gael set the letters down and opened the side window to gain more light. The battered trunk caught a beam of sun and invited Gael to come closer. She hurried to it and removed stashes of clothing and a few blankets that blocked her curiosity. Once unburdened, she lifted the lid gingerly, expecting something or someone to leap out and startle her, but what she found instead only fascinated. A few silk chemises topped a pile of clothing and when she dug deeper she found a glut of gowns—silk as well. She removed them as cautiously as she would remove an ancient parchment, and held one crimson one up to the light to view fully its exquisiteness. Maura had told her of the short time she'd lived a sumptuous existence at Winchester Castle, and the gowns proved evidence of her claim. The material slid sensuously between her fingers as she grasped the frock's shoulders and fashioned it to the front of her. She laughed at the hem running well beyond her boot. Maura had offered Gael her pick of the gowns for her wedding, though with the copious alterations that were necessary, Maura being at least two hands taller and much slimmer, the extra work seemed ludicrous for such an unheralded event. Gael abandoned the scarlet frock and took up a pair of linen hose and a sleeveless, satiny chemise. For a brief moment, she considered the foolishness of her frivolity, then threw off her mantle, her belt and baggy tunic, and her shapeless shift. She stood naked and chattering, clad only in thick woolen hose, wrestling with and finally wriggling herself into the chemise. After a great deal of grunted readjustment and mild curses, she surveyed the stunning effect in a long looking glass, first with a rather disbelieving gaze, then with an awed touch. Her hands smoothed over her firm, though smallish breasts, slid the short length of her lean waist, and came to rest on the slight swell of her hips. She felt pride for the flatness of her belly and, as she sat and peeled away her moth eaten hose, also for the sinewy shapeliness of her legs. The stockings, sheer and luxuriant, clung rapturously to her skin, and tugging one the full length of her limb, her fingers happened to brush the inside of her thigh, quite near the soft pale down that graced the space between her legs. For an ecstatic moment she imagined a man's fingers, roughly tender, wandering there, eager to discover and please. An unexpected dizziness and quickened heart beat followed. Shamed, she forced her eyes to see only her hand and quickly snatched it away, and the hose off. How ridiculous she thought, to primp for a man she felt absolutely nothing for, and who considered her 'dull looking'. She struggled from the chemise, somberly pulled back on her own shift, and replaced the garments in the trunk.

About to close the lid, Gael spotted a pale blue brocade and dug furiously to set it free. The gown—Maura's wedding gown—emerged voluminous and immaculate. Gael drew in a marveled breath and draped it across the bed. As her fingers traveled admiringly over the peach colored embroidery worked into the dangling sleeves and yoke, the texture awoke in Gael's imagination visions of their illustrious union. How miraculous to be so close to someone in mind, in spirit, in body! Certainly everyone dreams of such a gift, but few are favored. And hadn't she come near to achieving that intimacy with Rhodri...and surely such a pairing would have been possible with Marc. She stood and hung out the window to see the cross denoting Rhodri's burial spot jutting out of the center of a tuft of compost. Oddly, her tears flowed freely as she impulsively cried aloud, "Why...why did you leave me?! Life was happily simple with you...and right now I need and crave simple...Maybe sometimes it was boring and maybe we could have tried harder to find excitement in each other, but I loved you and we miss you ever so much." Her sobs doubled her over and forced her back to the bed, where she allowed herself permission to continue mourning the ache that had tormented her heart for so very long.

*****

Simon and Maura stood in a dense grove of oaks, straining their doubtful stares straight ahead. They glanced at each other, shrugged their shoulders, and looked again, Simon uttering, "Where?"

"There..." answered Owain, perturbed and pointing rigidly, "beyond the clearing."

Maura considered her eyesight might be deteriorating, but she knew Simon's was still keen, when she complained, "You're fooling us."

"No...Come. I'll show you."

They ventured nearer, followed by the unusually silent children and Marc, guiding the horses. Suddenly, Maura caught sight of the cottage, laughed, and called out in amazement, "I see it! Owain! It's so well hidden. Simon, don't you see? It's tucked into the side of that hill."

Simon squinted strenuously at the hill, then slowly drew his eyes downward finally to see a wall of wooden planks stained the hues of dirt and moss supporting a cliff of thatch. Yes!" he spouted, "I do see it. How astonishingly mysterious, Owain."

Owain swelled with pride and waved them along the sinuous path that spun its way through the trees. They reached the clearing and, with the cottage so starkly evident before them, Simon and Maura wondered how they hadn't seen it before. The ledge of the cliff made the roof; planks and wattle, daubed with clay and dirt, served as the front wall, and faced south to catch the most sun. Shuttered windows had been cut into the planks on either side of the arched door, a Norman arch, Maura noted, as she smiled and eagerly insisted, "We'll go in now."

Owain ushered them through the door. Simon, the last in, hesitated on the stoop, recalling the atrocities that had taken place here ten years past. He knew from Owain and Marc's recounting of their reconstruction progress that not all of the house had been rebuilt, and he wondered what ghosts might linger. Maura tugged him inside, dispelling his gloom with her beaming effusiveness, "Oh Simon, look! It's magnificent, don't you agree?" He nodded as his wide eyes took in the hall—a tall ceilinged, long chamber with a planked floor dyed the color of cranberries and blanketed with thickly woven rush mats. Set into its center was a tiled hearth, each tile painted with a delicate design of swirling patterns. Similarly decorated smaller tiles were impressed into the border surrounding the door and windows. Owain thrust open the shutters, flooding the room with the day's brilliance, and shivered with nervousness and cold as he knelt to light the fire. He noticed with satisfaction that his visitors had broken apart and were singly discovering the wonders of his home. Maura waddled to a far corner where she found a boxed bed, stuffed with a down mattress and covered with an intricately embroidered quilt detailing a celestial scene of sparkling stars and bulging moon. A loom directly faced the bed with half a cloth still entwined in its threads. A spinning wheel sat close by, and a trunk Maura imagined contained untold treasures footed the bed.

Owain hauled the bag of foodstuffs to a trestle table hugging the far wall at the opposite end of the hall, and began unloading the contents. He glanced up and out the side window, bracing the table, and smiled in delight at the lulling view of the rolling, twisting hills, seemingly supported by tall, majestic blue stones, and touched gently by the late sun.

Simon and Gruffydd's intense scrutiny of the beams that supported the roof tickled them. Each pillar was intricately carved with designs of climbing vines and berries; every leaf or so, Simon pointed out to Gruffydd, a set of eyes peeked out. Owain grabbed a cauldron and started out to the stream that trickled near. He met Marc coming in from a modest sized stable hugging the east side of the building. "Well what do they think?" asked Marc anxiously.

"So far they're dumbstruck," answered Owain.

Owain continued to the stream, and Marc stepped inside and smiled hugely at Maura and Nia laughing, rolling, and sinking into the down bed; at Gruffydd exclaiming in delight to Simon, "I found a bug on this leaf!"; and at Cynan, gazing impatiently at the wattle and beams crisscrossing the ceiling, his foot tapping out his boredom.

Hunger grumbled Marc's belly and he headed for the trestle table to see how he could aid Owain's preparation of supper. Once there, he partly watched Simon tentatively fingering an assortment of musical instruments propped against the back wall. Simon stood to examine the construction of the wall and peeked through slits in the boards to see an approximate distance of a foot spanning the wood and the dirt. "Doesn't the dirt get awfully damp?" he asked Marc.

"Not with the space between. The air keeps it mostly dry, and the dirt insulates the heat."

Simon marveled, "When did you learn the arts of architecture and carpentry?"

338

"Owain taught me. He's not a very patient teacher, so under his instruction I had to learn quickly."

"Well, I must say I'm highly impressed. Where's Owain?"

"Gone to fetch water."

"Is there a stable?" asked Simon.

"Yes, attached to the side, but there's no entrance from inside. He thought it made the main room awfully smelly."

"Thoughtful of him."

Marc nodded and began slicing up a plucked chicken. Gruffydd had joined Maura and Nia's play, and Cynan complained to Simon, "Can't we go outside and explore? It's still light and warm enough. Please, Simon!"

"If you wish, but don't go alone. Who knows what sorts of wild beasts lurk in these hills?"

"Gruffydd, Nia!" Cynan shouted in a deafening tone. "Let's go outside. You can jump on the bed later."

Gruffydd and Nia exchanged excited glances and bounded off the bed for the door. "Take your cloaks and don't go far, it will soon be dark!" was Simon's caution as he smiled after them. Immediately out the door, they shrieked and scattered as they encountered their first wild beast—Owain. He abandoned the cauldron and, growling and flailing, charged the little ones.

After supper, some light remained, and Simon surreptitiously coaxed Owain outside with a request for a tour of the stable.

"Why do you want to see the stable?" wondered Owain. "It looks like any other stable."

"No..." answered Simon, excitedly. "The altar...You promised you'd show me the altar. I didn't know if you wanted anyone else seeing it."

"When did I promise you?"

"Directly before Maura got out of bed."

Owain turned reflective, then pursed his lips and narrowed his eyes to wonder, "Why do you want to see it?"

"I'm interested," said Simon. "No...more than interested...intrigued. Please, show me?"

"Come," Owain commanded.

Simon obediently followed close at his friend's heels. Heavily prejudiced tales of the pagans who had once inhabited this mystical land had been related to him by the Archbishop Lanfranc and he was hoping to hear from Owain an alternate point of view. The deeper into the woods they foraged, the more baleful the trees and scrub appeared. A tingling of regret began to crawl Simon's spine, yet before he had an opportunity to suggest they return to the cottage, Owain stopped short. Simon collided with his back, regained his balance, and peered warily at a grove of six trees standing in an almost perfect circle beyond Owain's shoulder.

Owain grinned at Simon's stark look of misgiving, and asked skeptically, "What have you been told of my people?"

"Very little...The gruesome bits mostly—human sacrifices, dismemberment, head-hunters, cannibalism."

"Cannibalism? That's a new one. What does it mean?"

"People eating people. A new one what?"

"Description."

"Are you saying the descriptions are all lies?"

"I'm not saying that at all," said Owain, "but I don't believe we ever ate each other, or our enemies. Come further inside the grove." Owain delighted in Simon's large furtive glances and hesitation, and teased, "Don't worry. I wasn't intending on eating you."

"I wasn't thinking that," said Simon with an uneasy laugh. "It's cold and getting dark, and maybe we should go back."

"You begged to see, and I'm going to show you. Come closer." Owain gripped Simon's elbow and brusquely guided him to the center of the trees.

Simon turned a slow circle as his wide stare swept over the yews and the ground around. Relieved that no skeletons lurked, he noticed a long stone altar sitting at the foot of one tree, with bunches of berried greenery strewn over it, and a scattering the moss at its base. Two fat candles adorned the smooth rock, their tallow thickly stacked. He knelt and fingered a white berry, exclaiming, "It's mistletoe!"

"A potent and regular ingredient in your recipes, correct?" asked Owain, crossing his arms and leaning complacently against a trunk.

"Yes indeed. So I practice Druidic medicine?"

"Yes indeed," Owain gently mocked. "Long, long past, the Druids were the elite of the Welsh society—physicians, bards, soothsayers, mediators, judges, and, yes, executioners. They believed in a life for a life, the same as your people, but also, they believed that if one is offered in sacrifice to appease an angry god, or cut down in war, one is reborn as a higher being."

"And your father believed this as well?" questioned Simon.

"Partly, but in not so violent a manner. Any bull he sacrificed we also ate. The old ways ran thick in his blood."

"And since these switches were obviously laid here recently," Simon noted, rising with the branch in hand, "the old ways run in your blood as well."

"Yes, but I don't believe in spilling blood. I prefer an offering of food, greenery, or jewelry. Does that offend you?"

"No...It fascinates me."

"Why?"

"Because you also claim to be a practicing Christian!" Simon burst out in astonishment. "How can you possibly reconcile the two philosophies?"

"It's not that difficult. My mother was daughter of a priest."

Simon's jaw slackened as he imagined, "How confused you must have been."

"Not at all. My parents reconciled their differences quite well and taught us a blend of the best of both liturgies. I hear you studied to become a priest."

"Yes...but everyone involved soon realized I had no true vocation. I had a tendency to ask too many questions." He charged suspiciously, "And don't try to turn this conversation on me. I'm wanting to know how you get past the first Commandment...the bit about not worshipping false gods."

"I don't consider any of my Gods false. And I definitely believe praying to more than one God can be nothing but beneficial. You have your saints. No one worships in exactly the same way, Simon." Owain shifted to his other foot, and asked with a sportive grin, "What do you require from your church?"

Simon pondered the question a moment, then answered assuredly, "Comfort, grace, forgiveness, and guidance."

"And do you always follow the guidance you receive?"

"When I believe it comes directly from God, I do. When I receive it from the clergy..." He paused and guiltily confessed, "...not always."

"You see! Even *you* doubt your beliefs when they're spouted by mere men."

Chastened, Simon muttered, "Does Sulien know this about you?"

"I imagine he suspects, but you must see, our church was founded on tolerance for the many religions thriving here before the Christian doctrine first arrived, so he would never condemn me for my extra beliefs. If he did, he'd have to excommunicate half the village as well."

"Truly? There's more than you who do this?"

"Truly."

"Have you told Marc?" Simon asked.

"He caught me here one afternoon," Owain related in a troubled voice. "He seemed upset, and didn't speak a word to me for the remainder of the day. So I thought it best not to try to explain."

"Marc is rigid in his beliefs," said Simon.

"Too rigid," stressed Owain.

"No...not for Marc," Simon readily countered. "It is his way, and I've always felt envious of his conviction."

"I've been guilty of rigidness, and I envy your acceptance."

"I appreciate your envy, Owain, but being overly accepting can make one's life dreadfully perplexing."

"I don't see you as perplexed," touted Owain. "Your values are well fixed, your goals heroic, your manner most times polite, and your loyalty unquestioned. I, however, am awfully perplexed." His confession weighted his shoulders, and slumped him heavily down upon the altar stone.

Concerned, Simon asked, "About what exactly?"

"What to do with myself. I've been replaced as Pennaeth, and can no longer see myself in combat. To be a constant soldier one has to be always angry. I don't feel that anger anymore."

"What about the prospect of mediator?" offered Simon.

Owain vigorously wagged his head. "Mediators speak fluent English, French, can read, and write."

"You've mastered English," rallied Simon. "We can teach you French, and reading and writing if you like."

"I'm too old for learning," Owain scoffed.

"No one's too old for learning. Maura learned Welsh quite quickly."

"She's not old, and she knew it before."

"What?" blurted Simon.

"I think when younger, she heard the language."

"Oh..." Simon sank down upon the altar as well. "If Rhys requested, you'd not consider acting as a mediator?"

"I'd love to have the power to end wars." Owain cringed as he admitted, "...but my temper flares too easily, I haven't the patience, and it's so damned frustrating."

"I was guilty of voicing the exact same complaints...numerous times," confessed Simon. "However, when what you advise is attended to, and respected, and carried forth, and you are certain that you've saved countless injuries and lives, nothing can be more exciting and satisfying."

Feeling terribly inadequate and uncomfortable with the gravity of their talk, Owain took an opportunity to lighten the subject with a taunt. It was such fun and amazingly easy to fluster Simon. "Nothing?" he quipped, brow arched steeply. "Many a night you sounded very excited and satisfied, and I don't think from mediating."

Even in the mounting dusk, Simon's deep blush was clearly evident as he faintly admitted, "Almost nothing."

Owain's unabashedly spilled, "And that's something else I know very little about."

Simon gaped again, wider, and stuttered, "You...you've never—"

"And what's wrong with that?" returned Owain, eyes flaring.

"No...nothing." Simon struggled more, "I just thought with...I mean, I thought—"

Owain pressed forward threateningly and persisted, "What did you think?"

"I don't know what I thought," Simon shot back. "I'm surprised."

"Why surprised?"

"You lived at Dinefwr. And the times I've visited there, matters between men and women appeared...lax."

"Appeared what?"

"Extremely friendly."

"Oh...I suppose." Owain deflated and mentioned with distaste, "I didn't indulge."

Simon trod carefully. "Was there a specific reason...you didn't?"

To which Owain swiftly assured. "It wasn't because of lack of want...I just didn't approve."

Pleased by his response, Simon uttered a simple, "I see."

"I've never felt comfortable with the lot that dwell at Dinefwr, and my parents taught us to keep ourselves pure for our intended. Unfortunately, my intended wasn't taught the same."

"That was admirable of your parents," Simon affirmed.

"You don't seem to me to be the sort who's lax in that way," surmised Owain. "You appreciate and respect women the same as you do men."

"If they are worthy of my respect, most certainly I do...and you're correct, I've never been the sort who's lax in that way."

Simon smiled at Owain's dreamy preference, "I like to imagine the first time I choose to be with a woman will have meaning."

"Meaning..." Simon sighed ecstatically in assent. "Yes, in that context meaning is highly important."

"Did yours?"

"Did my what?"

"Your first time have meaning?"

"With Maura everything has meaning."

"Oh...with Maura," nodded Owain. "Well put. I agree and again I envy you...her. I suspect most want someone close, someone they can freely choose, feel comfortable with, talk easily to, be with at the close of the day."

"I'm certain most do...and I feel extremely blest to have...her."

"Taredd is that way," Owain spurted, yanking off a mistletoe berry and lobbing it into the encroaching blackness.

Simon didn't notice his angry action, and responded lightly, "I'm happy he feels blest."

"No...he's lax."

"Oh...Well he'll surely halt that sort of thing now that he's wed, won't he?"

"I doubt it. He doesn't deserve one of Gael's sort."

Simon heedlessly took Owain's comment as a barb and hotly defended, "I'm through with your criticisms of her! She is my friend, and I won't have her slandered—"

Owain's rigid gesture hushed his harangue, and Owain carefully corrected, "What I meant, and should have said was, he doesn't deserve one of Gael's quality."

Simon chuckled, ashamed at his assumption. "And so what do you suggest Gael do to rein in her wayward husband?"

"Kick him in just the right spot."

"And I suspect you've dreamt of doing just that to him."

"Many times...Let's go back. I'm freezing, and I can barely see you. There's no moon."

Simon's eyes flicked mischief. "We could always light the candles."

"You'd join my ceremony?"

"I'll not go that far." Simon dragged his fingers through his hair, and added earnestly, "But Owain, when next you pray or whatever it is you do here, could you mention our names, especially Maura's and our child's, we aim to call her Elyn, and Marc's name as well. It couldn't hurt."

"I already do."

"I'm grateful," Simon answered with mild surprise.

"As am I," replied Owain. His next question arrived as an after-thought. "Gael's not lax, is she?"

"No."

"I didn't think so, for she said no to Rhys. Not many say no to Rhys. She spoke kindly to me today."

"Did she? I'm pleased, are you?"

"Yes...I believe I am."

"Good," beamed Simon.

On their return journey, Simon noticed a number of pairs of eyes studying him from behind and between scrubs of underbrush. He shivered, gathered his cloak closer, and chanced, "What sort of wild beasts roam these hills?"

"Mostly deer. I've seen a wild cat on occasion and, of course, wolves and badgers, boars...a few bear."

"Bear?" echoed Simon in a quaver. "Let's hurry." They hastened their pace and Simon rambled to mask his nervousness. "And what names do you call your gods?"

"That's personal," Owain tersely replied, then he softened to instruct, "Listen to my tale tonight, and you'll hear many of them spoken of, for their personalities are laced throughout our legends."

An excellent idea resounded in Simon's mind, and he spurted, "Have you thought of becoming a bard?"

"I hate to travel," groused Owain, "and loath talking to and performing for people I don't know."

"If we should need to leave here, perhaps you could act as physician."

"I don't like being around sick people, and you'll never need to leave here."

"The list of vocations grows ever shorter, Owain," Simon counseled.

"Of that fact I'm constantly aware."

They entered to a rousing game of dice, and as Owain caught a hurled die mid-air, he mumbled concernedly, "Cynan must be losing. These days he's often mad."

Maura rose awkwardly to greet them, fretting, "Where've you been? The stable couldn't have taken that long to tour."

"We...we...saw some deer," gibbered Simon, "and—"

Owain cut short Simon's difficulty, "You can tell her, Simon, just do it later."

"Tell me what?" Maura asked, piqued. "I don't want to wait."

"It's a secret," Simon whispered close. "I'll tell you when it's just us."

Maura surrendered not too happily, and suggested to the men, "You can take my place in the game. Owain, may I rummage in your trunk?"

"Of course, and pick something for yourself."

Her eyes sparkled like those of a child anticipating a sweet treat, and she hurried to inspect the trove. And upon lifting the lid, her discovery drew from her a gasped breath. She brushed an awed touch over several pieces of thick gold jewelry—a heavy neck torc; hammered wrist and ankle bracelets, intricately engraved with impressions of beasts. There were necklaces dangling with swirled circles, which she thought too cumbersome to wear; and rings, some plain, and one she carefully extracted, that appeared identical to the one Rhys had gifted them. She stuck it on her thumb, and decided to ask Owain about it later. As she dug deeper, Maura happened upon scads of woven cloths, all depicting amazingly detailed scenes of forest, sea, and sky. Lastly, she uncovered some personal items, hair combs, carving tools, and sewing utensils. Everything she touched warmed her heart and summoned forth in her mind a vision of each of Owain's family, his parents, Madawg and Indeg; his sister, Gwen; the next boy, Bryn; and the twins, Rhiannon and Rhun. Owain had spoken so many tales of their adventures that Maura felt she knew them intimately and was honored to be staying the night in their elegant, yet succoring home. Marc at her back startled her musing. "You scared me."

"I'm sorry. Have you found anything interesting?"

"Yes, much. Look, there's jewelry, and cloth, and—"

"I'll see later. Could I speak to you a moment?"

"I hope more than a moment."

He helped her up, and guided her to the bed. "You'll be more comfortable here."

"What is it, Marc?" she asked, suddenly worried. "You're very pale."

"No, I'm only tired. It was quite grueling this morning."

"Nothing too troublesome for you," complimented Maura. "You've been quieter than usual. Is it something to do with Olwen?"

"A bit...She wants to be closer than I'm ready to be. She thought if she came with us here, that I might feel uncomfortable."

"Is that true?"

"Yes. You know I still want to be with Gael."

Maura nodded, and finished for him, "And you don't want anyone else." He nodded back and heartened to her bolstering speech. "Never let any woman force you to do what you are not ready or wanting to do, and never feel embarrassed or guilty about your decision. You did what's noble, Marc, nothing less. And about Gael, we can only hope that Rhys eventually sees the error of his edict, dissolves the farce he's forced her into, and allows her to be with the man she wants..."

"But will that be *me*, Maura?"

"Only she can tell you that, Marc. Do you have the patience to wait?"

"I have nothing but patience...and time...and during the last two months I've spent a great deal of time reconsidering my future here."

"I thought you enjoyed being Simon's assistant."

"I'll always be that...but I want to be something more, something only for myself. I've met several times with Sulien."

"Sulien?"

"Yes...and we've decided that I should begin preparation for taking my orders into the priesthood."

What he'd decided fit superbly with his temperament and education, yet still she repeated aghast, "Priesthood?!"

"I don't see why you're so surprised. Simon once suggested I take my vows and, well, the Welsh church has its differences from the See of Rome. The difference most attractive to me is that priests are allowed to marry, so I can have my wish to be closer to God and still some day, I pray, have a family."

"I don't know what to say," said Maura.

"You disapprove?"

"No...not at all. It's just that I wasn't expecting you to tell me that..."

"What were you expecting?" he asked with an awkward grin.

"I honestly don't know...Have you told Simon?"

"No...I thought I'd get your reaction first."

She grew silent and, by the width of the crease between her brows, it was clear she was contemplating the subject thoroughly. The crease finally smoothed and she uttered, "I think..."

"You...you think what?" he pressed in suspense.

With a loving kiss to his cheek, Maura professed, "I think your idea is a perfect one, as are all your ideas."

"And you are too sweet, Sister."

She held him in her arms, profusely exclaiming, "I love you, and want you happy...I pray this will make you so."

His voice broke and hug tightened to his indulgent confession, "You make me so very happy."

The remainder of the evening proved joyous to all. The children, with Owain's flustered supervision, tampered with the musical instruments, Gruffydd showing slight promise on the harp. And after the concert, they sat entranced in Owain's rendition of an ancient rollicking tale stocked with many references to dragons and giants. Simon listened attentively for the names of mystical beings who might be gods. Maura sat half-hearing, while happily considering the comfort of sleeping on the down bed and discovering Owain and Simon's secret. Marc glowed in Maura's blessing and in the warmth and favor of good friends. He anticipated the morrow when he and Owain would present Maura and Simon the gift they so desperately deserved. Owain was blissful in the wide-eyed fascination given his story-telling and the miracle that his family's home was once more filled with smiles, laughter, and love.

As the hour grew late, the children at last dropped off to sleep, and Maura shortly followed. Simon couldn't leave her alone in the bed for long, and Marc and Owain stayed awake till the early morn bantering and conjuring solutions to the villagers' and commote's present and possible problems.

*****

Gael waited for Taredd, the top half of her body slumped over the table in the llys, her cheek resting on the back of her hand, her mind imprisoned in a harrowed sleep. In her dream, abandoned and humiliated by her husband, she sought out an elusive Marc, chasing, but never catching, constantly losing sight of his changing face. She ached with repressed passion, burning deep within, yearning to explode and express itself in a glorious pairing of lust and love with someone she cared for so dearly. Lips, sloppy and wet, woke her from her turmoil, and thrust her into a darker dilemma. Taredd's breath, fiercely hot and reeking of stale mead, flamed the skin on the back of her neck. She gasped, "No!" and started up with force, throwing him off her shoulders and into the rushes behind. The faint light and his mussed hair hid the demented fury flaming his eyes, yet she unmistakably heard the ominous hiss of his breaths quicken with rage. Frozen with terror, she could only cry out, "I've waited since dusk...Where've you been?!" He rose with frightening rigidity, his posture huge and threatening, and staggered toward her. His foot shot up and kicked her belly. A great gasped groan left her as she stumbled away, fighting to find her breath and her strength. She found it fast and raged at him, shrilling, "You're stinking drunk, you putrid pig! You'll not touch me, not this night, not ever!"

His guttural drawl spiked her fear, "Dru...drunk...Ye...yes, I'm drunk, for...for only drunk can I...I suffer you, you ugly crone." He lurched forward, his talon swinging and catching her shoulder. His mistake was to yank her near, for she arrived armed with balled fists and fitfully slammed her knuckles to his gut. She pummeled again and again, harder and harder, till with an agonized moan, he sank to his knees and hands. Gael never once looked back as she raced wildly from her demon husband; nor did she slacken her pace till she was safely locked behind the door of her own cottage. There she spent the short remainder of the dark night huddled and cowering in a corner, a dagger's hilt snug in her palm, her knees hugged protectively to her chest, and her eyes, stark with panic, riveted on the door.

*****

"She's done it again!" exclaimed Owain, working the arrow loose from the exact center of the circled target drawn half-way up a fat oak.

"We told you she was skilled," laughed Simon with pride.

Owain looked back over the long expanse of ground that separated him and Simon from Maura and the children. He shook his head in wonder, and praised, "Yes, but I never imagined *how* skilled. If she were Welsh I could understand her talent, but being a Norman woman. Well...we hear you Norman men keep them mostly as slaves and brood mares."

"Maura was raised quite differently than most, and I wish you wouldn't keep including me in the general scum you refer to as *Norman men*," answered Simon in offense. "We weren't all born with the exact same values, or prejudices. And furthermore, I am only half Norman."

"Saxon men are just as bad." Owain chuckled wickedly at the scarlet rising in Simon's cheeks. Simon rolled his eyes, snatched the arrow away from Owain and waved it high over his head for Maura.

At the victory gesture, Maura dropped her hand that shielded her eyes, and clapped it to the other, spouting, "I hit it again! Lack of practice hasn't hurt me as much as I feared."

"Can it be my turn now, Maura?" asked Gruffydd, looking about to burst and clutching his arrows close.

"Of course, but wait till Simon and Owain get back." She winked and smirked, "We wouldn't want to frighten them, would we?"

"I would, actually," Gruffydd smirked back.

She ruffled his hair, and bent to offer him advice. "Can you see the circle clearly?"

"Yes."

"When you're shooting such a long distance, you need to aim the arrowhead slightly higher than your target, to make up for the curve it makes through the air. Do you understand?"

"I think so."

"Pull the string taut and wide." Fondly, she watched his young features pinch along with his exertion. Simon and Owain strolled up beside them. The arrowhead, made of flint, sparkled in the sun's glint while Maura asked, "Is the arrowhead slightly higher?"

"Yes..."

"Then take a big breath, hold very still and—let go!"

On cue, the arrow flew. Gruffydd kept his breath in and stared after the arrow, his eyes huge with hope and promise. Maura regarded critically the burst of the launch and arch of the flight, her eyes also filling with eagerness and awe. Gruffydd closed his as the missile neared its target, then popped them wide when he heard his audience whoop in triumph. He raced forward and noticed with rapture that he'd not only hit the tree, but managed to stick the head within the outer circle. As he wrestled the flint from the bark, he whispered elatedly, "Wait till I tell Mam!"

The rest soon joined him, Owain lauding, "That was fine, Gruffydd. You'll try again?"

"No," he adamantly answered. "Next time I might miss."

His decision was accepted, and the group started back to the cottage.

"We should pack and be going," suggested Simon, eyeing the sky with suspicion. "I don't like the thickness of the clouds. If we wait longer we could be imprisoned in snow for days."

"Would that be such a bad thing?" asked Owain.

"No...but I'm wanting to see my patients."

Marc met them half-way to announce, "The packing's done."

"Why didn't you wait for help?" asked Maura.

"It wasn't hard." Marc glanced quizzically at Owain, who shrugged in response.

Simon grinned in summation. "Then we can go."

To which Marc replied, "We can. You, however, and Maura, will be staying longer."

"What?" asked Maura, not certain she'd heard correctly.

"Owain and I plan to return to the village with the children, and you two are welcome to stay here, alone, as long as you please which, based on the amount of food left, can be at least three more days."

"Stay here alone for three more days!" exclaimed Simon with glee. "When did you decide this?"

"Back a month past," said Owain.

In happy shock, Maura stammered, "But...but what if the baby decides to...and Simon must see to his patients."

"I hope he feels confident with me seeing to them for the next few days," said Marc, "and he told me this morning that you don't think the child will arrive for another couple of weeks."

"I don't know that for certain," she stressed.

"Enough arguing," Owain stridently cut in. "The two of you have had no true privacy for the past two months. Would you agree to suffer staying here for three days more? It would please Marc and me."

Simon and Maura exchanged bemused expressions that gradually softened to bashful smiles. They clutched hands, and Maura spoke indulgently, "We will stay and are most grateful for your generosity, Owain...and Marc."

"Then I'll come get you on the Sabbath," said Marc. "We don't want you traveling alone."

"Will you come as well, Owain?" asked Simon.

"No...I leave this day for the north."

They all responded aghast, "You what?!"

"Leave...Not permanently, I don't believe. I still have some family in the north, on the island of Mon. I go every year, they expect it. I plan to return in a fortnight."

They all slumped with relief and sadness. "We'll miss you terribly," offered Maura. "How will we ever get to sleep without your stories and whistling?"

To hide his sorrow, Owain spoke almost curtly, "You did fine without me—before. You'll do fine without me—now."

"We do better *with* you," said Simon.

He raised his hand to grasp Owain's, and was abruptly pulled into a rough hug. He exuberantly returned the gesture and, emerging, nodded humbly to Owain's quavered order, "You watch over her always. And Maura—"

She disappeared as willingly into his robust hold, and heard, "I expect you to keep that child inside till I return. What a fine Christmas present it will make."

"She," muttered Simon.

"You don't know that for certain," argued Owain.

"I have a hunch."

"And that's all it is."

"Would you two stop," complained Marc, wincing at the touch of a snowflake on his nose. "Or we'll all end up here for days." He quietly kissed Maura and Simon's cheeks, and whispered, "Take care and enjoy," as he strode to where the horses waited.

"We'll leave the cart and E'dain...in case you should have to return early." Owain waved at the children to approach, and they hurried forward eager for praise, kisses, and hugs.

Simon and Maura wistfully watched the men and the children disappear into the trees, Maura sighing alluringly, "What will we do, all alone for three days?"

Simon pretended not to notice her insinuation, and answered vaguely, "I honestly don't know...We'll have to think of something or we're bound to get terribly bored." His act broke apart to rakish laughter when she attacked him with tickles and he extolled, "No squabbling for three whole days!"

"I'll give you squabbling!" she promised, swatting him on the behind and chasing him back to the hut.

*****

Rose sat herself at the trestle table in Edith's cottage, and neatly spread her serviette upon her lap in preparation for the midday meal. Her mild gaze darkened with caution as Edith rose from her seat and accepted the cauldron of stew from Arthur. Arthur instinctively cupped her elbow, yet she shook from his support insisting, "No, my love, let me try on my own."

With great hesitation, Arthur obliged her request and sat to her wave. Rose lifted an inch from her chair, but sank back down to Edith's firm gesture and plea, "I beg of both of you. Let me have the honor of serving. You've done little but serve me these long months since—"

"Odo", grunted Rose. "If only I could be allowed a short audience with the Bishop, I'd show him what to do with a hot iron—"

"Rose...don't blaspheme," begged Edith as she hobbled in Rose's direction and ladled a spoonful of thick pork stew into her bowl.

"Blaspheme?" Rose returned in agitation. "It is impossible to blaspheme the Devil, Edith. And you are acting, as always, entirely too pious. William only presented the title Bishop to Odo to keep him from mischief. Unfortunately, he abused his position, and used it as license to flaunt his wickedness."

"Please, my dear ladies," interjected Arthur. "We'll speak of some merrier topic. Did Edith tell you, Rose, how we expect her to be able to return to marketing by Christmas?" He beamed proudly. "The past week, she's ridden the cart to our stall and managed a few half days of bargaining with her usual spritely flair."

Delight gleamed Rose's eyes; her smile and praise revealed practically all her stained and crooked teeth, "I'm so pleased for you, Edith! There was a doubt once that you'd ever walk again—"

"No one..." cut in Edith, ripping a hunk of bread from the loaf for emphasis, "...especially Odo, could lame me for long." Her stern expression decreed the discussion done, and a relaxed grin and sip of ale began her question, "So tell us, Rose, how goes the manoring?"

"I was about to mention my imminent plans."

"Plans?" piqued Arthur.

"Yes...Richard has departed for Normandy, permanently, to serve Duke Robert. He could not bring himself to do homage to that depraved beast, Rufus. Geoffrey never left Normandy after King William's death, and does not intend to do so presently. As such, I will be—"

"You're not leaving," Edith worried.

"No, Edith. What I was about to say was...with both my sons away and..." Her voice lowered in lament, "Alan, Adam and Almodis gone, there's absolutely no reason for me to ramble about in that huge shell of a shack feeling lonely and sorry for myself any longer. A week past, Avenal's son, who is now seneschal of Dunheved Castle, came to visit me. It seems Estrith left with Almodis and Adam to go to Mortain and they've found no one suitable to undertake Estrith's chores as Mistress Chamberlain."

"Estrith left with Almodis?" Edith said, her eyes wide with disbelief.

"Who's Estrith?" queried Arthur.

"A kindly matron who has served Robert's household at Dunheved for—"

While Edith mentally counted the years, Rose helped her finish, "Forever. What I find shocking is her decision to serve the Lady. I believed she possessed more pride and sense than to submit to that pompous, snide, spoiled—"

"Rose...stop!" returned Edith with force. "I sorely miss the Lady and won't have her slandered."

"And neither will I," offered Arthur as intensely.

"And I'm certain Estrith couldn't help but fall in love with the boy," added Edith.

All three sat a moment in somber reflection, then Rose resumed her haranguing, "But Almodis wrought so much hurt!"

"And sacrificed so very much...for the good of us all!" Arthur heartily defended.

"Well...I won't argue the Lady's goodness with you any longer," said Rose. "I have decided to move back to the castle and resume my former position as Mistress Chamberlain."

Both Edith and Arthur paused their meal and lifted amazed eyes. "Rose," worried Edith, "how could you return after the horrors that happened when last you lived there?"

Rose straightened and strove to banish the uncertainty in her answer, "I believe it's time to exorcise the horrors. Odo is away and, from what Richard told me, is totally immersed in advising Curthose. Lord Robert and his family reside, happily I pray, at Mortain. I aim to make Dunheved profitable and habitable once again. I know it may sound impossible, but the old moldy tomb may once more be capable of housing joy...and—"

"Yes?" both Edith and Arthur pressed.

Rose leant forward on her forearms and said urgently, "I'll know sooner if anyone contemplating treachery against Simon, Maura, or yourselves is encroaching. I'll feel useful again and maybe with God's blessing I will be honored with a glimpse of Adam...occasionally."

"It will be very difficult to go back," said Edith.

"Maura returned," countered Rose, "...and survived."

"And as we are all very well aware," returned Edith, "Maura is an incredibly strong-willed and bold woman. Are you as bold?"

"I sincerely doubt it, though I would gladly lay down my life for hers."

"You believe that decision will be forced upon you...shortly?" Arthur asked tensely.

"I don't know, and pray not. I will visit you both often and purchase our cloth and our bread solely from your stalls, for no burghers in Dunheved are your equals." As Rose rested her fretful gaze upon her dearest friends, she felt a twinge of remorse for reawakening the dread they jointly felt yet strove so hard to hide. She tried to pacify with one last hope, "It has to be favorable to know of the doings of Lord Robert's rapacious family. It has to be!"

*****

At the lavishly appointed dais located in the great hall of Berkhamstead Castle, Odo sat opposite the Lord's throne and supported his cheek with his fist, his knuckles twisting half his lip into a vicious snarl. His other hand stabbed a knife repeatedly into a slab of venison topping a blood-sopped trencher as he grumbled lowly to Will at his side, "I cannot abide the fiend for too much longer, Nephew. His slobbering dulls my appetite, his greasy guise repulses me, and his grotesque fondling of his *boys* makes me want to vomit. Please, I beg of you, find a way to rid us of this pestilence."

"He *is* the King," reminded Will, relaxed in his seat, and sipping claret. "He does what he pleases, where he pleases."

"Why does it please him to be suddenly here?" demanded Odo in a gritted whisper. "His presence is not a mere coincidence. If you don't swiftly discover us a way out of this situation, we will not arrive in Wales in time to capture your prisoner and deliver her to her husband. And if that sad mistake should occur, your fancy new home is gone forever from you."

"Never!" growled Will.

"Then get to it." A garish smile began Odo's charge. "His taunting me amuses you, doesn't it? It wouldn't do to test my loyalty, Will. You stand little chance of achieving your Byzantine mission without the aid of my ingenious martial skills, and my expertly trained army."

"What are you two hissing about?" commanded Rufus from the throne. With the back of his hand, he wiped gravy from his sparse, clumped, yellow beard, then grabbed and thrust out his goblet at the seemingly sexless youngster at his side. The child refilled Rufus' cup, then smiled radiantly at the oily touch administered to his cheek by his Lord. Rufus directed his smug and sardonic expression at Odo. "You haven't yet provided me with a believable answer, Uncle."

"Answer to what?" Odo retorted petulantly.

"Don't speak to me that way!" bellowed Rufus. "I asked you why you haven't visited me sooner. I've been King four months now, and I expected out of respect, and most certainly affection, to witness your groveling. And if not for love, surely you wish to lay claim once again to your fiefs."

"I didn't realize I needed your permission to regain what's already mine."

"Everyone needs *my* permission to do anything in *my* country, including shitting!" Rufus laughed uproariously at his lame joke while his two boys aped his hysterics. Will chuckled slavishly, and Odo fidgeted with disgust and impatience. Rufus abruptly halted his chortling to proclaim, "All of England—the land, the people, and the beasts—belongs to me. If you choose to swear me homage, you will be allowed to lease your former properties. I'll have half your army at my disposal, and taxes, newly calculated by my treasurer. If you care to remain Bishop, you will serve under Lanfranc's rule. If you refuse any of my demands, you will not be allowed to crush a single blade of grass on this—*my* isle."

Odo shifted angrily; his nostrils flared and snorted his disrespect. "Why you pumped up perverted viper! The Devil must have entered your father's rotted body when he made *you* King. If you truly believe I'd serve a pig like yourself, you're far more demented than I remember, and I remember you being extremely dim!"

Rufus heaved his huge bulk up, and, lurching forward to retaliate, knocked over his claret and jostled his jeweled crown low upon his brow, covering one eye. He batted it back, fixed upon Odo a lethal glare, and barked to his guards, "Hang him!"

Seemingly unaffected, Odo stretched back in his seat and set his boots upon the dais with an arrogant plop.

Will wasn't as composed as he shouted out to Odo, "Apologize, you fool!"

"And why should I degrade myself so?"

"Because he *will* hang you!"

"Don't speak nonsense, Will. The fop is nothing but a puppet to that odious pustule, Rannulf Flambard." Odo's speech was abruptly interrupted by the rapid approach of two monstrously intimidating guards. He choked his next thought, then croaked, "Yet then again, one must—" With a quick twist and jerk, the guards wrenched the Bishop from his seat and thrust him upon the dais. At first, Odo was shocked silent, uttering only grunts and gasps, yet as the men joined him on the great table, forced him to his feet, and wrapped a thick noose of rope round his neck, he began shrieking.

Will couldn't believe what he was seeing! He raced to his cousin, and on his knees, implored, "Please, my most gracious King! Don't do this! Let him go! He was only jesting. You know his ways. He doesn't truly mean his retorts. Rufus! *Please*! It will cause a war, and you'll lose. Don't—" Will dared to look, and saw to his horror, the rope had been looped over a bracing log that held the chandelier over the dais. Odo tried to wrestle his offenders, but his body seem to only twitch, flop, and his face, red as blood, looked about to burst. Grunts and gasps were the only sounds his body could make! One guard yanked the rope, stretching Odo onto his toes. Will gave up on his groveling and joined his uncle upon the dais, tugging the rope against the guards. He provided little help. "Don't Rufus! He's family, our uncle! You can't do this to family! Stop this madness, now!"

Rufus' austere nod stopped his henchmen, but they remained close and shadowing. The release of the rope slumped Odo to the dais in a swoon. Will swiped at the trenchers and cups and gently laid Odo on the table, frantically pressing, "Uncle Odo, talk to me! Can you breathe? Can you talk? *Please* speak to me!"

Odo woke from his swoon, coughing radically. "Wi...wine...ple—wine."

Will obeyed and help Odo slurp the reviving liquid. Odo wheezed, spat, and gasped more, "He...help...me, Wi—" he huffed and panted. "Ge...et...me from here! He's mad!"

"Have your squire take him from here," gritted Rufus, "quickly before I change my mind."

"Ralf! Ralf!" screamed Will. Ralf appeared, pale and shaking, waiting for instructions. "Take Odo to his chamber. Fetch him anything he needs. Stay with him to calm him. Hurry. I'll join you both as soon as I'm able."

As Will and Ralf struggled to help Odo from the dais, they noticed his tunic skirt was damp, and from the repulsive odor emanating from Odo, that he had also soiled himself. With much trouble, they managed to get him on his feet and, as Will shifted Odo's weight to Ralf, he was astonished that the lean lad balanced the Bishop firmly in his hold. "Uncle," Will whispered with compassion, "I will come to you shortly. First I must calm Rufus down or our plan will never come to fruition. We'll both end up in Westminster's cells forever! Walk him carefully, Ralf."

"Wait!" roared Rufus. "Odo...Look at me!" Odo did and wheezed more to Rufus' posture, his stubby fingers pointing and trembling along with his hulk as he stuttered in rage, "Once...once more...If you dare insult me once more, I'll not hang you. *That*...that would be too neat. I'll cut your lips and tongue off, disembowel you, then let my swine chomp at your guts. Don't tempt me...for using you as pigs' fodder would bring me great joy. Clean yourself up, then return and address to me your heartrending apology. Is that clear?"

"A...as air, Sire."

Will slumped into the nearest chair, still in shock and quivering, and then he heard his cousin comment light and cheery as though nothing awry had occurred, "Will, you've grown soft and dull in the company of that dunghill. Come, I want to go hunting, you promised me hunting."

Will swallowed noisily and replied in a humble whisper, "My Lord, your soldiers burned down my hunting lodge last evening. They've ravaged my forests and my village. There are no deer left. Half the buildings are smoldering and I doubt I'll ever regain the respect and trust of my peasants."

"I regret my men's behavior, Cousin, but if I scold them too often, they will take their loyalty elsewhere. And they must practice their villainy—somewhere. Where do you and Odo intend to take your villainy next? Back to Normandy, I hope."

"Yes, that's exactly what we plan. How ingenious of you, my Lord! In fact, I have just this moment decided to leave directly after our meal."

"I want you with me," sneered Rufus. "You promised me hunting and more."

Will rapidly returned, "What if we accompany you back to Westminster where your deer reserve, I'm certain, is bulging in wait for slaughter? We'll both join your hunt, then the next day, we'll sail directly from your royal port. Do you agree, Sire?"

Rufus stood, his bottom lip thrust out in a pout, his bushy brows knitted in puzzlement. Will was purposely confusing him. Rufus wasn't good at games and hated confusion, and since becoming King there seemed no end to his bewilderment. He felt confident in ruling only when Flambard, his advisor, was near. He used to feel that way with Will, but he had wearied of his constant infirmities and complaints and sought out a younger, healthier, smarter advisor. Having mused too long, he forgot what he was contemplating before, and looked haplessly at Will's expectant expression. He'd feel foolish asking his cousin to repeat himself, so he restively sat and uttered, "Yes...whatever you say is fine."

"Sire," carefully stated Will. "I must go see to Uncle Odo. He is old and frail. Will you allow me to see him?"

"Why do you care?"

"We've always been close. I don't believe he truly meant his slur. His mind plays tricks on him at times. He says things to someone he believes is someone else."

"I don't want him to say anything to me ever again. Except an apology. He will return and apologize."

"He will, Sire. I will see to it personally. May I go?"

"I suppose. Hurry back."

"Ye...yes, my Lord," sputtered Will, moving slowly and backward through the great hall's doors. Once outside, he ran to Odo's chamber, praying fervently to himself, *Please God! Please let him be fine. I need him fine...to help me...find Maura!* He entered the room cautiously, and noticed to his great relief Odo laying on the bed in clean clothes, yet again in the queer position of being laid out for burial. "Uncle!" Will cried out, sprinting to his side. "Uncle! Speak to me!"

Odo opened his eyes and barked, "What!"

"Are you well? What damage has he done?!"

"Little. The rope burned my neck a bit."

Will slumped onto the bed with a deep sigh. "That's marvelous! I prayed for you!"

"Good," blurted Odo as he ominously raised himself up. "And you better pray more till the skin on your knees is raw. Pray that you back the correct family members, for this land will soon run red with blood! Rufus' blood and all who follow him. I'll kill the demon myself. No not now, I'm not ready now. We will carry out our game on your brother and his bitch, and then I will seek followers and when I feel the time is perfect, Rufus will fall, as will all who injure and defame me!"

"Yes, Uncle. Whatever you say, Uncle." Will tugged on his arm as he stood and declared, "Now you must apologize."

Instantly, the rigidness left Odo's body and he grabbed Will's hand to help him off the bed. He hurriedly whispered his plot to Will, "Yes, I must. And you as well will passionately pledge him eternal love and devotion. Convince him you'll be his spy and keep an eye on me. We'll leave for Westminster, spend a day hunting, then I'll escape. You will vow, for the sake of his security, to chase me. If we travel directly across the country to Roger's castle in Montgomery, it shouldn't take us more than two days to reach Menevia."

"Yes, Uncle, yes." Will paused a moment and remembered, "What have you done with Ralf? Where is he?"

"In some corner, cowering."

"What did you do to him?!"

"I might have kicked him."

"Ralf!" cried Will.

A tiny whine answered, "Yes, my Lord."

Will followed his squire's voice and found him in a corner...cowering. Annoyed, Will insisted, "What's the matter with you? You did not greet me when I entered."

"Don't hit me, my Lord. *Please!*" Ralf pleaded. "The Bishop kicked me many times...in my chest. It's hard to breathe or stand."

"God's blood!" cursed Will. "I wonder why I bother with you. You're a useless coward! Get yourself to the kitchens and find a chambermaid. Get her to clean you up. You stink! And have her wrap your ribs. I'll consider what's to become of you. Now go!"

Ralf did as told very slowly and moaned with each step. Will grasped Odo's arm to help him up. Odo batted away Will's aid. "Get off me!" he spurted and advised, "We must hurry, and let me speak first." Will only nodded.

Odo stood before the King with confidence, and spoke up loudly and with great passion, "Rufus!" His call was ignored, and he tried again, "Rufus!"

"What?!" Rufus shouted back, catching Odo's cloying gaze.

"I need to apologize for my rudeness, and then I'll ask your exalted permission to remove myself to my chamber."

Rufus' glared and spat, "You'll call me King William...I am William the second, King of England, and not Rufus anymore. Rufus is a child's name. Is that clear, Uncle?"

"Enormously...King William. May I go?"

Rufus' stupor continued awhile more, then he suddenly broke from his trance, brightened, and barked, "Yes...after you apologize! You forgot to apologize."

"Well then, King William," Odo promised carefully, "I am truly remorseful for my nasty blurt of before. I don't know what came over me. I forgot my manners and my homage, for my homage is to you and you only, my dear Lord and nephew. Will you see to your heart, your loving heart and soul to forgive me?"

Both Odo and Will waited with baited breath as Rufus jutted out his thick bottom lip for an interminable moment, then pulled it back in to stutter, "I...I'll con...consider it. Now get out and don't attempt anything sneaky. Know that my guards always watch you...always."

"And I'm honored to be under your royal surveillance, Sire. I bid you a good night. Will," he nodded.

"Uncle," Will nodded back.

The instant Rufus heard the hall's doors click shut, he lashed into Will, "God's teeth, Will, what are you doing with that rat?! He drives me mad with his fancy tunics, his ugly smile, his gloating. Why is he here, and why with you?! Henry sent a message and told me to watch Odo, that he was plotting mischief of some sort. You'll tell me what this mischief is right now!"

"Odo is in England simply to right a past wrong, and he does intend to return presently to Normandy. He's been restored to his See at Bayeux, and wants nothing

354

more than to return to a peaceful existence there as Bishop. You, Sire, are far too fidgety. Have some more claret to calm your jitters and confess, whom else do you assume is scheming to assassinate you?" Rufus waved his cup at his page, and uneasily shrugged, while Will suggested with an irked voice, "You ought to be trailing Henry. How do you know he didn't send you that note purposely to distract you, and is right this moment settling his skinny little ass into your throne at Westminster?"

"Henry loves me and has pledged his homage."

"As he did to Curthose, and anyone else who will supply him women, money, and land. Henry never hesitates to break a promise when it suits him, and it suits him often. Never trust him, my Lord." Will's bottom lip began to tremble expertly in time with his pained words, "I, however, remain your dearest friend when so many others have snubbed you...and you so maliciously passed me over for that sop Flambard! I'm hurt, Rufus, very hurt, and you didn't come to see me when I was so ill. My life was jeopardized by that bitch, Maura, and you abandoned me!"

Rufus' pout returned, dripping claret and remorse. He heaved one mighty sigh, and ruefully admitted, "I've been busy being King. It takes up a large part of my time. I heard of your illness and meant to visit, but my household needed arranging...and...well, Flambard was with me, Will, you weren't. He served Father quite well, and since I intend to continue with most of Father's rulings, appointing him as my chief advisor seemed at the time...shrewd. I'll find some place for you, Will, now that you're healthy again. You'd make a fine treasurer."

"Treasurer!" spat Will. "You insult me, you hideous slug. I should go join Curthose's household, and tattle all your secrets! I'm certain he's preparing to topple you and the mindless oafs you've employed, and could no doubt perform that feat quite easily with my—"

"No!" Rufus burst in. "You'll stay with me! No...nothing states I can't own two advisors. Will...will you please serve me equally with Flambard? I can't very well dismiss him. He's happy in his role and with the salary I pay him, and he helps me appear wise and gracious."

Will guffawed, then mimicked, "'Wise and gracious'? Oh, my dear, dear cousin, he's not helping you, he's mocking you and causing you to appear as what Odo claimed, 'a puppet'." Will grew morbid and almost managed to dribble a tear on cue as he sniffled, "I will consider your plea, Sire. Yet instead of advisor—I truly can't abide Flambard's presence. I would prefer the role of strategist."

"What in the holy face of Lucca is that?"

Confused, Will paused for a moment, then decided not to waste his time asking. Submission instantly left him; he puffed up huge and leant forward, excitement spiking his voice and glinting his eyes. "I'll plan your plots! I'll keep a keen eye on your adversaries. I'll arrange the imprisonment, punishment and, if need be, execution of anyone who dares slander you, in word, deed, or look. I'll manage the seedier side of your rule, Cousin, with an expertise only *you* know I possess. I'll find you presents of cloth, jewels, and—friends, young and willing friends. It's been far too long since we were evil together. I miss those times."

Rufus was practically moved to tears by Will's offer. They had indeed experienced countless exhilarating and wicked adventures—together. And in these troublesome days, he never could be truly certain who his true comrades were. In a shrill gush of emotion, he shoved up, knocking his crown off-center again, thrust out his arms, and blubbered, "Cousin! I've missed you so! No one else knows how hard a job it is to be King. But you will help me, listen to me, soothe me...as no one else is willing to do— and slaughter anyone who defies me. We will have fun again. Hunting...We'll go hunting!"

355

"Not here, Rufus. Remember, there are no deer here. Why don't we hunt at Westminster like I mentioned before? We'll bring Odo, so we can keep an eye on him. And I will return to Normandy with him for only a short while, entertain him, and hear all his secrets. I'll kiss each of my sisters, avoid my Father, his whore and their runt, and hasten back to the warmth of your bosom and abode."

"You'll stay with me at Westminster?" begged Rufus, his bottom lip trembling.

"Part of my time," appeased Will. "I do prefer my life here, and I will be needing to spend some time at Helmsley seeing to my borders. I implore you, Cousin, if you feel the urge to visit my home again, rein in your warriors. I do require a few peasants to work my fields and provide me taxes to pay into your coffers. But yes..." Will rose, reached long over the dais, grasped his cousin's shoulders, placed a neat, dry kiss on each scraggly cheek, and proclaimed, "I will serve you, Sire, with extreme pleasure and my deepest devotion. We will talk more on our journey to London, and after our hunt...Now I wish your permission to retire."

"You have it...and Will," Rufus' eyes brimmed affection as he gently offered, "If you like, one of my lads will gladly service you this night."

"How generous of you, Sire. Yet, alas, I must decline...I'm exhausted and must meet briefly with my seneschal."

"That woman?" scowled Rufus.

"Yes...And I don't appreciate your deprecating tone. She has proven herself invaluable to me."

Rufus asked with a leer, "In what way?"

"Not in *that* way, Rufus. Our doings are strictly platonic. She sees after my home and my health rather brilliantly."

"Perhaps you'll return from Normandy by Christmas?"

"Perhaps," said Will, "but I thought you didn't worship Christ anymore."

"I don't, but He's a marvelous excuse for a feast."

"Yes...I suppose He is that," chuckled Will. "We'll talk later. Good-night, Sire, and," he glanced delicately at each boy and sighed, "may you have the sweetest dreams."

*****

"Do you ever wonder what mischief Rufus is up to these days?" asked Maura, dripping melted cheese over a thick slice of bread. She caught the last fat drip, licked it from her finger, and then munched into a sumptuous bite.

"Sometimes..." mumbled Simon, his mouth full of bread as well. He took a swig of steaming mead, and swallowed to speak more clearly, "Actually, the thought of him makes me ill, so I don't wonder about him often. Yet I am astonished that England and Normandy remain under separate rule, and that we haven't received word of massive slaughter along the borders of Wales and Scotland. I suspected he'd try to grab everything for his own, and succeed."

"Yes...It is rather odd, isn't it? He couldn't have miraculously become placid and peaceful...could he?"

"No, my love, such a miracle is impossible. Here..." He leant close to steal a vagrant bit of cheese from the corner of her mouth. His lips lingered there, tasting more, and asked, "Do you need another pillow?"

Maura considered the plump down bed they had made for themselves from the many pillows located about the house. Cupped to Simon, she snuggled nearer and sighed, "I think we've gathered them all. It was so kind of Owain and Marc to let us stay here...alone. And it's so quiet."

"Almost too quiet," agreed Simon. They hushed a minute and heard only the faint crackling of the flames, the creaking of the wattle walls, and the whispering moan of the

356

wind as it stole its way between the bolted shutters. Both shivered and instinctively inched closer to each other and the bubbling cauldron full of mead. Simon noted to break the unnerving silence, "We've some dried apples left."

"No, my love...I've no room for any more food."

The play of her last word prompted him to ask, "And what is it you have room for?"

"I'll tell you...soon enough," she answered impishly, then asked, "What did you say when Marc told you his plans?"

"That I wholeheartedly agree!" he buoyantly answered. "What an absolutely perfect decision. I had suggested once that he take the robes."

"I know, he told me," said she.

"He's so suited to the role of priest, in its truest and most respectable form, and husband and father as well. That he can aspire to all three is simply marvelous. I believe we'll see a profound change in him once his training begins."

"That he'll be happier?"

"Happier, busier, full of knowledge to embrace and share."

She smiled contentedly to the thought, and wondered with a quirky grin, "Were you shocked when Owain showed you his altar?"

"Shocked? No...Fascinated, somewhat confused, but no, not shocked."

"When I was bedridden," Maura said, "he would sit with me and tell me tales abounding with goddesses—strong, wise, and sensual women worshipped by mortal men and women alike. I found that very appealing."

"Worshipping strong, wise, and sensual women," considered Simon, running his thumb along her jaw, then kissing the nape of her neck. He thought a moment more, then appraised with a lusty grin, "I also find that exquisitely appealing."

Maura beamed her delight and brightly remarked, "Owain's proven to be quite a surprise, hasn't he?"

"Yes...a welcomed one. He should stay Pennaeth."

Simon's bluntness fuddled Maura. She shifted onto her back and gazed questioningly upward into his intense expression. "But how could that happen? Gael chose Taredd."

"She should have chosen Owain."

"She hates Owain."

"Not anymore."

"Gael told you this?"

"No...but yesterday before we left and she wandered out to bid us good-bye, Owain rode up and her look was different."

"But to *marry* him, Simon?"

"So instead," he contended, "she marries a complete stranger, who upon first entering his new home, charges the bed suspecting his wife is committing adultery. Who knows what he might have done if I hadn't stopped him? What if his love of drink is chronic? Gruffydd and Owain have become great friends. At least in a marriage between Gael and Owain, they'd already know what they *dislike* about one another. The villagers trust Owain, and he's mighty skilled at leading peaceful folk. He's in a muddle as to what to do with himself, and I'm concerned that Rhys will insist he return to the battlefield. Nothing could make him more miserable."

"Not even marrying Gael?" asked Maura.

"Not even that."

"Marc loves her."

"I know he does."

The melancholy weighting his words worried Maura, and she chanced, "You don't think she loves him?"

"Not as intensely. And when he discovers this—" Simon's voice cracked as if he suffered from Marc's imminent turmoil. "He...he will be crushed. I...I don't want him hurt, Maura. I swore I'd never let anyone hurt him again! There is no man as good as Marc."

She reached a consoling touch to his cheek and, searching his pale gaze welling with sadness, whispered passionately, "I'm so lucky to love you, for no one is more caring. And if it happens that Marc is hurt, he knows to come to you for comfort. You've always given him the love he deserves and needs."

"As have you."

"But he's always aspired to be exactly like you."

"And that I've never understood...I do so admire him."

His sorrow endured. Her arms hugged his back and he rolled into her embrace. They shifted for comfort till he lay facing her, his knees slightly bent. She faced him as well, her legs draped over his as if she were sitting on his lap. So close and always touching, she remembered, "Once when we were sad, I don't recall exactly why, I asked you to take me back to a time when our life together was especially wondrous."

His eyes, still sparkling unspilt tears, smiled to the memory. "I reminded you of the storm and the barn."

"And we forgot the sadness."

"Yes," he sighed, "that we did."

"We'll spend our time here reliving those moments and creating new ones, Simon. That's what Marc wanted us to do, don't you think?"

He agreed with a shy smile, and melted more to her passionate appeal, "Let me give to *you*, my dearest love. You've done nothing but give to me these past long months and I want nothing more than to pleasure you, make you smile, hear you laugh."

He started to argue...then gazing upon her heartrending look, he instead nuzzled his cheek to hers, and began their rapture with a vehement kiss desperate to feel, to hear, and to know that her love would forever be his.

*****

Marc left Owain and the children at the bottom of the hill leading to the cottage. Owain, with Nia sharing his saddle, rode on, scolding the boys to rein in their ponies. After his yelling subsided, Nia chatted, "My mam says that I'll get my own pony soon. Then I'll get to race too."

"And I'm most certain you'll easily beat the lads," said Owain. "They show little control."

She looked thankfully up into his gentle gaze, her pale gray eyes swimming with innocence and delight, and asked, "Will you teach me to race?"

Reflecting on his humiliating jaunt on Henry's stallion, Owain smiled as he confessed, "Racing...I don't do well. But I've heard Maura is an expert horse woman, and I'm sure she will gladly teach you."

"Do we have to go to my hut? Can't we play more?"

Owain considered the toil he was about to endure, and sighed with discontent, "Actually, I'd love to play more. But there's something I must do, and your mam will be wanting to see you."

"She's always holding Morgan," Nia complained.

"If you couldn't walk," he returned, "she'd always be holding you."

"I guess. When will he walk?"

"Too soon," he answered with a laugh.

Owain looked up to see the welcoming sight of Olwen, an expectant beam splitting her comely face, standing at the roadside, jiggling a mewling Morgan in her arms, with her second youngest son, Maredudd, clinging to her skirts. Nia squirmed in Owain's hold; he reined in Ceffyl, and carefully set her on the ground, yet before she dashed to her mother, she glanced up again and proclaimed with a quick bow, "I thank you, Sir."

"As I thank you, my Lady." His formal response elicited from her a rash of giggles, and she bounded away. He rode nearer to greet and tell Olwen, "The children did well. Cynan and Gruffydd took the long way around and should arrive shortly."

"Has Marc returned?" she asked, not disguising her hope.

"Yes...he's at the cottage packing."

Her paleness worried Owain as she blurted, "He's not leaving, is he?"

"No," he assured. "It's best if he tells you his plans."

"Should I go to the cottage?"

"He'll come and explain all to you here." A nod and jerk of the reins took Owain back down the lane toward the llys. The boys trotted in his direction. He let Cynan pass, then blocked Gruffydd's advance with a grim look and command, "You'll come with me now."

Gruffydd returned a glare and a curt, "I'll go with Cynan." Owain grabbed Rhodri's harness, yanked the pony around, and kicked his own mare into a trot. Gruffydd promptly leapt from his saddle and took off running. Anticipating such an antic, Owain was instantly at his heels, caught him up by the waist, and hoisted him over his shoulder. To no avail, Gruffydd wriggled, bucked, and squawked miserably their entire journey to the llys. Owain purposely carried him to the rear of the building so as not to draw a crowd and, setting him on his feet, knelt to keep a restraining hold on his captive. He waited not so patiently till Gruffydd finished hurling his abuse, "Let me go! You're not my tad, you're not even Pennaeth anymore!"

"No, I'm neither your tad nor the Pennaeth. And the way you've behaved on our journey home, I'm glad I'm not your father." Owain's cutting comment struck Gruffydd still; Owain eased his grip and softened. "Why did you constantly ignore me?"

"Because I knew what you were going to say."

"And what was that?"

"That I should be understanding to my mam, and kind to my stepfather."

Owain swallowed his planned retort and confirmed instead, "Yes, that's what I was going to say."

"Well, I won't! No one asked me what I wanted, what I felt. And now I should be quiet and nice to everyone. I won't, I hate him...and I don't like my mam much either! I want to find Ella...I'll stay with her, or Simon, Maura and Marc, or Olwen. I won't live at the llys, not with them!"

Not accustomed to such parental dilemmas, Owain prayed for a placating and wise response, and when he chanced speaking again, he was grateful for the compassionate one that poured forth, "Your mam had no choice but to marry Taredd. Rhys told her if she didn't, he would take you away to live at Dinefwr. And that, for someone such as yourself, would be Hell. Your mam would do anything, even marry a man she doesn't know and may not care for to keep you safe and loved. She needs you most now, don't turn from her. Protect her as she protects you...love her, help her. I must leave awhile, and when I return I expect to hear that you've at least attempted what I've asked."

Gruffydd broke his narrow glare, and humbly dropped it to his feet, mumbling, "I'll try...but if he tries to hurt her, I'll kill him."

Owain lifted Gruffydd's chin and assured, "I know well your frustration...yet always remember, fight only to keep peace. When you feel you want to strike out and scream, think on your father's words and ways. They will calm you."

Gruffydd bit into his bottom lip and, with an awkward nod, implored, "You'll come back, soon?"

"I pray so...Yet when I *do* return, I don't know how long I'll be allowed to stay."

Alarm gripped and twisted Gruffydd's belly. For the past two months, Owain had been constantly about helping, playing, singing, whistling. He'd miss him sorely, and blurted with a broken voice, "Please come back to us. We'll find a way to keep you." He fell into his friend's taut hug, and when he finally eased back, swiped embarrassingly at an escaping tear.

Owain felt himself crumbling as well, and lightly suggested, "Go stable the horses, and then find your aunt. I'm sure she's wanting to see you. I need to talk to your mam and stepfather alone."

Gruffydd obediently slouched away, and Owain stood, straightened his mind and his clothes as best he could, and adhering to Maura's competent advice, took one very long deep breath. Upon entering the llys, he stopped short as he encountered through the misty light, a fondling couple. The man's back faced Owain; he recognized Taredd's blond greasy locks, and supposed the woman his body hid was Gael. Their suggestive snickers kindled within him a sense of rescue, quickly followed by guilt and a peculiar nausea. He cleared his throat to announce his presence. With drama, Taredd gasped and started back from his partner, who wasn't Gael at all, but Enid. She regarded Owain with a lofty sneer, cocked her chin, and flounced behind the tapestry.

Dumbstruck, Owain strove feverishly to conjure the proper curse and, during his struggled lapse, Taredd attacked. Taredd's fighting tactics were as unruly as his personal skills and Owain, even distracted, easily blocked his blow with a forceful parry to his jaw. The Pennaeth dropped to the rushes, groaning in misery. "Isn't this where I left you?" Owain gritted with revulsion, his color high and eyes flaming. He kicked out soundly, and fumed, "Get up, you fool! I have somewhere to go, and I won't be delayed...not by your failings. Where is your wife?"

"I do...don't know. She ran off last night, wouldn't let me touch her."

"And so you decided to touch someone else instead. You disgusting leech." He kicked once more, harder, and yelled, "I said get up!"

"Not till you swear to stop hitting and kicking me," groaned Taredd.

Owain grudgingly retreated one step and Taredd uncurled himself and struggled up, arms crossed and clutching his shoulders like a shield. "You filthy craven," spat Owain. "How did you convince Rhys that a moron like yourself could lead this village? Or should I ask how much you paid him?"

"You...you...have no right to complain," bumbled Taredd. "*You* were rejected."

"As it seems you were as well."

"We only had a slight disagreement."

Owain snorted in outrage, "I returned here to meet with you and your lady and discuss the status of the village! But as I see it, you have little interest in this village or your wife, and I won't waste my good time arguing with you further."

He whirled round to leave and was stalled by Gael. Her silhouette filled the door, and her voice, strained and faint, floated near, "Please...don't leave yet, Owain. I'm interested in your impressions of the village." As she came slowly forward, he noticed outright her paleness. Her eyes, darkly hollow, avoided his; she hugged herself self-consciously, and grew more ashen when she beheld Taredd. To cool the simmering tension, she gazed idly about, tugged her tangled braid, and wondered in a dull voice, "Where's Gruffydd?"

Owain didn't hear her question; instead he recalled how bright her eyes shone and her flush of embarrassment the morning before when she'd startled him at his wash. What had shaken her so? Then seeing how she shrank back as Taredd stepped forward confirmed his suspicion, that their tiff was more than slight. He wondered if voicing his concerns would help or hinder matters, then the fact of his imminent departure kept him silent. It wouldn't do to rile Taredd, then leave him to act out his rage on Gael. He snapped his head to Gael's call, "Owain. Where is my son?"

"Stabling the horses," he blurted. He quickly gulped a deep breath, and added, "I told him I would speak to you both alone, so he's gone to find your sister."

Gael seemed satisfied with his clumsy response. She shuffled to the trestle table and sagged down upon a bench, mumbling to, but not acknowledging, Taredd, "Is there mead or food? Owain is our guest and he should have been offered refreshment. Where is our servant?"

"As my wife, it is your role to handle the household, including our servant," returned Taredd with a humph as he slumped onto the bench opposite, arms crossed at his chest.

Owain snorted and rolled his eyes to Taredd's audacious comment, remembering how he found him happily handling the servant just a short while past.

"Enid!" Gael yelled and rose to search for her, but her quest ended abruptly when she yanked back the tapestry and discovered her maid stretched out upon the bed, wearing only her shift and a snide grin.

"Yes, my Lady," was Enid's twittery reply.

Gael exploded in a rash of expletives, "Damn you, you stinking whore! You may own my husband, but you don't yet own my bed!" Gael wrenched the woman off the bed and hurled her across the room, where Enid landed with a tremendous crash upon a tall stack of wood.

Owain covered his mouth to hide his gape, and balled his fists to keep from applauding. Enid flew at Taredd, clawed at his tunic, and wailed, "How can you let her hurt me this way! Hurt her back! Punish her, you coward!"

With a daunted exasperation, Taredd ripped her hands from his shirt and lunged from her swipe, screaming, "Get out, you crazed sows! Out of my house now!"

Taredd failed miserably to exert the mastery he aimed for, but Owain thought for everyone's sanity and safety, a break in the dispute was necessary. He spoke intensely with no sign of anger, "Gael, we'll speak outside." He'd countless times witnessed her fury, yet, in this instance, her wrath seemed fused with immense shame, and he felt an unfamiliar discomfort as his belly churned to her plight.

Gael averted her eyes and hesitantly trailed Owain out the back exit. In the courtyard between llys and stable, she fidgeted with her braid and fixed a lost look on moss climbing the base of an oak while sputtering, "I...I'm sorry...for...for my husband's and my childish behavior. Perchance if you come by later, he'll be prepared to listen." Her fleeting glance accidentally met his considerate gaze; though soft, his eyes nonetheless burned into her and the dreaded cramping tore again at her belly. Her hands left her hair to hug her waist and she stammered more, "Ple...please go, come later...I...I need to find Gruffydd...*Please*!"

Gael lurched to leave but Owain caught her wrist and found no resistance as he carefully explained, "I can't come later...And if I did he might be ready, but he won't listen to me. He hates me!"

"Why can't you come?!" she moaned.

"I won't be here...I'm leaving on a trip north...I'll be gone at least a fortnight."

"You have to tell him about the villagers, make him see his responsibilities!"

"You know the villagers better than I do. You tell him!"

Gael threw his hand away and despaired, "Do you truly believe I can tell him anything? He hates me as well!"

A screeching discord resounding from the llys tempered their banter. Horror replaced the frustration in Gael's expression and swelled Owain's concern. "You won't return to the llys," he firmly decided. "Fetch your things and move to Simon and Maura's cottage. Marc will watch over you."

The screams inside suddenly intensified, and Gael railed along with their rage, "I don't need watching over!"

"Then don't go to the cottage," he exasperated, "go to your own home, but I warn you...don't go near him...not tonight and not alone!"

"He is my husband, Owain."

"Not for much longer."

Panic banished her anger; she grabbed back his hand, squeezing and beseeching, "What will you do?"

"I'll complain to Rhys," he readily decided, "and have your union annulled."

"No!" she cried, her tone verging on hysteria. "You can't, you can't say anything. If you do, he'll take Gruffydd away, and send me back to my father. Swear you won't go to him, swear!"

"Something must be done to ensure your safety, and that of your son and sister and the village."

She jerked away; eerily, her posturing wilted and her voice lightened, "He won't really hurt me, or Gruffydd. He only blusters...We enjoyed a sweet night together last evening."

"That's not what *he* claims."

She turned only her head, her expression still wretched, and spurted, "What *did* he claim?"

"He said you wouldn't let him touch you."

Her false grin assured, "He's only being modest...Our marriage is at last a true union, legally and physically, and that's why I'm so weary this day. All couples quarrel, Owain. There's no need to tell Rhys otherwise." His leery eye told her she'd failed miserably in her act; she shook from the illusion, pulled herself tall, and soundly proclaimed, "I will make this match work...I have to. Say nothing."

"I don't see—"

"Swear!" she flared and pounced, her biting touch and pleading look igniting in Owain a burning that coursed crazily through his veins, rendering him weakened and speechless. He hung his head in assent, pried her fingers from his arm, and chanced leaving, stopping every few feet to glance back at her haunted features and defeated figure. She suddenly seemed so very small. He ducked into the stable, swiftly saddled Ceffyl and, tugging her outside, found the courtyard terribly empty.

He mounted in haste and urged his mare out onto the main road where he was promptly spotted and approached by Rhys. "Owain!" he called, trotting up to Ceffyl's side. "Are you away then?"

"I'm hoping to be very soon, but I keep getting interrupted," answered Owain pointedly.

"Did you speak to Taredd?"

"Not on the subject intended."

"Oh..." Rhys seemed confused, then hoped, "Well I'm certain he will prove me proud in his new role as leader."

Owain looked dubious but daren't reply. Instead he grimaced in relief at the saving sight of Marc sauntering up on Fulk.

"And Gael..." mentioned Rhys. "Have you talked to Gael?"

"Briefly," said Owain.

"Yes, between you two it would be brief. Does she appear pleased?"

"About what?"

"Her husband, you fool."

Owain wrestled with his retort, then sputtered, "De...determined."

"What are you talking about?" grunted Rhys.

"She spoke determinedly about her marriage and her husband."

"That doesn't sound overly passionate to me."

"It's suitable."

"What do you mean, suitable? Why don't you ever speak so people can understand you, Owain? How am I supposed to use you as mediator, when no one—"

"Marc...Marc's here."

"Oh yes...Marc..."

"Rhys...Owain..." greeted Marc.

Owain nodded and Rhys relayed, "I've heard from Sulien you begin your preparation this day. I am thrilled you've decided to join our clergy."

"I'm grateful, Sir," answered Marc.

"Where are Simon and that handsome sister of yours?"

"They are safely away," jumped in Owain, "as I must be. They will return on the Sabbath."

"But where've they gone? I may need Simon."

"I'm to see to the villagers' medical needs," stated Marc. "Will you be staying the week?"

"No...I plan to return to Dinefwr in the morning. Can I convince you, Owain, to remain till then?"

"No."

"We'll plan another feast," he enticed.

No," Owain stolidly tried again.

Rhys gestured sharply and huffed his frustration, "Then go visit your ancient ones. Such a trip seems entirely worthless to me."

Owain knew not to argue or agree, for if he did, he'd never escape his Prince. Rhys waited, then grew flustered at his soldier's deliberate quiet and barked to fill the void, "Where's Gael?"

"I don't know—" started Owain.

And Rhys angrily intruded, "No, you needn't finish...I know well enough you also don't care where she is. Well I'm weary of your rudeness, and shall go visit your successor. At least he knows and enjoys the art of conversation. You'll stop at Dinefwr on your return journey. By that time, I will have decided your future. Marc..."

"Rhys..." answered Marc as, puzzled, he watched Rhys stomp away toward the llys. "Owain, why do you purposely rile him?"

"I don't...Well, perhaps I did just now because I need to leave, and Rhys is highly skilled at delay." Owain abruptly switched thoughts and severely pressed, "I ask you not to question this request Marc, and beg you, while I'm gone, keep a keen watch over Taredd...and Gael."

Marc tensed and started gibbering just what Owain had forbade. "But...But—" He gulped the rest of his stammer, and confirmed instead, "Of course, I will." Awkwardly, he untethered a burlap sack from his pommel and offered it to Owain. "I've packed you food. It should serve you till you reach your first shelter."

Owain gratefully accepted the fare, and his meek smile showed abundant thanks. Their parting needed no words; saddened looks and a clenched hand clasp clearly affirmed their ever growing bond.

*****

Gael paced the skinny breadth of her hut, wringing her hands furiously, muttering curses and despair. What would she do, what could she do? If Owain betrayed her stormy home life, Rhys would surely punish her for not submitting properly to her fate

363

and her husband. Should she deny her pride and accept the humiliation dealt her? She'd never envisioned herself weak, yet now she felt horribly weak, feeble boned and minded. Somehow, she must heal her battered strength and fight back to regain her status and her esteem, and prepare to wage an eternal battle to keep what was most precious to her—her son.

Gruffydd peeked into the barely opened door and watched patiently his mam's fluster. She slowed her fury, clasped her hands together as in prayer, shut her eyes and loudly sighed. Such behavior usually signaled the end of her trouble, and Gruffydd felt safe in grasping Ella's hand and leading her cautiously inside the cottage. Gael opened her eyes to the welcoming sight of her family's cautious smiles, and greeted, "Gruffydd, Ella! I've missed you so!" She clutched her son in a smothering hug, and wondered too gaily, "Did you enjoy your trip to Owain's hut?"

Gruffydd noticed the quaver in her cheer and prayed his calm would infect her. "Yes...I did, very much. Simon and Maura stayed on and will return on the Sabbath. Marc is staying at the cathedral till they return, and I shot an arrow, Mam, that landed in the target, and it was much farther than I've ever shot before."

"I'm so very proud of you," she effused and hugged again, much harder.

Still in her arms, Gruffydd wriggled for comfort and spotted tears dotting her cheeks. His mam's praise didn't normally come with tears. He swelled protectively and demanded, "What's he done, Mam?"

"What's who done?" she dismissed with a crooked grin.

"My new tad...Has he hurt you?"

"No."

"Then why are you here and where is he?"

"I've come to fetch some of my things."

"All of your things are at the llys. Owain helped me move them."

Gael frantically scanned her surroundings, struggling for an excuse and, suddenly, not only did the excuse come to her but also a sobering bolt of fortitude and direction. "No, Gruffydd...You see I've come to fetch the rest of our things. All of us—me, you, and Ella—will move permanently into the llys." His questioning look rallied her reply, "And, I won't have an argument."

"I wasn't going to argue, Mam," assured Gruffydd.

"I wasn't speaking of you. Ella!" Gael called. The young woman readily stepped forward. Gael released Gruffydd and gently took her sister's hands. "We're going to live at the llys," Gael carefully explained. A spark of terror instantly flared the dullness of Ella's gaze. She tried to pull away; Gael firmed her grip and assured, "You will never be left alone with someone you don't trust...completely. No one will harm you again...I swear."

Ella's tenseness eased slightly, and with her hesitant nod came a look of tenuous relief and something else...Gael peered deeper into her sister's sea blue eyes and beheld shining there for the first time since her arrival—the tiniest speck of awareness.

The three strode resolutely, hand in hand, toward the llys, Gael's pony carrying the remaining pelts and various other household implements. Stinging, spitting hail forced them to seek shelter beneath their hoods and swiften their pace. As Gael ushered her family through the gate, she noticed Rhys' pony tethered to the fence. A winning smile graced her lips and straightened the caution of her posture. Her husband surely would show his most gracious behavior, however hypocritical, in the company of his Prince. She entered first, and the enlivening and calming strains of chuckling greeted her. As she stepped into the light of a wall-braced oil lamp, Rhys beamed and clumsily stood, his balance disturbed by an overabundance of mead. Taredd followed suit, his rising shakier and his expression curiously benign. "Come forward," she called softly to Gruffydd and Ella. "Prince Rhys is visiting."

Gael marveled at and envied Gruffydd's resolve. He appeared almost brazen, his chin cocked high, his gaze penetrating. He strode three long steps forward, bowed to his Prince, then at Rhys' awed nod, he turned to take pelts from his mother. "I'll make up beds for Ella and me. You talk to Rhys. He always makes you laugh."

Gael chucked softly, passed the furs to her son, and kissed his brow with a whisper, "Keep close to Ella, and talk to her sweetly as you do so very well."

He answered with a quick grin and happily left her to the adults. She strove to mimic her son's boldness as she approached the trestle table and swept herself gracefully onto the bench opposite the men. They plopped themselves down, Rhys pouring her a cup of mead, and booming, "Your husband has been expertly entertaining me. I'm delighted to hear how comfortably you've settled yourselves into your new union and home. Not so new a home for you, Gael, but appreciated, I'm certain, after living a year in that crowded box."

"I rather like my cottage..." she returned, then artfully added, "but I will enjoy the extra room and warmth of the llys. What else has my husband shared?" she asked with a suspicious smirk. Her narrow eye caught Taredd's bleary one, and she silently wondered *What was he thinking or playing at?* Or was he, in his present state of inebriation, capable of rational thought?

"As a gentleman, he refuses to divulge any of your private doings," begrudged Rhys. "But he spouts nothing but compliments for you and your son, and thanks to me for allowing him to compete for your home and heart."

At that most outrageous claim, Gael downed her entire cup of mead in three gulps, sat taller, and commented in a tone rivaling Rhys' in resonance, "I'm grateful for my husband's praise and generosity, for I know it was his idea to bring Enid from Dinefwr to assist me with our household. But I beg you, Sir, you know how I loathe to be waited on. It makes me feel foolish and inept. I wish to supervise my household solely on my own, and ask if you would be so kind as to escort Enid back to Dinefwr with you when you leave in the morn. She will be much more useful to you and your good Lady. Please, my Prince, see clear to granting my plea."

Rhys pondered groggily Gael's formal speech and odd appeal. Her request was simple enough; of course, he'd gladly take Enid home with him, for he missed her comely and giving presence. "Yes Gael," he answered, "I will grant your plea. Do you want for anything else?"

"No, my Prince, and I heartily thank you." Gael glanced to Taredd for his reaction, but his attention was directed elsewhere. She followed his pensive stare to the corner of the long house, where Gruffydd and Ella were busily laying pallets and pelts. Again she yearned and yet also dreaded discovering the peculiarities of his most volatile mind.

The girl is moving in here, Taredd discerned sourly to himself. Each day she unfortunately grew saner, and would soon be competent enough to accuse all involved in her assault, which he had begun quite harmlessly...He'd only asked her to lie on her back for him for a while, and in return he'd take her back to her lover on the border. Of course he'd lied, but she'd been too deranged to doubt his promise, and had freely consented. Then the others had come into the barn and demanded their time with the girl. He'd finished and had given her to them; she'd become frightened and tried to escape, but they wouldn't allow her leaving and forced her to submit. He'd stayed to watch for a time, then grew bored and left—left just before the raping was discovered by Rhys. His friends had been flogged and banished, and the fury Taredd felt over their punishment forever festered and now, watching Ella, threatened to erupt in revenge. Somehow, he had to silence her. If Rhys stayed the night at the llys, he'd pry from him information on her tryst with the Montgomery's squire. Perhaps it was possible to sell her to the Montgomerys or Taredd would consider offering a plump sum of money for her return. He'd never raped her, he'd only had some fun, yet he was certain once her wits returned she'd claim he'd instigated the entire crime, and he'd lose everything he had toiled so hard to attain. No...never would an addle-brained bitch spoil his achievements. She'd gladly go back to the Montgomerys, for he would ensure that her life here would be a horrid nightmare, and if she didn't agree to go voluntarily, well then, he'd have to quiet her some other way...permanently.

*****

Whipped by a furious north wind, hail rattled the shutters and battered the walls of Owain's cottage. A few vigorous crystals dashed their way through the roof vent, hissing and billowing steam as they plunged into the bubbling pot. Yet Simon and Maura failed to notice the tempest. They'd allow nothing to disturb their tenuous bliss; enchanted smiles, murmured memories, and stirring embraces had stolen them away to a secret paradise lush with ecstasy.

For two full glorious days and nights, Simon reveled in Maura's promised adoration. Not accustomed to such extravagance, he initially took uneasily to his spoiling, but soon found himself readily surrendering to her persistent pleasuring. She refused to let him perform any endeavor requiring effort; she cooked for him, bathed him, oft times fed him, and instilled in these usually simple acts a sensual opulence he found irresistible. And he was absolutely certain, he had to be the most fortunate and coveted man alive.

The wicked weather forced them inside, and they found little complaint with their confinement. Lolling upon their down bed, they gleefully reenacted the amorous adventures of their near and far past. Their gift of privacy allowed them to relish their loving with a fiery abandon they'd not enjoyed for far too long. They talked of everything and nothing, delighting each other with only favorable visions of their nebulous future. Bliss spilled from them in lilting laughter, endearing looks and touches, and during their frequent bouts of loving, rumbled forth with a new found intensity that not only thrilled, it also frightened.

Ecstatically spent and cupped together, they slept soundly their final night in Owain's home. The next morn, Maura was first to wake; for a long luxurious while. she lay very still, relishing the heat of his skin pressed against hers. Then ever so gently, she loosened his grip on her waist and studied the grace and length of his fingers. She felt him stir as her lips nipped the tip of each finger and caressed the taut and silky surface of his palm. He instinctively melded nearer, and she grew woozy to the sumptuous memory of what exquisite pleasure his beautiful hands had evoked in her the previous evening. He chuckled to her continued tickling, and gently urged her to her back. Their fingers laced together, and Simon murmured, his voice weary with happiness, "And how should we spend our last hours here?"

Jointly, they let go a rapturous sigh and began again their fondling. Simon paused his hand over her belly when he noticed a twinge of sadness in Maura's eyes and worried, "What is it, my love?"

Her hand covered his as she lamented, "I was hoping that Elyn would decide to arrive here and make our stay perfect."

He smiled tenderly. "Well we've done our utmost to jostle our chick from her nest. I honestly believe that after all her teasing, she's quite content to stay inside awhile longer. We can always return around Christmas and try again."

"Could we, Simon?!" Maura asked excitedly. "I would so love it if we could..."

"As would I...and Owain mentioned we could come again if we want or need to..." He nestled back beside her and reminded, "When we discussed all we longed to do

366

here, we mentioned exploring not only each other but the mountainside as well. Do you remember?"

"I think I do..." She crept over him, her eyes lust filled, and breathed between swooning kisses, "but we're always getting distracted. And the weather...the weather has been so terribly nasty..."

"I no longer hear the wind," he noticed, laughing to her nibbling attack on his ear.

She sat back on her heels, listened intently, and beheld glittering shafts of gold sneaking their way through the slits in the shutters. A sense of brilliance lured her from his warmth; she shivered from the morning chill and absence of a fire, grabbed up her chemise, and wriggled into the garment on her hurry to the door. Its opening produced a gasp from Maura and the exclamation, "Simon...I do believe we've found Heaven!"

Curiously, he struggled up, tripping into his braies on the way to her side and, once there, an awed sigh left him as he breathlessly agreed, "I do believe you're correct."

Virgin snow, piled near a foot deep and blinding in its pureness, blanketed the clearing and limbs and bushes of the forest; swords of ice shimmered from branches and glittered from the jutted roof of the cottage. Wisps of clouds whisked their iridescence between the trees and flickered rays of escaping sunlight across the pristine scene.

Their eyes met expectantly and Maura suggested, "We'll eat quickly, dress warmly, then go outside and play."

"I'll not argue," Simon exuberantly replied.

The door shut and when next it opened, Simon and Maura laughingly tumbled out, bundled in layer upon layer of coarse woolen clothing. Heaving mounds of snow at each other and their rampant chasing sufficiently heated them, and the layers briskly were peeled away. They boldly clambered the hill that backed the cottage and continued their difficult trek up its slick silvery surface to the summit of the mountain. From this eminent position they were able to view the entire range of the Cambrian peaks, the lush valleys between, and the sapphire sea beyond. They breathed deeply the crisp icy air and noticed, in the corner of the resplendent sight, a lone rider atop a gray gelding plodding toward the cottage. Marc had arrived to take them home and back to uncertainty. Facing each other, Simon and Maura were suddenly jolted by a crippling despair that rattled their minds and raced their hearts. The dread they constantly pondered, yet rarely spoke of, sank them to their knees and thrust them together, clutching and clawing to get closer. Maura let go her hug and took his damp face in her hands. "Si...Simon," she brokenly began. "You must swear—"

"No!" he wailed, knowing her plea.

He tried pulling away, but she held fast his hands and insisted, "You must! I can't leave here not knowing."

"You know...you have to know!" he stressed. "How can you doubt my love?"

"I don't...I'd never, but I do know how you will sacrifice all to keep me and Elyn alive!" Her plea swelled and stumbled with rising panic. "Swear...swear not to leave us, swear, Simon...You must take us with you wherever you go, swear this to me, to her...here and now! Please, my love, we can't, we won't be without you."

Great sobs shook them both as he buried his face in her hands and choked, "I...I swear to you and her, on my life and our love, I swear."

*****

367

CHAPTER TWENTY-ONE - DARK ILLUMINATING JOURNEYS

Bodeful was the night's blackness, and deadening the loneliness Owain suffered as he urged his straggling mare along the snow-stacked path that braced the blustery north shore of Gwynedd. Soon, he prayed, he'd reach Bangor where a raft awaited to cross him over to the isle of Mon, his family's homeland. Sleet pelted his head and shoulders, stung his face, and drenched his cloak. Rarely had he felt this wet, weary, and miserable. He'd grown accustomed to a daily wash and cringed in disgust to the constant itching roused by a thick layer of filth coating his skin...and by the bugs. The stable he'd been forced to sleep in the night before had been home to innumerable crawling critters and they'd happily found a new home on his and Ceffyl's hides. The saving thought of his great-grandparents' blazing hearth, warm water for washing, a hearty stew, and a soft pelted pallet to rest his worn bones upon, drove him onward on the blinding way he knew more from feel and scent than sight. To hasten his journey, he purposely bypassed the commote of Bangor and kept snug to the shore, where to his relief the waves lapped tamely. As he rode he distracted himself from discomfort by turning his thoughts to his mission thus far. He'd arrived just after dawn in Rhuddlan four days past and had begun a painstaking and ultimately frustrating search through its thirteen boroughs for information concerning battles waged in the early '70's between the Normans and Welsh. No one he'd spoken to had kept a memory of which commotes were razed, if any elite Normans were eliminated, who had survived, or who was victorious. He knew that the cruel Norman Baron, Hugh the Fat of Chester, had positioned himself on the border of North Wales soon after King William's Conquest of England. Hugh, when bored, employed the nasty habits of laying waste to Welsh villages simply because they irked him or sat in the way of a potential hunting preserve, and of kidnapping Welsh women from nearby settlements to serve as slaves in his harem. In the early 70's, however, the Welsh tired of his fickle rampages, and fought back with vigor. Hugh swiftly collected powerful allies for a reprisal and struck with zealous brutality, scorching to the earth all commotes in the vicinity of the border and ravaging deep into Gwynedd and along the Valley of Clywd. His forces had reached Bangor, intent on crossing the strait and ransacking Mon. To preserve his family's *gift* of prophesy, Owain, his sister Gwen, brother Bryn, the twins, and his parents had secretly stolen away by boat and landed a day later to seek refuge at Mynyw. Hugh failed in his attempt to subdue the natives and pulled his forces back to Chester, but not without wreaking numerous atrocities. Since that terrible time, skirmishes were constant though never of the same ferocity as the rebellion. No one Owain had spoken to could recall the tale of the Norman baron who'd been killed and the fate of his two orphaned children. Contrarily, what was remembered was the conspicuous absence of Norman women and children on the volatile border.

A hooded torch, whipped by raggling winds, shivered into view, and Owain thanked the Gods that he hadn't gotten himself lost in the gale. He dismounted and tugged Ceffyl through the soggy sand. Sloshing closer, he beheld the raft's pilot, huddled in his ramshackle shelter. So as not to startle, he called out in a friendly manner, "A passenger for you." The man turned to Owain's advancing dreary figure, waved his oil lamp in response, and smiled for the work and the coins to come.

A silken mist swirled ghostly over the black water, entrancing and chilling the raft's lone passenger. He loathed being on water, felt dizzy, sick, and frightened. What held them up, protected them from sinking into a smothering, choking death? Childhood nightmares of monsters angrily surfacing, hungry for human flesh, returned with a vivid vengeance. Screams of gulls lifted the hairs on the back of his neck and Owain squeezed shut his eyes and prayed vigorously and audibly for the island's shore to appear. A soft thumping told him his prayer had been answered. He felt faint with relief as he guided Ceffyl off the roped logs and onto a worm-eaten and rotten planked pier. He mounted his mare and shuddered to the realization that he still had much further to travel to the ancient village of Din Lligwy on the northeast coast of Mon.

Owain imagined it was halfway through the night when he at last encountered the timbered walls of the ancient village of Din Lligwy. He entered without question or opposition and steered his mount round swampy puddles, vagrant yapping dogs, and thatched timber and mud huts; he passed through a small copse of trees to an area filled with huts owning stone foundations, left, as the tale was told, by Roman and Welsh settlers centuries' past. Owain set his course to an especially tiny dwelling set far behind the other huts. Noting the abundance of smoke escaping the vent on its roof, he knew his great-grandparents were still awake, which was not unusual, and wondered if they ever slept. After tethering Ceffyl to a low bush, he knocked twice on the door, heard a rasped, "Enter..." and sucking a calming breath, boldly entered.

A shriveled old woman sat cross-legged by the hearth; her eyes, cloaked with a gray watery film, stared piercingly through and not at Owain. What little hair she still possessed was tightly trussed in two skinny white braids dangling to her waist. Her skin, ashen and mottled by brown stains, hung loosely from her hollowed cheeks, but tautened slightly as she strained a snarl and revealed her lack of teeth with the gripe, "You're late."

Owain tossed his saddlebag and promptly sat opposite her in the same cross-legged fashion. "I had business in Rhuddlan," he grunted back. He quickly searched his near surroundings, unique in that there was no furniture taller than a foot off the ground, and wondered, "Where's Tad-cu?"

"Dead..." bluntly announced Teleri, Owain's great-grandmother. She shivered from the breeze ushered in by Owain's arrival. He responded immediately by snatching up a pelt by his side and crawling round the pit to pile the fur upon the mound that already slumped her near skeletal figure.

"I'm sorry...about Tad-cu," he muttered, and he was sincere, since his great-grandfather had always been the one and only beam of light on Owain's bleak and dark journey north.

"You needn't be," she sniped. "He drove me mad with his complaining these past months. I'm glad for the quiet. Why were you in Rhuddlan? We've no kin there."

"No...nothing important," he awkwardly dismissed.

"Always know, Owain, you can't lie to me."

"I...I was searching for information about the wars in '70."

"Why?"

"I want to know the parentage of two friends I have in the south. They lost their family in the battles."

"Friends? You have friends? That's surprising."

He flushed to her sarcasm, and asked quickly to sway her thoughts. "Who is to be seer?"

"Not me," she scoffed in a laugh. "Our Pennaeth has brought in a bard from the mainland who claims to own the power. He's a trickster, nothing more, but our leader is very gullible. After all, he believed your tad-cu knew his future when all the while it was my sight that guided him." Her laugh continued long, rumbly, and gloating. It froze Owain's blood, and reinforced his extreme dislike for this grizzled, scathing creature sitting by him. He'd always despised her. She had never, to his memory, uttered a kindness to anyone, was always criticizing, belittling...and cruel. Now in her ninety-fifth year, Owain was certain, she lived only to spite the countless souls she'd harmed and harassed. During their brittle silence, she'd turned her unnerving, colorless stare upon him. He read caution and crept back to his spot opposite, where he abandoned his mantle and raked filthy fingers through his sopping hair and over his chafed cheeks. "There's warm water for your washing," she offered. "You may have your tad-cu's clothing. Your meal and your pallet are prepared. I've bought you a woman to keep you warm, cook for you, give you babies. You're far too thin and mean, and I figure since our last meeting, you've not done your duty and found a suitable woman for breeding. By your age, you should have a herd of children. You are the sole carrier of our gift, Owain and—"

"Why?!" he burst in frustration. "Why buy them when I don't want them?"

"Eventually I'll find one who suits you. You need watching over."

"I watch over myself," he retorted.

"Not well enough."

"You keep her."

"Heavens no...I've too many hens fussing over me, and I can't abide their squawking."

"I'll return her to her village."

"They don't want her back."

"Then let her serve someone else here!" flared Owain and he grumbled more as he crawled to a cauldron topped with soda and ash and angrily cast off his tunic and shirt.

The heat of her penetrating glower raised bumps on his bare skin and he winced to her crass compliment, "You're not ugly, I don't see why you have a problem finding women. You'll stay here and serve our Pennaeth as soldier or seer. I've been lonely since your tad-cu died. You'll keep me company, and I'll make certain you're content and that you don't waste your seed on some bitch who's not worthy of our family's sacredness."

He scrubbed hard to restrain the urge to scream and curse his pent up revulsion; convince her once and for all that he didn't own a *gift*, that he'd never sire children, never risk his heart on a woman, and most certainly, now that his great-grandfather was gone, never again visit this hateful, nosy, old crone.

"Owain!" she yelled, "Answer me!"

"What?!" he hurled back.

"Will you live here with me or do you want your own hut?"

"I won't be staying."

"Yes you will."

"No I won't...And if you keep on, I'll leave this night. I've rebuilt my family's home and intend to dwell there till Rhys decides a future for me."

"Is that putrid boar still alive? There are many that wish him dead. And you should never have raised your family's ashes. You've disturbed troubled souls and only tragedy can result from such defiling."

"I didn't defile anything," he gritted back, "and have slept there since its rebuilding. There was laughter and warmth...not tragedy."

"Who stayed with you?" Her look condemned before he could spout his answer, and the uneasiness that always accompanied her inquisitions began its creeping journey up his spine.

"Friends," he blurted, and tensed for her siege.

"Many or one?"

"Many."

Her glare darkened and pierced. "A Norman...You brought a stinking, gross, murdering Norman into the cottage!"

Her accusation shocked and confused Owain. How could she know, yet also be so wrong? He decided it best not to argue numbers, yet spoke up loudly in defense of Simon. "His loyalty lies solely with Rhys. He acts as court physician and practices our sort of healing."

"He's a Norman...and nothing good he does can wash away the evil in his blood. He must be destroyed. You will destroy him when you return."

He snorted to her absurd command, and answered with irony, "Actually, I tried to eliminate him once, but despite my effort, he instead saved *my* life. He is my friend and will remain so and will always be welcome in my home."

"If that is so," she replied in a snit, "you are no longer welcome in my home."

"Fine. I will eat and rest awhile before I go."

Teleri bristled to Owain's impudence. No one else owned the gall to question her eminence, for the consequence of such rudeness was conjured trouble of some sort, sometimes bothersome, sometimes lethal. Her incantations, though, had no damaging effect on her upstart grandson. And she knew why. Despite his refusal to acknowledge his gift, his power was the greater. That's why she needed him close. For if he were lured under the Norman's spell, they would abuse his force, and the results of such a calamity would devastate the remainder of their tribe, their traditions, and perhaps the whole of Wales. He was weak, vulnerable, owned questionable loyalties; he needed shaping, discipline. She could see little, but sensed much, and knew that during her pondering, he'd ended his wash and his meal, and was settling down to sleep. It wouldn't do to rile him more, for he might set a curse on her and she wasn't quite ready to pass on.

The morning after her husband's soul had flown, a huge black mongrel dog had arrived on her stoop and refused to leave. She knew Madawg had returned, obviously not as a higher being. But in revenge for her years of nagging, he'd purposely taken the form of the beast she most abhorred. She shuddered to the sound of the mutt's labored panting and the stench of his damp coat, and knew he lay just outside her door, always pestering.

While shifting on her pallet for comfort, Teleri inwardly lamented the misfortune constantly thrust upon her simply because she was of the chosen few. And as she did every night before reposing, she mumbled a quick prayer to the God of the Heavens that only when she was ready, he'd take her to his bosom, then set her free to fly. She'd always envied the grace and keen eyes of the gulls, and craved the knowledge they must possess, for didn't they see all from their lofty spot amid the clouds?

Someone entered the hut. Owain jerked up to see a dark, full-bodied young woman, dressed modestly and looking slavish. He watched tentatively as she knelt by Teleri and whispered, "Will you be wanting anything more, Madam?"

"No," she groused, "but you'll do for my grandson, and move with him to his own hut in the morning."

So this is the newest woman, sighed Owain to himself. She was pretty enough, they all were pretty, yet fairly vacant, and never said anything except to ask if they could serve. Teleri explained away their odd behavior with the outlandish claim that all the women she'd chosen were from a highly revered tribe whose sole purpose was to wait upon their betters.

The woman stood and, cracking a shy smile, crept his way. He abruptly rolled over, and squirmed deeper beneath his pelts, careful to cover all vestiges of nakedness. Pretending sleep, he squeezed shut his eyes, and faked a snore...badly. The woman snuggled down near Teleri, who promptly ruined Owain's act with the boomed command, "Play me something soothing on your whistle. All your talk of Normans has upset me. Play." He grunted and cursed and squirmed more, as his arm shot from under his blanket and his fingers groped about, found his saddlebag, and rummaged madly to produce the whistle. He blew a cleansing blow to rid the pipe of sand and bugs, then commenced trilling his most lulling tune, hoping to quiet Teleri and his own ravaged mind. His thoughts danced and tumbled with the melody, and a single solacing vision gradually emerged from his tangled musings...Faintly at first, then plainly, a face crystallized, one that he'd come to expect and vaguely anticipate round this time of evening, a comely face brimming innocence and fiery emotion. A twisting in his belly always followed its haunting, but he kept his eyes closed and focused on hers, colored the brilliant aqua of the sea, raging with denial and yearning. He played his tune over and over, enjoying a secret look and talk with the woman he never knew how to address properly in person, and wishing somehow she could hear his song and also be soothed.

"Owain!"

Teleri's shout made him choke on his next note and retort, "What?"

"You've lied to me!"

"I haven't!"

"You have...You don't want my women because you have one of your own."

"I don't!"

"Is she pregnant yet?"

"I don't have a woman."

"Maybe not in your bed...but certainly in your mind."

"Stop, Mam-gu...I won't hear more of your nonsense."

"Nonsense is it?" The massive wrinkles gouging her face scrunched together; she winced from the exertion of her trance and stuttered in a swoon, pieces of her vision, "...The look of a child, hair pale as straw, small, as fierce as you." A guttural laugh rocked her aware, and she sneeringly teased, "Oh, the sparks that flare between the two of you...Are they sparks that sear or sparks that meld? Tell me, Owain...Is it nonsense? Is it?"

"You guess."

"I never guess."

"But you do remember...well. I mentioned such a woman last visit, and made clear my dislike of her."

"Dislike no more," she leered toothlessly.

He huffed in exasperation, again rolled away, and hugged his whistle and his thoughts protectively. *Keep your mind empty and she'll sleep...empty, empty,* he repeated to himself, *and her prying will end.* He caught a wandering recollection and chuckled silently—her condemnation of Simon and his evil blood, cursed as such strictly by being Norman. His chuckling abruptly ended when he recalled fervently adhering to the same belief not three months past. He shuddered to the horrific memory of his fingers digging, hands squeezing, stealing away Simon's breath. A sharp pang ached his belly; he could force quiet his moan, yet couldn't banish the foreboding sense that he should race home and make certain Simon and Maura were safe and...hidden.

*****

Dawn brought havoc to the palace of Westminster; guards, soldiers, servants scuttled about in flustered confusion, straightening up after the departing royals, preparing for the arriving royals, and suffering the insistent abuse of the royal in residence. Alan loitered about the gatehouse, waiting as his companion hurried out to greet the entourage just docking. He'd slept the night in the guards' hut, as he'd done numerous times since his arrival in London two months past. His presence at the home of his brother Nicholas and his sister-in-law Judith seemed a constant intrusion, and he felt the need to allow them privacy whenever possible. Friends who'd once served with him as guards to King William now served his son Rufus, and warmly accepted Alan as their guest. Yet, so far, they'd failed to recruit him back to their ranks. Alan spread his palms over the meager fire built just inside the curtain wall, and shuddered to the raging squall that had dumped near a foot of snow over the night. It continued its onslaught this morn, and its fierceness raised in his mind a horrid memory—the night Maura had returned to Westminster from Normandy, bringing with her King William's reprieve for Simon's imprisonment. She'd confronted Rufus alone, a brazen and unfortunate act, and had been promptly tossed out into the crippling storm. Alan had discovered her, crouched and near frozen, beneath the stairs to the keep. They had ridden to Nicholas' house where Simon awaited her, near death as a result of the beating dealt him by his father.

The present abruptly returned in the lash of a freezing gust. Alan gravely felt the loss of Simon and Maura's presence, and offered a silent prayer for their safety. He abandoned the fire for the shelter of the gatehouse and, just inside the entrance, jumped to the screech of the rising portcullis. Bundled tighter in his cloak, he peered through the dense snow to distinguish faces of the approaching entourage. Guards, squires, and soldiers he did not recognize sauntered by, then his pinched expression dropped to a gape as he beheld Lord Robert, trailed closely by Henry FitzRoy. Alan rushed closer, startling a stallion, and receiving a reprimand from its rider, as his desperate eyes searched for Almodis and Adam. He loped along the line of riders, his heart near bursting. To his deep chagrin, he found no women or children traveling among the party. The last member of the troop disappeared beneath the curtain wall, and Alan forlornly rejoined his friend, Gilbert, guard to Rufus, and besieged him with questions, "Gilbert, why have Count Robert and Henry FitzRoy come?"

Gilbert, a chubby, squat fellow, hooded and dressed in chain mail, answered while swatting snow from his shoulders, "For Christmas feast, I suspect."

Another soldier joined their talk and corrected, "No...The Count's not staying. He's stopping only for a short rest, then leaving for Dunheved. I hear that trouble brews between the Count and his brother, the Bishop."

"Odo?" asked Alan.

"Yes...The Bishop was staying here, but slipped away two night's past. The King hates his Uncle Odo and has sent his cousin William to spy on him."

"Cousin William...Do you mean Count Robert's son, William?" exclaimed Alan.

"Yes," replied Gilbert.

Panic paled Alan and he quavered, "Are they all headed for Dunheved?"

"No one knows for certain where the Bishop is going. We thought he was headed to Normandy," said Gilbert, "but he was spotted traveling west."

The turmoil Alan had suffered his final week in Dunheved struck again with a force that weighted his back and quaked his knees. Yet his posture strengthened and his protective sense surged to the baleful thought that Odo, in his perpetual campaign to locate and destroy Simon, was returning to Dunheved to ply again his torture on the Lady Edith, and perhaps others as well.

Concerned by his friend's ashen silence, Gilbert worried, "What ails you, Alan?"

"Memories," struggled Alan, "and horrors sure to come." He squatted and swiftly gathered up his belongings. "I don't know when we'll meet again, Gilbert. There's business I must see to."

"At Nicholas'?" shouted Gilbert to Alan's departing figure.

"No," Alan yelled back over his shoulder, "...at Dunheved."

Gilbert cocked his head in question, then shrugged and assisted his fellow guard by grasping with him a fat dangling rope of hemp. Together they pulled and grunted, as, slowly and with great effort, they lowered the screeching iron meshed gate.

*****

Wrapped in his still damp mantle, Owain ducked out of the hut and scowled up into a dismal gray morning sky, spewing slushy rain. Despite the deluge, the occupants of the community slogged briskly about tending to their many chores. His thoughtful gaze then swept past the villagers to a long, heavily thatched building bracing the back timbered wall of the commote. While eating, Owain had recalled Teleri's complaint concerning the new seer, '...a bard who claims to own the power...a trickster, nothing more'. Well, Owain would discern for himself whether the man was indeed a trickster, but what intrigued him most was his former occupation—bard. As Owain skirted puddles, people, and huts, he sensed he was being trailed. He stopped and spun to confront his stalker. All he beheld was a huge, black dog with too fleshy a face, drooping ears, somber eyes, and possessing the silliest expression. Oddly, his great-grandfather's face instantly flashed in his mind, his expression just as silly, and eyes equally as sad. Owain walked a few feet ahead, turned, and saw the mutt had again followed. He swatted at the air and urged, "Go...get away. I don't want you with me."

The dog shook his head to rid it of slush and his motion appeared as a retort to Owain's dismissal.

Owain stepped cautiously closer and nudged the dog's shoulder, demanding louder, "Do what I ask and go."

The dog promptly slobbered his hand. Owain distastefully wiped the sticky spot on his cloak and hurried on; the mutt plodded behind. Grumbling under his breath, "I've trouble enough feeding and sheltering myself..." Owain rapped brusquely on the door to the llys. He jiggled a little dance for warmth and shifted from foot to foot nervously, wondering who might answer and how he could best offer his case. The latch was lifted and the door opened wide by a tall, silver-haired gentleman, with kind eyes and smiling mouth.

He stared curiously at Owain, waiting for a greeting. None came, so he took the initiative, "I'm Avaon, who might you be?"

"O...Owain ap Madawg," Owain stammered. "Soldier to Prince Rhys of Deheubarth, come north to visit my mam-gu Teleri."

"Well...you look mighty wet. Come in, but please leave your dog outside."

"He's not..." Owain glanced at the beast and felt his heart soften to the dejection pooling in the mutt's eyes. The dog cocked his head and dropped his frown longer; Owain simpered back and strode eagerly inside.

"I have some warm mead to offer you, and bread, meat, and cheese," offered Avaon.

"I'm grateful, but I've just eaten. Are you advisor to the Pennaeth?"

"Yes..." Avaon's smile soured and he surmised in a slightly accusatory tone, "Have you come to take my title, Sir?"

Owain snorted back, "I don't want your title and most certainly not the responsibility that comes with it. My father was advisor to Prince Rhys."

"So then, what is it you *do* want?"

"Right this moment, simply to sit awhile before your fire for my bones are brittle cold."

Avaon swung his arm invitingly toward the hearth. Owain strode directly there, and removed his cloak, which only chilled him more, as he sank to the rushes and chafed his hands over the flames.

"Perhaps this will help," offered Avaon, passing a cup of mead.

Owain strained a grin in thanks, gulped a mouthful, and sighed audibly to the nectar's rapid restorative properties.

Avaon sat cautiously by Owain's side, contemplating the motives of his peculiar visitor—Teleri's great-grandson. Since Avaon had been commissioned to his new home, Teleri had regularly harassed him with threats of her grandson's coming, and

Avaon's ultimate replacement. He'd been warned by the other villagers to humor the old one's eccentricities for, according to some, she did claim to hold questionable and potentially lethal powers. It seemed everyone was frightened of her, and her portent now sat beside him, with a dagger thrust in his belt, and his presence—starkly contrary. "I...I need to know your purpose, Sir, or I'll ask you to leave."

Owain eyed his host skeptically, and found fear in his darting gaze. He strove to quell the man's suspicions by softening his expression and gentling his voice. "I wish you no harm, Sir, only luck...And with my mam-gu's harping, you'll be needing more than luck." The relief was blatant in Avaon's knowing grin. "All I want from you, Sir, is the assurance that my mam-gu will be well seen to. She shouldn't be alive much longer to vex you...and the other villagers. I'd also ask..."

"Yes..." Avaon pressed expectantly.

"Information."

"Concerning?"

"The wars of the early '70's."

"I am a bard, Sir, not a soldier."

"Not tactical information," clarified Owain, "information of a personal sort. I have friends who lost their parents during the battles. They are eager to learn their history."

"I know stories of that time—nothing more."

"Stories?" wondered Owain.

"Tales that may hold truth...or may not."

"Are you busy this day?"

"Not till midday."

"Can you tell me these stories?"

"There are many, Sir."

"Please...I am Owain. Start telling," Owain abruptly directed, "I'll say when to stop."

To Avaon, it seemed he had no option but to appease his acerbic guest. He reached long to catch up two immense pillows, tossed one to Owain, and braced one behind his own back. He took a long steadying draught of mead, cleared his throat, and commenced his telling. Owain sipped his mead, intently listened, and quickly grew weary of the monotonous and similar themes of ravaging Normans and ever valiant Welsh, victorious in battle or perishing for the cause of freedom. Few contained children, and most of the women involved were revered as saints for fighting—being slain, kidnapped, or raped—or enduring all three scourges by the Normans. A few women had been condemned for selling their bodies to the Normans and luring them to their villages and encouraging their brutality, ultimately to be slain themselves. The notion brought briefly to Owain's mind his betrothed, and he chided himself for ever accusing her of such depravity. Soon names, locations, and descriptions began to slur together. Owain halted Avaon's droning with a gesture, asked for and received more mead, then requested, "Are there any that you recall that talk mainly of children?"

"Too many," sighed Avaon.

Owain shifted with impatience, and muttered discontentedly, "Then I'll hear only those." And so he carried on listening, nodded off several times; the bard didn't seem to notice. Then one curious tale wove its way among his sleepy thoughts. A village attacked by Normans—flames, smoke, a copper-haired Pennaeth named Emlyn, deprived of his army, forced along with his wife and the women and the children of the village to defend their commote against the treachery of Hugh the Fat and the Blighted Bishop. Owain started up from his pillow and blurted, "The who?"

"The Blighted Bishop."

"I'll have his true name."

"That I don't know."

"Why didn't this Emlyn have an army?" probed Owain.

"They'd been purposely poisoned."

"Poisoned!" Owain gasped, and added incredulously, "The whole lot of them? How?"

"Again Sir," Avaon cautioned, "don't take this as evidence. These are merely stories."

"Go on..."

"Hugh had invited Emlyn, his wife, and his army to Chester for a conciliatory feast. While the Pennaeth was being entertained in the great hall, the soldiers were fed separately a supper tainted by bane, the poison being slow acting so as not to alert the ones who ate last. His entire battalion perished over the night. Emlyn, drugged himself, barely escaped the following morn with his wife. But Hugh had taken a liking to the lady and craved her for his own. He took along a small battalion, thinking he'd encounter little resistance, and attacked the village. To Hugh's shock, the women of the village, highly skilled at battling and being so rudely deprived of their mates, soundly and victoriously raged back with swords, hatchets, and bows, rendering Hugh's army useless. In desperation, Hugh called on his Norman comrades, and they readily rallied to his defense."

"The Bishop came and who else?" asked Owain.

"I don't have any other names."

"And the Normans were successful?"

"They obliterated the entire commote within hours of their arrival."

"When Emlyn left Hugh's castle, did he take hostages?"

"Such as?"

"Children," stated Owain. "Did he take Hugh's children?"

"Hugh has never housed children within his castle."

"Then someone else's children—a steward, commander, fellow baron, anyone..."

"That is not part of the tale, Owain. Perhaps if you tell me your friends' tale, I can relate it to something more conclusive."

"My friends were children of a Norman baron situated on the north border of Wales. He was attacked by the Welsh and was cut down despite the help of his friends, as was his wife, and his children would have been had they not been rescued by another baron."

"I'm sorry Owain, there are no tales of—"

"I know, I know...no tales of Norman children on the border."

"And the only barons that have since the conquest dominated the north border of Wales are Hugh and his cousin, Robert of Rhuddlan."

"Does Robert have children?"

"If he does they do not reside with him and he arrived after the battles you allude to." Avaon sighed his atonement, "I'm sorry to have wasted your time, Owain."

"No...nothing's been wasted. This tale of Emlyn...I'd like to know it better. When and where did you learn it?"

"Where it claims to have occurred, in the town of Dinbych, not far down the river Clywd."

"Someone survived to tell the tale?"

"Not survived, returned too late. The woman who related the story is wife to the present Pennaeth."

"Is the present Pennaeth related to Emlyn?"

"No...though his wife was related to Emlyn's wife. A niece I believe. I must end our talk now for I'm sure it's nearing midday, and I have little voice left."

They both rose, Owain thrust out his hand in appreciation. It was warmly enclosed by Avaon's, who relayed his hope, "I wish you luck in your quest of history, Owain. Will you return to visit us again?"

"Mam-gu is my only surviving relative on my father's side of our family. I don't much like her, so I don't intend to come again."

"If you change your mind, you are always welcome."

Owain nodded shyly, swept up his cloak, and was about to depart when an idea stalled him. "Avaon...would you have need of a servant? My mam-gu employs too many for her tiny hut to hold and, if dismissed, this young woman has nowhere to go. She seems quite capable, and is good-natured."

Avaon wagged his head, and wryly answered, "I'll take her in. This village is full of your rejected mates, and kind souls and proficient workers they have all proven to be."

"I'm grateful..." Owain muttered as he departed the llys. The dog sat just where he'd been left, looking sad. Owain meant to leave immediately, for he'd suffer no more of Teleri's haranguing, and if he planned to stop in Dinbych, more days would have to be added to his already too long journey. The nagging need to hurry home still lurked, and Owain huffed with exasperation as he heard the dog's raspy breathing at his back.

The dog wisely stayed outside and, once inside Teleri's hut, Owain flinched to her command, "You'll celebrate the solstice with me."

"No...I haven't time."

"Then you'll make an offering at my altar before you leave."

"What do you suggest," he flippantly asked, "one of your servant girls?"

"Don't blaspheme, Owain! You are vile and *too* mean," she scowled. "And no one will ever choose to have you as husband and, if by your lapse, you cause our gift to die, I vow to haunt you forever."

"As what?"

"I'll think of something horrid."

"Not too difficult for you, I'm certain."

"Don't bother coming back," she growled. "The sight and sound of you sicken me. Go play with your Normans, and grovel to your Christ, you stinking traitor."

His pleasant expression never wavered to her abuse. Instead it grew more cheerful and his voice playfully teased, "I'll not come in the flesh, I'll send my spirit instead, Mam-gu, and be a bug in your ear, forever buzzing, driving you mad with insults."

"Get out!" She heaved a spoon at his back; it struck sharply its target, then bounced away to her curses, "Damn you, demon! I'll be a hawk and pluck out your eyes, nibble on your guts, and rip out your loins with my talons!"

Owain chose not to retaliate and, shielding his head, chuckled out the door, curses, spoons, and vexes soaring after him. He struggled and slipped his way over to Ceffyl, where he mounted and carefully maneuvered his mare through sucking mud and milling villagers to the village gate. As he cantered away toward the pier and the dreaded raft, Owain again sensed he had company. A deep resonant bark answered his wondering, and the huge black dog with the silly face loped up beside him. Owain grudgingly surrendered, "You can come with me, but only if you swear you are not one of Mam-gu's curses."

The mutt yipped brightly in response, which Owain took as a vow of innocence, and marveling again at the resemblance between the beast and his grandfather, gladly cantered on.

*****

Will and Joanna hustled down a dank, moldy passageway leading to the great hall of Roger of Montgomery's castle in the town of Shrewsbury, Will blatantly agitated with cold and wrath, and Joanna struggling to match his brisk pace. "Will!" she called in desperate concern, "Will, you mustn't present yourself this angry. You must try to calm yourself or there's chance of your mission being halted before it's begun!"

He shook from her grip on his shoulder, gestured madly, and gnashed back, "I'm absolutely enraged and will proudly show it to that bumbling, scheming bastard of a Bishop. How dare he desert me! *I*, who arranged his ingenious escape from Rufus and was forced to suffer his pompous diatribe for an entire fortnight...I should ride to Dunheved immediately and send word of Odo's plans to Father. He has the authority to arrest Odo on suspicion of planning Simon's murder, and will gladly dispense to Odo a fitting punishment. God damn him! I should have let Rufus hang him!"

Joanna waited till she was certain of Will's finishing, for before when she'd made the onerous mistake of interrupting, she'd received a sound cuffing. "I understand and share your rage," she spoke soothingly, "but Odo does own the larger and more skillful army. I've heard the Welsh are a ruthless lot, and if they aim to hold on to our Maura, they'll fight to the death to keep her. You need Odo. He will eliminate Simon for you, and I don't believe you'd want to confront your brother alone."

Will's ice blue eyes flared at her insinuation of cowardice, then cooled when he realized he'd been the one who'd confessed to her his fear of his sibling. He gasped twice more, a combination of latent temper and rabid disappointment, then deflated to concede, "I suppose you're correct...as always!" he added with a touch of spite. "But never leave me alone with the irreverent worm. I've brought my recipes and may sprinkle a nasty granule or two into his claret, by accident of course."

She flashed a cruel grin, he returned a scurrilous snarl and, with arms linked, they strolled and talked on. "He's purposely trying to rile you, leaving each proposed meeting place within an hour of your arrival, and he's succeeding beautifully," asserted Joanna. "Return the insult, Will. Pretend no notice of having been abandoned. Confuse and impress him with your determination and detachment, then never let him out of your sight."

"I won't sleep with him," Will muttered with distaste, "...he snores."

"Spies, Will. He uses them freely. You should as well."

"I do."

She stipulated, "Use them to watch after the Bishop."

"I didn't believe I had *need* to watch after the Bishop."

"Accept your mistake, and employ your men."

"Or woman?" Will replied, an impish twinkle in his eye. "You could sleep with him."

"Don't be revolting."

"It was just a thought."

"Think again...His squire, could he be bought?"

"Easily."

"Then do it..." She masterfully cocked her chin, retrieved her arm, and strutted forward alone; her dramatic approach faltered as the massive doors of the hall abruptly parted. She sucked a tight gasp as dozens of amply armed sentries poured out of the great room. In their center lumbered their burly lord—the infamous Roger of Montgomery, Earl of Shrewsbury. His guise was that of a crazed beast. Beady gray eyes peered out suspiciously from a mass of unruly hair that appeared to cloak his entire face, neck, and hands, and Joanna surmised probably the remainder of him as well, concealed beneath abundant pelts. She strained her sight to determine where the pelts ended and he began, and seeing no distinction, Joanna turned an anxious gaze on Will. The look he possessed—that of youthful exaltation—astounded her, for after months of service, she'd felt certain her lord had never known a day of innocence, and had been delivered into this world a sullied adult.

"Grandfather!" Will gushed, and rushed forward to disappear joyously into Roger's huge clutch.

"Willy, my Willy!" Roger blubbered. He rocked his grandson in his strenuous embrace, murmuring endearments, while Joanna stared aghast and wagged her head to relieve herself of this nauseating sight. But this was no act...The affection the relatives bestowed on one another was clearly true, though horribly exaggerated. She bowed and dropped her eyes in respect and embarrassment and, upon lifting them again, jumped at Roger's feral glare fixed directly on her. "And who is your pretty lass, my boy?" Roger asked with a rakish voice.

Will seemed hesitant to leave his grandfather's hug, but let go a moment to correct, "Not my lass, Grandfather, my seneschal."

"No!" Roger replied in shock. "A woman as seneschal? No."

"Yes..." answered Will, proudly. "And she performs her duties superbly."

"I imagine she does," said Roger with a sneering leer. "Let's take your lady—my pardon, Madam—your *seneschal* to my hall. You both look too cold and lean, and the evening needs brightening...Odo is here. He's gone quite peculiar, and is spouting chancy words."

"Such as?" prompted Will.

"Rebellion," Roger flatly obliged.

"Oh...He's most likely drunk too much claret...again. Come, Joanna," Will mumbled beneath his breath, "our happy presence will swiftly sober him."

Will winced to his grandfather's rough grip at his shoulder and stumbled forward to his shove, hearing Roger's barrage of questions, yet every time he'd open his lips to answer, another query was hurled. "What's kept you so long from us, lad? I pray not that bounder Rufus. And where's your father hiding? We've heard the rascal's gone and spawned himself another runt—a boy. Irks you a bit, I reckon. Don't worry yourself too long, for you'll get a bit of mine when I go. Which shouldn't be too much longer, and I have almost as much as Robert does."

Inside the hall's doors, Will finally grasped the chance to leap in, "I pray you stay with us a long while more, Grandfather..."

"And you are the sweetest of the lot," Roger mawkishly replied, taking Will's face between his hands and kissing noisily each cheek. "Mabel loved and admired you so."

"And I loved her, Grandfather, and miss her deeply."

Their soppy gazes blended, as they strode to the dais. Joanna padded close behind, quaking at the mention of the viperous Mabel of Belleme. Will had related her diabolical history, replete with gratuitous descriptions of her many victims' demises. She'd vomited at his story's completion, and worried he'd poisoned her during the telling, just a little as a warning. But he hadn't, and wouldn't, now that she'd convinced him she was every bit as wicked as he. Yet, for the sake of her continued health, a while back, when he'd journeyed a day from Berkhamstead, she'd secretly memorized his entire journal of recipes.

Odo sat half propped, half sprawled upon his seat, a waggish smile twisting his thin lips, cracked open just enough to dribble out a thin stream of wine. As his nephew loomed into view, Odo spilled forward and struggled up, spitting the pooling drink with his sputtered exclamation, "Wi...Will! What...whatever de...delayed you? Snow?" He tumbled back into his seat, and strained to hold his head erect, blinking furiously to focus.

"No...not snow..." Will answered with droll suspicion as he peeled away his gloves, tossed them to his squire, and yanked out first a chair for Joanna, then one for himself.

Trenchers heaped with a gelatinous slop, stinking vaguely of meat and onions, and huge tankards topped to the brim with mind numbing liquor instantly appeared before the new arrivals.

Roger loudly induced, "Drink, eat, and after we'll discuss your planned adventure, Will. Odo has furnished me with a few scanty details, and I have news that will make your scheme as simple as farting."

Desperate for this news, Will snapped his head expectantly to Odo, but the Bishop now snored in a puddle of spilt wine. Will looked back to Roger, eyes begging for elaboration. Roger waggled his finger and reproached, "Do what I say, eat, and drink...then talk."

Only Joanna caught Will's exasperated huff, and answered with a pained grin and wrinkled nose. Roger served only undiluted wine, and its effect instantly was telling on Will and Joanna. They stringently refused a refilling of their cups and, in unison, pushed their untouched putrid fare away. The hall was furnished with a raw simplicity—no tapestries, crude furniture, and soiled rushes. At its center, a towering pyre began to blur and spin, as Will strove to work his tongue. It flapped numbly, "Grand...Grandfather. I...I've done as told, and await your news."

Roger threw back his fifth cup and, seemingly unaffected, relayed with clear eye and head, "It's not that unusual hearing from the House of Dinefwr. We do so regularly, and Bernard, well, he had a tussle with them awhile back. Fierce warriors they are. He won't be returning there anytime soon, lost a great many men."

"What are you talking about Grandfather? Who is Dinefwr?"

"Not a who, a what. Rhys is Prince of Dehuebarth and lives at Dinefwr. He rules over Menevia. That is where you are headed, isn't it?"

"Yes. To find my slippery brother. How can you help?"

"I don't think you'll need my help," said Roger. "The new Chieftain of Menevia has contacted us with a request. I'm pleased and surprised the craven has risen to such a powerful position. When he resided on the border, he'd often spy for us for a fee. A bungling fool Taredd is, but he's asked for an audience and, for your convenience, we'll give him one. Seems he wants to rid himself of an irksome wench, who is now his sister-in-law and used to keep company with one of my squires. He talks of marriage. The girl's father is English, and holds a large property in Shrewsbury, which is tempting. Arnulf wants to take a part of Wales for his own, Pembroke, near Menevia, and this arrangement might make such a thing more likely. I'll make this squire a knight, give him his bitch, then wile my way into her family's trust. In good time, I hope to steal their property here...and Arnulf will take it there."

Roger's rambling faded, and Will leant near to Joanna, begging in a whisper, "Do you have any idea what he is talking about, or have I gone completely dull?"

"I believe..." Joanna strained so hard with her thinking that her eyes watered. "Someone from Menevia is coming to meet with Roger."

"He said that?!" answered Will, amazed. "When did he say that?"

"Ssshhh!" she chided, and nodded toward the aging Baron.

"So..." continued Roger after a long yawn and grunted stretch, "I'll send you with Arnulf...He loves this sort of thing."

"What sort of thing?" asked Will, more muddled.

"Wars, hacking, kidnapping."

"What war?!" panicked Will. "I only want Maura, and Odo wants Simon. We weren't planning on a war!"

"Perhaps it won't come to that. Taredd is easily bribed, but the rest of his village...if they like someone, they won't easily part with them. And your brother is well liked."

"You've heard talk of him...*here*?"

"Oh yes...The banished nephew of the late King, honored physician to the Welsh Prince, and lately another comment has surfaced which might prove troublesome for you."

"What's that, Grandfather?"

"Invincible warrior...But we've always known that, Will, haven't we?"

"I prefer dead warrior, don't you, Grandfather?"

"I don't particularly care. If that will make you happier, then I wish it as well. Why do you want Maura?"

"You've heard of her as well?"

"I remember her all too well, Will...She fairly ruined my chances of a profitable land alliance with your father. But yes, she has an excellent reputation as mediator for Rhys. She's never dealt with us, probably on account of your brother's hiding. Arnulf still is mighty attracted to the lady. You remember, they were once betrothed."

"Yes, I recall that dreadful time, Grandfather, and the Lady is legend with me only in that she brutally attacked me and left me wounded for life." He rubbed at his shoulder, hoping for sympathy, but Roger didn't seem to notice.

"So it's revenge you're wanting?" asked Roger.

"Not entirely. I've wed her by proxy to a gentleman knight in Yorkshire. It was necessary to acquire my manor in Helmsley."

"Your father doesn't know this, does he, lad?"

"I pray not, nor will he ever hear of it, will he, Grandfather?"

"I'll not spill a word."

"I just need to eliminate Simon," said Will simply, "and deliver Maura to her true husband."

"It all sounds easy enough, but take an army. Two days before Christmas, Taredd will meet with Arnulf at Llandovery, that's half-way between here and Menevia. Hide your men while Taredd's sister-in-law and her dowry are exchanged, then try to bribe Taredd to give you Simon and Maura. If he refuses, take him and his men hostage, lead them back to Menevia, and there demand Simon and Maura as your ransom. Shouldn't take more than that—the Welsh are ferociously tribal folk. Taredd is of their blood, Simon and Maura are not.

Slowly, Will's wine-fogged mind began to clear and Roger's advice began to make sense. "Yes." He beamed. "Simple...tribal loyalties, hostages, ransom. Simple. No war, just talk. Bribe them with what?"

"Taredd loves coins. I don't know what he does with all his silver. I'll let you have a bag or two, if you promise me one favor."

"What's that, Grandfather?"

"I'm looking for Maura's brother, Marc. I don't believe he died heroically for his King and Duke. I believe instead after William's death, he deserted across the channel, headed where I don't know, but I reckon his sister would know, don't you?"

"She'll confess, Grandfather," assured Will with a nasty grin. "Perhaps I'll let Arnulf coax Marc's secrets from her."

"Yes, he's looking mighty sour these days and needs cheering up."

Will settled a disdainful eye upon the still snoring Bishop, and grudgingly wondered, "What do we do with him?"

"Of course, he'll want to command everything and everybody. Humor him, let him strut around, flail, and spout sermons. Allow him the honor of removing your brother, for that's what he's been wanting to do for so very long. It will make him happy, and I'm certain many others will smile with Simon's passing. Will your father smile, lad? I've not spoken to him for ages. Last time we met, his hate for Simon was still rabid."

"They're friends again," spat Will as his fury blazed anew. "And with his new brother, Simon stands to inherit all Father's property in England. A far bigger slice than I'll ever see in Normandy, and after my greedy sisters grab a hide or two for themselves, I'll be lucky to own a shit house in a bog."

"Now, Will," consoled Roger, "remember Mabel left you money, and I won't forsake you, lad."

"I'm grateful, Grandfather, but I'm also tired and drunk. May I retire?"

"Why, of course. Do you require one or two rooms to be made ready?"

Again came Roger's leer, sickening Will's already sour belly. "Two..." he soundly retorted and shifted a side-long glance at Joanna to catch her response. Her eyes, however, penetrated the table top, her mind obviously absorbing, deciphering, and rearranging all that Roger had presented. She was expert at making unsolvable quandaries manageable, and he longed to hear her interpretation of the proceedings. He'd hear it though on the morrow, for in truth, he was horribly weary...and wanted only sleep.

*****

Owain arrived outside the palisade wall of the village of Dinbych late evening, exhausted and highly nervous. He'd rehearsed his greeting and request too many times, and each time it sounded more contrived and stupid. Perhaps the hopefully kind people leading this village would prefer honesty; he certainly would. So, sweeping his mind clear of unending and awkward sentences, he focused his thoughts on gaining entrance to this sleepy, seemingly placid place. His introduction as soldier to Rhys wishing to speak to the Pennaeth, was promptly accepted by a bored guard, and Owain was waved through the timbered gate and shown the direction to the long house. The village purred with complacency; clusters of folk loitered about open fires, drinking and chattering; children and dogs, despite it being far past dusk, scampered about, delighting in their noisy games. The hound still trod by Ceffyl's side, fascinated by the roaming sheep and chickens, but his nose was constantly distracted and danced about to catch the wafting odors lingering from supper. He whined a little, Owain guessed from hunger. "Food isn't far now, Dawg," Owain assured. Owain's belly rumbled in response as the llys came into view, brightly lit, and also bustling with people. He tethered Ceffyl to a fence a ways away, and advanced cautiously. No one seemed to notice he was a stranger; he received the same broad smiles and nods bestowed on the native inhabitants. Emboldened, he rapidly approached the main entrance to the llys and knocked with no thought as to what to say. The lovely vision that answered stole his breath and greeting. He blinked twice to clear his sight, then realized the fair lady standing before him—her skin pale as milk and sprinkled with peach freckles, and her hair, peach colored as well, trussed in two thick plaits that dangled down below her waist—eerily resembled Maura.

"Sir," she asked, gazing quizzically, yet kindly. "May I be of some help?"

"Ye...yes," he stumbled, then slowed his words to convey carefully, "I'm Owain ap Madawg, soldier to Prince Rhys of Dehuebarth, and have come in peace to speak to the Pennaeth and his wife.

"I am wife of the Pennaeth," she brightly replied. "I'm called Esyllht. My husband is due home in the morn, but Sir, please enter. You are welcome to stay the night." Esyllht spied Dawg, lurking behind Owain, tail woefully wagging, and expression dismal. She squatted, reached out, and sweetly greeted, "And you are also welcome..."

She glanced at Owain for a name; for a moment he hadn't a clue who she was speaking to, then turning to Dawg's solemn whine, he obliged, "Oh...I call him Dawg after my tad-cu, Madawg. Looks like him. He started trailing me this morning, and I hadn't the heart..." Owain paused suddenly realizing he was conversing with this

382

woman as if she were a long-time acquaintance. He wagged his head to dispel any doubts of her motives and finished, "...to refuse him my company."

She laughed a warm cozy sort of laugh, and Owain smiled with her and followed her inviting wave inside her home. Dawg was instantly investigated by two equally large hounds. No animosity ensued, so Owain's concern switched to wonder as he swept an awed gaze round the illustrious ruling household of Dinbych. Modest yet engaging, the ambiance instilled in him a sense of solace and safety. "We've just finished our feast we hold each Sabbath," remarked Esyllht, motioning two youngsters up from their places at a trestle table set at the far end of the hall. "Please enjoy what food remains, Owain, and we've warm honey mead. I expect you're parched."

"Yes, please," he responded.

The two children reluctantly wiggled up and clutched at Esyllht's tunic as she gently prodded them forward, and gaily introduced, "And these are our children, Tally," she patted the tow-headed boy's head, "who's six years old, and...Elyn..." Her fingers affectionately stroked the copper colored locks of the young girl child. "She's just turned three."

"Tally and..." Owain stopped as Simon's comment, 'We aim to call her Elyn...' echoed in his mind. He swiftly convinced himself that the uncanny resemblance the child and her mother bore to Maura was only a coincidence...and the name Elyn, it wasn't such an unusual name.

"Are you well Owain?" asked Esyllht concernedly.

"What?"

"You've gone awfully white."

"I'm well...only tired. I'm sorry for my rudeness and I'm pleased to know you Tally and Elyn."

Radiant with pride, Esyllht patted her belly and mentioned, "We've another due to arrive round Easter."

"I'm glad for you," said Owain.

"And I'm sorry for my rudeness, and will presently fetch your food and I'll have my servant wash your feet," said Esyllht. "Morvudd," she called.

A tall, ruddy looking, young woman entered from a back room, bowed slightly, and asked, "What is it you need, Madam?"

Owain interrupted with a deep blush, "I don't need my feet washed, though I'm greatly honored you thought of it."

"Of course, Owain. Morvudd, if you'd entertain the children awhile, I'll see to our guest's comfort. And Alarch..."

Another young woman, this one chestnut-haired with choleric skin, and owning deep, dark eyes, answered, "Yes, Madam?"

"Could you please play awhile more? Owain, Alarch works magic with her harp. You wouldn't mind, would you? Music soothes me when my man is away."

"I don't mind at all," said Owain.

"Then settle yourself before the fire and I'll fetch your supper."

"You needn't—"

Owain tried to argue, but Esyllht hushed him with a tender look and admonishment, "Settle yourself." And soon he was munching away on a chicken leg, and bread oozing sweet butter, and sipping the most exquisitely seasoned honey-mead, feeling especially warm and wondrous, and relishing the most appealing manner and chatter of his hostess. "My husband, Taliesen, is visiting a neighboring village in hope of arranging a trade agreement. Whatever you need to discuss though, may be discussed with me for we lead this village equally. It is our tradition. You said you serve Prince Rhys in the south, but you speak with a northern accent."

"My family hails from Mon," explained Owain, "and I was visiting a relative there when I met a bard who serves their Pennaeth. He told me a tale, and I'm wanting and needing to hear more of it...He claimed *you* had passed him the story."

She looked fuddled, and Owain helped, "The story of Hugh the Fat, and your village's destruction."

"Oh..." she replied limply. "I do recall the bard."

"If it isn't too painful for you, I was hoping you'd tell *me* the tale. He said you had survived only because you'd arrived home too late."

"Yes, my parents had taken me to the sea. I'd always begged to go and we came home to—"

Owain instantly regretted the upset he had upturned and suggested, "Perhaps we should wait till tomorrow."

Jostled by squealing laughter, they turned to see the children and their nurse romping with Dawg. Elyn tugged at his ears, Tally chased his tail, and Dawg appeared elated, yipping and pawing, prancing, and near to smiling. "My tad-cu had the same effect on children," said Owain. "He always seemed to have a young one hanging off him."

"He sounds wonderful."

"He was."

Esyllht studied Owain as he continued to enjoy the children; he owned a handsome, fascinating face full of mysteries, yet of one thing she was certain, he had only honorable reasons for his visit and inquiry of the demise of her friends, her family, and her history. "Owain," she indulgently began, "I will tell you the entire story now, but first tell me why you need to know."

"I have friends in the south whose parents were slain during the wars of the early '70's. I'm searching for their past, and something, I'm not certain what, but something about your story rings familiar."

"Then I will strive to help...A survivor who has since passed on related the tale quite precisely...The year was 1070, near Christmas. Emlyn, Pennaeth and husband to my aunt, Gwaeddan, was called to a holiday feast at Chester Castle on the ruse of forging a lasting peace between our people and Lord Hugh. Emlyn took along his elite force in case Hugh proved untrustworthy, and was hoping for an end to the Baron's relentless treachery..."

During this telling, Owain remained on alert for any inconsistency, overshadowing, or favoring, but he could find little difference, except for the extreme emotionality provided by Esyllht that gave the story an excruciating reality, and numerous times lured him to the brink of tears. Yet at its end, he felt no nearer to a solution and, desperately beseeched, "My dear Lady, my friends are the orphaned children of a Norman baron. Their father and mother were slain before their eyes by the Welsh. They lived only because of the intervention of their father's ally. I ask this question not out of meanness, but of the need for the truth. Did Emlyn kidnap children from the castle, in revenge for the murder of his soldiers?"

"Emlyn kidnap children?!" she exclaimed, wounded. "Oh no, Owain, he was a father himself, and would never have harmed a child, or used one in such a ruthless way. I've not heard a tale of a murdered Norman baron. Only two Norman barons have dominated the north since the Conquest—"

"Yes, I know that much."

The frustration that sagged Owain's face pained Esyllht's heart. "I'm sorry Owain. It seems you've come here for nothing."

"No," he readily argued. "You've been overly good to me, and I couldn't have imagined a nicer shelter in which to spend this night."

384

"I'll arrange for your pallet to be set out."

"And I'm sorry for your family's suffering," said he.

"I'm grateful," she answered with a dour grin.

The mead, the harp, and the warmth of Dawg pressed to his back, all lulled Owain quickly asleep, yet close to morning his dreams became a mass of horrors—fire, smoke, silver clad beasts swinging deadly sticks, flaming birds alighting on and igniting the huts, Maura's face or was it Elyn's, wailing for help, and Marc just a babe, overcome from smoke, dangling lifelessly in her clutch. Pieces of women's bodies lay strewn amongst slaughtered livestock, all gushing blood collecting in pools across the courtyard. Owain became part of the terror and chased the young girl and her brother to the llys. Once inside, he gasped to the cloaking, choking smoke; his limbs stiffened to stone and, paralyzed, he strained to find her. She stumbled to a corner where something or someone writhed on the floor, moaning, grasping out for her ankle. She whirled round...Owain thought to look at him, but no, she gaped past him at a woman spilling in the door, golden-haired, eyes huge with terror. After her raged a beast, metal clad and swinging a sword. Maura screamed to the woman and Owain understood perfectly her calls for help. The woman heard as well, but too late...Her severed head dropped to the charred rushes and rolled to Maura's feet. *The Norman!* Owain screamed in his mind, *the Norman will save Maura and Marc, steal them away from this carnage!* The soldier charged the children, and Owain cried out from his heart, "Please take them from this hell, save them!" Maura cowered to the man's approach, and Owain yelled, yet failed to convince, "He won't hurt you, go with him, please go with him!" Maura shrank further into the corner, Marc still senseless and clasped tightly in her lap. The abomination playing out before him turned all too real. Flames exploded from the walls, devoured the rushes, licked at the toes of his boots; and the heat, the horrid heat suffocated! Owain gasped for air, gagged, and screamed for rescue as the flames engulfed him and the Norman's sword plummeted over the children...

"Owain! Owain, wake up! It's a nightmare, please wake up!"

Soft cool hands on his face and a gentle voice captured him to safety. "Maura!" he cried, jolting up and grasping the arms of his succorer. "He'll kill you, kill you!"

"I'm not Maura, I'm Esyllht...And no one will kill anyone here."

The soft glow of the fire illuminated a halo round Esyllht's silhouette and if he knew her better, he would have grabbed hold of her and never let go. The fright he felt was horrendous. His heart's pounding ached his chest and deafened his ears. Ghosts had been awakened and he still heard their screams. He clasped his ears and croaked, "Their screams, I still hear their screams!"

"So do we..." she said with an eerie calm, "all too often. They died here, Emlyn in the corner, his throat slashed, and Gwaeddan, her body by the door, her head by her husband."

"My friends!" he yelled and gripped her forearms. "They were here! Maura has told me her nightmare. I became part of it this night and I'm certain it happened here. Your Uncle stole the Norman children! No matter what you've been told, he must have stolen them."

His hysteria frightened Esyllht. A quick whistle brought her two hounds bounding from a corner, snarling in warning. Dawg postured in defense of his master, and Owain pleaded, "I mean you no harm, my Lady, but I *will* have the truth!"

"Come and walk with me," said Esyllht, hand determinedly extended. Owain grasped hold, straggled up, and meekly obeyed. His harrowed mind cleared slightly to the jarring taste of the cold mead she offered. When he'd emptied his drink, she led him out the rear of the llys and through a postern door carved into the palisade. The strength of the morning sun coaxed a thick mist up from the damp ground; it curled round their feet, as she led their mournful stroll across a fallow field. In the distance, Owain glimpsed cows lolling and children racing ponies along the river. All seemed tranquil, yet he sensed more bleakness awaited him. They stopped at what seemed nowhere. Esyllht let go his hand and, snatching up a discarded branch, waved it vigorously over the ground, sweeping away the mist and illuminating crosses planted in a distinct pattern. She kept sweeping and there seemed to be no end to the graves. Finally, her gloomy task done, she stood tall, spread wide her arms, and tearfully defended, "This was my village, my family, my people, except for the men. We never were able to reclaim their bodies. These good people died innocently. They were cut down for greed and lust by a cruel devil, a blighted Bishop, and their fellow demons. Emlyn was a man of peace, he would never have purposely harmed anyone, especially a child! My Aunt and Uncle will never know peace, for they walk every night, crying, endlessly searching for *their* children." She stopped her tears with anger. "You've come to the wrong village, Owain, and I won't have my relatives slandered more!"

The shame Owain felt soured his belly and cracked his heart. He looked away, hoping for a saving sight, some distraction from the desolation, but there was just the sight of the children, boys and girls alike, racing wildly on their horses. To lift Esyllht's spirits, he tried sounding cheerful, "Aren't they awfully young to be riding that fast?"

Esyllht shook from her dirge and wondered faintly, "Sorry?"

"The children." He pointed. "Their racing. How old are they?"

"All ages. There are some between one and two," she answered.

"One and two?!" he echoed in alarm. "It's too dangerous."

She wandered to his side and flatly explained, "It is our custom to train both our women and men as warriors and start them on horseback when they begin to walk."

He watched the riders awhile more, then restively shifted his attention back to the crosses. Two larger crosses fronted the grave site, on their wood was carved the names Emlyn and Gwaeddon. There were no crosses to either side of their resting spots, and he absently asked, "Where are their children buried?"

Her reply, "Their bodies were never found," struck a pain in his mind that unleashed a glut of distorted and jolting images. Behind his closed eyes, the nightmare flared again. He moaned and cradled his skull as he saw clearly the hand, glittering with a ring of entwined circles, gripping Maura's ankle, not barring her from escape, straining to save her from death! There was the soldier, face smudged black from smoke, and his pale, limpid blue eyes glaring with ire. Another soldier lurched near and shoved him away before his sword struck its target—a brother, stopping a brother from committing the most heinous of crimes, the murder of children, but not Norman children—Welsh children!

Owain's eyes bulged wide. He fell to his knees and his fists hammered at the sky. "By the Gods!" he anguished aloud. "*He* kidnapped them. Lord Robert kidnapped Emlyn and Gwaeddon's children to save them from Bishop Odo!"

Esyllht's arm held tight to his shoulder as she begged, "What are you saying? Please tell me, Owain, what do you see?!"

And when he raised his woeful eyes to hers, she heard the broken conclusion of her family's torment. "My...my friends who are searching for their parents, I...I believe they are your lost cousins. How old were they when they disappeared?"

"Elyn was five..." she began and Owain's head swam again.

The pain was unbearable, and he intruded, "Please, may we go inside?"

"Of course."

Esyllht cupped Owain's elbow; she helped him up, and her excitement helped hurry them across the fields and inside the llys. Once seated and fortified with more mead,

Owain's nightmares and hurt eased enough for him to spill coherently, "Maura is twenty-two, looks so much like you. And Marc—"

Her beam practically blinded Owain as she barged in, "He was two, and already the kindest soul, his hair a tangle of gold curls, eyes of the deepest blue. Elyn was blue-eyed as well, and copper-haired, identical to her father, for whom she was justly named. I've named my daughter after her, for Elyn was my dearest companion." She swiped a tear and mused, "Marc and Maura, such strange names."

"They were named by their adopted parents and raised as Normans. And what was Marc called?"

"The same as you."

He didn't catch her meaning at first, and asked, "I don't understand?"

"He was called Owain, after his grandfather."

"The same as me," laughed Owain, shaking his head and adding, "Seems fitting, somehow."

"When can I see them?" prodded Esyllht.

"I don't know."

"Why are they in Wales?"

"Strangely enough, they are hiding from the family that saved them. Maura's wed to a Norman, a good one, who is also hiding, and Marc's about to take his vows at the Cathedral of St. Davids."

"He's to be a priest!" exclaimed Esyllht.

"Yes."

"As his father wished him to be. And is Elyn happy in her marriage?"

"Extremely so. Simon is son to Robert, the Norman who rescued them from the Bishop. Simon and Maura were raised together and they fought long and hard to remain together. She's to have their first child very soon. It's not easy or safe for them to travel."

"I'm afraid it isn't safe for me either, but surely, Owain, you will relate my joy and desire to see them as soon as I'm able. Does she ever speak of me?"

"The shock of that time left only a memory of her parents' death. She was told, and believes, her parents were Normans. Why Robert hasn't told her the truth is curious, for surely his action was heroic, to defy his brother and rescue and provide for the orphans. I'm certain though, when she sees and speaks to you, all the memories will come back."

"I pray so...I've missed her."

A clearing throat disturbed their elation, and they lifted their damp happy eyes up to a stern looking fellow, black-haired and bearded, elegantly handsome. "And who is your friend, Elsie?" he asked, askance.

"Oh, Tally!" she cried, grabbing her husband's offered hand, and rising awkwardly. "This is Owain, a soldier of Prince Rhys' from the south. He's come with the most amazingly wonderful news!"

Owain scrambled up, nodded with respect, and mumbled with hand outstretched, "I'm...I'm honored to know you, Sir. Your wife has been the most gracious hostess, and has helped me solve a most troubling mystery."

"Elyn and Owain!" she burst as she flung herself into Tally's hug. "Elyn and Owain, they are alive!"

Tally pulled back, his expression stark and dubious. "But where? How could they be alive?"

"They were kidnapped and now are hiding in Wales...Mynyw. Owain knows them! They're well and I pray happy."

Owain nodded his head in assent, while Tally continued to sift through this most startling revelation. "Well Sir, I hope you will stay longer and tell us all you know of my wife's lost family."

Owain exuberantly accepted the invitation for he liked these people tremendously, and was glad his talk of their relatives would bring them such joy.

The time whisked away as they leisurely toured the village, strolled the river, frolicked with the children and the dogs, and talked on and on about Elyn and Owain. Owain was surprised by the extensive amount of information he was able to provide about his friends and, of course, their rather fractious adopted family.

Early that evening after Owain had packed his belongings, he, Esyllht, and Tally, settled down to a succulent supper. During their lively repast, Esyllht stopped mid-sip, and repeated in an incredulous voice, "Elyn was betrothed once to the present King William. What a horrific thought."

"Luckily," stressed Owain, "the engagement was short lived and Maura doesn't speak much about her time with Rufus."

"Maura..." echoed Tally, setting his drink down. "Who is Maura?"

Owain realized the entire day they had spoken of Maura and Marc only by their Welsh names. "I'm sorry," he said, "Maura is Elyn's Norman name, Marc is Owain's."

Tally sat still and pensive, then pressed, "You don't speak of Maura, the Norman mediator who serves Prince Rhys?"

"I do," answered Owain with some wonder.

Tally stood and stipulated more, "She's wife to Rhys' Norman physician called Simon."

"Yes," granted Esyllht, "...and Marc is to be—" Tally's ashen countenance hushed Esyllht's praise, and she warily asked, "What is it, my love?"

"Rumors..." Tally's entire body tensed as he continued, "Newly spread and rampant...The Montgomerys and the Bishop Odo are combining forces to capture this Simon and Maura. You'd best get yourself quickly home, Owain, and warn them to find themselves a new and impenetrable hiding place, for their current location has been betrayed."

"Henry!" Owain leapt up to shout furiously, "Henry's told them, just as Simon said he would! Have the Montgomerys left for Mynyw?"

"I don't have that information, Sir, but if they are in a rush, it won't take them but two days to reach the shore."

"I must...I must..." Owain tripped out of his seat in his rush to reach his saddlebag.

Esyllht hastened to help and finished for him, "Yes, you must go..."

Owain turned in the door, reached long for his new friends' hands, squeezed fast, and vehemently pronounced, "I thank you, Tally, and you, Elsie for everything. I will relate your message, Elsie. They're to hide in my home. I'll make certain they are safe. Henry won't hurt them again, nor will the Bishop, never again!"

Esyllht clutched at her husband for strength, and whispered with dread as they watched from the door, "Don't let them be taken away, not so soon after we've found them again...*Please*!"

Owain swung up upon his mare, whistled for his mutt, and galloped madly away through the timbered gates of Dinbych.

*****

By the meager glow of dying coals, Taredd stood by the bed and scrutinized the outlines of the bodies snuggled beneath the rumpled pelts. It had to be this night and this time if he were to meet the Montgomerys at their decided rallying place. He'd been astonished by their willingness to accommodate his humble request to marry off Ella and his offer of only a measly dowry. His former alliance with the powerful family had, he supposed, given him credence and in but two days' time, he'd be rid of his problem. He'd neglected mentioning the minor point that the bride was damaged, and hoped they'd interpret her dullness as shyness. The past few days when Ella had not known him near, Taredd had noticed her mood disturbingly animated and he reckoned soon she'd be aware enough to remember and accuse.

Ella slept nearest him, Gruffydd occupied the middle of the bed, and Taredd's shrew of a wife lay on the far side; lucky for him, she was a sound sleeper. Delicately, he knelt and with gentle pressure to Ella's shoulder, nudged the girl awake. She opened confused and sleepy eyes and, as he expected, gasped in recognition. He hushed her protest with a terse, "Ssshhh!" strengthened his hold, and whispered swiftly, "I'm to do as I promised. I'll take you to your man, but your sister mustn't know. She wouldn't approve. Your love awaits you not a day and a half ride from here. You'll come with me now." He tentatively lessened the pressure and waited with bated breath for her response. She lay still, rigid, and silent for what seemed forever, then with an eerie sureness, rose from under the pelts. He grinned with wicked satisfaction and considerately offered her a tunic, helped her into her mantle and slippers, and passed her a satchel stuffed with her very few belongings. Already cloaked himself, Taredd cupped Ella's elbow and hastened her from the llys. A modest contingent of soldiers sat mounted in wait.

Ella stumbled from excitement and her sudden waking, but the words he had promised, 'I'll take you to your man' shouted to her from deep within her clouded mind. She'd been waiting to hear just that promise, and really hadn't cared about hearing anything or anyone else. With one foot poised in the stirrup, she hesitated a moment and looked back to the llys' door. Her reluctance worried Taredd; a firm grasp to her waist hoisted her into the saddle and he swiftly swung up behind, kicked his steed forward, and waved his men to follow.

Two narrow eyes peered from the dark of the door, growing ever rounder with the realization that they were witnessing a kidnapping. They shifted back to the bed and, once assured its lone occupant was still asleep, hardened with a bold notion. Gruffydd slipped back inside the llys, resolutely snatched up and donned his cloak, tugged on his boots, and fastened his cluster of arrows over his back. He grabbed his bow and glanced back one last time to his mother's coiled figure. There was no need to tell her what had happened or what he planned to do about it. He'd only worry her, and surely he'd have Ella back home safely by dawn. His mam would never know that they'd been gone.

*****

"I won't be treated this way!" Henry railed to the mold covered ceiling of his chamber tucked deep inside Dunheved Castle. He jerked to his side on his thin, moth eaten pallet, dribbled foam, and gnashed more, "The old goat watches my every move, I'm constantly smothered by his smelly, reechy guards, my rations are an insult...There must be some way to escape, there has to be some way!" Henry shoved up on his elbow and cried lowly, "John, John! Wake up, you lazy pig! I need you." He kicked out into the darkness, and smiled as his boot tip met its mark.

"Ow!" came the wounded call. "Why did you kick me?" John whined. "I'm tired. We rode all day and it took me an awfully long while to fall asleep on this lumpy mat. Leave me alone, Henry."

"Wake up!" Henry growled, and kicked again harder. "We have to escape."

"We can't escape," John vacantly replied. "Now go back to sleep."

"We can and will," determined Henry, rising and pacing. Lack of any light caused him to trip over John's foot; he tumbled into the rock wall and cursed, "God damn you, you insipid bastard! Get up and help me think!"

John obliged and dizzily watched Henry's faint outline rage back and forth, waiting for his master to spout, as he did every evening, his endless recital of ingenious, yet futile plots.

Henry rambled pieces of thoughts, hoping one would eventually fit the piece missing from his puzzle. "Simon's mother still lives here. Perhaps we could send her a message? If she hasn't spoken to Simon lately, she may still like me. There's no one I'm allied with nearby. Maybe Robert's servants are susceptible to bribery."

"And what would you bribe them with?" drawled John with a yawn.

"I'll promise them great wealth, some are stupid enough to believe me, for I'm still thought of as the good and kindly royal brother."

"The servants here look mighty mean, Henry. I wouldn't toy with their loyalties."

"I think you're enjoying our captivity, you slothful shit!" Henry berated. "Why I suffer you near, I'll never understand. Think, you empty-headed weasel!"

"I don't want to think, I want to sleep, and are you seriously contemplating not aiding Simon?"

"Compared to my present unfortunate situation, Simon is residing in Heaven. Only if I'm set free will I travel to Dinefwr, but I refuse to lead Robert there. If I did, that warty old toad would receive all the glory for saving his too virtuous son. I alone will gain that glory and won't allow Robert a word of praise, not after the despicable way he's treated me."

"And me," John limply added.

"You were born to it and deserve it, but not me, never me. I am a FitzRoy, and now also a Count! Robert can't wield any more prestige, he can only claim more years." Something in Henry's last statement prompted an extra thought, and he connived, "Maybe I can pay someone to assassinate him. Yes, maybe I'll convince Rhys that Robert is planning an attack and he'll kill him for me."

"Can I lie back down now, Henry?" croaked John.

"No. You'll pace with me. Perhaps walking will jostle some idea worth considering in that dormant mind of yours. There must be a sentry or a slave who hates Robert. Have you heard any dissension spoken?"

"No, everyone seems quite fond of him, actually."

An enlightened notion lit Henry's eyes. "A woman, some servant. If I can just get an hour with a pliable bitch, I can get us out of here." He stopped pacing to direct, his voice shrill with suspense, "Tomorrow morning, when we're allowed breakfast in the great hall, make the excuse to use the garderobe and find me a willing wench. Robert trusts you, knows you wouldn't dare try to run off without me."

"What would I say to her?"

"Most have an inkling of my reputation as an accomplished lover, so tell her I caught a glimpse of her ravishing self when entering the bailey, and my heart hasn't stopped fluttering with admiration, or if she's low-born, tell her my loins burn with lust, whatever, I don't care, just get her up here after breakfast on the ruse that I've fallen ill and need constant tending."

"I don't believe any woman is as gullible as you portray, Henry."

"I'll wager you anything, John, that she'll come when she hears it's me who wants her. She will most definitely come...Eventually, they all do."

John dryly reminded, "Except for Maura, that is."

Henry's abrupt blow to John's belly knocked him on his backside. He gasped and groaned for air and freedom as Henry dropped heavily upon his chest and pinned his shoulders to the rushes. "You'll never mention that witch's name again in my presence," Henry gnashed, his nose touching John's and spittle stinging his cheeks. "Swear!" He slammed John upon the cold stones and raved louder, "Swear!"

"I swear, I swear!" John wailed.

"She's the sole reason we're locked up in this pest hole. She is the cause of all the hardship and torment I've been forced to endure these past months." Suddenly, Henry's grip lightened, and his tone turned eerily rueful. "If she'd only surrendered to my wishes, none of this would have happened. We'd be free and she'd be content...with me. I hope Will feeds her one of his slow acting poisons and that I get the honor of overseeing her misery."

"Stop Henry..." John wriggled beneath Henry's weight and beseeched, "Get up. You're becoming far too morbid. Let me up. I'm not your enemy."

Henry gave John a final warning cuff and threatened, "You surely will be if you ever spout her cursed name again."

"I vow to *never* spout it, ever...Now, please let me sleep."

With a loud discontented grunt, Henry flopped off John and onto his mat. He wouldn't sleep, hadn't slept for days. He'd been too cold, too mad, too busy pondering how to escape. Maybe this newest ploy would prove successful? Since leaving Mortain more than a week past, he hadn't encountered any women till arriving here. The ones he'd spotted in the bailey were truly daughters of hounds, but, Hell, he'd suffer anything or anybody to escape Robert.

The morning of the twenty-third of December came quickly enough, but Henry's plot still had not advanced with any fruition. He lay upon his pallet inwardly cursing John, his confinement, and any woman who had ever lived. What had become of John and the whore, he scurrilously wondered? A knock on the door launched him into his drama, replete with writhes and moans. "Come," he croaked. When the door swung wide, Henry's most cloying look switched to pale shock as he encountered not a sympathetic maid, but a stony faced Uncle Robert glaring down at him.

"John says you're ill," said Robert, clearly irked.

"I am, Uncle!" groaned Henry, clutching at his belly. "Food poisoning, I suspect."

"Not poisoning, over eating, I suspect. You made quite a pig of yourself last evening, and ate far too many lampreys. I'll call in my physician to mix you up a draught."

"No!" wailed Henry. He struggled to sit, and anguished, moaning at every break in his plea. "He'll bleed me dry! Take me to the village leech. Your son taught me who's competent to heal and who's not. Only the leeches know the proper recipes to tame the fire in my belly. Take me to the village!"

"Don't be ridiculous, Henry. My man will cure you just fine."

"Not if you want me well...fast...I can't lead you anywhere in this sort of pain and I figure Will and Odo have reached the border and are well on their way to annihilating your son and his wife...Only the leech has the herbs to enable me to ride by mid-morning. I beg of you, Uncle, take me to her at once!"

"I don't know where there's a leech..."

"Your Saxon servants will surely know."

"I'll have them bring her here."

"No. She won't enter your castle. If she dared such a blunder, the villagers will forever shun her. You'll take me to her hut."

"I don't think so, Henry."

"My belly bulges, the pain grows more severe...If I die in your home without receiving proper medical treatment, my brothers will view my death as murder, and they still hold a great fondness for me. So, Uncle Robert, I highly suggest you get me to the leech...soon."

"I'll ask about, then return with my decision. I'll send in your man to look after you till then."

"I thank you, Uncle...God bless you, Uncle."

Still sporting a suspicious eye, Robert left Henry to his astute performance, and grumbled loudly to himself as he marched down the passageway searching for a Saxon servant. John dodged by him wearing a submissive grin, and slunk his way past the guards and into the chamber.

Henry leapt up to chastise, "Where have you been, you clod, and where is the woman?"

"Lord Robert caught me before I had an opportunity to escape the hall. I told him you were ill and I was off to find a nurse. He said he'd discover for himself how ill you truly were, and left before I could stall him further."

"You bungle everything, but there is hope...I believe I've convinced him to take me to the village leech. Once I get there, I'm not certain what to do, but I'll think of something."

"My...my Lord," stuttered John with excited pride, "I did find a woman. She wouldn't risk coming to nurse you, but she did provide me with the means to rid you of your misery."

"What means?"

"This..." Beaming victory, John produced from the folds of his tunic a dagger with a curved blade and razor sharp point.

As if gazing upon some exquisite woman, Henry's eyes pooled with delight. He reached a cautious touch, and ran his finger up one side of the blade. At the fat drop of blood that emerged from the tip of his finger, he exhaled, "Aaahhh! My lad, you may own a bit of promise after all. Whatever did you say to receive such a treasure?"

"Nothing special. I explained your...our plight, she looked queerly at me, and touched me here." He motioned to his cheek. "Then she drew me back to her chamber and presented me the knife."

Henry chuckled, "Is that all she presented?"

"Pardon, my Lord?"

"Never mind..." Rumbling voices approached; Henry recognized one as Robert's. He clumsily stuck the dagger back in John's belt, rearranged his tunic to hide its glint, and dropped back upon the pelt to continue his role as invalid. John knelt at his side, laid his palm across Henry's brow, and slyly became part of the charade.

Robert entered, and failed to hide his chagrin as he reported, "They've told me where she resides. There's a cart awaiting you at the keep's stairs. I will accompany you to her hut and see for myself what magic she conjures. Then Henry..." Robert resignedly stressed, "there will be *no* more delays. We must leave presently if we are to arrive at the Welsh Prince's residence by tomorrow evening."

"No...no more delays, Uncle," Henry strained. "But we must make haste...I fear I'm weakening."

"Guards," Robert barked. "Take him to the bailey where a cart awaits. And never take your eyes off his hide."

The cart rambled along the highroad into town. John shifted to keep the dagger from sticking his belly, leant close to Henry's beckoning finger, and attended to his whisper. "While the leech mixes my tonic, I'll distract Robert by asking him what she's doing. Keep as close to him as possible, and when I snap my fingers, press the dagger to his back, and warn him loudly that if he chooses to move, he dies. I'll take over custody of the dagger and handle the remainder of the threat. We'll steal the guard's horses, and when I yell run, you run! I reckon when Guy and my mercenaries hear we've escaped, they'll catch up to us quickly enough."

"And why won't Robert catch us quickly?"

"We'll steal all the guards' horses, and Robert's as well."

"I've never held a dagger to anyone, Henry."

"Then it's long past time you learned."

As Robert neared Edith's hut, he felt a faintness overtaking him. He wondered how much she knew of her son's imminent danger, and considered, only briefly, sharing the wretched turn of events with her. He paused his horse a moment before the sturdy structure and curiously noticed the door and windows nailed shut. Had she left to warn Simon, or perhaps, because of her episode with Odo, she'd felt forced to move? A sadness joined his lightheadedness, and guilt—the damned unrelenting and inescapable guilt. He soundly kicked his mount to a trot and hurried to join his exasperating nephew and his simpering cohort. They must remedy Henry's ailment and leave Dunheved soon. After he'd alerted the Welsh Prince, perchance the guilt would at last go away.

Henry lay deathly limp upon a pallet, swooning distress, and flinching to the leech's prodding fingers. Robert paced above, sneering distrust. John stood only feet away, appearing more ashen than his lord, dripping sweat and swallowing far too often. Two guards manned the door, two more held the horses just outside. The leech rose, and mutely began preparing a draught from a multitude of vials gracing a small trestle table. Henry struggled to sit, and grimacing from hurt, implored, "What's she doing, Uncle Robert? How will she poison me?"

"It was your cursed idea to come here," Robert scowled back, "and you'll drink whatever she mixes." Robert warily eyed the strange one's preparation and alerted, "She's adding something black to boiling water, some leaves, and something orange. It's foaming higher."

Henry groaned to his uncle's description, and wailed, "Don't make me drink it...She knows who I am and aims to do me in!"

"Quiet Henry! It doesn't look too terrible and she's adding honey."

Robert peered closer, and his guards joined in his fascination. Henry surmised the moment perfect—he snapped his fingers, but received no response from John. He glared John's way, and noticed his butler too had become entranced. Henry grunted loudly, shifted his ire, and snapped again. John turned a dull expression Henry's way, witnessed his Lord's snarl, and fumbled for the dagger. He pressed its tip barely into Robert's mantle, yet Robert made no indication of sensing the attack. Henry encouraged with a mouthed, "Deeper!"

John did as told successfully, for Robert suddenly stiffened and sucked an alarmed breath, cursing, "God's breath! What the—"

John forgot what he was supposed to say, and sighed in huge relief when Henry sprang up from the pallet and rescued the dagger with a graceful maneuver. "I'll stick you, Uncle," he precisely vowed. "You know I will, so come carefully with me...outside."

Robert's firm gesture held his guards at bay, while he obeyed his wily nephew. Once outside, Robert's posturing instantly alerted his guards to his danger, and their hands flew to their hilts. He stopped their retaliation with a broken, "N...no! Don't fight him, for I'll be the first one to suffer."

"I'll have your stallions, Uncle," crowed Henry, "and your blessing, for I'm off to save your son...alas, without your help. John, take the beasts, mount one, and bring one close."

John fumbled with the reins of the three extra steeds, while clambering aboard another, and guided Robert's stallion nearer to Henry.

"Take heed of my vow, Uncle," Henry spoke with deft clarity, "and never a truer vow have you witnessed. I will alert Rhys' household to your son's impending capture, and though Simon doesn't deserve my gallantry, be assured I will act to preserve his life and his happiness. I won't return to boast of my success, yet know I won't fail, I never fail. If you choose, foolishly, to chase me, I will ride straight for Normandy, and you and you alone will hold responsibility for your son's and your ward's deaths, and no doubt their child's as well." Still brandishing his weapon, Henry used his free hand to scramble up into the saddle. His howl, "Run!" startled the gawking villagers, and all scuttled away from the FitzRoy and his butler's thundering gait as they raced crazily from the burgh of Dunheved.

*****

CHAPTER TWENTY-TWO - CEREMONIES

Maura stopped short of Gael's cottage, her expression pinched with doubt. Simon stopped with her and asked, a touch annoyed, "What now?"

"I don't like this idea," said she.

"And what's wrong with it?"

"I'll get tremendously bored, Simon, there's nothing left in Gael's hut. At least in our home I can cut out drawers for the baby, or write more notes to Rose, or cook..."

"I want you close to me right now," Simon argued. "There are only two days left till Christmas. I won't have you delivering our child up the hill while I'm down here swabbing throats. Just for the day," he pleaded. "At night we'll go back home."

"Why can't I stay in the llys?" she asked, hesitantly entering.

He followed her in, and prodded her deeper into the room. "Because Gael asked Taredd and he refused us. Not that his refusal mattered one bit to Gael, she heartily welcomes you. I fear you'll become upset if Taredd decides to grace us with another one of his raving rampages. Gael, Gruffydd, and Marc promise to visit as often as they're able. And Rhys is due to arrive from Ireland any hour now, and is to stay through Christmas. He'll delight in entertaining you." Maura still didn't appear convinced, and Simon wondered in a wounded tone, "Don't you want me with you when—"

"Of course, I do," she earnestly intruded, squeezing his hands. "It isn't that, Simon, it's just that...that..."

"That what?"

"I love you terribly, but you worry *too* much," she said almost embarrassingly.

"Would you have me worry too little?"

"No," she flared in a fluster, "I'm tired of being pregnant and I want her to be born now in our own home where her cradle is!"

And he softly conceded, "I'm afraid she'll be born when and where she chooses."

Maura's hands left his and gripped at her lower back; she arched with discomfort and looked sorely about for somewhere to sit. There was only the floor, and she knew once she'd lowered herself down, it would take forever to stand again. Simon's expression reeked sympathy as he came close and wrapped his arm round her back to ease her strain. His fingers tenderly brushed her cheek and he asked, "Why don't you come with me on my rounds? No one has anything that's catching and it's bound to be a diversion."

She kissed his pout and murmured, "I'd like that, and I'm sorry for my mood."

"There's no need to apologize, and I marvel at your patience. I couldn't possibly know for certain what you're feeling, but since helping with pregnancies and the endless complaints I've heard, I can well imagine your discomfort. Come, my love..." He swung his bag over his shoulder and wove his arm with hers. "We'll walk. All my patients ask about you, now you'll get the chance to answer them yourself."

"Who are you to see today?" she asked, managing some cheer to her words as they emerged once again into the grayish, chilly morn.

"Today I'm to see practically the entire village. Over the past week, I've been fairly successful at ridding the afflicted ones of their coughs and belly aches. Now it's time to pass out fortifying tonics to maintain their good health."

"Like my oak beer."

"Precisely."

"What tonic do you have to encourage stubborn babies—out?"

"None," he regretted. "Do you remember Adela's labor?"

"*That* I will never forget."

"When her pains became sluggishly dangerous, you convinced her to drink a draught I'd mixed of molded rye and savory that strengthened her labor. I'd never subject you to that sort of torture in order to start something that is bound to begin quite naturally on its own."

"But *when* will it begin, Simon?"

"Soon...I can only predict...soon."

Maura let out a long, loud and frustrated breath, firmed their hold, then surmised, "Then walking can only help."

Not long after, Marc entered Gael's hut from the stables, anticipating finding his sister in the dimly lit, bare room. Seeing no one, he turned to leave, then paused to a light rapping on the main door. He eagerly opened it to Gael, looking cold and harried. "Marc," she greeted in slight surprise. "I didn't expect you. Is Maura inside?"

"No...but she may arrive shortly." His expression mirrored her worry, as he urged, "Come in and tell what's happened."

She entered, and shuddered involuntarily to the emptiness she felt inside and out. "Nothing's happened," she spurted. "At least nothing that I'm certain of...yet. Have you seen Gruffydd this morning, or Ella?"

"No...I've only just risen myself and came directly to your hut. I'd planned to stay with Maura awhile, but I believe Simon and Maura may have gotten here before me. Perhaps she's gone with him on his rounds."

"Have you eaten?" Gael asked.

"No..."

"Then come back to the llys with me, I'll fix you something warm, and we'll wait there for Gruffydd, Ella, and Maura. It's far more comfortable...and Taredd is nowhere to be seen. Will you come?"

Marc needed no more prodding, clasped her hand in assent, and beamed to her comfortable smile as they started for the llys.

*****

Directly over the llys of Llandovery, the sun's rays fought their way through a mass of black and threatening clouds. Inside, Arnulf FitzRoger, almost an exact replica of his bushy father, except younger and hairier, shifted for comfort upon a rock-hard bench before an elaborately decorated trestle table. Cadell, the current Pennaeth of the commote, occupied the seat to his right, the Bishop Odo held the one to his left. Will, blatantly irritated, paced behind the three; Joanna kept herself in the shadows, and winced to Will's tirade, "He won't come...After riding a bleeding twelve hours through this relentless quagmire of a country, and being forced to ingest this puke these heathens call food, it is my luck that the laggard won't show!"

Arnulf, not known for his extensive vocabulary, barked, "He'll come, or we'll go get him *and* her."

A strikingly pretty lad called Donald, owning a look of sublime innocence, sat taller in his seat at the end of the table, and announced with trepidation, "My Lord Arnulf, Ella will come if she's been told what we plan. She traveled to Shrewsbury many times on her own, and has no fear—"

"Quiet," rumbled Arnulf. "I don't know why Father's giving you, a mere simp, this girl and a knighthood. He's not given me a wife. He hasn't given me anything lately."

"Keep quiet yourself, Arnulf," mumbled Odo, oozing an overabundance of self-confidence. "He's allowing you to participate in our little game, isn't he?"

"What game? We're only sitting here arguing. I think we've been tricked."

"For what ends?" asked Odo. "This Chieftain...Taredd, has excellent motives for handing over the girl and providing us Simon and Maura. He keeps his title, and acquires a good deal of wealth in the process. And whether he comes or not, we can easily subdue the village of Menevia and take our prisoners. Remember the size and expertise of the armies we have amassed outside the village walls." Odo's hand stilled Arnulf's drumming fingers, he squeezed affectionately and simplified his language, "Arnulf...there is absolutely nothing to worry over. We will win, so calm yourself, have some more of this rancid mead, and strive to be patient. I recommend you do the same, Will."

Will only sneered in response to his uncle's command and paced faster. How could he be calm and patient when only a fortnight remained for him to deliver Maura to her rightful husband? The weather had proven treacherous and Yorkshire seemed a million miles away. If Maura caused him difficulty again, he'd have no choice but to eliminate her, along with his obdurate pest of a brother.

Sounds of an arriving party emanated through the open doorway and opened windows. All inside stood in anticipation as a gaggle of rugged guards, clad in thick leather armor, sworded and arrowed, stomped their way inside. Taredd followed, armored as well and seeming tentative. He spotted Arnulf and immediately straightened. A sly grin split his face, he strutted forward, sidled the blazing hearth, and thrust both arms out in a lavish greeting. "My dear Lord Arnulf," he spouted in perfect Norman French, "I've missed you so!"

Arnulf cheerily lumbered round the end of the dais, and bestowed on his supposed enemy an abundant hug and two huge kisses to his cheeks. "I've missed you too, Taredd, and I'm pleased you are Chieftain now, for I've been wanting to come south. You'll help me?"

"I'll do all that I can," Taredd flaunted, and turned his practiced radiance to the table of elite visitors. He pried loose from Arnulf and greeted first, in his native tongue, the Welsh Pennaeth Cadell, then smoothly switched to French to present himself to Odo and Will. Both seemed impressed by the Welshman's impeccably polished etiquette. Taredd waited till the Normans and Cadell sat, then motioned to one of his guards, and announced, "And now, my Lords, the bride."

Donald bolted up and strained his neck; his enthusiasm thrust him from the table as he beheld his love, looking lost and being tugged through the door by the guard. Surrounded by such prominent personalities Ella appeared a tiny, frightened mouse. Then as her terrified eyes finally found Donald, she burst an exclamation of brilliant joy. She threw herself into her lover's embrace, whimpering as her fingers crawled over and pinched at his face and his hair, making certain he was real. He squeezed her as vehemently, kissing everything his lips could reach. Yet when his wet, grateful eyes searched her tormented ones, he tensed, clutched her protectively, and to Taredd accused, "What have you done to her? Someone's hurt her. You've hurt her!"

"Not I, lad," Taredd assured, his manner verging on maudlin. "I'm sad to admit it was her father who punished her. Over the past month, she's made great progress in her healing, and will soon be whole again. She'll prove a grand wife, for she loves you dearly, as it appears you do her."

Donald grudgingly accepted Taredd's explanation, and guided Ella gently back to his seat, where he murmured endearments, hugged and rocked her on his lap.

Odo scowled to their soppy show of love, and grunted to Arnulf, "Let's get this done. I'm eager to visit my nephew—*the doctor*."

Arnulf returned to his seat, and ordered, "Taredd, I'll have the dowry." A dense leather sack of coins was tossed upon the table. Arnulf spilled the silver and, with excruciating slowness, began counting aloud the entire amount.

Will plopped his restlessness in a seat at the opposite end of the table from Donald's, threw back a cup of mead, rolled his eyes in exasperation, and groused to himself, *The world is populated with entirely too many idiots, and I'm related to the majority of them!*

Content with the total, Arnulf nodded to Odo, who clasped up his bible, stood and beckoned the lovers to, "Kneel before me, my children."

Donald readily advanced, helping Ella along; they knelt, and each kissed Odo's offered ring. Donald lifted eager eyes, and Ella kept her bemused yet oddly pleased expression as Odo muttered his prayers, and motioned numerous crosses over their heads. He recited the chosen litany swiftly, yet succinctly, and, with one final encompassing gesture, proclaimed with little emotion, "You are now wed, and may you be fruitful in your blest union."

Donald gushed, "We are most obliged, my Lord Bishop!"

Odo cast him a condescending look and dismissed them back to their seat, while Arnulf stood and bellowed, "Now we eat!"

On his cue, a line of serving maids paraded into the hall, balancing platters piled high with a blandly styled assortment of meats, cheeses, breads and cakes. More mead followed, and all commenced eating, except Will. He slipped into the chair by Taredd's and began his persuasive role in the game. "Taredd, we hear you now rule Menevia, and I have a personal interest in your village, for I'm concerned for the fate of my brother, who I'm told resides there. Do you know of him? He's called Simon, and has acquired the reputation of a skilled healer."

"Yes, he resides in my village..."

Taredd's testy tone betrayed an intense dislike of Simon and, encouraged, Will continued, "We...his Uncle Odo and myself, would like nothing more than to accept him back into our family. We are worried my father, Robert, is intent on murdering Simon. They've been rabid enemies for years. Robert is the sole reason Simon is in hiding, and a dreadful rumor recently has surfaced that his location has been betrayed and Robert is at this moment headed to your village to remove his son. Help us Taredd. We crave Simon's safety. He is a dear brother, who deserves my pride and protection and has suffered too long by our father's hand."

"What would you have me do about this?" asked Taredd skeptically.

"Lead us to Menevia, and help us accomplish our reunion."

"Rhys would be displeased if Simon were to leave. Simon tends to our Prince. I couldn't let him go without Rhys' permission."

Will replied with a hint of sarcasm, "You speak as if your Prince *owns* Simon."

"In a way he does. I will not madden my Prince."

Will's mawkish grin turned calculating, "It sounds to me that you'd rather Simon's father find him, and eliminate him permanently."

His secret discovered, Taredd shifted indignantly, and countered, "Maybe I would."

"Then perhaps, I should alter my request—" While Will paused a moment to compose a new approach, he noticed Donald lead Ella behind Arnulf toward the back entrance. He suspected they couldn't wait till evening to consummate their union. Joanna stepped out from the dark to say something to the bubbling couple. A distinct whirring drowned her words and her calm as an arrow whizzed through the window, flew between Odo and Arnulf, and grazed Donald's skull before embedding itself deep into the rushes! Everyone instantly dove to the floor, shielding themselves beneath the table or against the walls.

Donald threw Ella to the ground, dropped on top of her, and rolled them into the shadows. Another missile struck the back of Arnulf's chair; one more pierced Odo's bible. Arnulf screamed, "Call for the army! Seize Taredd and his guards!"

Donald used the chaos to accomplish what he prayed for since he'd been kidnapped eight years past. He crawled, then scrambled up and dragged Ella out through the stables, catching up his mount's reins on his way. "I'll take her to safety!" he called to Arnulf's guards, who were already mounted and leaving to fetch the army. Yet he murmured something quite different to his wife as he helped her into the saddle and swung up snugly behind her. "I'll take you to my parents in Scotland. They'll love you as I do, and will help you recover. Lord Roger won't bother looking for us, and Arnulf has his money. Come my love, we'll go home." They galloped away through the advancing army, and never once looked back. The arrows' onslaught abruptly ceased. Arnulf was first to rise, and cautiously spread his arms in a motion for all to follow. The guard securing Taredd to the floor pushed to his knees and swiftly trussed Taredd's wrists with a leather cord. Taredd's men, along with Cadell and his servants, were herded on their knees into a corner, Norman swords brandished precariously at the height of their necks. In the courtyard, the remainder of Taredd's scant battalion was corralled within a circle of Norman knights.

A wretched squawking ensued as the door burst wide and in struggled a guard, wrestling a flailing boy slung over his shoulder. The man bent to set Gruffydd on the floor, but Gruffydd leapt down first, kicked the sentry soundly in the groin, and bit into his hand, drawing from his victim a scream and much blood. Before Gruffydd could strike again, the guard landed a swift blow to his jaw, catapulting him onto a chair which promptly tipped backwards and sprawled him senseless to the floor.

Odo gaped at the skinny and ragged youngster. "This is our attacker?" he hooted incredulously. "So Taredd, you employ midgets in your army."

Arnulf's men chuckled along, and Taredd vigorously defended, "He's not mine, he's Ella's nephew!"

Joanna, who'd spent her idle time at Shrewsbury schooling herself in the familial relationships at Menevia, stepped forward in contest, "And as such is *your* step-son. How conniving and despicable of you to employ your son to launch an attack on the Montgomery household."

Amazed again at her genius, Will joined his steward, praising, "How astonishing your mind, Joanna," and suggested with aplomb to Arnulf, "Uncle Arnulf, let us cease this ridiculous charade and get on with our mission to capture Simon and Maura."

"I heartily agree, Will," said Odo, with a fond pat to his nephew's shoulder.

"I'll finish eating first," protested Arnulf in a furious huff. "And there will be a wedding feast!"

"But the happy couple has vanished," mentioned Will.

"They are most likely rutting in the stable," grunted Arnulf. "We'll celebrate their coupling!"

"Why not," appeased Will, with a guffaw. "I've celebrated stranger events. What do we do with the boy?"

"Keep him, of course," decided Odo. "He's mighty handy with a bow and could prove useful for bargaining when we arrive at Menevia."

Will kindly instructed, "Joanna, will you see to the lad? It appears he requires a woman's touch."

"Gladly, my Lord," she said and cunningly added, "and I believe it is worth knowing that the boy is the true son of the former Chieftain of Menevia, and will rightfully attain that position himself someday." Her statement caused all the barons' eyes to shift with menacing connivance.

Arnulf shouted to his expectant soldiers, "Lock the Welsh in the stable, but leave the servants to tend us. Then you may return to the feast. You've done well this day."

*****

Robert sat slumped upon his bed, bemoaning that once again he'd been tricked and beaten. Henry had literally tied his hands, and he could manage little more to save his son and ward. If chased, Henry would most certainly carry out his threat not to alert Simon, just as he would have murdered Robert as easily as he kissed him. With wounded heart, Robert pondered the viciousness of his family, and his cursed luck to be always caught in the middle of the good and the evil, most often manipulated by the bad, never gaining the trust of the virtuous. Edith couldn't tell him where Simon was now. She was gone and, if she were here, she'd never confess and he wouldn't blame her. And Rose...He'd sent a squire to her son's manor and found no one at home. His seneschal at Dunheved, who knew much about the Welsh, had known the location of the residence of the Prince of South Wales, and Robert had sent Benjamin and a few of his other soldiers to the place called Dinefwr. They would take a different route from Henry, stay land born and arrive sometime after the FitzRoy. Hopefully, Benjamin would discover for Robert the final ramifications of Odo's debacle. Robert dropped back upon his pillow, yearning for the comfort of Almodis' and Adam's presence, for Edith's sympathy and forgiveness, for Simon's lost love. What more could he have done to save his son? And wasn't it far too late for him to aspire to the accolade—hero?

*****

Sitting a cautious foot away from her guest, Gael absently stirred her bowl of honeyed oats, while chuckling to Marc's account of a flurried morning, "And then Clyde took a liking to some herb in Simon's bags, the ones he'd spent most of the evening preparing. Sometime during the night, the kitten removed all the bags from his satchel and hid them all over the garden, the stable, the corral. Maude trod on some, the horses mangled the others. Simon was none too happy this morning, and Maura, she's been a bit grumbly these days herself, not that I blame her."

"You couldn't get near me the last few days before Gruffydd's birth," Gael wistfully recalled. "I was constantly snarling, more from fear than meanness. I hope it happens soon for her, and after all the suffering she's already endured, is relatively easy. And what did Simon do to Clyde?"

"Oh he made great threats," said Marc, "but then the kitten wrapped himself around Simon's legs, and he crumbled."

"As usual. And did Maura's mood lighten at all?"

"No, she didn't want to come down to the village."

"I meant to tell her she could stay here with me," said Gael. "I don't think Taredd will return anytime soon."

"Where *does* he go?" asked Marc.

"I haven't a clue, nor do I care. I'm glad for his absence." The sour subject of her farce of a marriage shoved Gael from her seat at the trestle table and over to a shuttered window. She cracked it wide enough to contemplate the deluge of slushy rain that poured down from the gloomy heavens. "Gruffydd's been gone half the day now and couldn't be fishing," she noted absently. "Not even he would fish in *this* weather."

"He's probably with Cynan and Nia at Olwen's hut."

"And where's Ella?"

"With him there."

Gael pressed with tinge of worry, "Do you really think so, Marc?"

"I'll check now if you wish."

"No...you're most likely correct." Gael didn't want to search actively, not yet, for if she didn't find them, then her deepest fears would be confirmed. She stopped wringing her hands and dragged them over her face, asking as a distraction, "Will you be wanting more oats, or mead?"

"No...I'm fine." Now, Marc clearly noticed her turmoil, which she was most times fairly successful masking even from him. He felt concern and also anger at Gruffydd's odd desertion, and severe self-consciousness at her piercing stare. "Gael..." He called again to interrupt her trance, "Gael...Is there something else wrong?"

She hadn't realized her rudeness, for her mind was a tumult of vexing emotions, all upturned by this very simple man. "Wrong?" she asked, sounding exhausted. "No...I was only thinking about the last two weeks, how Simon and Maura and you especially have kept me company, and cheered me so. And last evening, you made Ella laugh. No one's been able to do that since she arrived here, not even Gruffydd. I'm grateful to you. You make me feel..." She lost the words, but not the sensation as she boldly strode to Marc's side, sat so their thighs touched, and laced her fingers with his. She held her damp gaze on their hands and, relieved that he didn't pull away, confessed, "You are so good...and kind...and so very handsome...I—"

His fingers stiffened, yet she firmed their grip and raised pleading eyes. "Don't Marc, don't leave me...not now, *please*. Sometimes I feel so very alone."

"I won't leave you, but you shouldn't be speaking—"

"Speaking what...the truth? I care for you, you know I do. Why can't I tell you?"

"Because you are married to another."

"No...*not* married. You can't call the horror Taredd and I share a marriage. It is an obscene nightmare that I can't wake from, for if I do, my son will be gone." She implored, helpless as a child, "You care for me, don't you?"

"More than I can ever say."

"And you don't think me dull looking, do you?"

He paused at her odd appeal, then easily pledged, "You are nothing but beautiful."

"You'll show me...how beautiful?" Her nearness burned and her breathy, "*Please*..." tickled his skin and sped his heart. All he need do to prove his love was close the space between their lips...close that tiny yet seemingly impenetrable distance.

At the crush of her mouth on his, the trepidation he'd felt magically vanished. A racing hunger fed from an eternity of loneliness and frustration thrust them up from the bench. Her warmth and eagerness flowed and flared with his as they stumbled everywhere and finally surrendered to the soft of the rushes. There a raging calm overtook them; they paused their kisses and, clenching tight for a long ponderous moment, considered the peril their recklessness might evoke. And although their eyes darkened to the dread, their hands, mouths, and bodies took no heed, and surged together again, discovering, clutching, and tasting what neither had savored before.

A shout resounded within Marc's mind, telling him of his sin, grievous enough to condemn him to Hell, but he found with amazement that he didn't really care and would gladly suffer the Devil's scourge for the love of this wondrous lady. He slowed his passion, and happily found a control that he strove to pass to her; yet she kept her fevered pace, groping at his clothes, moaning her rasped "*Please*..." endlessly.

Gently he restrained her grasp between his, and beseeched, "Slow, my sweet love, slow! I want to love you how I've dreamt..."

Gael tried terribly hard to oblige, yet she still shuddered violently beneath his reverent touch as his fingers danced their way through her pale locks, caressed her damp brow, and brushed over her wet and swollen lips. They singed the skin along her neck and easily nudged the loose neckline of her tunic off her shoulders. She helped strip him from his shirt and, naked to the waist, they knelt in an enduring and desperate clasp. In time and ever so hesitantly, they eased apart; their gazes pooled with wonder, and their touches tingled with awe as they began exploring each other's secrets.

Humbled by the preciousness before him, Marc hung his head and drew her close. His cheek he pressed to her breast; Gael's arms surrounded his shoulders and cuddled him nearer. She kissed his head and combed fingers through his thick burnished hair and, hugging him so, felt truly confident of his love, of hers—Her thoughts blurred and head lolled to the luscious sensations roused by his lips. She closed her eyes, whimpered, and willingly sank back with him into ecstasy...

What she beheld in that blinding instant forced from her a startled gasp. Marc heard her cry and felt her racing chill; it stiffened her limbs and doused her joy. He raised up alarmed, and gasped with her, "What is it?! What have I done—"

She searched his tortured expression, and strove to kiss away his worry, yet as her eyes closed again, the face came again, clearer, so intense and threatening that she cried aloud, "No, not him, never him!"

"Who?!" Marc anguished. "Who upsets you? Me?!"

"No...I..." She wrenched from his fervid hold and struggled back into her tunic, swiping at crazed tears. "I can't," she muttered madly, "...I can't—"

"Can't what?!" he cried, stealing back her hands.

They hung limply in his clench, and she sobbed, "I can't do this to you...I won't lie, not to you."

"Why would it be a lie?!" he assailed. "You care for me! You said you cared—"

"I do...I may even love you...But, when I close my eyes, I don't see you. My God, Marc, I don't see you!"

His confusion flared, and he lashed out, "Who?! Who do you see?!"

"I can't say! I won't—"

"You have to tell me!" His fingers bit her shoulders and yanked her weightlessly forward. "I'm dying inside! You have to tell me!"

"I can't, it will only hurt you more...I can't!"

Marc released her to the rushes and squeezed together his palms till his nails stabbed. He howled in misery; she panicked and moaned with him as he batted her consoling reach and scrambled up, snatching his shirt, racing from her dejection, her pity. She raced after, crying out, "Don't leave this way, please Marc, I didn't mean...I didn't...Please, stay, talk to me...hear me out! *Please!*"

At the bottom step, he turned her a face wet and wretched with devastation. The rain mingled with his tears, and he fought hard to find and hurl the curses that rumbled and ripped at his gut. Yet he could only strain the whisper, "I love you...only you...only you." Marc staggered away and slipped through pools of mud in a frantic struggle to reach his sanctuary—the cathedral. The sheltered stairs saved him from the elements, but not his crippling emotions. He slumped, gasping for breath upon the bottom step, and prayed for an end to the hurt—yet it only ravaged deeper, crushing his heart, his soul, his trust. He sensed a hovering presence and jerked anguished eyes up to see Sulien. Marc choked on the glut of words stuck somewhere between his heart and throat...Here stood the one person he could tell all and not be judged, the only one who owned the power to absolve his sin.

Sulien concernedly traveled the four stairs and crouched at Marc's side, imploring, "What is it, lad? What's happened?!"

Marc tried once more his confession, and one phrase finally emerged, cracked and aching, "I'm not fit to be a priest."

Sulien's compassionate touch helped lift Marc up from the stone. The Bishop gently guided him inside the church with the repeated assurance, "We'll go to my chamber and talk...We'll talk."

Gael sagged upon the top step of the llys, heaving and glaring at the wall of wet that matted her hair, soaked her tunic, and washed away her tears. She didn't want them washed away, she wanted them to drip down forever, and remind her always of the terrible torture she had just inflicted. Somewhere in her shattered mind she heard

402

laughing, wicked cackling. It was him. *He* had caused this tragedy. What she suspected was true. He did indeed possess the power to invade one's mind, and an evil, wounding power it had proven to be. Her loathing for Owain surged anew, bubbled over, and exploded in a rash of screamed curses. She raged up and lurched back inside the llys, flinging crockery and oats, overturning benches, ripping curtains. The intensity of her fit tripped her to the rushes, where she cradled her head between her hands, and rocked to and fro, her wails and stammers of hate growing ever meaner, ever louder. Surely, she'd go mad, and deserved it, deserved any punishment that God deemed appropriate for, despite her need to blame Owain, this disaster was entirely her doing. Her hands gripped at the cramping in her belly as she groaned and retched into the rushes, already soaked by her tears, thick and constant tears shed for the only man deserving of, yet so cruelly denied her love.

*****

Simon and Maura hustled up the sheltered stairs of the cathedral, shaking themselves, while Simon groused, "We should have stayed longer at Hywel's. Now you're soaked, and chilled, and—"

"I'm perfectly fine," Maura laughed. "And Hywel wouldn't have let us stay. Though, I must say, he was infinitely more kind than I've ever seen him."

"I think he misses Owain and is lonely." Simon helped her to sit on the top stair; he sat himself, and clutching hands they stared dreamily out into the shower.

Maura sighed contentedly and squeezed his palm. "I am highly impressed."

"With what?"

"You."

"Me?"

"Yes..."

"Heavens why?"

"It's been ages since I accompanied you on your rounds and I'd forgotten how skilled and caring a doctor you are."

"I do what I can, and you, my love, are too sweet."

"No...It's true." Her hand swept to encompass the entire village spread before them. "You are thoroughly loved by these good people, and as such you should be the one wearing this." She unclasped the chain around her neck, slid off Rhys' ring and presented it to her husband.

Simon waved away her offer. "I told Rhys when he gave it to me that I was no leader."

"I disagree, but whatever, I'm convinced it's *not* only a token a leadership." She glanced down at the similar ring adorning the third finger of her right hand, and mused, "I've yet to ask Owain about *this* ring, but I believe it was a gift given by Rhys to Owain's father for his service as ovate. The service you provide Rhys and the village is just as valuable—no, far more so, for many wouldn't have a chance for a future if not for your care. Please wear it, my love. I have your wedding ring, and I want you to have this one...Think of it as my gift to you."

"Then how can I resist." Simon's indulgent smile hinted a certain sadness as he accepted her gift and placed it where his wedding ring once resided. The rain lessened, and Simon eagerly suggested, "Come, let's go to Gael's hut. We must get you dry."

"And once there, will you impress me more?"

"I'll do what I can," he chuckled as they left the shelter and scuttled round puddles and mud, teasing and laughing along their way.

*****

403

Marc sat by the hearth in Sulien's chamber, his sanity somewhat restored by hours of attending to the Bishop's astute advice. "Before I leave," Marc asked, "can you say if a sin of thought is as damaging as a sin of the flesh?"

"If that were so," reckoned Sulien, "I fear we'd all be damned to Hell. Taming the hate you feel will be the hardest chore of your absolution."

"It's not that I hate her," Marc countered. "I couldn't *hate* her. I don't understand her."

"Again, I offer the notion that she was helping and not hurting you."

"Saving my soul?" asked Marc dubiously.

"In a sense...yes," replied Sulien.

"I don't feel saved."

"In time you will, and you'll also feel grateful. Marc, of all the people I've met in my lifetime, you are without challenge, the most thoroughly good individual I have had the luck to know. If you are not fit to be a priest, then the rest of us need discard our robes. Always remember, in our role as spiritual leaders we are asked to emulate Christ, not to *be* Christ. Be gentler on yourself. Search elsewhere and you'll find a suitable woman to wed, one who'll care for you as comfortably as you care for her. And I need not say how many are eager for you to begin your search."

Marc managed to mirror Sulien's slim smile and, rising, quietly admitted with a blush, "I don't know where to go. I don't want to be alone."

"You're welcome to stay here as long as you please, but I have some visits to make."

"I was supposed to entertain my sister. She's staying at Gael's old hut while Simon sees to his patients."

"And how does it feel to be almost an uncle?" asked Sulien, rising as well.

"It feels fine, but I'd rather be a father."

"And a fine father you'll make...someday."

"Someday..." Marc wistfully repeated. "I thank you, your Grace. I thank you ever so much for your time and your wisdom."

Sulien enclosed Marc's offered hand, and scoffed, "No, I thank you, my son, for I'm always learning from you and replenished by your enviable innocent view of life. When you return tonight to your chamber, I'll visit again to see how you fare."

*****

Marc stood atop the cathedral's stairs a long contemplative while, considering the village, which did appear somewhat brighter than when he'd left the llys. He wondered where Gael was, for he wasn't capable of facing her just now. Sulien's words, '...begin your search,' repeated themselves, and he knew he didn't have to waste his heart and time searching. There was someone waiting whom he could comfortably care for, and who already cared for him, perhaps more than Gael claimed to. As he trudged down the stairs, confident in his mission, he thought briefly on Gruffydd and Ella, and his promise to look for them. Along the lane leading to the village wall, he knocked upon each hut's door and asked every occupant if they'd seen or heard from either or both. 'No, not this day,' was the recurrent answer he received. Finally, he arrived at his destination, and again raised his fist to knock. An unbidden doubt mixed with a stabbing pain paused his rapping, shook his posture and faltered his resolve. He steeled himself, knowing he'd surely find happiness inside—a happiness he'd not yet allowed himself to acknowledge or nourish.

Olwen raised smiling eyes to the light tapping. She welcomed the disruption for the weather had forced her entire brood inside, and a whining lot they were fast becoming. She lay Morgan in his cradle and skirted her way between toys and youngsters to the door. Expecting to see Gruffydd, she beamed with gladdened surprise, "Marc! Please come inside. Children, it's Marc!"

Nia promptly jumped into Marc's snug embrace; Maredudd toddled up close, holding out his cup of milk; Morgan wailed; and Cynan stayed back, his expression suspicious. "I'm so glad you've come!" Olwen gushed, fussing with a thick plait of nearly white hair. "You'll eat with us. We've not much, but enough to share. Have you been to the cathedral?"

"Yes," answered Marc with noticeable tension. He set Nia down, and his long reach asked for Olwen's hand, which she readily provided. "The entire afternoon actually. I've spoken to Sulien about some...matters, and now I wish to speak to you."

"About the same matters?" she cautiously pressed.

"Yes, in a way." The infant raged louder, and Marc suggested, "If you're busy, I can return later—"

"No," she soundly protested. "He's only hungry. You don't mind?"

"No, of course I don't."

She smiled a relieved smile and hastened to cheer her son. "Please do sit and pour yourself mead." She plopped down herself, parted the front of her tunic, and glanced up from her fumbling child. "You look troubled, Marc," she chanced. "What you're wanting to say, will it upset—"

"I don't think so..." Marc assured.

Bored with her games, Nia wandered over and, with Marc's aid, clambered up upon his knee; Maredudd followed and perched himself happily upon Marc's other leg. Marc cast a smile to Cynan, who returned a sneer. Olwen, busy feeding Morgan, didn't notice the animosity and, finally achieving quiet, meekly asked, "What is it you're wanting to say?"

Marc took a moment to compose himself and his speech and settled a marveled gaze upon this remarkable woman. Her iridescent colorless locks and translucently ashen skin and features made her appear older than her true age of twenty, yet her voice and manner betrayed a childlike quality. Her own youth had been stolen from her—married at twelve, a mother by thirteen, and held hostage by a brutal husband the whole of their married life. Only in the past year had she enjoyed a tenuous freedom. Her strength of mind and body was unquestionable, for she managed her family with a strict, yet gentle command, and they all appeared exceptionally well cared for, cheerful, and loved. She was taller than Gael, her figure fuller, her fairness not as interesting, yet she had been blest with the sweetest smile, the most giving soul, and the grace to make even the most timid feel solace and safety in her humble presence.

"Marc," she said softly.

Her call and the shock of cold milk splashed upon his leg woke him from his musing. Maredudd clapped his cup against his other hand and, spilling more, squealed with glee.

"I'm so sorry," Olwen fretted.

"You needn't be," smiled Marc. "I'll need to become accustomed to such spills."

"Yes...When Maura's baby comes you'll—"

"I wasn't speaking of that time."

Olwen didn't answer his odd response, she only gazed quizzically, a long piercing, slightly hopeful stare, that caused Marc to shift awkwardly and stammer on. "I...I was speaking of a time...I pray in the near future...when we...we might be married."

Morgan lurched; Olwen started from his bite and stuttered, "Ma...married? We...we married?"

"Yes...I'm hoping you'll agree to marrying me. You needn't tell me now."

405

Cynan abruptly rose and stormed to his mother's side. "He's a Norman, Mam. You can't marry him," he stated nastily. "Rhys won't let you."

"Hush, Cynan, you're being rude," she chided, and to Marc asked, "Have you spoken to Prince Rhys about this, Marc?"

"No, but I plan to when he returns from Ireland, which he's due to do any moment."

"He'll say no," Cynan sternly decided.

"I don't think so," retaliated Marc.

"Cynan, please see to the stew and the children. I would talk to Marc, alone."

Cynan ignored her plea, till he met her formidable glare. He shrank off, performed a slight bow, and gathered up the youngsters from Marc's lap.

"I don't know what I've done to make him hate me," worried Marc.

"It doesn't matter...not now. He's bored and lonely for Gruffydd and doesn't like looking after his brothers and sister." Her little finger broke Morgan's hold on her nipple; she covered herself and lay the sleeping child back down in his cradle. Olwen hooked her arm in Marc's and hustled him outside her door. The rain trickled down, but not with the same urgency as before. Her pleas though were spiked with urgency and choler, "Why now, Marc?! Why do you ask me *this*, now? You've rejected my attentions, and now you ask me to wed you. How am I supposed to feel, what am I to think?!"

"I thought you knew exactly how you felt," he stressed back, "and it was me who was horribly confused."

"*She* told you no."

"What?"

"Gael...She told you no."

He gulped along with his guilty nod and was glad he didn't need to detail his upset with Gael.

"And so, you've come to me for comfort and kisses, to hear vows she can't give you."

"And will I get them?"

His request held no ill-will, no disrespect, instead it was spoken with the most sincere innocence and need that she could feel his despair. Olwen stared away for a long searing moment and pondered the amazingly gentle, perplexing man by her side. She didn't care about his heritage, and realized, neither did she care about his motives. He'd been honest, and she did love him, had loved him for months, and would make him a perfect wife, and in time perhaps he would come to love her. *Perhaps* was all she could pray for, and wasn't that more than most were granted? She turned a positive expression, spoiled by a few escaping tears, caused by sadness or glee, Marc couldn't tell. "I will marry you, Marc, as soon as you please," she spouted. "And you are right, I *am* certain of how I feel...I do love you. And I pray someday you'll love me."

Olwen wrapped her arms round his back and rested her head upon his chest. He hugged her as well, a hug firm with gratitude and caring, then letting go, he raised her chin, and tasted her eager lips. He broke their chaste kiss to swear, "I pray I will love you, Olwen, I pray so too."

"I must go to the children. You may return this night...if you wish," she excused, slipping her hands from his and wiping them self-consciously on her skirt.

"And I must go to Maura," he returned, feeling clumsy as well. He'd strode only two steps away, when her grab spun him back round. She threw herself into his arms and kissed him with a vehemence that made him swoon, and grasp hold of her for balance.

"I will make you happy, Marc," she passionately pledged, "believe I will!" As quickly as she'd pounced, she flitted away, leaving him nothing but more bewildered.

*****

Entering Gael's former hut from the stable, Marc intruded on Simon and Maura's intimate moment. "I'm sorry," he sighed, "I'll come back."

"No...Marc," said Maura. "We were only kissing and as much as we kiss, I'm surprised you still feel embarrassed."

"I'm not embarrassed."

"Well you're a much deeper shade of red than you were when I last saw you this morning."

"I'm not embarrassed," he repeated in a bit of a huff, and with each word his tone gathered more ire, "And where have you been? You said you'd be here...I waited for you here and at the llys."

"I went with Simon," she answered carefully, wary of his eruptive mood. "I didn't ask you to wait, you offered, and I'm sorry—"

"We came back here a number of times today and never saw you," intruded Simon with no caution. "Where have *you* been?"

Marc wagged his head, and mumbled flatly, "Around."

But not flat enough to discourage Maura's fretting. "Around where?"

"Why do you need to know?" he almost shouted.

Her concern vanished, and she returned his sharpness, "I don't need to know, not if you're not wanting to tell me!"

"I'm not wanting to tell you!"

"Fine," she snapped back.

"Stop, you two," declared Simon. "Why your anger, Marc?"

"You..." he directed to Maura, "were supposed to stay here."

"What difference does it make where she stayed?" asked Simon.

Marc wanted to rail, *Because, if you'd been here, I would never have gone to the llys!* Instead he awkwardly accused, "You should be where you'll say you'll be. Especially now!"

Simon noticed Maura's color rising, and chest heaving, and tried to intervene with the demand, "What's happened Marc?"

"Why should anything have happened?"

"No specific reason...It's just that you're not normally contrary."

"I'm not being *contrary*," Marc flippantly replied. "On the *con*trary I'm quite pleased with myself. Something has happened, something to celebrate."

"Celebrate..." Maura leerily echoed.

"Yes...As soon as Rhys agrees, I'm to marry Olwen." He looked upon their stunned expressions, and unabashedly asked, "Why are you surprised? Surely you know we care for each other. I asked her, and she agreed."

Maura blatantly burst, "We're shocked because you love Gael!"

"And I was a fool to do so."

"No, not a fool," parried Simon.

"You can't marry Olwen," blurted Maura.

"And why can't I?"

"Because a union with her would be a lie..."

Marc wagged an accusing finger. "You don't know everything, Maura!"

He flew from her haggling to the far side of the room, yet she raged at his heels, "But I do know you'd be lying with her and thinking about Gael and—"

He whirled, almost sparking a collision. "Stop, Maura! You are my sister, not my mother."

"I won't let you make this horrible mistake!"

"You can't stop me!"

"I'll tell Olwen how you truly feel."

"She knows the truth and will marry me anyway."

"Then she's the fool, and I mean to tell her."

Marc flagrantly swept his arm to the door, exasperating, "Go...go tell her...tell the world...I don't care, and neither will she...We *will* be wed, and nothing you do or say will stop us!"

Maura accepted his invitation. She paused and turned in the doorway, loudly affirming, "We'll see how matters change, after I've spoken to—Gael."

"Stop and hear yourselves!" shouted Simon, finally barging into the fray. "You're being ridiculously horrid. Both of you..."

"Not horrid, Simon," clarified Maura. "I'll not have Marc hurt, nor Olwen." Maura charged out the door, slamming the barrier with a force that rattled the hut's entire structure.

Simon sprang at Marc, grabbed at his shoulders, and demanded, "I have a hunch as to why Maura is acting crazed but why you? Why do you attack your sister?!"

"Because she attacked me!" Marc defended limply. "Your saintly wife isn't as sweet and tender as you believe, Brother."

"She loves you and only wants to save you!" rallied Simon.

"Save me from what, from whom?"

"From yourself, and your rashness."

"I'm not the one who acts first and thinks later," Marc cruelly contended. "*That* you're guilty of, not me!"

Simon raised his hands for peace, and strenuously concluded, "And that's why we're so concerned. You've never been rash! Don't fight me, Marc. I know you're grown, Maura has a harder time seeing that. You can love and marry whom you like, and they may or may not be the same person, but please don't punish your sister for your decision. She only loves you."

Marc blanched with remorse and stuttered his shame, "I...I'm sorry. I can't believe I said those things to Maura...Will you go find her, Simon? If she speaks to Gael, she'll fight with her, and only upset herself more."

Simon's tone and posture softened. "I don't know what's happened to you this day, and I'm sorry Marc for your obvious hurt, but it's not Maura's fault."

"Go," Marc stressed, "*please* find her! We'll talk later about Olwen and Gael, now you must find Maura."

"What will *you* do?" Simon asked worriedly.

"I'll fetch Gruffydd and Ella and bring them to the llys. There's something I need to say to Gael."

Simon engulfed Marc in a bracing hug. He experienced an uneasy twinge to the stronger pressure of Marc's return hold, and assured with a pat and a touch of woe, "You'll do fine with Olwen, you'll do fine."

*****

Maura's austere shadow fell over Gael, slumped upon the table, cheek pressed to the back of one hand, the fingers of the other clutching her fourth cup of mead. Without looking up, she slurred, "I was wondering when you'd come."

"Why were you expecting me?" requested Maura, a tad too formally.

"I figured by now you'd been told the torrid tale."

"What tale and why torrid?"

"The tale of a denied woman, who wickedly lured an innocent lad into her lair, and tried her utmost to seduce him, and almost succeeded...but...but..." She buried her remorse in her crossed arms and said no more.

Maura's rising ire sputtered away to her friend's distress. She brushed fingers over Gael's mussed hair and consoled, "I've heard no such tale, and wouldn't believe it if I did hear it."

Gael lifted shamed eyes. "But you've seen Marc?"

"Yes."

"And he's upset?"

"He yelled a bit...at me."

"Why you?"

"Because he's angry at someone else," returned Maura, "someone he doesn't feel he *can* yell at."

"Then his anger was meant for me."

Maura descended onto the bench opposite Gael's and conceded, "It might have been."

Their hands met, and Gael gripped hard. "I hurt him badly, Maura."

Maura's hold assured, "He will recover, but will you?"

"I don't know...I don't know if I want to recover. I seem to have acquired a unique power to make other people's lives totally miserable."

"Yours, no one else's," contradicted Maura.

"I imagine that you've noticed I made a foul choice of a husband."

"You didn't feel you *had* a choice."

"Perhaps I didn't when I made it, but things have change so drastically since that night. Sometimes I think I must be dreaming when Taredd screams at me. He's hit me over the past two weeks, I never told anyone. Gruffydd saw it happen once, and hit him back as hard. I'm frightened for my son, Maura, more than for myself, afraid that he'll turn as hard and violent as his step-father. I wanted more children, I'll never have them now. The last thing in the world I wanted was to hurt Marc. I suppose I had a notion he could somehow save me, take me away from my sordid life. Was it wrong to want to be happy if only for an instant?"

"But you're not happy, neither is he. You're both only more miserable."

"I do love Marc, maybe not as he loves me, but I do love him!" Gael passionately assailed. "You believe me, don't you?"

"Yes, of course, I believe you."

"If only I could have chosen him."

"Would you have?"

"Why do you ask?" Gael probed, askance.

"I wonder, that's all."

"So do I," she faintly confessed, "all the time."

"He's to wed Olwen."

Gael nodded as if she already knew, and her voice lightened as if relieved of a ponderous burden. "It's the right and proper thing for him to do. Olwen is a fine woman, and she'll love him more than anyone could, including me. You needn't fret for him, Maura. He's made the right decision."

Maura firmly contested, "But it's only fair that Olwen knows how he feels for you."

"She does," blurted Gael, "completely, and doesn't care, or if she does, she won't say. She'll have him under any conditions. That's how blindly she loves him."

"Then my anger was for nothing," regretted Maura.

"Not your anger, your caring, and caring is never for nothing."

Maura stiffened, released Gael, and pressed, "I must say I'm sorry...I must..."

Simon entered the llys and, kicking away rubble blocking his path, approached the two solemn souls before him with much caution. Maura saw him coming, lurched forward, and soundly atoned, "I'm sorry I yelled at Marc, Simon, and I must find him and tell him so. Where has he gone?"

"He's gone to fetch Gruffydd and Ella," he answered and, still confused, fretted, "Gael, has Taredd been here?"

"No..." Gael frankly replied. "It was my temper that made the mess." She suddenly comprehended his first statement; a rush of color drove the gray from her cheeks as she leapt up and cried, "Marc's found them!"

"So he implied," said Simon. "He rode off out of town, heading east, but he was too far down the road to hear me yell *why*. He said he'd bring them here. Why did you make this mess, Gael? Are you not well?"

"As well as I could be, considering. Simon and Maura, please stay and wait with me. I have a dire need to tell you both all that happened this day between Marc and me...here."

*****

Astride Fulk, Marc galloped out through the opened gate of the stone boundary, his ire festering, his mind juggling mysteries. On his way to the llys, without Gruffydd and Ella, he'd encountered a few of Taredd's men, drunk and loitering around the courtyard of the llys, their loose tongues bragging to each other. They knew where their lurid leader had gone—to a wedding in Llandovery, that he'd taken Ella with him, and Gruffydd had followed. They gave no other clues, and immediately vanished for fear of retribution for their betrayal. Marc would have asked Simon to ride with him to Llandovery, but his responsibilities lay here in Mynyw. And this was one rescue Marc preferred to accomplish on his own. Returning Ella and Gruffydd, and ridding Gael forever of her nasty mistake of a husband would no doubt please her, and perhaps help mend the gaping, ragged wound that was once their friendship.

*****

She was going lame; Owain felt certain Ceffyl was favoring her right leg over the last tedious and torturous hours of their journey down the coast—a trip that had thus far endured a full night and day. A constant battering of storms had slowed their course and they'd only managed to reach mid-way to Mynyw. He'd have to stop at least for the night, find some camphor, nurse and bind Ceffyl's leg, and force himself to rest so he didn't get them lost. Then, with the Gods' joint blessing, and favorable weather, they'd be able to continue by morn. Dawg whined as Owain dismounted within the walls of a nameless village. "We'll find food," muttered Owain tiredly, "and, if luck's with us, lodgings. We must tend to Ceffyl first. She's most important now." The mutt didn't agree and howled, raising the pitch of his protest to an unbearable whine. "Shush!" groused his master. "Shush, or I'll ride you the rest of the way." Dawg started to Owain's threat and, with eyes widened, crept to a supine position and remained obediently silent.

*****

Henry stood meek and quaking before the towering timbered palisade of Dinefwr Castle, his mind swimming with dread, his palms damp with sweat, throat parched, and belly aching. Too many 'ifs' with no certain answers wreaked havoc with his tenacity. If only he had Simon with him now, he would know exactly what to say, how to phrase it, and what expression he should don to convince the Prince of his unwavering loyalty to his luckless cousin. But Rhys certainly knew of Henry's unfortunate episode with Maura, and perhaps was prepared to exact punishment. He twisted a doubtful expression to John, waiting patiently and looking exhausted by his side. "I don't know

410

if we *should* enter...There's no guarantee that we can help Simon, and the Welsh may not react kindly to our visit."

"You can stay out here in the rain if you wish, my Lord. But I'm too tired, hungry, wet, and cold to care how the Welsh respond." John pounded the door and yelled, "Open for Henry FitzRoy!" He received no answer and yelled and pounded again and again, till finally the gates opened stealthily inward. Two enormous guards sloshed forward, hands on hilts, each sporting a starkly peeved look, most likely from having been wakened at such a late hour and forced out into the rain.

Henry froze to their fractious guises, grabbed hold of John's upper arm, and whispered his frantic decision, "I'm not the FitzRoy...We are messengers sent by Rufus to alert Simon. My name is Walter. You learned some Welsh...Talk to them, pacify them."

Henry shoved John into the sentries' path and took a dry swallow as he listened to his man appease the monsters in ragged Welsh, "Sirs, we are messengers...sent by King William to alert his cousin Simon, Rhys' Norman physician who lives in Mynyw, to...to trouble."

"What sort of trouble?" grunted the larger guard.

"Simon's Uncle Odo, Bishop of Bayeux, and his brother William are in route to Mynyw to capture Simon and his wife and take them back to England."

"Then all you need is a map to Mynyw."

Henry took a broad step toward John; a kick to his calf restarted his butler bumbling, "No...no, Sir. We have no guards, few weapons, it is not safe for us to travel alone through your hostile country. We...we were hoping that your Prince, or maybe one or two of his soldiers, would agree to travel to Mynyw and tell Simon of the approaching danger."

"Tell him what?!"

John's trembling intensified as he burst back, "Tell him his life is in danger! Please Sir...Help us to help Simon and the Lady Maura. *Please*."

Henry stalled his fear long enough to offer a word of praise to his man, inwardly of course. There was no sense in swelling the lad's head.

The guard's sharp nod brought them inside the gates, and they continued submissively at his heels to the stables. Perplexed, John asked, "Shouldn't we go to the llys and speak personally to Prince Rhys?"

"Our Prince is in Mynyw." The man kicked at two sentries snoring by the entrance.

He muttered John's request swiftly to the men, their faces bland and drowsy, and Henry complained to John, "I loathe this language, it's so bestial. What's he saying?"

"Mostly what I said to him," said John. To their alarm, the soldiers mumbled something unintelligible in any language, twisted for comfort and flopped back into the straw. Their snores resumed, and John panicked to the guard, "Will they go?!"

"Yes...But in the morning."

"What did he say?" pressed Henry.

"They might go in the morning."

"Tell him they need to go immediately!"

John attempted to demand, "They need to go now!"

"They won't go now, not for Simon, and neither will I or anyone else here, not unless our Prince tells us to," hollered the guard. "We don't like Simon."

One soldier struggled up and sleepily relayed, "I'll go. The Prince will want Simon to know. You can sleep in the stable with us, or I don't think Prince Rhys will mind if you bed down in the llys. There are no servants to serve you, they've all gone with him. But there's food, pallets, and pelts."

"We're grateful, Sir," submitted John.

"No we're not!" flared Henry.

John yanked Henry across the courtyard and stridently argued, "Yes we are...One soldier will go tomorrow and I'm grateful I still have a head, and get to sleep on a dry pallet, and partake of some nourishment, no matter how disgusting. And you should be as well. Come, you need food and sleep."

Henry shoved John away, stood firm and fumed more as he watched his butler lope toward the long house. He felt himself growing shorter and stared down at his boots disappearing beneath a pond of mud. Swiftly, he reappraised beneath his breath, "I remember the long house as being immensely cozy, and I *am* a bit hungry, and thirsty. They'll go, which is acceptable, I suppose it's acceptable, and surprising that they're willing to go at all."

*****

The sun had barely peeked above the horizon as, from the door of the llys, Maura blearily watched Simon stride back down the lane that led from the village. This was the sixth time he'd made the mucky trek, each one more frantic than the one before. They were sick with worry. The entire night they'd spent fretting, consoling, pacing, and interrogating Taredd's men, Olwen, Sulien, anyone who'd wandered by or spoken to Marc during the day. Simon had repeatedly searched the village, and kept steadfastly returning to the stone wall, waiting there for Marc, Ella, and Gruffydd's return that never came. Beyond weary, Maura would instantly dream at the close of her eyes— odious dreams tangling together the horrors of her childhood with the dread of her present. She fought sleep; a dull constant pain in her belly helped, but it also stole away her hunger and left only nausea. Her child shared her torment and thrashed inside her as she waited upon the step, bent with discomfort and crippling guilt, her hope dwindling. She spied Simon's dour return. He limped from his exhausting effort, his head hanging low and his heart hurting. Maura strangled her skirt and gulped back her tears. She'd strive to be strong and hopeful for him...for the missing ones. She glanced to the bed and saw Gael still sleeping, a drug-like sleep she'd lapsed into directly after telling of her upset with Marc. Soon, they would have the terrible task of waking her and fueling her dread with the news that he'd not returned, nor had her son, nor her sister.

*****

Hooded and hunched atop Fulk, Marc trepidly entered the stone walls of Llandovery. The villagers strolled about as if nothing were amiss; dawn's misty fog and smoke hung in a desolate low cloud choking the air, and an eerie quiet reigned. He'd not encountered the Montgomery's army along the high road, so he felt encouraged that he could put an end to their plans here before they became inevitable. He figured the Normans and Welsh would most likely be conducting the wedding ceremony at the llys. As he spurred Fulk along to the llys, Marc fingered the hilt of his dagger for assurance. Since studying for his priestly orders, he'd been forbidden to raise a weapon in any capacity. This rule had been waived for his practice with Simon, and he hoped Sulien would overlook this weapon's potential success in the rescue of Ella and Gruffydd.

Marc reined Fulk in a clump of trees, out of sight of the llys, yet near enough to distinguish clearly what was occurring directly at its fore. He noted nothing but three snoozing guards—Norman guards—sprawled at the steps' base. Marc dismounted, tethered Fulk to a tree limb, stole round the perimeter wall, and squatted behind a fat tree trunk not ten feet from the door. He started as the door burst open. A maid stepped out and dumped a pail of some brownish liquid off the top step, scarcely missing the guards. His pinched gaze strained to see beyond her figure and into the hall. He beheld no one else up and about and prayed most were still sleeping as he crept in a crouch to the north end of the building. His blood raced with exhilaration, and his heart thudded with a force that wavered his balance. He had to grip tight the wattle ends sticking from

412

the wall's daub, as he flattened himself against the wall and inched his way round to the front. The window shutter gaped enough for him to peek inside, and ever so carefully, he nudged it wider. Directly below the window lay stretched a number of bodies, presumably asleep. His creeping stare moved further along the floor and scaled the legs of a long table. Someone slept on its top surrounded by a mass of upturned tankards. The maid he'd viewed before was cautiously collecting rubbish and didn't notice his spying eye. To the right of the table, he craned his neck to see Taredd, trussed and propped upright, surprisingly asleep. *Gruffydd...Where is Gruffydd?! Ella?!* Marc ducked down and crawled through an opening beneath the stairs to another window. He darted a wary eye back to where Fulk stood and sighed to the hint of gray shifting behind the brown of the branches. Noiselessly, he raised up and peered through the gap in the shutters. No torch illuminated the left side of the trestle table, and as he surreptitiously pried the window open more, he prayed he'd discover the boy in the blackened corner.

Will and Joanna sat at the left end of the trestle table, enjoying the early quiet and an undisturbed cup of claret from a flask Will had packed along. Will settled a distasteful sneer on Arnulf's bulk spread over the table and muttered, "He likely won't wake till noon. And I haven't encountered the Bishop since midnight. Have you?"

"No," drawled Joanna with a yawn. "I've been tending to the boy most of the night."

"How is he?"

"He wakes sporadically, but he's never fully aware," she reported. "He cries out for his mam, then goes senseless again. It's quite sad, actually."

Will didn't care for her tender tone, and firmly contended, "We'll give him back to his mam, when and if we reach Menevia. I despise children, they only make trouble, and this one seems capable of committing atrocities."

Joanna shrewdly switched thoughts. "What will happen when and if we capture Simon and Maura?"

"Odo's planned an itinerary of what he repeatedly refers to as *'the ceremony'*. He hasn't felt obliged to share the details with me as yet, but promised when his show is done, I'll have Maura for myself and Simon will be ready for burial."

"*'The ceremony'*" repeated Joanna with distaste. "A strange phrasing for murder."

"He's a priest," excused Will. "Everything they do reeks of ritual."

"Arnulf wants Maura as well," she warned.

"I know, and that makes me more than a little nervous. Roger told him he could interrogate her as to Marc's whereabouts, yet it seems Arnulf now wants her for his wife. They were once betrothed."

"And what happened to break their betrothal?"

"The bride-to-be happened to be pregnant. I helped Father abort the abomination, but alas too late. Roger discovered her condition and annulled the engagement."

Joanna bluntly pried, "How did you abort the child?"

"An herb called savin. It's a deadly poison, but when dosed in the correct amount can achieve a swift termination without causing too much damage to the mother."

"And what if she's pregnant again?"

"I don't believe she can be, though I have brought some along...in case."

Joanna nodded and shifted with impatience. This mission that had begun so excitedly seemed now to be crumbling to a drunken halt. Discord between those in charge caused most of the hampering. If *she* were in command, Maura would this moment be tucked up beside Hugh in their marriage bed, and there would be plants sprouting atop Simon's grave. She was surprised and slightly irked by Will's nonchalance, but also grateful that he had so graciously allowed her, despite the heated objections of his uncles, to accompany him. Her keen eye caught movement; she tensed and hunted for its origin. Nothing inside moved, so her search swept from the back entrance, over the walls and ceiling, and lastly lit upon the window. Ever so subtly the shutter was opening. She immediately looked away so as not to alert the intruder, and whispered beneath her breath to Will, "Someone's watching us through the far window."

He started to look, but she gasped, "No, don't look up! Pretend you've not noticed a thing. He's opening the window."

Will's fingers strangled the handle of his tankard as he fought to appear oblivious. "What's happened to the guards?"

"Drunk and, I suppose, sleeping. Who could it be?"

"Word spreads rapidly across this bog and Dinefwr is only a short length down the road. Perhaps..." He wet his dry mouth with a gulp, and tremulously surmised, "it...it's one of Rhys' men."

She added her guess, "Then there could be others...waiting."

"Yes, there very well could be others...I'll wake Arnulf, you find Odo."

They rose casually and faked a kiss to mask their true tie. Will stiffly wobbled to Arnulf's side and prodded him sharply, at last managing to extract from him a sputtered, "Go...go away," a swipe from his fist, and a disgorge of spit.

Will leant close to his ear and whispered his alarm, "We've a visitor...a spy...and I reckon there's more come with him...from Dinefwr."

Arnulf flailed and fumbled his way up, whipping his head side to side in a vain attempt to dispel clouds of inebriation and discover the scout. "Where?" he growled. "Where's the scoundrel?"

"Hush!" Will insisted. "Or he will know *we* know he's here. I want you to come with me into the stables. That will give him the opportunity to open the window completely and hopefully risk entering. Now, Uncle Arnulf...hold tight to my arm, and walk with me."

In a stable stall, Joanna disrupted Odo's haranguing abuse of a soldier with her stark announcement, "We're being watched!"

Odo pitched the young man out of the stall, and argued, "Impossible!"

"Not impossible..."

"We've captured everyone who knows our scheme. Even the villagers believe we're peacefully engaging in wedding revelry."

Will arrived and interjected his plan, "We'll let the bastard make himself visible, then strike."

Marc watched Will leave the hall with Arnulf. Taredd's men had mentioned nothing about Will and Odo...and he knew only too well what they wanted. Three barons, and he guessed their three armies, all headed for Mynyw with one despicable goal. The thought made him woozy and he swiftly reassessed his plan to tackle the mission on his own. He recalled the onerous fact that Prince Rhys and his troops were returning from Ireland and not at Dinefwr. He'd have to return to Mynyw to alert Simon, the Prince, and his army. But he'd ride in warning only after finding Gruffydd and Ella. They had to be here! Ella's wedding must be the ruse for the meeting! Now that Will, Arnulf, and the woman were gone he could chance opening the window a tad more. He wedged his toe onto a jutting piece of wattle and hoisted himself higher to see over the table and into the blind corner. Someone squirmed among the rushes, someone small. Marc stretched himself taller, and saw to his relief, Gruffydd, unguarded, horribly bruised, yet alive. Nowhere was Ella to be seen. There was no time for fancy schemes. He'd attempt entering by the front door, keep near the floor, grab the boy, and run. Marc started lowering himself and found his boot stuck in the splintered branch; he kicked at the wall and frantically wriggled for freedom, managing only to slip against the window frame. He grabbed the sill for balance and cursed down at his still captured boot. A warm and rigid grip covered his and held tight. He gasped up into Arnulf's rabid glower and wicked mutter, "My...my...I've caught myself a coward."

Marc wrenched his foot loose and kicked both boots into the wall. His powerful shove freed his hands, but landed him defenseless on his back. He flipped, scrambled up, and raced for the grove of trees and Fulk. At Arnulf's shouted command, soldiers charged out from behind the stables and through the hall. They leapt the trestle table, bounded out the door and down the stairs. Fulk bolted to Marc's sudden weight and galloped for the wall. Marc braced himself for the sheer jump and flew. At the crest of the leap, a jolting thud struck the back of his shoulder and slammed him forward onto Fulk's neck. A searing agony followed and he grabbed hold for his life. Fulk never faltered his graceful gallop, holding his wounded rider aloft, and at the cross-roads turned determinedly south onto the road home.

"Did you hit him?" yelled Will to his soldier nearest the trees.

"I think I did, my Lord, but I can't know for certain."

"When we find his body on the road, we'll know for certain. If he arrives in Menevia before us, then I'll torch your body while you're still alive. Gather the armies. We leave now!"

All scuttled to obey their Lord's bellow and, in little time, the villagers scurried off the path leading to the village gate and froze awestruck to the ominous sight of the earth-shaking armies, astoundingly leaving their domain intact.

*****

Nesta straggled across the courtyard, sore and depressed by her long and uneventful journey home. She tried futilely to neaten her disheveled bud of a braid and straighten her soiled cloak and tunic, but soon surrendered to being unkempt till she could sink into a hot bath. The past week, she'd suffered nothing but travel from the boggy depths of Ireland to Mynyw where, to her chagrin, her father had kept her constantly surrounded by guards. 'So as not to cause mischief,' was his lame excuse. And then she was immediately ridden back to Dinefwr. To her father, she would eternally be a baby, capable of nothing but mischief. She was glad to be rid of him for awhile and was slightly pleased he'd received an injury to his leg in Ireland. His mishap would keep him at Mynyw longer in Simon's care. How she'd love to be in Simon's care...forever.

As she neared the entrance to the llys, one of her serving maids flew out the door, warning, "My Lady...my Lady! There are strangers inside!"

"Pardon?"

"Two men. One lies sleeping in the main hall, and one, my Lady, one has stolen *your* bed!"

"Truly?" Nesta asked, breaking a wry grin.

The maid restrained Nesta from entering. "No, my Lady. I'll find a guard. You'll not enter alone."

Too irked to argue, Nesta slapped her maid's face with a force that plunged her into a nearby puddle and strictly affirmed, "*I* will see to our visitors." Then, sporting an expectant eye and impish smirk, Nesta slipped stealthily into the hall, leaving the door ajar to allow in light. She minced her way to the first snoring figure, crouched, and studied him intently. His black locks hung long and loose across his face, too thin, youngish and pale; his tunic was fashioned in the Norman style, and he appeared vaguely familiar. Nesta didn't rouse him and straightened in preparation for her next mystery. She sucked a steadying breath and peeked round her tapestry. Stretched long upon her bed was an angel. Nesta crept closer and reached out, craving to examine the beauty before her. Her fingers paused an inch from his enticing lips and instead brushed

415

back his neatly trimmed bangs, black as well, that tumbled over his brow. She clearly and admirably recalled her curious gift—the FitzRoy—briefly reflecting on his night spent on the opposite side of her tapestry, filled with drunken bragging, and his clumsy apology to her father at Mynyw. She'd lately heard the rumor that he'd injured Maura, and she didn't mind, though doubted its truth, for Maura was such a vile liar. Her maid chanced a look, and gaped aghast as Nesta shed her mantle, wriggled from her tunic, and slipped out of her shift. Naked, Nesta whirled to her woman, and yelled in a fierce whisper, "Quiet! You'll bring me hot water for bathing, then leave this house, and don't dare return till morning. I alone will entertain the Prince!"

The maid knew better than to protest, and fluttered away, wringing her hands and mumbling frets. Nesta clasped her hands together, glanced reverently upward, and emoted, "I thank you, my Lord, for your gracious gift, and will be forever in your debt!" With that, she sat beside the FitzRoy and scrutinized his every comely feature, desperate to touch, yet holding back for the perfect moment. A disembodied hand hauling a sudsy pail of steaming water, broke through the tapestries. Nesta caught up the handle and, snatching up a soaked linen cloth floating on the surface, began her wash. Every bend, twist, and turn she performed as a sensual dance staged exclusively for the FitzRoy. She imagined him watching her, his eyes swimming with desire, hands tensing and dying to caress, that secret part of him hardening, lengthening. A sadness spoiled her show, as she noticed him snoring. Nesta grabbed up her wooden comb and, huffing a bitter sigh, commenced battling her tangled tresses. At long last satisfied with her lithe and seductive appearance, she tapped the contents of a small vase into her palm, lifted the pelts and scattered a fistful of dried violets over the sheet. She blew the stubborn ones off her palm, and onto Henry, producing from him a sneeze but not much more. She stifled a giggle and, glowing with anticipation, slid tentatively in beside her present.

*****

Stretched out upon a cot in the infirmary of St. Davids Cathedral, Rhys pushed up on his elbows, regarded Simon concernedly, and wondered, "You look wretched, lad. Tell me why?"

Simon briefly glanced up from his study of Rhys' leg wound, tensed a taut grin, then resumed his examination with the sighed explanation, "It's been a very long night."

"What's your diagnosis?"

"Pardon?"

"The cut on my leg...I'd like your opinion."

"Oh, it's festering and needs cleansing and watching. How did you cut yourself again?"

"On a blasted nail when I was boarding the ship in Ireland."

Simon nodded and stood faintly to say, "I need to fetch a few supplies. You stay prone, it's festering."

"You said that." Rhys piqued to Simon's dullness and insisted, "Why was it a very long night?"

Simon rubbed the back of his neck and quavered with concern, "Marc, Gruffydd, Ella, and Taredd have all gone missing."

"Who's gone to find them?"

"No one...as yet. I'll talk to Hywel again today, and try to convince—"

"My men will go find them," Rhys sturdily offered. "Which way?"

"We're not certain, but we suspect the road to Dinefwr."

"Then I'll send them north on the coast road, south on the road to Carew, and off to Dinefwr."

"I thank you, Sir," Simon said with audible relief. "We're mighty worried."

416

"How long have they been gone?"

"Taredd, Ella, and Gruffydd, two nights and a full day. Marc, a full night. He aimed to find Ella and Gruffydd. I'm certain something has happened—" He dropped down hard onto the bed, weighted partly with exhaustion, but mostly with dread.

Rhys hoisted himself up and rested a comforting hand on Simon's shoulder. "You go, lad, you go tell my men what to do."

"They won't listen to me," Simon scoffed with a snort. "They despise me!"

"They'll listen to you, or I'll beat them raw." He noticed Simon wore his ring and softened to suggest, "If at first they refuse, show them the ring."

Simon cocked his head in question, but Rhys urged him up with a bolstering look and a gentle shove. An argument would not be tolerated, so Simon warily accepted his role as commander, and added vacantly, "I'll fetch my herbs first."

Clutching hands and gasping hope, Gael and Olwen both leapt up from a bench as Simon entered the llys. He swiftly eased their suspense with the news, "Rhys is sending men north, south, and to Dinefwr."

Relieved, Olwen plopped back down. Gael stayed standing and anxious. "Have they left?"

"No..." Simon wagged his head to the queer image evoked by his next statement, "I'm to command them."

"You won't leave here?!" panicked Gael.

"No...I won't leave. I'm to direct them where to go."

She half nodded, and prodded, "Now?"

"As soon as I check on Maura and fetch my supplies from your hut."

"She's sleeping at last," Olwen warned, "...but ever so lightly. Her dreams trouble her..."

Simon echoed, "Dreams..." as he sank onto the bed and worriedly watched Maura sleep. She'd thrashed off her blanket; he gently covered her, smoothed her knitted brow, and listened to her fitful mumblings. Though relieved she finally slept, he feared her dreams, feared them as terribly as he fretted for Marc and the children. "Has she eaten?" he asked no one in particular.

"Not a bit," fretted Olwen. She wandered to his side and surmised, "I think the child will come today." He raised a look of dire fear, and she soothed it a little with the vow, "We'll watch over her. You see to Rhys and his men."

A lingering kiss to Maura's brow, a swift one to Olwen's hand, and a squeeze to Gael's shoulder took Simon off and into the courtyard leading to the stables. The bulk of Rhys' men were loosely assembled there, engaged in fights and games, or lolling about doing nothing. They averted their eyes from Simon as he wove his way through their ranks. He stumbled from a push, he reckoned not an accident, straightened taller in defense, and elbowed the remaining way to a flattened stump of tree. On it he stood and, dragging fingers through his mussed locks and over his beard, settled over the ranks an austere look, hinting concern, but no fright. "Sirs..." he resounded in perfect Welsh. "Your Prince's wound will heal only if he stays abed, so he's sent me here to relay his orders." A few guffaws sounded. In response, Simon's piercing glare swiftly produced a respectful silence. The intense quiet unnerved the men; they shifted, shuffled, waited, and soberly attended as Simon related, "Three regiments are needed, one to travel north along the coast, one south to Carew, and one east to Dinefwr."

"Why?!" came a sharp shout.

"Villagers and Taredd are missing and must be found."

"Which villagers?" snidely asked the same soldier.

"Gael's son Gruffydd and her sister Ella. My brother-in-law Marc left last night to find them."

Discordant muttering abounded, and Simon strode to the edge of his circular stage and implored, still in a commanding tone, "If someone knows where or why Ella and Gruffydd were taken, please speak now! No harm will come to you. You will be rewarded for your knowledge!"

All held sincere expressions of ignorance. Simon's sadness and frustration overwhelmed him, deflating his mastery, rendering him light-headed. Yet he mustered enough strength to finish, "Groups of seven to ten soldiers in each regiment should suffice. Stop in every village you encounter, ask who's been seen, who's visited, who's heard rumors, anything that will aid our search."

"Why didn't Marc bring them home?" goaded one rude sentry.

The dampness in his glare blotted Simon's rage and wavered his reply, "Since he's not returned, we fear he's come to some harm."

"Will you lead our battalion, Sir? We'll gladly follow," boldly stated a man at the fore of the throng.

Simon strained a bleak grin, stepped down, and excused with difficulty, "I'm thankful for your trust, Sir, but I must remain here. My wife...my wife will deliver our child very soon. If you have need of me, or discover anything of use, you'll find me either in the cathedral or the llys."

A path quickly parted for his exit, and as he walked between the curious crew, he heard his name spoken with mumbled oaths of certain success, and felt his dolefulness lighten with a twinge of promise. The soldier who'd expressed faith jumped onto the trunk and began barking orders, the others hurried to obey, and Simon headed for Gael's hut to fetch his herbs.

*****

Marc, his breath labored and hurting intense, collapsed off Fulk onto a small mound of frigid moss set within a dense thicket of oaks. He jerked to his knees and stretched backward, grasped the arrow, and yanked fiercely. His tortured cry answered the effort, and his pull broke off the missile inches from its head. He tried again, choking on the pain, but achieved nothing. Deep gulps of air settled Marc's mind enough for him to try to ponder a plan. He could not reach Mynyw before the armies, Fulk couldn't hold his gallop, and he had to rest as well, or he'd not make it back alive to help save his family and Gruffydd. *I will save them*, he swore, as he lay carefully on the spongy ground and pressed his cheek to its coolness. He had to accomplish something worthwhile before he died...

*****

Long excruciating hours passed with no change, and the sky cried more tears and blackened. Gael sat by Maura, muttering vague assurances to her still sleeping figure. Olwen waited at the table for word of her betrothed, her hand slowly rocking Morgan's cradle. Growing feeble-boned and minded, Simon dragged himself between the cathedral, the llys, the north and east stone walls, feeling terribly discouraged and useless. His mounting torment finally drove him to the small chapel attached to the cathedral, where during previous troubled times he had attained a sense of peace and direction. He knelt upon the cold stones, swiped at a tear, clasped his hands together, and uttered a simple but fervent prayer, "*Please* Lord, keep Marc, Gruffydd, and Ella safe. Bring them home to us soon. Don't...don't let Maura, Gael, or Olwen suffer for very much longer, and I beseech you...*please* grant me the strength not to fail them again."

*****

The storm didn't slow the devils' armies. Led by the Bishop and Arnulf, they moved malignantly southward, acquiring more wrath, treachery, and fortitude with each advancing mile. In a frozen stupor, Gruffydd sat astride Will's guard's saddle, imprisoned in the giant's steely grip. He couldn't think, speak, or pray; he could only shake. Taredd rode piteously trussed and bent, his steed squeezed between the barons' guards' horses. His guards followed in a group, trussed as well, with confining ropes tied from horse to horse. They'd found no Marc, and Will smoldered with rage and consternation, certain that Simon had been alerted and lay in wait to slit his throat. Surely, his uncles wouldn't allow such a catastrophe, he hoped, as he slowed his mount near the end of the line and into pace with Joanna's. She noted his paleness and asked, "What is it, Will?" What's gone wrong?"

"We haven't yet found the spy. Arnulf believes he recognized Maura's brother, Marc," he warily complained. "We can only assume he's made it back alive to Menevia."

"He could be rotting in the woods, wolves gnawing on his bones!" she returned forcefully. "You can't get weak-kneed now! We're nearly there. Look before you, my Lord."

He did as ordered, and in the gloaming, he could not see the fore of the troops.

"Menevia employs a battalion of pathetic old men," his steward lectured. "Rhys is visiting Ireland. The elite of his army lounges at Dinefwr, and they don't particularly care for your brother. There will be no fight, no arguments, probably not even a harsh word spoken. The villagers will beg your mercy and, to save their hides and homes, willingly hand over your brother and his wife."

"You're certain of this?" Will asked with quivered speculation.

"Absolutely certain," she staunchly asserted.

"Well, I pray you are correct, as you've always been before, yet...till we reach our destination, I prefer riding here in the back by you."

She simpered to his whine and guided her horse near enough to his for their girths to touch.

*****

Rhys' guard from Dinefwr, who'd been chosen to ride the alarm to Mynyw, had begun his journey late morning and found himself trailing the massive force. He escaped to the woods where his Welsh pony endured the miles and speed far more ably than the destriers on the cleared road. He'd even managed to gallop past their armies, and overtake them by near an hour.

Not far from the soldier's location, Marc woke to a disturbance rumbling from the direction of the road, and supposed it must be Will, Odo, and Arnulf. Miraculously, he found his head and sight clear, and only a mild pain plaguing his shoulder. He stood carefully and, wavering, failed in his first attempt to mount. He succeeded with the second, and urged Fulk further from the road, certain that his safest route home lay within the camouflage of the forest.

*****

Simon and Maura both dreamt of Marc...Simon lay sprawled at the base of the altar. His dream had thrust him back to his twelfth year and Marc's sixth, the boy then pale-haired, skinny, and clumsy; a virtual shadow, with envious eyes and too somber a manner. Flashes of their frolicking joyously played in Simon's mind. They raced along the beaches of Cornwall, battled imaginary foes amidst Saxon ruins near Dunheved, wrestled in mud, slept beneath glittering stars, and talked forever. Simon had reveled in Marc's mimicry and adulation, readily performing the satisfying task of teaching and shaping the youngster in his own image. Yet, strangely, as Marc grew, Simon found himself being molded as well, and learning from his adoptive brother the invaluable virtues of kindness and humility...

A troubling image began to crystallize in Maura's mind and spiked her turmoil. In a great room, Marc, just a babe, toddled behind her, tugging on her skirt and swiping at

419

her straw doll. Something sweet stuck to his hand and now to her tunic as well. Bothered, she brushed him away, and he tumbled to the floor, squalling misery. The oft repeated command, "Help your brother up," came to her, not spoken in French, but in rapid Welsh.

She glanced guiltily up into her mother's dark, reproving gaze, and instantly changed it to loving by picking up the boy, setting him on her lap, and rocking and murmuring, "You'll be fine. I'm sorry, I'm so sorry, do you forgive me?" Marc clung to her and laughed as she presented him his wooden horse. Her mother, golden and statuesque, sweet smelling and ever so soft, squatted with them, and gathered them both in her loving arms.

"May I join you?" The distinct, intimate voice loomed from above. The three lifted endearing eyes to a richly handsome man, tall and winsome, copper-haired and bearded. They stood and clutched at him and, in turn, he embraced them each separately. When Maura's moment came, she buried her head in her father's neck, and began to cry copious tears. Alarmed, he hugged tighter and worried, "What is it my angel, why your tears?"

"I hurt Owain, Tad," she whimpered, "I hurt him."

He set her down and gently cradled her small face in his huge hands. "Sometimes, I know," he soothed, "your brother seems a pest, but, when he's most like that, always remember, he only wants to be just like you—the bravest, wisest, and fairest child your mother and I know and love so very much." Cold metal touched her cheek. Maura removed her father's hand, and as she'd done countless times before, found and fingered his gold ring, carved with intricate circles. She abruptly stopped, and lifted horror-filled eyes to his wary ones. "What is it, my angel? What frightens you?

She crushed herself to his chest and wept more. She'd stay safe and snug in her father's warm hold and never leave, for when she left, he'd be gone...murdered. She felt her mother's arms wrap her shoulders from behind, and answered her sweetness, "Don't let go," Maura languished, "don't ever let me go! He'll kill you, kill us all!"

"Who, who will kill us, my sweet?" her mam implored. "Who?"

"No one..." duly answered her father. "We'll let no one hurt you...or your brother...no one...ever!"

Hell descended as flames raged round Maura's crouched figure huddled in a corner of the same room, Marc's limp body clutched fast in her lap. A hand gripped her ankle, keeping her from escape. Terrified, she glanced down to see her father's hand, his fingers long, graceful, unmistakable; and his ring, the entwined circles glittering from the advancing pyre. And she finally knew he hadn't held her from escape, he'd kept her from certain death. His beautiful eyes, now glazed and lifeless, stared nowhere. She frantically searched and found her mam tangled in combat with her father's assassin. Her mother jerked to Maura's warning cry. In that terrible instant a flash of silver cut her down. Her head rolled to Maura's feet, golden hair melting to char, mouth still twitching from the swiftness of death. Paralyzed, Maura could only grip Marc tighter and scream, but her screams were heard by no one. Everyone who could help, who would help, was dead. The man lorded above, face veiled with smoke, eyes limpid pools of pale blue. She screamed a last time and dropped over Marc as his reddened sword plummeted...

Maura's eyes half opened to the saving sight of the blazing hearth, and she partly heard ragged, intense voices surrounding her, loudening, then fading. She fought to sweep her mind of any remnants of her nightmare and listened.

Loud boot steps preceded an urgent shout, "Where's Prince Rhys?"

Was it Gael? No, someone else answered, "In the cathedral, injured."

More male voices clamored in, one asking loudly, "Have his regiments returned?"

The first voice answered, "I know nothing of regiments...I've come from Dinefwr with news from a Norman messenger. And I've seen his warning myself! A Norman army at least two hundred strong is but an hour away on the east road! They're wanting the doctor and his wife! They've already caught Taredd! I must alert Prince Rhys. We've no defense, not against the Bishop!" His footfalls faded. Maura tried to sit, but her heavy head dropped her back upon the pillow. She wasn't certain what she thought she'd heard, only that someone was coming here...*A bishop...What bishop?*"

"They must be hidden..." stated a female voice, not Gael's...Olwen's? "They're to go to Owain's."

A new voice insisted, "There's no time. We'll take the Lady to the cathedral, her husband we'll take north by boat."

Maura was sure it was Hywel who argued, "No boat can stay afloat in this storm, and the coast road's been washed away."

"Then take him by the south coast."

"They'll force him off the cliff," retorted Hywel.

A most calming voice intruded, "Then he'll ride south to Carew. Rhys has kin there. They will agree to hide him. If the Bishop finds them here, he'll slaughter us all!"

"He'll likely slaughter us anyway," humphed Hywel.

"There's no time for arguing! Fetch the Lady to the cathedral. We'll see to her husband."

Gentle, caring fingers patted Maura's cheek, waking her more fully. "Maura," called Olwen, as tranquilly as the situation allowed. "Maura...Hywel and these soldiers will take you to the cathedral. There's little time. For your safety and your child's, you must go to the cathedral."

"What...what soldiers? Where's Hywel? Where's Gael?" stuttered Maura, wagging her head in her hands, trying futilely to banish the true nightmare she awakened to.

"Rhys' soldiers. Hywel's here...Gael's watching my other children with Angharad. The men will take you to the cathedral. There you will be safe."

Maura's voice rang clear and frantic, "Safe from what, from whom?!"

"An army advancing...A Norman army, the messenger claims comes for you and Simon."

"Henry..." Maura hissed in a heated whisper. "Henry's come." The room's commotion crept in her direction, and she cried out, "Where is Simon?!"

"I don't know," said Olwen, stepping away for the men's advance.

"Simon!" Maura squalled to their severe expressions. "I won't go anywhere without Simon. Where's he gone? I must find him!"

They seemed not to hear her; she recoiled from their rigid reaches, clambered to the opposite side of the bed, and inched along the wall, her eyes stark with terror.

"Come, my Lady," the confident one assured, "we'll help you. It's but a short walk to the cathedral."

"No!" she groaned and lurched past them. "Not without Simon!"

"He's being hidden elsewhere, my Lady." His arm caught hers, and gently restrained her attempt to jerk away.

Hywel strode closer, grunting, "It's for the best."

"No!" she wailed back, then quick and panicked, gritted, "He swore! You won't take him from me! I'll go to him, now. You'll take me to him, now!"

Hywel's inescapable grip came at her; she spun, twisting the soldiers' arm so he had no option but to let her go, batted away Hywel's lunging arm, and raced furiously out the door.

*****

"Simon...Simon, wake up...Wake up!"

421

Simon woke abruptly to the urgent shake and summons delivered by a shadowed face haloed by a torch on the facing wall. "Marc!" he cried, surging up.

Only it wasn't Marc, it was Sulien's pinched face that greeted him, stuttering dread, "It...It's time to go, Simon."

Simon swept a fuddled gaze round his surroundings, and rose unsteadily, atoning, "I'm sorry I fell asleep here, your Grace. I'll go, I'll go."

"No..." Sulien's rigid grip betrayed apprehension and much danger. "It's time for you to leave Mynyw. The Bishop of Bayeux and his army are only an hour away on the east road. We're to ride you south to Carew. Come, there's no time to waste."

Shock constricted Simon's reply. He staggered forward to obey, coughing to regain his voice and stability, while inwardly wrestling his panic—*It couldn't be true, he couldn't be coming here, how could he know...Henry told him...Henry's with him, come to watch his murder and take Maura for himself!* He didn't know where the saneness came from, but he stopped, cradled his brow in his palm, and said with eerie calm, "We are to go to Owain's."

Sulien grabbed at Simon's elbow and steered him for the door, muttering, "There's no time to go to Owain's."

"Then I'll fetch Maura."

"It's best if you leave her here, Simon. She will be well seen to and—"

Simon's tenacity finally flared, "No! She'll ride with me, or we both stay. I'll fetch Maura."

"I don't know where they've taken her."

"Taken her!" raved Simon, seizing the Bishop's robe and yanking him near. "Who's taken her?!"

"Rhys' soldiers."

Dark suspicion clouded Simon's eye; his grip twisted as he forced, "You know where they've taken her, and you'll tell me!"

Sulien easily loosened Simon's fingers and sulked with remorse, "They are taking her to the cathedral." Simon dashed away and Sulien suffered a sudden debilitating pang of woe, wondering if he'd ever see his dear friends alive again.

Simon screamed, "Maura!" into the black and wet and wretched night. Villagers ran haphazardly from their huts and along the lane in their haste to seek shelter within the cathedral walls. Simon frenziedly followed, near hysterical, repeatedly crying out her name, till his throat could cry no more. So near to the church, he slipped in a puddle and slid to his knees. Too many people blocked his way, hindered his rising! There was no time to find her, to escape, to save these good people from Odo's savagery! He howled again, not her name, but in frustration and misery, and had all but given up hope when...

A hand firmly enveloped his and he found himself miraculously rising and sinking into Maura's smothering clutch. Her indomitable strength entered him and as they held each other's faces in their hands, the resolution seemed so simple. "We'll go now," said Simon.

She pressed her cheek to his palm and faintly added, "Rhys has offered us his pony and his sword." Reluctant to let go, their fingers lingered lovingly over cheeks, lips, then knitted and clamped tightly together as they swept away to the steps of the cathedral.

Gael hustled Olwen's older children from Angharad's hut. Someone sped by and almost trampled Nia; Gael cursed his back and Ahgharad looked past his racing figure and beheld there—chaos. Torches blazed, alighting the road between llys and cathedral; people scurried about like startled rodents; and an armored soldier bore down upon the two women, shouting, "To the cathedral with you. An army is advancing. Get yourselves to the cathedral!"

Gael, clutching Maredudd in her arms, scuttled to the sanctuary, glancing worriedly back to see Angharad close behind, hauling Nia and dragging Cynan. They reached the steps where a dense crowd of soldiers was amassing. Angharad took charge of the children's safety while Gael's fitful gaze darted about seeking her son, Marc, Simon, and Maura. She spotted Rhys hobbling back and forth across the landing, gesturing and booming orders. Shoving and cursing, she forged her way to his side, wailing over the deafening din, "What's happening, Rhys?!"

"We're preparing for war. You'd best get yourself inside."

"War with whom?"

"The Bishop of Bayeux."

"Why here? Why is he coming here?!"

"He comes for Simon."

All her blood drained away, buckling her knees, making her swoon. Rhys easily caught her slump and propped her in his hold while continuing to bellow commands. Somehow, through the uproar, she heard and strengthened to a critical cry. She stood on her own and fervidly searched, responding with intensity, "Simon! Maura!" Suddenly they were before her, mounted on Rhys' pony, and reaching out desperate hands. She sobbed and tripped to their side, clawing at the saddle to join them, weeping, "Don't leave me...*Please*, don't go! Don't leave me alone!"

Maura touched Gael's wet cheek, a slight hint of hope glinting the tears in her red, swollen eyes. Simon squeezed and kissed Gael's hand, deepening her sobs as he choked on his promise, "We...we love you and we *will* return. Always believe we will return. Tell Owain the same."

Their hands ripped apart to the shouted order, "Come!" The pony bounded forward to meet the escort troop, and Gael stumbled after. The surrounding tumult knocked her to the mud and there she stayed, too sad to cry more, too desolate to rise, too bitter to pray. Soldiers and villagers raged everywhere around, yet in her grieving soul she was horribly and utterly alone.

*****

CHAPTER TWENTY-THREE — MELEE

𝔄 thick deluge of sleet and rain poured from Heaven hiding Simon and Maura as she coaxed from Rhys' pony a terrifying, treacherous speed. Simon clutched his wife and the pony in a wrenching grip, astounded they still remained upright. Their escorts strove valiantly to match their breakneck pace yet began lagging far behind. One scout, sent ahead, approached and slowed their escape with a dire shout, "The armies are too close. They've blocked the entrance to the south road!"

Two of the escort troop trotted alongside, one yelling to Maura, "Don't stop! We'll distract them. Head through the forest and meet the road further down."

Maura never questioned his advice and sharply veered their mount off the road, kicking him directly toward a vertical wall of monstrous trees. Simon could only gasp, strengthen his hold, and pray as they flew between a dizzying blur of brown posts; branches lunged out, yanked at their mantles, stabbed and scraped their faces. He could feel Maura's heartbeat, his own, and he was certain their child's as well, thudding to burst, but Maura stayed rigidly focused, never betraying fear or indecision, never wavering in her mission to ride her family to safety.

Odo paused his troops at the entrance to the south road and blared to his lead knights, "We'll split our ranks here. I want twenty men to accompany me south. We'll stop at the first intact building and prepare for the melee. Fifty will advance on the village, find our prisoners, make the exchange, and then join us. Keep the boy. I want him for my own. If my nephew has managed to escape, threaten their Chieftain's life till the villagers confess Simon's whereabouts. Don't hesitate to behead Taredd and his guards, or raze the village," Odo gnashed. "I'll have my nephew and no one will deter me from my mission—no one! The remaining troops hold the road here. Arnulf!" he called.

His fellow baron sauntered forward and snarled, "I won't be ordered by you, Odo, nor will my men."

Odo simpered a placating grin. "I was only going to request that your men patrol the north forest and road."

"I want to attack the village and take Maura for my own."

"That matter you need to discuss with Will. *Will* your men watch the forest and the road?"

"I suppose," submitted Arnulf. "What's the melee?"

"Once the preparations are concluded, I will allow you the honor of viewing, perhaps even participating in, my long-awaited and overdue ceremony."

Arnulf's furrowed brow revealed distrust and hate as he jerked his mount around and grunted instructions to his men. They trailed him in a canter off the road and into the north woods.

A loud, grating, and demented howling rumbled from the direction of the village. Odo and his men tensed and brandished their weapons, yet as soon as the howler's faint outlines appeared in the thick downpour, they noiselessly darted away. Horses' manes bristled, and feet danced; soldiers ruffled and jerked their wide eyes every which way, wondering who or what would strike and from where. The berserk cries rallied again, nearer, more deafening, seemingly emitted by ghosts. Odo blanched, his resolve quavered, "The heathens have set demons upon us. We'll wait no longer. Fetch Taredd and approach the village. Will," he hollered toward the rear of the horde. "Hold this line! And I'll warn only once, if you fail me, you'll share your brother's fate. Is that clear?"

"I won't fail," Will shouted back with a gob of spit.

With the next yowling assault from nowhere, Joanna felt the hairs on the back of her neck prick straight up. "Who is it, Will?!" she called. "What is it!?"

"I...I don't know, and I'm not keen on finding out," he bleated. "Stay close by me...We'll command this line together."

With pride, Joanna realized she had come to represent the strength Will could never fully muster in himself. With a loving caress, she stroked the dagger stuck in her belt, and excitedly spurred her stallion alongside her Lord's.

*****

Rhys dragged and tugged Gael through sucking puddles down the road to the llys. She limply resisted his pull, and promptly tripped to her knees on the bottom step. With one grunted and mighty haul, Rhys yanked her off the wood up the remaining four stairs and thrust her inside the structure. He rummaged a stick madly through the glowing coals, stirring from them much smoke, and finally a few new flames. A blazing rush extracted from the hearth lit the oil lamp upon the trestle table, and when Rhys finally turned to face her, his breath hissed vaporous clouds and his fearsome countenance sent a tremor through her as he roared, "Do you know where your husband is at this very moment?!"

"No!" she wailed into her hands.

He stomped near and grabbed her shoulders; she hung in his hold, and jerked her eyes from his tirade, "I picked you to wed the new Pennaeth for a reason...I knew your strength, your ability to keep the villagers safe and content! I'd hoped you'd do the same for your husband. You'll tell me, Gael...Why is your husband being held hostage by the largest Norman contingent ever to encroach this far into Welsh territory? Tell me!" He shook her once and demanded more, "And where is your son and sister?"

"I don't know," she languished, gushing tears. "My God, I don't know!"

Rhys roughly released her, and she sank once again to her knees. He flailed about aimlessly, knowing he had to leave, wanting to stay angry, wanting to punish her for not knowing, but looking on her piteous state, he found his heart and rage melting. "Get up!" he ordered, his expression a mess of disgust and sympathy. She ignored him, so he hiked his request, "I said get up!" Gael complied shakily and swiped at her cheeks with her sleeve. She couldn't bring herself to meet his glower, hugged her waist, and nodded meekly to his decree, "Till I can find someone more suitable, you will remain in the llys as the village's leader through the whole of this crisis. Do you understand what that means, Gael?"

"I believe so, my Prince."

"You will command the force I leave behind, you will ensure the safety of the villagers, and you will take up arms if need be for the survival of our people."

"I will do all that you ask and more, my Prince."

"Then I will take my leave and attempt to rescue your lout of a husband, your sister, your son, and your friends with, I pray, little bloodshed." She didn't comment, nor did she move. He knew she'd watched Simon and Maura ride away to certain disaster and could only imagine the terror and despair that gnawed at her gut. His bolstering grip squeezed her shoulders, and his fervid embrace gathered her close. Slowly, she unlocked her arms from her belly and returned his hug as fiercely. He kissed her brow, pried her hands from his arms, and grudgingly left her with a mumbled, "I had total faith in you, my Lady. Show me that it wasn't for naught."

Again, she found herself alone in this hall that before had exuded peace and laughter and happiness; now it knew only pain and sadness. Somehow, she would find the strength to defend her people and her friends, to find her family and, when the opportunity presented itself—murder her husband.

On the south road, Odo's troops spied the pony barreling out of the woods. Maura spotted them as well and yanked the horse into a perilous turn, trying to return to the trees. The pony balked in protest, then readily responded to Maura's altered command; he leapt the ditch between woods and lane, and bounded away down the road, the soldiers in swift and close pursuit. Simon chanced a look back, and noticed they kept their lead, though tremulously. He could feel the pony's hold on the ground wavering, weakening. When would they stop, could they ever stop?! And if they fell...He couldn't bring himself even to imagine such a catastrophe! They wouldn't die this way, not broken and trampled, not when there was the slightest chance of surviving a duel with his uncle. He covered Maura's rigid grip with his own. She felt him tug backward and at first wrestled his madness. But his wise whisper, "We'll stop, my love, we'll stop. There's nowhere left to run...nowhere. We'll stop and see what the Bishop wants," caused her to surrender to the virtue of his decision and gently ease the reins back. The pony slowed to a trot, then he heaved and snorted as she urged him round boldly to confront the entourage's approach. The storm had ceased, and a shimmering moonlight gleamed the road and its travelers within a silver aura. Maura and Simon clenched hands, glanced at one another for strength, and then shifted bold looks toward their nemesis.

"I'm disappointed, mongrel," sniped Odo, sauntering up close on his stallion. "You've surrendered far too quickly and ruined our fun. We still have quite a bit of road to race. I'd have thought you'd at least give us the pleasure of a mile or so more."

"We won't die beneath your boots...Uncle," Simon returned as snidely. "We'll know your plans for us."

"Plans..." Odo sighed toward Heaven. "Yes, I've spent years concocting my many plans for *you*. First I thought we'd—"

Hoof beats travelling from the south intruded, and all jerked their heads to see a smaller contingent of Norman knights reining in their steeds. Their leader, hooded in chain mail, approached Odo, cast a startled eye at Simon and Maura, and reported to his Lord, "We've found a deserted, good-sized stable a mile down the road and a ways into the wood."

"Is there sufficient room for our ceremony?" asked Odo.

"More than sufficient, my Lord. My men are preparing the structure for the melee."

"Fine, we'll follow you." He shifted in his saddle and ordered backward, "Two of you return to the crossroads, fetch Lord William's and Lord Arnulf's armies."

"What do we do with the hostages, my Lord?"

"Release Taredd and his men. Arnulf will have use for them in the future. Keep the boy."

"And the village?"

"Harass them so our memory stays emblazoned on their minds." He snickered inwardly to his word play and attended back to his prisoners. "So...Mongrel, you and your whore will accompany us to the stables where we will have a little chat."

Having listened carefully to the Bishop's decrees, Simon swept a furtive glance over the hooded command and returned with force, "I'll see Will now!"

"He's up the road and—"

"You bring us Henry, the boy, and the young woman!"

"Henry?" piqued Odo. "Henry who?"

"Henry FitzRoy."

"I wouldn't allow that scrawny, incompetent toad to follow me to the garderobe. Thank the Lord, he's nowhere near."

"I don't believe you," returned Simon.

"Believe what you like."

"Where's the boy and the woman and Marc?"

"The boy is with Will, the woman left with her husband yesterday...Marc...Will's man thinks he hit him with an arrow. We don't know where he's gone."

Simon and Maura froze in panic, yet there was no time to ask more or worry about Marc and Ella. Simon worried, "The boy, is he hurt?"

"Not as severely as the knight he mangled."

"You have us, so let him go."

"Oh, he's dear to you," sneered Odo, "...how touching." He waggled a finger and roughened his tone, "He stays our prisoner, and you'll address me with respect, you mangy rodent! I'll not bargain with you...*I* rule here and aim to play a game with you. Will wants your woman."

"For what purpose?"

"To punish her, I believe for some former wrongdoing. Then he's to grant her to someone...I forget precisely whom."

"Henry..."

"It is conceivable...No more questions, no more delays. We'll go to the stable."

"Your prisoner is armed, my Lord," mentioned a nearby sentry.

"As he needs to be for our ceremony...And though lowly scum, he's not stupid enough to risk striking me down. Isn't that correct, Nephew?"

"As you, Uncle, are not stupid enough to murder us, for despite your intimate ties to the Devil, even *you* wouldn't risk eternal Hellfire."

"God damn you, you impudent runt!" flared Odo, his sword inches from Simon's mouth. He trembled and hissed with barely controlled fury, "Keep your vile tongue still, or I'll slice it out!"

Simon didn't flinch; Maura reached back to stroke and ease his solid grip on the hilt of Rhys' sword, and both started as their pony jaunted forward to catch the small troop guiding the way to the stable.

*****

Outside the stone wall, Rhys gathered and roused his troops, bolstering, "They outnumber us so don't fight them. Use your mischief instead to deafen and separate them. Grab Taredd, his men, Gruffydd, Ella, and Marc, then scatter and get yourselves away to the forest." Rhys noticed a number of competent women had joined his force. He smirked with renewed confidence, knowing their valuable presence would further confuse the enemy. He briefly recalled the old adage—Welsh men by themselves were easily vanquished, but with their women battling by their sides, they became invincible. "Listen for our whistle," he finished, "then and only then may you safely return." His long, stark rallying howl prodded the small ferocious troop on its way.

Gruffydd perked up his ears and, beyond the clamoring of his heart, heard the war cries. He shook away the clouds that frequently plagued his sight, straightened in the clutch of his keeper, and chanced a tentative look around. Silver-clad and hooded soldiers crowded the road as far as he could see. He knew the village lay just around the bend, yet had no clue what the armies planned once they arrived there. The harshness of their speech, to each other and to Taredd, told him what they aimed to do wouldn't be kind, but he'd keep praying and praying some more that they'd give him back to his mam. She must be awfully worried by now, and maybe he shouldn't have gone to rescue his aunt on his own. Since he'd shot the arrows, he'd not seen Ella, and what was most confusing of all was that the fellow she held hands with seemed to make her very happy. He heard Rhys' unmistakable war cry again, and his chest swelled with pride and promise. His Prince was coming, and would surely take him back home, back to his mam, his beasts, and his friends!

A messenger from Odo's contingent barged into the congested swarm, and cried, "Lord William! Lord William!"

"Over here!" Will called from behind his helm.

The knight urged his mount to Will's side and breathlessly relayed, "The Bishop wants you and the remaining armies south. They've caught your brother and his woman. There's no need for bargaining."

"But a troop is this moment entering the village with the Chieftain!" Will railed in exasperation. "They'll be slaughtered! We've heard the Welsh war cries! Run, catch up to them before they're murdered! Hurry!"

Joanna trotted up, pressing, "What now, Will?"

"None of this ridiculous posturing was needed," he replied with disgust. "Odo has Simon and Maura. Get the boy. We're going south to see what further nonsense the Bishop intends." He shouted to the surrounding troops, "Follow me! You," he pointed to Gruffydd's guardian, "hand the boy over to my steward and go find Arnulf and his men. Lead them down the south road. We'll intercept you there." Gruffydd was passed between the mounts; his struggling moans were instantly quelled by a sound strike to his jaw. Joanna shifted his limp body in her grasp and excitedly spurred her horse after Will's.

Ahead of the soldiers advancing on the village, the baleful noise of thundering hooves rocked the earth. Beastly yowling pained their ears and faltered their hearts. Behind them came the critical call, "Stop! Stop! Let the Chieftain go and follow me...The doctor and his lady are caught!" The messenger squalled once more to the befuddled group, "Let Taredd and his men go! Listen! There are thousands of them and they'll kill you all! Release him and follow me!"

The troop's leader briefly considered the approaching cacophony, and promptly and loudly decided, "Drive the Chieftain into the Welsh army! Retreat...Retreat!" His men slapped Taredd's pony forward into a full gallop and raced to catch their leader.

At the fore of his meager, yet strikingly riotous battalion, Rhys beheld the bewildering sight of a small troop charging in their direction. The moon's radiance betrayed their lack of armor; they brandished no weapons, made no sound. As they bounded nearer he noticed connecting ropes stretched between their saddles and calmed his force with raised arms and the order, "Slow yourselves! These attackers aren't Normans...I'm not certain who..." He peered intently through the silvery mist, mumbling his confusion, "But whoever, they're insane to take us on...By the God's!" he bellowed in disbelief. "It's Taredd and his men, alone and still roped! Come," Rhys muttered to the soldiers at his sides. "Let's go fetch the fools," and he added in hindsight, "carefully, and leave them trussed. We'll take them to the llys for questioning. Three of you ride on a few miles and discover what's become of our enemy."

*****

They were retreating...*Why are they suddenly retreating?* wondered Owain as he squatted behind a thick thatch of scrub oak, his hand resting on the snout of his kneeling horse, keeping her silent, and his mutt peeking with him and sharing his incredulous expression. He'd hidden for hours, certain the Normans would soon discover his ragged barrow and promptly murder him, steal his horse, and torture his dog. The simple answer suddenly crystallized—they'd gotten what they wanted and were leaving. A vague pain erupted deep inside him, and he knew someone dear to him experienced the same hurt, though much more intensely. He had to get back to the llys and discover the results of the treacherous portent he'd dreamt so often, yet clearly couldn't reach in time to prevent.

Not far away Marc hid as well and deduced a similar conclusion—Simon and Maura were captured, but they couldn't have been taken far. He'd follow Arnulf's men, find and disrupt the Bishop's plans, and in the ensuing chaos, rescue his family and Gruffydd. He still had strength, and his thoughts and sight remained astutely clear. Once they were all safely back in Mynyw, he'd take time to rest and heal...once they were back.

Owain and Marc simultaneously embarked on their missions, Owain approaching the village from the northeast, and Marc following the straggling troops south from a hidden distance inside the forest. Rhys' scouts also trailed Arnulf's men from off the road, directly across from Marc. None of them noticed the others.

Ceffyl kept her frantic gait directly up to the barred gate; she easily soared over the barrier and carried Owain at racing speed along the deserted lane till the queer sight of Rhys' soldiers circling a trussed Taredd came into view. Owain jerked her to a sliding halt as the most gruesome vision thus far shuddered his frame—Taredd had murdered Gael, maybe Gruffydd, and also Ella! He forsook his fellow sentries and raced instead for the llys. Nearing the house, Owain flew off his mare before she could fully stop, splashed through puddles and leapt the fence, slipped and stumbled up the stairs. Gael, daunted by the advancing commotion, grabbed up a long sword she'd pulled from the storage space beneath the floor, and wielded its cumbersome weight as best she knew how, convinced it was her time to die. Owain burst inside, wailing her name...But she saw only a horribly deranged beast, drenched and mud-covered, intent on slaughter. She squeezed shut her eyes, howled as loudly as he, and mightily swung her weapon. Luckily for Owain, the muted glow of an oil lamp lit her brazen effort; he sprang away, eluding the sword's tip by a hair. The force of her swing swung her as well. She spun and dropped heavily with her weapon to the floor, and there she coiled her body and shielded her head from the lethal assault sure to come.

Owain stayed flattened to the door, dazed and heaving shock, relieved to find her alive, yet abashed by her attack. He dragged his hands over his face, hoping to wipe away the bafflement he suffered, and discovered mud from his face smearing his palms. *She doesn't know,* he almost laughed, *she doesn't know it's me!* He lurched toward her, stuttering to keep from shouting and scaring her more, "Ga...Gael! It's Owain...Gael, you've nothing to fear, it's Owain!"

His greeting instantly switched her fright to fury. She unfolded her cramped body and menacingly rose, trembling now from only temper. Her eyes spit fire and her hiss sparked shivers along his skin, "Where in the bleeding hell have you been?"

"You know where I've been," he countered cautiously, noticing she still clenched the sword. "Up north visiting kin. What's happened? What's Taredd done? Why is Rhys holding him prisoner?"

Owain's odd barrage of questions muffled her ferocity; Gael let the sword fall, and besieged, "Where?! Where is Rhys, where is Taredd? Is *Gruffydd* with them...Ella?!"

The answers came quickly as the door burst wide. Sentries stomped in, followed by a stumbling Taredd, his guards, and finally Rhys, blaring ire and orders, "Rope him to a chair...I'll get my answers if I have to peel the skin off his stinking hide!" Rhys whipped his head round, searching and squalling, "Gael...Gael, where are you? Gael!" He spotted her in a darkened corner and his eyes bulged disbelief as they crept up the scraggly figure at her side. "By the God's..." Rhys whispered in awe, "what swamp have you crawled out from?"

"I've come from up north," blurted Owain.

"When did you get here?"

"Just now."

"Do you know what's happened?"

"No."

"Well, you'll soon find out."

Gael didn't hear their banter. All she heard were curses screeching in her mind, and all she saw was her husband, head hung low in humiliation, trussed and defenseless. The glint sticking from Owain's belt beckoned to her fingers and surged her gall; she snatched his dagger and had already reached her husband before Owain noticed the weapon gone. He shoved Rhys aside and flew after Gael, catching her up by the waist as the blade plummeted. Taredd's piercing scream ripped through the llys, and his wild gyrations toppled his chair backward. Owain fought passionately to restrain Gael, yowling with her as she thrashed against him, pummeled and kicked, and flourished the knife with deft precision. She nicked his hand. As if he'd received a mortal blow, he thrust her away; she whirled, lunged back, and beat savagely his face, chest, and shoulders. He stood sturdy as a statue, never flinching, never retaliating, accepting her blows as punishment and exhausting her rage till it crumpled her to the floor at his feet. She lay there quivering, panting, and flaccid, her eyes engorged with madness. Owain crouched, effortlessly lifted and carried her to the bed, gently set her there, and bundled her against the chill of the room and its occupants. His mud-stained fingers brushed back an escaped lock of hair that blocked her sight of her husband. Then he strode purposefully to where his dagger lay and retrieved it. One broad vicious step took him to Taredd's now upright chair, and the strike of the back of his hand forced from Taredd another scream and the plea, "Don't kill me Owain...*Please*, Rhys get him away! He'll kill me quick as she would. Please get him away!"

Rhys didn't move to save the pathetic Pennaeth. He stood nearby, arms crossed and expression grimly smug. Owain slapped again, harder, and Taredd shook with sobs which tightened to panicked groans as he beheld the dagger inching perilously toward his neck. He felt its prick, squeezed shut his eyes, and froze.

Owain knelt on one knee and pressed threateningly forward till the tip of his nose met Taredd's. The trembling in Owain's voice infected his hand and Taredd gasped to a stinging sensation of wetness trickling down his neck. "If I talk too long," cautioned Owain, "I'll get too mad, and when I get too mad, I shake a lot...So you'll tell us all very quickly what harm you've done. Rhys," he called with brittle control, "come close and ask what you need to know." Owain briefly glanced Gael's way, and noticed with satisfaction that she remained alert enough to witness the interrogation.

"How," roared Rhys, "did you end up the Normans' prisoner?!"

Taredd considered lying, but he knew Gael would dispute any untruth he spouted, so he strained instead, "I...I arranged a marriage between Ella and her lover, a squire in the Montgomery's household...I didn't know they planned to use me to get the doctor. I truly didn't know!"

Owain's hand jerked to the sudden sense of Simon's absence and turmoil. Taredd moaned at the resultant pain, and Rhys warned, "Still, Owain, keep still. I must know all that has happened. Where's Ella now?!" he railed to Taredd.

Taredd almost chuckled, but stopped knowing it could kill him, and answered in a slightly deranged way, "She's run off, happy with her love."

"And Gruffydd..."

Gael rose stiffly up on one arm, and leant forward on the other, awaiting the worst.

And it came with his rending statement, "The Normans aim to keep him for their own. It's his own fault, everything's his fault, he shot arrows at them, made them mad...It's *he* that should be punished, not me...not me!"

Gael strangled the bedclothes and wailed her grief to the heavens. Owain shared her anguish and as Taredd's features blurred before his glistening eyes, he considered jabbing deeper.

Rhys' glare of caution stopped him, and Rhys queried on, "Where have all the Normans gone?"

"South...They've caught Simon and Maura. The Bishop wasn't clear what he plans to do with them."

"Where's Marc?"

Owain reeled from the name's potent impact...They were all gone, gone, and maybe dead! He glanced back to Gael, craving some sanity, some hope, yet she lay slumped and seemingly unconscious.

"I didn't know he was missing," Taredd answered aloofly. "The Normans shot someone who disrupted their meeting at Llandovery. It could have been Marc."

Owain begged, "Rhys please take my knife before I kill him."

Rhys carefully obliged and directed his soldiers to imprison Taredd and his men. Owain pulled himself up onto a bench, and cradled his heavy head, wrestling misery and shame, and striving to make some sense of this tragedy. Rhys' command intruded on his suffering, "Owain, you'll stay here as Pennaeth. I have to discover what damage the Normans left in their wake. The villagers will remain in the cathedral till I'm certain the danger is truly done. Taredd will be locked in the stables till my return. Amazingly, no one has yet died from his foolishness, so don't execute him while I'm gone. If his death is warranted, I'll allow you the honor later in my presence...And keep her locked in here, or she'll gladly carry out the deed for us. Look after her, she's not well, understandably."

"But what of Gruffydd, Maura, Simon, and Marc?" Owain croaked. "You can't just desert them!"

"And what do you suggest I do to rescue them from an army three times the size of mine?"

"There has to be something..."

"Maybe there is...I'll send men down the south road to see what's taking place there, then we'll act, if we're able, to get them back."

Owain's limp nod sent Rhys, his men, and Taredd away. He dragged his pained and weary sight from the open door and across the floor. He saw the abandoned sword, drops of blood staining the leg of Taredd's chair, Gael's lone slipper, and not far away, a small wooden statue of a pony whittled by Gruffydd and knocked from its honored spot on a trunk. The misery pooling in his eyes, he finally let splash to his cheeks. It was safe, no one would see, no one would know his hurting. But someone *was* watching, someone he didn't mind knowing. Owain's tormented gaze met Dawg's pitying expression. The dog padded over to his master, whimpering, his tail barely swaying, and rested his head in Owain's lap.

*****

Maura and Simon rode behind Odo's white steed in the direction of a large stable engulfed in a garish glow. Their grip on one another strengthened as they paused before the double doors of the stable. To the guard's cry "Open for the Bishop!" the apertures swung wide, revealing a large, dry structure, blaring with light provided by too many torches. The ground was cleared of hay, with some bales stacked neatly in empty stalls and others arranged at the far end of the room into a make-shift throne.

"The horses will stay outside," directed Odo, dismounting. "Mongrel...get down and come with me...If you please, the rest of you may enter and view our ceremony. Some of you are to remain outside on alert for any interruption."

Simon slipped from their pony and helped Maura down. His eyes spoke to her, telling her plainly his plans for their escape; no violence, cunning was their only feasible option. To keep their child alive was all she would offer in defense. She marveled at their combined sense of calm and knew it couldn't last, but here, at this

431

moment, it was most crucially required—calm for decision, for tactics, for survival. They lingered awhile in each other's arms, shared a solemn, passionate kiss, and murmured vows they feared might be their last. "Maura," whispered Simon, "whatever happens in there, always know and remember how very much I love you." His hands covered her belly, and he brokenly begged, "And...and Elyn, you'll tell her about me?"

"I won't need to tell her," assured Maura with faint hope and a touch to his cheek, "for you'll be by us always. I love—" Her profession was cut short by a sentry's cuff to Simon's shoulder, knocking him forward and after the Bishop. But she was able to finish her thought after punching the bounder as severely and regaining her hug on Simon's arm. "—you...And no one will force our parting...no one."

Odo glided majestically toward his throne, chin cocked high, mantle billowing from the mounting breeze moaning in through an open shutter cut in the opposite wall of the stable. He reached his seat, turned with flair, and struck a regal pose, one hand grasping the hilt of his bejeweled sword, one sweeping the length of his line of subjects. All slavishly hung their heads, and he contentedly sat. His squire arranged Odo's mantle for comfort, produced a silver chalice from a satchel, and poured ruby red claret from a leather flask. Odo accepted the wine, relished one sip, then smiled waggishly at the curious couple standing in a gripping clutch before him. Studying Simon first, Odo felt his choler bubble at his tenacious and unwavering glower. With vivid clarity, Odo recalled that insidious look, a look he couldn't beat out of the bastard, and he'd tried, oh Lord, how he tried to save this wretch from his indomitable pride! Yet, he admitted to himself and all those inside the barn, with bitter remorse, "There are some heathens who are so vile that they can't be saved, and it is my duty to God, my church and country, and my dear, dear brother, to rid the earth of such virulence. The woman...Well, like all women, she no doubt encouraged the destruction of the bastard's soul. Born a pagan witch with devious powers, she eagerly lured Simon into the Devil's army. What a treacherous mistake Robert made years' past, keeping me from eliminating her...And what's this?" His pale, limpid blue eyes fixed upon her belly. He should have guessed. Fornicators beget monsters, and their monster could prove most dangerous.

"What's he doing, Simon?" Maura asked trepidly.

"Remembering." Simon surged forward, demanding with frustration, "What will you do with us, Uncle?"

Odo shook from his reverie and to Simon's gall, shrank slightly backward. A snap of his fingers fetched forth two immense soldiers. They flanked his sides, brandishing swords.

Simon instinctively made a grab for his, but instead, he gulped a steadying breath, focused a blank stare on the Bishop, and asked with stronger deliberation, "What will you do?"

Feeling secure, Odo toyed, "We must wait for the spectators."

"My brother?"

"Yes."

"And Henry?"

"I told you, Henry is not with us."

"He has to be."

"Well he's not."

"But he told you where we were."

"No actually he didn't...A friend of his did."

Simon's eyes grew round with shock, for he knew Odo meant John. Never would he have guessed John's betrayal, but then he recalled personally Odo's coercion tactics.

A great discord resounded from the rear of the building. Maura and Simon whirled round, agape at the frantic influx of soldiers shouting, forcing, and shoving their way inside the stable, all hooded and indistinguishable. Odo smirked and stood, squawking, "Quiet! Quiet! You'll frighten our guests with your scurrilous behavior. Find a spot and hush."

Simon's nostrils and mettle flared. Will was here, he could smell his stench, his fear. And he knew Odo hadn't lied, Henry wasn't present, but then he had numerous times proven himself far more a craven than Will. Yet there was someone else—someone as powerful and potently evil. His assumptions were stopped short by Odo's instructions, "Simon, you'll come forward and kneel before me. Before we proceed with our ceremony you must swear me the homage I never received and most rightly deserve."

Simon didn't budge and snorted a strict, "Never!"

Maura's mind tumbled with rank confusion; there were too many soldiers, too many swords! What perverse torture was Odo preparing to stage? The Bishop settled his sharp glare upon her, she felt the stab, and defiantly returned its fierceness. Instantly, horror seized Maura, and forced from her a harrowed groan; she gripped at her belly and at Simon for support. They both sagged to their knees, she burying her face in his tunic, he beseeching, "What? What, Maura? Is it the child? Tell me, please!"

Bits of her choked response gradually connected and became clear, "He...he's the one...He...my parents...he's the man, Simon. My dream...*He* murdered them, tried to murder me and Marc! It was him! He murdered them, and he'll murder you!"

"No...not me, not you, no one...never again!" Simon vowed as he staunchly rose, unsheathed his sword, and rushed forward, wielding and declaring, "I challenge you, Uncle, and only you. We'll play no more. Take up your sword and fight me!"

"Don't be ridiculous," Odo scoffed, unruffled. "I'm too ancient to take you on, even though you've done nothing but wipe noses, and soothe upset bellies for the past year. If you truly want to fight someone, I'll let you fight," Odo sulked with feigned pity, "for you did miss your knighthood ceremony, didn't you? If you recall, the final examination requires the squire to battle three of my most prestigious knights. I've altered the rules a little, you'll be allotted no armor, and I've instructed three of my best to strive their utmost to kill you...Whether or not you choose to dispose of them, that's entirely your decision."

Will and Joanna, both hooded, elbowed their way to the fore of the festive audience. Will's chief guard held Gruffydd still and stifled directly behind them, and their whispering bristled with exhilaration, puzzlement, and also a twinge of dismay. "What's he doing?" quibbled Will. "Why doesn't he just hack off his head and have done with it? Why all this drama? He's not impressing me, he's making me mighty angry." His ire leapt to Maura, rising awkwardly from the ground, one hand supporting her belly and one reaching out for Simon's. "God's teeth!" he cursed in a gasp. "She's done it again!"

"What?" asked Joanna, "What's she done?"

"Are you blind?! She's gotten herself pregnant."

"That's not impossible to remedy. You said so yourself."

Will scornfully clarified, "If I don't return the bitch to your brother in less than a fortnight, I lose Helmsley, and you, my loyal steward, are steward no longer. You'll go back to poverty, to nursing that decrepit sod, your father, and that sickening sweet little cretin, your niece. I can't return her pregnant, and if Odo doesn't kill Simon—"

"What happens then? Tell me!"

"Even if we manage to kidnap Maura, and get rid of the child, Simon is a stubborn fellow and highly possessive. He'll come to fetch her back and he's capable of wreaking enormous damage."

"But he's a physician. What does he know about fighting?"

Will's debacle in Normandy flashed in his mind, stuck to the ground by Simon's sword, humiliated, dung covered, and he practically whimpered, "Grandfather mentioned something the night we arrived...a rumor circulating about an invincible warrior...And my father...my father likes Simon again...All my dreams, our dreams, gone to Robert's new runt and his bastard. It isn't fair...and...and it can't happen, Joanna," he blubbered, "not when I'm so close to succeeding. Simon can't triumph this time, he can't!"

"Then for God's holy sake," imparted Joanna with force, "do something to stop him!"

While Will struggled for a solution requiring no danger on his part, Simon stepped back, helped Maura back into his hold, and requested to Odo, "What besides a cuff on the neck do I get if I defeat your best?"

"*You* beat my best?" Odo mocked with a snicker. "Humble you're not, but then you never were. If by chance, you manage to survive the bouts, I'll allow you to pick your final contender, and if your success reigns complete...I'll let you go."

"Go where?"

"Wherever you please."

"And Maura..."

"I've promised her to Will. You'll have to deal with him about her future, and I dare say Arnulf as well. Seems he wants to renew their betrothal."

Simon inwardly cringed—Arnulf Montgomery—ferocious, base, and immensely more stupid than Rufus, yet equally as indestructible. How did he become involved in this travesty? Simon spoke up, "Uncle, do you still honestly believe it was strictly my accusation that imprisoned you?"

"Of course, it was...You'd always planned to ruin me."

"How could I betray plans I knew nothing about?"

"You were always lurking about, listening, tattling."

Simon beamed, shook his head in disgust, and devised, "You've just confessed to your crime, Uncle."

"What?!" flared Odo. "What crime? I was innocent of the charges."

"The crime you were justly imprisoned for—seduction of the King's legions and plotting to usurp the Pope."

"I did no such thing. I confessed nothing."

"If I was lurking about and listening, the plans I heard and revealed must have come from your mouth and not my imagination. On the contrary, I only heard you had planned a visit to Rome for religious guidance, and that's exactly what I told Uncle William. Someone else alerted the King to your true offense."

"And that someone was?" goaded Odo.

"I'll never tell."

"You don't need to...Your mother mentioned that someone."

Simon stiffened with panic and hotly demanded, "When did you see my mother?!"

"Three or four months past. We had such a nice visit. Unfortunately, she's as pompous and stubborn as you. Wouldn't tell me your location. No matter what coercion I inflicted, she refused to say."

"Why you stinking fiend!" Simon urged Maura away and swung his sword to kill; his precise attempt was barred by two sentries' shields.

Odo sprang to his feet and burbled with jittery excitement, "Now that I've got him fired up, bring on the first knight! His lady will sit here by me."

Simon whirled and lunged at three guards heading for Maura. His concern almost cost him his head; he felt the wind of the swipe as the sword's slice passed by his skull.

He spun back, his attention darting between Maura and the pouncing knight. He noticed the guards hadn't hurt her or trussed her, they'd only guided her to the bales of straw and hovered near to keep her still. Of that he was glad, for if she tried to intervene, and she most certainly would, she'd instantly be cut down. He presented her an intrepid expression and bearing, hoping to still her terror, and convince her of the confidence he held for himself and for her. He'd not fail her or their child, not this time, not ever again!

The crowd hooted and cheered the contestants, marveling at their agility and grace. It seemed more of a dance than a duel; a jig to a din of clanging metal, grunts, and groans. The strikes rarely hit their intended mark, and soon the on-lookers started jeering impatience. Simon noticed his opponent tiring; his swings became clumsy and faltered his balance. In swift return, Simon exaggerated and broke open their game. He battered and chased the man the entire length of the room, circling endlessly, then speedily retreating the same distance; he forced the knight to jump higher, to skirt and duck quicker. The throng's excitement and loudness spiked to the doctor's unexpected and laudable prowess. His rival finally stumbled from a dodged thrust and landed heavily on one knee. At his back, Simon's sword cut through the air, sharpened edge aligned directly with his neck, yet inches before impact, Simon turned the blade flat and slammed the soldier face down to the ground.

Instantly, the second man was upon him, twice the bulk of the first. Simon's mind flashed back to the squabble where Hywel had attacked using nothing but brute force. With Simon's slim build, tricks, diversions, and strategically placed kicks had been his only recourse. He jumped the giant's first flagrant sweep and, while the knight's blade was still in motion, Simon soundly kicked the soldier's groin. The man grabbed his genitals, lurched forward, then howled in pain as Simon's up thrust knee cracked his nose with tremendous force. His head whipped, and arms swam backward; he teetered woozily, spurting blood till a kick to his chest stole his balance, his air, and his sense. Like a felled tree, the knight tipped to the dirt and remained there, sprawled and still.

The throng swiftly hushed, and Odo's smug expression creased with concern. This was not what he had envisioned! A quick study of his remaining knights drew his stern call, "Geoffrey, come onto the field!"

Simon sized up the approaching warrior, approximately his size, perhaps younger, and excruciatingly loud. A vociferous yowl preceded the knight's wanton charge. Simon staggered from Geoffrey's stunning flurry of blows, then rebounded with equal vehemence, clashing iron, and dashing sparks from his rival's hauberk and helmet.

Maura could only spy occasional flashes of silver, the pale blue of Simon's tunic, a shock of his flaxen hair, yet she acutely suffered his cries of pain and triumph. The Bishop frequently spouted derision her way; his vicious comments repulsed her to the point of weakness, so she refused to acknowledge his insults. Instead she folded her fingers over her palm, tapped the hilt of the dagger lodged up her sleeve, and kept her fitful gaze stuck on her looming guards, waiting for the perfect moment to wound the Bishop and escape. At Simon's anguished wail, her heart lurched to her throat, and she heaved up from her bale. She almost lost her weapon in her frantic fight to reach him. The guards barred her flailing surge, catching her arms between theirs as she stretched out, clawing and groping at nothing but air.

Odo snickered at the thrilling dissonance playing out beside and before him. Simon's ruin was near, so near, he squirmed uncontrollably for the chance to take up a sword and mete out the final blow himself! Blood stained the entire sleeve of the bastard's tunic, leaking from a gash sliced into his forearm. He'd lost his sword, and was visibly disabled, scurrying in retreat like a startled mouse. Odo couldn't keep his seat and bolted upward as Simon lapsed to the ground. He balled his fists, ready to burst, "Finish him!" But as Geoffrey brandished his weapon for the mortal blow, Simon suddenly rolled and kept rolling, Geoffrey scuttling after, jabbing his sword again and again into only dirt. His frustration drove from him a demented howl and a reckless swing. Simon abruptly reversed his roll, rammed into Geoffrey's legs, and easily knocked the knight to his knees. He threw his body upward, flipping the soldier to his side, and a swift and powerful kick to his jaw knocked him senseless.

Simon stole up Geoffrey's sword—Its red and lethal tip he didn't thrust at his opponent, but at the perpetrator of this insanity. "Now...now," he stuttered between gasps, "it's my turn, Uncle. And I choose...you."

"I said no!" quavered the Bishop, at last exhibiting fear. "A Bishop battles only when necessary. Choose someone else."

The audience couldn't contain itself, each one craving the opportunity to fight this wounded yet exceptional warrior. They pressed dangerously forward, hooting and howling their desire. Odo bellowed for restraint, which was promptly enforced by his elite guard.

Simon cast Maura a weak yet hopeful glance; her straining eased, and her narrow gaze told him his choice.

At the call of his name, Will's blood froze to ice. He wagged his head furiously trying to stave off his faint, and swiftly decided he'd bolt from this wretched place and blood-hungry demons, and run back to Helmsley, and the rain and the boredom. But— the truth tragically dawned—if he ran, he'd have no Maura, so no Helmsley.

"Kill him, Will," gritted Joanna, "Now's your chance, he's wounded, tired, incompetent. For you, the perfect rival. Kill him!"

Will snarled in response and wrenched from her grip. He stayed perfectly still and quiet, hiding behind his helmet, praying she wouldn't betray his presence. His name was shouted three more times, each call shortening his stature.

Finally, Odo shook his head, his expression soured by disgust and exasperation as he decided, "He won't answer, so I'll pick."

"That's not what you proposed, Uncle," parried Simon. "I've defeated your best, so I'll pick my contender and then I leave. The coward is here, I smell him, and I'll soon find him!" Simon loped for the front line and began stripping soldiers of their helms. A great ruckus arose as the men commenced wrestling amongst themselves and with Simon. His eyes bulging terror, Will noted Simon's raging and rapid advance, and minced his way backward. Joanna extracted her dagger, and slyly planted it in Will's sweaty grip.

Gruffydd, a palm smothering his mouth, spied the exchange. He also spotted Simon's perilous approach, bit into the guard's palm, and screamed into a sudden chill of air, "He's here, Simon! He's here, and—" The hand slapped his mouth shut, and twisted his neck sideways, exacting horrible pain. The boy writhed and silently sobbed, as Simon hastened to his call.

Odo urgently boomed, "Arnulf! Arnulf! Stop this nonsense. He'll cause a riot. Drag him here to me!" Odo raised himself and his sword tall; poised and stoic, he prepared to execute.

Marc, in a low squat, deftly wove his way between horses' quivering flanks to the rear of the building. Guards held only the front entrance of the structure and appeared more intent on focusing on the uproar inside than disabling intruders. He stood cautiously, hauled himself up, and peeked inside the window. At first glance, he could make little sense of the clamor, then his eye lit upon Simon's blue tunic, and darted over the floor to Maura's copper hair. Odo, not three feet from the window, stood stiff as a statue, sword clenched, obviously braced for combat. Arnulf, whom Marc recognized from the long, burnished curls dangling from his helm, also wielded a sword—at Simon's unprotected back! Marc vaulted through the window, crying out, "Simon! At your back, Simon!" Marc swung his sword at the Bishop's neck. A blow from his side toppled him from his target. Odo stumbled bug-eyed and shaken from the fray erupting between his chief guard and an unknown assailant. How many more waited outside, he fretted as he shuffled to the now undisturbed center of the room.

Simon whirled to Marc's caution and leapt back from Arnulf's strike. Joanna ignored Will's whining protest, grabbed his hand, and thrust it mightily upward. The blade jolted Simon, he felt its punch, then realized with horror he couldn't breathe. He strained horrible breaths, choked on blood, then arched and cried out in desperation as a second hit seared deep into his back. Simon reeled a turn, swiped out, and caught hold of the nose shield of his murderer. He yanked, and Will's stupefied gape appeared, blanched with panic that twisted in a shrill scream as his hand involuntarily jerked out once more. Simon sagged onto the dagger embedded in his gut, and ripped it from Will's rigid clench as he slid to his brother's feet and rasped for only God to hear, "Don't...don't take her from me...ple...*please* don't..."

A formidable silence fell as all eyes froze on Simon's coiled, bloodied, and too still figure. Will's widened more as they rose up and fixed warily upon the Bishop, colored a vivid scarlet and trembling with rage. He stiffly strode toward the crime, his sword steeled, finger accusing, tone raving, "What have you done, William?!"

"I...I...I didn't," Will blundered miserably, "He...he backed into my weapon...I didn't..."

"You've killed my dream! So, I've no other choice than to—" Odo's brutal cry, "Kill Lord William...and his men!" exploded the melee into total war. Odo hacked his way through the crowd back to his throne and there discovered his incompetent guards strewn and groaning from many wounds. The red-haired witch had flown! He dodged and skewered one of Will's guards, and from the corner of his eye beheld Maura kneeling and hovering, pawing at and kissing her mate...*Most likely sucking out the remainder of his soul*, he surmised to himself, snorting disgust. *I'll take her head home as a trophy, and the bastard's as well, hang them in my sleeping chamber, spit and snicker at them each and every morning!* He swept their way, skittering over and between bodies. His laughing crazed to hysterics, then quickly quieted as the stranger from the window leapt between him and the witch.

Maura tugged and tore at Simon's gouged tunic, frantically kissed his blood soaked lips, and nuzzled his blue tinged cheek. "Simon...Simon!" she ardently begged. "Please wake up! We'll run now. They've forgotten us. *Please*, I can't carry you! Open your eyes, my love, and look at me! You have to help me...Simon!" Maura forced her quaking hand quiet and tapped his face lightly, then slapped harder, but still he wouldn't rouse. She chafed feverishly his frigid hands between her own and as one of his slipped limply to the ground, her desperate whimpers spiraled to panicked moans. She curled by his side, sobbing, "I won't leave you...I'll never leave you...never," and gripped and gathered his coldness near, praying for a sword to drop and forever end their torment.

Harsh words fell instead...Snide, devious words, hurled by a woman, "It's too late for comforting, bitch...he's dead...dead!" Maura briefly raised her swollen eyes, saw first the hilt of a sword plummeting, then only blackness.

Marc's ravaging assault drove Odo across the room, but the Bishop's superb prowess kept Marc locked fast in combat. As he whacked at the Priest, he prayed vehemently for Simon to keep breathing, to keep faith, for he needed only a few moments more to incapacitate the Prelate...Miraculously, Odo's too long tunic snagged the tip of a downed soldier's dagger; he stumbled backward, rolled from Marc's cutting sweep, yet couldn't tear loose his robe. His cackling returned, almost deranged as he glared up and threatened, "Kill me, you vile heathen! Kill me and you'll roast in Hell, while I dine in Heaven...Kill me!" he screeched. "I dare you to kill me!"

Marc swung his sword vigorously to oblige yet paused his blade mid-air as the stench of smoke filled his head. Dense white clouds poured in through the back window and swirled down through holes in the roof. The front doors burst wide and a mass of screeching black-faced ghouls rampaged inward, torching the straw, flailing swords, hatchets, and knives. Marc recognized Rhys' men, and feared their zeal would annihilate not only the enemy but also everyone they aimed to save. Odo took advantage of Marc's distraction and crawled away. Once out of danger, he whisked up his sword and leapt a fiery timber as he absconded out a side door. Marc spun round and raced in pursuit of his family, yet batting through the cloaking smoke, he found only Simon. He dashed and darted every which way, fervently searching amid the chaos, dodging and parrying slices. He found Maura nowhere.

Flaming thatch and timbers rained down, the Bishop's throne burst into flames, pillars toppled. Screams of "Run! It's crumbling, crumbling!" came too late for some crushed under the grinding weight of the collapsing roof. Marc grabbed Simon's hands and dragged him beside the last standing pillar. Careful not to nudge the knife, he draped his mantle over his brother, gripped hold of the pole, and while shielding Simon from dropping debris, stared aghast at the surrounding desolation. The oppressive heat singed his skin and eyes. The horrendous sounds of raging flames, horrified yowls, and tortured wails wrenched his belly and wounded his ears. Pain from his shoulder wound flared and convulsed his entire body, blotting his thoughts and sapping his strength. He slumped over Simon, barely missing the protruding weapon, and readily surrendered to a calmer place deep within his ravaged mind.

*****

The cart's rapid lurching in and out of pot holes stirred Maura nearly awake. The moon's glow illuminated the silhouette of a body hidden beneath the same blanket that covered her. She jerked up her head; a stabbing, torturous pain dropped it immediately back upon the padding straw, and drew from her a long, grievous groan. After she'd regained some sense, her hand jutted out, hoping to unveil her husband. Nudging the blanket aside, she discovered Gruffydd instead, unconscious and horribly battered. She groaned again, protectively grabbed him up, and held him fast. Despite her misery, she forced herself up onto one elbow, desperate to determine where they were headed, who was their jailer, and how they could get away. She could tell little, only that her captors wore Norman armor. Her eyesight and resolve began to fade, yet she managed one final glance backward and witnessed through fluttering lids the horrific, fiery destruction of the stable. Maura gasped racking sobs of despair and crushing guilt—She'd sworn never to leave him, but she was here, and he was...Her mind darkened, yet before she could succumb to total oblivion, the woman's fatal voice sneered the end to her tragedy, "He's in there, my Lady, dead, and he'll soon be only ashes!"

*****

When Marc next woke, the fire had mostly died, its demise owing to a lack of fuel. No living troops remained, several small fires still flickered, and the stench of burned flesh permeated the wreckage. His weakness worried him, and another more paralyzing fright seized hold as he tugged the cloak off Simon. He lay still as death, his face a grisly gray, his lips blackened by dried blood. Marc's fingers gingerly hovered over Simon's chest, but they paused their descent as his pain stabbed again and forced closed his eyes. He pried them wide and firmly pressed his palm onto Simon's tunic. His grimace gradually eased to a tenuous, almost imperceptible pulse. Heartened, he lowered his ear to Simon's mouth and felt a faint tickle of air, nowhere near enough to survive. "Breathe!" he shouted to his brother. "Breathe for me, Simon!" A sound slap produced no notice, so

Marc grasped up his mantle, tore off two long stretches of material, molded one to a ball, then grasped hold the dagger's handle, and extracted the blade. The surge of blood he curbed by pushing the balled material onto the wound; he secured it with the other strip, and carefully rolled Simon to his belly. Marc's hope sagged to the vicious wounds and profuse blood he encountered drenching Simon's back. His mind raved—nothing could be done to save his brother, nothing—while his hands worked feverishly in protest. More mantle was ripped and tied. He wedged his finger into the highest gash, determined its depth, and guessed the blade may have nicked, but not likely punctured his lung. With renewed conviction, Marc straddled Simon's waist, spread his palms over his ribs and shoved his entire weight down and forward. No response followed his effort, so he sucked a fortifying breath, and shoved again...This time he gasped to a perceived resistance, and his elation practically toppled him from his perch. He thrust again and again, weeping freely to Simon's gurgling, choking reply. Tentatively he paused, crawled off his brother, wrapped the final bandage, and turned him again to his back. Overcome with relief and fatigue, he sank down beside his brother, cried more, and thanked God for the miraculous hint of color rising in Simon's cheeks, his heart's vibrant thumping that rivaled Marc's own, and the mist that arose from his labored but ample breathing. Still, Simon showed no consciousness, but that most surely would come later. Marc swiftly considered the smoldering, scattered ruins of the upheaval, deciding the safest and quickest route out and to Fulk, tethered a ways up north. He stood with purpose, yet as he hoisted Simon over his shoulder, he winced and wavered with hurt. He inhaled a deep and restorative breath, mustered his diminishing strength, and swore passionately his promise, "I'll take you home, then I'll go fetch Maura and Gruffydd and Ella and bring them home as well. Don't worry, Simon, all's not lost, nothing's lost, nothing...yet."

*****

To be continued in the final volume of the Trilogy—

Domesday Tales

A Web of Tyrants

HISTORICAL NOTES

The biggest change I made to known history in <u>A Plague of Devils</u> was to Nesta, daughter of Rhys ap Tewdwr. I have not been able to find a definite birth date for her; I usually see circa 1080. I, however, have made her near sixteen in the year 1087. Why, you ask? I wanted to make her a young woman on the cusp of a sexual awakening. Also, when it comes to Nesta, I am certain some people who may read this and my last novel in the trilogy, <u>A Web of Tyrants</u>, will argue that she was called Nest, not Nesta. I have seen both names used in history books and family trees, and I like Nesta better.

Also, concerning Henry's other women, I mention one in particular in this book and in <u>A Domesday Tale</u>. I initially made up a woman named Sybil, who was Henry's young mistress in Normandy. I subsequently read that one of his most frequented mistresses was, in fact, named Sybil. This was also after I married Sybil to a man named Herbert. The true Sybil married a man named Herbert. Her father, though, I named Ralph, not Robert, and I've decided not to change that since one of my main characters is called Robert. I have, however, named Henry and Sybil's children the names listed in the book, <u>The Royal Bastards of Medieval England</u>. How about that for coincidences?

Since Simon is now a full-time doctor, I want to repeat in these notes the short history of the Physicians of Myddfai. The first recorded Physicians of Myddfai were 'mediciners' to Rhys Gryg, in 1234. Rhys Gryg was Prince of Deheubarth, grandson of 'The Lord Rhys', who was grandson of Rhys ap Tewdwr. Rhys ap Tewdwr is one of my main characters in <u>A Plague of Devils</u>. Simon becomes Rhys ap Tewdwr's Court physician, and head physician to St. Davids Cathedral and its village, Mynyw. Court physicians were already common in Wales before <u>The Laws of Hywel Dda</u> were written in 930. This system of Welsh laws was named after Hywel Dda, who reigned as King of Wales circa 942-950, and who is credited with the laws' codification. Druidic and Galenic medicine seem to be a basis for the Myddfai remedies, and medicinal plants used by the Romans may have been utilized in their concoctions as well. Thus, in reality, Simon would not have been called a Physician of Myddfai but would have used remedies similar to theirs. I've used their title with his name to show reverence to the Welsh family of Physicians whose influence was known far and wide throughout history, and also to the present day.

I have also in this novel started to depict the crumbling of Henry's soul. Henry has been described as a cunning, though ruthless monarch, and I follow his moral decay as he emerges from his adolescence and becomes a mature man. My future novels, adult and young adult, will continue to focus on Henry, his reign, and his relatives. I am fascinated by the man and his times and I hope all will find my tales of him and his family worthwhile reads.

Robert, Count of Mortain and Earl of Cornwall may not have had a residence in Tintagel, though the first Norman castle appears to have been built in the early 1200's. A few of Robert's manor homes are still standing in Cornwall, so I used my imagination and gave him one in Tintagel.

I took license in giving Simon and Maura their own warm springs. The only warm springs known in Wales is at Ffynnon Taf, north of Cardiff.

I have studied the family of William the Conqueror for the past forty years. I feel I know his family as intimately as I know my own. From the inconclusive and contrary research I have read, I believe I have created real identities and personalities for all the

440

characters involved in the everyday lives of this iconic family. Contrary research does not necessarily hinder the creation of believable characters; instead, it tends to make them richer, more colorful, and multi-faceted. So please enjoy this rollicking tale of the adventures of William's highly dysfunctional family, and the sweeping and heartrending love story of Maura and Simon. And tell your friends all about it as well!

*****

ABOUT THE AUTHOR

M. (Maggie) Garfield was born in Alexandria, Virginia. An author, historian, editor and educator, she has lived and traveled throughout the world. Presently, she lives in Lafayette, Colorado.

Maggie's greatest joy is her family. Her second joy is writing for adults and young adults, who wish to learn and dream of living in a time of history that was frequently tragic, challenging, fulfilling, and always fascinating.

****

BIBLIOGRAPHY

Andrews, William. Old Time Punishments. New York: Dorset Press, 1991.

Arano, Luisa Cogliati. The Medieval Health Handbook. George Braziller, New York, 1976.

Aries, Philippe. A History of Private Life, Revelations of the Medieval World. Cambridge: The Belknap Press of Harvard University Press, 1988.

Ashley, Maurice. The Life and Times of William I. New York: Cross River Press, a division of Abbeville Press, Inc. 1992.

Barlow, Frank. William Rufus. Berkeley and Los Angeles, California: University of California Press, 1983.

Barrow, G.W.S. Feudal Britain. London: Edward Arnold Ltd., 1956.

Breverton, Terry. The Physicians of Myddfai. Carmarthenshire, Wales: Cambria Books, 2012.

Bridgeford, Andrew. 1066 The Hidden History in the Bayeux Tapestry. New York: Walker Publishing Company, Inc., 2006.

Bowen, John T. and Rhys Jones, T.J. Teach Yourself Welsh. London: The English Universities Press, 1960.

Brochard, Phillip. Castles of the Middle Ages. Morrison, New Jersey, Adapted U.S. Silver Burdett: Librairie Hechette, 1980.

Brooke, Christopher. From Alfred to Henry III 871-1272. New York and London: W.W. Norton & Company, 1961.

Brooke, Christopher. The Saxon and Norman Kings. Fontana/Collins, 1963.

Brown, R. Allen. Castles, A History and Guide. New York: Greenwich House, 1980.

Brown, R. Allen. The Normans. New York: St. Martin's Press, 1984.

Brown, R. Allen. The Normans and the Norman Conquest. Woodbridge, Suffolk: The Boydell Press, 1985.

Burke, John. Life in the Castle in Medieval England. New York: British Heritage Press, 1978.

Charles-Edwards, T.M.; Owen, Morfydd E.; Russell, Paul, Editors. The Welsh King and His Court. Cardiff: University of Wales Press, 2000.

Chibnall, Marjorie. Anglo-Norman England 1066-1166. Oxford: Basil Blackwell, 1986.

443

Chibnall, Marjorie, Editor. The Ecclesiastical History of Orderic Vitalis, Volume II, Books III and IV. Oxford: Clarendon Press, 1969.

Costain, Thomas B. The Conquerors. New York: Doubleday & Company, 1949.

Crouch, David. The Normans. London: Hambledon Continuum, 2007.

Davies, John. A History of Wales. Penguin Books, 1990.

Davies, R.R. The Age of Conquest, Wales 1063-1415. Oxford University Press, 1987.

Douglas, David C. The Norman Achievement 1050-1100. Berkeley: University of California Press, 1969.

Douglas, David C. William the Conqueror. Berkeley and Los Angeles: University of California Press, 1964.

Evans, Gwynfor. Land of My Fathers. Yllolfa, 1974.

Ford, Boris, Editor. Early Britain, The Cultural History. Cambridge University Press, 1988.

Gantz, Jeffrey. The Mabinogion. Penguin Books, 1976.

Gies, Joseph & Frances. Life in a Medieval Castle. New York, Hagerstown, San Francisco, London: Harper Colophon Books, 1974.

Gies, Joseph & Frances. Women in the Middle Ages. New York: Thomas Y. Crowell Company, 1978.

Given-Wilson, Chris and Alice Custeis. The Royal Bastards of Medieval England. New York: Barnes and Noble Books, 1984.

Green, Judith A. Henry I. Cambridge University Press, 2009

Hartley, Dorothy. Lost Country Life. New York: Pantheon Books, 1979.

Haskins, Charles Homer. The Normans in European History. New York: Barnes and Noble Books, 1995.

Herm, Gerhard. The Celts. New York: St. Martin's Press, 1975.

Higham, Robert and Philip Barker. Timber Castles. Stackpole Books, 1995.

Hollister, C. Warren. Henry I. New Haven and London: Yale University Press, 2001.

Jones, T.J. Rhys. Teach Yourself Welsh. NTC Publishing Group, 1992.

Kerr, Nigel and Mary. A Guide to Medieval Sites in Britain. London: Diamond Books, 1992.

Kightly, Charles. A Mirror of Medieval Wales. Cardiff, Wales: Cadw: Welsh Historic Monuments, 1988.

Kightly, Charles. A Traveller's Guide to Royal Roads. London: Spectator Publications, 1985.

Labarge, Margaret Wade. A Small Sound of the Trumpet, Women in Medieval Life. Boston: Beacon Press, 1986.

Le Goff, Jacques, Editor. The Medieval World. Collins & Brown, 1990.

Lewis, D. Geraint. Welsh Names. Scotland: Geddes & Grosset, 2001.

Leyser, Henrietta. Medieval Women, A Social History of Women in England 450-1500. London: Phoenix Press, 1996.

Lloyd, J.E., Sir. A History of Wales. Golden Grove Editions, 1989.

MacDonald, Fiona. A Medieval Castle. New York: Peter Bedrick Books, 1990.

Matarasso, Francois. The English Castle. London: Cassell Books, 1993.

Mennell, Stephen. All Manners of Food. University of Illinois Press, 1996.

Morgan, Gwyneth. Life in a Medieval Village. Minneapolis, Minnesota: Lerner Publication Co. by permission from Cambridge University Press, 1982.

Morris, Marc. William I, England's Conqueror. UK: Penguin, Random House, 2016.

Nelson, Lynn H. The Normans in South Wales, 1070-1171. Austin & London: The University of Texas Press, 1966.

Peacock, John. Costume 1066-1966. London: Thames and Hudson, Ltd., 1986.

Pelner Cosman, Madeleine. Medieval Wordbook. New York: Barnes & Noble, 1996.

Pine, L.G. They Came With the Conqueror. London: Evans Brothers Limited, 1966.

Poole, A.L. Domesday Book to Magna Carta 1087-1216. Oxford University Press, 1955.

Pounds, N.J.G. The Medieval Castle in England and Wales. Cambridge: Cambridge University Press, 1990.

Power, Eileen. Medieval Women. Cambridge University Press, 1975.

Pryor, Francis. Britain in the Middle Ages. London: Harper Perennial, 2006.

Pughe, John, Translator. The Herbal Remedies of the Physicians of Myddfai. Edited by Derek Bryce, Felinfach, 1987.

Rawson, Hugh. Wicked Words. New York: Crown Publishers, Inc., 1989.

Renn, D.F. Norman Castles in Britain. John Baker, Humanities Press, 1968.

Rhys, John and David Brynmor-Jones. The Welsh People. London: T. Fisher Unwin Paternoster Square, 1900.

Rowley, Trevor. A Traveller's Guide to Norman Britain. London: Spectator Publications, 1986.

Rowley, Trevor. The Man Behind the Bayeux Tapestry. Gloucestershire: The History Press, 2013.

Rowley, Trevor. The Norman Heritage 1066-1200. London: Routledge & Kegan Paul, 1983.

Rowling, Marjorie. Everyday Life in Medieval Times. New York: Dorset Press, 1968.

Shorter, Edward. A History of Women's Bodies. New York: Basic Books, 1982.

Slocombe, George. Sons of the Conqueror. London: Hutchinson & Co. Ltd., 1960.

Smith, Charles Hamilton. Ancient Costumes of Great Britain and Ireland. London: Bracken Books, 1989.

Stafford, Pauline. Unification and Conquest. London: Edward Arnold, 1989.

Steane, John M. The Archaeology of Medieval England and Wales. The University of Georgia Press, 1984.

Steane, John M. The Archaeology of Medieval English Monarchy. London: B.T. Batsford Ltd., 1993.

Stenton, Doris Mary. English Society in the Early Middle Ages. Penguin Books, 1951.

Stephenson, Carl. Medieaval Feudalism. Ithaca, New York: Cornell University Press, 1942.

Strickland, Matthew, Editor. Anglo-Norman Warfare. Suffolk: The Boydell Press, 1992.

Talbot, Charles H. Medieval Medicine. London: Oldbourne, 1967.

Thompson, C.J.S. Magic and Healing. New York: Bell Publishing Co., 1989.

Thorpe, Lewis, Translator. Gerald of Wales, The Journey through Wales and The Description of Wales. Penguin Books, 1978.

Toy, Sidney. Castles, Their Construction and History. New York: Dover Publications, Inc., 1985.

Turvey, Roger. Twenty-one Welsh Princes. Wales: Gwasg Carreg Gwalch, 2010.

Turvey, Roger. Pembrokeshire, The Concise History. Wales: University of Wales Press, Cardiff, 2007.

Van Houts, Elisabeth M.C., Editor. The Gesta Normannorum Ducum of William of Jumieges, Orderic Vitalis, and Robert of Torigni, Volume I. Oxford: Clarendon Press, 1992.

Van Houts, Elisabeth M.C., Editor. The Gesta Normannorum Ducum of William of Jumieges, Orderic Vitalis, and Robert of Torigni, Volume II. Oxford: Clarendon Press, 1992.

Vander Zee, Barbara. Green Pharmacy; A History of Herbal Medicine. New York: Viking Press, 1982.

Venning, Timothy. The Kings and Queens of Wales. Gloucestershire: Amberley Publishing, 2012.

Walker, David. Medieval Wales. Cambridge: Cambridge Medieval Press, 1990.

Warner, Philip. Famous Welsh Battles. New York: Barnes and Noble Books, 1977.

Warner, Philip. The Medieval Castle. New York: Barnes and Noble Books, 1971.

Williams, A.H., M.A. An Introduction to the History of Wales, Volume I. Cardiff, University of Wales Press, 1949.

Williams, A.H., M.A. An Introduction to the History of Wales, Volume II. Cardiff, University of Wales Press, 1948.

William, John. Brut Y Tywysogion: The Chronicles of the Princes of Wales. Cambridge: Cambridge University Press, 2012.

Williams, Moelwyn. The South Wales Landscape. Hodder and Stoughton, 1975.

*****

www.ingramcontent.com/pod-product-compliance
Lightning Source LLC
Chambersburg PA
CBHW060339260626
47160CB00006B/2130